More Praise for
The Circle: The Engelsfors Trilogy, Book I

"A beautiful, frightening, empowering novel reminiscent of the best of Scott Westerfeld or Anne Rice, *The Circle* puts its mismatched heroines — and readers — at the center of an ancient conspiracy of magic as terrifying as it is realistic. Enthralling from start to finish." **—Elizabeth Hand, bestselling author of *Available Dark* and *Waking the Moon***

"The six protagonists are dynamic heroines with dark motivations, conflicting desires, and plenty of secrets. When the demons finally threaten to kill off the girls one by one, tension climbs sharply toward a suspenseful conclusion, leaving fans eager for the next book in the series."
—*The Horn Book Magazine*

"A dark story of struggling teens and a rash of suicides; the multilayered, cinematic plot is buoyed by the girls' determination, as well as the understated and idiosyncratic presence of magic." **—*Booklist***

"…Ambitious, with much to please fans of character-driven fantasy." **—*Kirkus Reviews***

"A great book that adds magical elements with real life challenges and features an amazing cast of heroines."
—Teenreads.com

"Elfgren and Strandberg weave a thrilling web of ancient magic and teenage issues in this first book of the Engelsfors Trilogy." **—Kim Krajniak, for Indie Next**

An Indie Next Pick
and soon to be a major film!

SARA B. ELFGREN
MATS STRANDBERG

FIRE

THE ENGELSFORS TRILOGY
BOOK II

TRANSLATED FROM THE SWEDISH BY ANNA PATERSON

THE OVERLOOK PRESS
NEW YORK, NY

This edition first published in hardcover in the United States in 2014 by

The Overlook Press, Peter Mayer Publishers, Inc.
141 Wooster Street
New York, NY 10012
www.overlookpress.com

For bulk and special sales, please contact sales@overlookny.com,
or write us at the above address.

Library of Congress Cataloging-in-Publication Data

Elfgren, Sara B.
[Eld. English]
Fire / Sara B. Elfgren and Mats Strandberg ; translated from the Swedish by
Anna Paterson.
pages cm. -- (Engelsfors trilogy ; book 2)
ISBN 978-1-4683-0672-9 (hardback)
[1. Fantasy.] I. Strandberg, Mats, 1976- II. Paterson, Anna. III. Title.
PZ7.E386Fir 2014
[Fic]--dc23
2013044050

Manufactured in the United States of America
ISBN 978-1-4683-0672-9
2 4 6 8 10 9 7 5 3 1

This book is dedicated to those of you who were our friends when we were teenagers.

A NOTE ON THE SWEDISH SCHOOL SYSTEM

In Sweden, grades 1-9 comprise primary school, and secondary school (high school) lasts for three years, the equivalent of US grades 10-12. The main characters in *Fire* are therefore beginning eleventh grade, their second year of high school.

Part I

CHAPTER 1

Sunlight floods in through the tall windows and picks out every dirty old stain on the white textured wallpaper. A fan on the floor is slowly turning from side to side. The room is still unbearably hot.

'How did your summer go?'

Jakob, the shrink, is wearing shorts, and sitting back in the brown leather armchair.

Linnéa can't resist a little probe into his thoughts. She registers his discomfort at the leather of the chair seat sticking to the backs of his thighs and then his genuine pleasure at seeing her again. She backs off instantly. Feels a bit ashamed.

'Fine, thank you,' she replies. It's been horrible, she thinks.

She focuses on the framed poster behind Jakob. All pastelly geometric shapes. She can't imagine anything blander and wonders what point Jakob wanted to make by hanging it just there.

'Has anything special happened that you would like to talk about?' he asks.

Define 'special', Linnéa thinks and glares at the blue triangle that hovers above his shaved skull.

'Not really.'

Jakob nods and doesn't say anything more. Ever since she realized that she is a mind-reader, Linnéa has now and then asked herself if he might not have a milder variant of her power, if he isn't somehow able to sense what is going on in her head. He always seems to know when to be silent in a way that makes her want to talk. Mostly, she resists, but this time the words bubble up.

'I've had a fight with one of my friends. Several of them, actually.'

Linnéa lets one of her flip-flops dangle. She hates sandals. But when it's this damn hot you have no choice.

'So, what happened?' Jakob's tone is neutral.

'I was keeping something secret. Something the others should have known, but I kept it to myself. And then, when I finally told them they got furious with me because I hadn't let them in on it earlier. And now they don't trust me.'

'Can you tell me the secret?'

'No.'

Jakob just nods. She wonders what would happen to his professional composure if she told him the truth. He wouldn't believe her at first, obviously. But she could go on to describe how, before she learned to control her ability better, she sometimes, against her will, picked up what he was thinking. Which is how she knows that he was unfaithful to his wife last autumn. He was sleeping with a coworker. His darkest secret.

Jakob would become anxious. Always ill at ease whenever she was around. Just like the Chosen Ones.

A few days after the end-of-semester assembly, they finally revealed their secrets to each other. Minoo told them the whole truth about what happened that night in the school dining area, about the black smoke that no one else could see and that came pouring out of her and Max, who had been blessed by the demons. Anna-Karin described how she had cast a spell over her mother that lasted all of fall semester, and admitted how far she had gone with Jari. Heavy secrets, but nothing in comparison with what Linnéa had to confess.

4

That she could read their minds. And that she had been doing it for almost a year. Without saying anything.

Since then, nothing has been the same. They have been meeting regularly all summer to practice their magic skills and, each time, Linnéa has been aware of the others avoiding her eyes. Throughout the summer vacation, Vanessa has hardly said a word to her. When Linnéa thinks about that, she feels as if a super-sharp electric whisk has been thrust through her chest, churning her heart to mush.

'How did you react when they turned on you?' Jakob asks.

'I tried to defend myself. But I understood why they did, of course. I mean...like, if I had been one of them, I would've been so fucking angry.'

'Why didn't you tell them the truth before?'

'I knew they'd freak out.'

Once more, that psychologist-style silence. Linnéa stares hard at her feet. The polish on her toenails is black.

'Anyway, it felt kind of good, too,' she went on.

'What felt good?'

'It felt like having the upper hand.'

'It can be tough to let other people come close, truly close to you. There are times when being alone gives one a sense of security.'

Linnéa can't stop the laughter. It erupts with a snort.

'What's so funny?' Jakob asks.

She looks up and sees his gentle smile. What does he know about being alone? Not alone, as in everyone else is busy tonight, or alone, as in your wife is away at a conference. But utterly, painfully alone, so lonely it's as if the atoms in your body are pulling away from each other and you're about to dissolve into one great Nothing. So lonely you have to scream just to hear that you still exist. Alone, as in nobody would care if you disappeared.

Inside Linnéa's head, the list pops up. It has been there for as long as she can remember. It's the list titled *Who Would Care if I Died?* Since Elias's murder, there have been no obvious names left.

Jakob clearly realizes that she isn't going to reply, because he changes the subject.

'Before summer vacation, you told me that you had met someone you felt fond of.'

That murderously sharp, fast whisk starts up again.

'I'm over it,' she lies. 'It got too complicated.'

Flipping, flopping, her sandal keeps dangling. She avoids looking at Jakob.

He asks more questions and she answers mechanically, feeding him a small truth here, a large lie there.

There's so much she can't tell him. Like: 'The world is not the way you think it is. It's full of magic. Engelsfors will be the center of a battle that's going to cross the boundaries between the dimensions. Good pitted against evil. I and a handful of other high-school girls are up against the demons. And another thing: I'm a witch. You see, I've been chosen to vanquish evil and prevent the apocalypse. Any more questions?'

Besides, there are just as many not-magical secrets that Jakob will never hear about: 'After Elias's death, I started sleeping with Jonte. Sure, the same old Jonte, my ex-dealer friend. And, yes, we smoked together, but I've stopped now. I won't ever do it again, promise. I'm responsible enough to have an apartment of my own. You and Diana believe me, don't you?'

Any of that stuff would be a one-way ticket to another institution. Or to new foster parents. Foster parents who wouldn't be like Ulf and Tina. Those two never tried molding her into somebody she wasn't, never tried to play at being a perfect family. They understood that she hadn't been a child for many, many years – perhaps never. If they hadn't gotten it into their heads to go to Botswana and start a school, she would've liked to stay on with them.

'How do you feel about starting school again?' Jakob says and Linnéa realizes that she has been silent for a long while.

'No problem.'

'Do you think a lot about Elias?'

It surprises her sometimes how much it still hurts to hear his name mentioned.

'Of course I do,' she snaps, even though she knows that Jakob didn't intend to get at her. 'I think of him every day. Especially today.'

'Why just today?'

Inside Linnéa, the sense of loss beats like a pulse and she has to concentrate on not bursting into tears.

'It's his birthday today.'

Jakob nods and looks compassionately at her. Linnéa hates him. She doesn't want to be one of the sad sacks who everyone feels sorry for. She's damaged goods, she knows that, but detests seeing it reflected in other people's eyes, resents the way they can't wait to try fitting the broken bits together, get out the superglue and start mending until they think she looks whole.

She probes again and notices that Jakob feels hopeful, believes that he has connected with her and that she is about to open up, tell him more about Elias.

She takes revenge by keeping her mouth shut for the last ten minutes of their session.

I miss you so much. It doesn't pass. The pain feels less bad sometimes, that's all.

I hate remembering the last time we met, the fight we

had. The real reason was simply that I was worried about what was happening to you. Now, I understand what you were going through. I think so, anyway. You had begun to discover new, inexplicable changes in yourself, just like I had.

I thought I was losing my mind and you must have been afraid of that, too. You must have been so frightened.

If only we'd talked, told each other our secrets. Maybe everything would have been different then. If only you'd been born anywhere except in this fucking hole. Maybe you would still have been alive.

I know it's pointless to think these things, but I can't stop myself.

I draw up lists of all the tiny details that were part of you.

Like the way you always picked the pickles out of the veggie burger. I never figured out why you didn't ask them not to add it. And your favorite authors were Poppy Z. Brite and Edgar Allan Poe and Oscar Wilde. I've underlined the passages you read aloud to me when you phoned me at night. You promised to take me on a trip to Japan before our thirtieth birthdays. Once, you said that if you were a girl you would've liked to be called Lucretia. Where in the world did you get that from? You never had crushes on real-life celebs, only on fantasy people like Misa Amane, even though she's so annoying, and Edward Scissorhands.

And you asked me not to forget you if you died before I did. Such a truly typically fucking stupid thing to say. As if I could ever forget you.

You are my brother in everything but blood. I love you and will love you for ever.

Linnéa carefully rips out the diary page and folds it. She digs a small, deep hollow in the light soil by the rose bush next to the stone on Elias's grave. The white shrub roses are faded already and the leaves have ugly, dried-out edges. She pushes the folded paper into the hole. Buries it. Wipes her hands on her black skirt and sits back.

She can see the rectory between the old lime trees on the far side of the graveyard. Linnéa observes the window of the room that used to be Elias's. The panes reflect the bright blue sky. Elias loved the view over the graveyard. Imagine if he had realized that he was looking at the plot of his own grave.

The air is very still. Within the walled cemetery, the baking sun heats the gravestones. The grass is yellowing and the parched ground criss-crossed with cracks. In June, the *Engelsfors Herald* ran euphoric headlines about the record-breaking summer. Now, in August, the record figures are the numbers of old folks dying of dehydration and of farmers having their finances ruined.

Linnéa's phone pings, but she can't even be bothered to check. Olivia, the only one in the old gang who's still her friend, has been texting like crazy all morning. The summer vacation has passed without a sign of life from Olivia, but now that it suits her, she expects Linnéa to jump. No such luck.

She unscrews the top of the water bottle in her fabric carrier. It makes no difference how much she drinks, she's still thirsty afterwards. All the same, the rose bush gets the last few drops.

She puts the bottle back and pulls out the three red roses from the flower bed in Storvall Park. Their heads are drooping already. She puts one rose on Elias's grave. Then she goes along to place another one on a nearby grave, where the stone bears Rebecka's name.

Linnéa looks back at Elias's grave. In the beginning she had hoped to be able to pick up the thoughts of the dead.

To contact them. But she hasn't succeeded in even sensing whether they are there at all, let alone what might be going on in their minds.

Linnéa used to believe that when a person died, that was it. End of story. Now, she knows that at least souls exist.

They're where they should be, Minoo had said when, after the end-of-semester assembly, they had met up here, by the graves.

Linnéa hopes that it is true, that Elias exists somewhere else, in a better place.

She remembers meeting Max in the dining area and what he said when he was trying to make her reveal who the other Chosen Ones were.

Elias is waiting for you, Linnéa.

A tiny part of her is tempted to find out if Max, ally of the demons, is telling the truth.

You can be together again.

Now she can no longer hold back the tears. She lets them run down her cheeks as she walks away. So fucking what? Since when aren't you allowed to cry in a graveyard?

One red rose is left in her carrier bag. It is for her mom.

Linnéa is just about to take the path leading to the Memorial Wood when she catches sight of a black shadow moving close to the ground between the gravestones.

She stops.

With a plaintive meow, Nicolaus's familiar slips on to the path ahead of her. Cat, who has no other name, seems to have lost even more fur during the summer. Its single, green eye is fixed on her.

Linnéa has never managed to read the mind of an animal, but it's easy to grasp that Cat wants something from her. It stretches itself and meows, then pads along a narrow path leading to the oldest part of the graveyard. Now and then, it stops to make sure that Linnéa is following.

The cemetery is surrounded by a low stone wall. Cat stops in its shadow, next to a tall headstone almost a yard high and covered with mosses and pale gray lichens.

Cat meows shrilly, noisily, and gently butts its head against the stone.

'Yes, yes,' Linnéa says and kneels.

The ground feels surprisingly cool against her bare legs. She leans forward, scrapes some of the moss off the stone and tries to make out the crumbling letters.

NICOLAUS ELINGIUS
MEMENTO MORI

A chill makes Linnéa's whole body shiver, as if the souls of the dead were present here after all and reaching for her through the soil.

Chapter 2

Minoo has made one corner of the garden into her own, where she can sit with her books. She has placed a deckchair in the shade of a sycamore at the back of the house and as far away from it as you can get. Too bad that it isn't far enough for her to ignore what's going on inside it.

Minoo glimpses the outline of Dad through the kitchen window. He crosses the floor with long, clumping steps. Out of sight, he roars something. He's so loud he could make the windowpanes rattle. Mom shrieks something back at him. Minoo pulls her earphones down and tries to lose herself in a Nick Drake song, but music simply makes her even more aware of the sounds she is trying to exclude.

Mom and Dad always used to deny that they argued, called it 'discussions' when they fought about Dad's health or about all the time he spent at work. But this summer, at some point, they had stopped pretending.

Perhaps it would be kind of grown-up to think of their fights as normal. Whatever has been simmering under the surface for so long has finally found an outlet. But Minoo feels like a scared little kid whenever she thinks of the word 'divorce'. Maybe it wouldn't have felt so bad if she had had brothers or sisters. But what is at risk now is the only family she has ever known. Mom, Dad and herself.

Minoo tries to concentrate on the book in her lap. It's a

mystery by Georges Simenon that she found on Dad's book-shelf. Its back has split, and yellowing pages sometimes drop out when she leafs through it. The book is really good. At least, she imagines so. There's no way she can engage with the story. She feels shut out of the world in the book.

Minoo catches a glimpse of brightness in the corner of her eye. She quickly pulls off her earphones and turns around.

Gustaf is wearing a white T-shirt. It enhances his tanned skin and the golden sheen of his sun-bleached hair. Some people seem made for summer. Minoo definitely isn't one of them.

'Hi, Minoo,' he says.

'Hi,' she replies.

She glances nervously towards the house. All quiet in there now. But for how long?

'You look surprised,' Gustaf is saying. 'Did you forget we were meeting up today?'

'Oh, no. I'd just lost track of the time.'

Inside the house, a door slams and Dad roars at top volume. Mom's response has a lot of swearing in it. Gustaf's face is blank, but he must have heard them. Minoo stands up so quickly the book falls on to the lawn. She leaves it there.

'Come on,' she says and walks off quickly.

At the end of the garden, she turns impatiently. Gustaf has picked up the book and is putting it on the deckchair. He looks at her, smiles, then hurries to catch up.

Side by side, they amble through Engelsfors. It is impossible to move at anything like a normal pace. The heat is pressing them down to the ground, as if the gravitational pull had been magnified by a factor of ten.

Minoo has never seen the point of lying around on a beach. That is, not until just this summer, when she has been thinking seriously of going to Dammsjön Lake where the rest of Engelsfors goes to cool down. But the mere thought of undressing in front of other people has always made her stay away. She can hardly bear to show her face in public. The heatwave hasn't exactly done wonders for her skin. A particularly hyper pimple is throbbing at her temple and she tries to pull a strand of hair over it so that Gustaf won't notice.

Just as it is hard for her to put her finger on exactly when Mom and Dad started fighting openly, it is hard for her to pinpoint when she and Gustaf became friends.

When Minoo finally dared to tell the other Chosen Ones about the black smoke, her alienation from the world of other people felt a little less paralyzing. But she was not the same Minoo as before. Her friend Rebecka had died. Killed by Max, the man Minoo had loved more than anyone else. Max, who claimed that the demons had a plan for her. She had no idea what the plan might be, just as she knew nothing about the powers held inside her.

But in the middle of her confusion, Gustaf had been there for her. Early on in summer vacation, he tried to persuade her to come along to Dammsjön Lake but, when she kept being evasive, they went for walks instead. Or else talked, read or played cards in his garden.

Gustaf is the local soccer star and one of the most popular boys in the school. Through the years, Minoo has heard so much praise of him, usually over-the-top variants on what a perfect guy he is. As for Minoo, the word she feels describes him best is 'easy-going'. He makes everything seem simple. Since her life generally is the total opposite of simple, the time spent with Gustaf has become a rare zone of ease.

But when she is not with him, paranoia lurks. She wonders why he cares enough to be with her. Maybe she's some kind of charitable project.

They stroll across Canal Bridge, then follow the swirling flow of black water past the lock gates and take a path underneath the canopies of the trees. A wasp is buzzing around Minoo and she flicks it away.

'How are things with you? Honestly?' Gustaf asks.

The wasp disappears among the trees. Minoo understands that he means what he had heard from inside her house. He has probably sensed all summer that something was up.

'Look, I'm sorry, maybe you'd rather not talk about it?'

Minoo hesitates. He is her escape route and she doesn't want to mess that up.

'Do your parents fight like that?'

'They did when I was little. Now they never do,' Gustaf says and then doesn't speak for a moment. 'But now, I don't think they care enough any more.'

Astonished, Minoo glances at him. She always had the impression that Gustaf's family was like one of these sweet'n'cozy ones in sappy American comedies, the kind where people get mad at each other because of some crazy misunderstanding. And when everything's sorted out in the end, cue for hugs all around as everyone agrees they've learned a lesson.

'I try not to think too much about it, but I'm pretty sure they'll get divorced as soon as I'm out of their way,' Gustaf says. 'I'm the last of their kids who's still at home. I leave and that's it. Nothing left to hold them together.'

'Do you really believe that?'

'You notice when two people are in love, I think. It's like...a kind of energy between them. Do you know what I mean?'

Minoo mumbles agreement. She knows exactly what he means. She once felt an energy field between herself and Max. That is, before she found out who he actually was. That he was Rebecka's killer.

15

'There's nothing like that between my parents,' Gustaf continues. 'I realized that once I'd fallen in love.'

He falls silent. Minoo knows that he is thinking about Rebecka.

Her death had brought them together. Now they talk less and less about her. It is Minoo who avoids the subject. As she gets closer to Gustaf, it is more and more difficult to play along with the lie that the death of his girlfriend was suicide.

She sees a familiar shadow sweep across his face and wants to ask him how he feels. Does he still have nightmares about when he watched Rebecka die? Does he still blame himself? She wants to be the friend he deserves.

But how can she be a true friend at the same time as she keeps lying about something so important?

If only it were possible to tell him the truth. But she knows that she couldn't, not ever.

The woodland opens up into a meadow where the summer flowers have faded and died. The old abandoned manor house stands on the far side of the meadow.

'Did you know that building was an inn once?' Minoo asks to change the subject.

'No, I didn't. When?'

'In the nineties. Dad told me about it. A couple of Stockholm restaurant owners bought the whole thing, moved in and refurbished it. They spent serious money, apparently. And then they opened a restaurant. It got rave reviews but, even so, they had to close the place down after about a year. Zero customers. Dad said the talk in town was all about how they'd show the city folk that in Engelsfors there was no money to be had just for the asking. So there. As if everyone wouldn't have gained by something actually happening here.'

Gustaf laughs.

'Engelsfors strikes again. Typical.'

Part One

For a while, they stand looking at the house. It's a grand two-story building made of white-painted wood. Definitely the largest and most beautiful building in the town. Not that the competition is so hot. A wide flight of stone steps leads from the overgrown garden to a veranda where two massive pillars support a large balcony on the first floor.

'Let's check it out,' Gustaf says.

'Sure.'

They start crossing the meadow. The brittle, crackling stems of dry grass reach up to Minoo's knees and she thinks nervously about hordes of starving ticks scenting blood.

'Do you want to stay on in Engelsfors?' she asks. 'I mean, after leaving school?'

'I suppose I'll have to study first. Then...I don't know. In some ways, I really like the town. It's home. But there's no future here. On the other hand, maybe that's exactly why people ought to come back later in life. To build something new.'

'What, like opening a restaurant?'

'Do you think they'd come if I were the owner?'

Yes, Minoo thinks. They'd come all right. Because you're you.

'I guess so. You're no city slicker.'

Close up, it's easy to see how run-down the house is. The paint is flaking off the walls and here and there patches of bare wood show. The ground-floor windows are shuttered. Minoo thinks of the work done by the previous owners. Now the old place is decaying again.

Gustaf starts climbing the steps to the veranda, but stops halfway. Listens.

'What's the matter?' Minoo asks.

'I think there's someone in there,' he says quietly.

He sets out along one of the wings. Minoo trails after him, nervously eyeing the first-floor windows. They swing

17

around the gable end and step out in front of the house.

A dark green car is parked on the graveled area near the main entrance. The passenger side door is wide open. Minoo makes out a man seated inside.

He notices them and gets out of the car in one agile movement.

The man is young, their own age, and taller than Gustaf. Wavy, ash-blonde hair frames his face. His features are near-perfect and so is his smooth skin. His looks would fit just right in one of those high-end ads where everyone is sailing or playing golf non-stop.

'Hi,' Gustaf says. 'Sorry, we thought the house was empty...'

'You're mistaken, obviously,' the guy says.

He speaks with exactly the kind of 'posh' Stockholm accent that instantly gets under the skin of most Engelsforsers, regardless of how nice the speaker is. In this case, there isn't a trace of niceness in his voice.

Gustaf stares at him in blank amazement.

Of course he's baffled, Minoo thinks. Gustaf must be totally unused to people being rude to him.

'Sure, yes, our mistake,' Gustaf replies. 'Are you moving in?'

'Yeah, that's right,' the stranger drawls, sounding utterly fed up.

Minoo's ears are glowing. She wants to leave. Now. No point in trying to chat, not even Gustaf's charm will have any effect on this guy. He slams the car door shut, flattens the creases in his slacks. Then he looks up and stares intently at Minoo.

She feels as though he can see straight through her and that he isn't impressed.

'Come on. Let's go,' she mutters and grabs Gustaf's arm to pull him along.

'Hardly the type to improve the reputation of Stockholm folk around here,' Gustaf says as they cross back over the meadow.

'Too true.'

When they reach the edge of the wood, Minoo turns for a last view of the manor house. She catches a glimpse of what might have been someone moving upstairs.

'What would you like to do now?' Gustaf asks.

'I don't know.'

Her phone pings in the pocket of her skirt. She checks it. It's a text from Linnéa.

'Has anything happened?' Gustaf asks.

'No,' she lies. 'Nothing at all.'

CHAPTER 3

Under the large trees the ground is in the shade, but it is not cool. On the contrary, the heat feels more oppressive in the forest. The air is heavy to breathe and smells of resin, needles and sun-warmed wood. And that special forest scent, too, which Anna-Karin can't quite define in words. She inhales deeply as she walks along a narrow path through the blueberry shrub between the rough tree trunks.

Around her, the forest is completely still. But she doesn't feel the peace of mind she has come here to find.

Anna-Karin's safe places have always been with animals, with her grandfather and in the forest. But she only understood how much these places of refuge truly mattered after she and her mother had moved into an apartment in the center of Engelsfors.

The farm is sold. Grandpa has moved to Sunny Side Nursing Home. But the forest still belongs to her. Anna-Karin has been here practically every day of the summer vacation. Hiding away from other people who are crowding in on her, away from their eyes and from the town, its asphalt and bricks and concrete and ugliness. Here, she breathes more easily. She even dares to dream.

Yes. That is how it is, *usually*. But today is different.

Every single child in Engelsfors learns that 'you must stick to the forest paths'. It is part of growing up. Maps and compasses don't seem to function as they should and all attempts to organize orienteering on field days were abandoned long ago. In the past, such efforts had invariably ended with search parties being mobilized. The forest seems somehow larger when you are in it than when you look at it from the outside.

Several people disappeared without a trace during Anna-Karin's childhood. Even so, this is the first time she feels the typical Engelsfors response to the forest: a sense of unease. It dawns on her that she has heard not one note of birdsong, not one buzz of an insect.

But she walks deeper into the forest, allows herself to become engulfed.

Sweat starts trickling down her temples. The slope she has been walking up is too gradual for her to have noticed it at first, but now she feels it in her legs. To her right, the sun gleams on a water-filled mining hole. The luminous surface reminds her of how thirsty she is. How could she forget about bringing something to drink?

The path becomes steeper and stonier. It feels as if someone has turned the heat up higher still. Dry leaves are rustling as she pushes branches out of the way. She tastes the salty sweat on her lips and hears her own heavy breathing.

Near the top of the hill the ground flattens and the trees are fewer. Gasping for breath, she sits down on a rotten tree stump. Her lips feel dry under the film of sweat. She is thirstier than ever and dizzy if she closes her eyes. Trying to breathe deeply and slowly doesn't help, it just feels like breathing the same old stale air over and over again.

She opens her eyes.

The air is shimmering. Colors suddenly seem stronger, smells more distinct.

A dead tree stands in front of her. It looks like a human

21

being who is stretching his arms towards the sky. A hole in the trunk is like a mouth. The flaking bark is the color of ash.

That tree was not there before.

Obviously, that's ridiculous. Trees don't sneak up on you. Let alone dead trees.

Anna-Karin gets up. The dizziness hits her again. She must get back home. Must find some water.

But the dead tree beckons her. She leaves the path and walks towards it. Dead branches crackle under her feet. The sound is loud in the heavy silence. Drooping branches of blueberry bushes are so tinder dry they pulverize when she steps on them. She reaches out, touches the hot tree trunk, then keeps walking as if in a dream.

Behind the ghostly tree, the ground falls away abruptly, precipitously. She can see the chimneys of the closed-down factory in the distance.

There is a scattering of other lifeless trees. Tall trunks, bleached bone white by the sun.

It is not only the drought that's killing the forest, she realizes, without knowing how she knows. The forest is dying for another reason.

She turns slowly. It takes her a few seconds to discover the fox standing very still, close to the tree stump she had been sitting on. Its amber eyes coolly meet hers.

The sun on Anna-Karin's skull feels like a burning hot weight. As she and the fox watch each other, the sweat is nearly blinding her. She doesn't dare move, doesn't want to alarm it.

But in the end she must rub her eyes to try to remove the stinging saltiness.

When she takes her hands away, the fox is gone.

*

Anna-Karin steps out of the elevator in the Sunny Side home. The soles of her shoes make sucking noises against the linoleum flooring in the corridor. Her grandpa is sitting in a wheelchair near the window in the day room. He is so thin. Every time she sees him, he seems to have shrunk a little more.

An old lady with old-lady-style permed curls is snoozing in an armchair. She is the only other person in the room. Grandpa spots Anna-Karin and recognizes her. He smiles at her, his eyes are bright. He is having a good day. Anna-Karin's heart swells with love for him, almost bursting her ribcage.

She hands him the crossword magazine she bought for him at Leffe's kiosk.

'What, no hug today?' he says and puts the magazine down on the little table-top attached to his wheelchair.

'You wouldn't want to. I'm covered in sweat.'

'Silly girl! Come here.'

Grandpa used not to like hugs. But he is changing in so many ways. Anna-Karin puts her arms gently around the old man's frail body.

'Have you eaten anything today, Grandpa?' she asks once they let go of each other.

'I don't get hungry now that I'm not allowed to move around. All I do is sit or lie down.'

Guilt instantly overwhelms her. She will never forgive herself. It had been her fault that the barn caught fire. It had led to Grandpa's injuries.

'Besides, it's far too damn hot.'

'But you're drinking properly, right?' she adds, eyeing the half-empty glass of apple juice on the side table.

'Yes, yes, of course.' He waves away her question.

Anna-Karin makes a mental note that she must quiz the

staff. Is Grandpa really getting enough to drink? Earlier this summer, he was so badly dehydrated they had to put him on a drip.

'What have you been up to today, Anna-Karin? Have you been in the forest?'

'Yes, I have…'

She hesitates. Every time she visits him in Sunny Side, he asks her to describe every detail, all the scents, sounds and small changes that she has observed in nature. But she is not sure that it would be right to tell him what she has seen today in the forest. She doesn't want to worry him.

'What's troubling you, my dear?'

She makes up her mind. She will tell Grandpa about the ominous silence and the dieback in the forest. After all, if there's anything that makes Grandpa perk up, it is feeling useful. Feeling needed by someone who is eager to find out what he has to say.

As Anna-Karin describes the forest, Grandpa's face is expressionless but she realizes how tense he is from the way he sits.

When she begins to speak about that dead tree, he takes her hand.

'You had left the path,' he says. 'And that you mustn't do.'

'Just a tiny bit.'

'A step is enough in the forest. It will take you. Something is going on in there. Stick to the path, Anna-Karin.'

She looks at him, full of concern. He has taught her to respect nature, but never tried to frighten her.

'What do you mean?' she asks.

But he doesn't reply. He is looking towards the corridor. Åke, one of his oldest friends, comes in, waving happily. Anna-Karin notes the confusion in her grandpa's eyes.

'Oh, there's Åke,' she says.

Grandpa clears his throat.

'Ah, yes. Hello, Åke. Good to see you.'

Anna-Karin smiles at the visitor.

'Dear girl, you're becoming more and more like your mother every time I see you,' Åke tells her.

Anna-Karin forces herself to keep smiling.

A ping from the pocket of her sweatshirt. She fumbles for her phone.

A text from Minoo.

CHAPTER 4

Ida goes outside to stand on the terrace at the back of the house. The wooden decking is soft against the soles of her feet. She leans against the railing and breathes in deeply. The air is heavy with sweetish perfume.

The Holmström family's garden looks suspiciously green and flourishing. The city council issued a water restriction, but at night Ida's father runs the sprinklers all the same. It had worried her mother who mumbled about the neighbors noticing, but in the end she decided to look the other way. When all is said and done, why should she allow her select, specially ordered and rather expensive roses be sacrificed just because the Engelsfors council is too incompetent to provide enough water?

Right now, Mom is kneeling by one of the flowering shrubs with a basket full of gardening tools next to her. She attacks the weeds with focused fury.

'Mom-my!' Lotta shouts. She is bouncing up and down, down and up, on the huge trampoline further away in the garden. 'Mom-my, we are hung-ry!'

'There's milk and cereal in the kitchen,' Mom shouts back as she tugs at a tough root system in the border.

'We don't want milk! We want bang-cakes!' Rasmus screams. He is bouncing too, next to his big sister.

Mom sighs, pulls off her gardening gloves and dumps them in the basket.

'You want "bang-cakes", do you? Oh, all right then,' she says.

The kids, eight and six respectively, howl with delight.

'We love Mommy! We love Mommy!' they shout in time as they bounce, blonde hair flying around their heads.

'My little sweethearts!' Mom is laughing as she gets up.

Ida tries to suppress her irritation. It is childish and silly, she realizes that, but the feeling is strong. When she was little, no way did Mom run around frying 'bang-cakes' on demand. Besides, Ida thinks, at their age I could speak properly.

'Aren't you off to the lake yet?' Mom asks on her way into the house.

'You know I'm waiting for you.'

'But, darling, I'm so busy today.'

Mom pulls off her sandals, walks through the open French windows to the terrace and then, on light bare feet, across the white-stained floorboards. Ida follows her to the kitchen.

'But we were going for a practice drive,' Ida says.

'We talked about it but didn't actually make any plans.'

She pulls a white bowl out of one of the white-painted cupboards and puts it down on the white marble countertop. The words HOPE and LOVE, against a white background, hang on the wall above the counter. Mom owns an interior-decorating boutique in Borlänge and has turned their home into a three-dimensional sales catalogue.

'We did so.'

Ida realizes that she is whining and sounds just like Lotta and Rasmus.

'We'll have to do it some other day,' Mom says and takes eggs and milk from the fridge.

'But we hardly ever go for drives. Julia and Felicia will get their licenses before me.'

'Of course they won't. Neither of them is as disciplined as

you are. Nor has your will to win.' Mom turns, looks at Ida and smiles. 'You're like me when I was your age.'

Ida can't be mad any more. Julia and Felicia moan and groan about their mothers all the time, but Carina Holmström is one of Ida's role models. Her mother is always the best-looking and the most beautifully dressed, without being one of those embarrassing MILF types who put on far too young clothes and try to be best friends with their kids.

'Isn't Erik waiting for you?' Mom asks.

'Sure.'

'So why are you staying in here then?'

She turns on the radio and 'Hello to the Summer' booms from the wall-mounted loudspeakers. Mom starts whisking pancake batter at the same frenzied pace as her weed pulling earlier.

Ida goes outside to pick her bike up from the garage. Wheeling it through the garden, she passes her little brother and sister.

'Trampolining can make you incontinent,' she tells them.

'What's that?' Lotta asks.

'You'll find out soon enough.'

Vanessa is woken when Melvin starts screaming somewhere in the apartment.

She sits up and the headache does a somersault inside her cranium. The shuttered Viennese blinds leave the room in semi-darkness.

She stands on shaky legs and catches sight of herself in the full-length mirror that is leaning against the wall.

Her eyes are bloodshot. Her face is smeared with a mixture of sweat and what is left of her make-up, and when she runs her tongue over her teeth they're coated with something that feels like felt. The dark roots look worse than ever now that her hair is all greasy and messed up. And on top of it all, her right big toe is inexplicably painful.

Vanessa picks up her dressing gown from the chair in front of the desk and turns the radio on. An intense dance hit fills the space. Fragments of memories from the night before are flickering past. They played Truth or Dare and she kissed Evelina. Michelle stood in Jonte's kitchen and wept over Mehmet. Vanessa and Wille had sex on the ping-pong table. And then she remembers why her toe hurts. She stumbled over the vacuum cleaner in the hall when she came home last night.

Vanessa pulls her fingers through her hair, ties it up in a ponytail. A deep breath before she opens the door to the kitchen.

Mom and Nicke are sitting at the table with their mugs of coffee. Vanessa's baby brother Melvin is lying on the floor without a stitch on. As always after his tantrums, his face is bright red. Frasse, the German shepherd, lies next to Melvin. The dog's tongue is practically touching the floor.

'Good morning,' Vanessa says.

Nicke looks up from the *Engelsfors Herald* and drinks a mouthful of coffee. She suspects him of hiding a superior grin behind the mug.

'If it's still morning,' he says.

Vanessa glances at the clock. Not even half past ten yet.

'You do look tired,' Nicke tells her.

'It's too hot to sleep.'

He puts his mug down. Definitely sneering. Had he heard her stumble on the vacuum cleaner? And then she realizes what's up. Nicke was on the night shift last night. He must have come home just a few hours ago.

Ever since Vanessa moved back home, she and Nicke have tried to tolerate each other after a fashion. Unspoken hatred separates them like a minefield, but they step with caution, each watching out for the other's move. Vanessa pretends to accept Mom's rules of engagement and Nicke pretends to believe that she's sticking to the rules. But Vanessa knows that he's just waiting to catch her in the wrong. Like the cop he is.

Melvin cries a little, as he wants to remind everyone that he exists.

'What's up with Melvin?' Vanessa asks.

'He simply won't get dressed,' Mom says with a sigh and fingers the tattoo on her upper arm. A snake swallowing its tail. 'I gave up in the end. Look, I see his point. When it's this hot I'd like to run around naked, too.'

'Suits me,' Nicke grins.

Mom giggles. Vanessa rolls her eyes heavenwards.

'What are you up to today?' Mom asks.

'Off to Dammsjön Lake. With Michelle and Evelina.'

'Isn't Wille coming?' Nicke asks innocently.

'Yes, he's coming along as well,' Vanessa replies with a pretty smile. And thinks, *Die, die, die, you fucking loser.* 'Right. I'm going for a shower.'

After a long, cool shower, she brushes her teeth and then slaps ice-cold water on her face. Swallows a couple of paracetamols. Back in her room, she has already started sweating again but after putting on make-up she at least looks a little more like a human being.

She checks her phone. Text from Wille to say they're on their way. She puts on her turquoise bikini, then a loose top and cut-off jeans. Then packs her beach bag with a bath towel, a pillow and a book.

She fills her water bottle in the kitchen.

'I'm off now,' she says.

'What, aren't you going to have breakfast?' Mom asks.

'No time. But Michelle will bring picnic stuff.'

'Sure you don't want me to come along? Wouldn't it be great to bring your mother?'

This totally lame joke has been repeated all summer but Mom never seems to tire of it. Vanessa has had enough and more. But she has no time to reply. Her beach bag falls over and the book ends up on the kitchen floor.

'Oops,' Melvin says and laughs.

'What are you reading?'

Vanessa quickly holds the book up before stuffing it back into her bag.

'*The Stand*? Oh, my God, Nessa. Why read Stephen King? Isn't there death and misery enough in this world?'

'I took it from your bookshelf!'

'It's actually your book, Jannike,' Nicke says, sounding amused.

Mom shakes her head.

'Reading that kind of book you fill your head with a lot of rubbish. It ruins your mind. I really ought to weed them out of the bookshelf. I don't even want to have them in the house.'

Vanessa sighs. Mom has been like this ever since she took that latest course and found the meaning of life. Again. This time, her instructor is Helena Malmgren. Elias's mother stopped being a vicar and has turned herself into a self-help guru instead.

'Every one of us is responsible for the energies that are let into our lives,' Mom goes on. 'It is really true that you can choose to affirm either the positive or the negative energies in the universe. Keep thinking positively and most problems will solve themselves. But if you only have negative thoughts, well, no surprise that nothing works out for you.'

Vanessa loses her temper. She is so fed up with this crap.

'Oh, stop it. If people are sick or have a hard time, is that supposed to be their fault? Is that what you're saying? Are

African children starving because they have negative ener-gies? Or maybe the universe operates by different rules depending on which part of the world you live in?'

Mom looks annoyed.

'That's not at all what I meant.' Her usual way out of trouble.

Vanessa bends down and tickles Melvin's soft baby-belly until he gurgles with laughter.

'Bye,' she says and leaves.

'All my best to Wille!' Nicke shouts after her.

At the number 5 bus stop, Wille's car is waiting with the engine running. Vanessa jumps in at the passenger side and slams the door.

'Hi, hun,' Wille says and kisses her cheek before starting.

'Such a weird night, last night,' Michelle comments from the back.

'I remember…like, nothing,' Evelina says and giggles.

'You do, it's just that you won't admit it.' Vanessa catches Evelina's eye in the mirror and licks her lips suggestively.

They laugh and Vanessa leans against the backrest. She puts her hand out of the car window and feels the rushing air push against the palm of her hand.

'Please drive by the Sun Grill. I haven't eaten a thing. No time,' she says to Wille.

'Sure. But we'll have to pick up Jonte and Lucky first.'

'How are you going to pack them in? Lucky alone is at least three ordinary people.'

'The girls will have to sit on the guys' laps.'

Michelle and Evelina protest loudly.

'Hey, look in the glove compartment,' Wille tells her.

Vanessa spots a hint of a smile at the corner of his mouth. She opens the glove compartment and finds a small white teddy bear inside. The bear is clinging to a large silk-covered heart with the text *To the Best Girlfriend in the World*.

'Thank you,' Vanessa says.

She is really touched. The teddy is so silly and so sweet at the same time.

'Oh, my God! It's soooo cute,' Evelina shrieks.

'I *never* get any sort of present from Mehmet,' Michelle says.

Out on the main road, Wille speeds up.

'I love you,' he says and looks at Vanessa.

'And I love you,' she replies.

She twists her engagement ring and feels that what she's said is really the truth.

This is such non-stop exercise, Ida thinks as she opens the tube of sunscreen and squeezes out a large dollop into her hand.

It feels like you have acres and acres of skin when you rub it in. If you go in for a swim you've got to repeat the whole process from the beginning. Besides, this repulsive heat will make you sweat it all off in five minutes even if you don't go near the water.

Ida is longing for rain, a cloudy sky, the slightest little breath of wind. Sounds hang suspended in the still air. The children's shouting and splashing at the water's edge. Julia and Felicia's chatter. Robin and Erik's shitty hip hop from a cracked loudspeaker.

Ida finds a sunblock lip salve and smears it across her lips. The whitish, elastic substance reminds her of ectoplasm, the stuff she apparently dribbles when she gets possessed. The thought is irritating, so she rejects it and lies down on the beach towel. She tries to relax but her body is slippery and messy from all the cream. And now Erik is moving in, pushing his sweaty thigh against hers.

'Christ, can't you stop sticking to me like some kind of wart?' she says.

Julia and Felicia stop talking and Ida doesn't need to see them to know that they are exchanging nervous glances.

'Is it your period, or what?' Erik mutters but at least he moves away a little.

Julia and Felicia start talking to each other again. Saying things like how today is the last day of summer vacation and how inhuman it is to have to go to school when it's this hot. Julia starts on a story about meeting the principal, Adriana Lopez, in that hocus-pocus shop in the City Mall.

Ida tries not to hear. She doesn't want to think about the principal and that horrible scar on her chest. Sitting up, she reaches for her water bottle and unscrews the top with sticky hands. The water is tepid and tastes of plastic. It's disgusting, disgusting, everything is totally disgusting.

She peers at the others. Julia is holding forth, now and then tugging at the T-shirt to cover her bikini. Felicia pretends to listen, but she is completely focused on Robin who doesn't notice a thing. Must be the only one who hasn't figured out that Felicia is crazy about him.

'I wonder who of the mental cases are going to off themselves this year,' Robin says suddenly. The others cackle at this, Felicia louder than anyone else.

Ida avoids having to laugh along with them by swallowing another mouthful of the dregs in the water bottle. She certainly doesn't want to think about the so-called suicides of Elias and Rebecka. Why does everything and everyone have to remind her about the Chosen Ones and all the shit that happened last year?

'There can't be that many left by now,' Felicia says to Robin.

But his attention is directed elsewhere. He thumps Erik's chest.

Erik snorts and sits up.

'What now?'

Then he sees what Robin sees and goes quiet.

Ida doesn't even have to look to know that it's Vanessa Dahl. If only Ida had been more alert she would have registered from hundreds of yards away the hyped-up mini-tornado that is Vanessa's energy. Ida knows it only too well from their training sessions in magic.

She turns around. Vanessa has brought her entire following of pathetic no-hopers.

'I bet she slept with every one of them,' Felicia says. 'That fatso, too.'

Ida and Julia giggle. But the guys stay silent. Fixed on Vanessa, who bends over, in her minuscule bikini bottoms, to spread the beach towel. Her tan is perfect in the way Ida's pigmentation will never allow.

'Check out those roots,' Ida comments.

Vanessa's pale blonde mass of hair ends in several inches of dark brown hair close to her head. Ida touches a naturally pale blonde strand of hair that has worked free from her own ponytail. It reassures her. Vanessa turns and for one brief moment, Ida feels sure that she will say something, like 'Hi'.

But instead Vanessa silently lies down on the towel. That's a relief. Of course, there is no longer any reason for the five Chosen Ones to try to hide that they know each other. The demons already know who they are. But should it get around in Engelsfors that Ida and Vanessa had something in common...well, regrettably, Ida would have to kill herself.

Vanessa's boyfriend, the drug-pusher one, lies down next to Vanessa. It takes about, say, half a second before they start making out.

Ida glances at Erik. She would dearly like to scream at him to stop ogling Vanessa, but doesn't want to seem to care one way or the other.

Instead she puts her head to the side and stares at his thick dark hair until he senses her eyes on him.

'What is it?' he asks irritably.

Clearly, he isn't the slightest bit ashamed of being fixated on Vanessa. Ida keeps her voice as calm as she can.

'How weird that I haven't noticed it before,' she says.

'What?'

'Oh, nothing,' Ida mumbles and looks away.

'Out with it, for fuck's sake.'

Ida looks at him full on. Smiles.

'You know, it's just that when you're sitting here in the sun, it's obvious that you'll go bald super early.'

Robin howls with laughter. Julia and Felicia giggle hysterically.

'No way,' Erik says and his eyes darken.

'Oh, don't fret. It will be years before it really shows. It's just that in this light…'

Robin gives Erik's scalp a hard rub.

'Let's see if it comes off,' he says. Erik slaps his hand away and glares at Ida furiously.

She raises her eyebrows.

'What's wrong with you? You asked, after all. I'm just telling you the facts.'

In her beach bag, the phone pings and, at that instant, a signal rings out from somewhere else on the beach. She notes that Vanessa is checking her phone.

A sinking feeling somewhere inside Ida. This isn't a coincidence.

She pulls her phone out. The display is streaked with white sunscreen from her fingers.

A text message from Minoo. She opens it and reads, sensing that Vanessa, still on her towel, is watching her.

Ida deletes the text. Then stands, straightens her bikini and walks towards the water.

'You going for a swim?' Felicia calls out after her.

'What do you think?' Ida replies without stopping.

She navigates between the shouting kids and their over-protective parents, who are at least as noisy.

The water feels warm against her calves. She keeps going, then dives and swims until she finds one of the chilly currents running through the lake. She stays there. All the time, one sentence echoes through her body.

I don't want to be part of this. I don't want to be part of this. I don't want to be part of this.

But she knows that she will do as she has been told.

Like the others, she will turn up in the cemetery tonight. Not because she gives a damn about some old gravestone bearing Nicolaus's name, but because she must keep her promise to the *Book of Patterns*.

CHAPTER 5

Anna-Karin's mother made dinner. Deep-frozen meat-balls heated in the microwave and canned fruit salad with mayonnaise dressing. They eat in front of the TV set, as usual. Mom would have liked to do this even when they lived on the farm. It was Grandpa who insisted that they should sit together around the kitchen table.

Anna-Karin and her mom don't speak to each other, not once. The TV is on some show about a millionaire who pretends to be poor. Later on, the millionaire reveals who he is and gives away tons of money to truly poor people who become so pleased and grateful, they are crying with happiness. The program makes Anna-Karin feel a little nauseated. Or maybe it's just that salady thing. Once again, she has eaten too much and it wasn't even tasty.

'Thanks for the dinner,' Anna-Karin says and gets up.

'Sure,' Mom says absently and lights a cigarette.

Her eyes stay fixed on the TV screen.

Anna-Karin goes to her room, turns on the computer. With Pepper purring in her lap, she starts chasing information about forest death but nothing fits with what she has seen. Instead she drifts away on the Internet, looking up veterinary schools in places far away from Engelsfors. But what matters is doing well enough this high-school year. And the next one. And hope the apocalypse doesn't get in the way.

Part One

She looks at her watch. Time, she realizes, to set out for Nicolaus's place. She's told him that she wants a ride to the cemetery, but actually she wants to find out how he reacted to Linnéa's find.

The TV is still on when Anna-Karin pads through the living room. Mom is lying on her side and snoring a little. Anna-Karin tiptoes over to the sofa, picks up the ashtray and takes it to the kitchen to soak the butts under the tap.

As Anna-Karin leaves their block, she takes a look at the house across the road, the shut-down library. They have been refurbishing it all summer. The large windows are covered in brown paper, but light is seeping out through the gaps.

Anna-Karin wonders who is going to set up shop there and is feeling sorry for the owners already. They'll do well if they can hang on for a year.

She starts walking through the center of town.

It is Monday night and not a soul is around, as usual. Here and there, the blue light of a TV lights up a window. The August moon is like a fat, bright yellow cheese. The outside air is still warm and Anna-Karin longs for the end of this seemingly endless summer.

She crosses Storvall Square and turns into Gnejsgatan, where she stops in front of the three-story building covered in green-painted render.

The front door slides open after just a slight push. Anna-Karin walks up to the only door on the ground floor and presses the doorbell.

'Good evening, Anna-Karin,' Nicolaus says when he opens the door.

She hasn't seen him for a week and since then, he has tanned a little. His ice-blue eyes seem to glitter more brightly

39

than usual. He is neatly dressed in slacks and shirt, but his gray-streaked hair is long and tousled.

He is quite good-looking.

If only Mom would fall for someone like him, Anna-Karin thinks.

'Sorry...am I too early?' she asks.

'You're always welcome here,' Nicolaus says as he ushers her in.

When she enters the living room the first thing she notices is the fern. Apart from the old town map and the beautiful silver crucifix on the wall, Nicolaus's apartment is completely bare. No rugs, no curtains, nothing to cover up the worn coffee table and no books in the bookshelf. But a fern in a white plastic pot has been placed on the window-sill. It's heartbreaking to think of Nicolaus going out to get something to brighten his lonely rooms.

'That's a nice fern,' she says.

Nicolaus's face lights up.

'Isn't it? I felt something green was called for. You know, in the middle of this drought.'

Anna-Karin nearly says something about the dieback in the forest, but doesn't. Nicolaus is surely under enough stress already.

'You look preoccupied,' he says.

'Mostly because I was wondering how you would respond. I mean, to this gravestone thing.'

Nicolaus's smile seems slightly forced.

'It has its morbid sides, I must admit.'

The doorbell rings and Nicolaus answers the door.

Minoo's voice comes floating in from the stairwell.

'Hi, Nicolaus.'

She looks surprised at finding Anna-Karin in the living room.

'Are you, too...?'

Anna-Karin ends her sentence for her.

'Here to hitch a ride? Yes, I am.'

They exchange a glance. The same reason has brought them here. Anna-Karin asks herself if Nicolaus realizes.

Vanessa opens the windows wide even though she knows it's pointless. Outside, the air is as warm and muggy as in Jonte's living room. Not improved, of course, by Jonte, Lucky and Wille trying to break some record for being stoned.

But Wille has promised Vanessa that now she's going back to school, he'll lay off smoking most of the time and find himself a job. Vanessa has made up her mind to believe him.

Back on the sofa next to Wille, she relaxes. But she must set out for the cemetery soon. Mom thinks that she's staying the night with Evelina, who naturally agreed straight away to provide an alibi because it would allow Vanessa to be with Wille. Meanwhile, Wille has been told that she has to stay at home. Tomorrow morning, at breakfast, she will have to tell Mom that she came home in the middle of the night because she and Evelina had fallen out about something. In fact, Vanessa is preparing to lie to her mother, her boyfriend and her best friend, all in the same evening. Since she became one of the Chosen Ones, she has had to lie more than ever before in her life. It's getting hard to keep track of all the fibs.

'Wow...it's so fucking nice.' Lucky is moaning with pleasure as he stuffs his face with lemon curd biscuits.

Crumbs spray from his lips in a fine shower. Lucky's insatiable hunger after smoking weed reminds Vanessa of what it used to be like when the Chosen Ones had been practicing magic and simply had to gobble food and sweets afterwards.

'Nessa, have a beer at least,' Wille says, enveloping her in a cloud of sweet smoke. 'It makes me tense when you just sit around.'

'Don't be uptight,' Lucky says and jabs her arm. 'You're missing out on having a good time. You should've come along to Götis last Saturday. Totally sick night.'

'I can live with missing one night at Götis.'

'Just as well. I mean, it's not like you've much choice.'

He looks very full of himself because, for once, he has the upper hand. After the end of the school year, Vanessa and Evelina had managed to get banned from Götvändaren, the only hotel and hanging-out venue in town. A broken toilet and extensive water damage were part of the picture. The owners would definitely have pressed charges if they hadn't been underage and shouldn't have been admitted to the nightclub in the first place.

'You should've seen Wille—' Lucky goes on, but Jonte interrupts him.

'Shut it.'

It silences Lucky instantly. He starts fiddling with a new joint.

'Nessa...' Wille says, putting his head to the side in an attempt to look cute and succeeding very nicely. 'Why don't you want to party with us?'

'Because tonight, I turn into a superhero with a secret mission,' she tells him gravely. 'Sooo sorry.'

Wille just laughs, oblivious to any subtexts.

Vanessa catches Jonte watching her with his dark, intense eyes. At times, she feels that he knows too much about what is going on. Or, at least, that he's somehow more aware than he should be.

The ugly cuckoo clock starts calling the hour. Vanessa has to leave.

'You're so lovely,' Wille says. 'Out-of-this-world lovely. You know that, don't you? The best fiancée a man could hope for. The best in the entire world. Too good for me.'

Vanessa looks at him. Maybe his unruly blonde hair needs a cut, but Vanessa likes the way he looks. She kisses him before getting up from the sofa, a lingering kiss.

'I'm off home now,' she says and turns to Jonte. 'OK if I borrow your bike?'

He nods, tugs at his cap. Jonte can't refuse her anything. Vanessa knows too much about him. Things that he wants to stay secret and fears that she will give away to Wille. Like: Jonte has slept with Linnéa, Wille's ex. And Linnéa pocketed Jonte's handgun. And that was the gun found this winter in the dining area, next to Max.

Vanessa zooms along the road with soft air rushing past her bare legs. It feels good but is nowhere near enough to cool her. More than anything she'd like to lie down in a deep freeze, hands crossed on her breast, like a vampire in a coffin.

The bike is just as useless as its owner. The handlebars are wonky and pull to the left, and the whole thing rattles alarmingly at the slightest hole in the road. Vanessa is positive she hears lots of little tinkling noises, as if she's leaving a trail of lost bits like screws and nuts.

The white, rendered stone wall around the cemetery glows spookily in the strong moonlight. The others are already there, waiting by the gate.

They all look tense.

Vanessa, on the other hand, feels almost relieved. At last, something is happening. They will have something to worry about, other than when the demons will strike next.

The bike bumps on something and wobbles. Vanessa is nearly catapulted off before she manages to swing it around and skid to a halt in front of the others. Fucking bike from hell! She kicks it as she jumps off. She feels a sharp pain in her big toe and swears some more under her breath.

Vanessa doesn't even have to look at Linnéa to know that she's grinning. She longs achingly for the old days when she would have shared the joke with her.

Linnéa has promised them that she no longer reads their thoughts. Explained that she only kept her power a secret because she didn't want them to be scared of her. But nothing she can say will ever heal the wound. Vanessa now questions every good moment they have spent together. Did Linnéa read her mind all the time? Was that why she always seemed to know what to say? After the dining hall fight against Max the two of them had become so close. Or had their friendship started even earlier?

Vanessa often thinks of the Saturday night when she had turned up in Linnéa's apartment. They had been laughing together at everything sick and bizarre that had happened in their lives. She only realized how much that memory meant when it was ruined for her.

At first, she had been furious with Linnéa and that made ignoring her much easier. Later, it became harder and harder. Vanessa is amazed at how much she misses her. But as soon as she considers forgiving her, what Linnéa did comes back to her and the old anger erupts again.

It's all so awful. To be without Linnéa is as impossible as to forgive her.

'Now what? Are we supposed to stand around here all night?' Ida asks.

Nicolaus looks stern.

'You're right, Miss Holmström. Let's get this over and done with.'

They enter the cemetery. Their shoes make crunching

noises on the gravel. Vanessa is staring straight ahead when Linnéa comes alongside her.

'Hi. How are you?' Linnéa says.

'Fine.' Vanessa makes the short word sound dismissive.

If only Linnéa would stop looking at her like that. Vanessa repeats Melvin's favorite tune as a mantra to prevent herself from accidental thoughts that Linnéa might listen in on.

Twinkle, twinkle, little star, how I wonder what you are! Up above the world so high, like a diamond in the sky!

After a sidelong glance at Vanessa, Linnéa moves on to the front of the group. She waves to the others, a signal that they are to follow her into the old part of the cemetery.

A narrow path runs between crumbling blocks of stone and heavy cast-iron crosses. For several hundred years now, no one has known what the people buried here looked like while they were alive, or what kind of people they were. It is a strangely fascinating, dizzying thought.

'Here it is,' Linnéa says.

She stops at a gravestone that looks unimpressive compared with the grander memorials. She lights a torch and directs the beam at Nicolaus's name.

Minoo observes Nicolaus. He stands absolutely still, like one of those ghastly mime characters at festivals who pretend to be statues. She wonders what he's feeling.

Ida breaks the silence.

'So, Nicolaus had an ancestor with the same name. What I don't get is, why do we check out a graveyard in the middle of the night? Does Cat want us to take up genealogy? Or what?'

Ida's tone of voice makes Minoo cringe.

'*Memento mori*,' she says, fighting to control her voice. '*Remember you must die*. It said so in the letter Nicolaus wrote to himself. We have been wondering about it all this time. Now, maybe, we'll find out.'

Ida raises her eyebrows and looks at Nicolaus, who still hasn't said a word.

'Fine. You'd better tell us then,' she says. 'What is so special about this grave?'

He simply shakes his head.

Minoo realizes that she's being unfair but, at this moment, he is so frustrating. She had no idea what she'd expected from him when he confronted the grave. But *something*, at least.

'What do you think, maybe we should carry out a ritual?' Anna-Karin asks.

Everyone looks at Minoo and she can't help wondering why it has come to this. Why is she supposed to have the answers, she who can't read the *Book of Patterns* and doesn't even have her own element?

'I don't know. We could seek guidance from the book...'

'I've tried already and didn't find anything useful,' Linnéa says. 'Besides, what we have to do is perfectly obvious.'

She pauses, looks at the others.

'We have to start digging.'

It has occurred to Minoo, too, but she has dismissed the idea. They have done quite a few bizarre things together. Conducted magic rituals, fought demons – but to dig up a grave...

Still, she can't come up with an alternative.

'That's simply disgusting,' Ida says. 'Do you want us to start clawing at the ground here and now?'

'You will absolutely not break the peace of the grave,' Nicolaus says suddenly.

Minoo glances at him. His face has taken on a determined, authoritarian look. A look that won't allow you to argue. This is a side of Nicolaus that she hasn't seen before.

'What do you suggest we do?' Minoo asks feebly.

'Nothing. You do nothing. It is a mystery, I concede that. So it should remain. This is consecrated ground.'

'But...'

'No ifs, no buts!'

'What is your problem?' Linnéa asks. 'It was *your* familiar that led us to this grave. It was *you* who wrote that letter to *yourself*, complete with the clue *memento mori*. Therefore, *you* made us come here. Back when you still remembered things, this was exactly what you wanted us to do. So why hold us back now?'

Nicolaus just looks at her. Then he turns away and leaves.

Anna-Karin runs after Nicolaus as he crosses the cemetery.

He takes such long strides it's hard to catch up with him. Finally, she can reach out and put her hand on his shoulder. He stops instantly.

'Wait!' she says.

He turns to face her.

'Please don't go. We've got to talk about this.'

'There's nothing to discuss. Anna-Karin, I beg you. You must stop the others.'

His eyes plead, almost in desperation. And she wants to be on his side.

If Nicolaus doesn't want them to dig up the grave, why should they do it? He is their guide. And, besides, he is her...

Her what? Her friend?

Can she call him that? She likes him. At times, she has felt more strongly than that. She might even love him, as the father she was never allowed to know.

'But what are we supposed to do then?' she asks. 'We can't drop the whole thing. It might mean something. Cat seems to think so anyway.'

Nicolaus shakes his head and starts walking again. She wants to call out after him, but it would be stupid to go off like a bullhorn when you're sneaking around a cemetery in the middle of the night.

When she returns to the graveside, everybody is still there, standing around and talking.

'He's right, it's totally sick to dig up a grave,' Ida announces irritably to no one in particular. 'They could put you in prison for doing it.'

But none of the Chosen Ones cares to listen to Ida, as usual. Instead they decide to meet up here tomorrow night. And start discussing who can bring spades.

CHAPTER 6

Vanessa cycles home along the empty streets of Engelsfors.

As she pedals along under the viaduct, the echo makes the rattling of the chain and the whooshing of the tires against the asphalt bounce back at her. When she comes out on the other side, the silence is astonishing, as if she's the sole survivor in a disaster movie.

To get up the slope that starts when you're past the disused gas pumps, she has to stand and pedal. She feels drained but her longing to get home drives her despite the exhaustion.

Not far to Törnrosvägen now. She takes the short cut through bits of woodland, along the overgrown soccer field and the small playground where she sometimes takes Melvin...

She brakes so hard that the bike threatens to go to pieces once and for all.

Partly hidden by a shrubbery, a police car has pulled up on the far side of the sandpit and the swings.

Vanessa stays still. Is Nicke in the car or out prowling nearby?

Gripping the handlebars firmly, she focuses until the familiar wafts flow across her skin. During the summer, she practiced bringing bigger and bigger objects with her into a state of invisibility. Just now, she is truly grateful for what she has learned.

Fire

She starts pushing the bike towards the car until she is about ten yards away from it. The front windows are open. Somebody is in the driver's seat, a uniformed officer with close-cropped hair. Is it Nicke? Invisibility makes her movements soundless, but she steals forward all the same, almost holding her breath as she gets closer to the car.

Yes, it's him.

What is he doing here? Vanessa thinks. She stops again.

Nicke's head is thrown back, and he doesn't move at all. He is so still she thinks he might be dead. Her brain goes into overdrive – call 911, then Nicke's colleagues will come to the door to tell Mom and she will break down and, when Melvin asks at bedtime what death is, Vanessa must try to explain – and then she spots a little smile flickering around Nicke's mouth. One of his hands grips the steering wheel.

Then Nicke happens to hit the horn. Vanessa jumps. The bike nearly falls over when the handlebars slip out of her sweaty hand.

Nicke chuckles and looks down at his knees. He speaks in a low voice but is clearly audible in the still air.

'Hey! You are really something else,' he says, addressing his lap.

By now, Vanessa has to fight not to understand. Hopeless, it's like fighting off an eighteen-wheeler with a flyswatter.

A dark head suddenly pops up next to the dashboard.

It is a woman, who slides up onto the passenger seat and kisses Nicke on the mouth. He shakes his head and laughs. And then kisses her back.

Vanessa retreats. She can't stand watching this for another instant. She clenches her jaw to keep her nausea down, turns her bike, leaps into the seat and pedals away with an energy she lacked just moments ago.

CHAPTER 7

The black smoke is whirling around Minoo.

Anna-Karin, Ida, Linnéa and Vanessa are somewhere nearby. All helpless. Everything depends on Minoo now. She alone is left.

Alone with Max.

He stands in front of her with the black smoke eddying around him. Dark waves of hair frame his beautiful face.

'I know you don't understand now,' he says, 'but all I want…the only thing I've ever wanted…is for us to be together.'

The smoke swirls, grows denser around them. They are pulled towards each other and Minoo knows now that something isn't working the way it should. At this point she should resist and the battle shift in her favor.

But it isn't happening.

She tries to put up a fight, but is powerless. And suddenly Max is standing very close to her. His eyes are black and shiny, like a bird's.

'We belong together.'

He bends over her and kisses her with ice-cold, moist lips.

Minoo opens her eyes. Woken by a kiss.

It wasn't like that at all, she tries to persuade herself. I was victorious. I saved the others.

She turns to lie on her side and stares out into the dark room.

Is something moving over there? Have the shadows of the night taken on a deeper shade of darkness?

The black smoke.

Minoo sits up in bed.

She can see it clearly now. A black cloud, shuddering as it hangs in the air. A long tentacle of smoke is creeping out of the room and into the corridor.

Minoo's feet are caught in the ruffled sheet and she has to struggle to free herself before she can follow the black smoke. It has wound its way along the white wall of the corridor outside her room and crawled across the floorboards towards Mom and Dad's bedroom.

Minoo goes to look in through the open door.

Mom and Dad are lying on their backs in bed. The smoke envelops them, pulsating as if it were alive. But her parents' eyes are staring unseeing into the darkness.

'You killed them.'

Minoo turns around.

Max is standing in the corridor. He looks at her with the black eyes of a bird.

'You knew all along that this would happen. You haven't even tried to get the measure of your powers, because you guessed what you would discover.'

He holds out his hand.

'We belong together.'

And she knows it is true.

The alarm from Minoo's cell phone pulls her out of her sleep.

She sits up in bed and scrutinizes her room.

No black smoke anywhere.

She gets up and walks along the corridor. Noises from the kitchen. Everything as usual.

It didn't happen. Not for real, she thinks.

But she cannot make the dream go away.

Anna-Karin's mom is reading at the kitchen table. Her dark hair is pulled back in a bunch. The smoke from her cigarette is snaking upwards through the already stale air. Opposite her, Anna-Karin is prodding at her yogurt, watching as tiny air bubbles rise.

The *Engelsfors Herald* rustles as Mom slowly turns the pages. She sucks up every word, as eagerly as she sucks up the poisons in her smokes.

The silence in the kitchen is somehow made more tangible by the noises of traffic and people in the street outside. Being alone in town feels so much lonelier than being alone in the countryside.

Pepper pads into the kitchen and sniffs at his food bowl without much interest. Then he wanders off into the hall where he navigates between the movers' boxes, still not unpacked after months and months. Anna-Karin feels a pang of bad conscience. It was selfish of her to bring him here instead of giving him away to someone with a house and a garden. He should be free to run in and out as he pleases, and has been used to. But she couldn't have survived without him, not now when she has to live alone with Mom.

'Well, now. Monika has had to shut up shop, too,' Mom says.

Her eyes shine as they follow the lines of print under a photo of a grim-looking Monika standing in front of her closed café. Nothing excites Mom more than other people's bad-luck stories. Probably her greatest pleasure, up there with smoking. Anna-Karin isn't sure which of her mom's addictions is the most harmful. It's no comfort to know that you can't die from secondhand *Schadenfreude*.

Anna-Karin gets up and noisily dumps her plate in the sink.

'Are you just leaving it there?' Mom asks.

'I'll do it later,' Anna-Karin says and walks out into the hall.

'If you leave it there you might as well wash it up.'

Mom makes it sound as if *she's* the one who usually does the dishes.

'No time,' Anna-Karin says before going to the bathroom to brush her teeth.

They live off the money left from the farm sale and the compensation eventually paid by the insurers after the fire in the barn. Anna-Karin doesn't know how long this stash will last. Mom often talks about getting a job. But when Anna-Karin comes back from school, her mother has often not even managed to drag herself out to shop for the basics.

Anna-Karin would rather not admit to herself that she's disappointed. It would be the same as admitting that she had hoped for things to get better, that moving into town would inject new life into Mom. The fact is that she at least had work to do on the farm. Now, she's more isolated than ever before and Anna-Karin hates seeing her mother sinking deeper and deeper into paralyzing depression.

But she gets into black panics herself when she thinks about the future and what will happen when the money runs out.

The air shivers above the hot asphalt. In the distance, the school looks like a mirage.

Minoo walks past the gas station where she once bought an evening paper running a feature on the 'suicide pact' in Engelsfors. So unbelievably much has happened since she read the interview with Gustaf. Back then, she felt that she could never forgive him. A friendship between them was even less likely.

Her thoughts are interrupted by the sound of a car horn. Three short blasts. A dark blue Mercedes pulls up on the verge of the road. The woman driver leans across the passenger seat as the window slides down soundlessly.

'Hello, Minoo. Have you had a good summer?'

It is Adriana Lopez, the principal. They exchange small talk, but there is a slightly haunted look in Lopez's eyes.

'We will continue with the lessons in the fairground on Saturday,' she says. 'Do tell the others. We'll meet there at the usual time.'

'Okay. Of course,' Minoo replies.

Adriana lightly pats her black page-styled mane, though not one hair is out of place.

'In the near future, there will be certain...changes,' she says, avoiding Minoo's eyes.

'What changes?'

The principal seems to hesitate.

'Wait and see. Just until Saturday. Now I've got to move on. How would it look if the principal were late on the first day of school?'

Adriana pulls out and the car accelerates away. Minoo watches it go. And feels that she can see her principal adjust the rear mirror, as if to look back at Minoo.

A rat-ta-tat of Kevin Månsson's moped is closing in and Minoo has to jump clear when he almost drives it alongside her. He laughs out loud.

Nope, he still hasn't grown up, Minoo thinks.

She joins the stream of students flowing towards the dull brick building that houses the Engelsfors high school. The filled-in crack in the pavement runs across the school yard like a dark scar. The dead trees look somehow even more dead, as if utterly desiccated by the merciless sun.

Walking towards the main entrance, she feels the hot surface burning under the soles of her sandals. Here and there she registers new faces or, rather, new-old ones. Out of sight for just one year when Minoo had started high school and they stayed behind in the last year of middle school. Now they're back together again.

How young they look, Minoo thinks.

It feels like ages ago that she started here, but of course it's only one year. Back then, she felt she was so mature, so grown-up and ready for a new life. Full of hope and expectation, too. The future would surely bring something huge. If only she had known how her wishes were to be met she would definitely have taken it all back.

Minoo pushes her way into the dense crowd in the entrance lobby. She catches sight of one of the senior boys who is pinning up a large poster on the bulletin board.

He turns, spots her and smiles radiantly. He has dark hair, wears steel-rimmed glasses. Minoo searches her memory feverishly for his name. Rickard, maybe. One of the soccer guys in Engelsfors FC.

'You don't want to miss this!' he says.

This is the first thing he has ever said to her. He doesn't wait for a reply, just disappears into the crowd. Minoo looks at the poster. Under the large, red letters forming the word 'COMMUNITY', a group of young people are lined up in a summer meadow. Their arms are around each other's shoulders and they are all laughing, bursting with self-assurance in their out-of-date clothes and fluffy hairdos. Mouths full of gleaming white teeth. Cutely wrinkled noses. Some of them even do thumbs-up.

'BECOME PART OF POSITIVE ENGELSFORS!' the caption under the jaunty team shouts in block capitals.

Whatever, Minoo is definitely skipping this.

There is a small photo at the bottom of the poster showing a smiling, middle-aged woman with curly, carrot-colored hair.

It takes a second before Minoo makes the connection. The woman is Helena Malmgren. Elias's mother.

Elias.

She feels herself breaking out in a cold sweat, despite the heat. Memories of what happened in this school last year rush back at her.

The blood on the floor of the bathroom. Elias, his dead eyes staring at the ceiling.

His soul when she freed him from Max.

Already, it is too much for her. But then, Max's memories begin to infiltrate hers until she can hardly keep anything apart. She'll never be able to rid herself of what she has seen in Max's consciousness.

Minoo forces herself back to the present.

She follows the hallway leading to the janitor's office and knocks on the door. It takes a little while and then Nicolaus cautiously opens the door and puts his head around it. He is wearing a mustard-yellow shirt and brown corduroy pants. Minoo has a vivid idea of what Ida would say about his outfit.

'Come in,' he says.

She follows him into his small office and closes the door behind her. The stale air smells of dust. The *Book of Patterns* is open on the desk and the silvery Pattern Finder is placed neatly next to it.

'I very much regret my behavior last night,' Nicolaus says. 'I was excessively brusque. Still, I stand by my view. You must not dig up that grave, under any circumstances.'

There are dark rings under his eyes, but his gaze is steady as he looks at Minoo. As if he already knew that the others have sent her on a mission to persuade him to agree to Project Grave Opening. She grasps at once that it is pointless to try.

'Did you find anything?' she asks instead and nods towards the *Book of Patterns*.

Nicolaus shakes his head.

'It remains silent.'

'Do you think the book might be damaged in some way?' Minoo asks. 'What I mean is, Linnéa and Ida haven't seen anything new since the winter. And it wasn't as if it worked all that well before then.'

'I don't know whether it is the book that is flawed or our capacity for interpreting its messages,' Nicolaus says, twirling the Pattern Finder. 'Sometimes, I feel that it is trying to reach me. It could be that I was once able to read it, but if so, I have lost that skill now.'

He looks up.

'Which reminds me…have you arrived at any new insights into your own gifts?'

We belong together.

'No. But I dreamed about Max again,' Minoo says.

'What happened in your dream?'

Minoo thinks about the vision of her mom and dad in bed. It had seemed so real. She doesn't want to talk about it.

'Just the usual. I lost the fight. He said that we belonged together and that my powers are not for good.'

'Your powers are not *good*,' Nicolaus explains patiently. 'Nor are Anna-Karin's. Nor Linnéa's. Nor are Vanessa's and Ida's. What matters is how you use them.'

'But my powers aren't like any of theirs. I have no element. My magic takes the shape of black smoke, just like

Max's demonic magic. It seems I'm the only one who can see it. Besides, I can't understand how the power to suck the souls from people's bodies and root around in their memories can *ever* be good. Especially since Max said the demons had a plan for me.'

'That's what the demons told him, of course,' Nicolaus says. 'They may well be peddling untruths. They're demons, after all. Did you see any details of this alleged plan when you had access to Max's memories?'

'No, but then, I didn't see everything in his memory. Maybe, if I had been looking for...'

'Exactly so!' Nicolaus responds. 'You must explore your powers so that you become able to use them constructively.'

'No,' Minoo says in a firm tone, because she knows already what Nicolaus is going to say next.

'Minoo, you must,' he pleads. 'I know that my memories exist somewhere, but out of my reach. You could help me disperse the thick mists of forgetfulness.'

'So you end up in a coma, too?'

'You broke the demons' blessing of Max and I believe this was the actual cause of—'

'I will not experiment with your life,' Minoo interrupts.

Nicolaus sighs deeply. This summer, they have been through this discussion several times and Minoo senses that they are both equally frustrated. She decides to change the subject.

'There is one thing I've been wondering about. Why can't Cat tell you why that grave is so important? It is your familiar after all. How can it know things about you that you don't know yourself? I mean, first the bank deposit box and now this.'

'I so wish I knew,' Nicolaus says and pulls his fingers through his hair. 'Don't misunderstand me. I do believe that the gravestone is significant. Otherwise, Cat would not have led the way for Linnéa Wallin. But, no, to start digging in consecrated ground...'

He stops and lowers his voice.

'I don't know what is concealed in that grave. But please promise me not to interfere with it. *Promise.*'

Minoo can't make herself say the words needed for a lie. Instead, she nods quickly and leaves, hurrying back down the corridor.

When Minoo returns to the hall, she sees Linnéa, who stands in front of the bulletinboard and examines the 'COMMUNITY' poster. She is wearing a black dress with puff sleeves and a long necklace that looks like barbed wire.

Minoo goes to look at the poster over Linnéa's shoulder.

'Have you heard anything about this?' Minoo asks.

'No. But "Positive Engelsfors" sounds so typically Helena,' Linnéa says and points with a bright green nail at the picture of Elias's mother. 'That's how she was going on all the time. Like, you know, "Pull yourself together" and "When a door closes a window opens". Or "Look on the bright side of life". People with real problems unnerved her completely.'

'People like...Elias?' Minoo suggests cautiously.

Linnéa nods.

'People like Elias.'

'Strange that she decided to become a minister.'

'I don't know if you've noticed, but most people are so fucking strange,' Linnéa says.

Adriana Lopez is on her way down the stairs. She is moving quickly and passes them. She looks like her usual composed self as she hurries towards the assembly hall where she'll soon be welcoming the new students to the high school.

'We're supposed to meet in the fairground this Saturday and start the lessons again,' Minoo says.

Linnéa rolls her eyes skywards.

'Oh, yeah. Great. We'll be allowed to start on "defensive magic" at last.'

'Not sure,' Minoo says. 'She seemed like she was up to something. Talked about how there would be changes.'

'Whatever. The magic lessons could hardly get *more* pointless. Have you talked with Nicolaus, by the way?'

'Yes, I have. He'll never agree to do it.'

'He's scared. He doesn't know what's in the grave but he's afraid of what we might find,' Linnéa says and then adds quickly: 'It isn't as if I read his mind on purpose...but sometimes I'm not quite in control.'

Minoo looks into the other girl's dark eyes. She feels ill at ease, as always when Linnéa's capacity for mind-reading is mentioned. She can still recall painful moments when Linnéa must have known what Minoo thought.

'But we have no choice,' Linnéa continues. 'We'll have to do it without telling Nicolaus.'

As Vanessa steps inside the classroom, she looks around for Evelina and Michelle. They haven't turned up yet. It makes her unreasonably irritated. After all, they don't know that she's just about to boil over and simply has to talk to them about what she saw last night.

When she left for school this morning, Nicke still hadn't come home. Vanessa couldn't bear meeting Mom's eyes across the breakfast table. Part of her wanted to shout out what she had witnessed. This was her chance to get rid of him. At last. But there was another part of her, a side of herself she hardly recognized, that made Vanessa hold her tongue. That part of herself could not endure the thought of her mother's grief.

Vanessa collapses on a seat at the very back. Just then,

Evelina and Michelle, clinging theatrically onto each other, make an entrance into the classroom.

They sit down on either side of Vanessa. Evelina draws a deep sigh.

'Christ, I'm exhausted. Didn't sleep last night.'

'Her parents have been on the phone again, talking to each other,' Michelle explains.

'I thought the whole point of divorce was that people didn't have to fight each other all night long any more,' Evelina says.

Evelina's parents divorced several years ago. Since then, she has been living with her mom. Her dad is a long-distance trucker and hardly ever back in Engelsfors. Which doesn't stop him phoning up from all over Europe to voice his opinions about how Evelina's mom is bringing up his daughter.

'Are you all right now?' Vanessa asks.

Once more, Evelina sighs from the bottom of an abyss.

'Must it take, like, a hundred years before we're supposed to be real adults?'

'We should live together, the three of us,' Michelle says. 'As soon as we're eighteen. Do you realize what a good time we'd have!'

'You wouldn't have to put up with Nicke,' Evelina adds.

'But I might get rid of him anyway,' Vanessa replies.

'What's that?' Michelle asks. 'What do you mean?'

Vanessa observes the curiosity in her friends' faces.

They will say that she must tell Mom. And even though they would realize that her mom would be very upset, they wouldn't see any other problems with the tell-Mom scenario. Like the fact that Vanessa could be the messenger everyone wants to shoot. Besides, Mom might not even believe her.

There is an alternative, Vanessa thinks. Tell Nicke instead. Force him to admit all of it to Mom.

That seems to her to be the best option. But she hasn't slept all night and doesn't trust her judgment in the slightest.

She looks at Michelle and Evelina. She loves them but can't talk to them about this.

'What are you talking about?' Michelle asks again and twists a dark wavy strand of hair between her fingers.

'Nothing, really,' Vanessa replies. 'Just wishful thinking.'

CHAPTER 8

Linnéa manages to slip inside the classroom just before Petter Backman comes plodding along and closes the door behind him. She can sense him ogling her from behind her back and wishes she could shake off his sleazy eyes.

As soon as she had received her power, the art lessons became almost more than she could stand. Backman has always had a reputation for putting his arm around female students, rubbing up against them in a creepy way, but Linnéa has never actually caught him at it. He's presumably too smart. But when he's sitting at the teacher's desk or patrolling the art room, he allows his mind free rein instead, with very detailed fantasies.

Olivia is sitting at the back, doodling on her sketchpad. Linnéa goes over to sit next to her. Might as well get this out of the way.

'Where the fuck were you yesterday?' Olivia whispers. 'Why didn't you text me back?'

Her blue hair looks like radioactive spun sugar. Her heavily made-up face is paler than ever. Sweat has formed tiny runnels in the powder.

'I forgot,' Linnéa says.

'Not answering is so mean.'

'But you've hardly been in touch all summer.'

'Can I help it that my parents force me to stay in the

country the entire freaking summer?' Olivia looks hurt as she stares at Linnéa with big brown eyes that would look perfect in a Manga figure's face. Linnéa can't be bothered to say that she knows Olivia is lying. She has been spotted several times in the center of town. Blue-haired girls aren't that common in Engelsfors.

'You went to Elias yesterday, didn't you?' Olivia asks.

'Yes.'

Olivia carries on doodling in her sketchbook. Always the same kind of picture. A girl with huge eyes weeping black tears.

'You might've called,' she says quietly. 'I was a good friend of his, too. I've been so anguished about having to go back to school. Like, it happened here.'

Linnéa notes the irony of having to carry on avoiding Olivia in order to be alone with Elias, even after his death.

The three of them got to know each other at the same time. They belonged to the same group and went to the same parties. Linnéa and Elias had been spontaneously attracted to each other, as if their friendship was predestined. But Olivia clung to them, shadowed them like a tiresome little sister who tries to be like her older siblings. And who is so eager to do the right thing that she always comes across as slightly off-key, slightly embarrassing.

If Elias talked about a band he had just found out about, Olivia would turn up in school the next day with its name inscribed on her arm in black ink, claiming that she had been listening to that band *like forever*.

It was so easy to see through Olivia that Linnéa in the end stopped minding about her. Except that it still maddens her when Olivia chatters about her 'anguish' and her 'problems', like they're cool accessories. In fact, her background is a Brady Bunch-style idyll. Mom, Dad and her two older brothers have all treated her as their sweet baby, the favorite, the little princess.

There are moments when Linnéa feels that Olivia uses Elias and his alleged suicide to boost her status. As if the connection with him made *her* more authentic.

But at other times, like now, this line of thought gives Linnéa a guilty conscience. Olivia is the only one of the old crew who still keeps in touch with Linnéa, now that she has stopped partying. And they do have fun together now and then, although right now Linnéa can't recall the last time.

The chains on Olivia's tank top are tinkling as she bends to get closer to Linnéa.

'I don't want us to fight.'

'We haven't.'

'Good. You see, there's something I want to tell you. I met your dad last Saturday, in Västerås.'

Linnéa stiffens.

'And do you know what he said?' Olivia goes on.

'I don't want to know.'

'You've got to listen to this, honestly. It's good news.'

'Nothing to do with my dad is ever good news.'

'He's sober now.'

Linnéa's eyes are fixed on the desktop, where someone has carved *EFC Rulez.*

'He told me and I really believe him,' Olivia continues. 'He didn't smell like alcohol or anything like that. And he looked kind of *neat.*'

I can't bear this again, Linnéa thinks. Not again.

'Look, what's *wrong* with you?' Olivia whispers and now she sounds upset again. 'I thought you'd be *happy.*'

*

Part One

Last autumn, Minoo had been keeping the place next to her free for just one, special person. For Rebecka.

Now, the place next to Minoo is empty.

It is true that they had been friends for just a very short time, but that wasn't how it felt. Did Minoo care so much for Rebecka because of the bond between the Chosen Ones? Or was it because Rebecka was the first real friend Minoo had ever had?

Ylva, the new teacher, is checking attendance.

'Minoo Falk Karimi?' Ylva asks.

Minoo puts her hand up and her name is ticked off.

Ylva is in her thirties. She has thin, blonde hair, round glasses and all the charisma of a cheese sandwich.

Minoo suddenly realizes that she misses Max. Just for a moment. And not Max the killer, but Max the teacher.

Now, he lies immobile in a hospital bed, just a few miles away but still unreachable. No one knows if he will ever come out of his coma.

Ylva finishes the register and instead starts to scare them systematically with tales of all the hard work they will have to do this year.

Minoo loses herself in memories again. In memories of Max. This time she doesn't fight them. She looks for clues that she might have missed, but soon she can't control the direction of her thoughts. Her memories lead their own lives. And suddenly she is there. She sees Alice, Max's first girlfriend, in her room. Alice, who is so like Minoo.

'Please, Max, go away,' she is saying. 'Didn't you hear what I said? I never want to see you again.'

Minoo senses anger welling up inside Max. He wants Alice dead. He wants it passionately. And it is in this moment that his powers are aroused. He makes her climb up and stand on the windowsill, then makes her jump. The intoxicating feeling of power that fills Max also rushes into Minoo's mind, although she only wants to scream.

Minoo grips the edge of the desk. The floor seems to be swaying under her feet. She closes her eyes, breathes deeply a couple of times until the world comes to rest around her again.

When she looks up, he is standing at the teacher's desk. She knows him. He's the guy from the manor house.

'I'm sorry I'm late,' he says and smiles towards Ylva.

'That's all right just this once. Since you're new to the school.'

She tries to look strict, but can't hide a little smile. And she is blushing.

'Class, this is Viktor Ehrenskiöld. He has just moved to this area and I hope you'll all do your best to make him feel at home,' Ylva says and then turns to Viktor. 'Just find a spare place, please, and settle down.'

Viktor looks straight at Minoo. Despite the heat, he is wearing slacks, a shirt and a thin blue cardigan. Its color enhances his eyes, makes them glow with an almost unreal, intense blue. Cornflower blue. He nods to Ylva, then goes and sits down next to Minoo.

'I'll take this opportunity to remind you that the places you have chosen today will be yours for the rest of the term. At least during my lessons,' Ylva says.

Kevin protests from the far end of the classroom.

'Hey, miss! Is this effing kindergarten, or what? I don't want to sit *here* all term!'

Levan, who is sitting next to Kevin, fiddles with his glasses but doesn't say anything.

'Well, we've all got our crosses to bear,' Ylva says absently, as she skims through some papers in front of her. 'But if not, how am I going to learn your names? Answer me that, eh...Kevin?'

Viktor opens his brown leather satchel and lines up notebook, mechanical pencil and eraser on the desktop. Shifts the eraser along a few millimeters. Fascinated, Minoo observes him out of the corner of an eye.

Even at close proximity he might have come straight out of an advertisement. He is fully dressed but shows not the slightest sign of sweating. He doesn't even smell. Not of sweat, not of perfume, nothing. As if there were no human body inside his clothes. Minoo suddenly feels acutely aware of being moist and sticky all over.

Viktor, finally satisfied with his little desktop arrangement, turns to her.

'It seems like we'll have to put up with each other for a while,' he says.

There might have been a hint of a smile around the corners of his mouth, but the impression fades so quickly she thinks it must have been her imagination. Then Viktor turns to Ylva once more and seems to pay attention

The bell rings for the break. Anna-Karin sees Minoo rise and hurries to catch up with her.

'Do you have time to talk?' Anna-Karin asks quietly.

Minoo nods and glances meaningfully towards the staircase up to the top floor.

They start walking without looking at each other, pretending not to be going to the same place. It is hard to get rid of last year's fear that they might give themselves away to the demons.

Anna-Karin sneaks a sideways glance at Minoo. She asks herself if they are friends now, after all they have been through together, all they have been made to reveal to each other. Or is it simply fate that has forced them into each other's company? Made them some kind of…allies in the struggle against the apocalypse?

New messages have been scribbled all over the door to the bathroom. Students still make a pilgrimage to this place in order to write messages for Elias and Rebecka, or just to make some general point by leaving their marks. But the bathroom is hardly ever used. Rumor has it that the place is haunted.

As Anna-Karin opens the door, her eye is caught by a couple of lines written in round letters.

DON'T WORRY!

BE HAPPY! ☺

Anna-Karin steps inside and checks the cubicles.

'No one here,' she says. 'Except us, that is.'

Her voice echoes against the tiled walls. Minoo doesn't reply. She stands silently, looking at the window. Then at the sinks. Along the wall where the mirrors used to be. The screw-holes in the tiles are still there.

'How are things?' Anna-Karin asks.

'All right. It just feels strange to be here. What did you want to talk about?' she says, fixing her eyes on Anna-Karin.

It's her laser-beam gaze that looks capable of cutting through stone and steel. Anna-Karin clears her throat.

'The forest,' she manages to say. 'It's dying.'

Minoo looks confused.

'But not because of the drought,' Anna-Karin continues. 'Something else is going on. Something is wrong.'

'What do you mean?'

Anna-Karin feels frustrated. She wants to make Minoo understand. But how to go about it, since she herself hardly understands? She starts over again.

'Something is going wrong with the forest and it might have to do with the dry hot weather, of course. But what if it is the other way around? What I'm trying to say is, could it be that the bad things happening to the forest are also causing the drought?'

Anna-Karin tries to interpret the look on Minoo's face. Pitying? Thoughtful? Irritated?

'All I thought was...well, that it might be worth thinking about,' Anna-Karin says. 'You know how everyone is talking about the unnatural heat...what if it really *is* unnatural? Like, supernatural?'

She shrugs, looks away. Regrets that she started on all this.

'Forget it,' she says.

'No, don't say that, it's fine,' Minoo replies. 'We know nothing about what the demons are planning. We must be alert to everything.'

Anna-Karin wonders if she says this only to make the situation less embarrassing for them both.

'Have you talked to Nicolaus?' she asks.

Minoo nods.

'We'll have to go ahead without him. Even though it feels all wrong.'

A small chilly lump begins to wriggle in Anna-Karin's belly.

'He'll surely understand that we have to,' she says. 'That we're doing it for his sake as well.'

'I hope so,' Minoo says. 'Besides, maybe we won't find a thing. And then he doesn't need to know. Our best option now is to take one step at a time and not plan ages ahead.'

It sounds very much as if she's trying to convince herself and Anna-Karin realizes that Minoo cares as much for Nicolaus as she does. They have that in common, at least, and it is a good feeling.

CHAPTER 9

Ida looks up at the school clock.

She almost hopes that Erik won't turn up. If he doesn't, she'll cycle to the stables right away. She longs to be with Troja. Longs to hear him neigh when she steps into his box. Longs to go riding on him in the forest, losing herself in their shared rhythm.

'I'll give Erik exactly three minutes. Then I'm off,' she says.

'It's good that you're so strict with him,' Felicia replies.

'However else would he learn to behave?'

Felicia giggles in agreement. As if she knew the score about how to manage a boyfriend, even though she has never had one. Ida gives her sunglasses a push – they keep slipping down the sweaty ridge of her nose. Checks her phone again. No sign of life. And now the stream of students on their way out of school is thinning.

'Don't feel you have to wait with me,' Ida says.

'No problem,' Felicia replies, then tugs at the shoulder strap on her bra.

Of course it's no problem, Ida thinks. Felicia would wait however long it takes just to make sure she could breathe the same air as Robin for a few seconds.

'Listen, you've got to let go of this thing about Robin,' Ida tells her. 'Or at least do something about it. Like I did about Erik.'

Which isn't entirely true. When Erik kissed her at Hanna H's spring party, Ida had simply let him. Just as she let him hold her hand in school the next day and let him announce a week later that they were going out together. The thing was, she couldn't bear to wait around any longer. And she hoped that Erik could make her stop yearning for the person she really wanted.

'But maybe I'm not as brave as you are,' Felicia answers.

The front door of the school is thrown open. Ida feels the familiar small tug at her heartstrings when he steps outside into the sunshine.

G.

A huge wave of tiredness floods through her. Why won't it ever pass? Why doesn't her body stop reacting like this every time she sees Gustaf?

Then, a couple of paces behind him, Minoo. As she walks down the front steps, her black curls bounce around her head.

'Do you think what Julia said is true? You know, that they were making out down by the docks?' Felicia whispers.

'Oh, come on,' Ida snaps. 'Why would G make out with someone like Minoo?'

If only she were as sure as she pretends to be.

Ida tries to interpret the body language between Minoo and Gustaf. Aren't they walking closer to each other than they need to?

When Gustaf started going out with Rebecka last summer, she was devastated. And now, he's with Minoo? Seriously?

Ida has felt like this about Gustaf ever since elementary school. Now, her only comfort is that she hasn't told anyone. No one except Troja, that is. But not Julia or Felicia. Not even Mom. The rule is never to admit to wanting something until you're a hundred percent certain you can have it.

'I'm off now,' she says.

'Sure you shouldn't wait just a little longer?'

Ida's only reply is a snort. She bends to pick up her bag and her sunglasses slip off her nose. They hit the asphalt with a plasticky tinkle. She'd happily stomp on them.

'Oh, look, there's Erik,' Felicia says.

The disappointment in her voice is palpable. In other words, Erik is alone. Ida doesn't turn to look. She picks the glasses up, puts them on, then pretends to look for something in her bag. When Erik reaches them and tries to kiss her cheek, she twists her head away.

'You're late,' she says.

'Sorry.'

'No point in saying sorry, just stop being late all the time.'

'Kevin was doing this totally insane thing, we—'

Ida cuts him short.

'Forget it. Not interested.'

Ida turns to Felicia, who won't meet her eyes.

'We'll be in touch tonight.'

Felicia hesitates for another second.

'It won't do you any good to hang out here, Robin won't come,' Ida says.

Felicia forces her face into a surprised smile, as if ready to deny that she had thought of Robin at all. But she doesn't dare challenge Ida, so she retreats with a little laugh and a quick hug. And almost runs away across the schoolyard.

'What was all that about?' Erik asks.

'What was what?'

'All that about Robin?'

Now, at last, Ida looks at him.

'Don't say you haven't noticed that she obsesses about Robin all the time? Christ, she's so embarrassing!'

'Is she *in love* with him?'

'Can't we talk about something else? I want an ice cream before I go to the stables.'

'Noooo, not again,' Erik groans. 'Can't you forget about the fucking stables just for once? You're too old to keep on cuddling your horse.'

Ida has given up trying to explain to Erik that going to the stables isn't about being cuddly. It is a tough place and the work can be heavy and exhausting. Dangerous, even. At least as dangerous as his ice hockey. And she loves it.

'He's not even your horse,' Erik says.

'I'm joint rider. So I'm *responsible* for him.'

'I'd planned that we'd go to my place for a while. We'd have an hour before my parents come home.'

She hates the whining note in his voice. She's positive G would never sound like that.

'Really? Whatever you thought is hardly my problem. I never promised anything.'

Erik groans again. Ida picks up her bag and they start walking towards the bicycle racks. In silence. She has no intention of speaking first.

They unlock their bikes. Glancing his way, Ida realizes that Erik is looking at her. He is about to give in.

'Robin likes Felicia, too,' he says.

This is his little peace pipe, his way of saying that a possible fight is now behind them.

Ida fumbles for the silver heart on a chain that is always around her neck and starts twisting the chain around her fingers.

'No way,' she says. 'He hardly even looks at her. Last time we went to the lake he seemed fixated on Vanessa Dahl. Like *certain* other people.'

She can't be sure whether Erik hasn't noticed the edge in her voice, or just pretends he hasn't.

'You know what Robin is like. He has to be tanked up before he'll even talk to a girl...shit, I've got to tell him.'

He starts rooting around for his phone, but Ida puts her hand on his arm. She's got to buy some time. Work out what the consequences might be.

'Don't, not yet,' she says. 'Promise not to. I'd better talk to Felicia first.'

Ida is soaked in sweat after the ride through the forest. She brushes Troja and cleans out his hooves before taking him back into his box. Then she puts her cheek to his muzzle and strokes his neck.

'Aren't you the best horse in the world?' she whispers. 'And you love me, too, don't you?'

She blows gently into one of his nostrils and gets a warm gust against her face in response.

Sometimes, her love for him is so strong she is close to tears. They're the same age, she and Troja. It's so strange to imagine that he's well past middle age while she's still young.

'You mustn't die, not ever,' she whispers.

He buffets her belly with his muzzle.

While she changes afterwards, she becomes conscious of the world outside the stables. Perhaps she will never have to see Troja die. Tonight she will be in the cemetery and helping dig up a grave. And then they're supposed to prevent an apocalypse as well. Troja's chance of reaching twenty-five is better than hers.

She leaves the stables. One of the annoying little girls who usually hang around Troja is staring at her. Ida shoots her an icy glance.

She gets her phone out and scrolls down to find Felicia's number.

Felicia has always specialized in being unlucky in love. As far as Ida knows, this is the first time her feelings have been reciprocated.

Felicia and Julia have been her best friends for as long as she can remember. Sometimes she wonders if they would even be friends if they hadn't grown up in the same neighborhood and if their mothers hadn't been friends. Sometimes, she isn't even sure that she *likes* Julia and Felicia. Still, she knows one thing: she never again wants to feel as lonely as she did last autumn, when Anna-Karin stole them from her.

If Felicia starts going out with Robin, Ida's world will become unbalanced. She has fought long and hard to make it perfect. She has no intention of taking any risks with it now.

She puts her phone back in the bag.

CHAPTER 10

Vanessa has settled in Wille's mom's living room and is pushing the controller to the limit, slaughtering enemy soldiers as they rush at her on the TV screen.

She let herself in with the key she has kept since she stayed here last winter. Wille promised to be home when she finished school, but she has waited for hours by now. His phone is in his room. She heard it when she tried to call him.

Vanessa selects the flame-thrower and pretends that the soldier she aims it at is Nicke.

The secret has swelled inside her all day. By now, it feels fit to burst any minute.

She *must* talk to somebody. And Wille is her only option.

When she hears the key in the lock, she leaps up from the leather sofa and runs into the hall. Wille looks surprised to see her.

'Oh, Nessa...shit, I forgot...'

'It doesn't matter,' she says quickly. She is angry, but her need to talk is more urgent. 'Listen. We've got to talk.'

'All right if I get a glass of water first?'

'No!'

Wille looks scared. He kicks off his sandals and follows her into the living room.

She turns the TV off and they sit down on the sofa together.

'Nessa, what's up?' he says. 'What's happened?'

Suddenly she can't say a word, even though she tries. Wille's eyes widen.

'What's happened?' he says again.

She just shakes her head. He puts his arms around her and she leans her head against his chest.

'Nessa...' he says. 'You've got to talk to me. What's the matter? I'm getting worried.'

And she explodes. Her head is a mushroom cloud, a mass of snot and tears. She sobs so hard she becomes breathless. This is crying of the kind that makes your whole body hurt. And yet it is such a wonderful release. Wille strokes her hair, pats her back. It's enough just that he's there for her.

Then it's all over. The weeping ceases as suddenly as it began. Vanessa feels utterly empty, drained of both tears and energy. She quickly dries her eyes and straightens up.

Wille still looks quite terrified. He must think that she's crazy. Perhaps he's right.

'Is it something someone's said?' he asks.

'Something someone's said?'

Vanessa wipes her eyes and cheeks again. Her fingers go black with mascara, diluted with tears. Snot clogs her palate. She clears her throat.

'No, but I saw something...' she begins.

Wille suddenly gets up, walks to the kitchen and comes back with his mom's cigarettes and an ashtray. He hardly ever smokes ordinary cigarettes, only sometimes, at parties. His hands are shaking a little as he sits down again and lights one of Sirpa's menthol cigarettes.

'I really wish I hadn't seen it,' she says. 'I so wish I'd just fucked off.'

He inhales without looking at her.

'I saw Nicke,' she explains. 'With a...some female. They were having...like, she was...'

Talking about sex normally is no problem at all for Vanessa, but the combination of sex and Nicke feels totally different.

'He was unfaithful,' she finally said.

'Oh, Christ,' Wille says. 'And you *saw* it?'

'I saw enough to be certain. They were going at it when I got there.'

Vanessa shudders, remembering the smirk on Nicke's face as he sat back in the driver's seat.

'It's such a fucking awful thing to do,' she continues. 'Why bother about a relationship if you want to get with other people? I mean, why not be honest about it? Why do people have to lie?'

Wille mumbles in agreement.

'It probably isn't the first time, either. Mom's rotten luck with guys strikes again. And then *she* tries to tell *me* who I should go out with. Imagine her meeting someone who is the tiniest fraction as good for her as you are for me. Like, in her dreams.'

Wille nods. He is turning his engagement ring around and around.

'I don't know what to do,' Vanessa says. 'I'm not even sure what Mom would believe if I told her…And *if* she'd believed me…You've never seen her the way she is when one of her men walks out on her and I can't help worrying about Melvin…But on the other hand, I can't just shut up about something like this. Or, can I? What I can't bear is the thought of having to see that swine every day if I…'

Her flow of words stops. Wille is crying.

'Oh, Christ…Nessa,' he moans. 'Fuck it…I've done something so totally fucking stupid.'

He hides his face in his hands. Vanessa's heart is racing.

'Wille, what have you done?'

Thump-thump-thump inside her ribcage.

'I don't deserve you!'

'What have you done?' she repeats.

'I've been with someone else.'

His hands muffle his words but they cut right through her all the same. They slice her world into strips.

And then it stops hurting. As if emotional overload has blown a fuse. She feels numb. As if none of this has anything to do with her, as if it concerns another Vanessa. It is a good feeling.

Wille is howling now.

'I've been so scared you'd find out. I thought that was what had happened now, when you were so upset. You have no idea how awful I've been feeling!'

He lowers his hands. His face is bright red.

'Why are you telling me this?' she asks.

Because, so far as she has any feelings left, she feels that she didn't want to know this.

'I just wanted to be honest.'

'Honest? It would've been more honest not to screw someone behind my back, don't you think?'

'Yes, it would.' Wille's voice is thick with sobbing. 'But ask me anything you want to know now. I'll answer.'

'Was it just once?'

When Wille hesitates, she has her answer.

'How many times?'

'Twice. Just twice. Once last winter. Just when you'd moved out from here,' Wille says. 'The second time was last Saturday.'

'When you went to Götis?'

He nods.

Suddenly everything seems so obvious she cannot think how she has failed to see it.

'Was it the same chick both times?'

'I'll never see her again,' Wille assures her. 'I promise. If she calls, I won't even answer.'

'What? You gave her your number?'

'I was drunk. It meant nothing.'

'Why do it twice, then?'

Vanessa stands. Her legs are wobbly, but she must get out of here. Now.

'Please forgive me, Nessa. Please don't go.'

'There's only one more thing I want to know.'

'Anything,' he says and stands, too. Starts coming closer.

She backs away, out into the hall.

'What's her name?'

Don't say Linnéa, she thinks. Not Linnéa, not Linnéa.

'Elin,' Wille tells her. 'She's older than us. You don't know her.'

She stays silent, just nods. Feeling almost absurdly relieved.

'Nessa...'

She pulls the ring off her finger and wonders what she should do with it. Throw it at him, like someone in a B-movie?

'I'll do anything if only you'll forgive me,' he sobs.

She lets the ring fall. It rolls across the floor and disappears in under the chest of drawers in the hall.

And then she leaves.

The sun has almost set. The sky above the Holmström family home is a cascade, a cloudburst in pink and violet.

'Fuckingstupidassmachine!'

Ida's father kicks the lawnmower. It stands mute and immobile in the middle of the lawn.

'Hi, Dad,' Ida says as she pushes her bike into the garage.

'Hello there,' her father says wearily and bends over the mower. 'How was school?'

'The usual,' Ida replies.

Her father hums absent-mindedly as he starts poking about in the mushy grass that is sticking to the cutting blades.

Suddenly, Ida has a vision of the engine starting and blood spurting all over the lawn as her father's hands are ground to mincemeat.

She closes her eyes, opens them again. Her father is still crouching by the machine, muttering threats. There is an elongated sweaty patch on the back of his shirt.

It was just a fantasy. A sick quirk of her mind. Or was it? So far, Ida has only seen into the past and never had any visions of the future. So far.

She lets the bike fall to the garage floor and runs straight upstairs to her room to unlock the old hope chest at the foot of her bed. That's where she keeps the *Book of Patterns* and the Pattern Finder.

Lying on her front on the carpet, she opens the book and focuses with her eye pressed close up to the gleaming silver loupe. Twists the segments.

Was that a real vision I just had? Showing the future? Will that thing with Dad and the mower come about?

The signs on the page tremble. Some become fluid and look like ink spreading in water. Others develop sharper outlines, form a pattern. Once Ida learned to interpret the book, she felt that she had access to an utterly new alphabet, forming new words with new meanings. She doesn't receive messages as strings of words. They arrive directly into her brain. Sometimes they are completely incomprehensible.

This time, the book's answer is perfectly clear.

No.

A huge wave of relief. Ida is just about to shut the book when the signs tremble again.

The future is uncertain.

Ida's forehead wrinkles as she concentrates on the open page.

What does that mean? she asks herself. *That nothing is certain? Isn't it certain that the apocalypse will come?*

The book takes its time to formulate the answer.

The final battle will take place.

After that, it becomes vague. Fragments of information materialize in Ida's consciousness and she tries to fit them together. Something about possible choices of road. Greater or lesser probabilities.

She leafs onwards and twists the Pattern Finder. Concentrates on her next question.

So, there are several possible futures?

The book replies almost instantly.

Yes.

And then:

No.

Hey, make up your mind, Ida thinks before she can stop herself.

The signs dissolve, run into each other and turn into an unreadable mess. She worries that she has angered the book and focuses again, as hard as she can.

If there are different futures…will I be together with G in one of them?

The book is still. And then the signs move again.

You are special, Ida. Do not forget our agreement. You must collaborate with the Circle until the last battle has been fought. Then you will get your reward. Keep your promise to me, and I will keep mine to you.

Ida sighs.

She has told the others that she can no longer see anything in the *Book of Patterns*. And, strictly speaking, she hasn't.

At least, nothing that the others need to know. Nothing that might help them.

Ever since she learned to read the book it has made her the same promise: she *will* be relieved of her powers and all that has to do with the Chosen Ones. She only has to put up with everything until they have stopped the apocalypse.

Darkness has fallen by the time Vanessa reaches the apartment block. She wonders if Linnéa is at home and looks up at the windows on the top floor.

She has been walking through Engelsfors, still in the grip of that unreal feeling. The town is like a large movie set and the few people she encounters are extras.

A few hours to go and then they are to meet in the cemetery again. Vanessa has played another one of her alibi cards and told her mother that she is sleeping over at Michelle's.

Suddenly, a red light comes on in a window on the seventh floor and Vanessa knows that Linnéa is there. She might have seen her from above. Listened in on her thoughts, perhaps? Sensed that it was Vanessa down there?

There is nothing Vanessa wants more than a chance to forgive Linnéa. She longs for this so much it hurts. Linnéa is the only one in the whole world to whom she doesn't need to lie.

A wind rushes along the street. It stirs up dust that starts whirling around Vanessa. Small grains of gravel roll across the pavement at her feet. She glances at the shrubs between the apartments. They are quite still.

The wind blows only around Vanessa. She gets goosebumps when she feels it wafting across her skin, playing with her hair. It feels the way it does when she becomes invisible, but this sensation is stronger.

Fire

The wind blows only for a few more moments and then it dies down.

Vanessa walks away, after looking up at Linnéa's window once more.

CHAPTER 11

Minoo can't figure out which is worse. Is it when her mom and dad are screaming at each other, or the moments just before they start? Suppressed irritation is simmering inside every sentence. One word, one look can be the spark that ignites the blaze.

There was a time when she looked forward to their meals together. These days, she is relieved every time Mom is on the night shift at the hospital or Dad works overtime. Dinner with the two of them is just about as nice and relaxing as a picnic in the trenches.

'This damned heat,' Dad says and wipes his forehead with the napkin. 'Pass me the salt, Minoo, please.'

Mechanically, she hands him the salt mill. No need to look at Mom to realize that her face registers disapproval. And no need to look at Dad to know that he replies with a glance that says it's his decision, no one else's. He seems to twist the salt mill a few extra turns to underline that he won't be bossed around. The silence at the table is so total that the mill sounds like a stone crusher.

White flakes scatter over the fish and the potatoes. Her father will be fifty-four soon. Minoo's paternal grandfather died from a heart attack at just that age.

Minoo prods the dry piece of salmon with her fork and hopes that Mom won't say anything about the salt or the fact that Dad hasn't put any of the vegetables on his plate.

'How was your first day back at school?' Mom asks.

'Fine. We've got a new homeroom teacher, Ylva, who seems pretty boring. We'll have her in math and physics.'

'She can't measure up to Max, can she? Teachers like him don't come along often.'

Mom looks understanding, but understands nothing. Minoo drinks water, several mouthfuls to wash the salmon down.

'Such a sad business,' Mom continues. 'He must have been lying there, what is it – half a year? Or even longer...'

'Could we please talk about something else?' Minoo says.

'Yes, you leave her be. Minoo doesn't want to think about all that,' Dad says.

'Of course I will,' Mom replies softly, but her glance in Dad's direction is razor-sharp. 'All I meant was that I understand how hard it must be for Ylva to be compared with a teacher Minoo liked so much. And unlike you, Erik, I must say I think it's important to talk about difficult subjects once in a while.'

'And there's a new guy in the class as well,' Minoo says before Dad has time to respond. 'Viktor Ehrenskiöld. He's from Stockholm.'

'Ehrenskiöld, now. That's the name of the people who bought the manor house,' Dad says.

As editor of the *Engelsfors Herald*, Minoo's father finds out about everything that happens in the town, every squabble between neighbors and every item of expenditure, however small, in the local government budget.

'Do you know anything about them?' Minoo asks.

'Father and son. Ehrenskiöld senior is a day trader. Wired into the markets twenty-four hours at a time, buys and sells stocks and whatever else. And earns serious amounts of money. I was talking to Bertil, who's selling the manor, and he told me that both father and son are upper-class bullies.'

'I didn't know the world according to Bertil featured any other kind of Stockholmers,' Mom sneers.

'Actually, he does come across as kind of overbearing,' Minoo says quickly. 'I mean Viktor.'

'He might just feel insecure, Minoo.'

'Or else he's just some stuck-up bastard,' Dad says. 'Not everything can be psychoanalyzed and explained away.'

'Oh dear, no...*why* should one try to understand other human beings?' Mom says. 'And especially *Stockholm folk*. Honestly, Erik, you're becoming more of an Engelsforser with every passing year.'

There it is. The spark. Their eyes lock. Dad's face shifts from pink to traffic-light red in an instant.

'And your point is, Farnaz?'

'No need to shout,' Mom says in that superior, frozen voice that they take turns to use when they fight. When one of them shouts, the other one is as cold as ice.

'I'm not shouting!' Dad bellows and throws his fork down.

It flies across the table and lands with a ringing noise on the floor near Minoo.

She'd like to throw it back at him. Instead she gets up and takes her plate to the counter by the sink. Her mother and father don't seem to notice when she leaves the kitchen.

Minoo runs upstairs to her room, closes the door and turns on some music. Ups the volume until she can no longer hear the voices that find their way up through the floorboards.

She sinks down on the bed, tries to calm her breathing and concentrate on the song.

Is there any love left between her mother and father?

Over the years, they have both hugged and kissed her but they don't touch each other very often, or ever say: 'I love you.'

Maybe they hang on for my sake, Minoo thinks. Like Gustaf's parents. What if they're just waiting for me to move out so they can divorce at last?

It is a terrible, shaming thought. As if she was a shackle that chained them together.

On the ground floor, the door of her father's study slams and the bang echoes right through Minoo. Her mother shrieks something after him. They behave more like teenagers than Minoo ever has.

She looks at the large sports bag on the floor. In it, she has packed three spades, a couple of torches, a crowbar and a large bottle of water. She had never imagined that, just to get away from home, she would happily run off to dig up a grave in the middle of the night.

But she must wait until they've gone to sleep.

She opens the drawer in the bedside table and takes out the *Book of Patterns* and the Pattern Finder. Maybe something has gone wrong with the book, but she won't give up.

She slides her fingers over the worn, black cover. Two circles, a smaller one inside a larger, have been embossed into the leather. She opens the book and lets her fingers leaf through it while she concentrates on her question.

What is my power?

She puts the Pattern Finder to her eye and starts twisting the different segments.

What is my power?

Something flits through her consciousness. She fixes her eyes on the page again. Waits. But nothing happens.

*

Linnéa walks along the lit street leading to the cemetery, taking in the sounds of the night. The crickets playing in the dry grass. The distant rumble of a train on its way southwards.

Then, behind her, a sudden something. A shuffling sound on the pavement.

Linnéa turns around.

Nobody there.

But she was so convinced that she had heard something.

Linnéa focuses her magic. When she knows whose mind she is reading it is easier to catch hold of thoughts but, even so, she projects a few probes into the shadows.

Nothing there.

Linnéa starts walking again, in a hurry now.

No one else has arrived at the cemetery yet. She settles down to wait by the wall, looking up at the starry sky.

She is thinking of all the nights she spent with Elias, nights when they wandered together through the most abandoned quarters of Engelsfors. They could keep talking for hours on end. Elias never tried to give upbeat advice, but he made things seem easier. He was the only one she allowed to see her cry. The only one she allowed to comfort her. But he needed her, too. She wants to feel needed again.

If only he were here now. If only she could tell him …

Linnéa goes rigid when she senses Vanessa's energy coming closer. Soon afterwards, a pale figure materializes on the road.

Linnéa stands up. Thoughts flow quickly through her head. She has been hoping all summer for a chance to have a moment alone with Vanessa. But now, when the opportunity is at hand, she doesn't know how to deal with it.

She goes to meet her.

'Hi, Vanessa.'

Vanessa slows down, then stops. Her eyes are shiny. The mascara has run a little.

'Hi,' she mumbles.

Linnéa wants nothing except to touch Vanessa, hold her close and comfort her.

'What's happened?'

'I don't want to talk about it.'

But Linnéa has noticed already. The thin engagement ring is gone.

'Have you broken up with Wille?' she asks.

And regrets it instantly. But it is too late. Vanessa's eyes become hard.

'Stop poking around in my mind, would you?'

Linnéa could explain about the ring, that she has no need to read Vanessa's mind, but she is suddenly far too angry. Vanessa has judged her in advance.

If only Vanessa knew what an effort it takes not to pick up her thoughts. How hard it is to resist the temptation, even though she could find out what Vanessa truly feels about her, if there were any hope at all ...

'It's hardly necessary to read your mind to work out that it's over between you,' Linnéa hears herself say.

Vanessa stares at her. And abruptly turns around. Not quickly enough, though. Linnéa has time to see that Vanessa has started crying again.

Fuck, fuck, fuck...why did it end up like this?

Linnéa clenches her hand so hard that the nails cut into her palm. This was her chance to talk with Vanessa, reach out to her and apologize, and instead she has ruined the moment. Typical, she ruins everything – whatever she touches seems to break.

Vanessa's shoulders are heaving. Every sob cuts into Linnéa. She usually hates asking to be forgiven, but now she wants to say sorry until there are no more sorries left in the universe.

Suddenly, Vanessa falls silent. Minoo and Anna-Karin are coming along the road, still at a distance. They are carrying a large sports bag between them. Ida, with a spade in her hand, is following a little way behind them.

When they are close, Minoo and Anna-Karin glance at Vanessa and look bewildered.

But Ida smirks. She had the same look on her face when she watched while Erik Forslund, Robin Zetterqvist and Kevin Månsson cornered Elias. The same smile as when she starts off lies and half-truths that are going to spread throughout the school like bubonic plague. Linnéa feels like grabbing Ida's spade and hacking that sneer from her face.

She knows that she must accept that Ida is in the Circle, but she will never forget who Ida truly is: somebody at least as vicious as anyone that the Chosen Ones should stop.

'What are we waiting for?' Vanessa asks in a throaty voice. 'Are we supposed to dig up a grave, or what?'

CHAPTER 12

Ida watches as Minoo's face takes on its self-important, professorial look.

'I've brought three spades and Ida has one,' she announces.

As if the fact that Ida is standing there with exactly *one* spade in her hand weren't instantly obvious.

'So we don't have one spade each, but someone's got to keep a lookout anyway.'

'I'll do that,' Linnéa says.

Nobody minds, Ida least of all. She is simply grateful to lose that mind-reading freak.

It's fair to say that there's no one Ida detests more. Linnéa gives her a headache, she's always shouty and annoying. Above all, totally mental. She thinks she's so special with her offbeat clothes and make-up and has obviously missed the point that normal people think all weirdos look identical.

As Ida follows the others towards the grave, her hand clutches the wooden handle of the spade. She's last in line and feels prickly, as if the back of her neck were being tickled by a feather, as she senses the darkness behind her and all that might be hiding in it.

She fixes her eyes on Vanessa's blonde head. Doesn't want to look at the gravestones as they walk past. And especially doesn't want to think about the corpses that are rotting down there, worms crawling through eye sockets and between ribs. Doesn't want to think what might have been buried in the grave they are going to dig up. Doesn't want to think ahead about them digging up a horrible stinking grave at all.

I don't want to be part of this. I don't want to be part of this. I don't want to be part of this.

Ida has always hated the dark. When she was little it could take hours before she went to sleep. She would lie in bed, listening out for the slightest sound, carefully wrapping herself up in the duvet, not daring to have an arm or leg uncovered. Too scared to close her eyes, too scared to get out of bed, too scared to stay put.

Sometimes she would call out for her mom or dad. One of them would turn up in the doorway, sighing, still half asleep and tell her that the dark wasn't dangerous. That everything was just the same as during the day.

As if daytime life were totally safe and didn't hold anything frightening. As if it isn't worse when someone out to do something bad to you can hide away, concealed in the darkness. Like murderers and pedophiles. Rabid fighting dogs and drug addicts.

Erik, Julia and Felicia have never noticed this. Ida has become an expert at pretending to sleep. On taking deep, regular, sleepy breaths as she lies with her eyes wide open, scanning the darkness.

She has no intention whatsoever of letting the others in the Circle notice that she is afraid of the dark, but is prepared to bet that Linnéa has been fishing in her mind already and picked it up.

It makes sense. Obviously, Linnéa would use her power to get at Ida.

Vanessa stops so suddenly that Ida nearly walks into her.

They have arrived at the grave.

Everyone holds still for a moment. Ida feels the feather on the back of her neck again. She takes a few steps towards the gravestone so that Vanessa stands between her and the dark.

Minoo opens the sports bag.

'I did a search online and it seems the coffin should be about six feet below ground,' Minoo says and grabs a spade.

'*Six feet,*' Vanessa groans as she too takes a spade and probes the ground tentatively. 'Shit. Anna-Karin, since earth is your element, can't you just say abracadabra and make the soil disappear?'

'Yours is air, so you might as well blow it away,' Anna-Karin replies quietly.

Vanessa puts her foot on the spade and lifts a large lump of dry soil with scorched grass on top. Ida shivers despite the warm summer night. In this case, anyway, she is with Nicolaus. It's all so wrong, for lots of reasons.

Anna-Karin and Minoo push their spades in, too.

Ida swallows hard, reminds herself why she is here and what the book has promised her. She goes next to Minoo and starts digging.

It's much harder work than she had expected. Their spades get in each other's way all the time. But, just as when she's riding, the physical effort creates a kind of trance. She becomes a digging robot that pulls the spade up, drives it in, heaves at the dried-out, lumpy soil and throws it to the side.

The deeper they dig, the moister and heavier the soil becomes. Earthworms and insects try to crawl and creep away, but they have no hope against Ida's spade. She crushes each one she can reach, pretending they are her enemies whom she exterminates, one after the other.

Felicia. Robin.

Linnéa. All the Chosen Ones get a taste of her spade.

Erik, too. And Julia, because she's so annoying.

As the hole grows deeper, they have to take turns, two at a time. Naturally fatso Anna-Karin is panting and wheezing. Minoo presumably never exercises except for lifting books.

In the end, only Ida and Vanessa carry on digging. It has turned into a competition. The only sounds are their heavy breathing and the rasping of metal against grit.

Ida homes in on an unusually fat earthworm and drives the edge of the spade down to chop it up. The spade hits a hard surface. Both Ida and Vanessa stiffen.

'The coffin,' Minoo whispers.

Ida panics. She has to get out of the grave. Now, now, now! She jettisons the spade, holds up her hands.

'Help me up!' she hisses.

Minoo and Anna-Karin hesitate. They exchange a glance, then Minoo kneels and lets Ida grip her hands. She clings to them, scrabbles for footholds on the walls of the hole while clods of earth loosen and fall to the bottom. Finally, she is on firm ground, feeling the rough grass against her bare knees. Her heart is galloping.

Vanessa carries on clearing the lid of the coffin, cool as anything; must be violating graves on a weekly basis at least.

'Take care, you might break through it,' Minoo says. 'Old wood can be brittle.'

'It doesn't look that old,' Vanessa replies.

She is right. The dark wood of the coffin lid gleams in the moonlight. It looks as good as new, as if the coffin were buried only a few hours earlier.

Vanessa throws her spade up on the grass and bends over the coffin, letting her hands slide over the smooth surface.

'There's magic here. I sense it,' she says as her fingers fumble along the edges. 'How are we supposed to open this damn thing?'

'Can't you see how sick all this is?' Ida says. 'We can't open a coffin just like that! I don't feel like checking out some rotting corpse!'

When she gets to the bit about the corpse, her voice cracks. It always gives her away when she's upset.

'What did you think you'd find in a grave, huh? An Easter egg?' Vanessa snaps.

Her legs and arms are streaked with soil. There is a grimy line across her forehead, where she has wiped sweat off with a dirty hand.

Minoo extracts a crowbar from her bag and hands it to Vanessa.

'We don't know what's in that coffin. Maybe it isn't a corpse,' Minoo says.

But Ida hears the dread under Minoo's preachy tones.

Vanessa takes the crowbar and tries to lever the lid open. 'It's stuck!'

Suddenly Ida feels something soft against her leg. She can't hold back her scream. It echoes across the cemetery. She stamps wildly up and down with her feet and stares at the ground. The green eye of Cat stares back at her. It is grinning. Cats normally don't grin, but Ida is positive this fucking awful animal is doing exactly that.

'What's your problem?' Vanessa asks, as she throws the crowbar out of the grave before clambering up.

Ida feels her rage coming to the boil. More than anything she would like to kick Cat, it's so revolting. But it is an animal after all, though a shabby, ugly one.

Anna-Karin picks up Cat and holds it in her arms. Her fingers stroke the tufty fur and bare patches of skin. Ida simply can't bear to watch.

'What are you up to, pussy cat?' Anna-Karin coos.

Then she suddenly stops talking.

Something has caught her eye. Ida turns to look and immediately feels enormously relieved.

Nicolaus.

He will put a stop to all this.

Cat begins to twist in Anna-Karin's arms and she lets it down at once. It sneaks in behind the gravestone. Anna-Karin wishes that she could hide, too.

Nicolaus is walking across the cemetery. Linnéa is jogging along after him.

No one speaks. There is nothing to say. They have gone behind Nicolaus's back. Lied to him. Nicolaus, who has never betrayed them.

He stops at the edge of the gaping hole. Stares at it, standing still, as if frozen to the ground.

'Forgive us,' Anna-Karin says.

'Honestly, we had no choice,' Linnéa says breathlessly.

Nicolaus looks up and meets Anna-Karin's eyes. He doesn't seem angry, only resigned.

'I cannot criticize you for this,' he says. 'And I realize I ought not to have attempted to hinder you. My courage failed me. But not without reason. I do not know what is in that coffin, but whatever it is terrifies me to the depths of my soul.' He sighs heavily. 'But, whatever it is, I must have wanted to find it. I cannot escape.'

Cat interrupts by drawn-out meowing. It emerges from behind the gravestone and pads towards Nicolaus, sits down just in front of the grave and looks up at him. Its tail twitches from side to side. Nicolaus kneels down.

Around them, the silence seems to grow thicker. Nicolaus reaches out and Cat rubs its head against his hand. Anna-Karin can almost see the magic bond between them.

'No,' Nicolaus mumbles and lifts his hand to his throat, as

if he suddenly finds breathing difficult. 'No, no, I cannot...'

Cat meows again. Tears are streaming from Nicolaus's eyes.

'No,' he whispers. 'I cannot...'

'What's going on?' Ida asks impatiently.

Nicolaus looks up, but seems evasive, even ashamed.

'You must all leave this place. Please. I beg you.'

Anna-Karin feels as cold as ice. She doesn't want to walk away. She wants to *run* away from here. Something is very wrong.

'We're going nowhere,' Linnéa says.

Cat rubs itself against Nicolaus's knees and begins to purr softly.

Nicolaus closes his eyes and bends his neck. He lifts Cat and holds it in his arms as if it were a baby. Its purring gets louder.

'Forgive me, forgive, forgive...' Nicolaus whispers over and over again, his lips pressed close to Cat's ear.

He places his hand over Cat's eyes.

Cat's meowing sounds pained. The paws shudder a few times. Then its body goes limp and its head slumps. The bond between Cat and Nicolaus is broken for ever.

Anna-Karin's eyes fill with tears as Nicolaus lowers the lifeless body to the ground in front of the grave. Cat's single eye is still wide open.

'*Memento mori,*' Nicolaus whispers.

A crackling noise comes from inside the hole. Then one more. And another. It sounds like hailstones pattering against a roof.

Anna-Karin takes a few steps closer to the open grave. The others follow her.

The lid of the coffin is cracking and falling apart. Torn chunks of wood become sticks that become flakes that dissolve into nothingness. Anna-Karin is aware of the magic flowing out of the grave. She senses something in the air, something shimmering. It whirls toward Nicolaus and wraps him in a swarm of sparks that gradually fade.

Anna-Karin leans forward over the hole again.

Left inside the coffin are only shards of bone, blackened and porous. As she watches, they, too, fall apart into a fine dust. Instinctively, Anna-Karin covers her nose and mouth with her hands to keep herself from breathing in dust and death.

She casts a sidelong glance at Nicolaus, who is sitting curled up near the grave and staring into it.

'Nicolaus? What's happened?'

Nicolaus takes his time to answer.

'I remember,' he says in the end.

'What do you remember?'

Nicolaus slowly straightens up and looks at her.

It is Nicolaus and yet it is not. The uncertain look has gone. It has been replaced by infinite suffering.

'Everything,' he replies.

CHAPTER 13

Minoo observes Nicolaus. He gets up, drags his hand through his hair. That gesture is so characteristic of him. And yet, he is not really the same.

'My entire life,' he says. 'Everything has come back to me.'

He falls silent. Sways.

'It's too much to...'

'Just try to keep calm,' Anna-Karin says.

Nicolaus laughs briefly. It is an alien sound.

Minoo still observes him. She is worried. Better than most, she knows the power of memories. And to have your whole life back in one go...perhaps Nicolaus is suffering a massive brain overload?

'You will learn all,' he assures them. 'But not here, where anyone might be listening.'

He gently lifts Cat's dead body, slowly strokes its ragged fur.

'It wanted you to, didn't it?' Anna-Karin asks in a choked voice. 'What I mean is, it asked you to do this.'

'It's true,' Nicolaus replies. 'The life of my familiar should have ended long ago. But it stayed behind faithfully. Now, it can finally find rest.'

Nicolaus carefully places the small body in the grave. Then he takes a spade and starts shoveling down earth. Minoo gets hold of a spade, too, even though she has hardly any strength left in her arms. Together with Vanessa and Linnéa, the hole is quickly filled in. When that is finished, they try to smooth the top layer of soil as best they can.

'Terrific,' Ida says. 'You can see from miles away that this grave has been messed with.'

'Wait,' Nicolaus says.

He kneels once more and pushes his fingers into the soil. At first, nothing happens. Then, small green dots appear on the disturbed surface. The dots grow. Minoo can smell the grass. It is spreading over the grave. Minoo watches Nicolaus who trembles with the effort as the blades of grass grow taller, inch by inch, until the grave has become covered by a mat of fresh green grass.

They can 'shape and control different kinds of living material'. That is how the principal had described the power of the element wood. Elias's element. And Nicolaus's.

Nicolaus stands on shaky legs, brushing his pants with his hands.

Who is he, truly? Minoo thinks.

And what if the Nicolaus who has regained his memories is someone she cannot like?

They are scattered in Nicolaus's living room. Linnéa is sitting cross-legged on the small sofa. Nicolaus has not uttered a word since they left the cemetery. Now he is standing in front of the silver crucifix, looking at it in silence.

Linnéa is not reading his mind, but senses that his consciousness has changed. As if it has healed.

'I don't know where I should begin,' he says.

'The beginning seems a good place,' Linnéa says.

He turns to her.

'I shall try. Of course I shall. You have already had to wait for too long for answers from your guide.'

He looks at them, one by one.

'The beginning,' he repeats. 'Yes. Almost four centuries have passed since then.'

'What do you mean?' Minoo asks.

'Since I was born. And I should have died...I should have died more than three hundred years ago.'

A deep silence fills the room.

Linnéa tries to take on board what Nicolaus is saying. It is impossible.

Ida opens her mouth before anyone else.

'What are you telling us?' she asks shrilly. 'Are you a *vampire*?'

'Of course he isn't,' Anna-Karin says.

'How do you know?' Ida snaps. 'Witches and demons exist. Why not vampires?'

Linnéa moves in.

'Like I said, it would be good if you started from the beginning, Nicolaus.'

It would be faster to read his mind. But she has promised never to do that again.

He nods and wearily goes to sit down on the empty wooden chair next to Minoo.

'I was born here in Engelsfors. My father was the minister and it followed that I should take the cloth as well. When my father died, I took over his parish. I liked the post and married the woman who was selected for me. Hedvig. She, too, was one of us...What I mean is...One of the families that belonged to the Council.'

'Are you a member of the *Council*?' Linnéa asks, uncrossing her legs and putting her feet on the floor.

If Nicolaus is one of them, she'll get out of here and never come back.

'Not any more,' Nicolaus replies.

Linnéa scrutinizes him. Is he lying? The temptation to read his thoughts is stronger than ever.

'But I was one of the most faithful of the Councilors,' he continues. 'Then, as now, the members controlled all use of magic powers. But their primary function was to find, protect and train the Chosen One. There were various prophecies pointing to different places all over the world where the Chosen One might be found. Engelsfors was one such place. It was my family that was given the honorable task to watch over the region. We were to await the next era of magic and see if the Chosen One was here.'

'And so she was,' Minoo says. 'Did you know her?'

Nicolaus nods slowly. Lowers his eyes.

'She was my daughter.'

Linnéa doesn't quite believe her ears.

'Your daughter?'

'Matilda. She was our third child. The first two were dead at birth. Matilda meant everything to us. She was intelligent and strong-willed. And beautiful. Hedvig and I were both natural witches and, from early on, we realized that Matilda, too, had a powerful, inborn talent for magic. But it was when she was fifteen that her powers truly blossomed. We didn't dare let her leave the house because she saw visions and caused supernatural phenomena. She started a rainstorm in our bedroom once. We couldn't risk letting something like that happen in public. In those days, people were hunting for witches everywhere.'

Linnéa looks at him, trying to imagine him as a father of a family and a minister of the church. As someone alive in the seventeenth century. It is amazingly easy.

'One morning, we found her, outside the vicarage, frozen to the bone and covered in dirt. She was raving about a blood-red moon, about walking out into the forest and having had her fate foretold. We immediately informed the leader of the Council in the capital city. They arrived here a few days later and, after certain ... trials ... it was proven that ... Matilda was the Chosen One.'

A scene, an image in Nicolaus's memory, flickers briefly to life in Linnéa's consciousness. A girl screams. Blood splatters on a stone floor. Linnéa shies away, won't know, won't see.

'They carried out some kinds of test, right? Like the school principal, with our hairs?' Minoo asks and Linnéa could shake her for being so naïve.

'The Council has adopted more refined methods since then,' Nicolaus replies. 'In those days, they were more ... primitive. I ought to have intervened at that stage. But I was blind. I believed it was to be for the good of mankind. The good of Matilda. She was already close to sinking, forced under by her powers.'

In Linnéa's judgment, this sounds like a poor excuse. But she decides to give him a chance. Let him finish his story.

'How do you mean?' Minoo asks.

'You now know, of course, that a witch can master only one of the elements,' Nicolaus says. 'But it isn't quite true. The Chosen One controls every one of them. All six elements.'

'Shouldn't the principal have said something about this?' Minoo asks.

'She might have good reasons to conceal it from you,' Nicolaus replies. 'Or else the Council has forgotten. That wouldn't surprise me in the slightest.'

'But if Matilda was in control of all six elements ... wouldn't she be, like, about to explode?' Vanessa asks.

The grimy streak across her forehead, left when she wiped the sweat off during the dig, is still there.

'Theoretically, yes,' Nicolaus says. 'But, as you also know, the Chosen One is surrounded by a special, protective magic that keeps her powers together and keeps her from being found by the demons. Still, it was a heavy burden to bear. The Council claimed that they could help her and I was forced to trust them.'

Linnéa can't keep quiet any more.

'You were not forced. You chose to do what you did.'

A shadow passes over Nicolaus's face.

'Yes, I did. I made a choice. And, for all eternity, will wish I'd chosen differently, believe me.'

Nicolaus's remorse is so great that Linnéa can't avoid capturing a sense of how he feels. And the expression 'all eternity' takes on a special status when it is uttered by some-one who has lived for four hundred years.

'One night, I woke suddenly. I felt that something had happened to Matilda,' Nicolaus continues. 'She wasn't in her bed. I found her at a place in the forest where she used to go when she was little. She was barely alive, in a much worse state than during the night of the blood-red moon. I carried her home. And, already, I felt sure of a difference in her. When she woke, I became certain. Her magic was exhausted.'

'Exhausted?' Ida asks quickly. 'In what way "exhausted"?'

'She had no powers left.'

'So it can be done! One can get rid of one's powers!' Ida exclaims.

Linnéa glances crossly at her. No one has failed to notice that Ida wants to get out of being one of the Chosen. And, as ever, Ida's first concern is Ida.

'Yes, it's possible,' Nicolaus says. 'But I don't know what brought it about. She refused to tell Hedvig and me about it. She only insisted that she had acted for the good of everyone, that she was herself too weak to fight the battle. Then, the Council's emissaries arrived...'

He falls silent. Looks down at his hands. And Linnéa goes cold inside. Even though she doesn't know exactly what happened, she has followed Matilda on her journey to death. The others have done this, too, in their dreams.

'I was a fool,' Nicolaus says. His voice is very quiet. 'I ought to have hidden her, protected her. Instead, I left her in the hands of the Council. They accused her of gambling with the fate of the entire world. Matilda insisted that another Chosen One would be born sometime in the future and that he or she would be stronger than her and defeat the demons once and for all time. But the Council argued that she had betrayed them. And disloyalty is the one thing they will not tolerate...'

Nicolaus pauses briefly.

'In those days, witch-hunting was at its height in this country. It goes without saying that no real witches were affected. That is, except those who the Council wanted to dispose of. They saw to it that Matilda was imprisoned and tried, accused of having learned her witchcraft from Satan. The court found her guilty.'

Now, the guilt that fills Nicolaus so overwhelms him that it flows into Linnéa and she has to fight to keep her mind clear of it.

'I had known the judge since my student days. He was a very senior Council official, though of course the rest of the court had no idea. I begged him to be lenient and he told me that if Matilda confessed, mercy would be shown and the execution called off...I and my wife trusted my old friend.'

Nicolaus falls silent again and swallows hard before he can continue.

'In this country, the practice was to behead convicted

witches first and burn the body afterwards. But Matilda was marched straight to the pyre and tied to the stake…I went to speak to her. I said that they would set her free if only she would confess. And she obeyed me. I was so relieved. My friend nodded to the executioner. I was convinced that he would start to untie her ropes. Instead, he reached for the flaming torch…'

Tears are pouring down Nicolaus's cheeks. Linnéa can hardly breathe.

'I leapt towards the fire. The guards grabbed me and pinned me down. But they didn't catch Hedvig…She threw herself into the flames. Their screams…'

He presses the backs of his hands against his eyes. Linnéa smells smoke from a fire. She is not sure if it is her imagination or if it comes from Nicolaus's memory.

'That very night, I opened the *Book of Patterns* and asked it to show me how to atone for my crime, but also how I could avenge my wife and daughter. The book answered both pleas. It showed me how to live on and help the next Chosen One, in order to make up for my betrayal. But for such strong magic, great sacrifices are required.'

He wipes the tears off his cheeks.

'Matilda and Hedvig were not allowed to be buried in sacred ground. Not a witch and someone who had died by her own hands. But I bribed the executioner and he let me have their remains. The book instructed me to bury Matilda in the spot where I had found her that night when she lost her powers. The place you now call Kärrgruvan. I hid my wife's bones. The most powerful members of the Council had attended the session of the court and they still remained in Engelsfors. They gathered for a meeting in the church. I locked the doors and set fire to the building. It was a wooden church and burned quickly down to the ground. I had drawn circles around it and for every life that was consumed in the flames, my own life was lengthened. Then I torched the vicarage as well. The scorched bones that were buried in my name belonged to my wife.'

Linnéa recalls the words of the principal from just one year ago.

The church and vicarage burned down in 1675, and a great many very important documents were lost.

'The principal told us about the fire,' Minoo says.

'I heard her,' Nicolaus replies. 'You may remember that I stood outside her office and listened. But I am pretty sure that the Council is no longer aware that its leading figures died in the Engelsfors fire. Well, at least not members at Adriana's level.'

'But how could they forget?' Minoo asks. 'It must have been a huge trauma that affected the whole organization.'

'Maybe that's exactly why they've forgotten,' Linnéa says and looks at Nicolaus. 'Powerful people hate admitting that anyone can get at them.'

'Precisely so,' he says. 'The Council hates losing face. They want to be seen as invulnerable and all-knowing. The failure over the Chosen One was bad enough, inexplicable and embarrassing. As for the fire…I didn't dare go near the Council, of course, not after what I had done but, during my wanderings, rumors reached me now and then. New leaders stepped in and immediately suppressed all talk about the scandal in Engelsfors. Those who remembered kept their mouths shut. And grew old and died. The prophecy about the role of Engelsfors was just one among many prophecies. This must have been why the Council was so unprepared for all of you showing up just here. They had forgotten.'

Linnéa recalls how she picked up what went on in the principal's mind last year. And how, as time went by, she had realized that Adriana knew much less than she pretended.

'But what about your own memories?' Minoo asks. 'What happened at the grave?'

'Human beings are not meant to live for as long as I have,' Nicolaus says. 'I knew my forgetfulness would increase. That I would grow ever more lost. The book told me how to store magic in the grave, magic that would one day let me recover my memories. Some of them were stored in my familiar, memories that I hoped would lead me on the right way when the time came.'

'So you pulled together a backup copy of yourself and left it in safe storage here in Engelsfors?' Vanessa says. 'And then the magic kind of rebooted your brain?'

Some of the old confusion returns to Nicolaus's eyes.

'I am not entirely sure what you mean, but a copy kept safely ... yes, that is right.'

'So what have you been doing these past few centuries, then?' Linnéa asks.

'I drifted here and there, all over the world. Observed, as eras of war and peace passed. I carried the silver crucifix and it protected me. There were times when I became more lucid and remembered my task, and my crimes. Such periods allowed me to learn from my contemporaries, find out about their habits and language usage. Understand new things. But sooner or later I would slide back into the mist. I returned a few times to Engelsfors to store new clues for myself. Like that damned bank deposit box. And the letter.'

'But ...' Minoo says and Linnéa can almost see the cogs in her brain racing and throwing out sparks. 'When you wrote that letter to yourself, you did remember everything, but were scared that you would forget again. Why didn't you open the grave then?'

'Exactly,' Linnéa agrees. 'It would've been pretty useful

if you had remembered everything last autumn, when we were called.'

Nicolaus looks away.

'I don't know why I left the grave untouched.'

'So you remember everything else, but not that?' Linnéa asks.

Nicolaus meets her eyes.

'No, I don't remember. What matters is that now you know who I am as well as I do myself. That I'm a man who betrayed his wife and his daughter. Who murdered in cold blood and chose revenge instead of forgiveness. And I am deeply uncertain whether I can ever atone for my crimes.'

He looks unhappy and Linnéa understands why he was reluctant to open up the grave. His subconscious must have wanted to protect him from all these insights.

'I am sorry,' she says. 'I am sorry it happened and sorry that you were forced to remember.'

'Taking up the burden of these memories is hard,' Nicolaus says. 'That I admit. But I must choose light, not darkness, even if the light is merciless. Even if the memories are full of pain at least I recall *them* once more. My most dearly beloved. Hedvig. Matilda.'

Linnéa nods. She has to look away. She could have said this about herself, about Elias.

'I think she has forgiven you,' Anna-Karin says. 'I mean Matilda. She told us we could trust you on that very first night in Kärrgruvan.'

'I am not sure that I deserve to be forgiven,' Nicolaus says.

His body has been sagging more and more during the telling of his story. Now he almost seems about to faint.

'I'm afraid I must rest now,' he says.

'Thank you,' Minoo says. 'Thank you for telling us this.'

'I perfectly understand if you feel disappointed in me,'

Nicolaus says.

Anna-Karin shakes her head.

'It changes nothing,' she says. 'We know who you are. And we've known all the time.'

Chapter 14

Vanessa opens her eyes and sees a bird.

At first, she thinks it's part of a dream, but it's actually there, perched on her bedside table, looking at her.

It's a blue tit, one of the few bird species she recognizes. Blue skullcap and white face with a black brush stroke across it at eye level. Its chest is yellow, like a chicken's.

Vanessa waves sleepily at the wide-open window and tries to make it understand.

'Hey, you. Fly out,' she whispers hoarsely.

The blue tit puts its head to the side and peers at her with beady black eyes. Vanessa sighs. Starting the day by chasing a crazy bird around her room seems like hard work, and she'd only get bird shit all over her things.

She turns over and lies on her back, staring at the ceiling. She has only had a few hours' sleep.

When she came home, she had wanted a shower more than anything else but couldn't risk waking everyone. Instead, she grabbed a towel and, as best she could, wiped off the mixture of sweat and soil that coated her. Apart from the fact that she still feels dirty, her nightmares won't leave her in peace. The grave. Nicolaus's story. Fragments of last year's dreams, dreams that were haunted by Matilda's memories.

Then there is the different, more ordinary kind of evil that she has not yet had a chance to digest.

I've been with someone else.

Vanessa sits up abruptly, nausea rising into her throat. The bird flaps its wings, takes off to the ceiling, bumps into the lampshade and bounces out through the window. It disappears into the blue sky.

I've been with someone else.

She waits for the tears, but they don't come. She feels like that parched Russian lake they studied in geography. It was one of the biggest lakes in the world once, but now it has shrunk to a small puddle surrounded by desert.

A fucking useless puddle in the Russian desert. That's what she feels like.

Vanessa opens her wardrobe. The first thing she sees is the faded yellow T-shirt she usually sleeps in. Wille's. It has a washed-out print on the front that shows a bottle of ketchup high-fiving with a hot dog.

Vanessa stares at the T-shirt and thinks that something should happen inside her now. She should want to grab a pair of scissors and cut it into tiny, tiny pieces. Or set it on fire. Or soak it in her period blood and carry out some thoroughly wicked witch's ritual.

It should surely be possible to put a real curse on Wille. She could go to the Crystal Cave and bribe Mona Moonbeam to tell her how. Like sticking voodoo needles into that idiotic, ugly teddy bear Wille gave her. Or she could make herself go invisible, sneak into Wille's room and trash all his stuff. Or tell Nicke about Wille and Jonte dealing...

But revenge fantasies don't make her feel better. Instead, she starts thinking about her slippers, which have probably been kicked into the mess under Wille's bed.

She wants them back. And, come to think of it, she left her favorite lipgloss behind as well. She'll have to buy a new one now. Or should she ask him for it? No, better not. It isn't worth facing Wille just for that. She doesn't want to see him ever again. But she isn't sure if her special lipgloss is still in stores. Perhaps it's the last ever lipgloss of that type in the whole world and it's left in that repulsive shitface Wille's place, so she'll never get it back.

A sob, so sudden that at first she can't think who's crying.

'Nessa? Would you like an omelette?'

Vanessa turns around. Mom has opened the door a little to peep into the room.

'Oh no, darling girl...' she says when she sees Vanessa's face.

The puddle in the Russian desert suddenly fills and over-flows. Grows into a whole sea of salty water.

Mom comes in, closes the door behind her and stops, with one hand held out, as if she wants to touch Vanessa but doesn't quite dare.

'Darling, what's the matter?'

And Vanessa suddenly doesn't give a shit for her pride, doesn't give a shit that her mother might well say: 'I told you so.'

She starts talking. Has to take long pauses when her voice breaks.

Mom puts her arms around Vanessa, wraps her daughter into one of those long, warm Mommy hugs. Vanessa hugs her back, tightly, and burrows her head into Mom's dressing gown.

'My baby,' Mom says. 'My sweet baby.'

'I didn't want to let on because I know you don't like Wille,' Vanessa wails.

Mom strokes her hair.

'My lovely girl,' she says, with such feeling she seems about to burst into tears, too. 'Surely you know you can talk to me about everything?'

Vanessa thinks of Nicke and the woman in the car. Perhaps she ought to tell her mom now, perhaps this is the right opportunity, but then their roles would be reversed in an instant. She would have to comfort her mother.

Maybe it's selfish, but she couldn't cope. She feels small and vulnerable, and all she wants right now is for Mom just to be Mom.

Minoo examines her hands under the strong light of the bathroom lamp and notes that she still has soil stuck under her nails. For all her scrubbing, she can't get her hands clean.

And, for all her trying, she can't get her head around what happened last night.

She turns the tap on and puts more soap on the nailbrush.

All her dreams have been about Nicolaus and Matilda.

Minoo realizes now, more clearly than she ever has, that the previous Chosen One was a real person and not only some mysterious being who speaks to them through Ida and visits them all in their dreams.

Above all, she realizes how lonely Matilda must have been. A girl of Minoo's own age, who carried the entire world on her shoulders. Minoo and the others at least share the task.

The word *witch-hunt* keeps coming back to Minoo's mind. Suddenly, the witch trials have become real to her. Reality, instead of images in woodcuts remembered from history books. The trials happened. For real. Here in Engelsfors.

Minoo still remembers what it felt like to wake up with the smell of burning in her hair. She was with Matilda in the prison dungeon. She traveled in the cart with her, tied hand and foot, towards her death.

Fire

Burned alive.

The muscles in her arms ache after a night's digging, but she carries on scrubbing with the brush. Her fingertips go red, but the dirt is wedged in deep under her nails.

She had been given many answers last night, but also thought of new questions.

What took place the night when Matilda lost her powers? Why seven Chosen Ones this time instead of one?

Did Matilda *know* that this would happen? Was that why she did it, whatever it was? Because the burden was too heavy to bear alone? But why have seven, when there are only six elements?

Minoo scrubs and scrubs.

Of course, Matilda died before she had time to stop the apocalypse. Why didn't the demons take the world over there and then? Was the final battle postponed when Matilda left the game and dumped all the responsibility on the future Chosen Ones? If so, what does it mean that only five Chosen Ones are left? Do they have the slightest chance of winning?

And why can't she shake off the feeling that Nicolaus didn't tell them all he knows?

She walks into the passage and meets Mom. She is wrapped in the worn, red dressing gown she has used for as long as Minoo can remember.

'Bahar will come and see us in a few weeks,' Mom says happily. 'Shirin and Darya may be coming along, too.'

Minoo wishes she could share her pleasure. Even though she loves her aunt and her cousins, they are seriously exhausting to be with. And she has more than enough drama in her life right now.

'Isn't Darya in London?'

'No, she's back home and working as a trainee in some

sort of advertising agency. But Bahar is positive Darya will start her law course in the spring. Or maybe she'll do medicine. Or study for the Secretary Generalship in the United Nations.'

Mom rolls her eyes heavenwards and Minoo giggles. Bahar and her husband Reza have always had grandiose ambitions for their two daughters.

'Hurry up or you'll be late for school,' Mom adds as she disappears into the bathroom.

Minoo walks downstairs and picks up her backpack. As she steps outside, the sunlight dazzles her. She only spots Anna-Karin waiting for her after putting on her sunglasses.

'Hi, Minoo,' Anna-Karin says and they start walking to school together.

Anna-Karin wears a baggy black T-shirt and, despite the heat, a sweatshirt tied around her waist. As if ready for a sudden cold snap. She's wearing jogging shoes as well. Her feet must be boiling by now. Even Minoo has given in and shows off her abnormally big feet in sandals.

'Did you sleep at all?' Anna-Karin asks.

'Not much.'

Anna-Karin's face is hidden behind her mane of hair, but everything about her body language tells Minoo that she is keeping something back.

'I've been thinking…this stuff about the Council. Last year, the principal said that they'd set up a group to investigate me and everything I'd done…'

She falls silent. It dawns on Minoo that Nicolaus's story must have been especially terrifying for Anna-Karin.

Minoo is just about to say that the Council hardly goes around burning people at the stake any more, but then she remembers what they did to Adriana.

'But that was back in the seventeenth century,' she says,

trying to sound reassuring. 'And we haven't heard another thing about the investigation for almost a year.'

'No, that's true...' Anna-Karin says without conviction.

'Besides, you're not alone,' Minoo adds. 'We won't let anything happen to you.'

CHAPTER 15

Once in the school, Minoo and Anna-Karin go straight to the janitor's office and knock.

No response. The door is locked. It makes Minoo anxious, even though it would be perfectly reasonable for Nicolaus to stay at home today. Should they actually have left him alone in his apartment?

Anna-Karin must have had the same idea, because she calls his number.

'No reply,' she says and puts the phone away.

'I'm sure he'll be all right. Just needs time to get his head around everything.'

Anna-Karin nods. They stand together for a moment or two without speaking.

'Do you have that spare key?' Anna-Karin asks.

'Yes. And if he doesn't answer this evening, we'll go to his place.'

'Just to check that he's okay.'

'That's what I'm thinking.'

The first class that day is chemistry. When Minoo and Anna-Karin arrive upstairs, the class is waiting outside the locked laboratory. Anna-Karin mumbles something about going to the bathroom and disappears.

Minoo puts her bag down and leans against the wall.

She steals a look at Viktor, who is on his own. He is reading a book and seems oblivious to Hanna H and Hanna A who gaze adoringly at him. Actually, they are not the only ones. Every other female coming along the hallway glances longingly at Viktor.

At Engelsfors High School, a student from elsewhere is a rare enough specimen. A new student like Viktor is contrary to every law of nature. He doesn't belong, somehow. It is as if an exotic orchid has been planted in the local fir forest. Minoo looks at Erik and Robin. And Kevin, whose braying can be heard from a bit further away. She wonders for how long the orchid will survive.

Then she looks at Viktor again. To her surprise, he smiles and ambles over to see her.

'I must apologize,' he says. 'I must have sounded pretty arrogant, or worse, to you and your friend the other day. As it happened, you did turn up at a tricky time, but...it's probably better that I don't come up with any excuses. So, simply, please forgive me.'

Minoo can't think what to say. She is preoccupied with her feet and hopes that he hasn't noticed them. With any luck, the new zits on her forehead will distract him.

'It's all right,' she says.

'I don't want to criticize your home town. I'm sure Engelsfors is a really good place to live in. But it was such a sudden decision, what with leaving Stockholm and coming here, and somehow I hadn't taken on board what a...'

Viktor seems to search for the right word.

'... you know, *reorientation* it would be for me.'

'I understand how you feel. I mean, you must miss all your friends. Besides, this place isn't exactly Stockholm. Not that I don't like Stockholm. On the contrary,' she says and registers that her capacity for insane gabbling is in high gear. 'I always wanted to live in Stockholm. I've actually got relatives there.

I guess I'd have to rethink things, too, of course, but in a good way, if you see what I mean.'

Minoo doesn't know where to look. She catches sight of the title of the book under Victor's arm. It is a worn paperback edition of one of her favorites, Donna Tartt's *The Secret History*, in English.

'Do you like it?' she asks.

'Not exactly. I *love* it.'

There was a time when Minoo believed that anyone with good taste in books must automatically be a good human being. An illusion that Max trampled into the dust. Max, who despite his well-stocked bookshelf, was revealed as the demons' psychopathic menial.

But all the same, she can't help liking Viktor a little better than before.

'I love it, too,' she says. 'But I've never read it in English.'

'I only ever read books in the original language,' Viktor says and, for a moment, looks as condescending as he did when they met at the manor house. 'One loses such a lot otherwise. Translations do nothing but create barriers between you, the reader, and the author's real message.'

'I guess so...' Minoo says. 'You...read a lot, do you?'

Viktor is about to reply when an object comes flying through the air. It hits him in the back. A chemistry book.

Viktor doesn't look over. Instead he bends a little closer over Minoo.

'It was one of the Neanderthals over there, right?'

Minoo nods and looks across at them. Kevin stands a little apart. He is grinning. Robin and Erik seem rather impassive.

'Welcome to Engelsfors,' Minoo says to Viktor.

He sighs, picks up the book, opens it and reads out Kevin's name.

'Homo!' Kevin rasps.

Viktor closes the book, turns around and smiles.

'Do you want to talk to me, Kevin?' he says.

The two Hannas giggle. Viktor walks over to Kevin and hands him the book.

'Surely you're aware that you're in the eleventh grade? Throwing books isn't a—'

'Shut the fuck up, fucking Stockholmer,' Kevin grunts. 'You think you're all that, don't you.'

He turns to Erik and Robin for support but they're already off down the hall. Kevin suddenly looks nervous. Minoo almost feels sorry for him. Erik and Robin have always been the brains in the gang of three. Kevin is simply a blunt instrument that they use now and then. They would probably have bullied him if he hadn't been one of them.

Kevin sees her looking at him.

'Got a problem, slut?'

Minoos's sympathy evaporates instantly. Viktor stares at Kevin with distaste.

'Are you losing it 'cause I insulted your girlfriend here, or what?' Kevin asks.

'Am I supposed to be a queer or am I going out with Minoo? What's your angle?'

Kevin licks his front teeth, probes his mouth with his tongue to extract the wad of tobacco and spits it out. The brown spittle leaves a snail trail of mucus on Viktor's pale slacks.

Viktor looks quizzically at Kevin. At that moment, Inez, the chemistry teacher, walks briskly up to the classroom door, unlocks it and lets everybody in.

Inez is one of the best teachers at Engelsfors High School. She's pint-sized, but no one ever messes around with her. She starts handing out copies of the instructions for today's experiments straight away.

'You'll be working with acids today, so don't forget the acid-into-water rule,' she tells them. 'Acid-into-water means that you can add acid to water safely. The other way around is never safe!'

They all put on lab coats and safety goggles, then go off to collect the equipment. Minoo ends up in the same group as Anna-Karin and Levan.

Minoo has just gotten a good grip on the acid flask when a scream echoes through the room.

The entire class turns to see what is going on.

Hanna A and Hanna H are hysterical, but the loudest screams come from the third member of their lab group. Kevin.

'It splattered!' Hanna A screams. 'He got acid all over himself!'

'Fucking crap acid rule!' Kevin howls. 'I did it right!'

'It's true!' Hanna A shouts at top volume. 'I checked it too!'

Hanna H doesn't utter a word. She only shrieks.

Inez rushes up to them, grabs Kevin's lab coat and hauls him over to the emergency shower. She tugs at the handle and Kevin is instantly soaked.

Minoo looks away, lets her eyes scan the chaos in the lab. Everyone looks shocked.

Correction. *Nearly* everyone. Viktor is standing at the back of the room. He is calmly continuing with the experiment as if nothing is amiss. But he can't quite hide his smile.

'Oh, my God. Like, poor, poor Kevin,' Felicia says as she plonks her tray down next to Robin and opposite Ida. 'Totally awful!'

Ida spears a few peas on her fork. Whatever Felicia says or does today makes her shiver with irritation. Felicia has been messing around with both eyeliner and eyeshadow, and to cap it all she's wearing what she likes to call her 'cute vest'.

'I don't think it was that bad,' Erik says. 'He only got some stuff on his hand.'

He is stroking Ida's knee under the table and she lets him keep at it for now.

'But all the same...' Felicia won't let go. She takes a slice of toast from Julia's tray. 'I mean, what if his hand has to be amputated and he has to have a yucky plastic hand instead. Maybe it's the kind of acid that just bites into the skin and keeps on and on corroding. That kind really exists.'

'You'd almost think you passed chemistry,' Ida says and the others laugh.

Felicia goes quiet and starts breaking the toast into tiny fragments which she picks up and chews, one after the other.

'Lucky that Kevin has such great friends, anyway,' she says and smiles towards Robin.

'I guess you do your best,' he replies and smiles back at her.

'There are times I almost wish I were a guy,' Julia says. 'Girls are so mean to each other.'

Ida is just about to say something when her mouth goes as dry as sandpaper. A headache is beginning to pulsate behind her eyes. The smell of burning stings in her nose.

She recognizes what it is. It tries to seep into her and take her over. But this time, she has a name for it.

Matilda.

No, no, no! Not here! Not now!

She shuts her eyes tightly and musters all her defenses. She feels how the other one is trying to force her way in, but for once Ida manages to drive her back. And a moment later Matilda's gone.

Now, Ida is suddenly aware of how silent the group around

the table is.

She opens her eyes. The others stare at her.

'Ida, what's the matter?' Julia asks in a voice meant to be friendly but which mostly sounds frightened. 'Are you in pain or something?'

'Just a headache, that's all,' Ida says and pushes Erik's hand off her knee.

Linnéa pushes past the gaggle of first years at the school gates, where they hang out to smoke. They seem so young. But then, if she catches sight of herself in a mirror, Linnéa can sometimes be surprised at how young she looks. Inside, she feels ancient.

The air is a little cooler today. Not enough to make it bearable, just a shade less unbearable. She walks towards the center, past Leffe's kiosk. Leffe sits outside on a white plastic chair and smokes a pipe.

To stay out of the sun, Linnéa tacks between the patches of shade near the houses.

She lights the last cigarette in her pack and smokes it slowly. When she gets to the back of the City Mall, she stands still for a moment.

The seat where her father often sits is empty. Not a soul anywhere. Just two crows fighting over a piece of hot-dog bun.

She goes into the mall and looks for him in Sture & Co. He isn't there either. On her way out, she passes the Crystal Cave. The notice on the door states that it is 'CLOSED FOR INVENTORY'. Whatever, she can pick up a pungent smell of incense from inside.

When Linnéa steps into the street again, the sun dazzles her.

For a while, she is stuck behind three moms who walk

side by side, pushing their strollers. She has to jog a little to pass them and senses them checking her out, taking in her hair and make-up, what she wears, her shoes. All of her. In their worst nightmares, they must dread the prospect that their little darlings might grow up to look like her.

Some other day, she would have turned around and stared back at them, but not today. Not when she is trying to find him.

Linnéa did the same circuit yesterday, when Olivia had been telling her about Dad. Checked the City Mall. The local outlet for wines and spirits. Storvall Park. The Engelsfors winos' very own Bermuda triangle.

If she finds him anywhere here, she will know that Olivia was wrong. Which she almost hopes.

She has seen him 'sober up' so many times. Let herself believe him, only to have to stand by and watch as he breaks every single promise he has made, yet again. When everything collapsed and she had to be taken into care at the age of fourteen, she made up her mind never to trust him again. Never listen when he assures her that he will make it work this time.

Later, after Social Services let her have an apartment, she created a life of her own. The last thing she needs now is for him to ring her doorbell and offer her an awkwardly wrapped gift and a bunch of promises he can't keep. But if he does turn up, she wants at least to be prepared.

Linnéa has a last puff on the cigarette before throwing the butt away. She stops outside the closed and shuttered Café Monique.

Then she sees The Bag. He has parked himself outside the booze shop and is fermenting in the sun. He checks the shop door now and then. He is wearing sunglasses, so Linnéa isn't sure if he has noticed her. If he had, he'd have been sure to shout to her. Something like, Björn's girlie should come over and say hello. And then, when she didn't, start ranting about how effing stuck-up she's gotten lately.

Cautiously, Linnéa sends a probe into The Bag's ragged brain. He is impatient. Waiting for someone, but she can't make out who. Not now, when abstinence torments his mind.

Linnéa stays where she is until the booze shop's door swings open and Doris's bent figure emerges. She is pushing a trolley and bottles are clinking inside the basket. The Bag gives her the thumbs-up. He is thinking eagerly about the vodka he knows she has bought for him.

Linnéa walks on. Past Ingrid's Hidey-hole, the shop selling second-hand stuff where she sometimes works in exchange for fabrics and old clothes that she can make something from. Because Ingrid has so few customers, there's usually quite a lot for Linnéa to choose from. Her latest bargain is a big cloud of black tulle. She knows exactly what to do with it.

She glances at the disused library. The front door is wide open. Three men in blue overalls are shouting at each other over the noise of the drill. The windows are covered with brown paper.

Now she is almost at Storvall Park. Even from a distance, she spots the two figures on one of the park benches. One of them has got a radio and is turning the volume up and down, up and down. The loudspeaker grinds out an interminable report on wind speeds at sea.

'It's crap! Turn it off!' howls the other man, in a voice that slips and slides. Linnéa's heart does a somersault when she sees the flabby face and the slightly purplish hands that grab the radio and throw it on the ground. The shipping forecast stops. The owner of the radio roars with anger.

But neither of them is her father, Björn Wallin.

CHAPTER 16

'*Twinkle twinkle little star, how I wonder what you are...*'
Vanessa makes her voice fade and linger. Melvin has fallen asleep at last.

She stays by his bedside for a while. Listens to his hushed breathing and looks at the toy penguin cuddled in his arms. Recalls last winter, when she didn't see him for several months. It still pains her to think about how much her disappearance had confused him. She doesn't ever want to hurt him like that again. She would ruin Melvin's whole world if she were to tell her Mom about Nicke.

Tears are burning behind her eyelids. She gets up from the bed gently to avoid waking Melvin. He would see her cry and he mustn't.

She tiptoes across the floor and goes to the kitchen.

'All well?' Mom asks. She is sitting at the kitchen table, hunched over a sudoku.

'He's asleep now.'

'We'll see how long that lasts,' Mom says and smiles.

Her blonde hair is unwashed and she looks tired. But she's beautiful all the same, Vanessa thinks. She could have found someone better than Nicke. Much better, easily.

'What are you thinking?' Mom asks.

'That you're lovely,' Vanessa replies.

And regrets it instantly, because Mom's expression

brightens and she looks so happy that Vanessa almost starts crying again. She is saved by a key rattling in the front door lock.

Vanessa opens the dishwasher and tackles the mounds of dirty dishes piled up on the kitchen counter.

'It has been one fucking awful day,' Nicke says as he comes into the kitchen.

Mom welcomes him with a sloppy kiss and Vanessa's stomach turns. If only Mom knew where his mouth has been.

'Poor darling, you're so late home,' Mom says. 'You look all washed out.'

More squishy noises. Vanessa concentrates on the dishwasher. Competes with herself about fitting as many glasses as possible into the top drawer.

'I wonder sometimes what's going on in this town,' Nicke says and goes to the fridge to get a can of beer.

Vanessa turns icy cold. What if someone saw them in the cemetery yesterday and told the police about the violation of the grave?

'What's up this time?' Mom asks.

Vanessa tries to stack the dishes as quietly as possible. She doesn't want to draw attention to her listening.

'The autopsy results for that psychologist came through. It was an electric shock that did her in. Not a damn clue how it happened. But as luck would have it, she has no family so no one will demand answers,' Nicke says. There's a hiss as he opens his beer.

'Surely being *alone* can't ever be good luck?' Mom says.

'Come on, Jannike. You know what I mean. A bunch of determined relatives can make cases like this drag on for all eternity.'

He disgusts Vanessa so much that she can't stand being silent any more. She must find an outlet for her anger against him, her hatred. Even if it means that she's blamed for disturbing the family peace. Vanessa turns to him.

'It must be great to be you. I mean, it is so *tough* to keep trying to get one's head around other people's feelings.'

'Coming up for air now?' Nicke says.

He glances at her and his eyes are challenging. He doesn't know that she knows. And now she realizes that she *wants* him to know.

'You don't seem to care all that much about anybody's feelings, generally. Or who you're hurting,' Vanessa says.

'Please, you two. Don't start,' Mom says.

Vanessa tries to calm down. Reaches for a cloth and wipes the sink area slowly and thoroughly. It doesn't help much.

'I'd put my money on suicide,' Nicke says, swallowing the rest of the beer noisily and barely suppressing a burp. 'Everyone knows that psychologists have a hell of a lot of problems. Which is why they pick the job.'

'I'm not sure that has to be the case,' Mom says vaguely.

Vanessa throws the cloth into the sink.

'And that must be another great thing about being you,' she says. 'Being able to judge people without waiting for stuff like evidence. Everyone neatly pigeonholed, right?'

She felt sure, actually hoped, that Nicke would start a shouting match. That it would finally come to open warfare between them. But Nicke only smiles and looks superior.

'I don't prejudge anyone but I've learned something about how people's minds work,' he says. 'Like when I spotted straight away that it wouldn't work out for you and Wille.'

This silences Vanessa. And she gazes at her mother.

'Nessa, I haven't said a word. I promise you.'

'Then how does he know?'

Nicke waves his left hand about in a meaningful way, then points to his ring finger.

Vanessa looks at her own ring finger. At the thin line of pale skin showing where the summer sun has not reached. Of course. Now she sees just how obvious it is.

Maybe Linnéa noticed it when they met at the cemetery. And maybe didn't read Vanessa's mind.

'So next time you'd do well to listen to me and Jannike.'

'Oh, yes, please, why don't you give me tons of advice about relationships,' Vanessa sneers. 'You're such a terrific role model.'

'I can't bear another one of your shouting matches!' Mom says.

'Join the fucking crowd,' Vanessa says.

Mom spreads her arms in a resigned gesture and goes into the living room. Some crappy TV show starts up a few seconds later. Nicke grins arrogantly at Vanessa and also leaves the kitchen.

Fury is growing stronger inside her, but she doesn't dare let it out this time. She must think. Sort out her emotions. Decide what to do about her secret knowledge. Make up her mind, once and for all.

Vanessa goes to her room. Her phone pings. It's a text from Evelina.

Nessie, how are things? Call me!!!

Vanessa is glad that Evelina and Michelle are rooting for her. Truly, she is. But ever since she told them about Wille this morning, they've been like two small, caring leeches.

'Still hoping he'll call, or what?'

Vanessa turns around. Nicke stands in the doorway.

'Why don't you just fuck off, you creep.'

Nicke steps into the room and comes up close.

'You'd better watch it,' he says.

Vanessa's instinct tells her to back away, but she doesn't want to give him the pleasure. She crosses her arms.

133

'You're the one who should watch it,' she says quietly. 'I know what you've been up to.'

He snorts and a stale gust of beer wafts over her face.

'So what's that you reckon you know?'

Back in the living room, the audience is applauding wildly. Nicke is so close that his broad-shouldered body fills Vanessa's field of vision. She has to look up to meet his eyes.

'I saw you. In the police car. Your colleague was very obliging. What did you think, was she good at what she was doing?'

'I've no idea what you're talking about.'

But Nicke's eyes look shifty.

'That wasn't the first time, was it? And not the last time either, I bet. Was that the reason you were so late back from work tonight?'

And she can see from his expression that she has hit the bull's eye. His face goes bright red and she senses his body heat climbing several degrees.

'You're such a fucking repulsive creep,' she says and her voice cracks. 'How can you do this to Mom?'

The look in Nicke's eye changes. He could be hesitating about something.

An orchestra starts playing on TV. Cheerful trumpets and trombones. Then Nicke makes a decision.

'Whatever, it doesn't matter. You can't prove a thing. Why should Jannike believe you? She knows you're capable of dreaming up any old crap to ruin what's between us.'

'We'll see about that,' Vanessa says.

And wishes that she had sounded more convincing. Stronger.

'My advice to you is, forget what you saw,' Nicke tells her. 'If you don't, you'll be the one who gets it in the neck. In this family, you've used up any trust we've had in you. Got that? You little slut.'

He turns to leave, but stops in mid-step.

Mom is standing in the doorway, still and silent and pale. Her wide-open eyes have an empty look, as if all the life has seeped out of her.

'Jannike—'

'Oh, my God,' Mom says. 'I feel like such a fucking idiot.'

'Jannike, please calm down. She's just trying to ruin—'

'I should've known,' Mom whispers tonelessly, looking fixedly at the floor.

'You can't mean that you believe her?'

Nicke is speaking so loudly that the sound bounces off the walls.

Mom looks up at Nicke and there is determination in her eyes.

'Get out!'

'Fuck it ... you can't take her side!' Nicke bellows.

In the room next door, Melvin wakes up and starts calling out.

Vanessa would like to go to him, but that would mean having to push past Mom and Nicke. She doesn't dare to move an inch, hardly even to breathe.

'How can you turn against me like this?' Nicke shouts.

Melvin is crying loudly by now.

'I am going to Melvin,' Mom says evenly. 'And when I come back out, I don't want you to be in this apartment.'

'Is that so? And exactly where do you think I should fuck off to?'

'I'm sure you'll find somewhere to sleep. Or does Paula have someone around to be unfaithful to as well? I'm right, you're screwing Paula, aren't you?'

Nicke is speechless.

Mom vanishes from the doorway and Vanessa hears her go into Melvin's room, shush him and mumble soothingly.

Nicke glances at Vanessa and his eyes flash with anger.

'You'll regret this,' he says and turns to go.

Vanessa stands still and takes in the picture of his retreating back. She stays there, listening, until the front door slams shut.

She knows very well that his leaving is far from a solution and that the next stage will mean that they have to share the care of Melvin and deal with every other kind of hellish new problem.

But, for now, everything feels so damn good.

CHAPTER 17

Anna-Karin sits in Nicolaus's stairwell and waits. The automatic light has gone off but she hasn't got the energy to get up and switch it on one more time. After the gravedigging, muscles she didn't know she had are hurting.

She got here too early, of course. She still isn't used to living in the middle of town, so close to everywhere. Besides, she was far too restless to stay at home. Nicolaus hasn't answered his phone all day.

She considers ringing his doorbell again, but she's done that three times already. She has opened the letterbox and listened into the apartment three times, too. The silence in there makes her nervous. What if Nicolaus is crouching in the darkness, driven mad by his memories? What if he's done something stupid? Hurt himself?

At last, the door to the street opens. Minoo switches the light on, starts when she catches sight of Anna-Karin.

'Christ! You scared me,' she says.

'I'm sorry.'

Minoo takes the key from her pocket and twirls it in her hand.

'I've rung the doorbell lots of times,' Anna-Karin tells her.

'It feels so wrong just going in,' Minoo says. 'But we have to.'

She unlocks the door.

Fire

There's a piece of junkmail on the doormat, a flyer about something called *Positive Engelsfors*. The air is hot and stale.

Anna-Karin switches on the ceiling light. The venetian blinds are closed. On the windowsill the fern looks droopy.

'Nicolaus?' she calls out tentatively just as Minoo shuts the front door behind them.

No reply. The bathroom door is standing slightly open. Anna-Karin looks inside. No one. Minoo goes to the kitchen and comes back. Shakes her head. They look at the closed bedroom door.

'Nicolaus?' Minoo calls in her turn.

Silence.

Anna-Karin takes a few steps forward and knocks. Waits. No response. She pushes the handle down, opens the door.

The air is even staler in there and smells like unwashed bed linen. Anna-Karin gropes around for the light switch.

A shapeless black bulk lies on the floor next to the bed. Anna-Karin nearly screams before she realizes it's Nicolaus's winter coat.

The wardrobe is open. Someone has pulled at the clothes and dragged them out. Several shelves are empty.

Minoo walks over to the bed and picks up a white envelope placed on the pillow.

'Please, could you let me …?' Anna-Karin asks.

Minoo hands her the envelope and Anna-Karin rips it open with her index finger. Inside is a lined sheet torn from a notepad.

Dear children,
I must leave now. My reasons will stay secret for the time being. I can only assure you that one day you will understand why I have to go.

Take good care of the silver crucifix. It is charged with powerful magic that will protect you. I have always thought that it serves many functions. Perhaps it will be of use to you.

I have paid another year's rent for this residence. Please use it as you see fit. You will find cash to cover any other expenditure inside the mattress.

I beg you to believe me when I tell you that I have your best interests in mind when I leave Engelsfors. It would be selfish of me to remain.

There are difficult times ahead. You must stay together. Trust one other. And put your trust in Matilda and the Book of Patterns.

I hope and believe that I will return.
Ever yours, faithfully,
N.E.

Anna-Karin lowers the sheet of paper.

'What does it say?' Minoo asks.

Anna-Karin's head is thumping.

'What does it say?' Minoo repeats.

Anna-Karin hands her the letter.

Minoo reads and, when she has finished, turns the sheet of paper over as if looking for something more.

'But he can't simply leave like this...' Anna-Karin says, feeling her throat constrict.

Minoo glances knowingly at her and Anna-Karin realizes, yes, he can do that. He just has.

She walks back into the living room. Stops in front of the silver crucifix on the wall and looks at it. Minoo comes along to stand next to her.

'I might call Ida,' Minoo suggests. 'Ask her to try to find him with the pendulum.'

'No, it's pointless,' Anna-Karin replies. 'He'll have gotten out of town already. Besides, he doesn't want us to find him.'

'Do you believe everything he wrote? Like the bit about getting out of here for our sake?'

'Do *you* believe him?'

They look at each other.

'Yes, I do,' Minoo says. 'I believe him.'

Difficult times ahead.

Anna-Karin notices the big, black umbrella in the corner by the front door. That was the umbrella Nicolaus had held over them both that evening last autumn, only a few hours after Rebecka's death.

Anna-Karin remembers the sound of rain hammering against the umbrella. How safe she felt with Nicolaus.

Now he has disappeared. The Chosen Ones can only look to each other now.

CHAPTER 18

The psychologists' waiting room at the Child and Adolescent Mental Health clinic shouts institutional values at you. *We keep an eye on you! We watch every step you take!*

There are times when Linnéa wonders if she ever will be rid of this place. How she despises those wimps who whine about their parents acting like prison guards. At least they don't have to put their private life on show week after week and have it turned inside out just to prove that they're not on dope or about to have a nervous breakdown. If they break any rules, they get...what? A fight with Mom and Dad? But if Linnéa is caught in the wrong, she will lose her apartment and what little freedom she has.

Today, Diana should have come on one of her so-called 'home visits'. As if the whole idea were about sharing a nice cup of tea, and not about control. But she was off with food poisoning and canceled at the last minute.

Linnéa wouldn't mind in the slightest if Jakob canceled today, too.

Her need to talk about Vanessa is so strong that she is unsure if she will be able to stop herself. And she doesn't want to talk to Jakob about Vanessa, just as she doesn't want to tell him too much about Elias. She would rather keep harping on her father and her childhood and her dead mother, however long the therapy takes.

She treasures Vanessa and Elias, her only precious possessions, though they are stinging, painful wounds as well.

The door to one of the offices opens and Jakob comes out.

'Hi, Linnéa.'

He holds out his hand and Linnéa takes it in hers.

The grief that floods her is new and raw. It feels as if she's been thrown back to the time just after Elias's death. But this is not her grief. It is Jakob's.

... I can't cope with this session, I should've canceled ...

She pulls her hand back, but Jakob's emotions and thoughts still resound in her mind.

She follows him into the office and quickly sits down, trying to hide how shaken she is.

'How was your first week back at school?' Jakob asks.

'Terrific.'

The irony seems to pass Jakob by. He simply nods.

'Any recurrence of your panic attacks?'

'No, not for a while now.'

He doesn't reply and Linnéa cautiously sends a probe into his thoughts to find out if he thinks she's lying.

... this is going to be too much for me... Christ, how am I to help these kids, I should've called in sick ...

Linnéa observes his face. Pale under his tan. She notes his red-rimmed eyes. Notes the way he keeps picking at a loose thread in the hem of his shorts.

... why didn't I understand how strongly this would affect me? I'm a goddamn psychologist after all...she is dead...she really is dead ...

'How do *you* feel?' Linnéa asks.

'Oh, fine. Perhaps a little tired.'

Jakob looks guilty, as if he's been found out. She doesn't have to probe for his next thought, because it comes to her anyway.

... fuck, fuck, fuck, she's seeing straight through me, it's like in all these nightmares when they know exactly what I'm thinking ...

'Why do you want to know how I feel?' he says, probably unaware of the aggressive undertone in his voice.

'Surely I'm allowed to ask how you're feeling...?'

Jakob clears his throat. He is clearly trying to restore his grip on his role as psychologist.

'Of course you can,' he replies, but his eyes won't meet hers. 'What I meant was...You seem preoccupied. Maybe there's something you want to talk about?'

Linnéa can no longer hear herself think.

Jakob's thoughts have taken over her mind entirely.

His female colleague has died, the woman with whom he was unfaithful to his wife more than a year ago. Now, he regrets everything he didn't say and didn't do, as he remembers all the moments they had shared. Moments that Linnéa definitely doesn't want to see.

There is so much lurking under the surface of everyone's life. Before she was given the ability to read minds, Linnéa never grasped just *how much* is going on out of sight. She feels a whole lot less of a weirdo now that she has insight into other people, into their pain and dark secrets. Although right now, she would much prefer not to.

She feels a general anxiety about the future, she says, and talks on autopilot. Jakob is barely listening. But at least she manages to stay out of his head for the rest of the session.

It's last period on Friday and Minoo has a hard time concentrating in the hot classroom. She is not the only one. Her classmates' faces glisten; they sag in their seats, whisper to each other and ignore Ylva's attempts to make them focus on the joys of geometry. The air is thick with off-putting smells.

Sweat, moist clothing and, from Hanna A whose place is just in front of Minoo, far too much perfume on warm skin.

Hanna A leans against the backrest. Minoo holds her breath and sits back, too.

She thinks about Hanna's screaming in the chemistry lab. Viktor hasn't shown up in school since Wednesday, when it all happened. Minoo can't forget his smile when Kevin splashed acid over himself. What kind of person smiles at something like that?

Ylva draws a triangle on the blackboard, then turns to face the class.

'Listen, please be quiet,' she says.

There is a film of moisture over her glasses, just next to the base of her nose.

'Can't we do the rest of the lesson outside?' Kevin asks and people all around mumble in support. 'Hey, miss, what about it? I'll buy you an ice cream. A soooper-sized cone!'

There is some scattered laughter and Ylva's cheeks go even redder. Her hands go to her sides, her eyes fix on Kevin. Minoo has a feeling that Ylva must have practiced looking dignified in front of the mirror. If so, it hasn't done the trick.

'Come onnnn, it's too hot to think,' Kevin goes on.

Ylva shifts her weight from one foot to the other.

'Besides, it's the weekend soon...' Kevin says.

'That's enough!' Ylva shrieks. 'Get out!'

She points at the door. A large sweat stain in her armpit is now visible to all. The stain is Greenland-shaped.

'But, miss, he really hasn't done anything,' Hanna A says.

'All I wanted was to buy you an ice cream,' Kevin beams.

'OUT!'

It's a howl from the abyss. Minoo imagines she can see Greenland grow larger.

Kevin gets up to go, but stops in the doorway and waves

with his bandaged hand. Ylva almost pushes him out of the room. And locks the door.

'Oh, my God, she's totally hysterical,' someone whispers loudly.

Ylva's eyes search the room restlessly, but she can't identify the whisperer.

'Work independently for the rest of this class,' she says and settles down behind the teacher's desk.

Minoo stares at the lined notepaper in front of her. Ylva's outburst makes her feel terribly embarrassed. She doesn't care to begin to think what the rest of the school year will be like. Weak teachers can never keep order in class. But weak *and* easily provoked teachers create a special kind of chaos.

An eternity seems to pass before the bell rings.

Minoo is among the last to leave the classroom. Ylva sits at her desk, nodding rather stiffly as she says 'Have a nice weekend' to students who happen to look her way. Minoo feels sorry for her and smiles as pleasantly as she can. Ylva's expression is so grateful it hurts.

Minoo goes with the flow down the stairs, then stops at her locker to collect the books she'll need over the weekend. They make quite a pile. It seems true enough, what everybody said. Eleventh grade is a lot tougher than tenth. She'll need to bring a wheelbarrow to school soon.

As she walks towards the main entrance, she catches sight of Gustaf. He is standing at the bulletin board with a colorful sheet of paper in his hand.

'Hi, Minoo! I was just going to call you. Do you want to meet up this weekend?'

She is about to say yes, when she remembers tomorrow's meeting in the fairground. The principal had mentioned 'changes' in the fall. For all Minoo knew, it might mean lessons in magic throughout the weekend. Maybe second-year magic studies are tougher, too. Besides, she needs more time to think about all that happened concerning Nicolaus.

'I can't,' she says.

'What are you going to do?'

Minoo herself would never have dared to say that to someone who said he or she was busy, in case it was a lie and the person simply didn't *want* to see her. But Gustaf's gaze is unsuspecting. He really is so amazingly...*secure*.

'I've promised Mom to spend some time at home this weekend,' she says.

'What a pity. I was going to ask you along to this.'

He holds out the sheet of paper. It is the same advertising flyer that Minoo had noticed on the mat in Nicolaus's hallway. 'POSITIVE ENGELSFORS CENTER OPENS THIS WEEKEND' proclaims the text happily above a photo of peaceful-looking people watching a sunset. Minoo recognizes the address. The shut-down library in the town center. The invitation apparently includes food and music. And the obligatory free balloons for the kids.

'Where did you get this invite?' Minoo asks.

'My friend Rickard gave it to me. I've hardly seen him all summer. Frankly, I didn't think he was interested in anything except soccer.'

'Do you know what it's really about? It sounds kind of...cultish.'

'I don't think so. Rickard tells me it's great.'

'How is it great? I mean, what do they *do*?'

'I was going to find out. Aren't you coming?'

'I guess I'd better stay away. You know, so I can kidnap you and de-program you afterwards.'

She thought Gustaf would laugh, but he doesn't.

'After all, we talked about how this town needs something new to happen,' he says. 'And now there are people who're trying to create something good. No need to be critical and suspicious all the time, right?'

Minoo is surprised at how quickly irritation flares up. It is the first time Gustaf has made her feel like this. As if he has suddenly overdone the things she normally likes about him.

'No need at all, of course,' she replies. 'Of course one should believe the best about everyone and everything. It pays, doesn't it, since the world is such a terrifically kindly, nice place.'

Gustaf stares at her and Minoo realizes the impact of what she has just said. If there is one person who knows that the world is not a kindly, nice place, it is Gustaf. Gustaf, who watched as Rebecka, his girlfriend, fell from the school roof and was crushed against the asphalt. Who still believes that Rebecka took her own life.

'Enjoy your weekend with your mom,' he says and walks away.

She looks after him as he disappears in the crowd and wonders about what she just did. How she managed to ruin so much in such a short time.

Because she chases demons everywhere, why expect Gustaf to do the same? Who is she to judge him because he wants to see the light first, not the shadows?

CHAPTER 19

'G!' Ida calls to him the moment she spots Gustaf coming out of the school.

So what if she sounds pathetic, she doesn't care. The way she's lurking outside school is so pathetic to begin with. There is something about Gustaf that makes her endlessly willing to crawl to him.

After seeing Gustaf and Minoo talking in front of the bulletin board, she instantly came along to stand here and wait. They seemed to be arguing. Ida has no intention of missing her chance.

Now that he is walking towards her, she has to force herself to stand still and not run to meet him.

There are times when she worries about being too demonstrative and scaring G off. And, at other times, about not having made it clear *enough* how she feels about him. How is he supposed to know? Especially now, when she's going out with Erik?

But, whatever, she has to hold to being a winner. It's the right attitude. One day, Gustaf will realize that he and she belong together. They are made for each other, he can't stay blind to that for ever. All Ida needs to do is hang on and endure.

'Hi, Ida,' Gustaf says when he gets close.

He sounds weary and Ida's mind starts churning so fast she can barely keep up with her own thoughts.

Part One

What was his fight with Minoo about? Got to be a good sign – or is it? Maybe it's a bad sign. If Minoo can make G this bad-tempered, doesn't it mean that he cares for her seriously? Is he annoyed with Minoo, or maybe with someone else? What if it's me? No, surely not, why would he be annoyed with me? Anyway, who doesn't get irritated with Minoo?

Just now, Ida would give anything for Linnéa's mind-reading powers. Then she would at last know what he really thinks.

'Isn't it great it's the weekend now?' she says.

As she speaks, she lets her fingers slide over her collarbone. Only lightly, not so that it looks kind of porno or slutty. She read somewhere that men like it when they catch women touching themselves, because it signals sensuality and self-confidence.

'Yeah, it is,' Gustaf mumbles.

It is so rare for the two of them to talk alone like this. She wants to savor every second. Stretch the moment as far as possible.

'What are you doing? I mean, I know you have soccer practice, but apart from that?'

Does she come across like a stalker? Perhaps a little. But it shows that she pays attention to what he does and also how well she understands that his interests matter to him. Besides, Ida likes sports, too, especially soccer. So she obviously has the upper hand over Minoo.

'Rickard and I planned to check this thing out,' Gustaf says and hands Ida a flyer.

'Oh, gosh, that's so exciting,' she says while she pretends to read it.

But she can't get a single letter into her head; she is far too aware of his tanned arms and of his hands, which look masculine and somehow adult.

Fire

'But I'm not sure I'm going,' Gustaf adds. 'We'll see.'

'Umm, exactly,' Ida replies and twists the silver heart she wears on a chain around her neck. 'I've got a lot going on, too.'

A bit further away on the schoolyard, a glimpse of a mass of black curls. Minoo is hurrying towards the gates. She glances quickly in their direction.

Fucking Minoo. Minoo, who has been allowed to kiss G. True, she actually kissed Max wearing a magic disguise, but still. Kissing a copy of Gustaf just once would be better than kissing a thousand Eriks a hundred thousand times.

Anyway, Minoo might well have been kissing the real G all summer long.

Could it be true, that story of Julia's? That they were making out down by the canal docks?

Ida can't hold back. She must ask, must know.

'Are you and Minoo an item...or...?'

Gustaf looks wonderingly at her.

'Why do you ask?'

'No special reason, it's just that I heard...'

That you were making out down by the canal docks.

'... someone say you've been seen together in town. All I did was wonder a little.'

Before Gustaf can reply, she has realized that this is a mistake. He sighs.

'Christ, this town...what can I say? Why does everybody have to keep an eye on everything and everybody all the time?'

'It's so *true*,' Ida says quickly. 'That's what I said to the person who told me. To Julia. People ought to get a life instead of snooping on other people's. Totally typical Engelsfors.'

Gustaf shakes his head and smiles at Ida. His smile seems pitying. Something is cut, deep inside her.

'Have a nice weekend,' he says and walks away from her.

'You too!' she calls out after him, a little too loudly.

Ida stands still, almost as if she were paralyzed.

Gustaf never answered her question about Minoo.

A Knight Templar from Sweden rides across a desert landscape on a galloping horse. Ida is practically asleep; she has seen this movie before and it was deadly boring the first time. Dad's turn to choose, though, and he wouldn't listen when she protested.

Dad moves around on his dark blue leather armchair. It creaks and moans. Mom hates that chair because it looks like an ugly bruise on the smooth white surface of their home.

Rasmus and Lotta are sitting on the sofa next to Ida. Off and on, one of them mechanically gropes around for another handful of popcorn from the bowl that says POPCORN on its side.

As usual, Mom is up and about, puttering. She can't bear to stay still and watch.

'Carina, come back!' Dad calls after her. 'You're missing the whole film!'

'Coming!' she shouts from the kitchen.

Rasmus gobbles a handful of popcorn, licks his hand thoroughly and reaches for the bowl again.

'That's repulsive,' Ida says. 'Dad, did you see what Rasmus did?'

'Come on, folks. Quiet. Just watch the movie.'

Rasmus sticks his tongue out at Ida. It is coated with tiny, sticky popcorn crumbs.

'I think it's boring,' Lotta whines. 'Nothing is happening.'

'You only think that because you're too little to understand,' Ida sneers.

'I'm not too little!'

'No? Then you must be retarded, obviously.'

'Will you put a lid on it!' Dad says. 'For God's sake, it's hopeless watching a film with females around. Won't stop chattering, will they, eh, Rasmus?'

Rasmus looks pleased with himself, smiles and then licks his hand again with his eyes fixed on Ida. Dad doesn't pay attention, of course.

Mom comes back and sits down. She places an accounts folder on her lap.

'What's going on?' she asks. 'Have they left Sweden yet?'

'God, not again,' Dad groans. 'Either stay and keep your mind on the movie, or stop asking questions about it.'

'Sorry to trouble you, I'm sure,' Mom says sourly.

She exchanges a look with Ida and both of them roll their eyes heavenwards.

'Anyway, nothing's happened,' Lotta tells her. 'The film is total crap. They just talk and talk and ride and ride.'

'Don't use that word,' Mom says and starts leafing through the folder.

Ida suddenly realizes that her mouth is dry. The room begins to revolve around her. She feels giddy.

Abruptly, she gets up and hurries to the bathroom.

'Ida, what's wrong? Are you unwell?' Mom calls.

'Do you have the squishy squirts?' Rasmus shouts and Dad laughs.

Mom protests. Ida barely has time to hear Dad explain that the kid made it sound quite comical, the way he said it.

She closes the door, locks it. Then sinks on to the floor.

The bathroom walls are rotating around her. This is beyond dizziness. It's like being in free fall. Ida presses the palms of her hands against the tiled floor in an attempt to hold on to the real world. But the other one, Matilda, will not leave her in peace.

Ida fights her.

I don't want to be part of this. I don't want to be part of this. I don't want to be part of this.

She tries to draw strength from her anger and her hatred of what is being done to her.

Why should she always be the one who draws the short straw? Always! She was made to tell the truth, first by Anna-Karin in the fairground, and then again, with the truth serum. She was forced to wait alone in the dark when they broke into the principal's house. And she collapsed in the Lucia procession, in front of the entire school. And she wasn't allowed to join the others at their secret meetings. Rotten bullies, the lot of them. And why did she have to cope with the toughest, most humiliating of magic powers?

Leave me alone!!!

Glowing fragments dance in front of her eyes. Like sparklers.

Ida has lost. The uninvited guest, the familiar stranger, is forcing entry into her body.

A knock on the door. Dad's voice speaks to her.

'Ida, you're not dying in there, are you? Your mother seems to think so.'

Ida shuts her lips tightly. Will not utter the words of the other.

Then the floor disappears underneath her.

She falls through chaos, hurtling towards a distant surface. She might be crushed against it or it might not exist at all. Her speed is too high. She smells smoke from a fire, feels the grief of the betrayed, feels love turn into hatred and, then, confronted by an inescapable fate, senses the panic of the hunted turn into resignation. And then the scorching heat comes at her, a sea of flames engulfs her and for a brief moment she feels the fire burn off her skin, crack it open and make the flesh beneath sear and bubble.

Ida tries to scream but her open mouth fills with fire.

The last thing she sees is the *Book of Patterns* surrounded by flames.

She smells peppermint quite strongly.

Ida opens her eyes. Her left hand holds a tube of toothpaste and the fingers of her right hand are sticky.

She is standing in front of the bathroom mirror.

Six letters are written on the mirror glass with neon-blue toothpaste.

DANGER.

'Ida!' Dad's voice again and now he sounds anxious. 'What are you doing in there?'

'Go to hell!' she screams.

Ida screams at her father, at the Circle, at Matilda who dragged her into the darkness and the fire, at her entire shitty, awful life.

CHAPTER 20

The morning light filters through the lowered venetian blinds in Nicolaus's living room. As Ida changes position on her wooden chair, one of the lines of light makes her blue eyes flash. Minoo wonders, not for the first time, and hardly the last, what goes on behind those eyes. Who is Ida really?

'"Danger"? She couldn't have been a little bit less *precise*, could she?' Linnéa says.

'Are you sure it was Matilda?' Minoo asks.

Ida nods.

'I hate that fucking bitch. Why can't she go for one of you, just for a change?'

'Give it a rest,' Vanessa says. 'I think she's more to be pitied than you are.'

Ida snorts.

'What do you think she tried to tell you?' Minoo asks.

'Search me! I know no more than you do. Of course I realize that she had a hard time while she was alive but, honestly, it doesn't give her the right to invade me all the time! She had another run at me in the dining area, not too long ago but I managed to block her.'

'You did *what*?' Linnéa asks.

'Excuse me, but I didn't want to go apeshit in front of the entire school – not again!'

Linnéa groans.

'All right,' Minoo interrupts. 'We know that Nicolaus warned us of "difficult times". It seems Matilda is fearful too. But we have no idea where the threat is coming from.'

'Anyone else guessing the demons have something to do with it?' Linnéa says.

'Maybe we'd better ask her,' Vanessa suggests.

'Who?' Minoo asks.

'Matilda. Maybe we should have a séance.'

Minoo stares at her.

They know already that the dead can contact the living. But the other way around, is it possible? And if it can be done, what will it entail?

Despite the heat, Minoo's arms are covered in goose bumps.

Rebecka.

At the start of the summer, she had been convinced that Rebecka and Elias had left this world for good, that they were in the right place, wherever that might be. But what if it were possible to get in touch with them again? Perhaps talk with Rebecka? Just one last time?

It feels like a forbidden thought. But one she can't leave alone.

'A séance!' Ida says. Her voice is shrill. 'And of course you'll expect me to volunteer as your ghost magnet?'

'We haven't decided anything,' Minoo says. 'We don't even know how to.'

'And the *Book of Patterns* is no help, as far as we know,' Anna-Karin points out.

'But there's Mona Moonbeam as well,' Vanessa says. 'She'll help, at least for as long as she gets paid.'

'All right,' Minoo says again. 'Ida and Linnéa, you check the book just to make sure. Vanessa, you go to the Crystal Cave.'

'Why do I have to ...?' Vanessa begins, but falls silent and sighs. 'Yes, yes. All right.'

'Anyway, we're sure about one thing – that we can't trust the Council,' Linnéa says. 'So not one word to the principal about any of this or about what Nicolaus told us.'

'But Adriana is on our side,' Vanessa says. 'Well, sort of.'

'If there's one thing that Nicolaus's story confirms, it's that we can't trust any member of the Council.'

Minoo glances at her phone.

'We've got to go,' she says.

'True,' Vanessa says. 'We mustn't miss the fall semester's first lesson in magic.'

Minoo walks beside Linnéa on the way to Kärrgruvan. The others follow, each on her own.

Since they left Nicolaus's apartment, Linnéa hasn't said a word. Every so often, Minoo sneaks a look at her profile, with the black bangs, the shoulder-length black hair pulled up in two pigtails. Her heavily made-up eyes are hidden behind large sunglasses.

Minoo is often troubled by Linnéa's harshness and aggression, but she admires her, too. She is the kind of person Minoo would like to count as a friend. Only, their lives are so desperately different. Their talk never flows easily; there is always a watchful undertone.

'Do you think it can be done?' Linnéa asks suddenly. 'Contacting the dead?'

'I hope so. I mean, Matilda is obviously trying to contact us.'

'What about someone dead who isn't trying?'

She says this quickly, as if to conceal her feelings.

Minoo understands that she is thinking of Elias. Perhaps of her mother, too? Minoo wonders if Linnéa can even remember what her mother looked like. How old was Linnéa when her mother died?

'I don't know,' Minoo replies cautiously. 'Maybe you could ask the book?'

Linnéa doesn't answer.

They have almost reached Kärrgruvan. Minoo hasn't been to the fairground since the end of last semester. Everything looks the same. The broken fence. The ticket booth, with two planks nailed across the opening. The overgrown hedges. The dance pavilion under its pointy roof, which they can glimpse between the trees.

As they walk through the gate, the sense of an unchanging past grows even stronger. It's almost *too* unchanged. It's as if the abandoned fairground has been preserved in its state of decay. As if the whole place is holding its breath.

The principal waits, standing on the dance floor.

Adriana Lopez is wearing a tight skirt that ends above the knee and a creamy-white silk blouse, as ever buttoned up all the way. There is a patch of sweat on her chest. Minoo can't think why Adriana doesn't undo a few buttons. No need for her to hide anything now. They have already seen her scarred skin.

The raven, Adriana's familiar, caws loudly from its perch up on the roof.

Adriana looks up and waves to them. Her body language is stiffer than usual and her back even straighter.

Minoo and Linnéa step up on to the dance floor and the others join them, one by one.

He buried her somewhere here, Minoo thinks. Her eyes search the grounds. She wishes that they had asked Nicolaus exactly where Matilda's body has its resting place so that they could mark it out in some way only they would understand. In her honor.

'Girls, welcome back,' the principal says when they are all gathered around her.

Her smile is forced.

Minoo and Linnéa exchange glances. Both have observed it. Adriana is nervous.

'There is something I must tell you,' she continues, but falls silent when the sound of a car engine comes closer. Heavy tires crunch over the gravel on the roadway.

A dark green car pulls up just outside the gates.

The engine noise is cut and the driver, a tall man in a suit, climbs out. Then the passenger door opens. Viktor climbs out and slams the car door shut.

Kärrgruvan has been wiped from the collective consciousness in Engelsfors. People can't find their way here any longer. No one even remembers that it exists.

But now this stranger walks straight in, with Viktor in his wake.

Minoo observes the principal. Her face is blank, like a mask. She is transformed into the Adriana Lopez whom Minoo met a year ago. Back then, Minoo had found it impossible to imagine that Adriana had any emotional life whatsoever.

Adriana watches Viktor and the unknown man as they reach the pavilion.

The stranger is at least forty, Minoo guesses. Could he be Viktor's father? Only if some kind of genetic miracle had taken place. The man's skin has an olive tone, his hair is dark and his eyes are brown. Definitely different from pale, ash-blonde, blue-eyed Viktor.

And still they belong together. It shows, somehow.

Minoo tries to catch Viktor's eye, but he ignores her.

'Girls,' Adriana speaks loudly. 'Let me introduce Alexander and Viktor Ehrenskiöld. They are sent here to represent the Council.'

She steps aside. Minoo notes that Anna-Karin's face has turned green. She looks as if she is about to faint any minute, or throw up. Or both.

The Council. The authority whose rules Anna-Karin disobeyed throughout last year's fall semester, despite warnings. The authority that ordered the sign of Fire to be burned into the principal's skin to punish her defiance. That allowed the earlier Chosen One to be burned at the stake.

Minoo takes Anna-Karin's hand. She shudders at the touch at first, then returns it and squeezes Minoo's hand hard.

Alexander's gaze slides across their faces. Halts when it reaches Anna-Karin.

'Anna-Karin Nieminen?' Alexander Ehrenskiöld asks.

Anna-Karin is past speaking. It is as if she has forgotten how to. Mute, she nods instead.

'You will be tried in court for your crimes. As of now, and until further notice, you are not allowed to leave Engelsfors and must be available for interrogation. We would have preferred to keep you in custody, but Adriana has persuaded us that you will cooperate.'

His gaze leaves Anna-Karin and she at least dares to breathe again.

'Until the trial ends, your lessons in magic will be canceled. The rest of you must also be ready to be interrogated. I will prosecute. Viktor is my assistant—'

'Excuse me,' Vanessa interrupts, without a trace of apology in her voice. 'But this is so inappropriate. When somebody was trying to murder us, you guys didn't do anything at all. And now you're coming up here to take Anna-Karin to court?'

Anna-Karin tries to grasp what Vanessa is saying. Tries

to get into her head that she is not alone, exactly as Minoo said. She tightens her grip on Minoo's hand, despite worrying that her own is sweaty.

Alexander looks contemptuous as he turns to Vanessa.

'Who is this?' he asks Viktor.

'She is Vanessa Dahl,' Viktor replies promptly.

'"She" can speak for herself, just so you know,' Vanessa snaps.

'We are here to help you,' Alexander says. 'You are hugely important to us. Indeed, to the whole world.'

Anna-Karin realizes that he doesn't mean a word of all that. On the contrary. He doesn't even try to control the undertone of scorn in what he says.

'However, this trial is necessary,' Alexander continues. 'It is a consequence of the severe breaches that have been committed against the laws of magic.'

'What crimes is Anna-Karin actually charged with?' Minoo asks.

Alexander turns to stare at her.

'Minoo Falk Karimi,' Viktor prompts.

'Is that so?' Alexander says with a hint of interest in his dark brown eyes. 'Anna-Karin was told by Adriana Lopez to cease using magic for personal gain. She did not desist as ordered. You know the laws of the Council.'

Alexander turns to look at Anna-Karin and, once more, terror grabs her by the throat.

'Three laws, all straightforward,' he instructs. 'You are not allowed to practice magic without the permission of the Council. You are not allowed to use your magic powers to break non-magic laws. Finally, you are not allowed to reveal to the non-magic population that you are witches. In the case of Anna-Karin, we are certain that she is in breach of at least two of these laws. Probably all three.'

Fire

Anna-Karin is gasping for air. Just to escape that ice-cold, merciless gaze she would confess to practically anything.

'But, as a matter of fact, we were all given our powers before we even knew that the Council existed,' Minoo says. 'I'm saying that Anna-Karin hasn't committed any crime whatsoever, surely you can't be accused of breaking the laws of magic when you don't even know that such laws exist?'

Anna-Karin sneaks a glance at Minoo and sees that her cheeks are blushing bright red. Obviously, she is nearly as scared of Alexander as Anna-Karin. And yet she dares to contradict him.

'Naturally not,' Alexander replies coolly.

'Good,' Minoo says. 'I wanted that clarified.'

'I can assure you that the trial will be thorough and just, from beginning to end,' Alexander says. 'Afterwards, Adriana will continue to train you.'

Miss Lopez's face is immobile. She just stands there, like a wax doll.

'One more thing,' Alexander says. 'Until the Council has arrived at a sentence, you are all strictly forbidden to use magic. Viktor will keep you under surveillance at school and we have our methods for continuing to supervise you also during your leisure time. We will get in touch as and when you are required for interrogation.'

He walks towards the steps. But someone moves to block his way. Linnéa. Of course.

Anna-Karin's heart does a somersault inside her chest. She feels like screaming at Linnéa to keep out of this. Alexander is dangerous, can't she see that?

'Linnéa Wallin, I presume,' Alexander says. 'And what's on your mind?'

'Just a minor problem. The apocalypse.'

'We have plenty of time, enough to deal with the present case, as well as training you for future battles.'

'Why should we listen to you at all? You need us more than we need you.'

A faint smile flickers on Alexander's lips.

'Really? Well, if you believe that you must act accordingly. And be prepared to cope with the consequences.'

His eyes suddenly fix on Linnéa. She whimpers and puts her hands to her head as if a blow has been struck. Her sunglasses crash to the floor.

'So, I wouldn't try that kind of move again if I were you,' Alexander says.

These are his final words.

He walks to the car, closely followed by Viktor and Adriana.

CHAPTER 21

Linnéa's aching head stays painful for the time it takes her to walk along the gravel track and cross the main road. She ought not to have let herself be provoked by Alexander. He had of course worked out that she would try to find out what he was thinking and was ready for her. He flung back at her the power she had directed against him. Inside Linnéa's head, the feedback howl is tailing off but still reverberating.

They had scattered once the meeting was over. They had a lot to talk about, but didn't dare to do it openly. From now on, they have to stay alert not only for spies from the demons, but also from the Council.

Linnéa's phone pings. A message from Minoo to say that they should meet up in Nicolaus's apartment tomorrow night to decide on exactly what to say in the interrogations. Linnéa replies that she'll be there. Most of all, though, she would like to be rid of the whole scene.

'Linnéa!'

She turns when she hears the familiar voice.

Vanessa is jogging towards her.

Linnéa knows that hope can be a trap, but she can't help it. Vanessa wants to talk to her.

'All right if we walk together for a bit?' Vanessa asks.

'Sure,' Linnéa says, as coolly as she can.

For quite a long while, they walk along the main road in

silence. Linnéa doesn't dare to say anything, for fear that she might ruin this moment, manage to do something wrong now that Vanessa seems prepared once more to be close to her.

She is so, so lovely, Linnéa thinks.

Behind her sunglasses, she looks at Vanessa's brown legs and arms. Skin that she will never touch. Her neck, the contours of her body under the tight tank top that has ridden up a little and exposes part of the curve of the small of her back. Her freshly highlighted hair that glows against the dark trees along the road.

Of course, Vanessa knows that she looks great. To her, that's just a fact. But Linnéa believes that Vanessa hasn't understood what a beautiful *human being* she is.

At first, it was so easy to underestimate Vanessa. A chick with her hair dyed blonde, impossibly short skirts and thick layers of lipgloss. Wille's new squeeze. But Linnéa, who should know all there is to know about being judged without a hearing, was soon forced to accept that she, too, had been prejudiced.

Vanessa is brave. Smart. Honest. Instinctively, she's a good person. A true heroine. Wille is her one and only weakness, her kryptonite.

Wille is such a fucking creep. He never deserved her. Linnéa doesn't even want to think about Wille and Vanessa having sex, but because she has been with him, it is hard to prevent her brain projecting detailed images.

There is an ache inside Linnéa as she tries to imagine what putting her arm around Vanessa would feel like. Or kissing her lips, which look so soft. Jonte's party comes back to her, or rather, the moment when Vanessa came out of the bathroom and touched Linnéa's arm. Or when Vanessa came over to her place and they sat on the sofa. Their legs brushed against each other and everything felt, for once, as if the whole world were in harmony.

Linnéa should have kissed her, there and then.

But she has never picked up a single thought in Vanessa's mind that suggests that she feels the same way. And Vanessa's thoughts are so incredibly *clear*. There have been a few times when she thought that Linnéa looked good, but that means nothing. Linnéa has thought that lots of people look good without being in love with them.

In love.

The phrase seems too feeble.

'You know, there are times I wish *I* knew what *you* were thinking,' Vanessa says.

Linnéa is pulled back to reality. Vanessa smiles at her.

'Why do you say that?' Linnéa asks.

'You look so mysterious.'

'No mystery. Just a headache.'

Vanessa stops. Linnéa, too.

'I want to ask you to forgive me,' Vanessa says. 'That time at the cemetery. I overreacted. Later on, I realized you had seen that my ring wasn't there any more, and—'

'And I shouldn't have said what I did,' Linnéa says and steels herself. 'I'm sorry.'

Vanessa kicks a discarded beer can. It bounces across the asphalt, rattling as it goes.

'Is it all right with you if we don't have, like, a big heart-to-heart?' Vanessa asks. 'And instead just...have made up already?'

Linnéa is so relieved she feels about to lift off.

'Absolutely fine,' she says.

'I've missed you,' Vanessa tells her.

And I've missed you, Linnéa would like to say. And add, you have no idea how much.

But it is so terribly hard to say these very words, *and I've missed you*, without sounding false and artificial.

She is silent for a second too long and Vanessa seems to feel awkward, looks away. Linnéa's phone pings again. She pokes about, finds it. A text from Olivia.

Call me back OK?

Linnéa pretends to study this intently as they walk towards the center of town.

'Check that out,' Vanessa says after a while and points at the sky. It is covered by massive thunderclouds, so dark blue they are almost black.

'At last,' Linnéa says.

'Absolutely. Everyone had almost stopped believing it would happen,' Vanessa says, still looking upwards.

So that's how it goes. They're talking about the *weather*.

Linnéa would like to suggest that they might go to her apartment. Turn the lights off and sit by the windows up there and watch the flashes of lightning. But maybe all that would only scare Vanessa away?

She has no idea about what you're meant to do if you're actually in love with somebody. This is completely new to her. Usually, she hardly even *likes* the people she goes with. They simply surface in her life and she allows them to hang out with her to pass the time, to distract her restless mind for the time being. Fill the emptiness a little.

They reach the center of Engelsfors and Linnéa's eyes automatically scan the boozer seats as they pass by. She concentrates so hard on this that she almost misses him standing on the pavement a little further away.

Björn Wallin is wearing a bright yellow T-shirt with PE! printed on the chest. A laughing sun makes the dot of the exclamation mark. His hair is nicely combed. The look in his eye is alert and sober. And his front teeth are new, white and even, where before there were obvious gaps that caused the lower half of his face to sag.

A memory stirs in Linnéa.

Summer vacation. She and Elias had been in the forest. They had been playing – she couldn't remember what, apart from feeling it was a game they had really grown too old for. But they were happy. Still lots of days before school began. It had been great.

She had come back home and the apartment was dark. It smelled bad, so bad that she always worried that the smell would stick to her when she went outside. That it would follow her wherever she went and give her away for what she was. The smell of a drunk's kid.

She had called to her dad. Heard him mutter something in the bathroom.

And Linnéa remembers exactly how hard her heart had been beating when she opened the door. She remembers exactly how her father looked where he lay on the floor, his mouth sticky with vomit, every breath a snort. And the absence of life behind his eyes.

'Help me,' he whimpered.

For the first time, Linnéa had shut the door on him. She had seen this too often before.

And now he is standing right here, with a bundle of colorful flyers in his hand. He has spotted her already.

She can't get away.

'Linnéa?' he says and comes closer.

His voice sounds worn, the voice of a man who has had a hard life, but it is not slurred.

He hugs Linnéa and she picks up the smell of aftershave. But no alcohol, no ingrained cigarette smoke. No filthy clothes, lived in for too long. She stands quite still in his arms, her own arms hanging limply down her sides.

'Dearest child,' he mumbles in Linnéa's ear and now she backs away.

'Would you like me to …?' Vanessa asks, making a vague gesture that means *stay or go*?

'I'll be in touch soon,' Linnéa says.

Vanessa nods and walks off. There was understanding in her eyes, and pity, too. As always, that fucking pity. Linnéa swallows hard and turns to her father.

'You look well,' she says stiffly.

But would like to add, how long will it last this time? How long, before you're back ringing my doorbell because you want to borrow money?

'Linnéa,' he says and tries to hold her hands.

She pulls away.

'It's not just that I'm feeling well,' he tells her. 'I've become a completely new person. Sure, I know I've said that many times before. But this time I have changed fundamentally.'

He hands her one of the flyers and she notices that his nails are clean.

'Look. Helena Malmgren and Positive Engelsfors have saved my life.'

She studies the sheet of paper. Two middle-aged couples are sitting in a summer meadow, their faces glowing golden in the light of the setting sun. One of the women rests her head against her man's chest. Her eyes are dreamily shut and her smile radiates total peace.

The caption wishes everyone welcome to Positive Engelsfors. And then:

'MAN OR WOMAN, YOUNG OR OLD. POSITIVE ENGELSFORS – FOR A POSITIVE FUTURE!'

'They've offered me a job,' her father says. 'We open today.'

He nods over his shoulder and now Linnéa realizes that

the street ahead is packed with people. Children are running around waving bright yellow helium balloons.

A heavy drop falls on the flyer, spreads across the shiny print. Linnéa looks up at the sky. The thunderclouds hang above them like a lid.

'I've been offered an apartment as well,' he continues. 'You must come and see me.'

'Must? I don't think so.'

Her father nods.

'I understand why you feel that way. But give me a chance to prove that you can trust me now.'

'I won't give you any more chances.'

A part of her regrets this immediately. What if he really *is* serious this time? What if her refusal to believe in him drives him to start drinking again?

But she has believed him before and it didn't help at all.

'No, Linnéa, you don't owe me anything. But you do owe yourself to dare to believe that people *can* change. I will never need alcohol again. I *know* that this is the case, for the first time in my life. To help others gives a more satisfying high than any drugs in the world.'

She doesn't speak, only hands the sheet of paper back.

Several drops hit her now. Around them, the dusty pavement is covered in spots.

'When you're ready, you know where to find me,' he says, nodding again towards the center.

'Bye,' she says and starts walking.

When she passes the home of Positive Engelsfors, she has to push past a group of women. As Linnéa passes them, they are laughing and holding up the palms of their hands.

'Imagine us being this pleased that it's raining!' one of them says, beaming with delight.

They all burst out laughing again, as if this is the funniest thing ever. Linnéa keeps walking, but a panicky anguish comes alive inside her, roars inside her head.

CHAPTER 22

Anna-Karin registers the sounds first. The murmuring among the fir trees, the whispering high above her head in the canopy of the pines, the faint rustling noises of leaves touching. Then she feels it.

The wind.

When the first rumble of thunder comes, long and powerful, the storm is still far away. It is dark now, as if at dusk. A few drops of rain hit her forehead.

Anna-Karin feels that nature itself is watching the sky, as she is.

Another thunderclap. Closer now. The sound rolls across the sky, makes the ground tremble, invades Anna-Karin's body and becomes part of the terror that has been hammering inside her since the morning meeting in the fairground.

She should have stopped misusing her powers as soon as the principal told her to. The others had been warning her as well. But she kept on, lying to herself.

And so, all last year, she made up tales to tell herself. The Council never came, after all. She allowed herself to believe that they would overlook her breaches of the rules. Turn a blind eye, because they understood how Anna-Karin had already suffered for her mistakes.

But why should they?

Anna-Karin recalls the people she manipulated and

exploited. Julia, Felicia and all the others who became her 'friends'. How she had made Jari think that he was in love with her. Her mother, who had suddenly put her hands into boiling water. And her grandpa, who had never recovered his old self since he rescued her from the burning barn.

Now she wishes that they had never dug up that grave. If they hadn't, Nicolaus would have stayed. She needs him more than ever.

The sky roars again.

Sounds like a right big discharge, as Grandpa used to say.

He would also have urged her to hurry up and leave the forest before the storm breaks. But she is no longer sure about the way back home.

Warm rain is falling in heavy drops. The fir trees are rocking in the wind and the tall pines are swaying slowly.

Suddenly, it feels as if somebody is showing her the right way to go. Anna-Karin starts running.

Sometimes, she's close to stumbling over large stones that don't show under the moss. It grows all over the ground here and is so dry it crackles under the soles of her shoes.

A flash of lightning turns the whole world white and Anna-Karin counts.

Thousand-and-one, thousand—

That's as far as she gets. The thunder roars.

The air smells of electricity.

She has no idea where she is, but knows she must go on. Something is calling her and she has to obey the call.

Anna-Karin runs up a slope. A new flash – she can see it rippling across the sky – creates a glowing slash. The thunderclaps come in waves that rise, then withdraw, only to crash again just when Anna-Karin believes it is all over.

She is pushing her body to the limit but is carried forward

by the magnetic quality of the call and doesn't feel tired. And, now she realizes where she has come.

The ghostlike tree is silhouetted against the black sky. Another moment and it explodes in a shower of sparks. She falls, lands on her knees and elbows. Her jaws snap shut so hard she thinks her teeth will crack.

She sees the tree catch fire. Despite the rain, the flames quickly take hold in the dry branches.

Anna-Karin is in the eye of the storm now, completely unprotected at the top of a hill. She is deafened by the thunder. Flashes of lightning criss-cross the air.

She tries to get up, rests on her knees and pushes her rain-soaked hair out of her face. And picks up a movement in the corner of her eye. An undulation close to the ground.

A plaintive bark, barely audible over all the noise.

Anna-Karin wipes the rain from her eyelashes and squints her eyes to see.

The fox. She recognizes it at once. And it is coming straight at her, stepping delicately on its black paws.

It stops in front of her, puts its head to the side and observes her with its amber eyes. The fox's fur is wet. Thousands of droplets gleam in the light of the fire.

Then, suddenly, it leaps and digs its teeth into the fleshy part of Anna-Karin's hand, just at the base of the thumb, the place that always reminds her of a chicken drumstick. The pain and surprise make her scream out loud. She tries to pull her hand back but the fox has it in an iron grip. It draws its lips back to show rows of small, sharp teeth and Anna-Karin senses her skin being punctured.

All the time, the fox looks her straight in the eye.

Minoo is seated at her desk with her old notebook open in front of her.

None of Anna-Karin's actions before they were called in to see the principal can be regarded as a crime. Alexander himself said so. But they must not reveal anything of what happened afterwards. A great deal, in other words. How much is Alexander actually aware of? What kind of evidence does he have?

She goes through her notes, tries to decide what they can admit in the interrogations and what they must stay silent about.

She wants to have an overview ready when they meet tomorrow night to draw up a plan. They must create their own agreed version of the truth. And then they have to keep repeating it, over and over until they stay on message even if woken up in the middle of the night. They must spin a finely meshed safety net of lies to protect Anna-Karin.

Minoo wishes she could prepare herself even better.

How do you manage the defense when the prosecutor uses magic? The bottom line is, if there is a prosecutor, Anna-Karin surely ought to have someone pleading in her defence? But who knows how the Council's trials operate?

Nicolaus had told them that the Council's methods had become more refined since his days. But the principal's scorched skin tells another story. Besides, as far as Minoo knows, Adriana's only crime was trying to leave the Council.

And disloyalty is the one thing they will not tolerate ...

Was the Council in fact the 'danger' that Matilda warned them about? Did Nicolaus know that the Council was coming? Was that why he left Engelsfors? Or is there something even worse waiting for them?

Minoo would like to cry, it would be liberating. She feels the tears welling up, the first hint of a sob from the depth of her being. She tries to let it out and the tears immediately dry up.

The room is lit by the flash of lightning. The thunder booms.

Her phone rings.

Number not disclosed.

'Hello?' she says.

Scratchy noises on the line. Someone's breathing.

'Hello?' Minoo says again.

'Can you speak safely?' Adriana asks.

'Yes,' Minoo replies and moves away from the desk.

'This is my only chance to get to talk to you,' Adriana continues in a low voice. 'I wanted to warn you earlier but couldn't. I've risked too much already. Now that Alexander is in town, I can't carry on. You understand that, don't you?'

'Yes.'

At least, she thinks she understands. The principal is on their side but they must all pretend not to know. It is the first time this is mentioned openly.

'If the Council sends Alexander, it means that it takes the trial seriously,' Adriana explains. 'He is a high-ranking official and absolutely loyal to the Council. He is willing to sacrifice even his family, his friends. The people he claims to love.'

'You seem to know him well,' Minoo says.

The line stays silent for so long Minoo has time to think that the contact might be broken.

'He is my brother,' Adriana says finally.

Minoo becomes mute. She imagines Adriana and Alexander in front of her. So very alike. How come she didn't see it at once?

'You must be extremely cautious. Obey his orders in every detail. Minoo, make the others realize the importance of this. Do not oppose Alexander. And, whatever else, do not tell lies under interrogation! Tell the truth!'

Minoo feels a huge weight descend on her.

Adriana keeps talking.

'I cannot risk contacting you again and you must under no circumstances try to get in touch with me, regardless of what happens. Please, Minoo, promise me...Promise that you won't lie when you're interrogated.'

The desperation in her voice is unlike anything Minoo has heard from her before. It frightens her more than anything Adriana has said.

'I promise,' Minoo says.

'Thank you. I'll try to...'

The line goes dead. The entire sky is lit up by lightning and the thunderclap makes the windowpanes rattle.

In the next moment, the light goes out.

Minoo sits in the dark, very still, holding her phone.

She knows that she will never keep her promise to Adriana.

 Part 2

CHAPTER 23

Minoo makes a fist and flails about in the general direction of the big white ball that is coming at her.

She registers Viktor's grin on the other side of the net and feels certain that he aimed it at her on purpose.

The ball hits her knuckles and shoots off in the wrong direction. Bounces along for quite a ways outside the court. She runs to grab it and her teammates groan loudly.

She can feel their eyes on her back. She hates them. Hates the gym and everything else that goes with it; it's just one big, sweat-stinking torture chamber. The ball has rolled in under a row of seats. She reaches for it but only manages to push it even further in. No ball sense even when the ball is sitting still.

'Cool panties!' Kevin shouts and she tugs at her sweatpants that have slipped a bit.

Minoo squeezes in under the seats and manages in the end to get hold of the damn stinking ball. As she wriggles back out, she notes a pitying glance from Anna-Karin in the other court.

The apocalypse is a trifle compared to this. Volleyball is absolutely the worst thing anyone can be subjected to. In all other ball games, it's possible to get away with half-heartedly running up and down at the edge of the field, doing just enough to give Lollo, their gym teacher, the impression that

Minoo is 'really trying, at least'. But in volleyball, the teams are too small for her to hide in the crowd. And soon it is her turn to serve.

The ball flies back and forth across the net and Minoo wills it not to come near her again.

This time, fate is good to her. Her savior is Lollo, who blows her whistle.

'That's it for today! Thank you, everyone!' she shouts.

Minoo hurries off to the seats to pick up her bag and tries to avoid meeting other people's eyes.

But when she turns to go, she almost walks into Viktor, who is watching her with an amused smile on his face. Naturally, he hasn't got a drop of sweat anywhere.

He blocks her way.

'No one can be awesome at everything,' he says.

Minoo doesn't reply. Since the meeting in the fairground nearly three weeks ago, she hasn't answered his remarks once. It has been rather hard going, given that they sit next to each other in all Ylva's lessons.

'I happen to have ball sense but, you can take my word for it, I hate sports as much as you do,' he adds.

She can't bear to look at him. Her eyes wander upwards to the row of narrow windows near the ceiling. Outside, the sky is gray above the asphalt of the yard. A pair of jeans-clad legs hurries past.

'It's simply *pointless*, don't you think?' Viktor goes on. 'It's not like it *signifies* anything. I realize somebody like Kevin needs to feel he can win something now and then but…'

She pushes past him and walks towards the changing rooms.

'See you later,' he calls out after her.

*

Part Two

Vanessa frames her face with her hands and presses it close to the display window of the Crystal Cave. In the dim shop interior she spots dream catchers, Egyptian-style busts, dolphins.

'CLOSED FOR INVENTORY' is printed with letters in every shade of the rainbow on a note taped to the inside of the window. There is not the slightest sign of any activity inside. But a smell of incense is wafting out into the mall.

Vanessa has come here every day for the last few weeks. She has varied the times as much as she can, but the shop has been closed, regardless. And it's impossible to get hold of Mona Moonbeam. In fact, there seems to be no proof that she exists. Minoo even phoned the tax office and searched some kind of database at her father's job. Not a trace.

Vanessa sighs and leaves the window. Fuck it, what options do they have if Mona has vanished? The *Book of Patterns* of course refuses to reply to any of their questions about how to communicate with the dead. The great book behaves like a grumpy old hag, Vanessa thinks with a sense of déjà vu.

The already rather feeble light in the City Mall flickers and there is a sizzling sound. Ever since the big thunderstorm, electricity in Engelsfors has been wobbly. It's not just irritating; at times Vanessa feels it's rather too much like the horror movies.

She walks quickly out of the mall. Outside the supermarket, flags with its logo flutter disconsolately in the wind. It is the middle of September but still very hot.

Vanessa turns a corner at Storvall Square when she sees the first other person out walking. He is coming towards her.

And he is one of the last people she wants to meet just now.

Vanessa wonders if she can turn back, pretend she hasn't seen him. But they are the only living creatures in sight. He must have seen her, too. And he would realize if she tried to avoid him.

She carries on ahead.

About a hundred years pass before they finally meet. Jonte looks as awkward as she feels.

'Hi,' Vanessa says.

'Hi,' Jonte replies. 'How are things?'

'Good. Really good.'

'Right. That's great.'

Silence.

'And you?'

'Fine.' Jonte scans the surroundings, as if hoping that a rescuer will materialize from somewhere. 'Long time, no see.'

'Yes.'

For that is how it feels, even though she and Wille broke up only three weeks ago. When Wille left her life, his friends disappeared with him. She doesn't exactly miss them, but she misses the old simplicity of life. It was always easy to hang out in Jonte's house, always easy to convince him to throw a party. Without Wille she suddenly has too much time on her hands. She doesn't know what to do with it, and filling time in this town is so hard.

'Such a shame things turned out this way,' Jonte says. 'Everything is that much more boring now that you aren't around.'

He looks the other way, clearly embarrassed.

That's surprising. Vanessa never picked up any signs that Jonte enjoyed her company in any way. On the whole, he has seemed to tolerate her. Though it's a fact that she has never seen him show enthusiasm for anything much, except his cultivation of pot in the cellar.

'Did you know all along?' she asks. 'That he cheated on me, I mean.'

Jonte looks so guilty he doesn't need to answer.

Christ, how many of them had known? If Jonte knew, did *Lucky* know, too? Do they all think she's a brain-dead little bimbo who never could get a grip on anything? Vanessa feels ashamed and also hates the sense of shame because that's what Wille should feel, the rotten bastard.

'I hope you aren't angry with me,' Jonte says and tugs at his cap. 'You know, it's like, my fault it ended up like this.'

His fault? This is news to her. Jonte seems to think that Vanessa already knows all there is to know, or else he wouldn't have said what he just did.

She tries to keep her expression neutral and let him do the talking.

'Elin and I were classmates, of course. I've always liked her. That's why I asked her to my dad's cabin. I had no idea that she and Wille...'

In Vanessa's brain, pieces in a jigsaw puzzle are falling into place. *Click click click.* They form a pattern she hasn't seen before.

That weekend last year, when Wille just vanished. And then came back and said he had stayed in a cabin belonging to Jonte's father. He had told her that he had gone there alone to think, that the realization of how much he loved her had come to him. Then he had given her the engagement ring.

All lies.

He proposed to Vanessa out of a guilty conscience. He had slept with this *Elin* person. And Vanessa bought every single word. She had even abandoned Mom and Melvin for his sake.

He lied even when they sat together on Sirpa's sofa, when he wept and said that he only wanted 'to be honest'. He admitted to being unfaithful to her with Elin twice. But it was at least three times. Maybe more. Who knows how many?

Fire

Vanessa is suddenly about to throw up.

'I have to go,' she says. 'I've got…I've got to pick up Melvin.'

She sees panic in Jonte's eyes as the truth dawns on him.

'Shit! You didn't know. Forgive me.'

'I've had it with "forgiving",' she replies.

Naturally, Melvin is at his worst, sulky and peevish. First, he wants to sit in the stroller, then walk, then sit again. In the end, Vanessa can't take any more and, for the last stretch, sticks him in the stroller and tries to close her ears to his howling. When they arrive at the house he finally shuts up. She manages to get him into the elevator before he starts whining again.

'Where's Daddy?'

Great. That's all she needs.

'Your daddy's not at home.'

'Why?'

'You know why, Melvin. He isn't going to live with us any more. He lives somewhere else now.'

'Why?'

'Sometimes things just work out like that.'

'Why?'

She crouches down and looks him in the eyes.

'It will be so nice. Imagine what fun it's going to be to have two homes! Your daddy has found an apartment with a really great room for you.'

Melvin stares blankly at her. The elevator stops outside their apartment and Vanessa picks him up in her arms.

She unlocks the front door, opens it and hears the humming of the kitchen fan. She can smell the cigarette smoke even in the hall.

Vanessa sees a quick vision of Mom weeping over a wine

box and a packet of cigarettes. But then she hears laughter. Mom is laughing for the first time since Nicke moved out. And not on her own either. She is joined by a hoarse, smoke-raddled chuckle.

Vanessa knows of only one person who *chuckles*.

The moving company's boxes are stacked in the hall. She puts Melvin on top of one of them and helps him to pull off his shoes. Then they go to the kitchen together, just as Mom drags deeply on her cigarette, standing under the fan. When she sees them, her expression turns enormously guilty and she quickly stubs out her cigarette in the brimming ashtray.

'Oops, is that the time?' she says. 'We completely lost track.'

Vanessa turns to the kitchen table where Mona Moonbeam is sitting. She is smoking without any sign of inhibition. Her blonde hair, permed to within an inch of its life, is pulled back with a grip shaped like a butterfly. A wine box and two wine glasses are on the table in front of her. Mona's frosted lipstick has left a sticky mark on one of the glasses.

'Do you remember Mona?' Mom says. 'She told your fortune in the Crystal Cave once.'

Mona Moonbeam waves to Vanessa. It sets her thin silver bracelets tinkling.

'Vanessa's your name, right?' she says with a broad smile.

Vanessa watches in silence as Mom shows Melvin off to Mona, who pinches his cheeks hard and coos over him. Melvin looks ready to bite her and Vanessa hopes he will. Then he manages to wriggle free and runs off to the living room. Soon afterwards the TV starts up.

'What are you doing here?' Vanessa asks Mona, looking straight into her eyes.

'Jannike is one of my best customers. And definitely the

best company. I haven't met up with her for a long while so I felt I just had to phone and find out how she's getting on.'

Vanessa is convinced that Mona had felt she just had to earn some easy cash.

'Mona is so out of this world,' Mom says. 'She knew exactly what Nicke had been up to. And she says, give him a year and he'll be back with his tail between his legs. Not that it will do him any good.'

Typical. Mona's specialty is of course always to say exactly what her customers want to hear. That is her *real* talent, the skill that makes her so popular. Engelsfors is full of people in need of hope.

Mom puts her arm around Vanessa, her head close to her daughter's, but presses a little too hard. She smells of cigarettes and sour wine.

'Everything will turn out all right, Nessa. But now I must be off to the ladies'.'

She giggles suddenly and heads to the bathroom. Vanessa immediately sits down on the chair next to Mona.

'Where have you been?' she hisses. 'The shop has been closed for absolutely ages.'

'You're not to trouble yourself, sweetheart,' Mona says and lights another cigarette. Then she smiles at Vanessa. 'So, you're single again, I hear. You should've dumped him when I told you that you had no future as a couple. Would've saved yourself all this hassle. Tell you what, though. About that chick he cheated on you with. You have seen her once but she's never seen you.'

Vanessa can hear Mom rummaging in the bathroom. She has no time to figure out Mona's riddles.

'We need your help, Mona. How do you go about contacting the dead?'

Mona looks inquisitively at her.

'It depends,' she says, suddenly serious. 'It depends on whether the soul has passed on or is caught somewhere. And you must know the name of the dead person.'

'This soul has got caught, for sure. And we do know her name.'

There is the click from the lock on the bathroom door.

'We'll deal with this after the weekend,' Mona says.

'But it's urgent!'

'Not in my world. Come to the shop on Monday. And wear something classy.'

CHAPTER 24

Minoo clutches the red lunch tray and scans the dining area. The din hits her ears. Everyone is trying to be heard at the same time. Shouting, screeching laughter, ringing phones and clattering of cutlery on plates, chairs scraping against the floor.

There are of course plenty of free chairs, but where to sit without being made to feel an intruder?

She catches sight of Linnéa at a table in the middle of the room. She is with that blue-haired girl. They are surrounded by a whole crew of alternative types who just sit there and look aggressive. Minoo wishes that she too had a table where she belonged just as obviously.

She can't see Anna-Karin anywhere. Presumably she has already wolfed her food down and slunk off somewhere else. Minoo sympathizes. To have Viktor Ehrenskiöld watching you just about every class would drive anyone to the brink of a breakdown.

Minoo finally makes up her mind. She picks the table where a handful of gaming nerds from another class are already installed. They are so completely into their digital worlds they don't even look her way. Which is exactly how she wants it.

The potato patties are tough in the way they get when kept warm for hours. She is just chewing on her first bite when someone sits down opposite her. She looks up. It's Viktor.

'Hi,' he says.

She looks at her plate again.

'I must've become invisible?' he says, clearly trying to be amusing. 'Maybe Vanessa is infectious?'

Minoo concentrates on meticulously cutting the patties into small, neat pieces. It's pathetic, but she feels ashamed about eating in front of Viktor. His mere presence is enough to make her feel that everything she does is too *physical*. As if she were a big, lumpy human body with all these repulsive excretions, and he some ethereal being who floats through the air and sustains himself on flower nectar and birdsong. Does he really use the bathroom? She can't imagine it.

Viktor leans forward across the table. Once more, she is amazed at the absence of any smell. His lack of odor contributes to making him come across as unsettling. Skewed. Not quite human.

Who says, anyway, that Viktor actually *is* human?

Maybe Ida's right. Now that it's established that witches and demons exists, couldn't anything be true?

'I'm not your enemy, Minoo,' Viktor says quietly. 'I won't conduct the interrogations. I'm here simply to help my father. And he isn't your enemy either. He is in charge of seeing to it that everyone obeys the laws. That benefits all of us. Chaos would reign otherwise.'

Minoo stays silent. She is aware that the computer freaks at the other end of the table are eyeing her and Victor. No surprise if the gossip about them takes off, as of now.

'Come on, Minoo. Sooner or later you'll have to talk to me,' Viktor whispers.

Have to, will I? Minoo thinks and carries on dissecting the potato patties.

'Hello?' Viktor says and touches her hand.

She startles and drops the knife.

'I'm sorry,' he says and quickly pulls his hand away. 'But I don't understand why you keep on with this childish behavior. You're smarter than the rest of them. I don't mean just in your...circle of friends, but the entire school. Look around. You're the only one here who I could become friends with.'

'Am I meant to be *flattered* by all that?'

'All I'm doing is stating the facts,' Viktor says calmly.

'We will never be friends,' Minoo replies just as calmly. 'Anna-Karin is my friend.'

The instant she says this, she knows that it is the truth. The insight makes something slot into place in her mind. She cares for Anna-Karin. Not only because Anna-Karin is one of the Chosen Ones, but because she is Anna-Karin. Suddenly, Minoo is certain about this and equally certain that Viktor Ehrenskiöld is the enemy of them both.

She spears three pieces of patty on her fork, puts the lot in her mouth and chews.

'Bye-bye,' she says.

Before Viktor gets up and leaves, he shakes his head, pityingly.

Ida's voice soars towards the ceiling. It fills the music room.

Amazing grace, how sweet the sound, that saved a wretch like me. I once was lost but now am found, was blind, but now I see.

She shuts her eyes, feels that she can trust her voice to carry her all the way and increases the volume. The music class is transformed into an arena and she stands alone in the spotlights. She imagines the audience, the thousands of faces all turned towards her.

I shall possess within the veil, a life of joy and peace ...

Ida gives her voice a bit of vibrato towards the end and opens her eyes.

Julia and Felicia and all the others in the school choir are cheering and applauding. Ida sighs contentedly and thanks her audience.

And then she catches sight of Kerstin Stålnacke's worried-looking smile.

'Oh, for heaven's sake, Ida,' the choir's conductor says. 'What can we do with you?'

A knot tightens inside Ida's belly. She feels that every-body is staring at her.

'Did I make any mistakes?' she asks and smiles back.

She hit every note. What can the stupid hag be talking about now?

'Technically, you're outstanding. But you must let your *emotions* into your singing.'

Ida observes Kerstin's tent-style dress and obviously butch hairdo. She hasn't got the slightest wish even to imag-ine what kind of emotional display Kerstin has got in mind.

So effing typical that the conductor of the choir is this sad lezzy. Who clearly hasn't got a clue what she's talking about. *Everyone* knows that Ida is the best singer in the whole school, in all Engelsfors, probably. It's not being boastful, it's stating a fact.

And it is just so typical that the mediocre ones are trying to sit on the good ones, keep them down because the no-hopers can't bear to be as useless as they are, Ida thinks. Like Kerstin, who can't sing for beans.

'See!' Kerstin says and points at her.

'What?'

'You feel something. Anger. You're furious with me, Ida. I can see it in your eyes.'

'I'm not angry at all. Just focusing. I'm trying to listen properly to what you're telling me and take it on board.'

Kerstin marches up to Ida with the folds of her tent

fluttering. She grips Ida's shoulders and looks deep into her eyes.

'When you're singing, don't be afraid to show who you are. Let it out. What you feel, even if it's ugly. Or seems dangerous. Dare to let it out. Your sensibility. Your vulnerability. Dare to show *yourself* to the rest of us, Ida.'

Ida is so shocked she can't speak. As soon as Kerstin moves away, Ida walks across to Felicia and Julia. They whisper that Kerstin is a moron. It is exactly what Ida wants to hear, but it still doesn't feel right.

'Please, Alicja, your turn,' Kerstin says and waves to a slender little tenth-grader whose dark hair is in desperate need of an intensive repair treatment.

The ceiling lights flash as the power is cut and comes on again.

A nagging thought pesters Ida.

Maybe there's something wrong with me. Maybe that's why G doesn't love me.

But she rejects the thought. She must believe in herself.

It's not her that something's wrong with, it's Kerstin fucking Stålnacke.

Minoo takes her time before leaving the school library. She has a Swedish test to cram for, and she doesn't want to try to work in the middle of a fight at home.

But she isn't allowed much peace of mind in the library either. Some thoughts are pushy, insist that she pay attention, peck away like little woodpeckers. Viktor. The Council. Alexander. Adriana. Anna-Karin. Nicolaus. The demons. Matilda. The woodpeckers peck and peck, but her thinking doesn't lead anywhere.

'I'm sorry, I have to close now.'

Minoo looks up from her book. Johanna, the school

librarian, stands near the Drama section with an apologetic smile on her face. She is resting a pile of class copies of *Romeo and Juliet* on her pregnant belly.

'Oh, I'm sorry,' Minoo says. 'I'm going right now.'

She shuts the book and shoves it into her bag, which is already crammed.

'Have a nice weekend,' Johanna says as she locks the door.

Minoo stands still. A girl's voice echoes throughout the stairwell.

Ave Maria! Jungfrau mild, erhöre einer Jungfrau Flehen ...

Minoo runs through her usual options and dismisses them one after the other. Café Monique has shut up shop. On a Friday night, everyone says that Olsson's Hill is crawling with beer-swilling drunks and lots of people of her age as well. Minoo considers walking to the docks, but knows she won't be able to relax because it's too close to the manor house and Viktor. She wishes it were possible to go home to Gustaf, but he has avoided her ever since that 'discussion' about Positive Engelsfors. And she's too much of a coward to seek him out.

O Mutter, hör ein bittend Kind! Ave Maria!

The song ends, a short burst of applause and then the school falls completely silent.

There are no other alternatives. Minoo has to go home. With any luck, Mom and Dad will be so preoccupied with Aunt Bahar's arrival tomorrow that they'll forget about fighting each other. In any case, at least Minoo has her corner of the garden.

Like a dog in an exercise yard, she thinks.

Suddenly, a new voice breaks the silence. A woman is speaking loudly and excitedly, but the sound is interrupted when a door slams.

It takes only a second for Minoo to realize that she has heard the principal's voice.

She hurries to the spiral staircase and then downstairs, trying to step quietly so that her footsteps won't set up an echo. She opens the door to the office corridor.

'You have no right to do this!' Adriana exclaims behind the shut door of her office.

Another voice answers but is too low for Minoo to distinguish the words.

Minoo tiptoes over to Tommy Ekberg's office. The deputy principal's door is wide open. No one inside. But there is a connecting door to the principal's office. And it is open, just. The gap is narrow. But that's enough.

Minoo has never wished for Vanessa's powers as much as now. She doesn't really dare to spy. But to walk away without having tried to isn't possible either.

She sneaks into Tommy Ekberg's room. The desk is covered with piles of paper and opened folders. And, in the middle of the mess, a half-eaten chocolate bar.

Minoo takes the last few paces to the connecting door and crouches down to avoid being in someone's line of vision. And peeps through the gap.

The principal is standing behind her desk. The venetian blinds are drawn and the only light is filtered through the shade of her table lamp, a glass mosaic of dragonflies.

On the other side of the desk, three people are facing her. Tommy Ekberg, Petter Backman the creative arts teacher, and a blonde woman in a suit and with shoulder-length hair.

'This is utterly absurd,' Adriana says. 'Who is behind this?'

'The decision was made by the local authority,' the suit-lady says.

'The members of the teaching staff have also expressed

widespread disquiet,' Petter Backman says. 'As the union representative—'

'This is completely out of order,' Adriana says.

'You and your trade union are of course free to take your case to an employment tribunal,' the suit-lady says. 'But at this moment in time, we must insist that you collect your personal belongings and leave this office. Tommy Ekberg takes over as acting principal, at least for the duration.'

'Adriana, I truly regret…' Tommy mumbles, stroking his bushy moustache.

'I refuse to go,' she says.

'There are two options open to you,' the suit-lady goes on. 'Either you leave voluntarily. Or the police will remove you.'

'The police?'

'We need to establish the extent of your responsibility for the fatal incidents leading to the deaths of Elias Malmgren and Rebecka Mohlin. The first step will be an internal inquiry but if you prove uncooperative, we shall have to act accordingly. As I am sure you appreciate.'

Adriana looks as if she's about to faint. She supports herself by pressing the palms of her hands against the desktop.

Petter Backman turns around and Minoo barely has time to slide behind the door before he comes along to shut it properly. She slips out of Tommy's office without making a sound, hurries along the corridor and down the main staircase. She is so upset she can hardly breathe.

This is too awful. Too unfair.

And something is very, very wrong.

Anna-Karin is sitting on the old gray-blue kitchen sofa in Grandpa's little day room at Sunny Side. He brought some of his own furniture, but it still doesn't feel as if he really lives here.

Fire

Grandpa's index finger nudges cautiously the fiery red marks on Anna-Karin's left hand. The gashes where the fox bit her have still not healed properly. At night, her hand pulsates, dully and painfully. It itches during the day. Off and on, as in this moment, an icy sensation runs through her arm. It's like the spreading of frost. Anna-Karin has had a tetanus injection, but that chill frightens her. Words like 'cold gangrene' and 'amputation' haunt her.

'You'd better dress it again with broadleaf plantain,' Grandpa tells her. 'But remember to wash the leaves first, really carefully, to get rid of soil bacteria. And if the plantain doesn't work, ask your mother if she has any of my marigold ointment left.'

Anna-Karin hesitates for a moment.

She has told her grandpa a little about what happened last year, about her powers and how she used them. He seemed to have a shrewd idea anyway. But she has never spoken about the Chosen Ones. Or the Council. Or the apocalypse.

'How do you know all these things?' she asks.

'My father taught me about plants.'

'I didn't mean just plants. You've always … known a whole lot of things. Like, how to use a dowsing rod. You saw the blood moon. And you have these premonitions. When all these things happened around me last year … well, you knew that magic exists.'

Grandpa folds his hands on his lap and bends forward a little.

'Yes, some people would call it magic,' he says. 'I see it differently. It's always been part of nature. My family never thought it was peculiar. It is bred into the bone.'

'Have you heard of the Council?' Anna-Karin whispers.

She nearly holds her breath. But Grandpa looks uncomprehending.

'What council?'

'Oh, never mind. Anyway, it was just something…it doesn't matter,' she says with her eyes fixed on the floor.

'Tell me about the fox again.'

And she does. From the first time she saw it near the dead tree, then the second time on the day the thunderstorm came rolling in when the sky darkened and midday turned to dusk in just a few minutes.

'I can't understand why it acted like it did. The fox, I mean.'

'Do you remember the fox family that had made its lair where the forest began?' Grandpa asks.

Anna-Karin shivers, as if the chill from the sore hand has crept into the rest of her body. His story about the fox family is an old memory that has nothing to do with her.

'Grandpa, this is me. Anna-Karin. I was a baby when the foxes lived there.'

'I know that, child,' Grandpa replies impatiently. 'But it was surely decided back then. Foxes know a thing or two.'

She still isn't quite sure who he thinks he's talking to, her or Mom or even Grandma Gerda.

'How do you mean, Grandpa?'

'The forest knows,' he says quietly.

His eyes have an inwards look. He has disappeared to the place where she can't reach him. Anna-Karin gets up and hugs him gently.

'I must be off now,' she tells him. 'But I'll be back soon.'

She hopes that he, too, will come back. That he won't stay wandering, or even lose himself for good.

CHAPTER 25

Minoo wakes to voices coming from the garden. Two women are laughing and talking across each other.

Minoo promised to keep her mother company when she went to meet Bahar at the station. She dimly remembers mumbling that she was too sleepy when Mom came into her room to say it was time to go. A pang of guilty conscience makes her pull on her dressing gown and hurry down to the garden.

The two sisters are sitting in a hammock strung between two trees. They are swinging lightly and haven't noticed Minoo yet. She stands still, watching them.

Bahar is the older by just one year and Mom has said that people thought they were twins when they were little. Now Mom suddenly looks older than her big sister. Seeing them side by side makes Minoo realize how tired and worn Mom looks, even when she is laughing.

'Minoo!' Bahar has caught sight of her. '*Nazaninam, che-gad bozorgh shodi!* And so lovely to look at! You do resemble Darya and Shirin very much!'

Minoo goes along to hug her aunt. Takes the chance to hug her mother as well, and hold her half a second longer than usual. She looks up at Minoo as if she has noticed and been surprised.

'Is this the time of day to get up, *batcheye chabaloo?*'

Bahar says. 'This minute, we were ready to go inside for a cup of coffee. Are you a coffee drinker yet? Shirin started when she was thirteen. A bit too early if you ask me, but what can one do? She sends her love, by the way. And Darya, too. They wanted to come and see you but they're so busy, always so very busy. Has Shirin told you that she has been offered a film role?'

Bahar chatters on while they walk to the kitchen. Mom pours the three mugs of coffee and exchanges a knowing smile with Minoo, as Bahar heaps more unstinting praise on her daughters.

Suddenly Minoo feels enormously happy that Bahar is here. Exactly what Mom needs. And Dad, too. He and Bahar have vigorous discussions that always cheer both of them up, even though they never agree about anything.

'But what do you think, Minoo?'

Bahar is looking at her and seems to expect an answer. Minoo hasn't a clue what the question is about.

'What did you say, Auntie?'

'I said that you also ought to go to a school like Shirin's. Now up here, it can't be much of an education you're getting. And, as for friends...Na, aslan fekresh nemikham bokonam! Here, there's no culture! You don't even have a bookshop, right? It would be a wonderful thing for you to come to Stockholm.'

'Bahar, that's enough,' Mom says.

Minoo looks at her, surprised. Rushing to the defense of Engelsfors isn't her style. But then, Bahar's reaction is even more baffling. She falls silent at once. Very un-Bahar.

Dad enters the kitchen. Bahar's smile seems strained.

'Hello, Erik,' she says.

He greets her briskly and doesn't return her smile as he pours the last drops from the coffee maker into his mug.

Fire

'Good morning. Well, you must excuse me, I've got to work for a bit.'

'I understand,' Bahar replies and the strained smile stretches across her face again.

Mom says nothing. And she avoids Dad's glance.

Minoo looks from one to the other to the next. Now what's going on?

When Dad wanders off to his study, the atmosphere lightens at once.

'We were saying, what about a walk down to the docks before it gets too hot,' Mom says.

Minoo watches Dad retreat. He closes the study door behind him.

'Oh, my God, yes, isn't it hot! Apparently, this beats the former national record,' Bahar says. 'They were even discussing it on the radio.'

Mom turns to Minoo.

'Are you coming?'

'I need a shower. And I've got tons of homework.'

'There, you see. Kids get some kind of an education here as well,' Mom tells Bahar.

Minoo's hair is still damp when she knocks on the door to her father's study.

'Yes, what is it?' he says irritably.

'May I come in?'

'Of course, Minoo,' he says in a gentler voice.

Minoo opens the door and enters. Dad is bending over his desk, but looks up and smiles at her. He looks tired. His large hands are still now and rest on the keyboard of his laptop.

'What's on your mind, Minoo?'

'I just wanted to chat for a while.'

'About anything in particular?'

About you and Mom. About what your real quarrel is about. If you're planning to divorce. About the reason why you and Bahar are behaving so weirdly towards each other.

'Have you heard that they've fired the principal?' she asks.

Dad sits up. His face has the expression it always has when he scents news.

'When was this?'

'Yesterday afternoon. I guess it isn't official yet. But is it allowed? You know, to fire someone, just like that?'

Dad drinks a mouthful of coffee. He looks thoughtful now.

'Sounds irregular. And very odd. But, of course, there are always ways to get around the regulations.'

'I heard that it has something to do with Rebecka and Elias.'

'Did you, indeed? You've picked up a great deal. Where have you learned all this? I trust it isn't mere gossip?'

'I got the whole thing from ... I guess you'd call it "reliable sources".'

'Good. You might well become an investigative journalist one day, Minoo.'

Dad stands, pulls her into his arms and gives her a long, warm hug. Minoo realizes her eyes are full of tears. She loves him so very much. She loves them both very much. If only they would feel the same way about each other.

Maybe they do, Minoo thinks. In their heart of hearts.

She would really like to think so.

'What do you think?' Ida asks as she emerges into her room from the en-suite bathroom.

'Great,' Julia tells her. 'Perfect. Don't you think so?'

'Dunno.'

The back of the dress is cut really low. The black material

sways around Ida's legs when she sweeps around in a full circle.

'More a big party dress. Not so much a dress for a romantic dinner with your boyfriend. Don't you think?'

'Exactly,' Julia says and nods.

Ida sighs, annoyed. Totally pointless to ask for advice from someone who always agrees with you.

'If you really like it, would you like to borrow it?'

'One day, maybe,' Julia says and avoids Ida's eyes.

They both know that Julia would never wear it because her back is covered in pimples. Even on the lakeside beach she always wears a thin T-shirt over her bikini. And never goes in for a swim.

'I think this is more like it,' Ida says and pulls a flowery dress from the wardrobe.

She goes to the bathroom to change.

'Isn't it just sweet of Erik to invite you for dinner?' Julia calls after her. 'Imagine having the whole house to yourselves. Sheer luxury! I wish I had a boyfriend, too.'

'Maybe you can get with Kevin,' Ida teases her as she steps out of the black dress.

'Oh, my God, noo!' Julia shrieks. 'Do you know what he said the other day? That the best chicks have sexy bodies and ugly faces. That way you can bang them without falling in love.'

Ida giggles. As if Kevin has the faintest idea.

'The thing is, Robin and Erik were talking about him. Like, that Kevin is hopelessly immature,' Julia goes on. 'It's as if he sort of stopped developing at thirteen or so. They were wondering how long they could bear to have him hang out with them.'

'Robin and Erik said *that*?' Ida asks and pulls the dress with the flower pattern over her head.

Too tight-fitting around her hips.

'Well, sort of,' Julia replies.

Ida examines herself in the mirror. She looks like an over-stuffed flowery sausage. Either it's the heat that has made her swell like a balloon or else she's put on weight. Disgusted, she takes the dress off.

'I might be into Rickard,' Julia shouts.

'Which Rickard? Johnsson? The soccer player?'

'I think he's pretty hot.'

Ida and her image in the mirror roll their eyes in unison. Julia is incapable of expressing an opinion without scattering words like 'sort of' and 'maybe' and 'quite' all over her sentences. Just to be safe.

'Felicia thinks so too,' Julia adds.

'Felicia? I didn't think she'd even look at anyone except Robin, ever,' Ida says and puts the black dress back on.

Screw it, it doesn't matter if it's a little too flashy. It fits perfectly. And Mom always says that black is slimming.

'What happened to the one with flowers?' Julia asks when Ida is back in her room.

'You were right all along,' Ida says with a smile. 'This one is cool.'

Erik lives only a few blocks away and Ida walks slowly to avoid getting sweaty. At the front door, she pulls her fingers through her hair and gives her head a shake. Then she rings the doorbell.

Erik opens almost at once, as if he has been waiting on the doormat.

'You look great,' he says, pulling her close and kissing her hard on the lips. 'Sexy.'

'Thank you,' Ida says as she frees herself. 'Likewise.'

Erik looks pleased. He smells of aftershave and is wearing

a suit. He has combed his thick, dark hair straight back. He looks older, suddenly. More mature. Ida approves and tries to hang on to that feeling. Only to find that she suddenly remembers the time Anna-Karin made him pee himself in front of everyone in the school playground. She firmly rejects the memory. Why can't she be allowed to forget that incident when everybody else seems to?

'Come along to the living room. I'll fix us a couple of drinks.'

'Awesome,' Ida says and smiles.

The R&B from the loudspeakers is totally porny. Ida knows what the playlist is called. *ErikLove*. Too embarrassing. She doesn't want to think about it. She settles down on the sofa. Waits.

Erik's home smells funny.

Not nasty or anything bad, but *different*. Stale, with a hint of old-fashioned soap.

Ida's gaze stops at a large ball of fluff that has stuck to the hairy rug. Her mom has always said that Erik's parents ought to hire a cleaning service if they have a problem with keeping the place tidy.

When Ida and Erik were little, and Ida's family had been invited here, Mom and Dad used to start talking about the Forslunds the moment they got home. Mom would shake her head about their standard of cleaning and their furniture and clothes. Dad would criticize the food, the wines and the garden.

Ida used to wonder why they bothered to meet socially. Now that she is older, she understands. It's the way the system works. Anders Holmström owns the sawmill. Bosse Forslund owns a successful haulage firm. They do business together now, and when they were young they played ice hockey in the same team and saw quite a lot of each other.

Erik comes in carrying their drinks. He hands one to Ida.

'Cheers. A toast to us. Four months.'

Ida's parents also started going out together in high school. Sometimes, she thinks about this, tries to imagine Erik and herself as grown-ups, living in a house somewhere in this neighborhood. The images she creates are satisfying. Erik's older brother is studying medicine so Erik is destined to take over the haulage business and she could manage the sawmill. True, she isn't the slightest bit interested in it right now, but she knows that if she makes up her mind to take it on, everything will work out fine. Dad has always told her that she's got what it takes to run a business.

'Cheers,' she says, smiling.

The bitter taste burns her palate and all the way down to the stomach. She almost has to cough.

'Perhaps the mix is a bit on the strong side,' Erik says.

'The *tiniest* bit,' Ida says sharply.

But she softens her tone when she sees Erik's disappointed face.

'But amazing all the same. I just wasn't ready for it.'

She is determined to be nice tonight. *Not* think of Gustaf, not compare Erik with Gustaf all the time. Erik is here and now. And tonight he looks really good. And he is making an effort for her sake.

Erik and Ida Forslund.

The most successful couple of entrepreneurs in Engelsfors. Attractive. Owners of a newly built house. Two perfect kids, a boy and a girl.

They eat crisps and finish the drinks. Ida is feeling drunk already. She hates it; it's beyond her why everyone seems to want to feel as though they're losing control.

Erik serves wine with the food but she drinks only a few

mouthfuls. When he goes off to the loo, she pours the rest of her wine in the sink. He fills the glasses when he comes back and apparently doesn't notice.

They talk about the same things and the same people as always. The line that guys are not into talking behind people's backs is such total crap. The fact is that Erik obsesses at least as much as Ida about rumors and gossip, maybe even more. Ida tells the story about Kerstin Stålnacke and Erik agrees that she definitely must be a lezzy.

'The reason she's bitchy towards you has to be because she's hopelessly in love with you. Or something like that. You should report her for sexual harassment,' he jokes and Ida laughs.

It goes without saying that Ida would never take it that far. It would backfire on her. Vague rumors are something else and loose talk can easily undermine a person's position. They won't know a thing until suddenly everything collapses around them and the rumor changes into a generally accepted truth.

The question is whether Kerstin Stålnacke is worth the trouble. Could be, if Ida isn't chosen to lead the Lucia procession this year either.

By dessert time, they have run out of subjects to talk about. Erik has drunk almost the whole bottle of wine himself without noticing.

'Would you like to go to my room now?' he asks as soon as Ida has swallowed the last spoonful of ice cream.

'Umm,' she mumbles and looks away, because his smile makes her body crawl.

'Or my parents' room. What do you think? Their bed is bigger.'

'Yuck, that's such a creepy idea!'

He stiffens.

'What I mean is, I'd feel so out of it,' she adds in a milder tone and looks at him. 'I like *your* bed.'

They walk downstairs to the basement, which Erik has had to himself ever since his brother moved out. Ida often gets a touch of claustrophobia in his bedroom, what with its narrow windows placed high up under the ceiling.

ErikLove drifts down from the floor above. Erik has turned the volume up.

It feels faked to have sex to his 'sexy music', like a crappy erotic scene in a crappy film. But Ida doesn't comment. He was thinking about her when he spliced together the music on the list. He told her that he was, anyway.

'You're so gorgeous. The best-looking chick in Engelsfors,' Erik says.

He kisses her neck, nibbles at her earlobe.

Warmth is beginning to ooze through her body. She caresses his back, pulls him closer. Suddenly, Erik stops kissing her.

'Hey, you're ready to go, aren't you,' he beams. The warm feeling evaporates and vanishes.

But it's too late to back out. Ida starts wriggling out of her dress. She is not wearing a bra and Erik starts fondling her breasts at once, as well as carrying on kissing her neck. But her body no longer responds. She just wants it over and done with.

'Come on, get your clothes off,' Ida says.

He laughs.

'So ready,' he says as he fumbles with his fly zipper.

Soon, they are in Erik's bed, naked and turned towards each other. She tries to think sexy thoughts, but nothing catches hold, her mind just keeps going around, around, around. It seems disconnected from her body, from Erik.

'Have you got your new pills?' he asks.

Fire

Ida has no intention of taking contraceptive pills ever again. She had begun last summer, but all the time she was deathly scared of getting a blood clot. Apparently, it's a warning sign if one calf looks swollen compared with the other. After measuring her calves every evening for a month, she simply couldn't hack it any more. She had told Erik that she must have lost the pills somewhere and he has been nagging about them ever since.

'No, not yet. There's some hassle about the prescription,' she says.

Erik swears and starts rummaging for the condoms in the drawer of his bedside table.

Afterwards, she gets up to go to the bathroom, because it's important to have a pee immediately or you might get a urinary tract infection. She examines her face in the mirror while she is washing her hands.

Why does everyone pretend that sex is so simple and natural and fantastic?

It's exactly the other way around. The moment you start a sex life, a whole new world of problems opens. Hair or no hair? If hair, how much, how little, where? Am I supposed to move around? A lot? Or a little? How do I look when I do whatever it is? Is it normal that he tries whatever it is? Is it normal to feel like this? Do we have it too often, or not often enough? Can his parents hear us?

And if all that kind of thing wasn't enough, there are could-be fatal risks of taking certain contraceptives, abortion panics and sexually transmitted diseases.

If you have to worry about all that, how on earth are you meant to enjoy sex? Ida thinks as she returns to the bedroom.

Erik is in bed. There is a pleased smile on his face.

'Was that good for you?' he asks as she crawls in under the duvet.

'Mmmm, great,' she mumbles and leans her head against his shoulder.

He reaches for the remote and zaps the TV on. The set is mounted on the wall opposite the bed. Ida edges closer to him.

And now she can't keep her thoughts under control.

Surely, she thinks, it would be much better with Gustaf?

CHAPTER 26

Vanessa is dancing, but the living-room floor in Evelina's place is so crowded that dance moves are mostly about bouncing against other bodies that are sweating as much as hers is. The tune slips into a riff where only the underlying beat remains. The bass notes make the whole apartment shake. Expecting the chorus to explode again, Vanessa raises her arms. She feels like a space rocket just before lift-off.

'Happy birthday!' she screams to Evelina and gives her a smacking kiss on the mouth.

And *there* is the chorus. Vanessa and Evelina jump up and down like crazies.

Vanessa feels so terrifically alive. Why shouldn't she? Why should her life end, because Wille isn't in it? Wille is a loser. She stumbles over to the bookshelf where she left her glass of booze and Coke, drinks until she feels less thirsty and carries on dancing.

The tune ends and is followed by a track with a hip-hop beat. A girl is rapping about how she tastes just like candy. Vanessa looks around. Evelina has disappeared. But there's Jari, standing at the other end of the room. They were going to the same parties all summer, but she hasn't *seen* him the way she does now. He smiles at her and comes over her way.

'You're having a good time,' he says and pushes his dark bangs back from his face.

Instead of replying, Vanessa puts her glass down and drags him with her to the middle of the floor. With her arm around his neck, she moves to the beat of the music, so close to him that their bodies almost, but don't quite, touch.

Jari tries to follow her. He is a little clumsy but it doesn't matter, it's just sweet.

'Somebody told me you're single now,' he says.

She stumbles and their bodies are tightly pressed together. He puts his arm around her waist. Shit, he's so sexy.

'I had almost stopped hoping that you'd ever drop that idiot,' he says close to her ear.

'That makes two of us,' Vanessa replies.

Evelina comes back and sneaks along to stand next to them.

'Look, I'm sorry, but Michelle is practically freaking out,' she says. 'The usual.'

Vanessa rolls her eyes. Michelle and Mehmet have been on and off since they started dating. This week, it's off. So what? They'll be all over each other before the party ends.

She turns to Jari, tells him she'll be back soon, then takes Evelina's hand and pushes her way through the crowd.

'Is it true, it's you and Jari now?' Evelina says.

'We'll see.'

'My mom always says the best way to get over one man is to get under another.'

'So, *that's* how she got to sleep with half the town?' Vanessa says and they laugh and make yuck-noises.

The kitchen is if possible even more crowded. The music is drowned out by the loud, drunken voices. The sink is full of empty beer cans and plastic bottles and squeezed slices of lemon. Broken glass is crunching under Vanessa's high heels.

Evelina leads the way to the balcony where a lot of guys are hanging out. They push through to where Michelle sits, crouched in a corner. She is crying. Her eye make-up is in such a mess she looks like a grief-stricken panda.

Vanessa isn't absolutely certain that it isn't because she's drunk, but the floor seems to be at an angle. How many people can this rotten old balcony cope with? She doesn't want to think about it

'What happened?' she says and sits down next to Michelle.

Michelle throws herself around Vanessa's neck and sucks some snot up her nose with a moist sound.

'Fucking Mehmet, he doesn't give a shit about me!'

Vanessa strokes her back and glances upwards at Evelina.

'So don't give a shit about him,' Vanessa says.

'But...I...fucking...love...him!' Michelle sobs. She seems close to choking on snot and tears and has to swallow several times before she can speak again.

'He hasn't paid attention to me all evening, like, not given me a glance. He just talks with Rickard non-stop.'

Vanessa hasn't seen Mehmet for several hours and doesn't know which Rickard Michelle means.

Evelina points discreetly towards the bedroom window next to the balcony door and Vanessa, still crouching, straightens up to look inside.

Mehmet is sitting on the bed belonging to Evelina's mother, with one of the Engelsfors FC players next to him. Aha, *that* Rickard. A nice enough guy, with glasses, sort of good-looking but totally pointless, never known to talk about anything except soccer, protein drinks and match results. None of which is Mehmet's favorite subject, but he still looks absorbed by whatever Rickard has got to say.

Vanessa sinks down to be close to Michelle again.

'Who cares?' she says. 'Like, fuck it, Michelle. We are the best looking girls at the party...'

Michelle looks up. Her eyes are red from crying but a smile is spreading over her face.

'We are, aren't we? You, Evelina and me.'

'No question. And nobody, neither Mehmet nor Wille nor *anyone* can take that away from us. We are seventeen only once. A few years from now, do you think we'll even *remember* these guys?'

Michelle laughs a little, a small snorting noise that makes a big bubble of snot inflate in one of her nostrils. Vanessa wipes it away with the hem of her dress. Then she dries the tears from Michelle's cheeks. Vanessa's dress becomes streaked with mascara.

'Now, just chill,' she says.

Michelle nods and Evelina helps them both up on their feet. Vanessa's head suddenly goes into a spin.

'Do you know what we need, girls?' Evelina says. 'More booze!'

A couple of hours later, Vanessa is lying back on the tufty sofa in the living room. It is rocking her gently, as if it is afloat on a gentle sea. The voices and the music around her seem to be woven into a wall of sound that makes her drowsy. It's all Evelina's fault, her and her shots of whatever. Vanessa giggles. She loves her friends. Just now, she loves *everyone*.

'Feeling good?' someone says close to her ear and she slowly opens her eyes.

Jari. His face is very close to hers.

'Never better,' she replies and then, suddenly, feels completely awake.

Alert and somehow charged with energy that must have an outlet. Instantly. Time to test the validity of Evelina's mom's theory.

She lifts her head and kisses him. And he doesn't hesitate. Kisses her back.

Jari's mouth is warm and soft. Vanessa's lips start tingling in response. She relaxes back on the sofa again and he follows her, covers her body with his. She allows her hands to slip in under his T-shirt. Somebody wolf-whistles at them and they start laughing, still nuzzling each other's lips.

Hope Wille hears about this, she thinks.

And that's it.

One thought and the atmosphere is ruined. Her nerve endings stop reacting to Jari's touch. Now the only thing she can think about is how different his kisses are from Wille's, his lingering, firm lips.

Jari is too eager.

Vanessa shuts her eyes, tries to lose herself in the feeling that was so strong a moment ago. But when Jari's hand fumbles along her hip, she twists away.

Oh, fuck. This isn't working. Fuck Wille. Fuck everything.

Vanessa places one hand on Jari's chest and pushes him away. He looks surprised.

'What's the matter?'

'Nothing.'

Jari looks so anxious she tries to smile. She really likes him. Only, it isn't him she wants to kiss just now.

'I just realized I have to get home.'

Jari gets up from the sofa at the same time as Vanessa. She totters and he holds out his arm to support her.

'Will you be all right? Would you like me to walk you home?'

Vanessa shakes her head.

'I'll be fine,' she says and wishes it were true.

The night is dark and scented with decaying greenery.

Whatever the heat is trying to make the citizens believe, the fact is that autumn has come. September.

Vanessa has to cover one eye to make out what she is texting to Evelina.

wnt home <3 <3 <3

She can hear bellowing men and laughing women further along the street. Thumping music. The sounds from Götis. She screws up her eyes to read the time on her phone. Twelve-thirty. Half an hour to go before closing time. They'll be in top gear in there.

Groups of people are clustered near the entrance. They stumble, gabble, cling to each other. The middle-aged ones are the most sozzled, though they ought to have had enough time to learn to deal with alcohol. As she passes, Vanessa catches fragments of their talk. The negotiations are rolling. Who is going home with whom, who is throwing a late-nighter, who has to walk home alone?

Looking in through a window, Vanessa catches sight of a young couple in the bar. They are standing so close together they have surely just fallen in love. The girl's dark, shiny ponytail rocks when she starts laughing.

Vanessa wonders at how naïvely happy they are, asks herself how that can be. Is it possible to forget how microscopically small the chance is that a relationship will last? Will she ever be like those two again? As of now, she feels in a risk zone, about to start a lifetime of bitterness.

Then everything happens very quickly.

Jonte turns up in the bar.

The girl turns to him and smiles and there's something vaguely familiar about her profile.

Her boyfriend playfully puts his hand under her chin and kisses her on the lips.

Vanessa stops in mid-step when she sees his face.

Wille. It is *Wille*. His cheeks shaved, his hair cut in a new way. He is wearing a black T-shirt that fits more tightly than his old ones.

Vanessa's innards have transformed into a bunch of slithery, wet snakes that writhe around each other. She runs to the back of Götis, stops to lean forward over a small bush next to the parking lot. The retching is rough, even violent, but produces nothing except clear, rubbery saliva.

She straightens up. Aware that she has just had a terribly bad idea. But impossible to resist.

She shuts her eyes. Tries to focus on her power and notes that it's that much harder when you're drunk. She tries so hard she feels nauseous again, but then magic wafts over her skin. She slides into invisibility. One deep breath and then she walks towards the entrance to Götis.

The Council has forbidden them to use their magic. All magic. That rat Alexander tried to scare them, telling them that there were spies everywhere. But how are the spies, if there actually are any, meant to keep an eye on someone who is invisible? She sticks both her middle fingers up in the air and twirls in a full circle, just in case.

Vanessa glides past the bored bouncer who sits propped up on a tall stool and stares into the middle distance.

That's the one who threw her and Evelina out in the summer. Vanessa has to do something. She pinches his ear, fast and hard. He leaps up from his stool and looks wildly around. She laughs and walks past him into the nightclub.

In here, the heat is tropical. The air stinks of bodies, alcohol and desperation. The DJ is playing an old dance tune that Mom likes to listen to sometimes. Vanessa crosses the dance floor, where the strobe lights make everything dreamlike.

She pushes past a group of girls and accidentally bumps

into one of them so that she tumbles on to the floor in a bundle of long legs and flowery fabric.

The others are killing themselves laughing.

Sorry about that, Vanessa thinks and goes to the bar.

She sees Jonte in profile. He's drinking beer from the bottle.

Vanessa rounds a pillar and sees Wille and the girl with the dark hair. They're seated on bar stools now.

So this is Elin.

She is lovely. Fuck it, she is truly beautiful. High cheekbones, perfectly plucked eyebrows, skin that looks as if it is treated to expensive creams every evening.

And now Vanessa recognizes her. Elin works in the bank at Storvall Square. It was she who escorted Nicolaus and Vanessa down to the safe room with the bank deposit boxes.

Vanessa had been invisible that time, too.

The chick he cheated on you with. You have seen her once, but she's never seen you.

Vanessa is beginning to feel insanely fed up with Mona always being right, damn her.

She glides closer until she is standing next to them. Elin has turned towards Wille again. He looks fixedly at her, as if hypnotized.

Vanessa feels as if she has tumbled straight into a parallel universe. Only a few weeks ago, Wille was the most important human being in her life, the person her days were centered around. They were engaged; one day she would leave Engelsfors together with him. And now he's sitting here and looking at someone else with an expression on his face that Vanessa knows so very well, because that is how he used to look at her.

The snakes in Vanessa's belly are coming back to life. Her mouth fills with saliva and she swallows hard.

'What do you think? Time to go home?' Elin says. Her smile suggests only one thing.

And Wille, who never leaves a party if there are still drinks or drugs to be had, nods willingly and kisses her.

'I'll just go to the ladies',' Elin says and slides off the bar stool.

'We're off.' Wille shouts to be heard above the music. Jonte nods.

There you are, he and Elin are *we* already, Vanessa thinks. It is as if he doesn't even remember me.

'I'll stay here,' Jonte shouts back and turns to the bar to order.

The feeling between them seems tense.

Good, Vanessa thinks.

Wille sits down and stares in the direction of the bathrooms. Vanessa goes for it. She slides on to the stool next to him. The plastic mock-leather seat is still warm after Elin's butt.

Vanessa leans towards Wille. Feels his familiar smell. Tears are burning in the corners of her eyes. Her lips are close to his ear when he raises his glass of beer.

'How could you do this to me?' she whispers.

Wille twitches. A few drops of cold beer splat from his glass and land on Vanessa's thigh.

'Nessa?' he says hoarsely.

Jonte turns around.

'What's that?' he asks.

Wille opens his mouth to speak, but Vanessa is faster.

'Don't say a thing. He'll think you're crazy,' she whispers.

Wille shuts his mouth again, looks at Jonte and shakes his head.

'Maybe you *are* crazy?' Vanessa suggests and Wille goes pale. 'Or else, I'm really here and you can't do a thing about it. You choose what you'd rather believe. But I can see everything you do. I know it all. Every time you screw her, I'm there, watching. I hear everything you tell her.'

She blows lightly at his face and his eyes widen with terror.

'You will never have any more secrets from me,' she whispers. Her parting shot.

When she looks up, Jonte's eyes are turned on her.

No, of course not. Not straight at her. But in her direction. As if he senses that she is there.

Vanessa glances at Wille for a last time. He drains his beer in one go.

'How are things, man?' Jonte asks and Wille shakes his head again.

'I dunno, must have had some fucking flashback or something...'

Vanessa vanishes into the strobe flashes. An intoxicating joy at her victory is growing inside her.

She glimpses Elin emerging from the toilets. Vanessa can't help giggling. Laughter is bubbling and overflowing, but the music drowns the sound when she laughs out loud.

CHAPTER 27

The heavy supermarket bags bang against Anna-Karin's legs. She is walking with her mother, who carries just one half-full bag.

'Don't people have anything better to do than hang out here?' Mom says indignantly and looks along the street.

The pavement is packed with people. Many are wearing yellow T-shirts or sweaters. They have put up a new sign on the place just opposite the apartment block where Anna-Karin and Mom live. 'POSITIVE ENGELSFORS!' the sign says in purple letters against a yellow background.

This venue opened a couple of weeks earlier. Since then, every weekend has seemed like a festive party-time. And not one single minute has passed without Mom complaining about it.

'Mia!' calls a woman's voice just as Anna-Karin and Mom are about to cross the street.

Mom looks sort of found-out, almost frightened. A woman leaves her companions and walks towards them. She is familiar somehow. Her hair is gray, apart from a few blonde strands that look kind of forgotten and left behind.

The woman gives Mom a hug and doesn't seem to notice that Mom just stands there, stiff as a board. Then she holds out her hand to Anna-Karin and introduces herself as Sirpa.

'I was at school with your mother,' Sirpa explains. 'We've met in the supermarket a few times. I work there, you see.'

'Oh, yes,' Anna-Karin says.

'We arranged a little get-together at Positive Engelsfors today,' Sirpa says.

'Yes, I've noticed,' Mom says sourly and Anna-Karin feels ashamed of her.

'You really seem to have a good time,' she mumbles to make up for the rudeness.

Then she puts the bags down on the ground to try to rub some life back into her hands. The blood flow is practically static and the fox bite is starting to itch.

'Yes, such a wonderful atmosphere, don't you think?' Sirpa says and glances longingly at the center. 'That place is exactly what Engelsfors needed.'

She turns to Anna-Karin.

'It must be difficult to believe for someone as young as you, but Engelsfors was a flourishing town not too long ago. And we can make it flourish again, if only we learn to see all the opportunities around us. Won't you come along? Meet Helena? Helena Malmgren, I mean.'

'I know perfectly well which Helena you mean,' Mom says and begins to fumble for her cigarettes in her handbag.

'She is fantastic, Mia. Such a role model for us all. So strong, after all she's been through. She's changed my life. Like my neck, I've had trouble with it for years, but Helena proved to me that my attitude is the root of the problem. Obviously, it's going to hurt if I walk around full of negative, destructive thoughts all the time. If I think that I'm already well then the pain will go away.'

Anna-Karin observes her mother while Sirpa is talking. Mom is puffing furiously on her cigarette and refusing to take any of this to heart; that's only too obvious to Anna-Karin. Yes, of course it sounds rather woolly, but can't Mom see how happy Sirpa is?

'Maybe Helena can do something to help you with your back?' Anna-Karin says to her mother.

'We've got to go now,' she says abruptly. She throws away her cigarette.

'Mom, surely we're not in a hurry?' Anna-Karin says and tries to look innocent.

Mom looks crossly at her.

'You see!' Sirpa says cheerfully.

She leads them through the crowd on the pavement and shows the way into the Center for Positive Engelsfors. There are even more people inside. Happy faces everywhere. As if just by being here, they were sharing something big and important.

Anna-Karin spots Gustaf, who is talking with some of the boys in his soccer team. She recognizes other people from school. The two Hannas in her own class. The creative arts teacher and Tommy Ekberg, who Minoo said were there when the principal was fired.

Anna-Karin stops and her heart stops, too. She has seen Jari.

Jari, whom she has loved from afar for so many years. Periodically, she felt unable to think of anything except him. And then, after Jonte's party last Christmas, Jari was transformed into somebody she can hardly bear to think of at all.

Her body is screaming at her to beat it, now, but just then Jari catches sight of her.

His eyes rest on her for a moment and then he looks away, apparently uninterested. Several months have passed since they met. Perhaps all the inexplicable stuff that happened with Anna-Karin is hidden away in his subconscious. She hopes so.

She hurries to catch up with Mom and Sirpa.

'Helena! Someone wants to meet you!' Sirpa calls out.

Part Two

A woman turns around. Her hair is dyed orange.

Helena Malmgren. Elias's mother.

She is wearing a full-length dress in a thin, flowing material. Its strong shade of yellow lights up her face from below.

'Mia!' she says and her face splits into a wide smile, as if Mom's turning up here is a marvelous gift. 'It is so nice to see you!'

Mom grunts some kind of answer. Helena turns to Anna-Karin, examines her from top to toe. Anna-Karin feels both ill at ease and flattered by the attention.

'Stand tall, my girl,' Helena says. 'Smile and the world smiles with you.'

She winks at Anna-Karin, as if they share a secret. Then she turns back to Mom.

'I heard about the fire last winter,' she says.

Mom just nods.

'Now you must dare to believe that this is the beginning of something good,' Helena continues. 'There are always opportunities if only you choose to see them. A door might close, but at the same time a window is opened.'

'Easy for you to say,' Mom snaps. 'But my father became an invalid and I had to leave the farm where I grew up. And now I have to carry the responsibility for Anna-Karin on my own.'

What Mom is saying is like a disgusting, dirty stain spreading into the air. And the fury that is erupting inside Anna-Karin is so strong it takes almost physical effort to hold it back.

I could force you to tell the truth, she thinks and observes her mother. You take no responsibility for me. You don't even like me. You don't care much for Grandpa either. You have hardly ever gone to see him in Sunny Side. And it was always you who wanted to move into town. There was no need to. I bet you're *happy* about the fire.

A desire to use her magic, to force Mom to speak the truth, is so powerful inside Anna-Karin it feels as if it's about to boil over. Only her fear of the Council is stronger.

'I understand it has been very hard for you,' Helena says, still very friendly. 'But you might also see it as a chance of a new life. Of a new, exciting career.'

Anna-Karin glances gratefully at Helena. She is saying exactly what Mom needs to hear.

'I can't even get a job, what with my bad back.'

Mom sounds aggressive. But Helena won't be put off.

'That's exactly the kind of issue we in PE try to help each other out with,' she says, leaning a little closer and sniffing the air. 'Your smoking – we could do something about that as well.'

She winks again.

Obviously, this is the final straw.

'We've got to go now,' Mom says and pulls Anna-Karin away.

'Come again whenever you want to!' Helena says. 'Our doors, and our arms, will always be open to welcome you!'

Mom storms out, elbows her way through the crowd on the pavement and crosses the street with long steps.

'Nobody will tell me how to lead my life,' she mutters as she pushes the front door open. 'It's easy for her to say but…'

'*Easy*?' Anna-Karin screams so loudly it echoes in the stairwell. The front door slams shut behind them. 'Elias is dead! Helena's *son* died! And still she tries to help *you*!'

Her rage has finally reached boiling point. Mom stares at her, shocked.

'Even if you'd love to think so, you're not the most hard-done-by creature in the entire world,' Anna-Karin adds.

'You know nothing about what I've been through.'

'I know exactly what you've been through. Because I've been through the same things. And you've known that all along. But do you give a shit? No, you don't. You just feel sorry for yourself all the time!'

'So that's it, I'm a bad mother on top of everything else? Well, thank you very much, Anna-Karin. Thank you for kicking me when I'm down.'

This is a familiar tactic. Every time Anna-Karin gets anywhere near criticizing, this is what Mom does. Gives you a guilty conscience. You're supposed to take everything back. And even though you understand the strategy, it is effective.

Not this time, though.

'You should get some counseling,' Anna-Karin says and dumps the supermarket bags so that cans and soda bottles roll across the floor.

She leaves and doesn't turn around until she has walked quite a way down the street. Mom is nowhere to be seen, neither at the main entrance nor in the window of their apartment.

But Helena is there, outside Positive Engelsfors. She is surrounded by people but looks straight at Anna-Karin and smiles warmly.

Anna-Karin is about to smile back at her but Helena's husband, Krister Malmgren, comes out to join her. He puts his arm around his wife's shoulders. 'The great government boss himself,' as Mom used to say. He speaks to Helena and they walk back into the center.

CHAPTER 28

Vanessa is flying.

She is soaring through the air, higher and higher. She knows that the ground is far below, that she would die if she fell, but she is not afraid. She carries on. Upwards, upwards, ever upwards.

She passes through a cloud. It is like a mist. The sky is clear and blue again on the other side.

She allows her body to drift in the light breeze. All she needs to do is lean in a certain direction and the wind will carry her to where she wants to go. Flying is so *easy*. Why hasn't she understood this before?

Now she sees the dark forest way down there. The sun glitters on a water-filled mine hole and soon she also catches sight of the pointy roof of the dance pavilion.

Vanessa raises her eyes. Over there, at the horizon, she sees the school buildings.

The wind stops carrying her.

It feels like a crash landing in reality when she wakes up in bed. And then the memories of the night before tumble over her like a landslide and bury her.

'You look terrible,' Linnéa says with a smile and lets Vanessa into her apartment.

'I'm hungover,' Vanessa groans.

She goes into the living room and sinks down on to Linnéa's sofa. The worn velvet is smooth against Vanessa's bare legs.

On the sofa table is a pile of black tulle. Linnéa picks an armful and carries it into the bedroom, rummages near the sewing machine.

'Would you like some tea or something?' she says when she is back with Vanessa.

She has pulled her bangs back with a shocking pink headband. No make-up. Unlike her usual self, but lovely. Always lovely.

'Water, please,' Vanessa says. 'How can it still be this hot?'

'Anna-Karin must be right that the heatwave is supernatural,' Linnéa says on her way to the kitchen.

Vanessa looks at the chipped china panther next to the sofa and then lets her eyes wander to the beautiful and terrifying images that cover the walls. When it's dark outside, Linnéa turns on little red-shaded lamps that bathe the rooms in a warm glow. In daylight, it looks less mysterious but somehow more intriguing. More private and intimate. Like seeing Linnéa without make-up.

She brings a large glass of water and puts it on the table near Vanessa. Then Linnéa settles down, cross-legged like a tailor, at the other end of the sofa.

'Do you remember the time I came here to ask you for advice about Wille?' Vanessa asks.

She feels even warmer now. As if admitting that she has thought about that evening means that she has somehow exposed herself to Linnéa.

'Of course I do,' Linnéa says and briefly looks away. 'You were wrecked. Unforgettable, really,' she adds with a smile.

Vanessa laughs, then reaches for the glass of water and drinks deeply.

'Great that I'm a wreck every time I come to see you. Christ, I am so glad that you were home this time. I would've exploded if you hadn't been here. I need to talk to you.'

'Go for it,' Linnéa says and lights a cigarette.

She listens quietly while Vanessa tells her about her failed attempt to get some comfort sex with Jari. But when Vanessa goes on to describe how she spooked Wille, Linnéa bursts out laughing heartily. It's infectious. They both laugh so much they can't sit straight.

'Come on, be serious, we've got to stop,' Vanessa says. 'I'm finished.'

'All I'd want is to see his face,' Linnéa says and giggles again.

Vanessa imitates his expression and they laugh some more.

When they have finally stopped laughing, Vanessa feels that her facial muscles are fixed in an idiotic grin. She tries to relax. Linnéa must realize that she is serious now.

'What if the Council's spies saw me in Götis doing this comedy ghost stunt? Somehow, I don't think Alexander will buy the excuse that I was drunk.'

'He's so unlikely to find out about it.'

'But sometimes, when we've been practicing, you and the others have seen me even if I'm invisible.'

'Surely that's just because we are the Circle. Bonded together and all that.'

'And then there are animals, they can see me...one of the Council's familiars might have spotted me.'

'They simply can't check all of us out, all of the time,' Linnéa says.

'I do hope you're right,' Vanessa says and sighs. 'Listen, there's another important thing. It's Jari. What do you think? Should I give him another chance and try not to go all weird on him this time? He looks amazing. You should've felt his six-pack. And I like him.'

Linnéa's smile dies away. She looks at the window.

'Don't ask me,' she replies in a monotone. 'Sure, why not?'

'But if we sleep together, do you think he might fall totally in love with me? Because the last thing I could cope with now is someone who really loves me and wants a completely serious relationship.'

Linnéa produces a humming noise that could mean anything.

'I mean, I'm not positive that I don't still feel something for Wille,' Vanessa goes on. 'I don't *want* to miss him but I do, all the same. Even though I hate him for what he has done to me. And then I saw him with that chick...he had changed so much. And he seems to be utterly crazy about her...'

'What did you expect?' Linnéa interrupts. Vanessa is pulled up short.

'How do you mean, "expect"?'

'You know very well that Wille can't stand being alone. He needs someone to look after him. After I dumped him, how long did it take for him to find you?'

Vanessa doesn't know how to answer. She really hadn't believed that Wille would replace her quite that quickly. But when Linnéa is like this, Vanessa can't admit it.

'Besides, after you two got together, he kept phoning me,' Linnéa says. 'As if he wanted me to be a kind of fall-back if your affair turned sour. I guess it's only a matter of time before he starts calling you.'

Vanessa stares at her. Served up by Linnéa, the truth sounds so merciless. Also, Vanessa feels stupid. Stupid, because she still has feelings for Wille. Stupid, because she isn't as strong as Linnéa.

She shouldn't have talked to Linnéa about all this. She shouldn't have come here at all.

I shouldn't have come here at all.

Linnéa is unprepared for the energy of Vanessa's thought. It rushes into her head.

Why can't I ever keep my mouth shut? Linnéa thinks.

She mustn't even look at Vanessa. She is terrified that Vanessa will understand that Linnéa read that thought and perhaps think that she was listening in on purpose.

The doorbell rings.

'Back soon,' Linnéa says as she gets up.

There are only a few people who are likely to turn up without warning at Linnéa's front door, and she doesn't want to meet any of them.

And especially not the woman who stands outside on the landing. Her hair is a bleached blonde and she has a small, glittering stone in her pierced nostril.

Diana from Social Services.

'Hello, Linnéa,' she says.

Her face carries that concerned look. It terrifies Linnéa.

It's something about Dad, she thinks. Whatever else would make Diana call on a Sunday afternoon?

'May I come in?'

'Of course,' Linnéa replies and steps back from the door.

Diana walks straight in, doesn't even take her sneakers off. It is unlike her. Linnéa follows, stops to pick a jacket up from the floor and hang it on a hook.

Usually, she tidies up for hours before Diana's visits, airs the apartment to get rid of the smoke, polishes every spot of toothpaste from the bathroom mirror, exterminates every trace of dust balls and carries on until the entire apartment is a monument to Linnéa's capacity for clean living, good taste and neatness. And now it's like a bomb has hit it.

Vanessa looks up when they enter the living room.

'So you have a visitor,' Diana says.

'Diana, this is Vanessa. A friend from school.'

Diana holds out her hand and says hello.

'Linnéa and I must talk in private,' she announces.

'Yes, of course,' Vanessa says. 'I was on my way home anyway.' She glances quickly at Linnéa. 'See you.'

'Sure, see you,' Linnéa says. The super-sharp electric whisk is back, churning her heart to mush.

Diana settles down on the sofa. Scans the apartment. Linnéa takes the smoking cigarette from the ashtray and puts it out.

'She didn't look very happy,' Diana says.

'Her boyfriend left her a couple of weeks ago,' Linnéa replies.

'And you've had a little party here together?' Diana continues, as she slowly examines the room.

Linnéa feels even more ill at ease, if that's at all possible. What is this meeting supposed to be about?

'She might have, for all I know,' Linnéa says. 'Not me. I don't do "partying" any more.'

Diana's nose-jewel glitters when she turns her head to look straight at Linnéa.

'Would you trouble yourself to explain why you've opted out of our last three meetings?'

It takes a moment before Linnéa even understands the meaning of what she has said. It feels like being in one of those stage performances in nightmares, when you're the only one who doesn't know the lines.

'But...you canceled the visits,' Linnéa says.

Diana bends her neck a little sideways. Looks even more concerned. Linnéa senses an approaching panic attack. Unlike all the other ladies from Social Services, Diana has always stood up for Linnéa. It is thanks to her that Linnéa was allowed to live in a apartment on her own instead of being bundled off to another foster home.

But the apartment arrived in a package together with iron-clad rules about immaculate conduct. A single mistake could be enough for the whole arrangement to collapse.

'Our latest meeting was due last Friday,' Diana says.

'But they phoned from Social Services. Someone said you were off sick First, it was food poisoning. And then flu. I was waiting to hear how you were.'

Linnéa realizes all of it sounds like worthless excuses.

'Please, Linnéa. No barefaced lies.'

'No, I'm not lying…'

'I have not been ill at all, so why should someone phone and tell you so? On the other hand, I've left several messages on your voicemail and sent out notes which you have not responded to.'

Linnéa mustn't lose control now. The mere thought makes her feel even more panicky. She tries to sound calm and sensible. Adult. Responsible.

'I have not received any messages. Or any notes. Diana, please, you must believe me.'

'Is it this Vanessa who made you throw parties?'

'What parties?'

'Your neighbors have complained. What they say, in short, is that there has been non-stop mayhem. Even during weekday nights, and lasting well into the early hours.'

'But I've hardly got any neighbors!' Linnéa exclaims.

'So, you are not denying the parties?'

'Of course I am!'

Diana sighs.

Linnéa is suddenly aware of how heavily she is breathing.

Diana must listen to her, must believe her. She always has in the past.

'You insist that you are completely innocent?' Diana asks.

'Yes, I do.'

Diana's mouth tightens into a thin, straight line. Wrong answer.

'In other words, I am lying to you?'

'No, of course not. But maybe there's someone who hasn't told you the truth...'

'I see. You suggest there has been some sort of *conspiracy*?'

The nightmare is becoming worse and worse. Linnéa attempts to read Diana's mind; it isn't possible, her own panic overwhelms her, she can't concentrate.

'If you will not tell me the truth, I cannot help you,' Diana says and gets up.

Linnéa also gets up and follows Diana into the hall.

'This is a misunderstanding,' Linnéa says. 'Please give me a chance to prove it.'

Diana stops at the door and turns to her.

'It's always somebody else's fault, isn't that so? I like you, Linnéa. But I will not help you by letting you get away with this. You will have to learn to take responsibility for your own actions. You have reached a watershed. *You* will have to choose. See to it that you make the right choice.'

After Diana has left, Linnéa stands in the hall for a long while. She wants to scream out loud, throw things at the walls, break something, tear something to pieces. Everything that she must not do.

CHAPTER 29

Bahar parks her rolling suitcase on the platform and gives Minoo a long, warm hug.

'*Dokhtare azizam,*' she says. 'Take care, now. And we'll meet again very soon, I hope.'

'I hope so, too,' Minoo replies and really means it.

She doesn't want Bahar to leave. It's true that the atmosphere has been tense and weird during her visit, but at least Mom and Dad have behaved in a civilized way to each other.

Bahar turns to her sister and hugs her for even longer, whispers something in her ear. When they let each other go, both have tears in their eyes. They clasp each other's hands one last time and then Bahar climbs on board the train.

The doors shut with a shushing sound, the wheels start turning. Minoo and her mom stand and watch until the train has vanished from sight.

The silence between them is paralyzing. It follows them into the car and stays with them all the way as they drive from the station.

Mom parks a short distance from the school and switches the engine off. She faces Minoo and visibly pulls herself together. As if she is finally ready to speak the truth.

But that glued-on smile comes back on her face instead.

How can she believe that I'm tricked by that smile of

hers? Minoo thinks. She who's always going on about how one mustn't suppress one's emotions?

'There now, have a nice day, Minoo.'

Suddenly, Minoo isn't prepared to put up with this charade for a second longer.

'Are you getting divorced?' she asks.

Mom looks shocked. It makes Minoo even more furious. Did she imagine that this conversation could be avoided for ever?

'What is going on between you?' she asks when her mom doesn't answer.

'This is something for your father and me—'

'And Bahar.'

Mom goes rigid.

'Has she spoken to you?'

'No, she hasn't, but it's so obvious that she knows. And that Dad knows that she knows. Why should Bahar have a better grip on what happens in our family than I do?'

Minoo feels tears welling up. But she is not going to let herself go. She needs to demonstrate that she is strong enough to cope with the truth.

'I didn't want to burden you with all this,' Mom says.

'Don't you realize that *this* is a burden? You refuse to let me know anything about what the real issues are. I am simply supposed to accept that you two fight all the time. I do live in the same house as you. In case you hadn't noticed.'

Mom's hand clutches the steering wheel so hard her knuckles go white.

'My dearest child...' she says and her voice breaks. She is silent for a moment and then tries again. 'I understand you, of course. I truly do. And I'll tell you what there is to know. You are quite right to say that it affects you, too. Affects you very much. But I had to try sorting it all out in my own mind and that is why I spoke to Bahar. I can promise you one thing. The problems are entirely between your dad and me, it is not your fault—'

Minoo interrupts her.

'Of course it isn't! Do you think I'm a five-year-old, or what? I can't go on with things being like this. Fix your problems, go into therapy, whatever! Or just get a divorce!'

'Minoo...'

But Minoo throws the car door open and sets out to walk to school. She swallows her tears, swallows the hurt, the guilt and the anger. Swallows and swallows until the whole mess has become a hard little lump in her chest.

When she reaches the schoolyard, her first thought is that she must have missed something. Is it some kind of theme day?

Students in bright yellow polo shirts are clustered at the main entrance. Some of them are talking excitedly. Others are handing out flyers and stickers. Somebody has tied yellow helium balloons along the stair railings. More balloons are floating about, tied to the top bar of the solitary soccer goal and to the branches of the dead trees.

It doesn't dawn on Minoo what it is all about until she recognizes Rickard among the yellow-shirted crowd.

'Minoo!' Linnéa shouts.

She is just coming through the gate.

And she is the complete opposite of the army of baby chickens at the school entrance. Black hair, back-combed and held by a large bow made from a ribbon of black lace. Short black dress, torn net stockings and black ankle boots. Whole lakes of black make-up around her eyes.

'Yay, Positive Engelsfors,' Linnea says disgustedly as they walk towards the entrance. 'Their reproduction rate must be something else.'

Minoo tries to avoid the collective gaze of the yellow hordes as she and Linnéa come closer to the stairs. She is still feeling raw after the exchange in the car. Defenseless. Without any filters between herself and the rest of the world.

'Hello and welcome to the first day of the rest of your lives!' a rather good-looking guy says as he tries to push a flyer into Minoo's hand.

'No, thanks,' she says.

He beams at her.

'Why such a gloomy face? Have you had lemons for breakfast?'

'This is a bad day, that's all.'

'Only you yourself can change that!'

'Move over, Mehmet. And do your part by shutting up,' Linnéa says.

'Bad attitude, guys!' someone shouts at them as they enter the school.

Minoo and Linnéa look at each other.

'The first day of the rest of our lives?' Linnéa says. 'Seriously?'

'Sounds like a threat,' Minoo says.

Linnéa laughs and Minoo smiles. The jagged lump in her chest softens a little.

'Where are these people going?' Linnéa asks.

Minoo looks around and notices for the first time that around her and Linnéa people are drifting towards the assembly hall.

Except for that blue-haired girl. She is walking towards them.

'Linnéa!' she calls.

Her white foundation doesn't manage to hide the dark rings under her eyes. In fact, it enhances them. It might actually be the idea. She is wearing a long black T-shirt. On the chest, the words 'THE GOOD DIE YOUNG' are written in red, blood-spattered letters. The print looks home-made.

'Hi, Olivia,' Linnéa says. She suddenly sounds weary.

'Oh, hi,' says Olivia without looking at Minoo. 'The first period today is canceled – there's some kind of event in the assembly hall.'

Minoo exchanges a glance with Linnéa. Could it have something to do with Adriana?

'They say everybody has got to be there, like, it's mandatory, but they probably won't check,' Olivia continues. 'Wanna leave?'

'Can't,' Linnéa says.

Olivia lifts her vigorously penciled-in eyebrows.

'Diana is after me,' Linnéa says. 'From now on, I've got to be a good girl every single second.'

Olivia stares crossly at Minoo, as if she blames her for her bad influence making Linnéa refuse to play hooky. Then she walks away without saying another word.

Minoo and Linnéa go with the flow. The assembly hall is almost full and the only free seats are in the front rows. They sneak into the fourth row, just behind Vanessa and her friends.

When they settle down, Vanessa turns around.

'Do you know what this is for?

'No,' Minoo says.

Vanessa looks at Linnéa.

'How did things work out yesterday?' she asks. 'I tried to get hold of you—'

'I can't bear talking about it,' Linnéa interrupts without looking up.

'Fine by me.' Vanessa sounds fed up and turns away from them.

Minoo glances at Linnéa, who is absently fiddling with one of her cuticles.

Minoo wonders what happened. She doesn't dare ask. When Linnéa is in a mood, silence is the safest policy.

The yellow polo shirts march in and fill the half-empty front rows. There are more of them than just the group Minoo saw at the entrance. At least half of Engelsfors FC has changed their red-and-white colors for yellow. Minoo searches the lines and notices Kevin among them, but thankfully not Gustaf.

Applause starts up in the front rows when Tommy Ekberg steps out on the stage. For once, he is wearing a shirt that doesn't cause migraine straight away. He looks confused, as if uncertain whether to take the applause as ironic or genuinely encouraging. When he steps up to the lectern, the clapping stops abruptly. He clears his throat and leans towards the microphone. The spotlights make his bald head shine.

'Hello everyone. I don't know if the rumor has gone around already...But, I regret that I have to confirm the fact that our principal, Adriana Lopez, has left us '

A murmur fills the hall and Tommy Ekberg seems to suddenly realize his unhappy choice of words because he adds, speaking more loudly: 'No, no! What I meant to say was that she has left her post. For personal reasons. I am acting principal until...yes, well, simply until further notice.'

He strokes the back of his hand across his temple as if to wipe away drops of sweat. At least he doesn't seem to take pleasure in his new power.

'But I believe that, as with everything else that happens in one's life, it is important to see this change, not as negative, but instead as the beginning of a new and exciting stage. We must be forward-thinking. Together! And that is why we are all gathered here today. All of us at Engelsfors High School have joined in a unique collaborative project with a unique organization. Our school will offer a *positive* way forward.

And this new spirit of ours will inspire everything we teach, from social sciences, to sports, to mathematics.'

He takes a deep breath.

'However, in math we must surely still use negative numbers,' he adds, with a spasmodic wink.

Minoo wishes she had an I-am-embarrassed pillow to hide behind.

But the front rows laugh enthusiastically. Tommy looks more cheerful.

'And now, it is time for me to hand over to a pro! Ladies and gentlemen! I have the honor to present the lady who fired the shot that started the new future for Engelsfors – Helena Malmgren!'

CHAPTER 30

Vanessa has come across Elias's mother a couple of times in the past, at end-of-semester events and at Melvin's christening. She is the kind of person you remember, the kind whose face becomes etched into your memory.

But now, as she walks out on the stage wearing a yellow tunic over her jeans, her charisma seems to have been turned up several notches. It is somehow impossible *not* to look at her.

The yellow shirts start to applaud and shout happily. Helena stops at the center of the stage. Smiles. Her acolytes fall silent, as if on an agreed signal.

A giggly exchange of whispers can be heard from one of the back rows. Rickard stands and looks in that direction. The chatter ends abruptly and Rickard sits down again.

'Hi,' Helena says and looks out over the crowd, now dead silent.

Her smile broadens.

'Listen, everyone! I said "hi"!'

A fragmented 'hi' from here and there.

'And again! You can do better than that,' Helena says. 'Hi!'

She spreads her arms towards the crowd and it responds strongly, in unison.

'HI!'

Vanessa discovers that she has joined the shouting.

'That's more like it!' Helena says. 'But now we'll kick-start the energy in this hall. Stand up, everyone!'

Vanessa glances wearily at Evelina and Michelle who are sitting to her left. They get up, like everybody else. The folding seats rattle.

'Once again, now!' Helena calls out. 'Hi!'

'HI!' responds the hall.

'Hi!'

'HI!'

Up on the stage, Helena begins to clap her hands in a steady beat. The yellow rows follow her and soon the entire Engelsfors high school claps in the same rhythm.

Vanessa, too. But not very hard.

To do the same thing as a lot of other people gives a special feeling of strength. It is almost irresistible.

She can feel the energy in the room increasing. It has nothing to do with magic and that makes it even more sinister.

The tempo speeds up, faster, faster, faster until it turns into hysterical clatter. A cry goes up from the rows in front. Its volume grows and hands reach into the air.

'There, enough!' Helena shouts.

Vanessa lowers her hands. Looks disbelievingly at them.

She finds it hard to meet Evelina and Michelle's eyes when they all sit down again.

'Many of you know who I am,' Helena says. 'I used to be the vicar here in Engelsfors. Some will perhaps know me as Elias's mother.'

She pauses. The hall is completely silent once more. Vanessa remembers the school assembly after the death of Elias. The weeping and charged atmosphere before everything fell apart. She is certain that everyone who was here then will be thinking about the same thing.

'It is almost exactly a year since he died,' Helena continues.

'I felt swallowed up by a huge darkness. I thought I would never be able to carry on. But then I saw the light.'

Vanessa hears a sob from somewhere in the hall.

'My insight that bitterness and grief would not bring Elias back opened up, for the first time, a source of strength inside me. I realized that *I*, no one else, had the power to direct my own life. I understood that *I myself* must take control in order to *become the person I wanted to be*. I had to rethink and get it right. That is why I can stand here today and tell you that it really *does work*. Scientific evidence proves that the essence of our lives is of our own making. If you believe that life is all about misery and disappointment, then misery and disappointment will come your way. But if you believe that you are happy, doing well in school, loved by the boy or girl you love – *then it will happen*. That is guaranteed.'

Evelina rolls her eyes. 'Good news for those boys and girls,' she whispers.

Vanessa can't argue with that.

'I decided that Elias's death must be in some sense meaningful,' Helena continues. 'That is why I stand before you today and tell you that you can achieve anything you want if you are determined. And if you change your way of thinking.'

Vanessa tries to make sense of what Helena is actually saying. Is the idea that, before she changed her ways, her own thinking accidentally brought about the death of Elias? Or was it Elias who thought himself to death?

Helena steps forward to the edge of the stage. It feels as if she is looking into everyone's eyes at the same time. As if her every word, her every gesture is imbued with enormous significance.

'At your age, you are so busy sorting each other into boxes. Who is good-looking, who wears ugly clothes, who is popular and who is not. But all that is unimportant. Superficial.

All you need to keep in mind is that there are two types of people.'

'The ones who buy all this crap and the ones who don't?' Linnéa says loudly.

Vanessa giggles for a moment, proud to know Linnéa. She senses how, all around the hall, everyone catches their breath. But Helena just laughs.

'I actually meant those who have a positive attitude. And the others, who have a negative attitude,' she says and points at Linnéa.

The audience bursts into relieved laughter.

Vanessa turns around. Linnéa's face is immobile. But Minoo is blushing bright red.

'I do understand it can be difficult to believe what I tell you,' Helena continues smilingly. 'Some of you may even find it hard *to dare* to believe. But you mustn't judge anyone. Instead, you should focus on yourselves. I want you to remember the meaning of four letters: *WSOL. We Shape Our Lives.* Keep them in mind. We shape our lives, for better or for worse. It is up to each one of you. But Positive Engelsfors will help you to see the opportunities ahead, not the obstacles. You can become exactly that person you dream of being, if only you make the effort and stay focused on that goal. Just look at me. I would have sunk if I had clung to what I had lost. But I chose *something else.* What I chose was *the future.'*

She carries on with her lecture. Vanessa understands perfectly why her mom fell for Helena.

Everything she says sounds so obvious. So simple. One part of Vanessa would like to believe her. She is aware of a faint but nagging anxiety that maybe she *does* have the wrong attitude. Maybe she will lose out on all that is good in life, all those things that Helena says she can offer. Helena, who seems to have more precise contours than anyone else in the hall.

'I hope to have an opportunity to meet you all again. The Positive Engelsfors Center is open from nine in the morning until nine at night. You are always welcome. And, remember: smile and the world smiles with you.'

The applause breaks out from the front rows, washes over the hall like a flood wave and rises to a thunderous boom. Vanessa thinks it feels as if the floor is shaking and then, in the next instant, realizes that it actually is shaking. Hundreds of feet are stamping. And her own feet are moving to the same rhythm as the others.

Ida gives Erik a push to make him move on. They still haven't managed to get clear of the row they were in.

'Come on, there are masses of people ahead of me,' he says.

'But can't you even try to get somewhere?'

Ida sighs, annoyed that he won't answer her. She casually examines the group of yellow-shirted students that has gathered at the stage.

'Did you know that Kevin had joined that crowd?' she asks. He shrugs.

'So what, the entire soccer team joined. It isn't that odd.'

G didn't, Ida thinks.

'What do you think?' Erik asks.

'It's got to be good if people stop feeling sorry for themselves all the time.'

'That's just it.' Erik sounds as though he really means it. 'We ought to invite Helena to the hockey club and get her to give a pep talk to the team. All sports stars have coaches who've taught them to set goals and think of themselves as winners.'

At last, the blockage ahead of them gives way. Once in the aisle, Ida starts to edge towards the doors when she feels a hand on her shoulder. She turns around and sees Helena behind her.

'Ida Holmström,' Helena says. 'Such a long time ago.'

Ida manages to smile. She always feels uncomfortable about meeting Helena, even though she has never shown any sign of knowing how Elias did at school. Some people put it around that it was Ida and Erik's fault that he felt so bad about everything, but Ida insists that it was Elias's own problem if he got bullied. He had chosen not even to try to be more normal.

'Oh, hello!' Ida says and hears her voice go shrill in the way she detests.

'And Erik Forslund. As handsome as ever.'

'Thank you,' he laughs.

He is clearly not the slightest bit concerned about what Helena might know about what they did or didn't do to Elias. It calms Ida a little.

'Really nice to see you again,' Helena says, turning back to Ida. 'I haven't met Carina for ages. I'm really looking forward to seeing her, now that she's asked Krister and me to your autumn party. Usually, it's your mother and my husband who have dealings with each other.'

'Of course, that's how it often turns out,' Ida says and smiles.

'It is people like your parents who carry Engelsfors on their shoulders,' Helena goes on. 'I do very much hope that they will become involved with us in PE. And you two, as well. You would be such important role models. After all, your generation will shape the future of our town.'

Helena hands them two round yellow stickers. The text says 'I AM POSITIVE!' In the center, a happy purple sun.

'Thank you,' Erik says. 'It was very inspiring to listen to your speech.'

'It means a lot to me that you felt that, Erik. I do hope we will meet soon again and have another discussion. And bring your friends!'

Helena looks warmly at them both once more before she leaves them and disappears into the yellow sea behind her.

Linnéa hears that Minoo and Vanessa are calling her name, but she ignores them.

Inside her, a small quiet voice, which sounds suspiciously like Jakob's, tells her that this is a textbook example of the kind of situation she should avoid. That she must think first, not react impulsively, not be confrontational, that she must behave properly in school and especially now when social services is on the alert.

She refuses to listen to all that. Another voice is much stronger.

Elias's.

Elias, who cried when he spoke of how Helena and Krister didn't let him talk to them about being bullied. How he had known ever since he was a little boy that they were ashamed of him in front of their friends.

They were ashamed of him because he was not happy-clappy enough, not good enough at sports or academic work and didn't go around with a large enough group of the right kind of friends. Later on, they were ashamed of the way he dressed and dyed his hair black, and his use of make-up. The person he was did not sit easily with their idea of a successful Engelsfors family.

They didn't want to know about how badly he felt, didn't even want to see the scars on his arms. It was after Linnéa's phone call to tell them of his failed suicide attempt that they reluctantly opened their eyes for the first time and saw to it that he was given help.

And it was also the time when they began systematically to blame her for all his problems.

Some guy in a yellow polo shirt grabs hold of Linnéa's arm, but she keeps going, almost gets there. And then Helena suddenly turns around.

'Hi there, Linnéa,' she says with a brittle smile.

Linnéa would dearly like to read Helena's mind but she doesn't dare to take the risk in case Viktor is hovering nearby.

'Anything else you want to tell me?' Helena asks and some of the yellow shirts laugh.

'The couple you were schmoozing with, do you know who they were?' Linnéa asks. 'Ida and Erik, who made life worse for Elias than anybody else. It wasn't any kind of negative energy that ruined everything for him, but people like them.'

Helena's face is still lit up by her 10,000-watt smile, but she tilts her head a little sideways and sighs, as if steeling herself to cope with a cranky toddler.

'I'm sorry for you, Linnéa. You do let your destructive emotions run your life. Sadly, your approach infected my son's mind, too. If he had not kept company with friends who pulled him down, he might still have been alive today.'

The blow is too heavy. Linnéa can't utter words, hardly draw breath. Of course she had guessed that Helena would think along these lines, but to hear her say it is something else.

Helena stretches out her arms in a gesture to gather her flock. They all move off towards the main door. Linnéa just stands there. Tries to persuade her heart to start beating again, her lungs to remember how to breathe.

'Linnéa...'

Part Two

Vanessa's voice breaks the spell that turned her into stone.
Linnéa looks around and sees her standing there. Minoo is
with her. None of them speaks. There is no need.

CHAPTER 31

When Minoo steps out from the assembly hall, together with Vanessa and Linnéa, Anna-Karin is waiting for her. 'I was thinking, perhaps we'd better talk,' she says.

'You're right. But not here,' Minoo replies.

The students slowly drain away from the main lobby. Most people are dragging their feet as they drift along to their classrooms. Minoo feels a pang of anxiety about being late for her biology lesson, but the feeling is mostly an old conditioned reflex. Besides, Ove Post, the biology teacher, is so batty he'll probably never notice that she isn't there. He still believes that her name is Milou.

They walk downstairs to the girls' bathroom and check that they are alone.

'What's going on?' Minoo can't think of anything else to say.

'Something is up,' Vanessa says. 'But I didn't sense any magic. Did anyone else?'

Anna-Karin and Linnéa shake their heads. Minoo shrugs.

'I was in their center yesterday,' Anna-Karin says. 'Somebody who knows Mom took us along with her. I didn't pick anything up there either. Though it can be hard to work out what the difference is between what she's doing to people and actual magic. Do you know what I mean?'

Minoo understands very well what she means. She, too,

had felt how easy it was to be carried along by the mass hysteria in the hall. After this, Gustaf will surely realize that Positive Engelsfors is a cult?

'There's something very fishy about all this,' Linnéa says. 'Last Friday, Adriana is sacked. Today, Tommy Ekberg is principal and is already collaborating with Positive Engelsfors.'

'I saw him in the center,' Anna-Karin tells them.

'Do you think that Helena is behind the move to get rid of Adriana?' Minoo asks.

'Perhaps it's the Council,' Anna-Karin suggests.

'Why should the Council want her kicked out?' Vanessa asks.

'Maybe they suspect her of acting behind their backs,' Anna-Karin says. 'Like that time when she phoned Minoo.'

'I don't know,' Minoo says. 'But, if it had been the Council they would hardly have picked Tommy Ekberg as acting head. They would have wanted to control the school. Which is supposed to be the seat of evil and so forth.'

'Fuck!' Linnéa says. 'I'm so fucking stupid. Elias's father is the town hall super-boss. Of course it was no problem for him and Helena to fix it so that Adriana got the boot.'

Minoo feels that she has been just as dumb. Krister Malmgren is the local authority's 'strong man' and known for getting his way at all costs.

'That's so true,' Minoo says. 'They were saying to Adriana that it had been a local authority decision. And that the basis for it was what happened to Rebecka and Elias.'

'But Helena really wants to help people,' Anna-Karin says.

'How can you be so fucking naïve?' Linnéa snaps.

'Calm down,' Vanessa says. 'Anna-Karin doesn't know what happened after the meeting.'

Minoo tells Anna-Karin. It is hard to have to repeat what Helena had said.

'Why can't something that seems good actually *be* good, just for once?' Anna-Karin mumbles.

Perhaps because we live in Engelsfors, Minoo thinks.

'It must have been Helena that Matilda warned us about,' Linnéa says.

'Could be,' Vanessa says. 'Or else the Council. Or both one and the other. Or something else altogether that we haven't even caught a glimpse of yet.'

'Do you think one can see that this is me?' Olivia says and holds up her drawing.

Their task is to capture their mood on the paper and, as usual, Olivia has drawn a self-portrait. The face has only one set of features, two large eyes weeping black tears. A razor blade is suspended above her. The blade has slashed bloody lines across the sky.

'I'm sure. Only you would draw stuff like that,' Linnéa says.

Olivia looks at her in her typical Olivia way. It's as if she pauses briefly to work out if she's supposed to laugh or get angry.

This time, her face opens up in a big grin.

'Let me see yours,' she asks.

Linnéa pushes her drawing across, wishing she didn't have to, hoping that Olivia won't ask what it means.

She has drawn a heart-shaped flower arrangement, a romantic gift. But among all the flowers lies a bleeding, anatomically correct heart, as if just torn out of the body.

So maybe it's over the top, but it is how she feels when she thinks of Vanessa.

'Wow, you're so good,' Olivia sighs. 'When I see your work I never want to draw again.'

Linnéa rolls her eyes heavenwards.

'How did that assembly hall session go?' Olivia asks and

starts coloring in the hair on her self-portrait to make it look like flames of blue fire.

'Be happy you weren't there.'

Olivia doesn't speak for a long while.

'I've been thinking about something,' she says without taking her eyes off the paper. 'It feels as if we're slipping apart.'

Linnéa lowers her ink pen and looks at her.

'How do you mean?'

Olivia mixes the watercolor to get a darker shade of blue.

'We don't seem to care about the same things any more.'

'Are you mad because I wouldn't skip school and go with you?'

'It was the last straw.' Olivia looks up. 'I've given you lots of chances, Linnéa. Now I feel I can't keep doing that. I've got to learn to set boundaries. I don't mean we would be enemies or anything like that. But perhaps stop socializing.'

'Maybe it hasn't occurred to you, but we haven't actually *socialized* since the end of last term.'

'Exactly,' Olivia agrees seriously.

'Right. Let's decide to do what you say.'

'Listen, you two. Try to keep your minds on the job,' Backman calls from the teacher's desk.

Linnéa registers that his eyes are caressing Olivia's breasts and carefully avoids picking up any of his thoughts.

'I have to go to the bathroom,' she says, picks up her bag and walks out.

It is always a kind of liberation to leave the classroom, even just for a few minutes. As if you have managed to steal a little time for yourself, to take a break from reality.

Linnéa hurries upstairs and along the short passage that leads to the bathroom near the door to the attic.

She started to go up there again after the bathroom were reopened in the spring. She didn't want to keep being afraid to go there. It had been Elias's and her place during the few weeks when they were in high school together. Now, she has come to regard it as the place where he lived, not where he died.

She opens the door. A half-dead bouquet of flowers and burned-down candles on the windowsill. A photo of Elias in a cheap frame. Linnéa knows that Olivia and a few others from their old gang got together up here on the day Elias died to honor his memory. She had honored him in her own way by spending hours when she listened to his favorite songs and read through all the letters he had sent her when she was in the treatment center. She has saved them, a whole boxful. Long, funny, sad, page after page tightly filled with writing and with drawings in the margins.

She almost wishes that she could believe that Helena were right. That it were possible to focus only on the positive sides of life. To forget and carry on.

After Elias's death, Jakob went on about how she should enter into her grief and make it part of her. Let emotions out, instead of fleeing from them.

At first, she hadn't listened to him. Instead, she had rushed straight to Jonte and tried all the easy escape routes he had on offer. But she had finally understood that none of all that worked. The harder she tried to lock the monsters out, the bigger and stronger they grew.

This is how she came to know that to remind yourself of what is bright in life is a good thing to do. But it is totally different from pretending that the darkness does not exist.

She sits down on the toilet seat inside one of the cubicles. Then she takes the *Book of Patterns* and the Pattern Finder from her bag.

Part Two

She tries to work out how to ask the question in the best way. Then she opens the book, leafs through it and concentrates.

Is Helena our enemy?

She twists the Pattern Finder until it is focused. What she sees is like nothing else she has ever found in the book.

The signs are moving restlessly on the page, whirling and twisting in and out of each other. Linnéa turns the pages but wherever she looks, the signs are behaving the same way. They are rushing across the page as if about to overflow the edges.

She tries to concentrate on the question, but all it does is to create new waves of activity in the book.

In the end, she shuts it briskly, puts it back in her bag together with the Pattern Finder and opens the cubicle door.

Viktor Ehrenskiöld stands in front of the cubicle where Elias died. Linnéa had not even noticed him coming in. He looks paler than ever in the cold light from the window.

'It was here it happened, wasn't it?' he asks.

Linnéa doesn't reply. She wonders if he understands by some magic that she has tried to read the book.

'It is so tragic that Elias never found out why he died,' Viktor says thoughtfully. 'Or who he was.'

'He knew who he was.'

'You know what I'm talking about. Elias was one of the Chosen—'

'Don't speak his name,' she interrupts him. 'You have no right to.'

'Perhaps you'd better examine your attitude,' he says calmly.

'Perhaps you should join that yellow-shirt brigade.'

'Hardly my kind of crowd. My world view is rather more realistic than that. And I believe that is something we have in common, you and I.'

Fire

'I can't accept that the words "you", "I" and "have in common" could possibly exist in the same sentence,' Linnéa says.

Viktor stares straight at her with his dark blue eyes.

'I was adopted,' he says. 'My mother was a heroin addict. She died of an overdose when I was seven. No one knows who my biological father is. I had been through five foster homes before Alexander found me.'

Linnéa watches Viktor. She feels certain that he is lying, trying to manipulate her.

She sends out a probe, but he gets there first.

Linnéa. You know it counts as practicing magic, don't you?

A small smile curls one corner of Viktor's mouth.

'I promise not to tell,' he says. 'This time, that is.'

CHAPTER 32

The little brass bell rings when Vanessa steps into the Crystal Cave and shuts the door behind her. The shop is full of customers and Mona Moonbeam stares irritably at Kerstin Stålnacke who stands at the register rummaging in her purse.

'You're late,' Mona says to Vanessa when she catches sight of her. 'We're closing soon.'

'All you said was that I should turn up today. You didn't give me a time.'

Mona shuts her eyes tightly and sighs.

'Excuse me just one moment,' she says to Kerstin who nods and carries on putting coins down on the counter, one by one.

Mona picks up a cardboard box from the floor and comes over to Vanessa.

'And I told you to wear something classy,' she hisses.

Vanessa checks out Mona's baby-pink jeans skirt and glittery green top embroidered with a unicorn motif in gold thread. But she doesn't comment. They need Mona's help.

'Take this,' she says and places the box in Vanessa's arms.

It is surprisingly heavy and Vanessa's shoulder-bag slips down to her elbow and makes her drop almost everything.

'What am I supposed to do with this?'

'Unpack it, of course. Put them on the shelf next to the angels.'

Fire

Mona returns to the register. The spurs on her cowboy boots rattle as she walks.

Vanessa clenches her teeth. She carries the box to a corner, puts it down on the floor and starts trying to peel the brown tape off.

The box is full of mirrors set in garish, octagonal brass frames. The center of the round mirror glass is either bulging outwards or inwards.

Vanessa starts placing the mirrors on the shelf and glances at the china angels. The chubby one playing the harp is still there. A year has passed since she and Linnéa were laughing at it.

So ugly it's wonderful.

Vanessa smiles at the memory.

When the last customer has left, Mona locks the door and sighs heavily.

'I don't know, all these effing people,' she says and lights a cigarette. 'If I can't have a real vacation soon I don't know what I'll do.'

'But you have just had time off for, like, a century or something,' Vanessa says and lines up three mirrors.

'Time off?' Mona snorts as she returns to the register. 'That would be the day. Ever since I heard that the Council was coming to town I've been working like a slave to boost the protective magic around this place. And, honestly, what with this heatwave, it was no fun smuggling my entire stock of special items off into safe keeping.'

Mona blows out a big cloud of smoke and mutters something about fucking nursemaids.

'How did you come to hear that the Council was on its way?' Vanessa asks.

'Step on it, will you,' Mona says curtly. 'I want to get out of this hole sometime soon.'

'Can't you at least tell me what this crap I'm unpacking is all about?'

'Feng shui mirrors. One type amplifies positive energy, and the other transforms negative energy into positive. I can't remember which is supposed to be which. It hardly matters anyway as long as people believe that it works.'

At this point, Vanessa becomes aware for the first time that the word 'positive' can be found everywhere in the shop, on the backs of books, on coffee mugs and fridge magnets. And, in pride of place in a corner, an assortment of bright yellow scented candles, crystals and bath beads.

Say what you like about Mona, but she's a survivor, Vanessa thinks.

'Seems you've found a new lot of target customers for your merchandise,' she says.

'And they have plenty of money,' Mona says contentedly.

'What do you think about Positive Engelsfors?'

'That one can't have too many clients,' Mona says and shoots her a warning glance.

She has made it very clear to Vanessa that she never gossips about her customers. And that she doesn't give a damn who they are, as long as they pay up.

'But what do you make of what they're saying?' Vanessa asks all the same.

'Seems they're trying to find a short cut to an easier life. Most of us are, one way or another.'

Vanessa places the last of the mirrors on the shelf and takes the empty box to the counter.

'Fine. I've helped you,' she says. 'Now it's your turn.'

'I say, is that how an employee is meant to address the boss?'

'Excuse me?'

Mona chuckles and blows a cloud of smoke into Vanessa's face.

'You see, sweetie, hardly any of my suppliers dare to sell any ecto for as long as the Council is around. My stock is almost finished. You won't be able to afford my stuff in a month of Sundays. But if you work for me, maybe we can agree on a deal that suits us both.'

'Are you saying you want me to work here for free?'

'Not at all. You will get paid in kind. In magic materials.'

Vanessa puts her bag over her shoulder. She has been thinking about getting a part-time job. Mom hasn't said it in so many words, but since Nicke moved out, she's obviously been finding it hard to make ends meet.

'You need me as much as I need you,' Vanessa says and leans across the counter. 'You can't employ just anybody. And for another thing, I'm taking a risk by being linked to you while the Council is in town.'

Mona glares at her.

'What's your point?'

'If I'm to work here I want to get paid as well. And you are to give me all the information I need. I'm fed up with not getting any answers anywhere.'

Mona stares disbelievingly at her. Then she bursts out into one of her hoarse chuckles. She sounds exactly as Vanessa imagines witches should sound before she realizes that she is one herself.

'Right you are,' Mona says. 'It's a deal. Just don't expect too much. I'm not made of money.'

Mona's bracelets tinkle when they shake hands.

'Fine,' Vanessa says. 'Now, tell me how you go about getting in touch with a ghost.'

'Excuse me, but is this for real?' Ida says while trying to find a way to be comfortable on the wooden chair in Nicolaus's living room. 'Are you telling us we're supposed to do fairy-tale stuff, like, *the spirit in the bottle?'*

'Sort of,' Vanessa replies and twists the jar of ectoplasm in her hands. 'But this is the real deal.'

Ida changes position again. Her legs are really numb. Today she took Troja out in the forest and stayed for longer than usual. It had felt practically impossible for her to tear herself away from Troja, and from the stables, especially knowing she was due here later on.

'Sounds totally sicko,' Ida says. 'But whatever, I'll go for it as long as I'm not the one who has to do all the hard work again.'

In fact, she is more than willing to go for it. She is so relieved she can't express it in words.

'You have to help lay out the circles,' Vanessa says.

Ida shrugs. Anything, if only she gets away from the being-invaded-by-spirits shtick.

'You and Minoo,' Vanessa says.

Aha. So effing predictable. Nothing is ever just safe and simple.

Ida can't remember much of what happened in the dining area when Minoo defeated Max. But she heard about the black smoke and what Minoo did to him. Ever since, she has been scared to death when they practice magic, in case Minoo accidentally sucks out Ida's soul.

'I'm not sure that I feel totally safe with that,' Ida says.

All eyes turn to her now.

'What I mean is, we have no idea what kind of powers Minoo actually has. We could never be sure what she might let loose.'

Ida doesn't even look back at them. She knows what comes next. This is the point where they all jump up and down on her, because she dares to say what everyone is thinking.

But Minoo surprises her.

'Ida's right. Why do I have to do it?' she says, sounding nervous. Which is just common sense.

'Mona said she really doesn't know what you're supposed to be useful for,' Vanessa says. 'But she had this feeling that you ought to do it. Together with Ida.'

'*This feeling*...is that how we operate now?' Ida says. 'Am I the only one who realizes how dangerous it is?'

'Do we have a choice?' Linnéa says. 'What do you think? The book hasn't given me any answers. And not you, either...right?'

Ida doesn't reply. Tries to remember that the book has at least promised to liberate her from the freaks in the Circle when it is all over.

Vanessa places the ectoplasm jar on the table and starts reading aloud from a piece of paper headed with the ornate logo of the Crystal Cave.

'The ritual can be carried out only on a Saturday night between midnight and one o'clock in the morning,' she says. 'We need a large mirror. On it, we are to draw the letters of the alphabet with a black permanent marker.'

'Why does it have a mirror?' Anna-Karin asks.

'Apparently, spirits can't resist mirrors,' Vanessa explains. 'I guess they're vain, or something.'

Ida feels horror crawling like cold fingers over her face. She's got to start covering the bedroom mirror at night.

'Next, we need the ingredients for the circles. The ectoplasm, of course. We must all bury one nail clipping each near Matilda's grave. In Kärrgruvan, that is. The clippings are to be there for one night and then dug up again.'

'Does it matter whether it's a fingernail or a toenail?' Anna-Karin asks.

'Eww!' Ida says.

'I guess it doesn't matter,' Vanessa replies.

'Hey, it matters to *me*,' Ida says. 'I'm supposed to mess around with all this stuff.'

'We are to use some soil from Kärrgruvan as well,' Vanessa continues. 'And salt, and iron filings. All this to be added to the ectoplasm and mixed with it. Together with…' she pauses to look at Linnéa, who is sitting on the floor, and then at Minoo, 'the ashes of something created by Elias and Rebecka.'

'Created?' Minoo asks. What do you mean by *created*?'

'Some kind of physical object,' Vanessa explains. 'Something they have made with their hands.'

'Can it be something Rebecka has written?' Minoo asks.

'I think so.'

'And it is to be burned?' Linnéa asks.

Vanessa nods.

Linnéa is thinking about the box of letters from Elias. Every single one is precious to her. She wonders how she can possibly select one to sacrifice.

If only she could talk to him one final time. Say goodbye properly.

And if one can talk with the dead …

Linnéa has another box back home. It contains a washed-out T-shirt with Kurt Cobain on it. And a cassette tape with love songs, the label of which says *'TO BJÖRN FROM EMELIE'*. A letter from Mom written to Dad when he was in rehab and Linnéa stayed with foster parents who made her sleep on a mattress on the floor of their unheated cellar. Mom writes about how much she misses Dad, how utterly lost she feels without him. There is a collection of poems by Karin Boye, with an inscription in ink on the title page: *'BELONGS TO EMELIE LUNDÉN'*. A pair of green baby socks that Mom knitted. A photo of Mom, seated on a bench in Storvall

Park with her hands clasped over her gigantic belly. She was twenty years old when she became pregnant, but she looks almost younger than Linnéa. Her thick, black hair obscures her face so that her eyes are barely visible. But she is smiling. No idea of the bus accident that is waiting for her only a year ahead.

'Is it possible to contact anyone who has died?' Linnéa asks.

She avoids Minoo's eyes. She probably understands who Linnéa is thinking about. And perhaps Vanessa understands, too, because she looks gravely at Linnéa.

'Mona was very exact about how the ritual must only be used to contact spirits who are stuck in our world. You mustn't try to contact souls who have passed over to the other side. It can be dangerous both for us and for them...'

Everyone jumps when the sound of the doorbell slices through the air in the apartment. The bell rings again. And again. They stare at each other when someone tries the door handle. Then, scraping noises in the lock.

Linnéa looks at the silver crucifix on the wall. Because of its presence, Nicolaus claimed that the apartment would be a protected space. But if you take into account that Viktor and Alexander could march straight into Kärrgruvan, she can't help wondering how effective *this* protection is if this is someone from the Council. She'd prefer it to be an ordinary burglar.

Suddenly, the lock clicks and the door is opened. Vanessa jumps at the jar of ectoplasm and tries to get it back into her bag. Linnéa grabs Mona's list and pushes it into the top of her ankle boot.

'Now we've had it,' Ida mumbles.

Anna-Karin makes a small squeaky noise.

They hear Adriana's voice in the hall.

'What are we doing here?'

'We must tie up all loose ends,' a man's voice answers. Then Alexander stands in the doorway, with his sister close behind him.

Linnéa curses everything. This was their last hiding place and now it is taken from them.

Out of the corner of her eyes, she sees Ida get up from the wooden chair.

'We haven't done anything that's forbidden,' she says in a falsetto voice. 'Nothing magic at all!'

Alexander looks around.

'How can anyone live in a place like this?' he says contemptuously and wanders off to the bedroom.

Adriana stands still, looking after him.

Linnéa doesn't get it.

They can't see us!

Vanessa's thought is as clear as a bell inside Linnéa's head. She is right, of course, Linnéa realizes. It must be the protective magic of the crucifix that makes them invisible to the enemy.

Alexander comes back from the bedroom and goes to the kitchen. Linnéa hears cupboards and drawers being opened.

'He's been away for three weeks now,' Adriana says. She looks incredibly tired. 'I don't understand what you're looking for.'

Alexander returns to the living room and looks coldly at her.

'Nothing you need to know about,' he says.

Linnéa watches as Adriana wilts a little more and feels sorry for her. She remembers the man she caught a glimpse of in Adriana's memories, the man she had loved. As part of their punishment for trying to leave the Council together, Adriana had been forced to watch while he slowly choked to death.

Alexander walks along to the empty bookshelf. Linnéa has to move out of his way quickly or he'd step on her. He pulls the shelf a few inches away from the wall and has a look behind it. Then he pushes it back.

Minoo and Anna-Karin leap up from the sofa when Alexander comes straight at them and starts lifting the cushions. He comes up empty handed and kneels to look underneath the sofa instead. Then he gets up, looking disgusted as he brushes dust off his slacks.

'Can't we go now?' Adriana asks quietly.

'Not yet.'

Linnéa looks around at the others. Minoo and Anna-Karin stand pressed up against the windowsill. Anna-Karin holds both hands over her mouth as if to force a scream back into her body. Vanessa and Ida stand together, immobile.

Alexander's eyes travel slowly across the pale brown walls. He goes up to the map of Engelsfors and stares at it. But he doesn't seem to notice the silver crucifix. He turns to the window. Linnéa feels as if he is looking straight at her.

Then a smile spreads over his face.

'Three weeks, is it?' Alexander says.

Linnéa jumps aside when he comes up to the windowsill. He parts the bushy leaves of the fern and touches the soil. 'Somebody's been watering it.'

In her head, Linnéa curses. Why couldn't Anna-Karin let that fucking fern just die?

'Maybe one of the girls has a key?' Adriana says.

'I bet they get together here and practice magic when no one's looking.'

'Surely not.'

Alexander puts the pot down and faces her.

'Last year, you yourself said you suspected that. Then these reports ceased.'

Part Two

Adriana crosses her arms on her chest and looks down.

'You've let them get away with it all this time, haven't you?' he says. 'Allowed them to carry on experimenting with magic unsupervised?'

She shakes her head. Linnéa suddenly realizes what big risks Adriana must have run when she kept backing up the Chosen Ones. And how she is risking even more now.

'Can't you grasp that, at this point, control is more important than ever?' Alexander says. 'We are in the dawn of an age of magic. More and more natural witches emerge from nowhere. All young and silly and capable of causing immense harm...'

He comes closer to her.

'Everything worked out so well,' he says gently. 'You were completely rehabilitated. Our family's reputation was fully restored. And then you get lost in a morass once more.'

'I have no idea what you're talking about.'

Alexander sighs.

'Adriana. Can't you simply tell me what has been going on in this hopeless dump of a town?'

She raises her eyes to look at her brother. Suddenly Linnéa hardly recognizes her. But she knows what it is like to hate someone so intensely.

'Is this the point where you start to threaten me?' Adriana says.

'Will you never forgive me?' Alexander says. He sounds sad.

She doesn't reply.

'Do you think that was an easy decision for me to make?' he continues. 'It was a sacrifice for me, too. I did what I had to for the sake of our family. For your sake. Your suffering would have been even greater if it had been someone else who—'

Fire

'I'm too grateful for words,' Adriana says. 'Can we go now?'

Alexander sighs. He nods and they walk towards the hall.

Soon afterwards, the front door shuts, then something scrapes in the lock until it slowly clicks into place again.

Steps echo in the stairwell. The door to the street opens and shuts. Silence falls.

'Okay,' Vanessa says. 'Now you all know what it feels like to be invisible.'

CHAPTER 33

They agree to leave the apartment at five-minute intervals. Linnéa goes first. She waits for Vanessa in Storvall Square. When Vanessa finally arrives, Linnéa pulls a packet of cigarettes and a lighter from the pocket of her dress.

'Would you like one?' she asks, but Vanessa shakes her head.

Linnéa lights up and inhales the smoke deep into her lungs. She really should stop. If for no better reason than that she can't afford this garbage.

They walk through the center of Engelsfors. The evening sun warms their faces and gleams in the display windows of the abandoned shops.

They stop by a small playground. There are a couple of swings made from tires that dangle from creaking chains, and a climbing frame that looks like a death trap.

Vanessa crosses the sandy patch under the swings and pushes her legs through one of the tires. Linnéa settles on the rim of the other swing.

'What do you think Alexander and Adriana were talking about?' Vanessa says.

'Search me. But I wouldn't want to join their family get-togethers.'

Linnéa takes hold of the chains, leans back, and looks up at the sky.

'It is so typically Anna-Karin that she couldn't resist looking after Nicolaus's fern.'

'But she couldn't know that Alexander would turn up,' Vanessa says.

'No, I know. It's just that…Fuck it. Now and then I get so fed up with her.'

'How do you mean?'

'I don't know,' Linnéa says and lets the cigarette drop on the sand. She rubs the ashes out with her foot.

She knows exactly what it is. She can't stand Anna-Karin's soft, submissive naïveté. Her permanent victimhood. And the fact that Linnéa could so easily have become an Anna-Karin, if she hadn't made up her mind to be hard and aloof instead.

'Tell me, who was that visitor?' Vanessa asks. 'The woman who came to your place yesterday?'

Linnéa straightens up, sets the swing going and tells her about Diana's visit. Then she talks about her session with Jakob this afternoon and how she had to defend herself. He had of course heard all Diana's side of the story.

And Vanessa listens. Listens intently, as no one has since Elias died.

Linnéa loves her for that.

She loves Vanessa.

This insight strikes home with a massive impact. It isn't the first time, but the shock is always the same. A great rush of happiness that floods her body. She has to remind herself that it is just some neurotransmitter agents that cheat her brain into believing that everything is fantastic.

Because she knows of course that it is hopeless. And also knows that, all the same, she will never stop hoping.

'Think about it, Helena could be behind this as well, couldn't she?' Vanessa says.

Linnéa tries to focus again. She has almost forgotten what they were talking about.

'The way I see it, she really did think you were a bad influence on Elias,' Vanessa continues. 'If she's revenged herself on Adriana by getting her sacked, why wouldn't she do a similar thing to you? I bet that Diana person is also a member of Positive Engelsfors.'

'Isn't that a bit far-fetched?' Linnéa says and shoves her feet into the sand so that the swing stops with a jerk.

'I don't know,' Vanessa says. 'But it seems to me it's about as far-fetched as complaints about parties you haven't given made by neighbors you don't have.'

'I hope you're wrong,' Linnéa says. 'I'd so much prefer it to be some misunderstanding rather than a mega conspiracy.'

And something Elias used to say comes back to her.

Even if you're not paranoid, it doesn't mean they aren't out to get you.

The editorial staff at the *Engelsfors Herald* has finished work for the day. All except Dad, who is holed up in his office writing the editorial for the next issue. Minoo observes him through the panes of glass that make up part of the office wall. He sometimes raises his hands from the keyboard and stares at the screen. He looks discontented. His lips move without speaking. His forehead is wrinkled. He nods to himself. When Minoo was little, she used to laugh at the way Dad behaved when he wrote.

She is in the common room and leafs through the latest issue of the *Herald* while she is waiting. The reason she's here is to talk with him about Helena. He would soon be done, he had said, just another fifteen minutes. That was forty-five minutes ago.

It is Friday's paper. It's running a long piece about the

problems with the electricity supply these last few weeks. The people in charge are 'baffled', a headline explains. No one has been able to locate any faults in the hardware. Minoo turns the pages.

Helena Malmgren smiles at her from a double-page spread. The *Herald*'s trainee has done a personal interview. Minoo skims the totally uncritical text. Clearly, Helena has acquired yet another admirer in the course of the interview.

Minoo turns another page. An article about the continued high risk of forest fires. A road report and, to go with it, a photo of a lady who points accusingly at a pothole in the street outside her house. And someone has seen a lynx and taken a blurry picture on a cell phone.

Minoo leafs through the sports results, weather reports and school lunch menus. The classified ads with the announcements of deaths on the second-to-last page. She can't resist reading them. It is almost compulsive with her. She scans the images printed in each one: crosses, lilies of the valley, shining sunsets, boats, sports club logos …

Days when no one of Mom or Dad's age, or anyone younger than them, has died, always come as a huge relief. But this time, she spots a year of birth that upsets her and also a name she recognizes. Only forty-two years old. Leila Barsotti. Minoo's first teacher.

Minoo hasn't seen Leila for years, or even thought about her. But in elementary school, Leila was her idol. Minoo even burst into tears at her first end-of-semester assembly because she didn't want to leave her teacher and all her wonderful school books.

Leila leaves a husband and two children, it says in the paper. Minoo stops reading when Dad comes and sits down heavily at the table.

'How are things?' he asks.

'I just saw that Leila Barsotti has died.'

'Yes, of course. Leila. I'm sorry I didn't get around to telling you,' he says and looks sadly at her. 'We haven't talked much lately, not as much as we used to.'

'No, I guess we haven't,' she says, but feels she can't bear a repetition of what happened in the car this morning. She changes the subject.

'Did you know that Positive Engelsfors and my school are supposed to collaborate?'

Dad straightens his back and looks so intently at Minoo that someone who didn't know him might well think that he was angry.

'No, I didn't. Where did you hear that?'

'At assembly, this morning. Tommy Ekberg – he's the acting principal now – introduced our school's new "positive" approach. Helena came on stage afterwards and gave a speech. Urged everyone to come along to their center.'

By now, Dad looks angry for real.

'It's a local authority school, for heaven's sake.'

'She's married to Krister Malmgren, so presumably she can do what she likes,' Minoo says. 'Do you think she's behind Adriana Lopez being fired? As some kind of revenge for what happened to Elias?'

'Couldn't tell you,' Dad says between clenched teeth. 'But I'll make it my business to find out.'

Anna-Karin doesn't want to go home, but can't think of anywhere else. She doesn't dare to seek refuge in the forest, not any more. And it's too late to go and see Grandpa. Not even Nicolaus's apartment is a safe haven. And that's her fault. She should have taken the fern home instead.

She hasn't kept track of how long she has been drifting around in the narrow streets around the center of Engelsfors, but it's getting dark now and she's hungry. She has to go home, sooner or later. Since their fight yesterday, she and Mom haven't said a word to each other. The thought of returning to the apartment makes Anna-Karin claustrophobic before she even gets there.

When she crosses Storvall Square, she catches sight of Minoo standing below the blue neon sign saying *Engelsfors Herald*.

'Hi, Anna-Karin,' Minoo says and waves.

'Hello,' Anna-Karin says. 'Been visiting your dad?'

Minoo nods.

'He's bringing the car around. Would you like a lift?'

'No, I'm fine, thanks,' Anna-Karin says.

She would rather not have to meet Minoo's father again. Their stiff meeting last winter was quite enough.

'I live so near,' she adds and looks at the ground.

'How are you feeling?' Minoo asks.

Anna-Karin studies the cobbled paving on the square.

'So-so,' she mumbles.

They stand in silence for a while. A flock of rooks flies past above their heads. The birds are cawing noisily at each other.

'You see, when Mom and I went to the Positive Engelsfors Center,' Anna-Karin says, 'Mom...I don't know. She seems to hate the way her life has turned out but she still won't do anything about it. She hardly goes out at all. And Helena said exactly all the things Mom needed to hear. Well, I thought so anyway. But she didn't want to listen. And, besides...'

Anna-Karin stops. She very nearly began to explain how worried she is about money, but feels it would be too humiliating.

'I just don't get it,' she says instead. 'I've done everything I can think of, but it's as if she doesn't want to change. That was why I tried...to help her last autumn.'

Part Two

At last, Anna-Karin looks at Minoo. She has wrapped her arms around herself, as if cold inside her dark blue sweater.

'Listen, this isn't the same thing at all, but anyway...' she says. 'My dad is killing himself. His father died from a heart attack when he was Dad's age, but he – my dad, I mean – still carries on as if he'll live forever. He just eats and eats and never gets any exercise and his blood pressure is sky high, you only need to look at him to see that. And he and my mom are at each other's throats all the time and I think they're talking about divorce.'

Minoo is almost breathless when she pauses.

'I'm sorry,' she says in the next moment. 'You were telling me about your problems. And so I go gabbling on about mine instead.'

'That's all right. It's kind of comforting to know that other people have problems, too.'

'We could start an alternative to Positive Engelsfors,' Minoo says. '"Join Negative Engelsfors! Feel better after listening to people who are worse off than you!"'

They both laugh.

A car glides to a halt close to them. Anna-Karin looks quickly at it and notes that Minoo's father is driving. He is listening to the news with the car radio turned up high. They can easily hear the woman newsreader's calm voice.

'I've got to go,' Minoo says. 'But listen. It's not as if I know much about mental illness, but I think your mother is depressed. Would you like me to find the number to a helpline or something? So she can phone up and talk? My mom's bound to know who to contact.'

'Thanks, it's nice of you,' Anna-Karin says. 'But she'd never make that call.'

'Think about it, anyway.'

Fire

Minoo touches Anna-Karin's arm a little awkwardly. Anna-Karin is so amazed that she has no time to respond before Minoo is in the car.

CHAPTER 34

'Jesus, just look at these clowns,' Ida says. 'Such a poor show.'

'Maybe you should invite them to the party tonight?' Erik says.

He and Robin laugh. All three stand and watch Michelle and Evelina who are pretend-wrestling with a senior boy each at the far end of the corridor and shrieking with laughter at the tops of their voices.

Ida can't get her head around why Vanessa would want to be friends with those two. Compared to them, Vanessa is hyperintelligent and tastefully dressed. Michelle and Evelina are always clinging to older guys, always too scantily dressed with far too much make-up slapped on, and always laugh too often and too loudly. As if they hadn't ever needed to stop and think.

'Anybody read Evelina's blog?' Erik says. 'That chick is completely brain-dead.'

'Girls who look good are always brain-dead,' Robin announces, as if he's stating a fact, a law of nature established beyond doubt.

Ida swings around to face him.

'Exactly what is that supposed to mean?'

Robin's eyes swivel nervously.

'But it's how it is,' he says. 'The lookers don't have to be smart to get on in life, so their brains become, like, underdeveloped.'

'So, do you think I'm brain-dead?' Ida asks.

'Of course I don't.'

'Is that so? You must think I'm ugly, then?'

'Give it a rest, Ida,' Erik groans at the same time as Robin says something about how there are exceptions, really.

Ida remains cool, with an effort. No scenes, not now. She must pick her battles.

Especially keeping in mind that everyone is turning up at her parents' autumn party tonight. Mom has planned the evening meticulously. Nothing left to chance. Nothing must be allowed to spoil the atmosphere.

'I must go home now,' Ida says. 'Got to help with the preparations. Do be punctual, darlings.'

She smiles warmly to Erik and Robin to demonstrate that all is forgiven and leaves them.

As she walks down the corridor, sunny-looking yellow stickers radiate happiness from at least every tenth locker door. 'I AM POSITIVE! I AM POSITIVE! I AM POSITIVE!'

She carries on down the main staircase. In the entrance lobby, she catches sight of Viktor leaning against the wall near the stairs to the gym hall. He notices her and ambles over to intercept her. Has he been waiting for her?

Oh, shit, what now? Ida thinks.

It must be something special. It always is. Why couldn't the Council just carry Anna-Karin off and sort it once and for all, instead of wasting everybody's time? Ida is so fed up with all this. She would have had no problem whatsoever with telling all about what Anna-Karin got up to. But the book tells her to collaborate with the others.

'Looking forward to tonight?' Viktor asks when he has stopped in front of her.

'Why do you ask?' Ida says and puts on her sunglasses.

'Everyone who's anyone in Engelsfors seems to be going

to tonight's party at your place,' he says smilingly.

Why does everything he says sound insulting?

'Are you bitter because you weren't invited, or what?'

'Not at all. I would probably have found it a little hard to fit in.'

That sounds like an insult, too.

'Yeah, probably,' she says.

She quickly examines his expensive Stockholm clothes, his smooth face that seems to have no pores to speak of. What everyone says behind his back must be true, he has to be. Guys simply aren't that good-looking, with such immaculate hair, unless they are.

'What do you want?' she says. 'I'm busy.'

'I just thought I'd better check if you and the *Book of Patterns* have been chatting at all recently? Because you're apparently the only one who can read it?'

She doesn't know what he's after, but has no intention of being so easily tricked.

'No, I haven't. And, yes, I am the only one. Will that do?'

Viktor's smile becomes even broader.

'Perfect!' he says. 'Have a nice evening. I hope the party is a success.'

He disappears, walking towards the main staircase at the other side of the entrance lobby. Ida stands where she is for a while, filled with a weird feeling that she has been tricked somehow.

My only love, sprung from my only hate. Too early seen unknown, and known too late.

Minoo's finger follows Juliet's line on the page of the tattered library copy of the play.

Last year she lied to her parents about being absent because her grade was working on *Romeo and Juliet* in the

English classes. 'Rehearsing' was her alibi when she went to the fairground lessons in magic. Ironically, that lie has become the truth.

Now, Minoo wonders how Patrick, the uptight English teacher, is going to handle all the innuendo in the text. Romeo and his band of friends are of course exactly like any sex-fixated teenage guys anywhere. Not that their latter-day counterparts seem to have a clue. Kevin, for instance, has been moaning about how he can't relate to 'that moldy old play'.

There is something ironic, too, about the way Juliet's line about Romeo chimes so exactly with Minoo's feelings for Max.

Minoo knows what it is like to fall in love and then discover that the man of your dreams is a mortal enemy. But at least Romeo didn't set out to murder Juliet and her friends.

Minoo wonders if she will ever dare to fall in love again. It's unlikely, she thinks. If she doesn't, her worst enemy will be the only one she has ever loved.

Her backpack vibrates and she lets the book fall shut. It's a text from Vanessa to say that she has managed to pick the lock to the chemistry lab store and steal a jar of iron filings.

Minoo puts the phone back in her bag, pulls out the bottle of water and drinks a couple of mouthfuls. Then she rests her head in her hands. The school library is so peaceful. She knows that sleep would come easily, that she could slip into dreams and not have to think.

Her head feels heavier and heavier.

'This is nothing but cult propaganda!'

Minoo comes awake with a jerk.

Surely that was Johanna, the librarian?

Minoo gets up, carefully so that the chair legs don't scrape on the floor. She peeps cautiously between the rows of shelving and sees a fraction of a yellow shirt patterned with bright red maple leaves. It has to be Tommy Ekberg. Johanna faces him.

Minoo creeps closer, as silently as possible. Pretends to study the backs of the books, just in case they catch sight of her.

'I'm afraid I'm not happy about this,' Johanna says.

'We're following this new guideline—' Tommy starts to say.

Johanna interrupts him.

'Which was introduced overnight!'

'The teaching staff is with me all the way.'

'Half of them have already joined Positive Engelsfors and that hardly makes the issue any less problematic. This is a local public school, the only one in the whole district, but now we're suddenly meant to collaborate with a private organization. And here you are, already having opinions about the library's stock of books!'

Minoo glances at them and notices a stack of colorful books in Tommy's arms. The titles on the backs promise prescriptions for how to become wealthy, happy, healthy and generally a success in every way. He bends stiffly and puts the books on the floor at Johanna's feet.

'I'm just adding to what's on offer. The students are free to make up their own minds.' His back creaks as he straightens up.

'But that's exactly the point!' Johanna exclaims. 'How are they going to learn to think critically if they keep hearing sermons in school telling them to have a positive approach to everything and ignore anything difficult? How on earth are they going to learn to change things if they're taught that only their own attitude matters?'

'The positive approach is a scientifically proven method

that has led to success for groups like company directors and sports stars.'

'It is a method for turning people into acquiescent yes-sayers! The world around us can be a terrible place, it's a fact you can't just think away—'

Tommy interrupts her with a laugh.

'But dear Johanna, haven't you heard the song about *wiping away your sour face*? Maybe you'd better listen to it. Nobody likes to be around a killjoy.'

Johanna stares at him.

'Are you serious?' she says.

'If you're not happy here there's no need for you to return after your maternity leave. I am sure there are other librarians who will understand what we are trying to achieve here.'

'I have no intention of abandoning the students. And you can't make me go as quietly and obediently as Adriana.'

These are her last words. She disappears from sight and Minoo wishes she could run after Johanna and tell her how much she admires her, how much she is needed.

Tommy Ekberg stands looking at his stack of books for a moment. And then starts picking them up, one by one, and arranging them on a display table with a First World War theme.

Minoo has seen enough.

Back at her table, she finds Viktor with *Romeo and Juliet* open in front of him.

'Have you noticed that when the play starts, Romeo is pining for *another* girl?' he says and turns a page without looking up. 'And tells her that he'll never look at anyone but her. Only to stand and drool below Juliet's balcony a few hours later. It kind of leaves you with the impression that if they had survived, their relationship wouldn't have lasted all that long.'

'What do you want?' Minoo asks.

'Did you know that there are versions of this story with a happy ending? Maybe they'll force us to read it now that everything is so *positive...*'

Minoo closes the book. Viktor looks up at her, smiling a little. He holds a cell phone and it takes her a moment before she recognizes it as her own.

'I've sent a message to your mom. You'll be late back tonight because you're doing homework at a friend's house.'

Anger rushes through Minoo and shakes her.

'Give it back,' she says.

'You'll get it back when we're finished for tonight,' Viktor says. 'You're required for interrogation.'

They are sitting in Linnéa's freshly cleaned living room. From her end of the sofa, Diana is looking watchfully at Linnéa.

'I am truly, truly sorry,' Linnéa says. 'Please forgive me.'

She spots a satisfied spark in Diana's eyes and carries on apologizing.

'I haven't felt all that well lately. It's a year now since Elias died. And I've been thinking a lot about him. It's been hard to keep track of anything else.'

Diana raises her eyebrows.

'I meant that as an explanation, not an excuse,' Linnéa adds quickly. 'I have been doing things that are wrong, I know. But I feel better now. What I'm trying to say is, I still miss Elias, but it is as if I am beginning to...heal. Of course, it helps to talk to Jakob as well.'

She feels disgusting throughout all this. It's disgusting to use Elias in this way.

But he would understand. He knew how much the apartment means to her. That she would sink if she lost it.

'You're quite right to say that it's no excuse,' Diana says.

285

Linnéa wonders what has actually happened to her. She isn't like the old Diana at all. It's not only *what* she says but *how* she says it.

'Still, I'm glad that you've stopped lying to me,' Diana continues. 'So, for now, we'll let bygones be bygones.'

'Thank you.'

She wonders if Diana is actually out to get her or if someone is feeding her lies. Linnéa can't pick up any clues in her mind.

'We'll keep you under especially keen surveillance from now on,' Diana says. 'And if we receive just one more complaint from anyone in this house...'

She doesn't finish the sentence.

'Right,' Linnéa says. 'I hear what you're saying.'

A black car is parked a bit away from the school. Viktor unlocks the door with a remote and walks around to the passenger door to open it for Minoo.

She dislikes intensely being subjected to Viktor's old-fashioned manners and reaches for the door handle at the same time as he does. Their hands touch, but Minoo gets there first and opens the door herself. Viktor laughs a little and Minoo hopes he'll choke on his own tongue.

Inside, the car smells of newness and expense. Viktor starts the engine.

'Did you repeat a year in school?' she asks.

'Why do you ask?' Viktor says as he turns into the road.

'Obviously you've got a driver's license. I hope so, anyway. Which means you must be over eighteen, right?'

'I did tell you, you're smart,' Viktor says. 'Let's do it this way. I won't give anything away about my father or the Council, but I'll answer three questions about me. Ask what you like.'

Viktor stops for a red light. Minoo looks at him.

'You're assuming that I'm interested enough to ask you questions about yourself.'

'Haven't you come across the line, *Keep your friends close, and your enemies closer?*'

'Of course I have.'

'You seem convinced that I am your enemy. Now I'm offering you an opportunity to come closer,' he says and smiles broadly.

She looks away. She doesn't really want to join in his little game. But they know next to nothing about Viktor and Alexander. Just like Mona Moonbeam, they can't be traced in any public records. It should be impossible in highly organized Sweden. But do members of the Council follow any laws except their own? Who knows?

In Nicolaus's time, Council members clearly held superior posts in non-magic society. Perhaps they do nowadays as well.

The light changes to green and Viktor pulls away at high speed.

'Come on,' he says. 'Ask away.'

Minoo remembers the fairy-tale conundrum about when someone is given three wishes that will come true. And then the person always asks for the wrong things.

She must think out the right questions. The manor house isn't far now and she has a suspicion that Viktor's offer won't be open for ever.

'Who are you?'

Viktor grins.

'One of the great questions of philosophy, just for starters?'

'You know what I mean. The basic facts.'

'Viktor Ehrenskiöld, born Andersson,' he says and his fingers are drumming on the steering wheel. 'I assume that Linnéa has told you all about my background.'

'Yes, she has.'

'But she thought I was lying, didn't she?'

Minoo would dearly like to know if he lied, but doesn't want to waste a question on it.

'I was born in Stockholm,' he continues. 'I am nineteen years old. So, yes, I have already passed my baccalaureate exams. And, yes, I can think of more stimulating things to do than going back to school. But the Council needs me to keep an eye on you lot. And, of course, I've never attended an ordinary high school, so that's at least a new experience.'

'What do you mean?'

'That's question number two,' Viktor points out and Minoo curses herself for having made the same mistake as the characters in the fairy tales.

'The Council have their own schools,' he explains.

Naturally. Why shouldn't they?

They cross Canal Bridge and turn into the track leading to the manor house.

'One question to go,' Viktor says when they are within sight of the house. Minoo finally makes up her mind.

'What is your element?'

Viktor parks the car on the graveled area in front of the house and turns to her. He reaches for the backpack on the floor between her feet and pulls out the half-emptied water bottle. Holds it in front of her. The water crackles as it freezes. In a few seconds, it has become a lump of ice.

'I see. Water,' she says. 'So that's how you did it. In that chemistry lesson. You manipulated the acid and the water, made them change place somehow.'

Viktor gazes at her face as if he hasn't heard a word she said but instead is determined to observe every pore, every pimple, every unplucked eyebrow hair. She tries hard not to show that he has made her feel self-conscious.

'Kevin could have been seriously hurt and you found out as having caused it,' she says. 'You violated the rules laid down by the Council. How do you think they would respond if they were told?'

Viktor smiles.

'They wouldn't say a thing. Because I didn't do it.'

He climbs out of the car and Minoo realizes that threatening him will get her nowhere. She has no proof and the Council would never believe her.

CHAPTER 35

Seen from the outside, the manor house looks just as uninhabited as when Minoo saw it last. The ground-floor windows are still shuttered.

Viktor walks straight to the front door. He unlocks it and ushers her in with an old-fashioned, exaggerated gesture.

What was once the restaurant reception, a long, wooden counter and a shelf with pigeonholes for keys, is still in place at the far end of the grand entrance hall. The paint is coming off the walls and ceiling in large flakes. But it smells clean. Unnaturally clean. Just like Adriana's home.

'Follow me,' Viktor says.

He turns into a corridor and waves at her to come along.

She keeps two steps behind him in the semi-darkness. The only sound is the tapping of their shoes against the stone floor. Faint strips of light find their way through cracks around the window shutters.

When they come close to the end of the corridor, Viktor tells her to wait and disappears around the corner.

Minoo listens as his footsteps fade away. A door is opened somewhere, and closed. And then everything is silent.

She turns and looks towards the main door. Her chance to escape. What if she isn't here just for interrogation? What if Viktor and Alexander want to hurt her?

No one knows that I'm here, Minoo thinks and suddenly

feels as if the large house has swallowed her whole.

Adriana had seemed scared to death when she warned Minoo about Alexander, her own brother. Who knows how far he is prepared to go in order to extract the truth?

Do not oppose Alexander. And, whatever else, do not tell lies under interrogation!

But Minoo must tell lies. The Chosen Ones don't have a choice if they are to defend themselves, especially Anna-Karin.

They have agreed what to say and Minoo repeats the lies again, tries to make them feel like the truth.

From the hallway behind her, a shuffling noise. When she turns to look, all she sees are shadows, but she cannot persuade herself that the sound was just her imagination. The hallway is empty and yet Minoo feels acutely that she is being watched.

She has to force herself not to run to Viktor when he calls her name.

They go into a library. The floor is tiled in a checkerboard pattern and the walls are lined with crammed-full bookshelves that reach all the way to the ceiling. A few standard lamps cast a warm light. In different circumstances, this room would have been Minoo's heaven on earth.

Alexander is seated in an armchair placed in front of closed double doors. He nods to her and invites her to sit down in a similar armchair opposite him.

She sits down without a word. The armchair is soft as a sponge and she sinks so deep down inside it that she feels the size of a preschool kid. Presumably a part of their psychological warfare.

Viktor stands leaning against the fireplace just behind Minoo, and knowing that he observes her hardly makes her feel more at ease.

She thinks of the others. They will manage this together. For Anna-Karin's sake.

Minoo fixes her gaze on Alexander. She must stay as cold as he is, as inscrutable.

'A drink of water?' he asks and gestures at a jug and a couple of glasses on a small table at his side.

'No, thank you,' she replies, even though she is thirsty.

Who knows, they might well have doctored the water. After all, once she herself tricked Gustaf into taking truth serum …

Minoo cuts the thought short when it occurs to her that it's not enough for her to be careful about what she *says*. If Viktor's element is water, perhaps he can mind-read, just like Linnéa. Why didn't she think of that sooner?

'According to the protocol, I must begin with asking you if you are Minoo Falk Karimi,' Alexander says. His hands rest in his lap.

'Yes, I am,' she says and wonders fleetingly if that's the last true statement she will make in this room.

'This is an interrogation. But it is also a kind of test.'

Minoo shifts around in her chair and manages to burrow deeper into it.

'What are you going to test?' she asks.

'Your loyalty to the Council.'

It is getting harder and harder not to let them see how terrified she is. She tries to remind herself that since she found out that she was one of the Chosen Ones, she has done more dangerous things than this.

Things she absolutely mustn't think about, in case Viktor happens to register them.

'It is important that you speak the truth,' Alexander says. 'Do you intend to?'

'Yes,' Minoo replies.

Her first lie.

She hears a slight scratching noise. Viktor has produced a small black notebook and is making a note in it with a pencil. He might keep a record of everything she says.

Or thinks.

If only she could sense the presence of magic as acutely as the others. She doesn't even dare erect any magic defences. Just imagine that she let the black smoke out by mistake. The other Chosen Ones can't see it, but what if Viktor and Alexander can? Might they not *know* it, somehow, and just be waiting for it to happen?

'I want to make it quite clear that we punish those who betray us,' Alexander says. 'But also that we reward those who cooperate. Do you understand what I'm saying?'

Minoo nods.

'Answer yes or no,' Alexander demands.

'Yes.'

'Do you know where Nicolaus Elingius is at present?'

'No,' Minoo says, relieved to be able to tell the truth.

'What do you know about his background?'

'I know no more than you do,' she says and focuses on the base of Alexander's nose, hoping that he will get the impression that she is meeting his eyes directly.

'Have you met up in his apartment?'

Minoo is silent for a moment. She must be careful with her answer and remember what they decided together. How they should set about speaking the truth as much as possible before they have to lie.

'I have been there, off and on. You know, watered his plant and so on.'

Minoo's heart begins to beat faster.

'So you and the others have not met there and practiced magic?'

'No.'

Scratchy sounds as Viktor takes notes.

'From now on, you are forbidden to be in Nicolaus's apartment,' Alexander says. 'And, to repeat my previous instruction, you are not allowed to experiment with magic unsupervised, under any circumstances.'

Minoo tries to block out all thoughts about the séance they plan to carry out tomorrow. Only a few minutes into the questioning and she is feeling exhausted already.

'Now, tell me about the night of the blood-red moon,' Alexander says. 'And about how the others discovered their powers. Yes, and also the demise of Elias and Rebecka.'

Minoo takes a deep breath. Slowly and carefully, she sets out to feed Alexander a version that is as true as possible, without including the slightest hint that they acted against Adriana's orders, or that she knew but let them carry on all the same, and that they exposed Max's true identity and neutralized him.

It adds up to a story full of gaping holes.

When Minoo has finished speaking, Alexander sits in silence for a moment.

'When was Anna-Karin informed that she had broken the laws of the Council?' he finally asks.

'At the same time as we learned that the Council existed. At the time that Adriana told us we were witches.'

'Afterwards, did Anna-Karin continue to practice magic in such a manner as to break the laws of the Council?'

'No.'

'According to my sources, Anna-Karin maintained her...prominent position at school throughout the autumn term. Even after she had been informed by Adriana Lopez that it is forbidden to manipulate people around you in this manner.'

Minoo's mouth is so dry her tongue feels mummified. She looks longingly at the water jug.

'That's just the way things work out,' she says. 'Anna-Karin of course never used her powers on everyone, but lots of people attached themselves to her anyway. When someone is popular, other people feel attracted to them. This carried on long after she had stopped using magic.'

'Interesting. For how long did this effect last?'

'Until after Christmas vacation, maybe.'

'And around then, her "popularity" ceased? Just like that?'

'Yes.'

'Would you not agree that it sounds more plausible that her appeal faded when she stopped using her magic in school?'

'Maybe it sounds more plausible,' Minoo replies. 'But that was not the case.'

Minoo can feel her cheeks going hot. The only sound is the scraping of Viktor's pencil.

'I have a question for you,' Minoo says, trying to appear calm and collected. 'What will the trial procedure be like? We haven't been given any information at all.'

'You will receive all the information you require,' Alexander says.

Minoo feels it is too risky to ask any more questions. But she has to if they are to have any chance to prepare.

'But shouldn't Anna-Karin have access to someone who'll plead in her defense? We don't know anything about how it will be—'

'You will receive all the information you require,' Alexander repeats and his eyes darken.

He pours a glass of water for himself and empties it in a few swallows. Then he looks at Minoo again.

'Did you ever find the guilty one?' he asks. 'Whomever the demons had blessed?'

'No.'

'I see,' Alexander says. 'In fact, the attacks against you stopped just as suddenly as they had started?'

'Yes. Maybe the demons gave up.'

Alexander's smile is scornful.

'And your own powers. What can you tell me about them?'

It is as if her lungs have shrunk. Breathing in doesn't give her enough air.

'I don't know if I have any. I haven't noticed anything special, anyway.'

'Are you quite sure?'

'Yes.'

Alexander looks sharply at her.

'Very well. Now I want to return to talking about Anna-Karin. Tell me everything about her magic practices. From the beginning.'

When Minoo walks out through the front door, three hours have passed but it feels like twenty-four. Inside her head, everything is in a complete mess. Only one thing seems clear to her and that is the feeling that she has said too much, put it the wrong way, ruined everything, for all of them.

As promised, her phone was handed back to her after the interrogation. She panicked when she remembered Vanessa's text about iron filings. The Chosen Ones usually delete all each other's texts, but this time Minoo didn't have the time before Viktor pocketed her phone. She has not the slightest doubt that he has been checking through it.

Inwardly, Minoo curses. Before Vanessa is called in for questioning, they must invent an innocent, non-magical use of iron filings. Something in which Minoo and Vanessa might reasonably share an interest.

She walks across the gravelled yard and follows the road

down to the docks. She doesn't turn around, certain that Viktor is keeping an eye on her from one of the top-floor windows. He offered to drive her home, but she had had enough of the Council's representatives for now. Actually, for an entire lifetime. Viktor looked almost disappointed. Perhaps he was looking forward to having another go at winding her up.

Minoo walks along the edge of the canal. The evening sun makes the surface glitter. The ever-changing patterns nearly hypnotize her.

When she is within hearing distance of the water rushing through the locks, she suddenly sees Gustaf.

She slows down. Stops.

He is sitting on a bench, reading. He hasn't noticed her. She can still slip away.

But suddenly a great grief fills her. It was so improbable that they should become friends. And so terribly unnecessary that they should fall out.

She has missed him these last few weeks. She feels that clearly now when she sees him in the setting where they used to go for walks during the summer. There will never be a better opportunity to ask him to forgive her.

'Gustaf!' she calls and walks closer to him.

He looks up.

'Hi there,' he says and closes the biology textbook on his lap.

Minoo stands in front of the bench. She considers sitting down, but the empty part of the seat next to Gustaf is a moonscape of dried bird shit.

'What are you doing here?' he asks.

'Just out for a walk.'

'Right.'

Gustaf kicks a small stone and Minoo's eyes follow it. It

sails through the air and lands with a splat in the canal below the several-yards-high dock gates.

'I thought I saw you with Viktor earlier on,' Gustaf says. 'In a car. Was that you?'

'Yes.'

'So you're seeing that idiot *socially*?' Gustaf says. He sounds amazed.

'We're in the same class,' she says. 'As for socializing, I guess I can see who I like.'

She can't stop herself. She has had enough of having her behavior questioned for today. Especially questioned by people to whom she can't tell the truth.

'Fine, okay,' Gustaf says. 'Of course, I don't really know him. It's just that he comes across pretty badly.'

'Well, maybe. But then, you don't know him.'

It feels so absurd to be defending Viktor.

'Forget it. If you like him he must be...okay.'

Minoo looks at him. Realizes that he is trying. She mustn't mess this up again.

'Gustaf...please forgive me. Things just came out all wrong last time.'

'All forgotten,' he says, and seems to mean it.

'I don't want us to fight,' she says.

'I don't either.'

He seems to ponder over something. She waits hopefully.

'It just that I can't bear analyzing all the time,' he says eventually. 'Twisting and turning things until they break.'

Minoo nods. She knows exactly what he means. What he describes is her own speciality.

'I want to feel good about things again,' he continues. 'Get away from churning over the past. Get away from nightmares and all that fucking misery. And I've started to think that the ideas of Positive Engelsfors maybe can help me.'

He looks tentatively at her.

'And it might make you feel a whole lot better, too. Anyway, Rickard thinks so.'

Minoo stares at him.

'*Rickard* thinks so? But he doesn't know me.'

'I was telling him a few things...' Gustaf says and quickly looks away. 'About what we were talking about. Rickard said that it's hard to get by if you're surrounded by negative people.'

Minoo laughs, quite joylessly.

'That would be people like me, right?'

'I didn't mean it like that...' Gustaf says.

Minoo feels her face get hot. Or is it just the warm air around her? She can't sense any distinction. It is as if the boundaries between herself and the outside world are dissolving.

'What are you trying to tell me?' she says. 'That we shouldn't be friends any more?'

The words are hard to say. Her vocal cords are tensed to suppress crying.

'No. No, not at all. All I'm saying is that I want to give the PE ideas an honest chance.'

'But that means you'd better not be around "negative people".'

'Minoo...'

'Why won't you say it straight out?'

Gustaf has gone red in the face, too.

'All I want is some order in my life!'

'By letting Rickard decide what you're meant to think and believe and feel? Decide who's good company for you?'

'I'm not saying that he's right, I'm only telling you what he said...'

'And you had no opinion of your own, as usual? You're so *weak*.'

She knows she's crossing the mark, again. Weakness is exactly what Gustaf has been blaming himself for. For being too much of a coward to ask Rebecka about her problems, which he still believes led her to kill herself.

And yet, Minoo isn't sure that she can stop herself from going even further. She wants to ask him what he believes Rebecka would have to say about Rickard's philosophizing. For instance, that you should avoid people who aren't sufficiently happy and contented, people who face difficulties and feel rotten.

If she pulls Rebecka into all this, she knows she'll never forgive herself. But if she stays here for one second longer, she knows it will be impossible for her not to. She must leave.

But Gustaf gets there first.

'I'd better go home now.'

All she can do is nod. If she opens her mouth, the unforgivable words will come flying out and ruin everything.

Gustaf gets up.

'I didn't want things to be like this,' he says before he walks away.

She looks after him until she can't see him any more. It feels as if he has disappeared from her life for good.

A moist sound from the canal. Minoo looks that way.

A large bubble is rising to the surface of the water. Then it bursts, with a splash.

Chapter 36

A nna-Karin squeezes her phone in her hand.

She is standing in the small copse on the edge of Dammsjön Lake, while the dusk is spreading over the sky. She ought to go home now, before it gets dark, but moving seems impossible.

She appreciated that Minoo had been trying to tell her about the interrogation in a way that wouldn't drive her crazy with fear. Considerate, but pointless.

The interrogations have begun. It's really happening now.

She thinks about the money that Nicolaus hid in the mattress, cash that she is now hiding in the case in her wardrobe. What if she just ran away? The others would surely understand ...

But the Council would find me, she thinks. They are everywhere in the entire world. I could never hide from them.

She looks out over the still surface of Dammsjön Lake. It reflects the images of the trees on the other side of the lake.

She hasn't been here for several years. Not since some of the elementary-schoolers were made to come here to camp overnight. A twenty-four-hour nightmare of nature-quiz walks, sausage grilling and swimming, all for the sake of 'getting to know each other'. Anna-Karin was the only one who didn't have somebody to share her tent, and she lay awake all night because Erik and Ida had told her that they would set fire to her sleeping bag after she fell asleep.

The fox-bite part of her hand begins to throb and feel hot. Anna-Karin rubs the scar with the fingers of her other hand and ambles along the shore, looking for plantain leaves.

A loud splash from somewhere in the lake. Anna-Karin looks up.

Thin rings are forming far out and spreading over the water. Perhaps a fish leapt up. That must have been it.

Another splash.

Her eyes search the water. New rings are forming, closer to the shore where she stands.

Anna-Karin begins to back away towards the wood when a slurping noise from the other side of the lake sets up an echo.

Must be the fish at play, she tells herself. Normal, nothing to worry about.

In the middle of the lake, the water begins to move gently, around and around in a circle.

And then the water slowly retreats away from the shoreline and moves towards the center. Inch by inch, the wet sandy bottom of the lake is exposed.

Nothing odd about this, she thinks. Nothing weird at all.

She keeps going backwards until she stumbles and almost falls over into a lot of shrubs.

The lake withdraws from the land by a few more inches.

Utter stillness.

Only tiny ripples disturb the surface and make the reflected trees tremble.

And then, a horrible slurping noise resounds everywhere.

Anna-Karin doesn't even dare to look. She turns and runs until she reaches the road. Or track. It is little more than two wide furrows on either side of a ridge covered in yellowing grass. Around her, the night is drawing in.

She is just within sight of the main road when a shadow steals out in front of her.

Two amber eyes shine in the darkness. They are fixed on her and she stops instantly.

The fox.

Anna-Karin sees a white flash, then herself standing in the middle of the track. The perspective is obliquely from below and she is gigantic.

A new flash. Anna-Karin's legs fold under her. She goes down on her knees.

When she opens her eyes the fox is standing immediately in front of her.

Their eyes meet.

And, suddenly, Anna-Karin understands.

Through a complex process, a witch can create a connection with an animal.

Adriana's words, the first time she spoke to the Chosen Ones in her office.

I chose a raven. Or, rather, it chose me.

My familiar can act as my eyes or ears when my own aren't up to the task.

The fox is Anna-Karin's familiar.

It has chosen her.

Hesitantly, she holds out her hand. The fox observes her attentively. Then it barks. Sticks its nose out and licks her scar with its rough little tongue.

Anna-Karin lowers her hand.

'Hello,' she says.

The fox stares at her.

'Now what?' Anna-Karin asks it. 'I mean, should I do something?'

The fox barks again. Anna-Karin feels a new kind of ache

inside her. She longs to run through the forest, to sense moss and dry needles under her paws ...

'This is really strange,' she says.

She has a feeling that the fox agrees. Then it licks her hand once more and slips away into the forest.

'See you sometime, I suppose,' Anna-Karin says wonderingly.

Ida, Julia and Hanna H are standing side by side, leaning on the balustrade around the terrace at the Holmström home. They are gazing at the party-dressed people who throng the garden. Most of the guests are on their second or third drink and the atmosphere is becoming more relaxed and the laughs more boisterous. As the dusk grows darker, the light from colored lamps in the trees softens people's features.

Helena and Krister Malmgren have already gone home. But somehow it is as if Helena's spirit still hovers over the crowd. Positive Engelsfors is *the* topic, running like mercury in and out of the conversations.

... as we've been saying for ages, if people would only pull themselves together...

... she must be so strong, not to let something like that break her...

... it's up to everyone to make a choice ...

... you don't get something for nothing ...

... too much feather-bedding for some ...

... and ever since, I've never had any problems ...

... mustn't let negative people drag you down ...

Ida scans the scene until she locates her mom. Every time Ida finds her, she is talking to a new person, laughing, asking interested questions. But she also glances regularly at the table with nibbles to check if any of the dishes need replenishing. She keeps an eye on Dad to make sure he doesn't drink too much, and at the same time sees to it that none of the guests is holding an empty glass. Now and then, she slips into the bathroom to freshen her make-up. Ida's mother is the perfect hostess.

Dad is standing in a corner, next to the large freezer box of beer bottles. While Mom flutters among the guests, Dad is holding court. He is well-liked in Engelsfors. So well-liked, in fact, that he gets away with a great deal that most others wouldn't. Everyone knows that he's a cheerful guy who occasionally has a glass or two too many.

Lotta stands close to him, pressed against his leg. As always when many adults are around, she sounds more childish than usual. She seems to *act* the role of being a child. But it works really well. Mom and Dad's friends always go on about how Lotta is the most charming little girl they've ever met. One more checkmark on the Holmström family's social scorecard.

'Oh, Christ,' Julia whispers. 'Here comes that horrible wino.'

Robin's mother, Åsa Zetterqvist, envelops them in a cloud of alcohol-laden breath and heavy perfume.

'So, where are you hiding your fiancé, Ida?' Åsa says.

She obviously hopes that speaking very precisely will make her seem less drunk, but the effect is the exact opposite.

'He's gone to get me a drink,' Ida says.

'That's fine, exactly what one needs men for,' Åsa says and tosses back a mouthful of sparkling white from her frosted glass.

Julia and Hanna H exchange a glance.

'Are you enjoying yourself?' Ida asks and smiles.

She despises the old cow, but she can be just as good a hostess as her mom.

'I'm having a fine time, I really am,' Åsa replies with lots of emphasis. 'Everything here is just as perfect as usual. Even your lawn is a perfect green. Ours looks like an African plain.'

She chortles and Ida notices that Mom is looking their way, with panic in her eyes. Everyone knows that Åsa drinks too much, but it usually isn't obvious this early in the evening.

'Your parents have got a fantastic knack for inviting just the right people,' Åsa goes on. 'In this kind of company one feels proud of living in Engelsfors.'

She drains her glass and then leans towards Ida.

'This could be such a fine town if only we got rid of the rotten apples,' she says and her breath blows warm and moist against Ida's cheek. 'I really hope that Helena Malmgren will make everyone see sense. At last, we have somebody who speaks out. People who won't make a contribution have no business being here.'

Ida wonders if Helena has actually said anything of the sort. But perhaps everyone is so happy to take her message on board because it can be used to suit yourself.

Åsa raises the empty glass to her lips. When she tips her head back for another shot and only one solitary drop dribbles out of it, she looks peevishly at it, as if the lack of drink were the fault of the glass.

Julia and Hanna H giggle. Fortunately Åsa doesn't seem to notice.

Erik finally arrives and hands her a glass of cranberry juice with slices of lime. She sips it cautiously to check that he hasn't laced it with vodka. He and Robin have already sneaked off to the bottom of the garden with a stolen bottle several times this evening.

'Ida...' he says.

Now she registers the expression on his face for the first time.

Something has gone wrong.

'A small problem...' he says. 'Down by the kids' play-house. But it isn't my fault.'

'What are you talking about?'

Erik glances discreetly at Åsa and Ida takes the hint.

Something to do with Robin.

And where is Felicia? Ida hasn't actually seen her for a good half-hour.

'Wait here,' she says to Julia and Hanna H.

'You just toddle off, my little turtle doves,' says the old lush. 'Seize the day.'

Ida pulls Erik along into the garden.

'Hey, relax,' he says.

She sees Felicia and Robin sitting on the steps to the den.

He has put his arm around her and they're talking intensely. Ida quickly figures out what about.

He has to be tanked up before he'll even talk to a girl.

By now, Robin has had a lot to drink. And he and Felicia have obviously been chatting.

'You promised not to tell,' she snarls at Erik.

He begins to speak, but Ida holds up her hand.

'Let me deal with this.'

Rasmus and his friends are playing war on the lawn with small plastic robots. They make sound effects that are meant to be explosions and laser beams. When Ida walks past, her little brother looks up.

'They're angry with you, Ida,' he informs her.

He clearly loves telling her and she detests him with all her heart.

They have almost arrived at the den when Ida sees that Felicia has the empty vodka bottle in her hand. Felicia, who never drinks.

'You're such a fucking bitch,' she croaks when she catches sight of Ida.

Robin shifts a little to get even closer to Felicia and tries to look protective, even though he's quite cross-eyed.

'Oh, come on,' Ida says. 'What have I done now?'

'You *knew*,' Felicia says and snivels. 'You *knew* I was in love with Robin and you knew he was in love with me. And you didn't say. So fuuuuck you.'

'Erik said that he'd told you that I'd told him that I was interested in Felicia,' Robin gabbles and looks accusingly at her.

Ida twists the silver heart until it becomes warm from her touch. It's a catastrophe that she should have seen coming and prevented. Stupid fucking Erik.

'You're totally false,' Felicia says. 'You didn't want me to go out with Robin, admit it!'

'Why shouldn't I want that?'

'Because you don't want anyone else to be happy, of course,' Felicia mumbles and tries to hide a belch behind her hand. 'Just because you're engaged to a guy you don't love.'

Ida feels all the blood rush to her face.

'I have no idea what you're talking about,' she says. 'And neither do you, it seems.'

'Erik has got to be the only one in town who doesn't know that you're crazy about Gustaf Åhlander!'

It is as if Felicia has ripped all Ida's clothes off and left her naked for all the guests to see.

'Where the fuck did you get that idea from?' Ida says sharply.

'As if it weren't totally obvious,' Felicia says and makes her voice sound artificial and squeaky. '"Oh, G! G! Please, G, look at meee! May I lick your shoes, pleease G!"'

Ida draws a deep breath. She must not show any emotion. She must not allow herself to be provoked. That would seem to admit that Felicia is right.

'You're drunk,' she says.

'Piss off, Ida! Go away! Just go away!'

'You seem to have forgotten that you're at my home.'

Felicia stares at her with bloodshot eyes.

'Come on, Robin,' she says. She tries to stand upright and reaches for the wall of the den. 'Let's go to your place.' She leans against the wall and fixes her eyes on Ida again. 'Just wait until I tell Julia about this.'

'You've just misunderstood everything,' Ida says. 'We'll talk about it when you're sober. I haven't got the slightest desire to stand here and explain myself to someone as out of it as you are now. Tomorrow you wouldn't remember a thing I had said anyway.'

Robin and Felicia start staggering across the garden and almost bump into Erik. His eyes look piercingly into Ida's.

'What the fuck was all that about?' he hisses and comes closer.

'Don't ask me, she's totally off her head—'

'I mean, what she said about Gustaf Åhlander,' Erik interrupts. 'Are you *in love* with him?'

Ida opens her mouth to reassure Erik that she loves him, only him in the whole world.

But, suddenly, all her energy is gone. She can't think what to say and can't think why she should try.

Is it worth trying?

The thought buzzes around in her head like a captive fly against a windowpane.

Is it worth it? Is it worth it? Is it worth it?

'Are you?' Erik asks again. 'Are you in love with him?'

There is a gurgling sound from somewhere in the garden. Everyone stops what they are doing and listens.

Another gurgling sound, then a drawn-out slurping noise. The air fills with moisture. It is raining blood.

The drops hit Ida's hot face, fall on Rasmus and his friends, speckle the guests' best clothes with red.

The lawn sprinkler is bouncing across the grass, spitting long, fine streams of red fluid. The hose jumps and curls along after it.

The guests scream and run for shelter. Lotta stands stock-still with her eyes tightly shut and howls like a foghorn.

'Anders! Ida!' Mom shouts from inside the house.

Ida runs. She flies across the lawn, past the little kids, up the steps to the terrace.

'Excuse me!' Ida shouts as she pushes through the crowd that is trying to get into the house. '*Excuse me!*'

Mom stands bent over the kitchen sink with her hands clutching the spurting, spitting tap. Strong jets of fluid are spouting between her fingers and shooting into space as large sheets of liquid. In the overhead light Ida sees that the color isn't like blood, but a dirty, brownish red.

'What are we going to do?' a woman screams and Mom starts sobbing.

'Fuck! The toilet's flooded!' Dad shouts from somewhere inside the house.

A huge puddle is forming under the dishwasher. From inside the walls, the pipework makes mysterious coughing noises.

Ida takes in the chaotic scene.

Mom's panic-stricken face. Her fouled dress. The rusty-looking water that is spattered and dribbling down her perfect white walls, ceiling, kitchen cabinets. Dad's helpless calls from the bathroom.

Ida turns around and sees Åsa. She stands a bit away from everyone else and has pressed herself up against a wall. A big, happy grin lights up her whole face.

And, at that very moment, Ida understands exactly how she feels.

CHAPTER 37

'Anna-Karin!' Mom calls from the bathroom. 'That dreadful water is back! It's driving me crazy!'

Anna-Karin hurries to her. Mom is bending over the handbasin. Brownish-red water is bubbling up into the basin and then draining away. It leaves a reddish film where it has been. Rust, the local radio station has informed the town.

Almost exactly twenty-four hours have passed since the water supply in Engelsfors was wrecked. Rumor has it that a minor earthquake has disrupted deep aquifers.

'Maybe it's because of some aftershock,' Anna-Karin says.

Mom looks up and meets her eyes in the mirror.

'Yes, that might be it,' she says. 'Are you going out at this hour?'

This is the first time they have talked to each other since the visit to the Positive Engelsfors Center.

'I'm sleeping over at Minoo's,' Anna-Karin says. She is pleased that it wasn't her, just for once, who was the first to break the silence.

Mom raises her eyebrows.

'Erik Falk's daughter? Well, well. I didn't know that you were friends with her.'

'It's quite a new thing.'

Mom looks down at the sink again.

'Remember now, you mustn't drink the water,' she says. 'It's easy to forget.'

Her concern unsettles Anna-Karin and she hovers in the doorway, very nearly saying that she's sorry for what she said last week.

But she knows the kind of thing Mom would say. A sharply accusing *Of course I understand why you said what you said, it can't be easy to have a mother as useless as me.* Or a bitter *I already know I'm a bad mother so there was no need to tell me.*

'I'll remember, promise,' she says.

Pepper meows and rubs against her pant leg on his way towards the litter box.

'Bye then, Mom.'

'Bye-bye, Anna-Karin,' she says without looking up.

Vanessa weighs the silver crucifix in her hand. It is surprisingly heavy. And *warm.* As if it's been left in the sun.

She can sense the power it emits. Like very, very small but intense vibrations in the air. Like electricity. Or a magnetic field. That kind of thing but still not the same.

She hangs the crucifix on the nail that Linnéa hammered into the wall next to the wooden cross from Mexico. The cross was a gift from Elias. According to Mexican folk beliefs it would protect you against evil. And it's only too likely that they'll need all the protection they can get.

Vanessa helped Linnéa to carry all her furniture into the bedroom to give them enough space to conduct the ritual in the living room. Nicolaus's apartment is no longer safe. Maybe Linnéa's isn't either, but at least there are no parents or siblings around to disturb them.

The rectangular sheet of mirror glass, just removed from the inside of Linnéa's wardrobe door, is waiting on the floor. Using black markers, they have drawn circles all over its surface, one for every number between one and ten, one for every letter in the alphabet and two more circles, one for YES and one for NO.

'I hope they'll give us twice as much protection,' Linnéa says as she comes into the room.

She nods at the crosses.

'I'm guessing we'll need it.'

Vanessa looks at her.

'I thought exactly that, just now. It isn't as if you were … did you? I mean, I know you're not always aware of reading my thoughts but you do admit it just happens now and then?'

'Not this time.'

'I believe you. We must be thinking along the same lines then,' Vanessa smiles.

Linnéa glances at her, a strange look.

'Could be,' she says.

Vanessa is suddenly very aware of how close Linnéa is to her. The scooped-out neckline of Linnéa's T-shirt has slipped, leaving her shoulder and collarbone bare. Her skin seems so soft.

Vanessa wonders what it would be like to touch it.

She looks away, afraid that Linnéa will misunderstand the way she is being gazed at. That she'll think …

Think what? She can't put this into words and lets the thought go. It makes her nervous.

'But you will tell me?' she says instead.

Linnéa looks confused.

'If you happen to hear what I think,' Vanessa explains. 'I'd rather know than not.'

Linnéa nods.

'I promise.'

The doorbell rings.

'Honestly, I so don't want Ida to be in my home,' Linnéa says.

'If it's any comfort to you, I don't think she wants to be here either.'

Linnéa goes to the door. Inside, she is trembling. She came very close to telling Vanessa how she feels about her.

Far too close.

She takes a deep breath and unlocks the door, hoping that the first arrival won't be Ida. Her being in the apartment will somehow foul it. Linnéa doesn't even want to think about what Elias would say about Ida being here.

Elias.

For the thousandth time, she wonders how things would have worked out if he were still alive. If he had been at her side this last year, if they had been through everything together. But thinking like that gets you nowhere.

She opens the door.

Minoo and Anna-Karin.

Linnéa asks them in, feeling odd and uncomfortable. She doesn't like having anyone in her place. The one exception was on the night of the blood-red moon, when Vanessa came here for the first time. She'd felt so sorry for Vanessa, who'd appeared wearing nothing but a blanket and whose boyfriend was a loser. It's weird to remember that Vanessa was almost a stranger back then. Wille's new chick. That was all.

Minoo puts her backpack down on the floor and starts rooting around inside it. Anna-Karin stands still, her eyes sliding along the walls. Her jaw drops.

'Pretty,' Anna-Karin mumbles, unable to take her eyes off a depiction of hell by Hieronymus Bosch.

'Where are the rest of the ingredients?' Minoo asks and pulls a folded piece of checked notepaper from her bag.

'In the kitchen,' Linnéa says and shows the way.

'Your apartment's really nice,' Minoo says.

'It isn't my apartment, it belongs to Social Services.'

Off and on, she can't resist pushing the buttons that make Minoo so ill at ease, reminding her of how different their lives are. Linnéa can't quite work out why she does this. There is no special satisfaction in seeing Minoo's ears go bright red.

'The rest of the stuff is here,' Linnéa says and points at the counter by the sink, where the saucer with the dug-up nail clippings has been lined up next to the salt cellar, the iron filings, a bowl full of ashes and the ectoplasm jar.

Minoo adds her folded piece of paper.

'Rebecka and I used to scribble messages to each other during lessons,' she explains with a glance at Linnéa.

'I picked one of the postcards Elias sent to me when he was on vacation in Mexico. He hated every second of it. They were staying in one of those all-inclusive hotels where you don't even leave the grounds. He wrote to me every day.'

They are silent for a while.

'I'm so nervous,' Minoo says.

'I know. I thought I'd pee myself when we made the truth serum.'

'But this is something else. Not that what you did wasn't hard, but what scares me now is that I'm supposed to help draw the circles...' She stops speaking for a bit and then carries on. 'Because I don't know anything about my powers. I could hurt somebody.'

'I trust you. And the others do, too,' Linnéa says and hands her a lighter.

Minoo sighs.

'Do you have two bowls?' she says. And the doorbell rings.

They exchange a glance.

'Would you go, please?' Linnéa asks.

'Of course,' says Minoo.

Linnéa gets two pottery bowls from a cupboard. She tries

not to panic at the thought of Ida Holmström in her hall and about to enter the living room at any moment.

'What a cozy place,' she hears Ida say. 'If you're a serial killer, that is.'

Linnéa realizes she is grinning broadly. Because it was almost a funny thing to say. Almost.

CHAPTER 38

Ida holds the pottery bowl containing half of the revolting gray sludge. It looks like mud, stodgy and gooey. Minoo stands next to her, holding an identical bowl.

Mona Moonbeam instructed them to clear all electrical fittings out of the room before beginning the ritual. Vanessa and Anna-Karin have lit thick red candles and their flickering light makes shadows dance along the walls. The doorways gape like open mouths.

Minoo has brought an old-fashioned alarm clock and it is ticking loudly in the silence. Nearly midnight now.

'One minute to go,' Vanessa says in a low voice.

Vanessa, Anna-Karin and Linnéa sit cross-legged close to the mirror, ready to take each other's hands.

This ritual does not entail drawing an inner circle. The witches themselves form it. The outer circle, which will be drawn by Ida and Minoo, is there to protect outsiders, in case uninvited guests happen to turn up. But there is nothing to protect Ida.

Stories come back to her mind, all she has heard about what can happen to people who experiment with spirit-in-the-glass sessions. The stories invariably end with madness, spirit possession or death.

'Thirty seconds,' Vanessa says.

'Good luck,' Minoo whispers with a quick look at Ida.

She doesn't reply. The bowl feels warm against the palms of her hands.

'Twenty...'

Anna-Karin strangles a sneeze and Ida's flesh crawls with irritation.

'...ten...nine...eight...'

Ida tries to concentrate. She doesn't want to think about the darkness. And that they will be trying to make a ghost appear. In the dark. At midnight. The goddamn witching hour.

'...four...three...'

She thinks about the book's promise.

'...two...'

She thinks about G.

'Go.'

Ida dips the three middle fingers of her left hand into the bowl. The sludge is as cold as ice, so cold it almost hurts, though the outside of the bowl is warm.

'The circle that binds,' Vanessa says.

Ida kneels on the floor and starts drawing the circle. At her side, Minoo does the same. Each draws her part of the circle around the others in the opposite direction. All the time, they both take care to stay inside the circle themselves.

Ida can feel magic flow through her body, through her arm, out through her fingertips. They are tingling. As she slides her fingers over Linnéa's floor, the icy ectoplasm seems to be sucking magic out of her. She is sweating now. Her top sticks soggily to her back.

She dips her hand in the bowl again and carries on.

The room is completely silent. The air seems to absorb every sound, to grow denser the closer she and Minoo come to each other. Soon, the outer circle will be closed.

Please, let this pass, Ida thinks and dips her fingers in the bowl yet again. Just let it pass.

Minoo feels as if someone or something is steering her hand, making the ectoplasm arrange itself into a perfect line that will form a perfect circle.

The magic is in the air, she feels it radiating from herself. As if she is about to dissolve, become part of something greater.

Dissolve.

Fear is crawling into her.

It is a feeling she recognizes from the evening in the dining area when she defeated Max.

Minoo knows what is about to happen. The black smoke will be coming soon. She can almost sense it now, whirling at the very edge of her field of vision, spreading away from her towards the others.

She forces herself to go on. Once begun, the ritual must be completed, Mona Moonbeam has instructed them. If not, there is no telling what will be let out into our world.

She dips her left hand in the ice-cold goo again. Only a yard or so until she and Ida meet.

If she could, she would hurry up, but this is a process she cannot control. The circle is growing at its own pace.

A thin, black wisp of smoke snakes past in front of her eyes and she watches in terror as it tentatively throws out filaments towards Ida.

But no one else seems to notice what is about to happen. No one realizes that Minoo is about to become a monster. Panic hammers inside her, splashes through her blood vessels.

Ida is coming closer. Closer. Closer.

Their hands touch and the lines of goo melt and merge across the last inch. The circle is closed.

The black smoke disperses and vanishes.

Minoo stands up on shaky legs. She and Ida sit down with

the others. Together, they all grip the mirror and lift it, and then Ida stretches out her hand and draws the sign of metal with ectoplasm on the floor.

Ida nods and they carefully lower the mirror again.

'The circle that gives power,' Vanessa says.

Minoo takes a firm grip on Ida and Linnéa's hands.

'Okay. Good,' Vanessa whispers. 'Shall I ...?'

'Yes, yes, just go ahead,' Ida hisses.

'Everybody concentrate on the glass,' Vanessa says.

It is standing upside down inside an empty circle in the middle of the mirror. They have smeared the rim of the glass with pure ectoplasm. Minoo notes the IKEA logo stamped on the bottom of it.

'Uh ... hi there,' Vanessa says. 'We are trying to make contact with Matilda, daughter of Nicolaus Elingius and his wife Hedvig. Are you here?'

The glass jerks. And starts sliding across the mirror in a straight line towards YES.

'Holy shit,' Linnéa whispers.

Minoo swallows hard.

'We greet you and wish you welcome at this hour of midnight when the dead and the living can meet,' Vanessa says formally. 'Within this circle, we meet with mutual respect and deference.'

Apparently, it is important to say all this, word for word. In her instruction sheet, Mona Moonbeam has underlined this several times. But once it has been properly said, Vanessa seems to be at a loss. Minoo has to fight her know-it-all urge to take over.

'The introduction,' she whispers instead and Vanessa's face clears.

'My name is Vanessa Dahl and I speak for us all. To my left, you see Ida Holmström. To her left, Minoo Falk Karimi,

then Linnéa Wallin and then Anna-Karin Nieminen, who sits
to my right. Do you accept all the participants in this circle?'

The glass jerks again, but stays where it is. Once more, a
yes.

'The danger you warned us of – is that the Council?'

The glass jerks, stays in place. Yes. And then it slides along
to NO.

'What do you want to tell us?' Vanessa asks. 'Do you
mean that there are other dangers? Like Positive Engelsfors?'

The glass slides quickly over to the letters, trailing ectoplasm as it moves.

'M,' Vanessa reads. 'O-R-E. More. More dangers? In addition to Positive Engelsfors?'

The glass whizzes back to YES and stops with a grinding,
glass-against-glass sound that sets Minoo's teeth on edge.
Then it goes back to the letters, much more slowly now; it
almost looks laborious. It stops at the letter M.

'M…' Vanessa says. 'M?'

A piercing grinding sound that makes Minoo want to
cover her ears with her hands, but instead she grips Ida and
Linnéa's hands harder. They must not break the circle.

A snapping sound from the glass. Cracks spread all over it.

'Shut your eyes!' Minoo screams and shuts her own eyes
tightly.

She bows her head just as she hears the glass explode.
Shards land in her hair.

And then, *everything* explodes.

A white, dazzling light fills Minoo's head.

She sees the *Book of Patterns,* surrounded by flames.

She sees the grinning, toothless man who was Matilda's
prison guard.

She sees a dagger, its edge of dull silver.

She sees Nicolaus's face. He is younger than she has

known him. His hair is dark and he is wearing a long black coat with a white collar. His ice-blue eyes are full of grief.

She sees a face as if reflected in a watery surface, a girl in her teens, with long, reddish-blonde hair falling in curls around her freckled face. Instantly, Minoo knows who she is. The spirit they have sought. Matilda.

'I am here now.'

The voice uses Ida's vocal cords, but it is not Ida who is speaking.

A wave of electricity shoots through Minoo. She opens her eyes.

Ida's hand slips out of hers.

Ida, still cross-legged, is floating a few inches above the floor. A thin string of ectoplasm trickles from one of the corners of her mouth. Her pupils are so widely dilated that her blue eyes look almost black.

'My daughters,' she says.

'Matilda?' Anna-Karin says tentatively.

Ida sighs deeply, as if in relief. The breath from her mouth is like white vapor.

'It has been so long since I heard someone utter my name.'

'Nicolaus has spoken to us about everything,' Minoo says. 'He told us about you. About what happened.'

The candle flames gleam in Ida's pupils.

'I know.'

'We can't even begin to imagine all that you have been through—' Minoo begins.

'You must not pity me,' Matilda interrupts her. 'Centuries have passed since then. And I made my own choice.'

Minoo wants to ask her what her choice was, how it affected her powers. But Matilda continues.

'Time is out of joint. Events are moving too swiftly and you are not properly prepared. In many ways, I take a great risk to come here. I am not at all certain that you are mature enough for what I intend to tell you. It is taking a leap of faith. I hope you will show yourselves to be worthy.'

Matilda lets her gaze wander from one face to the next. It stays on Minoo.

'And especially you, Minoo,' she adds. 'You will learn the truth about your powers.'

The circle is silent. Goose bumps cover Minoo's arms.

CHAPTER 39

'You are not alone in your battle against the demons,' Matilda says. 'Humanity has guardians who have existed at our side since the beginning of time. They have watched over us. Sustained us. Tried to protect us from evil.'

'What kind of guardians?' Vanessa asks. 'Like, guardian angels, or something?'

'They have been called angels,' Matilda says. 'But they have been given many names. They prefer to be known as guardians. They taught us human beings to master magic in this world, gave us the *Book of Patterns* and the Pattern Finders.'

Minoo thinks that it should be a relief to know that they are not alone when they confront the demons. But right now, all she can do is wonder where these so-called guardians have been hiding.

Linnéa has obviously been thinking along the same lines.

'Our guardians have done such a fucking fantastic job so far,' she says. 'Like, first we were seven. And then six. Now, we're down to five and the demons know who we are. I feel so safe.'

'They have helped you as best they could,' Matilda replies. 'Once upon a time, they were stronger and lived closer to us. But their power has diminished and so has their ability to communicate with people. The guardians have their own

324

language, their own way of thinking. They hoped that the *Book of Patterns* would bridge that gap, but today, fewer and fewer human beings can read it.'

'So the guardians are the ones who communicate with us through the book, then?' Minoo asks.

'Yes,' Matilda answers. 'And also through me. I speak for them. We do all we can to help you, but we are not all-knowing, or all-powerful. Or all-seeing.'

'But the *Book of Patterns* contains prophecies, too,' Minoo says. 'Like the one about us.'

'The guardians can prophesy different *possible* future developments. But the future is in constant flux. It is influenced by the incalculable number of choices people make every day. Prophecies are unstable, they change. It is only the Council that has tied itself to particular interpretations.'

'Why have we not heard about the guardians before?' Anna-Karin asks. 'Adriana ought to have mentioned them.'

Matilda smiles sadly.

'The Council has forgotten. They had forgotten even when I was alive. Once, tasks were shared between the guardians and the Council. Together, they were to help the Chosen One. As the guardians' powers declined, the Council's grew steadily stronger. But with increasing strength went an increasing obsession with hierarchies and control. The Council slowly changed into a self-perpetuating organization with a single item on its agenda: to control all magic practice and all witches.'

'But how much does the Council really know?' Minoo says. 'About anything?'

'It is very difficult to say. The Council maintains a united front to the outside world, but internally there are ceaseless intrigues and power struggles. Knowledge is distorted to suit the goals of the powerful. A large majority of the

Council members know no more than they are told. If any real knowledge is still held within the Council it is in the possession of the elite. They have access to enormous libraries, where witches' accounts of their readings in the *Book of Patterns* are kept. The collections have been built up over many centuries.'

Minoo imagines the labyrinthine passages between shelves so tall you can't see where they end, filled with ancient books and rolls of parchment. How much simpler would everything become if only you could have access to such a library?

'I understand that you have many questions, but our time together is limited to this hour. And I must tell you about the demons,' Matilda says. 'From time to time, creatures from other dimensions make attempts to get into our world. The demons' attack has been the worst. They are entities capable of moving between different worlds. They exist to achieve just one goal and that is to eliminate chaos and establish order. When they discover life forms in other worlds, they see it as their foremost task to tame them, then mold them in their own image. The demons detest irrationality, emotions, discrepancies, change. They perceive themselves as flawless and eternal. No living beings can match the ideals of the demons. That is why their experiments always fail. And when they do, they move to the next stage.'

'What is their next stage?' Anna-Karin asks.

'Complete extinction of all living things on the planet,' Matilda replies evenly. 'In a dead world, nothing is left to offend the demons' sense of order.'

They feel a chill, as if the air in the room has grown colder. A chill that is finding its way even into Minoo's very soul.

She sees her own terror reflected in the eyes of the others. For the first time, the apocalypse feels real. All life on earth would be wiped out. No one doubts that humanity and its chaotic world would fail the tests set by the demons.

'When the demons discovered our world, they first tried to gain entrance and tame it,' Matilda continues. 'The guardians put up strong resistance and joined forces with powerful witches. They drove the demons into retreat, but during these battles, our reality was ripped in some places. The gaps serve as doors of a kind, openings into our world. There were seven of these gaps, or doors, in seven different places. The guardians and the witches managed to close but not to lock them, despite being aware that, for as long as the doors were left unlocked, the demons would keep trying to enter. They never give up.'

'What fun,' Linnéa says.

'The guardians realized that there was only one individual who could save us,' Matilda explains. 'A witch. They called her the Chosen One. She had to be a unique witch, in control of all the elements, and born near one of the doors during a magic age. The first Chosen One succeeded in locking the first door. But that magic age was fading and several centuries passed before the next Chosen One was born and could lock the second door.'

'Why didn't the first Chosen One bar all seven doors?' Minoo asks.

'The Chosen One, whoever he or she is, is always strongly tied to his or her birthplace, just as you are to Engelsfors. It follows that he or she can close only the nearby portal. It is a hard task, you need guidance and support. That was why the guardians decided to set up the Council. Its mission was to help the Chosen One and preserve all knowledge about the task.'

'I see. They were created to be there for us, but now they want us to exist for them,' Linnéa says.

'Yes.'

'How long has this been going on for?' Minoo says. 'What I mean is, for how long have there been Chosen Ones?'

'I don't know. Thousands of years, perhaps longer still. The guardians' notion of time is different from humans. All I know is what they have told me,' Matilda replies. 'But the previous Chosen Ones have managed to bar six doors.'

'That's to say, the Engelsfors door is the seventh? And last?' Minoo asks.

'Yes. Engelsfors is the last place where the demons can gain entrance to our world.'

Minoo checks the time. She must remember all the questions she wants Matilda to answer and get around to asking them before the hour is out.

'Forgive me, but I don't quite understand,' she says. 'You were previous Chosen One and born near this portal. But you died before you could close it...'

'Yes, exactly,' Vanessa says. 'How come we aren't overrun with demons by now?'

'The door can only be closed or opened at a certain time,' Matilda says. 'That time coincides with when the magic at the gap is at its strongest, when the veil separating the worlds is at its thinnest. That is when the door can be locked, and only then. Or else, opened wide. I died before that point in time.'

'But the demons didn't succeed in opening the portal?' Linnéa says.

'No, they didn't succeed.'

'Why not?' Minoo asks.

'I don't know. But that earlier magic age was not as dominant as this current one. And opening or closing the door can only be done from this world. It means that the demons are utterly dependent on those they have managed to bless. The unlocked gap in the veil is not wide enough for them to get in, but they can still reach out and seduce people who live nearby on our side. Once blessed with powers, these recruits can be used as demonic tools.'

Minoo is thinking about Max's memories. How he lay awake at night, speculating about the terrible things he had committed himself to carry out. The demons had promised him that, in return, he would get Alice back. The girl he loved. The girl he had murdered.

'Why don't they simply bless a whole army of recruits?' Linnéa says.

'Until the portal opens, they haven't enough power to do anything on a big scale. Besides, only a natural witch can endure living with the blessing of the demons. Natural witches are rare. There are more of them near the doors, but they are still rare.'

'And you died. But the demons still couldn't open the door,' Minoo says.

'That is so,' Matilda replies 'Then the magic age ebbed out. The guardians had to wait for the next inflow of magic and the next Chosen One. My soul stayed and waited with them.'

'And the demons, they had to wait as well,' Vanessa says.

'And the Council, too. They had time to forget even more of what they knew,' Linnéa says.

'And Nicolaus,' Anna-Karin whispers.

'Yes,' Matilda replies. 'We have all been waiting…for you.'

Minoo steels herself. This question is almost too frightening to ask, but she must know.

'Max said that the demons have a plan for me. What did he mean?'

Matilda's head turns to look directly at Minoo. For a brief moment, Ida's eyes go black and glisten, like crude oil. Like a bird's eyes. In the next moment, the blackness is gone.

Fire

It must have been my imagination, Minoo thinks.

'I don't know,' Matilda says. 'But they fear you.'

Linnéa laughs a little.

'I'm sorry, but honestly, it's so weird. The demons are afraid of Minoo?'

Minoo wishes she could laugh, too.

'Is that why they stopped persecuting us?' Anna-Karin asks.

'As I told you, the demons never give up. Instead they choose many different routes. It seems that they are trying to speed up the next inflow of magic. And it seems they are succeeding. We thought the final battle wouldn't come for at least another ten years, but events are progressing far too fast by now. You must have seen the signs.'

'The heat,' Minoo says. 'The dying forest. The erratic electricity. And the water...'

'Yes,' Matilda says. 'The veil separating the worlds is becoming thinner and that affects your physical reality. Something in Engelsfors is very wrong.'

'You don't say...' Vanessa mutters.

'But isn't it just as well that it is happening now?' Linnéa says.

Everyone's eyes fix on her.

'It's just that I don't like the idea of waiting for the apocalypse,' she shrugs. 'We might as well get it over and done with. Shut that portal, once and for all. Or, at least, try to shut it.'

'You don't understand,' Matilda says.

Minoo can't hold back a flood of questions any longer.

'But then, explain it to us. Why were we seven and not just one? What happened to your powers? How do we go about closing the portal? *Can* we actually do it, now that there are only five of us?'

A shiver runs through Ida's body. She shakes her head vigorously.

'You are not ready.'

'Surely you, if anyone, should do everything to help us!' Minoo says. 'After all, you have been in the same situation as we are now and—'

Matilda interrupts her.

'We have helped you, as much as we've been able to. And your situation is not comparable with mine. I was alone.'

Minoo is ashamed. She has thought of this herself. Also, Matilda has been waiting for them for centuries. All the time aware that the apocalypse is approaching.

'Forgive me,' Minoo says. 'You're right.'

'But what should we do now?' Anna-Karin asks.

Matilda looks at them gravely.

'We will try to help you about the current matter of the Council and its trial. You should collaborate as much as you can with the Council, but without giving each other away. Keep pretending that you are following all its laws. Try to endure. Use your magic sparingly. In the circumstances, it is difficult to foresee how your powers will develop. Handle them carefully or you could be harmed. That is true of you, Minoo, in particular.'

Minoo feels ice cold again.

'You don't belong to any one element, Minoo,' Matilda continues. 'The guardians have blessed you. That is how you are able to see the magic of the demons. That is why you can use it against them and against their human servants.'

Minoo has frozen to the floor. She feels like a pillar of ice. She registers that the others are looking at her, but she doesn't dare to meet their eyes. Why do Matilda's words frighten her so much? She should feel relieved. Her own suspicion had been so much worse. That she herself was some kind of demon.

'I understand how frightening it must be for you to learn

that your powers are so similar to those of the demons,' Matilda says. 'But it singles you out as someone who can defeat them. You have no reason to be fearful as long as you use your power responsibly, for good..And I know you will.'

And now Minoo realizes what truly terrifies her.

How can you know that you are good? How to be certain?

'The midnight hour will soon be over and I shall have to leave you,' Matilda says. 'The demons cannot single-handedly speed up the arrival of the apocalypse. They must have blessed a recruit here in Engelsfors, someone they can use. We don't know who it is. Do not trust anyone.'

'That doesn't sound at all familiar,' Vanessa says ironically.

'Helena,' Linnéa says. 'It has got to be her.'

'But none of us has sensed any magic in her,' Vanessa says and turns to Minoo. 'Look, if Helena had been oozing demonic magic you would have noticed when she spoke at assembly – wouldn't you?'

Minoo says nothing. She knows nothing, not any more. Thankfully, Matilda answers instead.

'Minoo can see demonic magic, but only when the Blessed One uses it. We don't know if Helena is blessed. But the movement she leads can be dangerous all the same. You must not, under any circumstances, approach her organization, or her, before we know more...'

Matilda falls silent and another shiver courses through Ida's body. It worries Minoo.

'Are you alright?' she asks.

'In the future, it will be difficult to communicate with you. The energies are out of kilter. I must leave you now.'

She shuts her eyes. Ectoplasm begins to dribble from a corner of Ida's mouth.

'I'm not trying to ruin the atmosphere or anything,

but someone ought to collect that stuff,' Vanessa whispers. 'Mona's prices have gone up...'

'Wait!' Linnéa cries and tears herself free from the circle, leans forward and grabs hold of Ida's arm. 'Who or what are you, truly? A ghost?'

Ida's eyes open again.

'I am a soul caught between worlds,' she says.

'Are there any others with you?'

Matilda looks sad.

'Elias is not with me. Nor is your mother, Linnéa. Nor Rebecka. Souls that pass on are no longer among us.'

Linnéa's eyes shine with tears.

'Where are they, then?' she asks.

'It is concealed, even to us,' Matilda replies. 'I myself do not know if another world is waiting, perhaps the heavenly world my father believed in. Or perhaps our consciousness will be extinguished for ever. I wish that I knew.'

Ida's eyes close once more. Her body sinks towards the floor and once down, she collapses like a rag doll.

The smoky smell of a burning fire sweeps through the rooms and quickly disappears.

CHAPTER 40

A magnificent September sky spans the tops of the trees. Violet shades into red that deepens at the horizon. The sun is setting, a peach-colored globe glowing behind the roofs of the houses.

Linnéa is crossing Storvall Park. She moves slowly and her head feels woolly, as always when she has slept a whole day away.

Last night, after the others had left, she stayed up. She listened to music, chain-smoked her last cigarettes, wrote in her diary for hours. Wrote, because of her need to try to deal with the overwhelming sense of hopelessness that always pours into her when she's alone, wrote in order to remind herself that oblivion solves nothing.

Though she longed for oblivion, more now than she had for a long time.

A call to Jonte would have been so simple.

Souls that can pass on are no longer among us.

It wasn't until she heard those words that she realized how hopeful she had been.

But they are gone for ever.

She fell asleep at dawn. And now the sun is setting.

Linnéa stops on the pavement just opposite the Positive Engelsfors Center. Fluorescent light streams out through the large windows.

She spots him at once. He is standing in the middle of the room, surrounded by people who just a few months ago would have avoided even looking at him. Now they're all chatting and laughing together as they help each other scrub a wall that has been splattered with rust-red water.

Dad.

He looks happy. Comfortable. He fits in well. He looks like the father she long since gave up dreaming that he would be.

All the way here, she has been speculating about what she should do. She thought, if only she saw him it would tell her if she ought to talk to him. To warn him about Helena. True, there is no proof that she is allied to the demons, but Linnéa needs no proof.

Now she has seen her father and knows what to do.

Nothing.

Perhaps this is his new addiction. Perhaps he has found something that makes him happy. Whatever it is, clearly nothing Linnéa can say would make him leave Positive Engelsfors.

She wants to walk away, but something makes her stop and turn around.

She sees Anna-Karin in a window in the house opposite the center. Her face is difficult to distinguish as the pane reflects the sunset.

Linnéa raises her hand in greeting and Anna-Karin waves back to her.

Anna-Karin stays at the kitchen window until Linnéa is out of sight. When she has disappeared, Anna-Karin leans her forehead against the glass and shuts her eyes. Tries to let go of all thoughts about Matilda, the Council, the guardians, the apocalypse, the demons and Positive Engelsfors.

Then she suddenly loses herself completely.

A flashing light flits past her eyes. The pressure against her forehead disappears.

She sees again.

And now, the scents and smells of the forest fill all her senses. She runs fast across the forest floor, down between the lowest parts of the tree trunks. She takes long leaps and her body stretches with each pace.

She is not happy, because happiness is not a concept she knows about or needs. She is free. She is whole. She *is*.

'What are you doing?'

Anna-Karin smells the kitchen odors again. Stale cigarette smoke and grease.

She opens her eyes and straightens up. Her forehead has left a sticky mark on the windowpane. Anna-Karin can see her mother reflected in the glass. She is standing in the kitchen doorway.

'Nothing,' Anna-Karin says and tries to calm her thumping heart, which still believes that she has been running in the forest. 'Just looking.'

'Goodness, people might think there's something wrong with you,' Mom says and puts her coffee mug in the sink before going back to the living room.

Soon afterwards, the sound of machine guns and swelling orchestral music.

Anna-Karin will tell the others about her familiar. Tomorrow. Tonight, it is her secret, like Pepper when he was a tiny kitten and she took him to school in her jacket pocket.

A secret friend, the only spark of light in the darkness that is closing in around her.

In the living room, a dance tune is playing at maximum volume.

Vanessa closes the door and lets Frasse off the leash. He

pads along to the kitchen to gobble whatever is in his food bowl.

'Vanessa, you two have been away for such ages!' Mom exclaims. She is sitting on the sofa, swaying to the music. 'Come here and sit down!'

She pats the seat next to her. Vanessa sneaks a glance at the box of rosé wine and the two glasses on the sofa table. One of the glasses is half full.

Mom grabs the box and fills both glasses to the brim with much splashing and dribbling.

'Isn't it cozy? Just us girls at home alone,' she says and hands Vanessa her glass.

Vanessa looks quizzically at her. What's this, a trap?

'I do think you should be allowed a few sips at home,' Mom says and winks. 'You're a big girl now. And I'm not as easily tricked as you think, Nessa. I know perfectly well you take a drink every now and then.'

Vanessa takes the glass and drinks. The wine tastes like ice-cold lingonberry juice.

She quickly checks the time on her phone. More than an hour to go before Mom is due to meet up with some friends from work and go to the 'Singles' Sunday Night' in Götis.

She drinks another mouthful of wine and puts the glass down. It's too weird, sitting here drinking with her mother.

'Just imagine, you'll be eighteen next year,' Mom says. 'Then we can do Götis nights together. Two cool single girls! We'll be *just devastating*!'

Great, Vanessa thinks. If I'm not banned for life from Götis, and if the apocalypse doesn't come before then, I have this fantastic chance to go out with my mom and pick up men. Just the kind of existence I dream about.

She picks up her phone. Starts writing a text, deletes, starts again. Finally decides.

Try again on a different sofa?

'Do I, do you think?' Mom asks.

'Do what?' Vanessa says and sends the text to Jari before she has time to regret it.

'Do I look good? I mean, do I look all right?'

She cautiously pats her hair. Vanessa feels strangely moved by the gesture. She has blow-dried her hair a little too much, it looks like a lion's mane. The style was probably right about fifteen years ago. But Mom's make-up is expertly applied and she is wearing a bright red top that shows off her impressive cleavage.

'You look fantastic,' Vanessa tells her.

Mom smiles gratefully and drinks some more wine.

'You know, Nessa, I really feel so good about everything,' she says and leans back on the sofa. 'I should have thrown Nicke out well before I did. Stole one's will to live, he did. Having a good time meant nothing to him! And he was so damn cheap! We never even took a vacation. Next year, we'll go for a vacation in the sun, you and I and Melvin. We can have fun without men. Don't you think so?'

'Suits me just fine,' Vanessa says and tries to look excited, but a wave of thoughts about the apocalypse flows into her mind.

In a dead world, nothing is left to offend the demons' sense of order.

How will it look? Will fire and ashes rain down? Black, smoke-filled skies loom over the ruins of the cities of the world? Will the seawater evaporate in the heat, leaving a dead ocean floor?

Vanessa wishes that she hadn't watched so many disaster movies. And that it were as easy to imagine the guardians who are supposed to protect humanity.

'There, we've decided,' Mom says and refills her glass. 'I'll start to save up straight away. It's important for us both to have something to look forward to.'

The playlist moves on to a slow tune. Mom changes to a faster one and talks on.

'Still, Nicke is a good father for Melvin. And I thought he would be good for you as well. I must have wanted to believe that a little too much. I've always felt so bad about you growing up without a male role model.'

'Doesn't matter any more,' Vanessa says. 'He's gone now.'

'Exactly,' Mom agrees. 'And this time, I'm going to enjoy being single, not get hitched with the first guy on the horizon. I have finally come to realize that love doesn't have to be so difficult and complicated to be for real. I know you're not too keen on Helena Malmgren, but she really has made me see my own worth. And that happiness will be there for me, too.'

Vanessa must have made a face unintentionally, because Mom smiles a little grimly.

'That's to say, I am very happy with what I've got just now,' she says and drains her glass. 'No regrets, either. If I hadn't met Nicke, I wouldn't have had Melvin. And then I look at my very wonderful daughter and I'm so proud of her. You have grown up to be really special. So mature and responsible. Just take your job at Mona's place...'

Her eyes are definitely tearful.

'I'm happy if you're happy,' Vanessa says quietly and Mom puts her arm around Vanessa and kisses her forehead.

The tune's refrain is starting and Mom shouts.

'Come on, Nessa, let's dance!'

Mom takes Vanessa's hands and tries to pull her up from the sofa. But Vanessa hangs back.

'Oh, Mom, stop that,' she says.

Mom just laughs, lets go and starts shaking her booty.

Vanessa catches sight of a blue tit perched on the window-sill, looking in. Even the bird looks embarrassed.

CHAPTER 41

Ida leans her cheek against Troja's muzzle and feels his calm filter into her. She would like to stand here all night.

'I should have known that I'd become possessed all the same,' she whispers to him. 'Whatever, it always ends with me in the shit.'

She recalls what she saw when she was possessed, a reflection on the surface of still water. So that's what Matilda looks like. Freckled face.

Ida's power is totally pointless. She would much rather be able to communicate with the living than with the dead.

If only she could make Gustaf's soul materialize and ask it a straight question.

Where would the glass go? YES or NO?

Mom and Dad were angry with her for coming here, instead of helping them to sort out the chaos left by the floods at home. But no way would she miss out on being with Troja. Not tonight. He is the antidote to all that has happened to her over the last twenty-four hours.

They have been out in the forest. She thought galloping could get her away from the filthy sensation that lingered in her body after the séance. The trail left by the other, who had ruled over Ida, taken control of her body, spoken through her mouth, seen through her eyes. Meanwhile, Ida herself had been dismissed into a corner where she had cowered, forced to experience everything from a distance.

Being stuck in that corner for ever is Ida's worst nightmare.

She strokes Troja's muzzle, then straightens up and starts scratching at that special place near his ear until sheer pleasure makes him close his eyes.

'It will be all right in the end,' Ida whispers. 'Julia is on my side. She totally sees it my way. Felicia is thick and it isn't my fault that she didn't speak out earlier about how she felt for Robin. Besides, whatever they've got won't last. And then she'll come crawling back.'

Troja's muzzle butts lightly against her.

'And I've fixed things with Erik, too. I called him today and he agrees that Felicia was drunk out of her mind and talking total nonsense.'

She has put her backpack in the corner of the stall. She gets a carrot for Troja. His lips nibble at it with tremendous delicacy. Always so careful not to hurt Ida.

She checks her bag again. A corner of the *Book of Patterns* sticks up. She has noticed scratches on the hope chest, suggesting that someone, probably Lotta, has tried to force it open. Ever since then, she has always taken the book and the Pattern Finder with her if she goes out.

'Maybe it will work better here?' she says. 'Hey, old boy?'

She picks up her bag and locks herself into one of the bathrooms, despite being certain that she is alone in the stables.

A handwritten note, taped to the wall above the toilet, forbids its use due to the water problems.

Someone hasn't taken the ban seriously enough, judging by the smell.

Ida sits down on the lid and opens the book on her lap.

Will I be together with G in the end?

When she queries the book, it's sometimes hard to focus her thoughts properly. But not this time.

She feels with all her heart that she must have an answer,

a straight, clear yes or no. The guardians must let her know how this will pan out – she can't waste more time on pursuing something that might be hopeless. She can't risk humiliation for no return.

The book does not answer. The signs remain motionless on the page. Apparently the guardians don't care to communicate.

The Pattern Finder makes a ringing noise as Ida puts it on the sink. She is just about to close the book and get up, when the familiar dizziness takes over, stronger than ever.

And in the next instant, she's *there*.

Close, close to Gustaf's face. His lips meet hers and they merge, until she can hardly tell Gustaf's mouth from her own.

She wants him so intensely it hurts.

Another split second passes and then she is back in the bathroom.

She fumbles for the Pattern Finder, drops it on the floor among the scrunched-up paper towels around the waste bin. When she's got a grip on it, she twists the segments and concentrates.

Was that a vision of the future?

The patterns shift across the pages, unbearably slowly.

Yes.

The book seems certain, but Ida doesn't quite dare to trust its glorious message. Not yet.

All right, but you said there are different futures. Is this the one that will be?

She stares impatiently at the book.

Yes. In all probability. If you keep true to our agreement. Collaborate with the others. And, whatever you do, don't join Positive Engelsfors.

Why would she even think about joining that pathetic cult?

'I promise,' she says loudly and has a strong sense of how satisfied the book is with her.

Don't say anything to the others. This is our secret.

Ida promises once more. She'll have no problem whatever with keeping this to herself.

For the first time this autumn, the evening air carries a hint of cold.

Minoo is curled up on the deckchair in her corner of the garden. *Romeo and Juliet* is next to her, closed.

She didn't wake up until the afternoon. Mom and Dad were not at home and after a walk around town, she returned to a house that was still empty and unlit.

A gust of wind. She shivers, but doesn't want to go inside into that silence.

Minoo thinks about everything that has happened since the night of the blood-red moon. She remembers Elias and Rebecka.

One of Max's memories bubbles up to the surface. A visual memory of Rebecka falling off the roof of the school, falling to her death.

Where were the guardians then?

It seems to her that they are harder to believe in than the demons. As hard as it is to believe that their powers belong also to her.

Matilda had said almost exactly what Nicolaus had told her earlier.

You have no reason to be fearful as long as you use your power responsibly, for good. And I know you will.

Why hasn't the book, and Matilda, told them earlier about the guardians and about Minoo's powers? Matilda had said that the guardians don't think in the human way, don't have the same notion of time and that they communicate in a different manner from humans. Is that the explanation? Couldn't they grasp how much it matters to know these things?

A car slows down outside, turns into the drive to their garage.

Minoo hears the car doors slam, hears Mom and Dad going into the house and watches as the lights come on in there.

Mom calls her name. Minoo will go indoors soon, but not quite yet.

First, she must pull herself together.

Gather the strength she needs to feel sure that she won't burst into tears and tell them that Engelsfors is a door and the demons are just outside, banging on it. That the apocalypse is approaching and is closing in fast. That they have no idea how to stop it.

'We're in the kitchen, Minoo. Come here, would you?' Mom calls when Minoo opens the front door.

They are sitting at the kitchen table and as soon as Minoo sees the expressions on their faces, she knows.

The time has come. They will tell her now. Naturally, they would pick today of all days.

'Sit down,' Mom says with a quick glance at Dad.

Minoo realizes that she's nervous. Meanwhile, Dad sweeps the crumbs on the table into a small pile, then stares fixedly at it.

Minoo crosses her arms on her chest. Steels herself. Right, let's get it over and done with.

'Just say what you've got to say.'

'I have been offered a consultant's post,' Mom says. 'In Stockholm.'

Minoo had been prepared for the word 'divorce'. But not for this.

'Actually, the offer came up early in the summer and I've been hesitating ever since, weighing up the pros and cons. But somewhere deep down, I knew all along that I would accept. It's the kind of opportunity you have only once in your life.'

Minoo can't process what she is being told. Her brain seems to have switched off.

'You see, Minoo, twenty years ago I followed Erik here because he was so fired up about running the local paper in the town where he grew up. It was important to him to make it a really lively, high-quality newspaper. And I wanted to try life in a smaller town, experience a calmer tempo. But I can't bear staying in Engelsfors much longer. That's how I've felt for years…Of course, I want you and your father to come with me, but he refuses to leave the paper.'

Dad sighs impatiently, strongly enough to scatter the crumbs again.

'In the end, I've made up my mind to make the move, come what may,' Mom continues. 'I must go for that job. I deserve it. And I know you'd like to complete your schooling in Stockholm. You've always talked about that, right through high school…'

Mom doesn't end the sentence and looks hopefully at Minoo instead.

She obviously expects Minoo to be overwhelmed, happy, ready to throw her arms around Mom's neck and thank her for this wonderful chance to change her life.

Minoo hates her. Hates them both, because they're only asking her now, for the first time, when it is too late.

She must stay in Engelsfors. Or else the world will end.

'I can't move anywhere,' she says.

Dad looks up from the tabletop with a glint of triumph in his eyes.

'But not because I want to be here with you,' she snarls and the glint disappears. 'That's not why I'm going to stay in this fucking awful dump.'

'Now I don't understand a thing,' Mom says.

'What is it you don't get?' Minoo yells. 'That you should've asked a year ago? Why not *ten* years ago? You've kept me prisoner here when I had no friends or anything. When I hated every second in this ghastly place!'

'What—' Dad begins.

'Shut up!' Minoo yells. 'I've had it with listening to you! You don't give a damn for either Mom or me, all you want is your stupid paper and working yourself to death!'

For once, her father seems at a loss for words. Minoo turns to her mother.

'Of course, you didn't think it mattered enough that *I've* always had a rotten time here, oh no, *you* had to get an offer of a top job. Then it's suddenly okay to move! And now you're going to leave me here!'

By now, Mom is screaming, too.

'I thought you wanted to come with me. I will not accept—'

'You don't get it! You never get a single thing!'

'All right, explain it!' Dad says.

Minoo stares at her parents. She will never be able to explain to them, will never be able to tell them the truth.

I must carry this burden alone, Minoo thinks. I have no choice.

She doesn't want to be left alone with Dad. Perhaps she could persuade Mom to stay. But that is as bad an alternative. Three unhappy people sharing a house.

'I would like to come with you,' she says and now her voice sounds quite dead. 'But I can't risk my grades by changing school in the middle of junior year. And I've found some friends here, at last. I don't want to leave them.'

347

'You don't have to decide straight away...' Mom begins.

'I have made my decision,' Minoo says and forces herself to meet her mother's eyes. 'I am not going to change my mind. But you go. I understand.'

Mom shakes her head.

'You can change your mind any time,' she says. 'For one thing, you can visit Stockholm whenever you like. And I promise to come home as often as possible. Your father and I are not divorcing. We'll just live in different places for some time.'

'Fine,' Minoo says and stares at the floor.

'Minoo—' Dad starts, but she interrupts him.

'I just want to be left alone for a while.'

She walks upstairs, stops briefly at the open bathroom door and looks at the bathtub. Thinks of what happened there last winter. The voice in her head saying that she had no idea of what was coming her way.

It's only going to get worse. Much, much worse.

Part 3

CHAPTER 42

Ida stops in the kitchen doorway.

It looks exactly the same as it did before the water damage six months earlier. The whole house is white and clean again.

Ida has always been proud of her family home. Lately, though, her perspective sometimes shifts. Then, all the whiteness makes the whole place seem soaked in milk. Together with the mist outside the large windows, it feels as if milk is oozing all over the world.

That mist. During the autumn and winter, it has been hanging over Engelsfors almost every morning. The snow lasted for a few days around the New Year, but the rest of the time it melted as soon as it landed on the ground.

Ida observes her family at the kitchen table. Mom and Dad are both eating their toasted sandwiches. Lotta has pulled her legs up so high her face is almost hidden behind her knees. She is chatting quietly with Rasmus, who is giggling at something she says.

Looking at them like this, at a distance, Ida feels it is easy to love them. Mother. Father. Sister. Brother. Standing here, she can sense the reality of her love. It is floating inside her, light and pure. She wishes that she could encapsulate the feeling and save it.

She clutches her French textbook closer to her chest and steps into the kitchen.

Fire

'Good morning.'

Mom and Dad mumble something in response.

Ida sticks a slice of bread in the toaster. And gets a shock when she accidentally touches the metal cover. She swears quietly under her breath. It's going to be one of those days. It started with the phone charger. Next, the hairdryer. Her metal element is running wild these lousy misty mornings.

Gingerly, she extracts the toast when it pops up, butters it thinly, and brings it to the table with her mug.

Mom pushes the teapot towards Ida.

'Did you sleep well?'

'I can't remember, so I guess I must have.'

She meant it humorously, but Mom looks irritated. Ida regrets it at once. Now this morning is ruined already.

'Are you working today or can I take the car to school?' she tries all the same.

'No, I have to go to the shop.'

Ida nods, opens her book and starts quizzing herself on irregular verbs.

'I don't like it when you read at the table,' Mom says. 'And you know it.'

'I've got a test coming up. Would you prefer me to fail, or what?'

'Mom, Ida's being negative again,' Rasmus says.

Dad lowers his sandwich and eyes her.

'Now, now. What kind of attitude is that, Ida?'

'You're supposed to imagine you get the test back and the teacher is happy and has checked off all your answers,' Lotta tells her.

'Or else I can study, like normal people,' Ida says.

She drinks some tea and tries to stay cool. But she can feel the others looking at her.

Please don't say anything about Positive Engelsfors, she thinks.

I'll simply die if I hear the words 'Positive Engelsfors' again.

Besides, is it really *normal* for people to study for a test these days? It seems at least half the town argues exactly as Lotta just did.

Mom and Dad joined Positive Engelsfors just a few weeks after the autumn party. Not that they seem to believe very much of what it preaches. Never mind, the PE philosophy is useful for a whole lot of reasons. For instance, it saves you from having to take complaints from employees seriously. Or you can explain that if Lotta is supposed to have bullied someone, the kid was spreading negative energy.

The fact is, being a member is a social 'must'. The Engelsfors elite are all followers of Helena and Krister Malmgren. If you don't join the movement you cease to exist. That's already happening to Ida.

Erik and Kevin hardly talk about anything besides PE. Robin and Felicia don't talk to Ida at all, but they are just as heavily into the PE thing. Julia is the only one Ida has persuaded not to go along with it yet, but it's obviously only a matter of time before she does.

And then Ida will be an outsider, all alone.

She has asked the book lots of times why she can't join. No answer. Apparently, the guardians don't want to communicate with her in any way.

Ida sometimes feels she is ready to dump all her promises to the book. Going against the flow simply isn't her. Rather, she'd want to be in the lead.

The doorbell rings. Lotta jumps from her chair and runs to the hall.

Ida drinks a large mouthful of tea. Pretends to be engrossed in French verbs.

'It's Erik!' Lotta shouts and dances into the kitchen in front of him.

353

'Hi, everyone,' he says and everyone greets him with enthusiasm. Except Ida.

'Well, now, Erik. All prepared for the Spring Revel?' Dad asks.

'Yes. Brighter times are ahead. In many ways!'

Erik's cheeks are red with cold and a large, clear drop of snot is dangling from his nose.

'I hear there'll be a huge crowd meeting up at the center,' Mom says.

'It's the same at school,' Erik says. 'Everyone I know is coming along. Except Ida, actually. Because only PE members are invited.'

All eyes are on Ida now.

She shuts her book.

'I just haven't made up my mind yet,' she says and gets up before they start discussing it. 'I'll just brush my teeth and then we'll go.'

Ida hurries upstairs to her room. She can hear how downstairs, in the kitchen, Erik, Mom and Dad are chatting about PE's Spring Revel. The center has put on a buffet and dancing to a live band. The high school group is throwing a party in the gym hall. Erik is one of the arrangers. Naturally. He has been one of Helena's favorites ever since last autumn, when he asked her along to do a coaching session with the hockey team.

Ida brushes her teeth briskly and examines her face in the mirror.

She hardly recognizes the Ida who is looking back at her. It is as if all the color has been drained out of her during the winter.

How did my life become like this? Ida thinks.

It is March now. You hated this time of year as much as I do.

Part Three

It is the worst time, when you've been wandering around in the dark and the cold for half a year and can't believe that light and warmth will ever come back again.

It's almost a year to the day since I took J's handgun. I'm not sure what I was thinking, I guess I didn't have a thought in my head, all I wanted was to kill the person who had taken you from me. And then, there he was, standing around in the dining area and pretending to be you. Looked like you, talked like you, remembered your memories. And even though he had murdered you, I was almost ready to buy it, never mind that he wasn't for real. That was how much I missed you.

I still miss you.

Just now it feels as if you were here, listening to me. It's probably just my imagination. I don't care. I need someone who listens to me or I'll explode.

Of course I know what I should do – I should keep away from V as much as possible. Sometimes, I almost believe it has passed, that the fire inside me has died down to a mild glow, but then I see her walk along a corridor, or we touch accidently when I'm unprepared for it, and it's like pouring a whole can of gasoline on the embers. I catch fire again.

Things might have been different if I hadn't gone to that party at J's. I remember exactly the moment it hit me. V had just emerged from the bathroom when I saw her. She looked so happy. I can't explain but, to me, a bright zone of energy seemed to surround her. I wanted to be near her always. A little later, when she touched my arm, I knew I was caught.

Imagine how stupid it felt when I realized. I did, you see, in that instant. Me, in love with W's new girlfriend? At J's party? Hey, business as usual, Linnéa. Why try to make your life easy?

I must stop soon, any minute now the bell will ring for the next class. Backman's, so guess how much I'm looking forward to it. I almost miss Olivia – at least she and I could make fun of him together. I think I saw her in town a few weeks ago, but can't be sure because the girl I saw wore a woolly hat. Olivia hasn't been in touch. She probably regrets quitting school at Christmas. At the time, she must have thought it was a really cool, rebellious decision.

In a way, I'm happy that you don't have to be around and see what's going on in this town. Our new, 'positive' Engelsfors. There's even less room for people like us now. And I'm happy, too, that you don't have to see your parents in action. If you thought this town was insane before ...

Must dash now, must be a good girl and do well at school, get along well with Jakob, get on well with Diana. She is almost back to her usual self, but I don't trust her any longer.

I love you, E. Wherever you are, I hope you're happy.

Linnéa closes her diary.

She pulls out her make-up bag, checks her face in the powder-compact mirror and touches up her jet-black eyeliner. Then she jumps down from the windowsill and leaves the bathroom. Ready to meet the day.

As ready as she can be.

Vanessa slams her locker door shut and locks it.

As she walks down the hallway, the Positive Engelsfors stickers are beaming at her from every other locker door. A huge, neon-bright yellow poster on the bulletin board trumpets out an announcement about some kind of spring party next week.

In the seating area, she sees Michelle, with Mehmet and Rickard on either side, perched on the table and dangling her legs.

She waves to Vanessa, who nods to them as she passes.

Ever since Michelle joined PE, her thing with Mehmet has been at boiling point. Michelle doesn't seem to care much for the movement – besides, she'd rather die than wear a yellow polo shirt – but she does like Mehmet a lot.

And because Vanessa and Evelina can't bear 'the cult', they take turns to avoid Michelle-with-Mehmet.

Vanessa has just pulled out her phone to text Evelina when she realizes that someone has arrived at her side.

'Hi, Vanessa,' Viktor says.

She looks at him. His black winter coat is covered in tiny glittering drops of moisture and his hair is damp.

'What do you want?' Vanessa asks.

'May I have a word with you? In private?'

He nods in the direction of a classroom door. Vanessa sighs and follows him in. The rain must be heavier now, going by the loud tapping on the windowpanes. Viktor closes the door, locks it and stands still for a moment. The drops of water on his coat evaporate and his hair suddenly looks newly blowdried.

How practical, Vanessa thinks.

Viktor pulls off his coat, hangs it over his arm. Seeing him close by, she observes two things that surely haven't affected him before. Tiredness. And just a hint of insecurity.

'Talk to me,' she says impatiently. 'What do you want?'

'It would be good if you told Anna-Karin from me that her interrogation is today,' Viktor says. 'I'll meet her after school and give her a lift.'

'Why not tell her yourself? You're in the same class, after all.'

'I know we are,' he replies.

She waits for an explanation, but Viktor offers none, only shifts his weight from one foot to the other.

Fire

'All right. I'll tell her,' she says.
'I thought it would be easier for her if it came from you.'
'So thoughtful of you. Charming,' she says.
Viktor looks hurt.

Not that Vanessa falls for his tricks. Doesn't he grasp that they talk about him and compare what he says to them? They got his number long ago. He plays all these different roles. With Vanessa, he is mostly quiet and serious. She assumes that he thinks this will make her nervous.

'I'm not…' he begins, then falls silent. 'Look, this investigation hasn't been much fun for me either, if that's what you think.'

'Bad luck that your crowd has been dragging it out for half a year, then.'

'We must be thorough,' he says. 'It doesn't mean I enjoy it.'
'Such a shame, Viktor. Poor you.'

He looks away, suddenly super-interested on the wall poster showing the periodic system.

'I get it. It doesn't matter what I say. We belong to different camps.'

'Have you realized that just this minute?'

'I truly wish the circumstances had been different,' Viktor says. He sounds almost sad. 'Very, very different.'

'So do I,' Vanessa says. 'I wish that you and your father had never come here at all. For your own sakes.'

Viktor looks surprised.

'You will make such a total fucking mess of this trial of yours. And lose so badly it will be an absolute catastrophe. You'll never recover. Do you know why?'

Viktor shakes his head.

'Because we are the Chosen Ones,' Vanessa says and smiles. 'And who the fuck are you?'

He seems to have no answer.

358

Part Three

Vanessa's hand trembles a little when she undoes the lock. She has no idea how they are to go about winning the trial, doesn't even know if it is possible.

But she does know that she will do *everything* to make it happen.

CHAPTER 43

Minoo walks heavily up the main school staircase. It feels like climbing a mountain. She is so tired she could lie down on the spot and fall asleep instantly. She has hardly slept at all for three nights running.

'WE GO TOWARDS BRIGHTER TIMES!' She passes one of the neon-yellow posters advertising that spring party.

A horde of Positive Engelsforsers are stampeding up the stairs and Minoo clings to the wall to avoid being trampled. Kevin is in the lead, as if he were the flock's alpha male. Minoo asks herself how many yellow polo shirts he has stocked up on. Hopefully more than one, because, like many of his PE friends, he has taken to wearing one every day, like a sort of school uniform.

She stops on the next floor up.

The new janitor is up a ladder, scraping gobs of chewing tobacco off the hallway ceiling. People throw them to see if they stick. She is so young you might take her for one of the students.

While Minoo gets her breath back, she watches the janitor. There is something mildly hypnotic about her grim cleaning job.

A sound like someone playing a xylophone starts up in Minoo's jacket pocket. It's so loud people turn to see. She pulls out her new phone and turns off the ringtone.

Part Three

Yesterday was her birthday and the phone is one of her presents. Whenever she's touched it, she can't resist wiping the screen so it won't be marked by a single fingerprint. Soon, it will be another ordinary accessory, but just now it feels sacrilegious even to use it.

She looks up the text.

Hope your present is of use to you, darling! Be in touch soon!

It is the first time that Mom has texted Minoo. Mom used to say that you should phone up with any messages. Yet another of the many small, but still gigantic, things that have changed in her mother since she moved to Stockholm. She wears her hair cut shorter. Uses another perfume. Lots of seemingly minor details that add up to the new life she leads somewhere else, a life that goes on without Minoo.

They often chat, but since she moved last autumn, Mom has only come to see them once a month. Dad is working harder than ever. Minoo sometimes feels both are equally absent.

She is happy with her phone. No question. But the mountain of gifts that Mom and Dad dumped on her bed yesterday morning smacked of guilty conscience.

She carries on up the next flight of stairs. She thought it would feel different to turn eighteen. Grown up. Her own person, in the eyes of others. But being allowed to buy alcoholic drinks in a bar is not such a treat when you have carried the fate of the whole world on your shoulder for a year and half.

When she comes into the classroom, Kevin is already in his seat. He is holding court among the people at the back of the room. Minoo sits down next to Anna-Karin, who looks up from her physics textbook.

'Did you enjoy your birthday?'

'It was all right. How was your weekend?'

Anna-Karin points at the page in her book and looks unhappily at Minoo.

'I will never understand this,' she says.

Minoo recognizes the problem. She has spent most of her weekend working through the more intricate aspects of magnetic fields. That is one of the reasons for her not sleeping.

'Let's go through this together after school today,' Minoo says. 'Maybe we'll get the hang of it together.'

Anna-Karin doesn't look cheered up at all.

'If even you don't get it, I don't have a hope,' she says.

'We'll make it.'

Minoo's past experience of studying with other people has been made up of the kind of group assignments that meant she did all the work while the rest of the group sat around gossiping about parties she hadn't been asked to.

But it is different with Anna-Karin. During the autumn term, the two of them started preparing for the semester exams. In a way, Anna-Karin is even *better* at studying than Minoo. She never gives up before she understands every last detail.

'Dad asked if you'd like to join us at home on Saturday night,' Minoo says.

Anna-Karin looks surprised. Just then, the bell goes for the start of lessons.

'Why?'

To do something about his guilty conscience about working all the time, Minoo thinks. Because when he is free for once, he wants to show off what an awesome father he is. And because it suited him to bring this idea up while Mom was at home to demonstrate to her that he really does care about me and my life.

'Well, why not?' she says.

'That would be really nice,' Anna-Karin says after a moment's hesitation.

She is just about to add something when Viktor enters the classroom. Minoo watches Anna-Karin shrink in her seat when he walks up to them. But Viktor doesn't even look at her.

'Did you get my present?' he asks Minoo.

'No, I haven't had a present from you. And if I had, I would've thrown it away.'

Viktor's package was in the mailbox yesterday. A beautifully wrapped first edition of *The Secret History* in English. Minoo definitely won't tell him that she's started to read it and has already gotten halfway through. Or that she agrees with him that it is a different experience to read it in the original.

'I don't think you would've,' Viktor says with his usual self-satisfied smirk.

Ylva enters with a bundle of papers in her arms.

'Sit down, class!'

Viktor wanders over to the empty seat next to Levan and starts lining his belongings up on the desk, following the same neat pattern as always.

Ylva puts her pile of papers on her desk with a bang.

'Excuse me, but you're late, actually,' Kevin says.

Here and there, people are giggling. Ylva's jaw muscles tense. She acts as if the final breakdown is lurking just below the surface and Minoo cannot think how Ylva has managed to keep going for this long.

'Or, is it like, okay for *you* to be late, but not for us?' Kevin goes on.

'That's right, Kevin. It is okay for me to be a few minutes late when the copier is playing up,' Ylva says and straightens her back.

But Minoo can see Ylva's hand shake as she writes 'INDUCTION' on the blackboard.

'We'll do some review today,' she says. 'Can anyone explain the concept of induction?'

As if on an agreed signal, both Minoo and Anna-Karin put up a hand.

Ylva looks disappointed and checks the classroom.

'Is there really nobody else who knows the answer?'

'Well, we think that we all ought to talk together about how this class doesn't have a good atmosphere,' Hanna A says. 'I think we should do some role-playing exercises to sort it out.'

Minoo lowers her hand. She recalls with horror the exercise they had tried in English class at the beginning of the spring semester. Everyone was supposed to 'talk freely' about their opinions of each other. The would-be exercise was quickly debased into covert bullying. All expressed in English and sanctioned by Patrick, the teacher, who seemed clueless about what was going on.

'You're here to learn—' Ylva begins.

'So you think it's more important to talk about induction than about how your students are feeling, right?' Hanna A says.

'The other teachers get what's really important,' Hanna H says.

'I'm uninterested in what other teachers might or might not "get". This is *my* lesson.'

'Come on, it's cool,' Kevin laughs. 'We're just trying to help you to help us.'

'Kind of you,' Ylva says through clenched teeth. 'Minoo, would you answer my question?'

The change that the arrival of Positive Engelsfors has brought about is most easily seen in the dining area. The most popular crowd is still hanging out in the small, partitioned-off room. The difference is that most of them wear yellow now.

They and their many fans are rooting for the PE spirit, which by now has percolated through the entire school.

While Minoo gets in line at the salad buffet she catches sight of Gustaf at Rickard's table. At least Gustaf isn't wearing a yellow shirt.

Not yet, anyway.

How did it happen? Her friend Gustaf, the same Gustaf who had been Rebecka's boyfriend, would never have subdivided the world into positive and negative, black and white, the way PE tells them to do.

Minoo piles grated carrots and white cabbage on her plate. Perhaps Gustaf was never the person she thought he was. What does she know about people? It took her six months to figure out that she had fallen in love with a murderer.

I loved Max, she thinks. And I thought he loved me and asked him to wait until I'm eighteen. And now I am eighteen and in the place where he tried to kill us all. What if Max is the only one who will ever love me? What if I'm the perfect love object for supernatural killers with severe personality disorders?

The thoughts are flying around in her head as she follows Anna-Karin to the table where Vanessa and Linnéa are already seated.

They're talking quietly with their heads close together. Minoo puts her tray down and checks that there is no chewing gum stuck to her chair.

Vanessa leans towards Anna-Karin.

'Has Viktor said anything to you?' she whispers.

Anna-Karin shakes her head.

'It's my turn now, is it?' she mumbles.

'Yes,' Vanessa says. 'He told me this morning. He'll drive you to the manor house after the last class today.'

'Why did Viktor tell *you*?' Minoo asks Vanessa.

'He said it was because it would be easier for Anna-Karin to hear it from me.'

'He could've told me in that case. We're in the same class, after all.'

'Oh, Minoo, are you jealous?' Linnéa says with a grin.

'So witty,' Minoo says. 'But you've got to admit it's weird.'

'What's *not* weird about that guy?' Vanessa says. 'Just thank your lucky stars you got out of talking with him.'

'I didn't, as a matter of fact,' Minoo says.

She steals a glance at Anna-Karin, who stares silently at the tabletop.

Minoo wishes she could think of something reassuring to say. But her own interrogation was nightmarish and she can't even imagine what it is going to be like for Anna-Karin.

'Afterwards, you'll feel like you said the wrong thing, however hard you tried,' Minoo says. 'That's how we all felt.'

'Remember, Alexander will do everything to break you. He asked me for ages, like, a quarter of an hour, about Minoo and the iron filings,' Vanessa says. 'Stick to what we've agreed and it will be all right.'

'Try to get some protection against magic ready,' Linnéa says. 'I don't think Viktor can read your thoughts, but he's up to *something*.'

'I know,' Anna-Karin says. 'I'm grateful. I understand that you're trying to help me—'

Vanessa interrupts her.

'Hi! What do you want?' she says quickly to someone standing behind Minoo's back.

When Minoo turns around, Evelina is there, holding a tray. She looks like a walking, talking reminder to Minoo of all her inferiority complexes. Evelina's dark skin is flawless, she carries off her tight outfit with confidence and her feet, at the ends of her impossibly long legs, definitely can't be bigger than size 6.

'Hi,' she says and sits down next to Vanessa.

Minoo doesn't even dare to look at the others. Could Evelina have heard anything?

'What a party atmosphere,' Evelina says and drinks some water.

'I thought you were going to eat with Michelle today,' Vanessa says.

'She wanted to go out to the diner and I'm broke. What's going on, have I disturbed some life-or-death talk?'

Minoo looks up, exchanges a glance with Vanessa. If only Evelina knew how right she is.

'No, we're just deadly boring,' Vanessa says. 'Tired out, all of us.'

'I know someone who doesn't think you're boring in the slightest,' Evelina grins and turns to the others. 'If you must know, I met Samir this weekend and he's like, totally obsessed with her.'

Vanessa laughs a little. Minoo has no idea who Samir is.

'Samir, as well as just about all other guys alive in Sweden today,' Evelina adds and spears a piece of hamburger. 'No one left for the rest of us, practically.'

fuck

Minoo jerks upright and almost spills her water when she hears the voice inside her head.

Her heart is racing at the same pace as her thoughts. It must be Max. He has waited for her eighteenth birthday and now he's back to reunite with her.

fuck fuck fuck fuck fuck fuck

Now she realizes that this is a completely different voice. A voice she knows well, even though she has never before heard it in this way.

Minoo observes Linnéa who is aimlessly prodding her portion of vegetarian casserole. She seems withdrawn into herself and unaware that Minoo is staring at her. And, still more so, unaware that her thoughts have leaked into Minoo's head.

fuck fuck I can't bear it fuck fuck

Minoo glances at the others. Is she the only one who hears this? Anna-Karin seems absorbed in her own thoughts and Vanessa's attention is fixed on Evelina, who keeps talking about Samir.

I can't bear listening to any more of this I can't bear it will someone make her shut her face

Minoo opens her mouth, but what can she say to Linnéa here, in front of Evelina?

Vanessa laughs and says something to Evelina about Samir's ugly underwear.

'I guess they looked better on his floor, right?' Evelina says.

Linnéa starts tearing her napkin into pieces, tiny, tiny ones, like snowflakes.

WHY CAN'T I SIMPLY STOP LOVING HER?

Her thought rings out thunderously inside Minoo's head. Then the world falls silent. All that is left is a faint ringing noise in Minoo's ears. She can see the mouths of the others moving, but doesn't grasp what they are saying.

She had not only heard Linnéa's thoughts, she had sensed an emotion. An emotion so powerful it was like being run over by a speeding freight train.

Linnéa loves Vanessa. Truly *loves* Vanessa.

And Minoo cannot think what she can do with that information.

CHAPTER 44

Anna-Karin is so nervous she nearly throws up. The movements of the car don't help. It runs across a pot-hole and her stomach seems to bounce up against her palate.

Viktor turns into the drive to the manor house. But instead of going on, he stops the car.

'Would you like a breath of fresh air?' he asks. 'You look as if it would do you good.'

Anna-Karin climbs out and takes deep breaths of the cool air. She looks out over the canal and tries to imagine that this is a quite ordinary day, tries to forget why they are here.

'It's nice here,' Viktor says.

She looks at him. He stands with his hands plunged into his coat pockets.

'It will all be over in a few hours,' he says and looks sympathetically at her.

Anna-Karin is far from convinced that she will manage to survive the first minute.

'I want you to know, I understand why you did it,' Viktor says. 'I'm sure no one could honestly swear that they wouldn't have done the same in your situation.'

All her life, Anna-Karin has kept in the background and observed other people. She is usually pretty good at working out who they really are. But she cannot read Viktor. He seems to mean what he says, but why should he? His mission here is to catch her out at breaking the law.

'When I arrived in town, I immediately felt my powers grow stronger,' he says. 'Engelsfors is like a big battery for all natural witches. And for you, who also has a special bond to the power source in this place...it must be intoxicating. Magic is hard to handle if you're not used to it. I know only too well how badly things can turn out when you suddenly have too much of it, too soon...'

He falls silent, stares blankly ahead.

'What did you do?' she asks, reluctantly curious.

'Not me. My twin sister.'

Anna-Karin is surprised. Tries to imagine a female version of Viktor.

'Her magic talents developed far too fast. She couldn't stop using them. It made her...sick.'

'What happened to her?'

Viktor smiles a little bitterly.

'Let's just say that she was never the same again.'

He pulls his left hand from his pocket and glances at his watch.

'I'm sorry, but we must move on.'

Minoo opens her locker and fills her backpack with textbooks. She tries to avoid thinking about Anna-Karin, who just now is being driven to the manor house by Viktor. She can't help her in any way. It is the worst thing about all this.

She hears familiar laughter. Vanessa and Evelina are strolling along the hallway together.

Minoo wonders about Vanessa. Does she know how Linnéa feels?

I must say something to Linnéa, Minoo thinks as she locks up. I must. Soon. She should know that I know.

She leaves school and walks to Storvall Square As she comes closer to the yellow house where the *Engelsfors*

Herald has its editorial office, she sees that the large window next to the entrance has been bashed. The cracked glass is kept in place with strips of duct tape. It must have been done last night.

Minoo has no doubt about who is behind this. The same people who phone them at home in the evenings. No one speaks, but the silence at the other end of the line is more frightening than words. The first call was in the autumn, the same day that the paper published its first investigative report on Positive Engelsfors. The frequency of the calls has kept pace with PE's rate of growth. Now it has organized a boycott of the paper and subscriptions have fallen off sharply. Not that Dad caves in to pressure. On the contrary. His editorials are evidence of a personal crusade.

This thing with the window is a straightforward escalation of the warfare. And Minoo dreads the next turn of the screw.

She walks into the editorial office. Dad is in the kitchen, pouring himself a large mugful of coffee as black as oil.

'Hello there,' he says absently and starts moving towards his office.

Minoo follows him. Watches the small sweat stains on the back of his shirt. His red neck. He is angry again. He is always angry these days.

'What happened to the window?' she says while Dad settles behind his desk.

'I reported it to the police this morning,' he replies and drinks a large mouthful of coffee. 'Probably won't get us anywhere. But it's on record if something else happens.'

'You should install cameras, CCTV or something,' she says.

Dad doesn't reply. He is focused on his computer again, starts reading something on the screen.

'Anna-Karin can come,' she says after a short while and he looks up, clearly lost.

So he has forgotten all about it.

'For dinner,' she adds.

It isn't easy to live with someone who is never with you, not even when you are in the same room. She understands better now why Mom got into the habit of slamming cupboard doors. You have to make yourself heard, one way or the other.

'Good, good,' Dad says and his eyes slip back to his computer.

Minoo feels like screaming at the top of her voice that she, too, is doing stuff. She still hangs on to top rankings in all her school subjects, though it's getting harder and harder. Meanwhile, she's trying to figure out if the demons are sponsoring Positive Engelsfors, as well as trying to prepare for a magic trial *and* the end of the world. But here she is, all the same, ready to play her part in her father's life, though you might think it should be the other way around.

Footsteps in the outer office. The steps are coming their way and Minoo turns around.

Helena Malmgren stops in the doorway. Close behind, Krister Malmgren towers over her. He is wearing a gray suit, but would look just as comfortable in workman's overalls. It isn't hard to see why people in this old industrial town love him. They both eye Minoo – who has to try hard not to show how much she hates them. And how much she fears them.

'May we come in?' Helena says.

Her tone of voice is pleasant, but she steps inside Dad's office without waiting for a reply.

Dad leans back in his chair.

'Well, this is a surprise,' he says.

Despite Matilda's warnings, the Chosen Ones have been

372

keeping an eye on Helena and Krister off and on during the autumn and winter, but have found no evidence that the Malmgren couple use magic.

Not that it proves anything, Minoo thinks. If they are in league with demons, they will have been warned about us. Told to be circumspect if they use magic.

'We decided we had better come and see you,' Krister says. 'You and I have always gotten along, Erik. You're a hard-hitting journalist, but fair. It's good for us politicians to have our decisions scrutinized.'

Dad says nothing.

'But I can't help wondering if you have a hidden agenda when it comes to my wife,' Krister goes on.

Dad looks straight at Helena.

'I have nothing against you personally,' he says. 'But I have strong reservations about the grip Positive Engelsfors has established on the whole town. And I'm very skeptical about the actual means used. Just recently, I was told that this new, positive spirit is set to spread through even the healthcare services. Perhaps that's something you'd like to comment on, now that you're here?'

'No problem,' Krister says. 'Positive attitudes have been shown to lead to excellent outcomes.'

'And the evidence is what, exactly?' Dad asks.

'Don't discuss this with him, Krister,' Helena says. 'It doesn't matter what you say, he'll turn it into something negative. Newspaper people are only interested in misery, anywhere in the world. That's how it is, wouldn't you agree, Erik? You want to expose faults in everything. But there is a new spirit all around in Engelsfors. We've had enough of this guzzling of pessimistic titbits. And, do you know? I believe that deep inside you are fed up with it, too. Wouldn't it be a great change for the better to write up good news instead?'

She smiles sweetly at Dad.

'For instance, rethink when it comes to our Spring Revel,' Krister says. 'We hope that you won't blacken it. Regardless of your views on PE, trade has in fact increased in town...'

'Thank you for reminding me,' Dad says frostily. 'I'll keep all this in mind.'

'Good,' Helena says. 'You know, I've got a strong feeling that more people would buy the paper if they approved of what they read.'

They leave and Minoo looks at her father. At his blood-shot eyes and sweating face. And she knows that Helena and Krister didn't come here just to ask Dad to write positively about the Spring Revel.

They came here to feast on his defeat, on his being about to lose control of the newspaper that has been his.

And Minoo hates them still more.

Vanessa goes up on tiptoe in front of the book display to reach as far as she can with the duster. She could have brought the small ladder from behind the register, but it's too much of a hassle.

One of the busts of Native Americans falls over when she dusts the top of the cupboard. She swears. If something breaks, Mona will take the price of it out of Vanessa's paycheck.

She carries on, dusting her way through the Crystal Cave to the accompaniment of the recorded sounds of harps and wind-chimes. When she checks the time on the dolphin clock, she thinks of Anna-Karin, who will have arrived at the manor house.

Vanessa doesn't want to think about all that. When they had lunch together, she had realized that Anna-Karin was already close to despair. Not a good sign.

Vanessa hadn't been all that nervous before her own inter-rogation. She knows that she is a good liar. But before the session was over, she had nearly broken down all the same. Despite not even being accused of anything.

The dark red curtain is drawn. Next to it hangs a small sign announcing that a fortune-telling consultation is under way. Mona's client is the head of Vanessa's middle school, a Mr. Svensson. Everyone called him Svensson and Vanessa still doesn't know his first name. An elderly nobody, with zero personality. As gray as the mist surrounding the City Mall.

Svensson definitely doesn't come across as the type who'd ask some spooky lady to foretell his future. But if there is one thing Vanessa has learned since she started in the Crystal Cave, it is that no such 'type' exists. Mona has many unexpected clients.

The telephone rings. Vanessa puts the duster on a table and hurries to the counter.

'The Crystal Cave,' she answers.

'Is that Vanessa?'

A young man's voice. It sounds a little familiar. The accent isn't quite right for Engelsfors.

'Yes?'

'I'm Isak. From Sala.'

Isak from Sala. The guy at the New Year's party. She had slept with him and then, afterwards, he admitted that he was only fifteen.

'Why are you calling me here?'

'I couldn't find your number anywhere,' Isak says. He sounds nervous. 'But then I remembered you speaking about this New Age-style shop you're working in...'

Vanessa leans across the counter, supports herself on her elbows. Wonders when she had gotten around to telling him about the Crystal Cave. It wasn't like they talked a lot that night.

'...but I wanted to check if you've got my emails and... you know,' Isak rounds off.

Fire

The doorbell tinkles and out of the corner of her eye, Vanessa sees a woman come into the shop.

'Yes, I've got your emails,' Vanessa says. 'I replied to the first one, didn't I?'

'Yes, you did.'

'Then you must know already that I'm not interested right now.'

'But I thought maybe you'd change your mind when you had read the other messages. But if you haven't gotten them...'

Vanessa looks into the shop. The woman has disappeared behind the shelves.

'I'm sure you're a great guy,' Vanessa says, speaking as quietly as she can without whispering. 'I really did have a great time with you. But, *as I wrote to you*, I don't want to start a relationship now. Not with you and not with anyone else.'

'But how can you say that when you don't know me?'

Vanessa groans and glances at the customer, who's now standing with her back to the register, examining the scented candles.

She suddenly turns around.

Sirpa. Wille's mother.

'Right, so now you know that we're not interested,' Vanessa says into the receiver. 'Thank you for calling. Goodbye.'

'Vanessa? Are you working here?'

Vanessa nods and mumbles something about persistent salesmen.

'How nice to see you!' Sirpa says.

'And you,' Vanessa says, wondering if it's all right to hug Sirpa, or if it would seem odd.

She would like to hug her. She has missed her. Sirpa, who allowed her to stay in her home for months. Sometimes, Vanessa wished Sirpa were her mother.

'Well, now...' Sirpa looks around the shop. 'I haven't been in here before, you know...'

The words peter out. It strikes Vanessa for the first time now that Sirpa looks sad.

Wille, Vanessa thinks. Please, don't let anything have happened to Wille.

It is a surprisingly strong feeling.

'How are you?' she asks.

'I'm fine!' Sirpa replies, with a feeble attempt at cheerfulness. 'Mustn't grumble!'

Tears well up in her eyes and she wipes them away with her hand, still in a woollen glove.

'Has something happened?'

'No, not at all,' Sirpa says and forces herself to laugh a little. 'If anything, that's the problem. *Nothing* has happened. I'm still in pain.'

At least, this hasn't to do with Wille.

Relief floods into Vanessa's mind, but is instantly changed to guilt when she meets Sirpa's eyes.

'Is it your neck?'

'Yes, you might remember it got worse last summer. When I joined PE, I really believed it could help me. Or, I should say, it would teach me something about how to help myself. To be my true self.'

'And your true self doesn't have a painful neck. Right?'

'No, exactly,' Sirpa says. Somehow it is hugely sad that she hasn't even understood the irony in what Vanessa said. 'Helena says that I don't really suffer pain. The thing is, I burden myself with negative thoughts and that makes me feel *as if* I hurt. If only I could change my way of thinking...but maybe I'm a hopeless case. Still, that's just the way one mustn't think. You see, I can't stop myself from getting myself down, and then I criticize myself for that as well.'

Sirpa forces another small burst of laughter and rolls her eyes.

Vanessa's heart goes out to her.

'So, the fact that you've been sitting at a supermarket checkout for something like thirty years has nothing to do with your neck hurting? Are you supposed to be kind of imagining it?'

'But Vanessa...' Sirpa laughs, then looks over her shoulder as if afraid that someone is listening to them. 'That's not what she means.'

'What does she mean?'

'Well, I would say that she means we should be able to control our own lives...that we've the power to shape them...'

'But we can't control *everything*, surely?' Vanessa says. 'Don't you agree?'

Sirpa looks anxious.

'Now, we mustn't talk about this any more,' she says. 'I came here to find some books that might help me. I've left the group for people with so-called physical problems. Only for a while, of course. They told me I wasn't advancing sufficiently. And it's true, I was dragging the others down. So instead I decided to carry on with the healing work on my own. Hopefully, I'll impress them, in time. I will think again and think the right way!'

Vanessa doesn't know what she wants most, to comfort Sirpa or to yell at her to wake up. One thing she knows for sure. She doesn't want to sell that sort of book to Sirpa.

'I don't think we have any books that would suit you.'

'Perhaps your boss has some ideas?'

'She is busy right now,' Vanessa says and points at the sign saying *'FUTURE FORETOLD NOW'*.

'Oh, I see,' Sirpa says. She seems to hesitate. 'Nice to see you, Vanessa.'

'It's good to see you, too.'

She has so many questions that she would like to ask Sirpa. About Positive Engelsfors. About Helena. And about Wille.

'Take care,' she says instead. Sirpa nods and leaves.

Vanessa stares at the shop door. Fury is hissing and bubbling inside her. How can Sirpa allow Helena to brainwash her?

Vanessa almost hopes that magic directs the behavior of the PE membership. It would be easier to understand. Easier to accept.

She has tried to ask Mona if Helena and Krister belong to her group of 'special clients' but Mona won't tell. She hasn't even shown Vanessa where her secret stashes are kept. And it isn't easy to be on the trail of a target with second sight. Mona has even managed to distract Anna-Karin's fox.

A rattling sound behind Vanessa tells her that the curtain is being pulled back. Svensson emerges with Mona immediately behind. He smiles happily and shakes her hand before holding out a wad of twenty-dollar bills.

'I am very grateful,' he says. 'I feel much better now.'

Mona peers at him over the rim of her glasses and offers him her most radiant smile. There are traces of lipstick on her teeth.

'Take care out there,' she says.

When Svensson has left, Mona stuffs the notes into a pocket of her snow-washed carpenter's pants, then takes her glasses off and puts them into another pocket.

'He's going to die pretty soon,' she says and lights a cigarette.

'Do you mean it the way you meant it when you said I would die?' Vanessa asks indifferently.

'No, I mean it literally,' Mona says and retrieves the red

marble ashtray from under the counter. 'Poor guy.'

This takes another moment to sink in.

'But he…he looked so happy. What did you tell him?'

Mona snorts.

'Nothing. What do you take me for?'

'But you've got to warn him!'

Mona shakes her head and sits down on the tall stool behind the counter.

Vanessa looks out through the window, but Svensson is not in sight.

'If I run, maybe I can catch up with him,' she says.

'Catch up to tell him what? "Excuse me, but Mona forget to say you're dying"?'

'But he must be allowed to know!'

'I can see when clients are fairly close to death, but not the cause,' Mona says and meets Vanessa's eyes seriously. 'Death is hovering above him, but can take the shape of a malignant tumor or an axe murderer or whatever. I don't know when. Mostly within the first six months. It seems the max level for how long death needs when it's got somebody in the crosshairs.'

The smoke from her cigarette rises like a pillar to the ceiling.

'Once, when I was young and silly, I made the mistake of telling a client that he was going to die soon. What good did it do him? The anguish ruined what was left of his life. And then he slipped in the shower and died anyway.'

'But the future isn't predetermined!' Vanessa exclaims. 'It can be changed.'

'Oh yes, if you know what to change,' Mona snaps. 'Believe me, sweetheart, I don't like all this either.'

'What do you tell them?'

'Three things. First, enjoy your life. Second, look after yourself and watch out in traffic. Then I can at least hope they will have that health check, or spot that car with enough seconds to spare.'

She stubs out her cigarette.

'And what's the third thing?' Vanessa asks.

'That they're coming back after half a year. And I promise the session will be free.'

The recorded wind-chimes tinkle gently.

'Do they? Come back?'

Mona's silence is a sufficient answer.

'They could've moved away, of course,' Vanessa says. 'Or forgotten.'

'Let's say that,' Mona says and lights another cigarette. 'Have you finished the dusting? I have to close earlier today.'

'Suits me.'

Mona vanishes behind the curtain again and Vanessa walks to the door and flips the sign from 'OPEN' to 'CLOSED'.

She thinks about her own future and the future of the Chosen Ones and of the whole world.

How much is already written.

And, perhaps, how little that can be changed.

Chapter 45

Alexander sits still for a long time and just looks at Anna-Karin.

She feels a solitary drop of sweat trickle down her back, all the way to the elastic of her underwear. She leans back in the soft leather armchair.

Behind her, Viktor is scribbling energetically in his notebook and Anna-Karin wonders what she is giving away by just sitting here.

It's true what Linnéa said in the dining area. He does do *something*. She can sense the magic flowing from him and fears she might not have the strength to keep her defenses up for as long as it takes. That's probably why the interrogations go on for hours.

She doesn't trust herself at all. She is aware of a strong temptation to allow herself to capitulate, admit everything, say anything to get out of here as soon as possible.

When she thinks she can't bear sitting there for one second longer, Alexander leans forward in his armchair and pours himself a glass of water from a beautiful carafe. He drinks and puts the glass down.

'For the record, I will begin by asking if you are Anna-Karin Nieminen?'

'Yes.'

'This is an interrogation. But it also tests your loyalty to the Council. Is that understood?'

'Yes.'

'It is important that you speak the truth,' Alexander says. 'Do you intend to do that?'

'Yes.'

The biggest lie of the lot.

'When did you discover your magic powers?'

'Just before the night of the blood-red moon,' Anna-Karin answers.

'What happened?'

'I accidentally made my mother lose her voice. I didn't intend to at all.'

'How did you bring this about?'

'I wished that she would stop talking. It was only a thought, sort of, but really, really strong...I wanted her to shut up. And then...she did.'

'I understand,' Alexander says. Viktor's pencil scratches away. 'And when was the first time you used your powers deliberately?'

'We had just held a silent minute for Elias in school. I became angry with a certain person...so I made him do something.'

'What did you make him do?'

She hesitates. But this had happened before Adriana told them about the laws of the Council. She doesn't need to lie about what she did, but dislikes talking about it.

'I made Erik Forslund pee himself in front of everyone. It actually wasn't...I didn't know that he would really do it. Or maybe I did know, in a way. It was all so new.'

Alexander's face is expressionless, but she hears Viktor trying to hold back a laugh.

'I understand,' Alexander says and sends Viktor a warning glance.

'No, I don't think you do,' Anna-Karin says before she can

stop herself. 'You don't understand what it was like, how it felt.'

Alexander raises his hand to silence her. It works. She shuts her mouth and swallows nervously.

'You are right,' he says. 'I don't understand everything. That is precisely why we conduct these interrogations. I ask questions and you answer them. I don't want any interruptions. And we will stick to the facts throughout. Is that clear?'

She nods.

Alexander continues his questioning. He wants the names of everyone she's used magic on at school, though that is almost impossible. Not only are there so many of them, but she is also unsure about where the borderline goes. She didn't consciously set about enticing everyone. Many were drawn to her when they realized how popular she had become.

Every answer she gives leads on to new questions. It seems to her that everything she says sounds wrong, piles on the guilt.

She feels tiredness creeping into her mind. At one point, a sudden flash in front of her eyes is followed by a view from the outside of the manor house and she understands that the fox is out there somewhere and offering to help her think of something else for a while. But she doesn't dare to go with it.

'Did you continue to practice magic at school after Adriana Lopez had drawn the Laws of the Council to your attention?' Alexander asks.

She cowers inside. It is such an enormous lie.

'No.'

Alexander exchanges a glance with Viktor, then looks coldly at her.

'You did not carry on breaking the rules laid down by the Council?'

She shakes her head.

'Yes or no?'

'No.'

'As I have understood it, other members of the group of Chosen Ones tried to make you stop,' Alexander says.

Anna-Karin looks up.

'But that was before we were told about the rules.'

Alexander smiles for the first time. As if Anna-Karin has just given herself away. Not only of being guilty as charged, but also ridiculously naïve.

She has no illusions about Ida. She will have said anything to save herself during the questioning. But surely none of the others would have snitched on her? Would they?

'Let us proceed,' Alexander says. 'Your family's farm building caught fire. What happened that night?'

Anna-Karin sticks her hands into the sleeves of her sweater. The magic in the air seems to become stronger all the time.

'I don't know,' she says. 'I woke in the middle of the night because it was so light outside my window. And I saw the barn was on fire...'

She tries to force out all thoughts about the real events. The voice in her head that said it was easier to die. She had listened to it, believed it.

'You didn't notice any magical activity?'

'No.'

'None at all?'

'No.'

'Interesting,' he says. 'Our analyses of the site showed unmistakable remains of magic around the barn. In other words, it was a magic fire.'

How much does Alexander know, really? She desperately tries to hide how upset this makes her.

'Really? I didn't know.'

'Carry on. What happened after you had seen the fire?'

She remembers the chaos. The heat and the roar of the fire. The cows panicking.

'I ran to the barn. My grandfather had already got there trying to rescue the cows.'

'Yes, your grandfather. He was close to becoming a fatality, isn't that so?'

She nods.

'And you have no notion of who started the fire?' Alexander asks.

'No. If it was a magic fire, then...there was someone who tried to kill us all last year...'

'But why should this individual set fire to the barn and not the house where you were sleeping?'

'I have no idea,' she says.

She feels as if she's treading water in a sea of lies. She is almost drowning.

Alexander has taken note. He is quite clearly enjoying himself.

'Who killed Elias and Rebecka?' he asks.

The question bowls her over.

'I don't know.'

'Do you think it could have been the same individual who was responsible for the fire?'

'Maybe. I don't know.'

'Aren't you anxious to know? Don't you care that your grandfather was badly injured?'

Anna-Karin becomes angry for the first time. Alexander doesn't know a thing about her feelings. He doesn't seem to know about feelings, period.

But she says nothing. And it is not only her fear that stops her. She is pretty sure that he *wants* to make her angry. Make her reveal her weak points.

Anna-Karin knows the method only too well. This was what Erik, Ida, Robin, Kevin and the rest of them did when they were bullying her.

When she has been silent for several minutes Alexander says: 'Well, now I would like to talk a little more about the week leading up to the night of the blood-red moon.'

And it starts all over again.

Hours later, Alexander gets up from his armchair and, at last, Anna-Karin dares to believe that the interrogation is over.

Her brain feels as if it has been boiled to mush. She gets up, too, but staggers and almost tumbles back into her armchair.

'I believe that by now we have assembled all the information we need,' Alexander says. 'The trial will take place this coming Saturday.'

Anna-Karin doesn't even react. All she wants is to leave.

'We have appointed someone to plead in your defense,' Alexander goes on.

Anna-Karin suddenly sees Adriana waiting in the door way. How long has she been standing there?

'Come in,' Alexander says.

She is wearing a severe suit in her usual style. But when she steps into the light, Anna-Karin sees how tired Adriana is. And how much weight she has lost.

But although she looks defeated, Anna-Karin feels a little relieved. She hadn't even dared to hope that she would be allowed anyone to defend her. And she knows that she can trust Adriana.

'Would you like me to drive you home?' Viktor asks Anna-Karin.

'I'd rather walk,' she says as she pulls on her duffel coat.

Adriana walks with her down the long corridor to the front door, with Viktor and Alexander following a few steps behind.

Fire

When they have reached the door, Anna-Karin opens it wide and breathes in the fresh outside air. It has just started to drizzle.

'Don't worry, it will all work out well for you,' Adriana says. Her voice lacks conviction as well as warmth.

She holds out her hand to Anna-Karin, an oddly formal gesture even for her.

Anna-Karin takes her hand and touches a small, folded piece of paper that is held tightly between Adriana's long finger and index finger. She glimpses the terror in Adriana's eyes.

Anna-Karin keeps clasping Adriana's hand until she is sure to have gotten a hold of the piece of paper. Then she plunges her hands clumsily into the pockets of her duffel coat. She feels that Viktor and Alexander must be watching everything she does, but doesn't dare look their way.

'Yes, thanks…bye-bye,' Anna-Karin says.

She walks down the steps. The door closes behind her and she relaxes, buttons her coat and starts walking across the yard. The raindrops are icy cold against her face, her jeans are quickly getting wet and she speeds up.

The fox is waiting for her near the docks and trots lightly at her side as she sets out for the town. When they are close to the center, he disappears out of sight but she feels his presence all the time. He follows her among the shadows, all the way home.

She is too scared to look at the piece of paper until she is in her own room. Adriana Lopez's handwriting is as neat as ever.

We must meet in the old fairground at midnight. It will be our only chance to talk before the trial. Tell the others.

CHAPTER 46

'Vanessa, you can't study at the same time as you watch movies and text your friends,' Mom says. She stands in the living-room doorway.

'I do that all the time,' Vanessa replies.

She quickly deletes the text from Anna-Karin and throws the phone on the sofa.

Trial. Now, this Saturday. And tonight, she has to go to the fairground. But she's in luck, her mom has the night shift in the old folks' home and Melvin is off to visit Nicke in his two-bedroom apartment near the station. No one will notice if she sneaks out.

Trasse is snoring on the rug in front of her and she eyes him, feeling jealous. No hope of any sleep for her.

The screen of her laptop shows a guy hung up on a meat-hook. He is trying to persuade his girlfriend to kill him and put an end to his suffering. She screams more than he does.

'But Nessa, what *are* you watching?'

'A romantic comedy,' Vanessa says.

Mom sighs. She seems resigned. At least she doesn't start another sermon.

'Maybe you'd get better grades if you tried out another study method,' she says.

'Come on, Mom, I know what works best for me.'

'Well, turn down the sound anyway,' Mom says and wanders off to the kitchen again.

Vanessa turns the volume down a few notches. And then turns it up again, just a little, hoping that Mom won't notice.

Studying in what people are fond of calling 'peace and quiet' only makes Vanessa so restless that she can't concentrate at all. She needs to be reminded all the time that there is another life out there, beyond the textbooks.

She sinks more deeply into the sofa cushions and puts her feet on the coffee table. Props up the open book against her thighs.

Mom pops her head around the door again.

'What are you working on anyway?' she asks.

'English grammar and it's totally pointless and I hate it,' Vanessa says tonelessly.

'It must be useful to know.'

'Why? Can you explain that for me? No one else has managed to.'

Impatiently, Vanessa taps her pen on the open book. She has no problem speaking English. Song lyrics and film subtitles have taught her everything she needs. The only snag is, she happens not to know all the *rules* or exactly *why* you're supposed to use this or that phrase.

'You're asking the wrong person,' Mom says and smiles.

Vanessa is just about to reply when her phone rings from somewhere among the cushions. Mom instantly turns on her severe face.

'Really, Nessa,' she says.

'I'm just going to check who it is,' she says and digs out the phone.

Wille.

She's deleted his number from her phone, but hasn't been able to delete it from her mind. Just about six months ago, a call from him around this time was a regular part of her day. Now it makes her heart beat double time.

The phone goes on ringing and Mom just stands there, staring at her.

'Aren't you going to answer?' she asks.

It feels as though it would be a mistake to answer. Is it a mistake she can resist making?

'I'll have to take this call,' she says and gets up from the sofa.

Mom sighs when Vanessa runs into her room. She presses the reply button at the same time as she shuts the door behind her.

'Hello?'

'Nessa, hi...' he says.

His voice makes her feel dizzy.

'Mom says she met you today,' he says.

'Yes?' Vanessa says, trying to sound indifferent but doubting the effect.

'I'm waiting at the usual place,' Wille says. 'Can you come?'

Seeing him would be the next mistake. An even bigger one.

'Why?'

'I just want to talk for a while. It's been a long time.'

Vanessa swings around to the full-length mirror and fluffs up her hair. And as soon as she does this she realizes that she has made up her mind.

'I'll be down soon,' she says.

She doesn't give him time to reply, just switches off the call, puts the phone in the pocket of her hoodie and goes back to the living room. She looks out through the window. Wille's car is parked at the bus stop.

She ought to text him to say she won't come after all.

Fire

'Are you working?' Mom shouts from the kitchen.

'Umm,' Vanessa mutters.

Wille is waiting for her in his car and it all feels so familiar, so *usual*, as if the last half-year never happened.

She finds herself wondering if she isn't ready to forgive him now. If he really, truly begged her maybe she would. Maybe.

Christ, Linnéa would think she's pathetic.

But it shouldn't matter what anyone else thinks, should it?

'I've got to take Frasse out,' she shouts to Mom.

'But you've already been out with him.'

'He's acting like it's totally urgent,' Vanessa says and tugs a little at his collar. Frasse reluctantly lifts his head and stares sleepily at her.

'Nessa, if this is a lousy excuse to get out of studying...'

Vanessa drags Frasse into the hall, clips on his lead and puts on her coat. The dog is alert by now and wags his tail happily, over the moon at the chance to go out again.

'Back soon,' Vanessa says.

The air is chilly, with a raw dampness about it. Vanessa starts feeling cold the moment she steps outside. Frasse sniffs the ground eagerly as they walk towards Wille's car.

They are almost there when Wille climbs out and Frasse starts tugging at the lead so energetically he almost rips off Vanessa's arm.

'Hiya, Frasse,' Wille says. 'Hi there, old pal.'

Frasse leaps up, puts his front paws on Wille's belly and allows himself to be patted and scratched behind his ears. Vanessa stands by silently, waiting. Wille avoids looking at her and she wonders if he feels as tense as she does.

Frasse finally calms down and settles back on all four paws. Wille looks at her.

And, yes. He is just as tense.

'I'm glad you came,' he says.

She hasn't seen him since she spooked him in Götis, but she has heard that he's moved in with Elin in Riddarhyttan, a village just outside Engelsfors.

And the transformation has clearly continued.

Wille's hair is cut shorter than she has ever seen it. His jacket is new. Wille, who had been putting on the same worn old outfit for as long as she had known him.

He looks more handsome than ever. One part of Vanessa wants to whimper a little and wag her tail, just like Frasse.

This is a mistake, she thinks as they look at each other for a long time. But I knew that already, didn't I?

'You look different,' she says.

'I've got myself a haircut and a job,' he says and smiles. 'Perhaps I'll buy myself a new car as well.' He kicks a front tire. 'This sad old heap has done its part.'

He might as well be talking about her. She has obviously been *exchanged*.

Suddenly she feels idiotic to have even considered forgiving Wille, since she hasn't a clue what *he* wants.

'Why are you here?' Vanessa asks.

Wille puts his hands into his jacket pockets and leans against the car. His breath forms a cloud in the light from the street lamps. She shivers.

'I wanted to see you,' he says. 'And thank you.'

'For what?'

'For your belief in me. Look, throughout our relationship I was a fucking loser, I know that. But you always believed that I could change. It's because of you that I began to believe it myself in the end. I smoke maybe only once or twice a month now. I've landed a job in a call center and it isn't too bad at all. And I've moved away from home.'

Vanessa senses her own bitterness as distinctly as a taste in her mouth.

Well, isn't that just fabulous, Wille, she wants to cry. Great to have had this fantastic opportunity to get you on the payroll. And such fun for me to struggle and nag and beg and deliver endless pep talks. Shame, isn't it, that somebody else will have the benefit of all that hard work? Still, that's the way it goes.

'You mean, you've moved in with Elin,' she says.

Wille nods, doesn't answer.

'Great,' Vanessa says. 'What do you want me to say? Congrats to your new, happy life?'

'I never said I was happy,' Wille says and looks at her. 'I should never have done what I did to you. I have never regretted anything so much in my whole life. I miss you.'

'What about Elin? What does she think about it?'

Wille's eyes fix on something else.

'Aha, she doesn't know a thing, does she?' Vanessa says. 'She thinks everything is fine now.'

She starts tugging at Frasse's lead. He just sits there.

'Come on, Frasse,' she says and he stands up at last.

She walks back to the front door. Frasse's claws are clicking against the asphalt. And then she hears Wille come running after her.

'Nessa!'

He swings her around half a turn, pulls her close and kisses her.

She wants to leave, but can't make herself do it. She can't even control her own mouth. It opens to receive his kiss, go further.

Wille's kiss is just as it always was, like nobody else's and she wants to stop thinking, stop feeling bitter and twisted. Fuck everything. She wants them to jump into his car and drive until they run out of gas.

'There's no one like you,' Wille whispers.

She does free herself now. Her treacherous body protests. It already misses having him so close. Her Wille addiction has come back to life and, just now, her body is on a high and would easily sell off her pride.

'I must go.'

'Nessa...'

She turns and starts walking away with Frasse at her heels.

'Don't you miss me, too?' Wille calls after her.

She doesn't answer him. She doesn't dare to answer, for fear of telling him the truth.

CHAPTER 47

Minoo cautiously opens the door to her room and slips out into the corridor.

Mom and Dad's bedroom door is slightly open. Dad's snoring sounds like low rumbling in there. Just as Minoo puts her foot on the top step of the stairs, the snores stop.

She listens, hears him turn heavily in bed. She holds her breath until the snoring starts again. She starts to walk downstairs. Since the night of the blood-red moon, she has sneaked down the staircase so many times that she knows exactly where to place her feet, which of the steps creak.

Minoo has just reached the ground floor when the house phone rings out shrilly. She rushes into the hall to pick it up, hoping that the signal hasn't woken Dad.

'Hello?' she whispers breathlessly.

No one answers. Only breathing, some scraping noises. Someone who listens and waits.

'Stop calling,' she says and puts the receiver down.

Cowardly shits, Minoo thinks.

She tries to work up some anger, but fails. Instead she hates them because they frighten her so badly. The calls make her feel as if someone is watching her, observing everything she does.

She switches off the ringtone. Listens out for sounds from

396

upstairs. Dad's snoring is perfectly audible even here. She pulls her coat on and leaves quickly.

The fog is so thick she can hardly see the gate on the other side of the lawn.

Someone is waiting on the pavement. That's just what they agreed. But Minoo can't be sure that the dim shape really is Anna-Karin until they are only a few yards apart.

'Hi,' Minoo says quietly.

'Hi,' Anna-Karin says and pushes a tangled strand of hair behind her ear.

They start walking along the street. The fog wraps Minoo's face like a cold, damp blanket.

'How are things?' she asks.

'I don't know. I just wish it would all be over soon.'

Minoo feels like saying that she's sure everything will be all right, but they both know that she has no idea, one way or the other. And it isn't empty phrases Anna-Karin needs just now.

They carry on walking in silence towards Kärrgruvan.

Now and then, Anna-Karin halts and closes her eyes. Her familiar is keeping watch down by the manor house. It will warn her if anyone leaves the house. But just in case, Anna-Karin gets in touch with it quite regularly.

'It must be such a strange feeling,' Minoo says at one point when Anna-Karin goes through this routine again. 'You know, like, being a fox.'

They have just arrived at the start of the dirt road to the fairground. Minoo lights her torch. Dense strands of fog dance slowly in the cone of light.

'I've gotten used to it,' Anna-Karin says and opens her eyes. 'He suddenly materialized from nowhere but now it feels as if he has been part of me always. Like the magic, if you see what I mean?'

Fire

Minoo nods but doesn't comment.

Magic has never felt part of her. Rather, it is like being occupied by a foreign power. Perhaps it would be like a more natural extension of her self if she knew what it could be used for.

Ever since she found out that the guardians are supporting her powers, she has dared to experiment a little. But she still can't make objects move, make herself invisible, read people's thoughts or affect the way they act. Her one talent seems to be an ability to haul souls out of bodies with her bare hands. She still can't see how this can be for good.

They walk on and finally the familiar shrubberies around Kärrgruvan emerge ghostlike out of the misty air.

The fog lifts as they enter through the gate.

Inside the fairground, the air is clear. High above them, the black night sky, scattered with stars, forms an arch without end.

A shimmering light flickers around the pavilion. Adriana's blue fire burns in the center of the dance floor. Minoo turns off the torch. They pass through the gleaming shell and feel the warmth of the fire.

The other Chosen Ones are seated. Adriana is the only one who is standing. Minoo hasn't seen her since she came with Alexander to inspect Nicolaus's apartment. Illuminated by the blue flames, she looks almost ill, but her eyes glitter with nervous energy.

'Join us and sit down,' she says. 'We are short of time.'

She tugs at a narrow leather strap around her neck. From it hangs a white piece of something that looks like bone. Red lines are growing slowly over its surface, branching like blood vessels across the white.

Minoo and Anna-Karin pull off their coats and sit down on the floor.

Minoo can't resist taking a quick look at Linnéa, who sits next to Vanessa. She can't understand how she failed to see this for so long. Now that she knows, it is unmistakable. Linnéa keeps glancing at Vanessa all the time, as if she doesn't want to miss one second of being with her.

I must talk to Linnéa, Minoo thinks.

But she can't work out how to handle it.

'I'll tell you everything, from the beginning, to make you understand how the Council functions,' Adriana says.

Minoo shudders once the words have fully sunk in. Adriana seems to have decided to reveal all there is to know. Chosen to be on their side, regardless.

'I was born to join the uppermost class of the Council hierarchy,' Adriana begins. 'Both my parents were immensely powerful witches. Both were descendants of families that had belonged to the Council for generations. It was clear from the start that I would follow in their footsteps.'

Her smile is sad.

'Unfortunately, it soon became obvious that I had no particular talent for magic. Neither my mother nor my father was a natural witch, but they were both very gifted and the gift for magic is often inherited. Given the history of my family, no one had expected me to be such a disappointment.'

Adriana's legs begin to fold under her and she sinks down to sit on the floor, too. She supports herself with one hand flat on the floor.

'Luckily for my parents, they had one child already, Alexander, who more than met their expectations. My father worshipped him and ignored me completely. My mother tried to share her love more fairly between her children, but she felt ashamed of me. I knew that she couldn't understand what they had done wrong to have a daughter like me. The Council despises weakness. Also, strength is measured in levels of magic talent and the contributions individuals can make. I tried to compensate in different ways. Above all, to balance my lack of innate ability with perfect behavior and devotion to my studies.'

Minoo notices Adriana's quick glance in her direction. Once, Adriana had said that Minoo reminded her of herself as a young woman.

'And then I met Simon,' Adriana continues. 'We were both nineteen. He and Alexander were friends. That was how we met. We soon fell in love. Deeply in love.'

She looks gravely at them. Her dark eyes shine in the light of the blue fire.

'The Council exerts incredibly tight control over its membership. Everyone is a potential informant. That means one's parents, siblings, children, friends, lovers. Everyone. But I trusted Simon. And he trusted me. For the first time in our lives we allowed ourselves to formulate in words a forbidden idea that we had both carried in our heads – that the Council was no better than a prison. Once we had taught each other to see, we could no longer shut our eyes to the truth. The Council de-humanized us. We decided to run away.'

'Why did you have to run away? Couldn't you simply...resign?' Vanessa asks.

Adriana shakes her head.

'Those of us who are born into Council membership have to choose on our eighteenth birthday if we want to join the Council formally or to leave forever. And I mean, *forever*. They sever all connections with dissenters. Extremely few have chosen that alternative. Even the doubters stay on. The Council is our family, our entire world. Both Simon and I had sworn an oath to stay faithful to the Council until death.'

Adriana turns her face towards the darkness that surrounds the dance floor, but she is looking at something else. She seems to search her mind for the right words.

'We planned our escape for months. I was to meet Simon in a hotel in Copenhagen. When I arrived, the representatives of the Council were waiting for me. They had taken Simon already, before he left Stockholm.'

She shuts her eyes, takes a deep breath.

'There was a court case. We couldn't deny our crime, of course. Simon was sentenced to death and I would have been executed, too, if it hadn't been for my mother's intervention. She sacrificed so much to save me, but I could not be grateful. I wanted to die, I...'

She falls silent again.

'They let me live, but saw to it that I would never forget my crime.'

She absently touches her left collarbone and Minoo feels a chill run down her spine as she thinks of the sign of fire, burned into skin that is hidden under her blouse.

'They punished me in a ritual that physically bound me to the Council. I could not do anything other than obey their commands. And after a while, I wanted nothing else. I allowed myself to be brainwashed again. I suppose it was weak and cowardly. I was so badly broken, I saw no other way out...but I realize that you would find it hard to grasp.'

Minoo shakes her head. Everyone is silent. The blue fire makes the shadows flutter over their faces.

It almost feels as if Adriana is a member of the Circle.

'I returned to the life that had been mine before I met Simon. To the books. As you know, by now most Council members find reading the *Book of Patterns* difficult. That's true even of the natural witches. But we do have access to huge library collections of knowledge about the book and interpretations of what has been seen in it. The accumulated work of untold generations.'

Minoo wishes she could tell Adriana that they already know about these libraries and that they actually have spoken with Matilda. When Adriana opens up to them in this way, it feels awful to keep so many secrets from her. Secrets about themselves, about the previous Chosen One, about the guardians, Nicolaus and the history of the Council.

'I was given the task of investigating how true various prophecies had been,' Adriana says. 'Vast numbers of prophecies are on record. They predict all sorts of things, from very minor to very important matters. A power shift in a country, a local magic phenomenon, the fate of a family. The Council studies the prophecies and attempts to use them to work out what the future will bring. Knowledge is power. And one thing you must understand is that, essentially, the Council is interested only in power.'

'We've all got the message by now, I think,' Linnéa says.

'A few years ago, I went to the Norwegian headquarters of the Council. In Trondheim. I was looking for an eighteenth-century text that was said to contain prophecies about harvest failures. The Council libraries are astonishingly poorly organized, mainly because of internal power struggles over many centuries. Some manuscripts would be banned from time to time. It took me weeks to find what I had been looking for. I skimmed the book and happened to find a reference to "the Chosen One in Engelsfors" and certain events in this part of the world that took place around the end of the seventeenth century. It caught my interest. The myth of the Chosen One has fascinated me ever since I was little. And now it seemed I had found indications that the myth was in fact a true historical account.'

'What do you mean? A *myth*?' Minoo says.

True, Matilda had said that the Council seemed to have forgotten most circumstances of its origin and most of its goals. But all the time, Adriana has spoken about the Chosen Ones as if she totally accepted them.

'Yes, what's that about a myth? Like, Santa Claus?' Vanessa asks.

Adriana smiles sadly.

'Council members regard the accounts of the Chosen One in ways similar to how many religions regard their ancient texts. As symbolic narratives or mythologized versions of historical events.'

Minoo tries to digest what Adriana has told them so far, but it's hard to fully comprehend that people see you as a kind of fairy-tale creature.

'I became curious and started digging deeper in the Trondheim archives,' Adriana says. 'Traces of the idea turned up here and there, but as little more than cautious hints. And then, finally, I located a badly worn copy of a prophecy from the thirteenth century and found that I could begin to work with it and the other sources to piece together a more complete picture. Everything pointed to a large explosion of magic in Engelsfors and the area around it, sometime between 1650 and 1700. A witch with special powers had lived here. A girl, said to be the only one who could stop the demons. She was the Chosen One. It was unclear what happened to her, but the prophecy foretold that a new Chosen One would be awakened in order to stop the apocalypse. It would happen here in Engelsfors, under a blood-red moon. Having been interested in the myth before, I now became obsessed with it. Especially when my research demonstrated that the next blood-red moon would soon rise over Engelsfors.

'Certain groups in the Council became very interested in my account, but others dismissed it as sheer superstition. The skeptics didn't care to believe in any of it, invading demons or an impending apocalypse or specially "chosen" witches. But I was permitted to make some preliminary measurements and soon showed that Engelsfors was an exceptionally magical place. Even the skeptics became interested then. They ordered me to come here and install myself as high school principal, since my findings indicated that the Chosen One would be in your age group. And that's how I found Elias.'

Her voice trembles and she has to pull herself together before she continues.

'As soon as we realized that there were seven of you, not just one, the debate in the Council flared up again. From the beginning, you were exceptions to the rule, as it were.'

Adriana smiles faintly.

'I had to fight to make them recognize you as the Chosen Ones and allow me to tell you about your situation. The analyses of hairs from your heads, which proved a never-before-observed magic potential, finally persuaded them. Although there were still those who didn't believe that you were the Chosen Ones, the consensus was that you could be very useful.'

Her eyes move to each one of them in turn.

'But you made me wake up. Especially you, Linnéa. And I would like to thank you.'

'Umm, okay,' Linnéa says uncertainly.

'It was you who all the time pointed out that your lives were at risk from the inhuman bureaucracy of the Council,' Adriana says. 'It reminded me of everything that Simon and I had been talking about. And made me realize that if I wanted to honor his memory I had to act. Or rather, *not* act, when it became clear that you were going behind my back.'

Minoo remembers the notes she had taken last year. She suddenly sees them in a new light. So much is explained by now. So many question marks have been straightened out.

'What do they think about us now?' Anna-Karin asks. 'Do they believe we are the Chosen Ones?'

'Officially, yes, that is the premise,' Adriana says. 'But the groups of skeptics are gaining influence. And Alexander definitely counts among them.'

Minoo recalls Alexander's sneering smile when she referred to the demons during the interrogation. His contemptuous tone when he came to the fairground and Linnéa mentioned the apocalypse. It seems quite logical now.

'But what if they're right?' Ida says. 'Perhaps we're not the Chosen Ones. Imagine, it might just be a misunderstanding...'

'Do you believe that?' Linnéa asks.

Ida shakes her head.

'Not really, no,' she says wearily. 'But admit it, it would be a relief.'

'But if you couldn't tell us all this before, how can you do it *now*?' Vanessa asks Adriana.

'Thanks to the exceptionally expensive magic I bought with Mona Moonbeam's help. I paid for it with information. Of course I couldn't tell her straight out that Alexander was about to arrive in town, but I put her on the right track. In return, she gave me this.'

Adriana tugs at the leather strap around her neck and Minoo sees the piece of bone. By now it looks more red than white. The process is taking place right before eyes, slowly but relentlessly.

'It has taken the best part of nine months to create an amulet that can block my connection to the Council for a few hours.'

'I'm guessing,' Vanessa says. 'When it's red all over, your time is up.'

Adriana nods.

'As you can all see, we must hurry,' she says and lets go of the strap. 'You'd better ask your questions now.'

'What do we need to know about Alexander and Viktor?' Minoo says.

'Like me, Alexander is a fire witch. He is as strong as a trained witch can be.'

'But we're natural witches, as well as the Chosen Ones and all that,' Anna-Karin says. 'Then we must surely be stronger than him.'

'You are *potentially* much stronger,' Adriana replies. 'But your powers are not yet fully engaged. Alexander has had many years of experience. He is utterly loyal to the Council. And utterly ruthless.'

She seems unaware that her fingers are moving up to touch her collarbone again. Minoo remembers what Adriana had said the first time she told them about Alexander.

He is willing to sacrifice even his family, his friends. The people he claims to love.

And her stomach churns when she suddenly understands the significance of what Alexander said in Nicolaus's apartment.

Will you never forgive me?

Your suffering would have been even greater if it had been someone else who—

'Did he do it?' she asks. 'Did he execute your punishment?' Adriana nods.

'He volunteered, to show where his loyalties lay. My parents were present throughout. It was too much for my mother and she died soon afterwards. That was when I changed my surname to hers.'

Alexander had terrified Minoo from when she first saw him. By now, he seems almost worse than the demons. And at least as inhuman.

'As for Viktor, I don't know all that much,' Adriana continues. 'Alexander adopted him. It is quite common for the Council to undertake adoptions when especially talented children are discovered growing up in non-magical families. Viktor's biological mother was a drug addict. He has a twin sister, but I have never met her. Both she and Viktor were educated in the boarding schools run by the Council.'

'Viktor has told us that he's a natural witch, and that water is his element,' Minoo says. 'Can he mind-read, like Linnéa?'

'No, he can't,' Adriana says. 'His talent is related to that, though. He can discern when people are lying.'

Minoo looks around the circle of Chosen Ones. Knows that they are all thinking the same thing. *We're done for.*

Suddenly, their attempts to prepare for the trial seem so obviously pathetic. Fancy them imagining that they could outwit the Council.

'So that's what Alexander meant when he said the interrogation was also a test,' she manages to say. 'We failed and are seen as disloyal. Because they know we've been lying.'

'Yes,' Adriana says.

'Can Viktor see through us and find out the truth as well?' Ida says.

'No. Thankfully. He functions more like a magical lie detector. Very reliable. And, as far as I know, you have all been lying under interrogation. Despite my warning to you,' Adriana says and looks at Minoo.

'We had no choice,' she says.

'I understand that you believe that,' Adriana says. 'But, if you had been honest when you answered the questions, they might have decided to treat you more considerately. Because during the trial, they will extract the truth from you, whether you like it or not. And tomorrow, reinforcements from the Council are due. On Saturday, you will confront them all, not only Alexander and Viktor.'

Minoo wants to clamp her hands over her ears to keep out any more bad news. But if they're to have any chance at all, she must ask about the procedure.

'The trial itself...how is it organized?' she asks.

'Alexander and Viktor have spent months preparing the courtroom. They've been thorough to say the least. No magic at all can be practiced in that room. For instance, Anna-Karin won't be able to influence anyone and Linnéa won't be able to read anyone's thoughts. Not that I would have recommended you to try anything of the sort. But it might have been a straw to cling to.'

'Who's the judge?' Linnéa asks.

'The bench will consist of five judges, all drawn from among the Council's oldest, most trusted members. Establishment figures, who are the least likely to show mercy. Alexander and I will question you.'

'But if no one can use magic in court, then Viktor won't be able to know if we're lying, right?' Vanessa asks.

'No, he will not. But that would have been preferable compared to the Council's standard practices in cases like this. They have very effective means to prevent lies being told.'

'Oh, can't you get to the point!' Ida shouts. 'What will they do to us?'

'Alexander and Viktor have collaborated on setting up very powerful circles in the courtroom,' Adriana says. 'Alexander is an expert on a technique that reflects witches' powers back on themselves. Linnéa, you'll remember what happened when you tried to read Alexander's mind?'

Linnéa makes a face.

'Yes.'

'That's what will happen to any one of you if you lie

during your witness statements. Your powers will be turned towards yourself. But the pain will be a thousand times worse than what you felt, Linnéa.'

Total silence in the dance pavilion.

It means that only two alternatives are left. To reveal all immediately, or to endure torture until they break down and then reveal all. That is, they will be convicted regardless.

'What kind of punishment should we expect?' Linnéa asks.

Naturally, she is the one who asks the straight question, the one Minoo hardly has dared to formulate even to herself.

'Let's not speculate about it,' Adriana says gravely.

'But there must be something we can do!' Ida says.

'Turn to the *Book of Patterns* for advice,' Adriana says. 'That's your only hope.'

Minoo swallows.

'Some kind of power fluctuation makes it not work the way it's supposed to,' she says.

Adriana suddenly turns very pale. She checks the amulet. The redness covers almost all of it now. Only a few white spots left.

Everyone who could help us seems to be prevented from doing anything, Minoo thinks. And everyone is short of time.

'I must leave now,' Adriana says, as she stands and brushes down her coat. 'But before I go, I want to ask you all to forgive me. If I had in any way been able to foresee all this...I wouldn't have started looking into the stories about Engelsfors. Much better if the Council had never heard of this town.'

'Surely it would've been worse if you had just ignored a prophecy that had predicted the apocalypse,' Vanessa says.

'And you really tried to help us, after all,' Anna-Karin says.

Adriana looks seriously at her.

'I will do everything in my power to help you during the trial. I'll do my best for all of you. But I can truly think of only one possible action you could take.'

'And what's that?' Ida says, feebly.

'Run away,' Adriana replies.

CHAPTER 48

The blue fire has died down slowly. Minoo is the only one left in the dance pavilion. She keeps the flashlight on. The dark is solid beyond the cone of light.

After Adriana's departure, they talked about what could be done, but it was no more than fumbling about blindly.

Of course, the others had wondered why Minoo wanted to stay, on her own and in the middle of the night. By now, she has begun to wonder too.

Her heart almost stops when she hears soft thumps somewhere in the forest outside the fence. She swings the flashlight that way and catches a brief glimpse of a deer before it vanishes into the mist.

Run away.

So, this was all Adriana could think of advising them to do. But they can't run away and just let the world end.

Minoo takes the *Book of Patterns* and the Pattern Finder from her backpack, puts them down in front of her and lets the beam of light play over them. She opens the book and places the Pattern Finder in front of her eyes. Twists it as she leafs through the pages, tries to concentrate on just one of the many questions whirling around in her head.

But the signs stay still. The book does not speak.

Nothing, nothing. As usual.

'Help us, please!' Minoo says aloud and stares into the

dark. 'Matilda said that you would help us to get through the trial!'

No one replies.

'We haven't got a hope on our own!'

She is speaking even louder now.

'If you are our guardians, protect us now.'

All Minoo hears is the wind rustling in the treetops. She slams the book shut. Throws the Pattern Finder into the darkness. A gleam, and it is gone. She is so frustrated she nearly bursts into tears.

'You have blessed me with your magic. Allow me to use it.'

She is going to pieces. Everything is breaking apart. Can't the guardians see it?

'If you exist, if you are on our side – show yourselves. Now!'

And something stirs inside her. Her pleas have triggered a response. Something flows through her. Spreads throughout her body, fills her.

It wants out.

And Minoo releases it. Lets the black smoke pour out. Dense, silky, it swiftly streams towards the *Book of Patterns*.

A sharp snap, when the book opens where it lies on the floor. The pages start turning on their own, faster and faster. Finally, they settle and stay still.

The black smoke swirls above the book. Hangs there, waiting.

And Minoo asks her question.

How are we to deal with the trial?

Suddenly Minoo sees the patterns form among the elementary signs.

She can see the signs, she can see beyond them.

When the answer emerges, she does not quite understand.

But she knows what they must do.

CHAPTER 49

'You know, I really hate this place,' Anna-Karin's mom says when she and Anna-Karin walk into the hall at Sunny Side. And Anna-Karin agrees. She always looks forward to seeing Grandpa but, even so, the actual nursing home is hopelessly depressing. The smells, the sounds, the bleak atmosphere. It all adds up to the message that Sunny Side is nothing more than a lock-up at the end of the road. The terminus.

When they step into the elevator, Mom is fiddling nervously with her rings.

'I'd rather die than end up in a home like this,' she mutters and pushes the Up button.

'Why do you make Grandpa stay here then?' Anna-Karin says. 'We do have a spare room, after all.'

Mom blinks. Quite a long time has passed since their last discussion about this.

'Our apartment isn't suitable for a handicapped person,' she says.

As the elevator rocks a little and stops, she moves ahead of Anna-Karin into the corridor.

'I've checked,' Anna-Karin says and follows on her heels. 'The doors are wide enough. All we need to do is remove the thresholds and—'

Mom interrupts her.

'Anna-Karin...' She stops. Sighs. Twists her rings some more. 'I can't.'

'But I—'

'You have your school,' Mom interrupts. 'And I...I can't cope.'

She looks up, meets Anna-Karin's eyes.

'I can't cope,' she repeats.

Anna-Karin doesn't know how to answer her. Because she knows it's the truth. Mom can't cope. However much Anna-Karin would like her to, she simply can't.

'I know,' Anna-Karin says.

Mom nods. In one of the nearby rooms, an old woman is speaking loudly into a phone.

'But, please, Mom,' Anna-Karin says, feeling that her voice is about to crack. 'Please. Can't you find someone who will help you? You don't have to go on like this.'

Mom shakes her head.

'This is me, the person I am. How I've always been. I can't help it. Just try to do my best.'

Thoughts are buzzing inside Anna-Karin's head. There are a thousand things she might say, but what's the point when Mom won't listen?

'I've got to have a smoke,' Mom says and quickly touches Anna-Karin's arm. 'You go ahead.'

'I will,' Anna-Karin replies and Mom walks back to the elevator.

Grandpa's living room is empty. Anna-Karin is just about to turn around and go looking for him when she hears him call her from the bedroom.

'Sweetheart, is that you?'

Anna-Karin goes to him. Grandpa is in bed, in his night-shirt, with the duvet pulled right up over his shoulders. The blind is drawn.

'Grandpa, are you still in bed? Haven't they helped you get up?'

'Yes, they did,' he says. 'I did get up. But I felt ever so tired.'

One of his hands comes out from under the duvet and beckons her closer. Anna-Karin sits down on the chair next to the bed. Tries not to think about how weak he looks, how much this reminds her of his time in hospital after the fire.

What will life be like for him if she never comes to see him any more? The guardians have told Minoo about a ritual that should help them to get through the trial, but the Chosen Ones aren't certain about how it will work. Or *if* it is going to work.

'Has Mia come with you today?'

'She'll be here soon. She just went off for a smoke.'

'Good. I must speak to you now,' he says and takes her hand. His fingers are cold as ice. 'Something is about to happen here in Engelsfors. Something that's not right. I've felt bad about it for a long time now and it's getting worse.'

She puts her other hand over his to try to warm it.

'And you know it, too, don't you? You know more than you want to tell me,' Grandpa says. 'Someone wants to harm you.'

Anna-Karin looks away. Grandpa's grip on her hand grows firmer.

'I would like nothing better than for you to speak to me about it, but I understand. There are things you have to bear alone. But listen to me...'

His tongue runs over his dry lips.

'Would you like a drink of water?' Anna-Karin asks, but he shakes his head impatiently.

'My father, he had dreams that came true,' he continues. 'Me, I've only had two of them. The first one was the night before you were born.'

Grandpa glances towards the open door. Then he lowers his voice until he is almost whispering.

Fire

'I dreamed of a moon that rose above Engelsfors. Red, it was, colored by the blood of a boy with black hair. And I dreamed of a fox and a girl with green eyes. A girl who would have to endure much. But she was strong. Stronger and braver than she herself realized. And she was not alone. She had friends. Do you know who I'm talking about, Anna-Karin?'

Anna-Karin's eyes are brimming with tears. All she can do is nod.

'Last night I dreamed again…a dream *that was not a dream*. I was in the no-man's-land between the living and the dead. I met a girl with a freckled face. She was alive many hundreds of years ago, but is held back in that boundary zone. She wanted to tell me many things, but couldn't. All she said was that you must be at peace with yourselves and each other, once and for all. You must all do it. The road you are following is dark and dangerous and you must be able to trust each other, know each other's secrets, if you are to face the one who has been blessed by the demons.'

'The demons?' Anna-Karin says. 'Grandpa, do you know anything about them?'

He glances at the door again.

'No, it was she who said this.'

'Did she say who that was? The one blessed by demons?'

'I don't know if she knew. Or maybe it was that she couldn't tell me.'

Anna-Karin recognizes her mother's heavy footsteps in the corridor.

'Thank you for telling me this, Grandpa,' she says quietly.

Ida knows that she shouldn't.

But she has been at dinner with Erik and his family. And then he asked her once more if she wouldn't let him take her to the center.

There was something about the way he said it that made her realize this was more than the usual question. If she said no again, it would have been one *no* too many. And then everything would've been over between them.

When she said yes, Erik suddenly looked happy and hugged her.

And now they are walking through Engelsfors towards the center. Hand in hand. Girlfriend and boyfriend.

Making him happy made her feel good. And it felt liberating to go 'fuck you' to the other Chosen Ones and ditch the book's warnings, and Matilda's, too. Decide what to do on your own, just for a change.

'Look at that,' Erik whispers, when they reach the center.

Ida looks where he is looking. Anna-Karin and her mother are about to go inside the house just opposite the center. The mother looks like a totally typical case of the kind of Engelsforser who has given up long ago. Characters who potter around town in sagging sweatpants, wearing socks with sandals and fuzz-covered old sweaters. Like they have zero self-respect.

'How the hell can they allow themselves to look like that?' Erik says. 'They could at least have *tried*.'

'I guess there's a lot of in-breeding among the rustics,' Ida says.

Erik laughs and gives her hand a squeeze. It feels good to be on his side, on the side of the strong, the winners. People who aren't always worrying, fearful of spooky mind invasions and the end of the world as we know it.

Tonight, Ida wants to pretend that she is her real, old self. It might soon be too late. Tomorrow might be too late. She has not the slightest confidence in the mysterious ritual that's supposed to be such a great idea.

The Positive Engelsfors Center is almost empty. Posters

advertising the Spring Revel beam at her from every wall. Erik lets go of her hand, kisses her cheek and wanders away to talk to Robin, who's hammering the game controls.

Ida catches sight of Julia. She's sitting on a sofa, doing something on her cell. When she sees Ida advancing, Julia stares wide-eyed at her and smiles nervously.

'Gosh, that's just terrific!' the little traitor says. 'So, you've joined, too?'

'*Too?*'

'Yes, the thing is, my mom really wanted me to become a member, she was going on at me all the time. And then Felicia said she'd be here tonight and you were with Erik...'

'Sure. I get it.'

And Ida means it. Given the choice, she too would have joined Positive Engelsfors.

'Is Felicia here?' she asks.

Julia's eyes look unsure.

'I don't see a lot of her, of course, only sometimes when you aren't around...'

By now, the lovely feeling of being on top of things has leached out of Ida. Left behind is only a great big hollow. And, echoing inside it, a small still voice that has grown more and more familiar recently.

is it worth it is it worth it is it worth it is it worth it is it worth it

It feels as if she has been playing a role all her life only to find that the play isn't right for her any more. The other actors have changed and don't behave the way they used to.

Or else, it's just about me, Ida thinks. I'm the one who's changed. I'm becoming a freak, like the other Chosen Ones.

'No problem,' she says. 'You and Felicia are free to hang

out. Comb each other's hair all day long, or whatever. It's fine by me.'

'You're mad now, I can see it,' Julia says uncertainly.

'No, honestly. I mean it. I can hardly remember why Felicia and I fell out.'

Julia watches her anxiously, as if she's standing on a trap-door, trying to work out whether Ida is going to press the button.

'Great,' she says and tests a cautious smile. 'Then all three of us can become friends again, at last. And now we're all PE members, too.'

Ida coolly returns the smile.

'I'll go and find Felicia, have a word so she knows you're here and that you'd like to be friends again and all that,' Julia says and hurries off.

Ida sighs and begins a tour of the room. An entire wall is covered with a display of drawings made by the kids in the Play'n'Learn group. Large, happy suns, smiling families of heads-on-feet people holding hands in front of their houses. Laughing bumblebees, cats and puppies. Rasmus has signed several of them, in proud crayon capitals.

A door is thrown wide open somewhere in the building. Ida turns to look and sees Gustaf crossing the room, striding angrily towards the exit. He doesn't even notice her.

G! she wants to cry out, but she chokes it back.

G! G! Please, G, look at meee! May I lick your shoes, pleease, G!

He sees her and stops.

'What next? Have you joined this outfit, too?'

He seems disgusted. Ida is at a loss for words. She has never seen him so furious.

'No, I...I just kept Erik company.'

Her voice sounds small and feeble. She hates it, clears her

throat and rather pointedly slaps her chest, as if to suggest that she has caught a cold.

'What happened?' she asks.

Gustaf glances in the direction he just came from. Rickard is standing in the doorway. He waves to Erik and Robin to get them to come along. Before Rickard shuts the door behind them, he smiles at Gustaf, then gives him a thumbs-up.

'Fucking bastard,' Gustaf mutters.

'What's going on?'

'He said something about Rebecka...' Gustaf stops, shakes his head. 'I can't talk to you about this.'

'Why can't you?'

He looks at her with a tired expression on his face.

'Because you're you,' he says before disappearing out into the street.

Ida looks after him. She must not run after him, must not cling to his leg, must not allow herself to be dragged along the streets of Engelsfors until he answers the question that has now taken over all of her being.

And what is wrong with me?

WHAT IS WRONG WITH ME?

Erik calls her name. She blinks the tears away before she turns to face him.

'Look, we're going to do some stuff,' Erik says. 'We'll be a bit late. You'd probably better go home now.'

'What are you going to do?'

'Just go home. We'll meet up tomorrow.'

She doesn't want to go home. Just the thought of being alone makes her panic. She doesn't know how to cope. Rejected twice, first by the love of her life, now by her boyfriend. Ida has never felt less like a winner.

'Can't I come along, too?'

'Only specially selected members are allowed.'

Part Three

Ida recognizes the look on Erik's face. That is exactly how he looked that time in elementary school when she handed him the scissors and he cut off Elias's hair. And later, when she gave him the password to Anna-Karin's social media account and together they wrote all sorts of things on her wall. She has observed Erik in this mood many times. It has always filled her with expectation, with the irresistible excitement of watching someone who is about to go too far.

Now for the first time his expression frightens her.

And, then, suddenly, she senses it.

The magic.

It wasn't here a moment ago, but now it sweeps around the room, rippling back and forth between the walls.

There is a witch somewhere in the building. A powerful witch.

Ida looks around.

'Who's here?' she asks.

'Rickard, Robin, Julia, Felicia...Helena and Krister are supposed to be upstairs, I think. I don't know of anybody else. Why do you ask?'

Ida feels the hairs on her arms stand on end, shivers run down her back and her chest, up across her neck and face. As if a fever has rushed into every part of her body in a few seconds. Around her, the air starts to sparkle.

'What's the matter?' Erik asks and reaches out for her.

Even before he touches her jacket, a small white flash of lightning shoots through the air. He nearly screams.

'Ouch, shit! You gave me a shock.'

The ceiling lights start going on and off, then the electricity supply fails altogether. The room goes completely dark and, outside, the street lights go off.

'Fucking hell, not again,' Erik groans.

The magic in the room has vanished as suddenly as it arrived.

'Erik!' Rickard calls from the room next door.

'I've got to go,' Erik says.

'Hang on.'

Ida wants to beg him not to do whatever it is they're planning.

'Don't do anything I wouldn't do,' she says, trying to sound light-hearted.

Erik laughs a little.

'I promise,' he says and leaves her alone in the dark.

CHAPTER 50

Minoo strikes a match and lights the array of tea lights on her desk. The power cuts have come and gone since the autumn and she has become used to them, almost grown fond of the sudden dark. She likes the stillness. The silence. But this time, the thought of the phone call she has to make kills any coziness stone dead.

Tonight, she's got to speak to Linnéa about Vanessa. This is the best opportunity, before the ritual, which must be before the trial.

Or does she really have to make the call?

I can give it a miss, she thinks and blows out the match. Not my problem, really.

But every individual problem in the group could become the problem of the entire group, she answers herself. And, if I were Linnéa … wouldn't I want to know? After all, *I* was angry when *she* didn't tell me that she could read *my* thoughts.

Minoo picks up her phone. And hesitates again. How is she supposed to know what Linnéa wants? Would it be better not to? Maybe this call will just make things worse?

No. This is her cowardly self talking. Also, there is another good reason for phoning. The most important one. Linnéa sounded desperate. And Minoo cares about her.

Her phone rings as she holds it. Ida's name glows on the screen and she feels relieved, as if given a brief respite.

'Hello?'

'It's me,' Ida says breathlessly. 'I was in the center just minutes ago and this thing happened.'

'Why were you—' Minoo begins, but Ida interrupts her.

'Yes, I know, but listen, don't yell at me now. It was the first time and the last. I'll never go there again.'

Ida is panting as she speaks. It sounds as if she's running.

'What happened?'

'Magic. Strong magic. The ceiling lights went on the fritz and then there was another goddamn power cut and now I have to walk home alone in the goddamn fucking awful dark.'

'Do you know who—'

'No. Don't you think I'd say if I did?' Ida snaps.

A witch in the Positive Engelsfors Center. Are they right in their suspicions? Have they been right all along? Is Helena the one the demons have blessed, the human being charged with helping to bring on the apocalypse? Or is it Krister? Or maybe someone else?

It could of course have been an ordinary witch, Minoo thinks. The species seems pretty over-represented in this town.

'Hello?' Ida says shrilly. 'Are you still there?'

'Yes, yes. I'm here. But listen, we need to concentrate on the trial now,' Minoo says. 'We can't fight two enemies at the same time.'

A sound in the phone, almost a sob.

'Is everything all right, Ida?' Minoo asks.

'What a fucking marvelous life!' Ida says. 'How I simply adore my wonderful rich life! My family, my boyfriend and all my friends have joined a demonic sect!'

Minoo almost corrects Ida, by telling her it might not be a demonic sect, just an ordinary one. But she suspects it would hardly make Ida feel any happier.

'Hello?' Ida says again. 'You're not ending the call, are you?'

'Well, no...'

'So...I'll soon be home,' Ida puffs. 'If we could just keep talking a little longer...'

'Of course. About what?'

'Not a clue. Just not the end of the world.'

'Ida,' Minoo says and knows the moment she begins that she will regret saying this. 'You know you have friends who are not members of PE. We could be your friends. If you only...'

'If I only...what? Why is it just me who's supposed to change all the time? Why is everyone complaining about me? What's actually wrong with me?'

'Maybe it would be a good idea to find out,' Minoo replies quietly.

Ida says nothing. Her panting is the only sound.

'I'm home now,' she says in the end.

Minoo hears her unlock a door.

'See you later,' Ida says and ends the call.

Minoo hangs on to the phone. Might as well deal with the next awkward call straight away

Ingrid comes out from the storeroom at the back carrying two hurricane lamps. She puts them on the counter in front of Linnéa. And then laughs a little.

'You look so funny,' she says.

Linnéa glances sideways at her.

'I guess so,' she says.

She's standing near the register, putting a few invoices into a folder in the light of a flashlight that she keeps squashed between her chin and her shoulder.

Ingrid stops in front of a mirror set in a frame made of corks from wine bottles.

'Typical, isn't it,' she says. 'Just when we'd decided to organize the storeroom at last. And there's no way of telling when the power will be back on. You don't have to stay. We can keep going tomorrow.'

'It's fine, I'll stay.'

Ingrid lets down her long white hair, then twists it and pins it up in a bun at the back of her head.

'You're a stubborn one, you are,' she says.

Maybe so, Linnéa thinks.

But above all, she doesn't like the idea of setting out into the darkness just yet. Or being alone for any longer than absolutely necessary on a night like this. Her body has been uncomfortably tense ever since she left school today. She's kept looking over her shoulder. Jumped at the slightest sound.

Ingrid walks over to one of the 'bargain shelves' and picks up a troll made of pine cones.

'Oh, dear, how long have you been standing around?' she asks the troll. 'Doesn't anybody want you? What do you think, time to throw you in the bin?'

She blows some of the dust off the gloomy little cone-creature and puts it back where it came from. It's safe enough on its shelf. Linnéa knows that Ingrid can't ever bring herself to get rid of anything.

'Didn't you want that white lace fabric that was just delivered?' Ingrid asks. 'With those stains it will never sell and you dye everything black anyway.'

'Thanks,' Linnéa says. 'Love it.'

It is utterly mysterious how Ingrid keeps the shop going since there are hardly ever any customers. Rumor has it that she lives off a big inheritance after her husband, who won a serious sum of money on a lottery ticket, died. The story is that Ingrid's adult children don't want to know about her any more. And that she was one of the steady visitors to the secret swingers' club in Lilla Lugnet before the house burned down.

But all Linnéa needs and wants to know about Ingrid is that she has always treated her well.

A piercing signal cuts the silence and Linnéa is so startled she drops the torch. It bounces on the counter, falls to the floor. And goes dark.

'Christ Almighty,' Ingrid says. 'Whoever is calling at this time?'

Linnéa lifts the receiver of the old-fashioned telephone on the wall.

'Ingrid's Hidey-hole.'

No response.

'Hello?' she says.

The line goes dead.

Linnéa looks at Ingrid and shrugs.

The next moment there is a ringtone from Linnéa's bag. She swears, starts rummaging. Her phone stops and then starts again just as she picks it up. It's Minoo. What new shit has hit the fan?

'Has something happened?' Linnéa says immediately.

'Yes, it has,' Minoo replies.

'Was it you who phoned the shop just now?'

'What shop?'

Linnéa sighs.

'Never mind.'

She looks apologetically at Ingrid, picks up one of the hurricane lamps and goes through to the storeroom as she listens to Minoo starting to tell her about Ida's evening in the center.

'I can't say it's a surprise,' Linnéa says when Minoo reaches the end of the story. 'But what you said is right. We must wait. One evil power at a time.'

'But there's something else,' Minoo says.

'Ah?'

Linnéa absently examines a table cluttered with collectors' china plates decorated with pictures of European royalty.

'Can't you come here?' Minoo says. 'When the power is off the newspaper office goes crazy and Dad doesn't come home for hours. So we'd be on our own. If you can make it, that is. It would be great if you could come.'

Linnéa can't think what Minoo might want, but she sounds really upset.

'Right, I'll come,' she says. 'As soon as I can.'

Linnéa plays the flashlight over the front of Minoo's house and confirms that it looks exactly the way she had imagined it. A large, detached villa on two floors. Several tall trees that lean protectively over the neat garden.

She goes rigid for a moment when she hears the rat-ta-tat of a moped engine start up on the road behind her. She thought she heard the same sound when she came out of Ingrid's Hidey-hole. Is somebody following her?

You're just paranoid, she tells herself. Let go.

A last drag on her cigarette. She throws it away and goes along to ring the doorbell.

Minoo opens the door.

'Come in.'

She's holding a four-armed candlestick. The candle flames flicker in the wind.

Linnéa steps inside, pulls off her coat of leopard-patterned fake fur and hangs it up among all the dark coats and jackets on the hall stand. Seemingly, the entire Falk Karimi family have the same boring taste in clothes.

Minoo leads the way into the living room. A pale brown teapot, two matching cups and saucers, sugar and milk, are set

out on the table by the sofa. Two kinds of cookies on a plate.
Lit candles everywhere. Whatever this is all about, clearly it
isn't so bad that Minoo was put off organizing a tea party.

Linnéa sits down on the sofa, scans the room.

It looks tasteful, impeccable. Nice, but anxiously restrained.
Only the books are likely to tell you something about the
personalities of the people who live here.

Minoo pours tea for two.

'I'm not sure how to tell you this,' Minoo says as she
pushes a cup across.

She sits down on the sofa, too, and turns to Linnéa.

'Do you remember when Vanessa could suddenly hear
you inside her head? The time Max held you prisoner in the
dining area?'

'Yes,' Linnéa says.

She cautiously sips her tea. Tries not to show how nervous
this is making her.

'You didn't know that you did it, right? That you sort of
cried out to her?'

'No, I didn't. Why are you asking about this?'

Minoo bites her lip.

'It happened again. This Monday. But it was me who heard
you this time. Heard your thought, that is.'

Linnéa almost spills the tea.

'Impossible,' she says. 'You must have imagined it.'

It is impossible, she repeats inwardly.

Surely it is? That time, with Max, she was so desperate, so
certain she would die.

'You thought about Vanessa,' Minoo says. 'You were
thinking that you…that she…'

Linnéa puts her cup down on the table with a bang. Tea
splashes onto the saucer.

'Linnéa…' Minoo says.

Fire

Linnéa gets up. Her heart thumps against her chest wall, so hard it will break her ribs any time now.

'I need to go home,' she says.

So, this is what it feels like when someone reads your mind. No wonder the others felt so awful when they found out about her magic power.

'Please, don't go,' Minoo says. 'You need to talk about this.'

'I need to do nothing,' Linnéa replies and walks into the hall, fumbling in the dark to find her fake fur coat.

Minoo catches up with her and grabs her arm.

'I truly believe you need to talk. Just like when you told me last spring that I had to tell someone about the black smoke. And you were right. What I'm trying to say is, I understand if you don't want to talk to me about Vanessa, but you must talk to somebody. Open up to someone. If you don't, it might bubble out of your head again.'

Linnéa can hardly follow all this because Minoo is speaking so quickly.

'Next time, maybe it'll be Vanessa who hears your thoughts,' Minoo continues. 'Is that really the way you want her to find out?'

'I don't want her to find out at all!' Linnéa snarls.

'Why not?'

'Because I haven't got a chance!'

The words hang in the air between them. Silent, they face each other in the dark hall.

'Shall we go back and sit down again?' Minoo suggests.

The tea has cooled down long ago, when Minoo swallows the last mouthful in her cup. She tries to look as if she doesn't think what Linnéa has just told her is strange in the slightest.

In fact, she doesn't think it is. But it's weird that Linnéa has told her any of this. Now, Minoo isn't sure how she should deal with this huge confession. This is a fragile moment. She feels awkward and is worried that Linnéa might misunderstand.

'What I don't get is, how can you bear listening to all this,' Linnéa says and rubs her forehead.

She is avoiding Minoo's eyes.

'I asked you,' Minoo says.

'Perhaps you got more than you asked for. I need a smoke now.'

'I'll come with you.'

Minoo picks up a couple of blankets and an ashtray and they go outside to sit on the front steps. Just as they settle down, the street lamps whir for a moment and start up again. The lamps inside the house also come on and the windows create lit rectangles on the grass. The mist is crawling out of the ground.

'You want one?' Linnéa says and waves the packet of cigarettes at Minoo.

'No, thanks.'

'I guessed,' Linnéa says with a grin.

'Nice of you to keep reminding me of what a wholesome person I am,' Minoo says and smiles back.

Linnéa lights her cigarette and inhales deeply.

'Not all that wholesome. You seduced a teacher, for instance.'

'And was punished for it,' Minoo points out. Linnéa laughs.

Their eyes meet and Minoo feels a sudden, overwhelming wave of warmth for Linnéa.

'Thank you for telling me,' Linnéa says seriously.

'I know what it's like to love somebody and not be able to mention it to anyone. Thank your lucky stars you've got better taste than me.'

Linnéa laughs a little again.

'Not usually, believe you me. You'd weep if you saw my list of exes. It's so typical that when I care for someone who makes sense, she doesn't want me. I've got to try to stop falling in love. For my own good.'

'Good luck,' Minoo says ironically.

It slips off her tongue so naturally and then, abruptly, she has to look away.

Good luck.

That's what Rebecka said, that autumn day when they met in the fairground. Same words, same ironic tone, when Minoo had said she would stop loving Max.

'Hello?' Linnéa says. 'Where did you disappear to?'

'I was just reminded of Rebecka,' Minoo says.

Linnéa looks searchingly at her.

'A shame I never got to know her better,' she says. 'And it's a shame, too, that you never got to know Elias. He would have liked you.'

Surely there can't be a better compliment, coming from Linnéa.

'I knew him, just for a few seconds. The time I liberated him from Max.'

Linnéa nods.

Minoo thinks about the child Elias, a classmate of hers in elementary school. It is only a faint memory. His hair, so blonde it was almost white, and the look in his eyes, always on his guard, that he kept throughout life.

Linnéa stubs her cigarette out and gets up.

'I'd better go home now.'

She folds the blanket she had wrapped herself in and hands it to Minoo.

'Are you absolutely sure that you know what Vanessa feels?' Minoo asks. 'She always comes across as if she likes you very much.'

'She does, I suppose, but as a friend. And you must have noticed that she likes men *very, very* much.'

'Perhaps it simply hasn't dawned on her yet.'

'I don't want to hope for anything,' Linnéa says. 'Then it hurts even more.'

Minoo nods. She knows exactly what Linnéa means. On the other hand, she isn't so sure that Linnéa is right about Vanessa.

CHAPTER 51

When Linnéa is nearly back in her part of town, she feels so tired she's almost sleepwalking.

But it is the right kind of tiredness. A load is lifted off her mind and, for the first time, she understands how heavy a burden the secrecy about her feelings for Vanessa has been.

The fog has swallowed up a large part of Linnéa's apartment block. It looks as if it is rising up from among the clouds. Someone in the area is throwing a party. The music is very loud, hard and aggressive. The sound echoes between the walls and grows more intense the closer Linnéa gets. She even recognizes the tune now, Elias used to like it.

At the front door, she hears the sound of glass breaking above her. Fragments are raining down from the sky. She just manages to wrap her arms protectively around her head when the largest shards hit the ground just next to her.

It must be that bunch of total idiots who've made Diana give her hell.

Linnéa tugs the door open. The music fills the entire stairwell, bouncing off the walls as she steps into the elevator. As it crawls upwards, she checks each landing through its window, trying to work out where the party is being held.

The music comes closer. The heavy beat thumps so hard that Linnéa's heart seems to follow the rhythm.

The elevator chugs past the fifth floor. Sixth. On the seventh floor, the music is howling at her. And she realizes where it is coming from.

Someone is in her apartment.

She isn't frightened but her fury is overpowering. A jerk as the elevator stops, a click from the automatic lock. Linnéa throws the door open and runs to the landing.

Her apartment is definitely the source. She pushes the door handle down, but the door is locked. She finds the keys, unlocks it with shaking hands.

She steps inside the hall. The music is so loud it makes her ears hurt. She stumbles on an empty bottle, picks up the stench of alcohol. Walks into the living room.

The sofa cover has been slashed all over and cream-colored stuffing bulges from the tears. All her pictures have been torn down, scrunched up, ripped to pieces. The lamps have been knocked over but are still on. Bathed in their blood-red light, Erik stands in front of the broken windows. He has a baseball bat in his hands.

Erik.

Splinters of glass glitter all over his black sweater. He looks straight at her.

You fucking cunt.

The hatred in his thought paralyzes her. And transforms her fury into fear.

Now, two guys, no, three, are entering from the bedroom and the kitchen. Kevin stares emptily at her. He seems almost in shock. Robin and Rickard pull balaclavas down over their faces, but she has seen them already and they know it. Their panic-stricken thoughts rush into her head.

Fuck it, where did she come from?
It's fucked up. We're in deep shit now.
Got to deal with it ... deal with it ...

We should've kept the balaclavas on, I should've stood guard, why don't they ever listen to me...

Erik's grip on the baseball bat tightens and he smiles at her. Kevin's terror is almost as palpable as Linnéa's own.

No, no, no, he's totally lost it, he's sick...

Rickard screams something, but Erik pulls the balaclava down over his face and starts walking towards her and her paralysis won't lift, she stands there as if frozen stiff even though panic is burning inside her body. She meets Robin's eyes and registers that he is making up his mind, that he will side with Erik.

We've got no choice. We've got no fucking choice.

Erik raises the baseball bat and at last, at last the world starts to turn. And she can control her body.

Linnéa runs from the apartment, slams the door behind her and turns the key in the lock before she starts down the stairs. Opening the lock from inside the apartment takes a special twist. It might gain her a few extra seconds.

She runs downstairs two steps at a time, holding her hand close to the handrail, terrified of slipping.

The music roars in the stairwell and her own footsteps echo against the concrete, she can't hear if someone is closing in. But suddenly Erik's thought is there.

That bitch won't get away!

Third floor. Second. First. Any time now, a kick in the back or a push between the shoulder blades, a crash as the baseball bat slams into her skull.

The thought fills her with such dread that she takes half the last flight in one long leap and when the soles of her boots slap loudly against the green concrete floor, she stumbles and drops her bag.

... I'll kill you, you fucking slut, you cunt, I'll fucking kill you ...

Part Three

She throws herself against the street door. A rush of cool night air. She runs into the mist. Now she can hear their steps behind her. The adrenalin is like fuel flowing through her veins and she runs faster than ever before in her life.

Robin thinks the whole thing has gone completely off the rails and he'll never do anything Erik says ever again, he'll never...He is afraid now, afraid of what will happen if they don't catch her, afraid of what will happen if they do.

Erik has stopped thinking altogether. He is hunting, that's all.

Linnéa runs into Storvall Park, crossing the damp lawns in the hope that the mist will hide her. Robin is somewhere off-course behind her, on her right, Erik somewhere on her left.

She leaves the park and carries on running down the abandoned Engelsfors streets.

'Fucking...bitch,' Erik pants behind her and his voice sounds close, far too close.

'Help!'

She screams with lungs that have little air left.

No one responds. Engelsfors is a silent creature, indifferently observing passing events. And her phone is inside the bag she dropped in the stairwell.

She screams again. Wordlessly this time. She sees the light from a TV screen in an apartment but no one comes to the window when she cries out and she must keep running, running.

Anna-Karin's house isn't far from here, but Robin could simply cut her off before she gets there. And even if she does reach the front door...what if it's locked?

No alternative, only running. Straight ahead.

A taste of blood in her mouth.

Linnéa runs.

Fire

*

Anna-Karin is sitting on the bed in her room. She senses the soft bulk of the mattress, the tightness of the stretched elastic in the waistband of her pajama bottoms, but she is seeing through the eyes of the fox. Hidden in the mist, they have dared to sneak up close to the illuminated facade of the manor house.

Several cars are parked on the graveled area in front of the house. Over the last few days, a steady stream of strangers has been arriving. Anna-Karin wishes she could see what's going on in there, behind the closed shutters.

She senses, too, how alert the fox is to the voles. They are puttering around by the overgrown shrubbery and his wish to hunt them is so strong it feels like her own.

Later, she promises him. *Later.*

Obediently, the fox stays put.

The doors open and Viktor comes out on the front steps. He walks down and across the driveway. Kicks at the gravel. Stops, and bends to inspect one of his shoes.

And suddenly straightens up again, as if he has heard something not even the fox's sensitive ears could pick up. Viktor shuts his eyes and seems to pull himself together before going back inside, shutting the door behind him.

All is quiet again.

Anna-Karin allows the fox to pad away towards the bushes to chase his dinner.

Linnéa feels that a heart attack is a certainty. Her heart cannot possibly keep beating at this rate for very much longer. She presses herself against the bridge support, covers her mouth with both hands and tries to breathe as quietly as she can although her body is screaming for oxygen.

The only sound is the faint slapping of canal water. She

can no longer hear Erik and Robin's thoughts and has no strength left to try to tune them in. All her energy is going into staying upright.

Above her head, the green-painted metal of the bridge swoops over the canal. Across the water, the lights of the manor house are gleaming through the mist.

Maybe she should try to get there. Seek protection in the enemy camp.

Canal Bridge is illuminated, but the mist is growing denser. She must risk it. Linnéa's whole body is shaking now. She is afraid of fainting. If they find her here, she's got no hope.

She looks around one last time and concentrates on listening into the darkness. Then she allows herself a few deep breaths and starts clambering up the slope. Thin branches scratch her face as she makes her way through the bushes. The ground is wet and slippery under her ankle boots. It smells of damp earth.

Linnéa's arms are trembling with the strain as she hauls herself up the last bit. She straightens up on shaky legs, stands bent forward in the poison-yellow light of the street lamps. Then she runs out on the bridge, into the bright light.

She knows that she has reached the top of the arch when the slight rise flattens out. Halfway. She must make it. Must.

Caught! She's so fucking caught!

Linnéa stops abruptly when she hears the thought in her head. She turns and sees through the mist the outline of a guy walking towards her. Holding a baseball bat.

So fucking caught!

She turns again and sees another shape materializing out of the haze on the other side of the bridge. Robin. She can hear his breathing in the distance, but he isn't running any more. He is walking, as calmly as Erik. They aren't bothered now, certain that she can't get away from them.

Their staring eyes gleam from the eye-holes in their bala-clavas. The fuckers. The cowardly fuckers. She won't show them how afraid she is.

'Hi there, Linnéa,' Erik says.

'Fuck off,' she says.

He laughs a little, lets the baseball bat drag on the ground as he walks. It rattles heavily against the asphalt, jumps and bounces over the uneven bits.

'This wasn't the idea from the start,' he says. 'You weren't supposed to come home that early. We thought whores like you worked all night. But it's fine by us. This is even *better*.'

They stop and stand on either side of her. Linnéa tries to run across the bridge. But Robin gets hold of her. Grabbing both her arms, he drags her towards Erik who waits calmly by the railing of the bridge.

'Fuck's sake, Linnéa, you're so boring,' he says. 'I thought you'd like a good time.'

Linnéa yells when Erik tugs at her bangs. The pain makes her eyes fill with tears. He bends her neck back and looks into her eyes.

'Aren't you frightened?'

'No,' she says.

She doesn't want to scream, but when he pulls her hair again the pain is too sharp. Suddenly, she hears Robin's thoughts perfectly clearly.

Let this be over, just let it stop, let it stop ...

'Robin, please let me go,' Linnéa whispers hoarsely. 'Let go of me, please, Robin...'

She hates herself for pleading and begging. But Robin hesitates. Erik sees it, too.

He raises the baseball bat.

'Jump in,' he says and nods his head towards the railing of the bridge.

Part Three

*

A white flash of lightning cuts through Anna-Karin's dream and she sits up in bed.

She is with the fox again. He is running along the canal with all his attention focused on the bridge. Three human shapes are standing on the top of the bridge, strongly lit but still unrecognizable in the mist. The fox's ears record their voices.

'Jump,' one of them says and Anna-Karin instantly recognizes Erik's voice. 'Or we'll throw you in.'

'Come on, I mean, seriously,' says another voice.

Robin's.

'*Come on, I mean, seriously,*' Erik imitates him. 'Be a man, you wimp. You hate this slut as much as I do.'

'Let me go, Robin, please, Robin,' Linnéa begs.

Linnéa.

Anna-Karin leaps out of bed. Police. Make an emergency call. Must stop this. She gets hold of her cell but holds back in mid-movement. What if they trace the call? How can she explain that she can see what is happening so far away? Perhaps they won't believe a word she says?

'You heard me. Jump,' Erik says. 'I thought all you psychos wanted to kill yourselves anyway. Here's your chance.'

He swings some heavy object through the air and Linnéa screams.

Anna-Karin pulls on a pair of jeans under her pajama top and runs into the hall, pushes her feet into a pair of worn sneakers, while Erik pulls Linnéa out of Robin's grip and presses her up against the railing.

'Someone should fuck you first but we'd rather not catch AIDS.'

Anna-Karin can't see what he does, but Linnéa screams again.

'I'll jump. I'll do it.'

'Fuck's sake, Erik…' Robin says.

Help her, Robin, Anna-Karin thinks. Why don't you help her!

She runs out on the square. The lights are on in the Positive Engelsfors place, but she can't see anyone inside. The telephone box is just around the corner. She grabs the receiver.

Part of her is not there, but watching by the canal. She has to blink several times before she can see the buttons well enough to dial.

Linnéa is sobbing, but she swings one leg across the railing and sits astride it.

'Please…'

Linnéa's eyes are fixed on Robin, but he looks the other way.

'Just do it,' he says hoarsely.

'That's right. Just do it, Linnéa,' Erik says.

Linnéa swings her other leg over the railing. Now she stands on the very edge of the bridge, holding on to the railing.

A female voice says, 'Emergency Services' in the receiver and Anna-Karin nearly shouts the words.

'You must send someone to Canal Bridge in Engelsfors! Erik Forslund and Robin Zetterqvist…they're trying to kill Linnéa Wallin!'

Linnéa looks down at the black water. If she survives the fall, the cold will get her anyway. She looks up at Erik and Robin. She hates them and hates the thought that these two are her last sight in life. Still, she forces herself to meet their eyes.

And then she jumps.

She falls. Falls and falls, hoping that Elias will be there for her on the other side.

Her only regret is that she never told Vanessa what she feels for her.

Why did that scare me so much? she thinks.

When Linnéa finally hits the water, the cold is such a shock that it knocks out all thought. And then she disappears under the surface, into the dark, silent depths.

CHAPTER 52

Vanessa is dreaming and she knows it. But still the dream feels utterly real.

She is trying to find Linnéa's apartment block, but wanders lost along streets she doesn't recognize. She tries to phone Linnéa, or one of the other Chosen Ones. Even Wille. But all the numbers are wiped off her phone list and she can't remember a single one.

And something makes the ground shake.

As if some force deep underneath is trying to find a way up. Crushing layers of rock, breaking through the asphalt.

Vanessa wakes. Her phone is vibrating on the floor beside her bed. She reaches out for it.

'Hello,' she says, her voice thick with sleep.

'Something has happened,' Anna-Karin says.

Vanessa can see the blue lights through the mist. They are blinking silently near Canal Bridge. People are milling around everywhere. All in uniform. Firefighters. Police. Paramedics. Beams from powerful flashlights slice through the dark along the banks and a large searchlight on the bridge is scanning the water.

Vanessa speeds up her run when she spots Minoo and Anna-Karin on the footpath.

'Where is she?' she asks as soon as she comes within speaking distance.

'We don't know,' Anna Karin replies quietly.

Minoo only shakes her head.

'I've tried to pick up her energy,' Anna-Karin continues. 'But I can't…locate her.'

'Ida, what about her? Where is Ida?' Vanessa says. 'Perhaps she can—'

'Her phone's off,' Minoo interrupts. 'We've tried to get hold of her, but—'

'Try her again!'

'No point,' Minoo says but makes the call anyway. She puts her phone down almost at once. 'I just get her voicemail.'

Vanessa shuts her eyes. Changes her mind's setting until she can sense the energies of the others. It works well. She registers Anna-Karin and Minoo clearly, but she can't find any trace of Linnéa in the night that surrounds them.

Among them all, Linnéa was the one she found most easily during their training sessions.

If she can't register her, then Linnéa is nowhere near.

Or else, only her body remains.

Vanessa opens her eyes. She attempts to force the visions out of her mind, images of Linnéa's pale face, her skin tinged with blue, her black hair waving in currents deep below the surface.

She must be strong. For Linnéa's sake. As long as there is a chance left she must not allow herself to break down.

If Linnéa has managed to haul herself out of the canal, she will be soaked and frozen. They have to find her. Find her *now*.

Vanessa looks towards the bridge. Nicke is not in sight. But close by the police car, a dark-haired, uniformed woman is standing guard. Paula.

'What do they know?' Vanessa asks. 'Have you talked to them?'

'No, we can't really tell them that we know because a fox saw it,' Minoo says. 'Anna-Karin made an anonymous call. Just named Linnéa and told them that she was forced to jump in. And that it was Erik and Robin who...who made her.'

Vanessa almost vomits at the sound of their names.

'I want to kill them,' she says bleakly. 'I *will* kill them.'

Minoo doesn't reply. She seems to hesitate, just for a moment. Then she puts her arms around Vanessa.

Vanessa reacts instantly. She sobs. The desire to let it all pour out is almost irresistible and she twists herself free.

'I mustn't,' she says. 'I mustn't...you see, it feels as if Linnéa really is dead...if I let go.'

She falls silent.

'I understand,' Minoo says.

Vanessa checks the police car again.

'Wait here,' she says and runs off before the others have time to say anything.

Paula catches sight of her, but doesn't seem to know who she is.

'Have you found her?' Vanessa asks.

'Was it you who raised the alarm?'

'No. I was just told...a girl had ended up in the canal. Is there any chance that she ...?'

Vanessa can't formulate the rest of her question.

'We're waiting for the divers. The fire brigade is sending a team, but it will be some time before it gets here,' Paula says. 'And we're looking for her on land as well. Hopefully she's managed to get up on the bank somewhere. We haven't given up hope.'

But Paula's tone of voice belies her words. And Vanessa looks down at the canal. On the black, cold water far down there.

She wants to scream. Scream until this nightmare has been ripped apart and she is back in reality, a reality that encompasses a living Linnéa, safe and sound.

Because that's what it is, right? It has to be a nightmare. Linnéa is fine, she must be. She *must*.

After all they have been through together, it simply can't be *Erik Forslund* and *Robin Zetterqvist* who ...

Vanessa walks away. Concentrates on counting her steps, one at a time, so she won't collapse.

'What did they say?' Minoo asks when she is back with them.

Vanessa can't reply. That scream is growing stronger inside her, tries to force its way up through her throat.

Her phone rings inside her jacket pocket. She pulls it out. *Unknown number.*

'Hello?' Vanessa says.

Time stretches into an eternal instant.

'It's me,' Linnéa says.

Vanessa can't utter a word.

'Hello? Vanessa?'

'Where are you?' she manages to make herself say at last.

'I've just come back home.'

Vanessa can't hold her tears back now.

'I thought you...' she sobs. 'I thought you...'

Minoo tugs at her jacket.

'Is it her?' she whispers and Vanessa nods.

'How do you...' Linnéa begins to say.

'Anna-Karin's fox saw what happened,' Vanessa says. 'Everyone's mobilized now, they're looking for you. I'm so unbelievably hugely glad you're alive. I...' She bursts into tears again, crying so hard she has to crouch. 'Are you sure you're all right?'

'Yes, I am,' Linnéa says and her voice sounds shaky. 'I'm

fine. Vanessa...Forgive me. I didn't know that you knew, that anyone knew. I should've phoned straight away, but...'

Vanessa can't talk any more, she is crying too much. She hands the phone to Minoo, who carries on speaking with Linnéa.

Linnéa is alive. She is alive.

CHAPTER 53

Linnéa hands Viktor his phone and walks ahead of him into her apartment.

First, the hall, where broken glass crunches under her feet, then the living room. She looks around.

The torn-down images rustle in the draught from the broken windows. The cross that Elias gave her is broken in two and the black china panther has ended up on the floor with its head cracked. She walks into the bedroom. The mattress has been tipped on to the floor, her clothes have been torn out of the wardrobe and scattered everywhere. Someone must have stomped on the laptop that was a gift from Ulf and Tina. The sewing machine has been opened up and systematically dismantled. And the contents of her memory boxes are spread all over the floor. Pictures, letters, mementos. Her entire past has been turned inside out. Rummaged in. Torn. Ruined.

But she is alive.

As she was sinking through the black water, something happened.

At first, with spasms in arms and legs, she was swept along by the currents below the surface. Her body struggled to survive and the breathing reflex grew so strong that it would soon open her mouth and pull water into her lungs.

But instead something new awoke inside her.

Linnéa had tried to influence water before, to make it

freeze or evaporate. It never worked. But down there in the canal, the energy started to stream out from her body and form a protective, warming shell around her. Like a kind of magic wetsuit. Suddenly, she was able to kick out with her legs. Her arms made breaststrokes, she seemed to be sucked upwards, as if she were buoyant like a cork, made not to sink.

When she broke through the surface and inhaled the cold night air, endorphins poured into her circulation. Then the cold settled over her face like a mask of ice.

Somehow, she got up on the bank. Coughed until she threw up. Every breath felt like icy needles piercing her lungs.

She crawled up the steep slope, her water-filled, heavy boots slipping on the wet mud and her stiff, cold fingers clawing to find purchase. And then, finally, she collapsed in a heap on the asphalt footpath.

It was Viktor's thought that returned her to consciousness. *Linnéa? What happened?*

Linnéa opened her eyes and couldn't make sense of the world as she saw it. She was lying on her side and her field of vision included only asphalt and a pair of legs in dark slacks, seen from a completely wrong angle.

Viktor bent over her, wrapped her in his coat and took her ice-cold hands in his. She could feel his magic streaming into her. It turned the water in her clothes and hair into vapor that rose around them. She was drying so fast she could watch it happen.

Come along.

He helped her up and half dragged, half carried her to his car which was parked in front of the manor house. She sank into the passenger seat, he shut the doors and turned the heater setting into the widest red band on the scale.

Linnéa pulled his coat closer around her. Slowly, her body relaxed and with relaxation came a deeply soothing tiredness.

What happened? Viktor asked inside her head.

They forced me to jump in, she replied, amazed at how easy it was to communicate like this.

Forced you? Who were they?

'Erik Forslund. Robin Zetterqvist.'

She almost slurred. Watched as Viktor pulled out his phone. Then she sat up and made herself come awake.

'Don't call the police,' she said.

'Of course we must.'

'I can promise you, here and now, these guys will have alibis. I heard their thoughts. Erik would never have risked doing it if he hadn't made sure that he wouldn't get caught. In the end, it will be my word against theirs.'

Viktor looked thoughtfully at her.

'You must know who the police tend to believe,' Linnéa went on. 'Hardly ever people like me, not in this town anyway.'

He put his phone away.

'Why did they do it?'

'They've hated me forever,' Linnéa said. 'They hate everyone who's different. Only, now they have a whole organization supporting them. I'm quite certain they did what they did because someone had told them to. But the plan probably wasn't meant to go this far.'

'Whose idea do you think it was?'

'I don't want to discuss that.'

Viktor was drumming with his fingers against the steering wheel.

'I'll have to ask Alexander if I really can omit calling the police,' he said. 'Still, I have a feeling he won't object. The Council's official position is, whenever possible, to avoid confrontations with the non-magic community.'

'So you usually don't intervene when someone tries to murder a witch?' Linnéa asked and managed to stop herself from going on to ask if perhaps it was just the Chosen Ones who didn't matter one way or the other.

Viktor glanced at her.

'Wait here while I get you some dry things to wear. Then I'll drive you back.'

Now, Linnéa stands here, in rolled-up sweatpants, a much-too-large woolly sweater and a pair of too-tight sneakers that belongs to someone she doesn't know.

Linnéa shuts her eyes. Doesn't want to see any more of the chaos that surrounds her.

The police are due any minute and Diana will hear all about it tomorrow morning. And Linnéa will be evicted and lose her independence. Has Helena intended this all along? Because it must be her who is behind this.

But Linnéa has no intention of giving in that easily. She opens her eyes again and begins to pick up the empty beer cans that have been thrown about in the room. Her thigh hurts where Erik hit her with the baseball bat. When she changed in the car, she saw the large purplish area spreading.

Erik. Robin.

In the car, she was curiously calm and collected. Now she feels the terror crawling all over her again, tightening her throat with its strong, slippery fingers.

She slowly sinks to the floor. The panic attack is advancing on her, booming in her head, making the room revolve, making her relive the fall. Erik wanted to break her and he succeeded.

'Linnéa?' Viktor says.

She wants to get away from herself, turn herself inside out and crawl out of her skin.

Breathe in…Breathe out…Breathe in …

'Linnéa?'

Viktor is crouching next to her, his hands are gripping her

shoulders. She concentrates on him and the panic slowly ebbs from her body. She doesn't want to lose it while he's watching.

They mustn't break me, they mustn't break me ...

She observes Viktor, who looks troubled. Then she realizes that her thought must have been projected straight into his head.

'How are you feeling now?' he asks.

'Just, you know...a fit of post-traumatic stress, that's all.'

Viktor straightens up, takes her hand and helps her up.

'Is there anything I can do for you now?'

'No, I'll fix all this.'

He looks searchingly at her.

'I trust you're not planning any kind of vendetta,' he says.

It hasn't even occurred to her. Her efforts not to crack up have consumed all her energy. That, and trying to work out how to keep her apartment. Now, Linnéa realizes that she wants Erik and Robin to pay for what they've done, but how to go about it defeats her.

'That is something the Council cannot sanction,' Viktor continues. 'The exact opposite, in fact. Alexander asked me to stress that.'

Linnéa remembers what Minoo told them about the chemistry lesson in the fall. What Viktor did to Kevin. He took revenge for a trifling annoyance.

'Of course, you always live as you preach, Viktor. Or do you?'

Viktor avoids her eyes. Prods a broken pottery bowl with the tip of his shoe.

'Alexander said that the Council will examine the events carefully. And we will not accuse you of using magic, despite the prohibition. After all, you weren't aware of what you were doing, just driven by the need to survive.'

Linnéa can only look at him.

Viktor bends and picks up the broken bowl. It had fallen on top of a sheet of paper and now Linnéa sees what it is. One of her many drawings of Vanessa. Viktor looks at it for a long while.

'You've really managed to capture something about her,' he says.

'You'd better go now,' Linnéa says as she takes the drawing from him and puts it in her pocket.

She follows him into the hall, unlocks and opens the door. The elevator is slowly coming up.

'Take care,' Viktor says.

'Thanks for all your help.'

Viktor nods and starts walking downstairs.

Linnéa senses Vanessa's energy vibrating in the air. It is coming closer and closer as the elevator creaks upwards. More faintly, in the background, she registers Anna-Karin and Minoo.

The elevator door opens.

Vanessa runs to Linnéa, throws her arms around her and hugs her suffocatingly tight. Not that it matters, Linnéa doesn't ever want to be set free. The coconut scent of Vanessa's hair is so familiar it makes her heart ache.

If she had drowned, she would never have experienced this moment. If her element hadn't been activated down there in the water. If Viktor hadn't found her. All her thoughts beginning with 'If' seem totally incomprehensible.

She ought not to be here. From now on, everything that happens is a bonus.

'I thought you'd died,' Vanessa whispers.

'So did I.'

When they see the living room, Vanessa squeezes Linnéa's hand.

'How awful. How simply fucking awful,' she says.

'Would you like to sleep at my place tonight?' Minoo asks.

'That would be great,' Linnéa replies.

'I can't get my head around all this,' Minoo says as she scans the room.

'I can,' Anna-Karin says.

Linnéa turns to her.

'I feel almost the opposite,' Anna-Karin continues. 'To me, the odd thing is that this kind of thing hasn't happened before. Erik has always been so close to crossing some boundary...He has always been the one who went the furthest. Don't you agree?'

Linnéa nods and tries to suppress another welling-up of the dread and anguish that lurks so close under her skin.

They step into the bedroom. Linnéa lets go of Vanessa's hand and picks up the photo of her mother in the park. It is crumpled but not torn.

All four jump at the hard knock on the front door. A male voice echoes in the stairwell.

'Police.'

'Damn, it's Nicke,' Vanessa says.

'Don't say a thing about the anonymous tip-off,' Linnéa says quickly. 'We have no idea. And I haven't been doing any swimming tonight.'

'What are you saying?' Vanessa asks. 'That they'll get away with it?'

Linnéa has no time to explain. She can hear the front door open.

'We're in here,' she calls, all the while looking from one to the other.

Let me do the talking. I can read his mind.

Surprised, the others stare at her when they hear her thought.

Yes, I know. Seems to be something you learn to do when you're just about to be murdered.

They troop back into the living room. Nicke enters and stares at the room with a look of distaste on his face.

Linnéa remembers when she faced him in the principal's office. She and Minoo had just found Elias's dead body. As Nicke went through his routine questions, she heard his thoughts, sensed his contempt. *Like father, like daughter. So this is the new hooligans generation in Engelsfors.*

He turns to Linnéa.

'Right, now. You seem to be alive and kicking. And you've thrown one hell of a party by the looks of it. Obviously following in your daddy's footsteps.'

He looks the rest of them over. Stops when he sees Vanessa.

'I should've guessed. You would hang out in this place.'

'There's been a break-in,' Linnéa says. 'I was just about to call the police.'

'No worries, we've been called in already. By your neighbors, for one thing. Even people in the other blocks around here.'

'I haven't been here all evening,' Linnéa says. 'I was at Minoo's house.'

Nicke produces a pad and chewed stump of a pencil.

'And when did you leave?'

'I couldn't tell you exactly. A couple of hours ago.'

'I can confirm that,' Minoo says and Nicke looks dissatisfied.

So much harder to dismiss statements made by the daughter of the editor of the *Engelsfors Herald*.

'Then what did you get up to?' he asks Linnéa.

'I was with Viktor Ehrenskiöld. He's a...friend from school. We went for a drive in his car and then he took me home.'

Part Three

It is very easy to read Nicke's thoughts. He might as well have shouted them out loud. He is recalling what was said in the talk he's just had with Erik's parents, how they confirmed that their son slept over in the Positive Engelsfors Center.

Then his thoughts shift to his visit to the center. Erik, Robin, Kevin and Rickard were there. Put up a show of innocence. Not that Nicke was looking for any kind of proof against them. On the contrary. All he wanted was to confirm that this was nothing worse than a wild bit of fun and games. And then Helena joined them and she said, sure enough, these guys had been there all night. They had been planning for the spring party and she had been sitting up late, working. If one's a night person, well, that's what one does.

'Half the neighborhood is complaining about your binge-ing,' Nicke says. 'And soon after the complaints stop flooding in, we have an anonymous tip-off that you're being pushed off Canal Bridge by a couple of guys. Guys you dislike heartily, that's well enough known. You have to agree it's a pretty peculiar story?'

'So true,' Linnéa says. 'Very peculiar.'

'This is how my thinking goes. You and your friends threw a party. It runs out of control. At some point, you decide now is the time to make life a misery for a group of poor lads you happen to hate.'

She can hear Erik's voice like an echo inside Nicke's head.

She's mentally unstable. In school, she attacked me and Robin, totally unprovoked. She is deranged and trying to pin something on us.

'It doesn't make sense, does it?' Linnéa says. 'Why should I spread the rumor that someone pushed me into the canal? It's totally easy to check, after all. What would be in it for me? And there's been no party here. I'm completely sober. Why don't you check that?'

457

'Which is what I'll do next. There's a breathalyzer in the car,' Nicke says.

Linnéa doesn't need mind-reading powers to notice his growing frustration.

'Sorry to interrupt,' Minoo says. 'Is Linnéa being charged for something?'

Nicke makes an annoyed face.

'How come you lot are here anyway?'

'I couldn't sleep,' Anna-Karin says. 'So I went out for a walk. When I was near the canal I heard someone say that Linnéa Wallin had been pushed in. I called Vanessa and Minoo. They came along straight away. We all wanted to help with the search.'

'Obviously, we tried to call Linnéa but we got no answer,' Minoo says.

'I'd left my phone at home and now it's lost,' Linnéa adds.

It's almost true. Her bag wasn't in the stairwell when she and Viktor arrived.

'Then Linnéa phoned us, using Viktor's phone,' Vanessa says. 'They'd just discovered the break-in.'

'So why didn't you inform the police immediately, if you were still hanging around near the canal?' Nicke asks.

He is looking at Vanessa, who meets his eyes unblinkingly.

I know you're lying, he thinks. *And I'll do all I can to show you up.*

'You must realize that Linnéa was, like, in shock. Everything in her apartment has been bashed to pieces,' Vanessa says. 'We just wanted to make sure she was all right before we called.'

'Neither here nor there. You should have contacted the police before we wasted any more resources on—'

'We were just about to call you,' Minoo says.

'Despite Linnéa's past experience of the local force, which hasn't been too great,' Vanessa says.

Nicke's eyes slide from one of them to the next. He's at a dead end.

They've caught him. It couldn't have worked out more neatly if they had spent their entire lives practicing to lie in harmony.

Linnéa smiles at him, a completely genuine smile that she can't hold back, because it feels so good to win, just for once.

'I'd like to report a break-in. Would that be in order, officer?'

CHAPTER 54

I da wakes when her mother pulls the door to her room open.
'Ida! I'm off to run with the kids now! Hurry up or you'll
be late!' she shouts, already on her way somewhere else.

Ida reaches for her phone and switches it on. It starts ping-
ing incessantly. Ida can't be bothered to open all these texts,
even less to listen to the voicemail messages.

She staggers out of bed. Meets her gaze in the bathroom mirror, notes how her face is still swollen with sleep.
Disgusted, she looks away.

Because you're you.

The force of Gustaf's remembered words almost makes her
sway and fall. They hurt as badly today as they did yesterday.

After the shower, she rubs in lotion, puts on make-up and
does her hair. Back in her room, she puts on the clothes she
laid out yesterday night. She decides to skip breakfast and
sets out for school.

The sky over Engelsfors is high and clear. She has almost
forgotten that mornings can be like this. Even so, she can't
enjoy it. Can't let go of the thoughts that revolve around
what happened yesterday. The magic flowing towards her in
the center. Erik's eyes. And G.

Because you're you.

When Ida turns into the schoolyard, she instantly senses
the subdued excitement in the air that is always generated

when everyone is talking about the same thing. In the usual run of things, it would have made her curious. Exalted, even. Now, she feels the exact opposite of that.

She sees Julia who is running to meet her.

'Shit, Ida, I just heard,' she says as soon as she is close enough.

'What's up? Has something happened?'

Julia's large eyes manage to grow even larger.

'But Erik must have gotten in touch ...?'

Ida regrets not checking her messages. What actually went on while she slept?

'What are you talking about?'

'Oh, my God. Poor love, so you really haven't heard?'

Julia puts her head at a sympathetic angle. But Ida sees straight through her. Julia is loving being the one to tell her about whatever has happened. She's loving it so much she's fit to spontaneously combust any second now.

'Linnéa Wallin is spreading a rumor about Erik and Robin. She says they pushed her into the canal,' Julia carries on. 'Like, an attempted murder! I mean, how sick is *that*?'

'I don't get it,' Ida says.

Something is stirring deep inside her. A sense of an approaching, unstoppable catastrophe.

'Exactly. Wild, isn't it?' Julia says.

She pulls Ida along with her through the front doors and into the entrance hall. Ida immediately spots Erik and Robin in the middle of a large group of students, mostly PE supporters. Kevin and Rickard are there. And Felicia, who is clinging to Robin with both arms around his waist, as if she thinks he might float off into the air if she lets him go.

Rickard is holding forth.

'Everyone knows that Linnéa hates PE. Remember the assembly last autumn?'

'I mean, she's totally buddy-buddy with Minoo Falk Karimi. And Minoo's old man is spreading lies about PE, like, non-stop,' Hanna A says.

'It isn't just about getting at Erik and Robin, it's an attack against the entire movement,' Rickard continues, just as Ida pushes her way through the crowd to Erik.

As soon as he sees her, he reaches out, grabs her jacket and pulls her close.

'Where have you been?' he hisses under his breath. 'I've been trying to phone you all morning.'

'I'd switched the phone off. What's happening?'

'It's a fucking mess,' Robin says and Ida turns around. He is stroking Felicia's head. 'We were in the center and the police turned up. Apparently someone had called the emergency services and said that we'd pushed Linnéa Wallin into the canal.'

'She made the call, obviously,' Erik says.

'Yeah, she's fucking mental,' Kevin says.

Ida looks at him. Then at Robin. And finally, at Erik.

She knows them so well, has known them all her life.

She knows them so well, and now she knows that they are all lying.

'But why should Linnéa invent something like that?' she asks.

'What, don't you believe us?' Erik says.

'Of course I do. All I meant was…she could've thought up a better lie than that. This one makes no sense. If you'd pushed her into the canal she would've died.'

'Who knows what goes on in her fucking mind, she's so deranged,' Robin says and begins to twist Felicia's blonde hair between his fingers, until it becomes more and more entangled.

'Look who's there!' Felicia whispers.

The whole group turns around when Linnéa steps inside. The talk dies down. Silence falls in the hall. People glance covertly in Linnéa's direction. A tenth-grade girl titters nervously.

'How dare she show her face around here?' Julia says.

'You lay off telling lies about my boyfriend, you crazy slut!' Felicia shouts.

Ida senses that Erik is looking at her, that several others are turning her way, and realizes they are expecting her to say something.

But not a word reaches her lips. Linnéa wanders off down the stairs, without a single sign of having heard what Felicia shouted, or having noticed that everyone is staring at her.

Ida!

Ida is startled when she hears Linnéa call her name. No one else seems to have heard, though.

'She'll be fucking sorry,' Robin says.

Meet me in the bathroom by the dining area. It's important.

And then Ida realizes that Linnéa's voice is only audible inside her own head.

Erik is still watching her. She gently prises herself free from his grip.

'Back soon,' she says and makes herself kiss him lightly on the cheek.

'Where are you off to?'

'The bathroom, that's all.'

She tries to smile before walking away.

Linnéa is waiting in the bathroom. She is wearing more make-up than ever. As if she's painted a warrior's mask on her face.

The cubicle doors are wide open. They are alone.

'What really happened?' Ida asks. 'What's all this about?'

Linnéa's lips tremble and, for a moment, Ida thinks that Linnéa is going to burst into tears.

'I can't...'

She leans against the wall, shuts her eyes.

I thought I'd faint when I saw them.

'Saw who?'

'Erik and Robin...'

'What's with them? Christ, what have you been saying about them?'

Linnéa opens her eyes and looks straight at Ida.

'They tried to kill me.'

Ida shakes her head.

'Of course they didn't! I don't want to listen to you!'

She walks towards the door, but Linnéa grabs her wrist, holds her there.

'Let me go, you freak!' Ida squeals and tries to pull free.

'Listen to me!'

'Leave me alone!'

Ida tries to tug herself free, but now all the strength is draining from her body. Her field of vision narrows, then goes dark.

Ida watches Erik as he pulls the balaclava over his face and starts walking towards her.

And she runs, runs for her life.

They are on the bridge now and she can see in Erik's eyes that he is prepared to kill her, that he *wants* to kill her.

Be a man, you wimp. You hate this slut as much as I do.

The baseball bat looks heavy in his hand.

You heard me. Jump. I thought all you psychos wanted to kill yourselves anyway.

The water is running so swiftly under the bridge, black and gleaming like oil.

Someone should fuck you first but we'd rather not catch AIDS.

Part Three

And she falls through the air, falls, falls and she knows she will die.

Ida gasps for breath when she hits the water.

Ida opens her eyes. She is lying on the cold floor of the bathroom. Linnéa's face is floating into sight above her.

'You saw,' Linnéa says with tears running down her face. 'You saw it, didn't you?'

Ida can still feel the icy-cold water closing around her. Her whole body is shaking, she can't stop shaking.

'No,' she hears herself say. 'He couldn't ever, he couldn't, not ever...'

But he could. She knows that now.

Ida stands up, then leaves quickly and runs back upstairs. She has to get away from Linnéa and from Erik, away from the whole school.

But Erik is waiting for her in the entrance hall. The bell has rung, the first class has started. He is alone, nobody else is there to watch them. He walks towards her and when Ida meets his eyes, she is on the bridge again and he wants to kill her.

'What's the matter with you?' Erik says.

One of his hands reaches for her.

'Don't touch me!'

Ida hears her own scream echo between the walls as Erik takes hold of her upper arms.

'Calm down!' he says.

She looks straight into his eyes and thinks that she no longer knows who he is.

Except, it's not true. She has known all along who Erik is. The difference between the past and this present moment is that she has never seen him like this, from the other side, as it were. The way his victims have always seen him.

So many victims over all these years. His, and *hers*, too. 'Come, come, kids must learn to put up with bit of rough and tumble,' as Ida's father used to say to the few parents who phoned up to complain. 'I bet it's just six of one and half a dozen of the other. As usual.' And Ida knew she would always get out of trouble for as long as she stayed among the winners. Belonged among those who count.

'Let me go!' she says.

Erik tightens his grip on her arms, so hard that her eyes fill with tears. She feels her magic power come alive inside her. It crackles around her as if she is fully charged with static electricity. Every hair on the back of her neck is standing on end.

'You're acting like a fucking psycho!' he says.

The discharge is so powerful that Erik is thrown backwards. He crashes into the wall and slumps to the floor. He stays there, looking around with a confused expression on his face.

Someone takes Ida's hand. Linnéa.

Come on, run. We can't stay here.

Linnéa pulls her along, out through the main entrance. They run together across the yard, past the dead trees and through the school gates.

There is no turning back.

Ida will never again be one of those who count.

She has crossed to the other side now.

CHAPTER 55

Minoo can hardly believe her eyes, when she is close enough to the dance pavilion. Many bizarre things have happened in the fairground, but this takes the cake.

Linnéa and Ida are sitting close together on the edge of the stage. Ida's head is resting on Linnéa's shoulder. True, Linnéa doesn't look exactly relaxed, but she seems to be tolerating the situation well enough.

Minoo heard that Ida and Linnéa left the school together suddenly that morning. Their disappearance is already part of the mythology that is growing around the recent events. It is the only subject people talked about today, in the hallways, classrooms and dining area.

At the end of the last lesson, Minoo heard Hanna H say that Ida had tried to push Erik down a flight of stairs. Apparently, Ida and Linnéa had been doing drugs together and Ida had a bad trip. Hanna H was so, so worried about Ida, of course. But, still, not really surprised because Ida has been behaving weirdly all through junior year, don't you agree?

Linnéa looks up when Minoo comes closer. Ida doesn't move. She looks quite haggard. Her eyes are swollen and red-rimmed.

'How are things?' Minoo asks cautiously.

Linnéa glances at Ida.

'It's been a long day,' she says and looks up at Minoo.

She hasn't said a word all day. I took her back to my place. She hasn't had anything to eat or drink. While I cleaned the apartment, she just sat staring at nothing. More or less like she is now.

Minoo nods, doesn't comment.

The ritual must be carried out at twilight and the sun is already low in the sky. They haven't got much time now.

She takes a quick look at Linnéa's heavily made-up face.

'How are you feeling?'

Linnéa chews on one of her nails. The black polish is flaking.

'I thought I saw Erik on the way here. I realized it wasn't him, but not soon enough. I went off into a real panic attack. That's the very worst thing, you know. They've managed to tunnel into my head, undo me.'

'You're in no way undone,' Minoo says.

Steps approach on the gravel and Minoo turns to see. Vanessa and Anna-Karin climb up on the dance floor.

Vanessa goes straight to Linnéa.

'How are you?'

'Dunno. But still alive.'

Vanessa hugs her. She shuts her eyes for a moment before she lets Linnéa go. When she sees them together like this, Minoo can't help hoping that Linnéa will dare to tell Vanessa about her feelings. She is quite certain that Vanessa's response would surprise Linnéa.

'Have you heard any more about the report of your break-in?' Vanessa asks. 'Like, have the police called or anything?'

'Nothing. I'm pretty sure they won't even bother to investigate. Anyway, Social Services has been in touch. Someone wants to see me tomorrow morning. I'm screwed, I guess.'

'It's not too late to tell them what really happened,' Minoo says. 'You could explain that you were afraid of the guys and that's why you didn't tell the full story. And if you need a witness that you were pushed in you could always get in touch with Viktor and…'

Minoo's sentence fades out. She can hear perfectly well how naïve it must sound to Linnéa. But it is very hard to accept that Erik and Robin won't be punished.

'That would be pointless,' Linnéa says. 'The entire town has made up its mind already. My word against Helena's. No contest. Besides, Viktor did save my life but I still don't trust him.'

'What about making Erik and Robin confess?' Anna-Karin says. 'I can make them. Just like we planned to do with Max.'

'It was a stupid plan back then,' Linnéa says. 'And still is. You haven't got the time to hang around controlling Erik and Robin throughout a long police investigation and then a trial. We need you for other things.'

Minoo looks at Ida again. After all, it is her boyfriend they're talking about. But her expression doesn't change at all. She hardly even blinks.

'I want them to die,' Vanessa says.

'Fine by me,' Linnéa says.

Minoo goes cold inside. Must they have this discussion? They had it a year ago, when they kept talking about what to do to Max.

'But then I'm not sure it is the best solution,' Linnéa says after a while. 'I was convinced I wanted to kill Max, but when I had a chance, I didn't. I couldn't. On the other hand, I don't know how I'll be able to bear seeing Erik and Robin around in Engelsfors.'

'We'll think of something,' Minoo says. 'Together.'

Linnéa nods.

'As soon as this show trial is over and done with, we'll sort

469

everything else, like Erik and Robin and Positive Engelsfors. And the demons,' she says. 'But now we've got to conduct this ritual.'

Vanessa roots around in her bag and produces a jar of ectoplasm.

'Are you all prepared?' Minoo asks.

'Hard to say since we don't have a clue what this ritual is for,' Vanessa says.

Cue Ida, Minoo thinks. She'll say something, come up with some objection, I-don't-want-to, why-should-I.

But Ida is silent, just sits there.

'All we need to know is that the ritual will help us get through the trial,' Minoo says, wishing that she felt as much in control as she sounds. 'All quiet back at the manor house?'

Anna-Karin nods. Her fox is keeping watch.

Vanessa hands Minoo the jar. Linnéa stands up and Ida hauls herself up after her.

'The circle that binds,' Minoo says and starts on the outer circle along the railing.

It feels quite different from the first time. Now, her hand slides easily across the worn wooden floor. It is *too* easy. Suddenly, she feels uncertain, as if she is only pretending.

The outer circle takes only a few minutes to complete. Nothing happens. She glances at the others.

'Anyone feel anything?'

Anna-Karin, Linnéa and Vanessa shake their heads. Ida doesn't even seem to have heard her.

'Are you sure you're doing it right?' Vanessa asks.

'There aren't all that many ways of doing it,' Minoo says as she goes to the center of the dance floor. 'The circle that gives power.'

She crouches to draw the inner circle. It forms perfectly, but still she cannot sense any magic.

'Over to you now,' she says and stands up.

One by one, they walk into the inner circle to draw the signs of their elements.

'The sun has almost set,' Anna-Karin observes.

Minoo takes the silver crucifix out of her backpack. She has kept it at home since the séance.

'Go and stand by the signs of your power,' she says.

Minoo walks towards the inner circle with the crucifix in her hand. And now she feels something. The cross is becoming warm, then almost hot.

There is a crackling noise as small, violet sparks start leaping about in the inner circle.

'Shit!' Vanessa says. 'Now what? Are you sure this is a good idea? Why didn't the guardians want to tell us what the ritual was supposed to do?'

'Maybe because if we'd known we'd never have joined in,' Linnéa says.

Sparks start flying again in the inner circle. The crucifix grows so hot that Minoo can barely hold on to it.

'Right, this is the right time,' she says. 'When I step inside the circle, take each other's hands. And shut your eyes when I tell you.'

Minoo takes a deep breath, steps into the inner circle and raises the crucifix in front of her, as the guardians ordered.

'Now,' she says.

Vanessa barely has time to close her eyes before a strong wind lifts her hair. It pushes itself in through her nose and mouth. Tugs at her clothes.

She almost loses her balance and worries that she is going to fall and pull Anna-Karin and Linnéa down with her. She fights to stay upright with the wind roaring in her ears. It feels as if it could tear her apart from the inside.

And then the wind stops blowing, as quickly as it began. The world falls silent again. Vanessa feels heavy. Her legs seem almost welded to the floor.

She hears the others breathe heavily.

'I'm exhausted,' Minoo mumbles.

'Did it work?' Ida says.

'I don't know,' Linnéa says. 'After all, the guardians never said how we would find out, one way or the other.'

'Can we open our eyes now?' Vanessa hears herself say.

But I didn't say that, she thinks. It was my voice. But I didn't do the speaking.

She gradually opens her eyes and realizes that she is looking at her own face.

Vanessa is standing next to herself and holds her own hand. She lets it go.

'What happened?' she says, quite shocked, and hears that her voice is not her own.

The palms of her hands are sweating heavily.

'Who are you?' Vanessa asks, staring at the Vanessa who is standing next to her and biting her nails.

'Linnéa,' she says.

Vanessa can't stop staring. It is like looking at yourself in the mirror but still not the same.

She looks down at the body she inhabits and sees a duffel coat, sweatpants and sneakers.

She observes Linnéa who is looking around, apparently confused.

'And who are you?' Vanessa asks.

'I'm Minoo,' she replies. 'But I'm sort of Linnéa, right? Who of you is me? Who is inside me, I mean?'

'I am,' Minoo says in a trembling voice. 'But I'm Ida.'

'What's happened?' Vanessa asks once more in desperation. Everyone turns to her.

'You're me,' Ida says gently. 'That is, I'm Anna-Karin now, and you're Vanessa, really, aren't you?'

Vanessa nods and a long, dark strand of hair falls into her eyes. She pushes it back.

'At least, I was Vanessa just moments ago,' she adds, speaking with Anna-Karin's voice.

Minoo puts her pen down and looks at the others. They are seated in a semicircle around her, looking at an open notebook and trying to get their heads around what she has written.

The sun is fully set by now, but the circle of ectoplasm is glowing around them.

Minoo = Linnéa's body
Linnéa = Vanessa's body
Vanessa = Anna-Karin's body
Anna-Karin = Ida's body
Ida = Minoo's body

'This is correct, right?' Minoo asks.

Her handwriting isn't the same as usual. Linnéa's hand has its own practiced grip on a pen and won't quite do what Minoo wants.

'Yes,' Vanessa says and starts fiddling with one of her cuticles.

She is Linnéa, of course.

And I'm inside Linnéa's body, Minoo thinks. *I'm inside somebody else's body!*

It's too weird. If she thinks too much about this, her head is going to explode. No, Linnéa's head.

I must see behind their faces, try to think of their real selves or I'll go completely out of my mind, she thinks.

'When the guardians showed me how to go about the ritual, I was told that the effect would last for three days and three nights,' she says. 'So that means that at sunset on the third day from now, we'll be back in our own bodies.'

'How can you be sure?' Minoo hears her own voice ask, but it sounds so different, like hearing your recorded voice. 'Imagine what might happen if something goes wrong and we're left in these bodies for ever. Or, think about it, we might end up in the wrong one when the whole thing goes in reverse. Or simply disappear. Or, what if *my* body dies because Anna-Karin crosses the street in front of a bus.'

Ida's panic is unmistakable. She is fumbling for the silver heart that isn't there.

Minoo, too, is scared half to death. But she mustn't allow fear to take over.

'I'm sure we'll be okay,' she says. 'The guardians are on our side. They want what's best for us. Matilda said they would help us with the trial, remember.'

She meets Ida's eyes. And looks into *her own* eyes. It all spins around and around inside her head.

'But how is changing about supposed to help us?' Ida asks.

'I don't know,' Minoo says. 'Not the faintest idea. But there will be a plan behind it all. We have to trust them.'

She shifts position to stand in a different way and happens to touch a bruise that seems to cover most of Linnéa's thigh.

'Minoo, you can't hear me, can you?'

Minoo looks up at Vanessa and that sets off another dizzying spin. Vanessa's eyes, but recognizably expressing Linnéa's mind at the same time.

'I'm trying to send you my thoughts just now. It doesn't work, does it?'

'No, it doesn't. I haven't picked up a thing.'

'So while I'm in Vanessa's body my magic is "out of order"?'

'Do you think that's the same for all of us?' Anna-Karin asks.

Minoo shuts her eyes and tries to release the black smoke. No effect. She can't locate that catch inside her. She feels totally...ordinary. Unmagical.

She opens her eyes again and looks searchingly at the others.

'It's like some kind of short circuit,' Vanessa says.

'I hope the guardians know what they're doing, because I can't see how we can cope with this,' Linnéa says. 'I don't just mean the trial. Look, we'll have to lead each other's *lives* now. Minoo, congrats! Now you're in my fantastic life.'

'We'd better swap all the information we might need about each other,' Minoo says. 'Tell each other about the most important things. Write lists.'

She starts pulling pages out of her notebook and hands them around. But she grasps the true significance of this for the first time when she sees her own hand take a piece of paper. She'll have to tell Ida *everything* about herself. Her habits and routines, all the little secrets that add up to a person's private life.

CHAPTER 56

Anna-Karin vaguely remembers that there's an old saying about how you learn to know your enemy by walking in his shoes.

So far, it has been surprisingly satisfying to be in Ida's shoes. To be in her body, generally.

Anna-Karin takes a few tentative running steps as she walks along the road through the posh residential district. And it feels as if she's flying. Her body is light and strong, ready to keep running for ages.

After a few blocks she sees Ida's home and walks the last bit up to the gate. She listens to her own breathing. Even that seems unfamiliar.

How many times has she wondered about what's going on inside that house? If there are any dark secrets hidden behind these green walls, secrets that might help to explain the mystery that is Ida Holmström?

Anna-Karin stops by the front door. She has forgotten which of the keys on the ring she should use. While trying them out, she runs through what she remembers of the things on Ida's list. Her father's name is Anders, her mother is Carina and the little kids are Rasmus and Lotta. Ida's room is nearest the top of the stairs. Her toothbrush is red. She always uses a special range of skincare products, which Anna-Karin can't pronounce the name of, and she always sleeps with a bra on to avoid droopy breasts when she is older.

Anna-Karin finds the door key at last and steps inside the hall. She hears voices and the clatter of cutlery from somewhere inside the house.

A woman's voice calls out.

'Ida?'

When Anna-Karin bends to pull her boots off, there is nothing in the way. As she straightens up, she marvels again at how different Ida's body feels. So much more...obedient.

Her own body, on the other hand, is more like an appendage to her head. A shapeless bulk that is essential to her when she needs to move from point A to point B. An object that is best kept hidden under layers of clothing.

'Ida?' the woman calls again

'Yes?' Anna-Karin replies hesitantly.

It still feels so odd to hear Ida's voice like this. It sounds deeper than usual.

'We've already eaten. Are you coming?'

Anna-Karin takes a deep breath and walks to the kitchen.

Everything in there is white. Just nudging something might leave dirty fingerprints, she thinks. The overall look is cool and expensive. And the family seated at the kitchen table projects the same image.

Anna-Karin has seen Ida's parents before and always thought them somehow *too* perfect. As if they've just been unpacked from their box. The kids are miniature copies of Ida. Anna-Karin shudders a little as her mind speeds through a montage of classic clips from her nastiest childhood memories. She wonders if Lotta and Rasmus are like their big sister in other ways, too.

Ida's father looks up and it strikes her how like Erik Forslund he is. A blonde, middle-aged Erik Forslund. She shudders again.

Fire

'Why are you looking at us like that?' Anders says.

'Your eyes will pop out of your head,' Rasmus says and then he and Lotta start to laugh in that exaggerated way kids sometimes do, as if they have to laugh just for the sake of laughing.

'*Rasmus*,' Ida's mother says in an admonishing tone.

'But her eyes looked like they would pop out,' Rasmus says sulkily. 'And there are dogs that can have their eyes falling out, honestly.'

Anna-Karin settles down on the free chair at the table. Ida's mother pushes a large bowl of salad towards her.

'The fish is keeping warm on the cooker,' she adds.

Anna-Karin serves herself salad, then goes to pick up the last piece of steamed fish from the pan.

As soon as she starts eating she realizes how hungry Ida's body is. The food is incredibly good, too. When was Anna-Karin last offered home-cooking?

'How are you?' Ida's mother asks.

Anna-Karin swallows a mouthful of fish, looks up and tries out a reply.

'Fine?'

But that isn't the right thing to say. She sees that from the wrinkles that appear on Carina Holmström's normally ever-so-smooth forehead.

'Right, children. You may leave the table now,' she says without taking her eyes off Anna-Karin.

Rasmus and Lotta bounce happily off their chairs and charge out of the kitchen and up the stairs.

'Darling, why haven't you told us about what's happened?' Ida's mother asks.

Anna-Karin looks at the two concerned parental faces.

If only they were horrible. It would make it so very much easier to understand Ida. So endlessly much easier to *forgive* her.

'You see, we've heard about Erik and that girl,' Anders says. 'Terrible.'

'Yes, it is. How *can* she go around spreading these tales?' Carina says. 'Of course, she must be mentally unstable.'

'That is no excuse at all,' the father says and glances at his wife. 'That kind of person isn't helped by being indulged all the time.'

'No, of course. That's true,' Carina says. 'You must be utterly distraught, Ida.'

They both look at Anna-Karin, waiting for an answer.

'Umm,' is all she can think of.

'The thing is, Erik is such a kind young man,' Carina says. 'Robin is different, of course. It isn't hard to see why the boy might be a bit difficult – his mother has her own problems to cope with. But Erik! How could anyone even think of it?'

'Erik is a born leader, just like Ida,' Anders says. 'Some people will always be envious of leaders, that's par for the course.'

Anna-Karin realizes there might be an explanation about why Ida is who she is, after all. She can't keep quiet any longer.

'Erik is not kind,' she says. 'Actually, neither am I, not all the time.'

'What *do* you mean?' Carina asks.

'Come on, one can't go through life being kind,' Anders says at the same time. 'Cows are kind, all the way to the slaughterhouse.'

Anna-Karin feels a crazy impulse to moo into his face, but the doorbell rings.

'I'll open the door!' Lotta shouts and comes running downstairs.

'Who can that be?' Ida's mother says and cranes her neck to try and catch a glimpse of the visitor through the window.

Fire

'It's Erik!' Lotta yells.

'Speak of the devil,' Anders says.

Anna-Karin stands up but forgets about Ida's muscular legs, pushes too hard and almost falls over backwards.

'I don't want to see him,' she says.

She hears Erik chatting with Lotta in the hall and he sounds convincingly nice. A mother's dream suitor for her daughter, which makes the whole thing even more terrifying.

Jump. Or we'll throw you in.

Anna-Karin hurries off towards a doorway that doesn't open into the hall.

'Ida! What are you doing?' Carina calls after her.

Anna-Karin finds herself in the living room. Desperate, she looks around. She hears Erik's voice from the kitchen, asking for Ida. She doesn't give herself time to find out what Ida's parents tell him. She pushes the French windows open, hurries out on to an expanse of decking, closes the doors quietly again and runs across the damp planks in her sock feet. Then, down some steps and into the garden.

The ground is wet and cold. Her feet soon become soaked but she hardly notices. She is aiming for the playhouse and runs as fast as she can. Now and then, she glances quickly over her shoulder at the towering bulk of the villa behind her. The living-room light is on and through a window she sees Erik come into the room.

Anna-Karin slips around the corner of the playhouse and presses herself against the wall.

Ida would never hide like this. Anna-Karin, on the other hand, can't face meeting Erik. He's always frightened her and now she knows he's a killer.

If he follows me I'll climb the fence and run for it, she promises herself. She hears the French windows opening and tenses her whole body, ready for flight.

Part Three

'Ida!' Erik shouts so loud it sends an echo around the gar
den. 'Come here!'

She feels sure she'll hear his footsteps on the deck any
moment now. Nothing happens. After a while the doors are
closed again.

Anna-Karin waits. She crosses her arms over her chest as
the cold, raw wind burrows through Ida's thin cardigan. She
wishes she could escape into the fox's mind but that bond has
been cut.

Finally, the front door of the house opens and she hears
Erik's footsteps fade away as he walks along the street.

At last it seems safe to go inside.

Her socks are wet, freezing rags by now and she leaves
foot-shaped marks on the white-limed living-room floor. She
rips her socks off.

Anders Holmström's bellowing voice shouts from the
kitchen.

'Ida! Come here at once and explain what you think
you're doing!'

Anna-Karin doesn't answer him. She runs upstairs, two
steps at a time, and slams the door to Ida's room after her. To
her huge relief she sees that there's a key in the lock.

'Ida!' Carina calls and Anna-Karin hears her come upstairs.

The angry knock on the door makes her back away. Carina
speaks from just outside.

'Erik told us you're *friendly* with that girl. And that she's
a *junkie*! Your dad and I don't want you to keep that kind of
company. Are you listening? Open the door!'

The door handle rattles.

'We will not tolerate you going around with criminals,'
Carina says.

'You don't know Erik! You have no idea who he really is!'

Another pull at the door handle. Much harder this time.

'Have it your own way, then,' Carina snarls. 'You'll have to stay here all evening.'

'Suits me!' Anna-Karin screeches. Ida's voice nearly hurts her ears.

'What's your problem? Have you started taking drugs, too? Do you?'

'Of course I don't!'

'You're too old for this kind of nonsense. We'll talk about it tomorrow.'

As Carina Holmström walks away, she manages to make the sound of her footsteps spell out her anger.

If only she knew who her darling Erik truly is, Anna-Karin thinks.

But Ida's mother would never believe the truth if she heard it.

She would simply refuse.

Linnéa drinks some of the tepid tea and observes herself sitting on the other side of the table.

She has wondered so many times about how Vanessa sees her. And now she is literally inside Vanessa's head and able to look at herself through Vanessa's eyes.

But, of course, it doesn't make her any wiser. She is not Vanessa. That is just a trick with smoke and mirrors. Just as it isn't actually herself she is looking at, but Minoo.

'Another sandwich, Nessa?' Jannike Dahl says, ready to hand her the bread basket.

'No, thank you,' Linnéa says.

'It's been so nice,' Minoo says. 'Really lovely tea as well.'

Her polite smile looks totally wrong in Linnéa's face, but Vanessa's mother hasn't got a clue, of course.

Linnéa drinks another mouthful and tries to ignore the dog who is sitting on the floor at her feet. Frasse is snuffling loudly and has angled his head so he can keep his eye on her.

Jannike doesn't seem to have sensed anything out of the ordinary about her daughter. The dog has, though. And Melvin as well. When Jannike asked 'Vanessa' to read him a bedtime story, the kid brother had yelled protestingly at the top of his voice.

'It's very kind of you to let me sleep over here tonight,' Minoo says.

'Goes without saying,' Jannike says. 'I'm really glad to meet Nessa's friends. And I've heard so much about you, Linnéa.'

Linnéa scrutinizes her teacup. Tries not to show how happy this makes her.

'That's nice,' Minoo says. 'Only good things, I hope.'

When she is chatting with Vanessa's mother, Minoo has this knack of making all her smarmy politeness sound quite natural. She must be used to grown-ups taking her seriously, even liking her.

'I hope it's okay with you to share a bed tonight,' Jannike says.

Linnéa and Minoo exchange a quick glance.

'Haven't we got a spare mattress?' Linnéa asks.

'Nicke took it with him when he moved out. There's the sofa, of course, but Melvin usually gets up really early. I think it'll be easier for you to get a good night's sleep if you can shut the door.'

'That's great, no problem at all,' Minoo says and gets up. 'Excuse me a moment.'

Linnéa tries not to think about her body being taken to the bathroom by Minoo. Another thing she doesn't want to think about is being left alone for the first time with this woman she has to pretend is her mother.

'Nessa,' Jannike says quietly when Minoo is out of ear-shot. 'Nicke phoned me this morning.'

'Did he?' Linnéa says and tries to sound neutral.

'He said he met you last night in Linnéa's place. He also said something about a party that had got out of hand. And now you turn up here with Linnéa in tow and tell me there was a break-in. I don't know what to think. Were you there, in the middle of the night? On a school night?'

Linnéa's immediate instinct is to be defensive. Let Jannike think what she likes. But what would Vanessa do?

'When I heard what had happened last night, I went over to see her,' she says and carries on, trying to feel her way. 'It was stupid of me. I should've told you first. But I was so terribly worried about Linnéa. And Nicke has got everything totally wrong.'

Jannike looks concerned but doesn't comment.

'There really had been a break-in,' Linnéa says. 'It's the truth.'

She stops and looks uncertainly at Jannike.

'I trust you,' Vanessa's mother says. 'I don't think you'd lie about something so serious. But if anything like that happens again, please tell me. Don't just sneak away.'

Linnéa nods. It is all she can do.

'I'm glad that you care about your friends, though,' Jannike continues. 'And Linnéa seems a very nice person. So polite. Tries a little too hard, perhaps, but a real sweetie.'

Minoo comes back into the kitchen. Jannike puts her arm around Linnéa's shoulders, kisses her forehead and leaves.

For a moment, Linnéa can't draw breath.

Vanessa's body responded to the intimate touch, it felt so natural and calming. But to Linnéa, it was a reminder of what she has never experienced. And never will, ever.

*

Minoo has borrowed an old T-shirt from Vanessa's wardrobe and scrubbed all the make-up from Linnéa's face. Now, she is patting it dry with a towel that smells strongly of some alien detergent.

She is jittery, every nerve in her body is vibrating. Even her fingertips are prickling. And she feels so restless she'd like to crawl out of her skin, this skin which after all isn't hers.

All this will drive me out of my mind, she thinks as she examines Linnéa's naked face in the mirror. I will probably go insane.

Everything is so confusing.

Minoo has never believed that body and soul can be separated, not completely anyway. Now, she knows for certain. Linnéa's feelings for Vanessa are part of her whole body. When she sees Vanessa, who isn't even the real Vanessa but Linnéa herself, Linnéa's body responds with deep-rooted longing. It is so powerful that Minoo almost feels that she is the one in love with Vanessa.

Her head spins and she has to look away from the mirror.

Who is she actually seeing there and whose mind is producing these thoughts? Shouldn't she be able to access Linnéa's memories and emotions, now that she is thinking with Linnéa's brain? Or does her awareness of being Minoo in fact come from her own brain, but somehow projected into Linnéa's body?

Whichever brain Minoo is using to think with, by now it's about to burst into flames.

'How goes it?' Linnéa asks when Minoo comes back to Vanessa's room.

'I don't know. I feel so odd. Dizzy. And my fingers are kind of prickly. I hope the ritual hasn't had any side effects.'

Linnéa watches her. And then bursts into laughter. Vanessa's laughter.

Fire

'You're dying for a smoke,' she says. 'Or, rather, I am.'

Linnéa lies awake in the dark while Minoo snores lightly next to her.

She had fallen asleep as soon as they had come back from having a cigarette outside. Linnéa had wanted one, too, but decided to spare Vanessa's lungs. Somehow, it was perfectly obvious that the need she felt was purely in the mind.

She had had to show her how to go about smoking. Minoo was disgusted.

'I just don't get it,' Minoo snorted. 'I think it's totally foul, but my body wants more of it all the same. Your body, that is.'

'Just be glad I don't do hard drugs anymore,' Linnéa said and laughed.

Minoo smiled and dragged clumsily on the cigarette.

'It must be extra strange for you, this exchange thing,' she said. 'I mean, that you ended up inside *Vanessa*. The person you love.'

'I try not to think about it,' Linnéa said. 'Everything seems deranged.'

It *is* totally deranged.

Here she is, sleeping in Vanessa's bed, wrapped in Vanessa's sheets. The bed is quite narrow and from close by she can feel the warmth of her own body.

Vanessa's body responds to the closeness.

Linnéa doesn't know what it means. Is it just being close that makes all the difference? Or is there some part of Vanessa that actually feels for her?

Whatever, it is as if Linnéa is aroused by herself, which is *beyond* deranged. So despite being very tired, she can't sleep.

She carries on staring into the dark. Listening to the wind outside. She has almost dropped off to sleep when Vanessa's phone starts vibrating.

She turns over in bed and starts fumbling for the phone on the floor. Next to her, Minoo mutters something inaudible.

Linnéa checks the phone.

It's a text.

Can't stop remembering that kiss. I want more. Wille

Linnéa gently puts the phone down.

Turns to lie on her back again.

If she wants a sign to indicate whether or not she has a chance to make it with Vanessa, well, there it is.

Linnéa shuts her eyes and two tears trail down her temples and disappear into her hair.

She is inside Vanessa's body, but Vanessa seems further away than ever.

CHAPTER 57

Vanessa walks slowly up the school stairs.

Anna-Karin's body is heavy in a way that has nothing to do with weight. It feels as if her blood doesn't flow. As if her feet don't lift clear off the ground when she walks.

She had thought it would be difficult to pretend to be Anna-Karin and mimic the way she moves, but being in her body is enough. It becomes automatic. Anna-Karin's spine protests when Vanessa tries to walk with a straight back. Her shoulders won't give up their hunched position. The natural shape of her neck is being bent forward.

So Vanessa pushes her hands into the pockets of her duffel coat and walks along, her hair dangling over her face, to find Anna-Karin's locker.

She doesn't look at anyone. And no one sees her. It's as close to being invisible as Vanessa has ever been.

Ida is waiting for her at the row of lockers. She holds up a sheet of paper covered in writing.

'Minoo has mailed me lists of *everything*,' she says and points to something in the middle of the mass of text. 'Look, it says here which books we should bring to the first lesson.'

Ida has Minoo's face. Minoo's voice. But no way Minoo's presence.

A shout echoes in the corridor.

'Nessa!'

Vanessa automatically turns around. She sees herself, then how Evelina puts her arm around that other Vanessa. Notes Linnéa's alarmed look in her own eyes.

'What have you done to your hair?' Evelina shrieks and kisses her cheek.

Linnéa drags her fingers nervously through Vanessa's hair that flops around her head, flat and lifeless.

'I just didn't have time this morning,' Linnéa says.

And Vanessa wonders if her voice always sounds that squeaky.

How are they going to pull off an entire fucking school day? Not to speak of the trial, when they are subjected to the scrutiny of the Council?

Evelina and Linnéa wander off together down the corridor.

Vanessa wonders what kind of discoveries Linnéa has made about her body. She had a really bad time herself this morning in the shower. Had to shut her eyes in the end, because it felt far too intimate to handle Anna-Karin's body like that.

Vanessa finds Anna-Karin's books and locks up. She walks along the corridor and up the stairs, side by side with Ida. Neither of them says a word.

When they step into the classroom, it is only half-full. Vanessa and Ida look out over the empty seats and exchange a quick glance.

'Did Minoo's list say where she usually sits?' Vanessa asks under her breath.

'No,' Ida replies. 'But if Minoo has anything to do with it it's got to be somewhere near the front.'

'And Anna-Karin would go for a place near a wall, so she can sit squeezed up against it,' Vanessa says.

There are only two free places that fit the bill and no one reacts when they settle down.

In the row of seats just behind theirs, Hanna A and Hanna H are whispering with their heads close together. At various points, Vanessa picks up names. Linnéa, Ida, Erik.

And, of course, Ida hears all this as well. She stares straight ahead and fingers the base of her throat, as if trying to touch her silver heart.

'Good for Erik to get shot of that bitch,' Kevin says when he and his crowd enter the classroom. 'Everyone knows she's frigid anyway.'

His friends laugh. Vanessa turns and sends Kevin a disgusted glance as he goes to sit down right at the back.

'You got a problem? Just say,' Kevin shouts.

'I have *nothing* to say to you,' Vanessa answers.

'That's dead right. Lezzies should just keep their traps shut.'

Vanessa turns to face forward again. The classroom is slowly filling up and she makes the mistake of meeting Viktor's eyes as he walks in. She tells herself it might be her imagination, but he seems to be baffled for a moment. Instantly, Anna-Karin's palms become moist.

Viktor's dark blue eyes scrutinize her in a way that makes Vanessa so nervous she has to look down. Her hair falls over her face. She feels very much like Anna-Karin.

'Right. Everyone settle down now, please,' a typical teacher's voice says.

Vanessa looks up cautiously. Over by the teacher's desk, a woman with spectacles is pulling a bundle of copied sheets from her briefcase.

'Today, I've got a surprise pretest for you on induction,' she says and the students groan in unison.

'You can't test us on something we haven't studied for,' Kevin brays.

'Oh, yes, I can,' the teacher says and Vanessa thinks she

sees a triumphant glint in her eyes. 'That's precisely why it's called a pretest.'

One of the question papers is plonked on her desk and Vanessa checks out the first page.

She understands nothing of what is written on it. Absolutely *nothing*. She says a prayer under her breath, begging Anna-Karin to forgive her.

Ida finds a seat in the dining area and looks herself over for the first time that day.

Anna-Karin has managed to match Ida's black skirt with that old bulky red sweater that makes her look such a fatso. But Ida hasn't got the energy to care, not even a little.

She is far too conscious of the whispering in the dining area. Mostly about her, she knows.

She glances at the side room. Robin, Felicia, Julia and Kevin are there. But not Erik.

Please please please, let him stay at home today, she thinks.

Yesterday, she used Minoo's computer to log into her account. Erik had not only ended their relationship, he had also de-friended her. Many others had followed his lead. That is, after they had posted foul comments about her on her wall. With plenty of relish. It seemed they had been wanting to say these things for ages but hadn't dared until now.

And then, Anna-Karin phoned.

Ida simply listened. She couldn't be sure that she would have acted differently. The mere thought of Erik fills her with greater terror than her old fear of the dark ever did.

She turns to the other Chosen Ones again. Drinks some water. Stares at the hand holding the glass. Her head goes into a spin every time she sees Minoo's hands instead of her own.

'I get a massive headache every time I try to figure out who's who,' Vanessa says.

No, she didn't, Ida quickly reminds herself. Linnéa said it. Linnéa, inside Vanessa's body.

'Actually, it's *my* head that hurts,' Anna-Karin says and giggles.

Of course, it's Vanessa who says it. Vanessa inside Anna-Karin's body.

Minoo stares at Ida from behind Linnéa's eyes.

'It's totally unreal. Like watching yourself in a movie.'

'The most advanced 3D-film in the world, though. And then there's this thing about being audience and actor at the same time,' Anna-Karin points out. Or, rather, Vanessa does.

Ida reaches for her knife and fork, and then puts the cutlery down when she sees Minoo's hands again. She won't ever be able to cope with this.

'Ida,' Linnéa's voice says and Ida looks her way.

And once more has to remind herself that it's Minoo who's talking.

'I think we'll have to try to see ourselves as the people we really are. Or we'll go crazy.'

Ida looks around the circle, at each one in turn. It can be done, with an effort. Although they're trying to play the right roles, all sorts of small mannerisms reveal who they are.

'We need to talk about what's happened since we last met,' Minoo says. 'Has anyone suspected anything?'

'Your cat hissed at me when I came home yesterday,' Vanessa says to Anna-Karin. 'But I don't think it'll tell on me. And I hardly saw your mother. She was at home, but in her room almost all the time.'

'Both Frasse and Melvin know that there's something wrong about me,' Linnéa says.

'Poor little Melvin—' Vanessa says, but Anna-Karin interrupts.

'Erik!' she whispers.

Ida's fear is mirrored in her face.

Anna-Karin sees Erik walking towards her.

His face is bright red and an angry flare has spread upwards from the neckline of his sweater and reached his prominent Adam's apple.

She has often been afraid of Erik, but only seen him watch her with cold calculation in his eyes or else with a glimpse of amused excitement. Tormenting her has been one of his hobbies. At times, it has even seemed to have turned into a kind of dull routine.

At the tables near theirs, all talk is dying down.

Erik squares up to Anna-Karin.

'Ida, what's your problem?'

By now the entire dining area is silent. Some people stand up to see better.

'Why do you want to sit with this bunch of sad retards?' Erik demands. 'Like that filthy slut there. She's been spreading rumors about me.'

Linnéa seems close to fainting. Vanessa reaches out across the table and takes her hand.

'Answer me!' Erik says.

Anna-Karin feels blocked. Her brain is unable to formulate a single thought. Let alone express it in spoken words.

'This is your *only* chance,' Erik says. 'It's all over if you don't leave these losers now and come away with me. Get my drift? I'm not just saying it's over between us. *It's all over for you.*'

Anna-Karin looks at the real Ida inside Minoo's body. Her

eyes have grown huge and fearful. But she nods lightly at Anna-Karin.

Gives her permission.

Once, Anna-Karin made Erik pee his pants in front of the entire school. Now, she has no access to her magic.

But she has a new option. She can be Ida. And being Ida means being capable of saying whatever comes to mind.

'Piss off, Piss-Erik,' she says.

'What the fuck did you say?'

His voice is so tense with fury that Anna-Karin's instinctive response is to run away. She suppresses it.

'You heard me,' she says. 'Surely you haven't forgotten how you peed yourself when the whole school was watching?'

'You have so lost it. You've gone insane,' Erik says, turning an even deeper shade of red.

'Not any more,' Anna-Karin says. 'It was being with you that screwed my mind up. You're a psychopath. People like you ought to be locked up.'

'If you believe that Julia or Felicia or anyone else will hang out with you ever again, you're making such a fucking big mistake,' Erik says. 'No one will want to have anything to do with you now.'

'What makes you think she cares?' Ida says.

Erik swings around to face her.

'Who the fuck are you? And who's asked for your fucking opinion about anything?'

'She doesn't even love you,' Ida continues. 'She never has.'

'So true,' Anna-Karin says and Erik turns back to her. 'You know why, don't you? You're utterly unlovable. There just isn't anything to like about you. Not when you know who you are.'

Erik's hands clench into fists and Anna-Karin is certain that he wants to hit her.

'Go ahead,' she says. 'Just show everybody who you really are.'

Erik's hands unclench.

'You've made your choice, Ida. Now live with it. Best of luck, you'll need it.'

He walks away. Around them, the talk immediately starts up again.

Anna-Karin looks at Ida.

'I couldn't have said it better myself,' Ida mutters.

CHAPTER 58

Walking through town as Linnéa is a strange experience for Minoo. She always wanted to try out an alternative style but never dared to look really different. Now she is wearing a skirt of black tulle covered with small, shiny metallic spiders that now and then clink against each other. Everyone is staring at her. A middle-aged man even shouted something after her. It sounded like 'Has the circus come to town?'

'How do you put up with everybody ogling you all the time?' Minoo asks as they walk to the social services office.

'It's a fail-safe idiot test,' Linnéa says. 'An instant check on who's a bigoted dumbass. The data is kind of depressing.'

The social services department is just a block away from the *Engelsfors Herald* office. Minoo has probably passed by hundreds of times, but never actually noticed. The name in black lettering on the white background doesn't signify anything that matters in her life.

Linnéa stops outside the entrance.

'Ready?'

'As ready as I'll ever be,' Minoo says. 'Anything else I should know about Diana?'

'*I* feel like I don't know a thing about her any more,' Linnéa says. 'She used to be on my side. I can't think what's changed her.'

'Maybe she's under a spell,' Minoo says. 'Seems possible,

now that we know they're into magic at PE. And we also know that Helena hates you.'

Linnéa looks at Minoo through Vanessa's brown eyes.

'I hope so. I hope it isn't Diana herself who's doing this to me.'

Minoo nods. Eyes the door.

'Feeling nervous?' Linnéa asks.

'Not at all. After all, it's just your life that hangs on how this ends.'

Linnéa smiles faintly, pushes a large button to make the glass door swing open and leads the way in.

Minoo shyly observes the people they meet and tries to work out who are members of staff and who are clients. Then tells herself off for presuming that it will show in their looks.

They walk through a long corridor painted in a shade of avocado-green that makes people's faces look mildly seasick. Then they stop at one of the doors. A white plastic sign says '*Diana Ehn*'.

Minoo knocks on the door and a woman opens it. Diana is younger than Minoo had imagined. But her face is deeply lined, as if she is constantly worried.

'Hi there, Linnéa,' she sighs.

Her tone of voice doesn't bode well. Then Diana turns to the real Linnéa.

'Vanessa has come along to give friendly support,' Minoo explains quickly.

'Sorry, but she'll have to wait outside,' Diana says.

'Oh, come on—' Linnéa says.

'No problem,' Minoo interrupts at once. 'I'll be fine.'

She follows Diana into her office. The door slams behind them.

'Sit down,' Diana says.

It sounds like an order and Minoo goes to sit down on the

hard sofa. Diana bends over her desk. She examines Minoo intently. Minoo has to take off Linnéa's fake fur coat because it suddenly feels like a live creature that is about to suffocate her.

'I am utterly disappointed in you,' Diana says.

'Please, just let me explain...'

Diana shakes her head.

'You've got to give me a chance to—' Minoo says.

'You missed your meetings with me,' Diana interrupts. 'You've thrown wild parties. Not to mention that hoax call to emergency services. On top of everything, you've spread slander about the two boys. You should be grateful they haven't charged you.'

'I'm not trying to explain anything away. I just want to tell you what really happened.'

'No.'

'But—'

'No more "buts", Linnéa. You've done enough.'

Minoo feels frustration growing inside her. Suddenly, she understands why Linnéa is always so angry, why she always seems to think attack is the best defense.

But she mustn't lose her temper. Her job is to try and sort this out for Linnéa.

'It *was* a break-in,' Minoo says. 'And I know nothing about the false alarm call, it was a shock to me, too.'

'You have to be out of that apartment by Monday.'

Feverishly, Minoo racks her brain for arguments to back her case. All she can think of is a question.

'Surely you can't throw me out just like that?'

'I can and I will. Also, you will be held financially responsible for any damages.'

'But where am I supposed to live?'

'We have been quite lucky this time. There is a place in a

special home that has just been freed up. The home specializes in girls with behavioral problems. Initially, you have to stay in a closed ward. That is, until your behavior has stabilized.'

Linnéa's heart is beating wildly now and Minoo feels sweat breaking out on her back. So, this is how a panic attack starts. She tries to breathe calmly, as Linnéa has advised her to do.

'But you can't have me locked up,' she manages to say.

'Of course I wish it weren't necessary, but you've brought it on yourself. Think of it as for your own good.'

'I can stay with a friend,' Minoo says. 'I have someone in mind who I can ask right away.' She'll persuade Dad to let Linnéa move in with them. And tell him what has happened. 'I'll be eighteen this summer. Let me stay with her until then, it's only a matter of a few months.'

'Is that the friend who's waiting for you in the hallway? You party together, don't you?'

'No—'

'Anyway, it's out of the question,' Diana interrupts. 'This discussion is over.'

She leans forward and fixes her eyes on Minoo.

'You are to present yourself here at nine o'clock tomorrow morning. If you don't, the police will come and pick you up.'

A small pendant on a silver chain around Diana's neck slips out from under the neckline of her T-shirt.

The pendant is the symbol of the metal element.

'I had hoped that you would prove yourself able to handle freedom responsibly,' Diana continues. 'Instead, you have abused my trust. I have no other choice.'

What is the significance of her pendant? It might easily mean nothing at all. Are there jewellery designers who think a triangle bisected by a vertical line is just the thing? Or is it really intended as the symbol of metal? If so, does it follow that Diana is a witch? Or is she *bewitched*? Could the necklace have something to do with her behaving so out of character?

The silver chain is very thin.

Minoo wonders if she can risk it. Then wonders if she can risk not to.

They are going to lock up Linnéa.

She has to do it.

Quick as a flash, Minoo reaches for the necklace. Gets a grip on it and tugs. The lock on the silver chain breaks instantly.

'Ouch!' Diana rubs the back of her neck. 'It felt like something bit me.'

She straightens up. Looks around, apparently confused.

'Now, what were we saying?' she asks.

She sees the pendant in Minoo's hand and stares at it blankly.

'Do you recognize this?' Minoo asks nervously.

Diana shakes her head.

'You know, I don't feel so well,' she says. 'Maybe we should reschedule this meeting, things have been so stressful recently…'

She stops speaking, shuffles the forms on her desk and glances at them quickly, as if trying to work out what's happened so far.

'What can we do about the apartment?' Minoo asks.

Diana stares at her, as if just woken from a dream.

Linnéa gets up from the floor as soon as the door to Diana's office opens. The butterflies in her stomach have razor-edged wings.

'What did she say?' she asks Minoo as soon as she is close enough.

The butterfly wings are beating more wildly than ever.

'I think the matter is resolved,' Minoo replies.

'How do you mean, "resolved"?'

'Let's go outside,' Minoo says. 'I've got something I need to show you.'

Once outside, Minoo pulls the packet of cigarettes from the top of one of her ankle boots. She lights a cigarette awkwardly and inhales so deeply she is practically sick on the spot. Linnéa is jumping with impatience.

'Now tell me,' she says.

'She was wearing this,' Minoo says and discreetly holds up a chain with the metal symbol dangling from it.

It glints, reflecting the sunshine. Linnéa touches it cautiously.

'Someone has been controlling Diana through the necklace,' Minoo says. 'When I pulled it off her she became quite—'

'When you *pulled it off* her?' Linnéa says disbelievingly.

Minoo grins suddenly, as if she, too, can't quite believe she did it.

'Seems that when I'm you, I take risks,' she says.

'*I* would never have dared to. Didn't it occur to you how dangerous it was?'

'I had no choice,' Minoo says and drags on her cigarette, so deeply that tears come to her eyes. 'They were going to lock you up in a home tomorrow.'

It pains Linnéa to hear this. But, above all, it is a relief to be reassured that she isn't paranoid. There *was* a conspiracy against her.

'What happened when you pulled the necklace off her?'

'She was so confused she didn't recognize it. And scared, too, really scared. I told her about the break-in, the same version you told the police. She said that she couldn't think how she'd arrived at a decision so fast.'

'But, tell me. What is she going to do about the apartment?'

'We agreed that you can keep it for now. I'm pretty sure she wants to forget about all this as soon as possible.'

'You *agreed*?'

Minoo nods and has a last drag on her cigarette.

'You're right about her,' she says. 'Diana is all right.'

'She believed you, then? I mean, me?'

'Actually, she didn't seem to know what to think about anything much,' Minoo says. 'But now we know that it wasn't Diana who did this to you. Someone's been controlling her. And we'll find out who it was.'

Linnéa looks at her friend. And asks herself if Minoo truly understands how huge this is, what a fantastic thing she has done.

The kitchen windows creak and rattle in the wind. Ida can't understand how Minoo copes with being on her own such a lot, all alone in this house.

Minoo's father phoned to say he would be late and she'd better order a pizza from Venezia. He sounded apologetic, reminded her that he will be a better dad and make up for it when he cooks dinner for her and Anna-Karin tomorrow.

Ida had almost managed to suppress all thoughts about that dinner. She had a sudden vision of what a disaster it could be, with herself and Vanessa acting madly as Minoo and Anna-Karin, with Minoo's father as the only one in the audience. For an entire evening. And immediately after the trial as well. So she told him that she had asked her friend Linnéa to join them. It would be good to have the real Minoo around to help her avoid the worst traps. And then she added that she had invited Ida Holmström, too. It felt safer to have her own body within sight.

Minoo's father sounded so pleasantly surprised it was almost sad. Obviously, Minoo doesn't have friends over a lot.

Ida pours herself a glass of juice and settles down at the kitchen table. Doesn't dare look at the darkness outside the windows.

Sitting here, she feels so exposed. But turning the light off would be even worse. Ida nervously twists a strand of Minoo's hair, so different from her own. Thicker, curlier and somehow rougher.

She wishes she could go to the stables, but has already phoned them to say that she's got flu. It seems that animals can sense when something isn't right and she doesn't want to risk alarming Troja. Any of the girls in his fan club will be only too willing to ride him.

Ida lifts the glass. And puts it down again when she hears footsteps in the garden. They're coming closer.

She gets up and tiptoes into the hall.

Most likely, it's Minoo's father who's decided to come home early tonight after all, she tells herself.

But he drives a car, her panicky mind points out instantly.

If only her powers were functioning she might be able to sense who's outside, but now she is as helpless as any non-magic person anywhere.

Feet are climbing the steps. And Ida remembers Minoo's stories about the anonymous phone calls. And the broken windows at the *Engelsfors Herald*'s office. The threatening letters that Minoo's father thinks she hasn't found out about.

Someone rings the doorbell. Ida jumps.

Whoever it is carries on ringing the bell while she stands pressed against the wall. She doesn't dare to move until she hears the steps walk away again.

She needs to make sure that the visitor really does leave

and doesn't sneak around looking for another way to get in. The house has too many windows. She *hates* it.

Ida hurries silently into the living room and peeps out from behind one of the curtains.

She instantly recognizes the figure just stepping out into the street. His upright posture. The cap and quilted jacket he wore last year as well.

G.

She runs out into the hall and throws the front door open. The chilly evening air flows in.

'Wait!' she calls.

Gustaf turns around.

'Hi,' he says as he starts walking back towards the house. 'I'm sorry if I disturbed you. Were you asleep or something?'

'Yup,' Ida says.

Gustaf's expression is so different from anything she has ever seen.

'May I come in?' he asks.

Something clicks for Ida. Gustaf is *nervous*.

'Of course you can.'

She moves out of the way.

Gustaf hangs up his jacket in a way that somehow shows he has been here before. The old jealousy starts gnawing at Ida's insides.

'Is your Dad at home?' he asks.

'No, he's working.'

'And your mom's in Stockholm now, right?'

'Yes.'

They just stand there. Their eyes meet. Both of them look away simultaneously.

'Would you like to have a cup of tea or something?' she asks.

'No, thanks, I'm fine. I just wanted to talk. If it's all right by you.'

'Of course it's all right,' Ida says a little too quickly.

'Sure. But...well, you know,' G says.

No, she doesn't know. The only thing that comes to mind is that she hasn't seen Gustaf and Minoo in each other's company for a long time. It would've been helpful if Minoo had included some info about her and G in her long list.

'Yup,' she says again.

She ushers Gustaf into the living room and they sit down on the sofa, side by side. She can feel Minoo's ears go bright red the way they always do, giving away how she feels.

She is sitting on a sofa.

Alone with G.

Despite all the time she's spent observing him, she has never before noticed the attractive *color* of his lips.

Is this it? Will it happen now? Will it come soon, the moment when he kisses her?

Better not, she reminds herself grudgingly. She doesn't want it to happen now. As far as he's concerned, she isn't Ida, she's Minoo. And she mustn't forget it.

'I feel so ashamed that I can't think where to start,' Gustaf says. 'I understand if you're angry with me. I had a feeling you wouldn't answer if I phoned. That's why I came here instead.'

Ida just nods. She must leave this to Gustaf, let him talk. Sooner or later, hopefully she'll work out what he's talking about.

'You were right all along about Positive Engelsfors,' he says. 'PE is a cult.'

He looks at her, as if to watch her reaction. It is instantaneous. Her ears go several hundred degrees hotter.

'I've felt lost ever since Rebecka died. But only now am I beginning to understand just *how* lost I've been,' he continues. 'I so wanted to believe that PE could help make me whole

505

again. Because you made me doubt them, I was angry with you. I want you to know that I've been very unhappy about the way I treated you. You used to be my best friend. The only one who really understood. And then I dumped you for...Rickard, of all people.'

Gustaf looks at Ida. His eyes are so beautiful. She wants to take him in her arms and tell him that she can forgive him anything.

'It's fine,' she says.

'It's not fine.'

'Yes, honestly. I understand that you broke down after Rebecka—'

'That's no excuse. I should have realized that there are no short cuts to being happy. Some things are *meant* to hurt. Perhaps I'll never quite get over what I felt for her. I can face that now. And...well, that's how it's got to be.'

Ida does something that, as herself, she would never have dared to do. She takes his hand and holds it tightly.

His hand is warm and smooth, just as she always imagined it. Touching him makes her vibrate.

'Right at the beginning, I had my doubts as to what they were about,' he says. 'But it is part of PE's teaching that doubt is the great enemy, exactly the thing that prevents you from being happy. So I shoved it out of my mind. Thought the answer was to work harder on myself. Then, just the other day, Rickard said something that made me wake up at last.'

He uses his free hand to rub away an angry tear.

'He said that the reason Rebecka killed herself was that she had opened herself up to the negative energies of the universe. That's why she was depressed. He went on to say that the same thing applied to people who die in natural disasters or in war. It happens because they've tuned into the wrong wavelength...fucking sick idea.'

'Yes,' Ida says. 'It is.'

Rebecka is someone Ida has avoided thinking about as much as possible. Now she can't stop herself. Last year, Ida had hated her intensely. Rebecka, who had come from nowhere and stolen Gustaf. But now, Ida realizes that she has never thought about *who* she was, as a person. While she was alive, Ida had seen Rebecka simply as an obstacle to getting Gustaf. And when she was killed, it was proof that Ida herself was in deep trouble.

Now, for the first time, she understands just how deeply Gustaf loved Rebecka. Which only makes her care *even more* for him.

'Rickard has tried for ages to persuade me to join "the innermost circle", but I've always backed away. I guess I didn't want to know what they were up to. I have no proof, but I have a suspicion that the rumor going around about Linnéa Wallin…you know, I think they might really have tried to do something to her.'

Ida wishes that she could tell him what happened, let him know about Erik, but they agreed to stick to the version Linnéa had told the police.

'Someone did break into Linnéa's apartment that night,' she says. 'She told the police.'

'I could swear the inner-circle boys are behind it. I was in the center that evening and they were definitely plotting something. I think they've lost all touch with reality. They think they can do whatever comes into their heads and no one can get back at them. It's fucking scary.'

'But now you've done the right thing? And left?'

'No, I haven't,' Gustaf replies. 'I phoned Rickard a little earlier and apologized for the way I'd reacted. And said I'd like to join the innermost circle after all.'

'But…'

'If I get in, I can dig up information to pass on to your dad. He might publish it. Someone has to expose these people before everything gets badly screwed up.'

'No, don't,' Ida says. 'It's far too dangerous!'

'I'm past caring,' Gustaf says. 'The PE jargon is all about helping others but somehow all the benefits go to people who are already strong and "successful". Just look at the members who front the organization. Like Erik and Ida.'

Ida pulls her hand away.

'Ida isn't even a member!'

'She was in the center that day.'

'I know, but just because she's going out with Erik, that's all. Was going out, I mean. It's over between them. She was never really in love with him.'

Gustaf laughs a little.

'It sounds almost as if you're defending her.'

'Why shouldn't I?'

'Are you serious?' he asks.

Ida swallows. This might well be her only chance of hearing the truth. Not that she's sure she wants to.

'What do you think is so bad about Ida, really?'

Confusion replaces Gustaf's smile.

'But you know as well as I do. She's totally false. She even bitches about her best friends. I honestly don't think Ida has any genuine feelings. Except for herself, that is.'

'Of course she does!' Ida says and, by now, her whole face is glowing. 'Of course she's got genuine feelings! Lots of them!'

'In that case she's managed to hide them pretty well,' Gustaf says.

'I think Ida is…different now,' Ida says. 'She kind of grasps that she's been wrong. At times.'

Gustaf looks searchingly at her.

'Like, I think she's trying to become a better person.'

'Do you mean it's true what they say about her backing Linnéa, instead of taking sides with Erik and his friends? Did she really?'

'Yes, she did. Honestly. So, you see, she's not all bad. It's just that she's had a hard time. It's all been, like, too much. Where to start, though?'

'What do you mean?'

'Where should Ida start? If she wanted to change?'

'What about stop bitching? Ask people she's insulted to forgive her? Though she'd better hurry up if she's going to get around to apologizing to everyone before she dies.'

Gustaf laughs.

And Ida bursts into tears. It is so sudden she doesn't have time to hold them back.

At least it isn't she who's making an idiot of herself in front of Gustaf, it's Minoo.

'What's the matter?' Gustaf asks.

Ida shakes her head.

'I'm so glad you're here,' she manages to say.

'Is this how you are when you're glad?' he smiles.

'I'm glad because we're talking, even if these are such difficult, sad subjects.'

'I know,' he says. 'I'm glad, too.'

Gustaf puts his arm around her and pulls her close. And even when she stops crying, he doesn't let go but carries on holding her.

In the night sky, the moon is hanging red and heavy, but its light shimmers like polished silver on the black surface of the stream. Minoo kneels on the damp ground of the bank. She looks at the face reflected back. The rippling water changes it constantly.

Suddenly, it is completely transformed.

Reddish-blonde curls frame a pale face. The eyes are closed. For a second, Minoo thinks it is Rebecka and reaches out to the image. Just before her fingers touch the water, the shifting outlines steady and she realizes who it is.

Her face flickered past them during the séance.

Matilda.

She opens her eyes and looks straight at Minoo.

You showed great courage today when you broke the magic bond.

Matilda's lips don't move when she speaks.

'Oh, you mean freeing Diana? Do you know anything about the necklace?'

An amulet. It was used to control her.

'But who by? Who controlled her?'

To use an amulet in that way requires powerful magic. Whoever managed Diana must have been blessed by the demons.

'But who is the Blessed One? The witch whose magic Ida felt in the Positive Engelsfors Center? Is it Helena? Or who?'

It is concealed from us.

Two black feathers come floating along. Matilda's face shivers when the feathers cross it.

The Blessed One has committed many crimes. You will soon become aware of them.

'How can you know that, when you don't know who the Blessed One is?'

Matilda only looks at her and Minoo feels increasingly frustrated. She has sympathized with the young girl who was Matilda once. But the Matilda who shows herself to them now has so little in common with a human being. She has been behaving like some elevated oracle all along, handing out the odd clue now and then. Is that what you become like after centuries on your own, with only the guardians for company?

'What should we do?' Minoo asks.

Matilda looks gravely at her.

After the trial you must identify and then stop the Blessed One.

In the sky, the red moon is extinguished. But the sprinkling of silver still glitters on the dark surface of the stream.

Time is running out.

Matilda's face shivers and then vanishes.

CHAPTER 59

Vanessa wakes up with panic shooting through her body. This is Saturday. The day of the trial. And she is the one who will take the stand as the defendant.

It is five o'clock in the morning, but she can't get back to sleep.

What happens if the body exchanges don't help? What if Anna-Karin is convicted? What will her sentence be? Will she be executed, like Simon? Or will she 'only' be tortured?

Vanessa twists and turns in bed while her thoughts whirl around in her head.

What will happen to her if Anna-Karin's body dies? Will Vanessa, her true self, also die? Or return to her own body? But then, where does Linnéa go, since she is in Vanessa's body now? And what will happen to Anna-Karin's soul …?

And a new line of thought begins. About her mom. And Melvin.

What if she never sees them again?

If she stays in bed for just one more second she'll never manage to get out of it. There's only one thing she can do. Prepare herself.

Vanessa pads across the cold floor in Anna-Karin's room and opens the door to the kitchen. The smell of cigarette smoke hits her. Anna-Karin's mother is already awake and seated at the kitchen table, puffing away and gazing absently at something outside the window. She doesn't notice Vanessa, who quietly goes into the bathroom.

Adriana phoned yesterday to remind them how important it is that they present themselves in the courtroom looking 'proper'. Vanessa has a long, hot shower, washes her hair and combs out the tangles. She finds a pair of scissors on the top shelf in the cabinet and trims the split ends.

Back in her bedroom, she puts on the only one of Anna-Karin's bras that seems to fit more or less okay. The fact is that she's using the wrong size altogether and Vanessa promises herself she'll tell Anna-Karin that. Later, if they get to live long enough.

When she starts a serious search in Anna-Karin's wardrobe she almost loses all hope. She keeps rummaging helplessly among old sweatsuits and saggy slacks.

She should have guessed. Cursing herself, she walks back to the kitchen.

'There you are. Up already?' Mia Nieminen says without looking at her daughter.

'Mom,' Vanessa says, despite the word feeling so utterly wrong, 'do you mind if I look around in your wardrobe?'

Baffled, Mia turns to look at her.

'What for?'

'I'm doing some stuff at school.'

Mia gets up and slowly leads the way into her own bedroom.

On the wall above the bed hangs a small embroidery sampler with the motto:

'There's no place like home.'

'But isn't it Saturday today?' she says as she opens the wardrobe doors.

'Yeah, but it's some special stuff.'

The contents of Mia's wardrobe are practically identical

with Anna-Karin's. But she finds a black skirt suit. Utterly boring and unfashionable, which is surely what's meant by 'proper'.

'May I borrow that suit?' Vanessa asks.

'What? Is it a funeral?'

I hope not, Vanessa thinks.

'It looks kind of grown-up, that's all,' she says.

Vanessa returns to the bathroom and puts Anna-Karin's hair up in a bun. After rooting around in the bathroom cabinet for a while, she locates a tube with nearly dried-out mascara and sharpens up the look of her lashes. She never realized before how green Anna-Karin's eyes are. Perfect, or would be if only she had a little lipgloss.

'Now we'll damn well show them,' Vanessa tells herself in the mirror.

When she walks into the kitchen, Mia stares at her.

'Goodness, you've tarted yourself up,' she says and sounds almost disapproving.

'Oh, thanks,' Vanessa says and edges past Mia to pour cornflakes and milk into a bowl.

Mia reaches for her packet of cigarettes and, at the same time, starts coughing chestily.

Christ, she smokes so much that her lungs must be full of tar, Vanessa thinks. She's a worse case than Mona Moonbeam.

Anna-Karin's mother has gone back to staring out through the window and Vanessa wonders what might actually be going on inside her head. On the surface, everything about her seems so empty and dead. Resigned. Inside her, what's it like? Just the same? All the time? Vanessa is sorry for her. But she is even sorrier for Anna-Karin.

Now she understands why Anna-Karin used her magic to change her mother. And if Vanessa had been given the same power, if she could have made her mother leave Nicke much sooner, would she have been able to resist the temptation?

She rinses her plate under the tap. Checks the time. Suddenly, she's in a hurry. Another couple of minutes and Adriana is due to collect her.

'I'm off now,' Vanessa says.

Mia doesn't even look her way. Vanessa suddenly asks herself what life would be like for Mia if something were to happen to Anna-Karin. This could be the last time she sees her daughter.

She goes to Mia and puts her arm around her. Anna-Karin's mother starts at the touch, but Vanessa doesn't back away.

'I hope you'll have a good day today, Mom,' she says. 'I care very much for you.'

She cannot make herself say that she loves her. But this is better than nothing. Mia looks down and makes a mumbling noise.

'Have a nice time,' she says, places her hand on top of Vanessa's and pats it a little awkwardly.

When Vanessa steps out into the street, the dark blue car is already there, waiting for her.

Adriana drives off the moment she shuts the car door.

'How do you feel?' Adriana asks.

'Not too bad,' Vanessa replies.

The car is warm and she pulls off Anna-Karin's duffel coat.

'You've dressed up,' Adriana says. 'Good for you.'

'If I get a death sentence I'll at least want to go out in style.'

Adriana glances at her, clearly confused. And Vanessa realizes that she sounded far too much like herself.

Driving through the center of town, Vanessa notes that yellow flags and bunting are flapping in the wind in front of the supermarket and that its window displays seem to consist mainly of posters advertising either 'POSITIVE PRICES' or 'THE SPRING REVEL'.

They drive over Canal Bridge and Vanessa stares down at the water.

She is filled with hatred for Erik and Robin. When all this is over we'll make them pay, she thinks.

And, in that instant, she realizes that she is no longer afraid. She is far too angry for that. Furious with the Council and everyone else who is against them.

Vanessa intends to win against these forces. No matter what the cost.

Anna-Karin is on her way to the manor house. She pedals Ida's bicycle as fast as she can.

She couldn't get out of the Holmström household fast enough. Carina and Anders tried to keep her at the breakfast table, intent on 'having a serious talk'. They were certainly not going to 'just stay on the sidelines' while she went about 'ruining' her 'future' and her 'whole social life'. Anna-Karin had a distinct feeling that, above all, it was their own social life they had in mind.

Cars have been parked all over the graveled area in front of the manor house but the only human beings within sight are Minoo, Linnéa and Ida. They look up when she comes.

'Where is …?' she begins as she brakes and stops near them.

'Vanessa has already gone inside. Adriana is with her,' Minoo says quickly. 'Are you ready to come along?'

Anna-Karin just nods.

She has dreaded this day for so long it's almost impossible to grasp that it has arrived.

When they walk into the grand entrance hall, the smell

of fresh paint is almost overwhelming. The window shutters are still closed, but this time lamps spread a warm light over newly painted white walls.

Viktor is waiting for them, standing at the old reception desk. His hair is combed straight back and he looks even more uptight than usual.

He greets them gravely.

'Why so gloomy?' Linnéa says. 'Surely you've been looking forward to this.'

'Not at all, Vanessa,' he replies. 'No, I haven't. Would you all please come with me.'

They walk along the hallway to the library and Anna-Karin can't stop herself from thinking of cows lining up for the slaughterhouse.

The double doors of the library are wide open and, standing guard on either side, two stony-faced men in suits. Their eyes follow Anna-Karin, Linnéa, Ida and Minoo as they walk across the black-and-white tiled floor. Anna-Karin thinks she sees a kind of gun-holster shape bulging under their jackets, but it could be that her imagination is accelerating at the same pace as her feelings of panic.

By now, there is no way back. They are caught. They have to participate in this, until the bitter end.

And it is all her fault.

Someone takes her hand. Minoo. Together, they walk through the double doors.

When Anna-Karin has tried to visualize the trial, she has imagined something like the courtrooms in crime dramas on TV, all dark wood paneling and judges in white wigs. This court sits in an ordinary conference hall, where everything is styled in white and birchwood veneer. The people who have come to watch look like any bunch of conference members. Men and women wearing businesslike outfits fill the rows of chairs.

Anna-Karin wonders if any of these people will side with her; perhaps every one of them would like nothing more than to hear her being found guilty.

Viktor ushers them to chairs at a table where Adriana is already seated. She turns and nods at them. A large antique silver brooch gleams on her sober jacket. She looks serious, but calm. It is impossible to see her now as the same woman who talked to them in the fairground just a few days ago. Her facade is intact once more. Anna-Karin would like to learn the trick.

She looks at the empty seat next to Adriana.

I ought to be sitting there, she thinks and feels her guilty fear grow stronger still.

Viktor sits down at the same table as Alexander, who's concentrating as he leafs through some documentation. Preparing for his big show. This is to be his opportunity to excel, to become even more approved of and even more loved by the Council. No wonder he seemed to revel in the interrogations, since he knew he was leading them straight into a trap.

There is a door at the very front of the courtroom, and next to it is a table with five chairs behind it. To the right of the table stands a solitary chair, unlike any of the others in the room. It is high-backed and made of some kind of metal that's blackened with age. Anna-Karin understands immediately. That chair is for the witnesses as they are being heard.

Anna-Karin squeezes Minoo's hand harder.

The door in front of them all opens and, as if on a given signal, everyone stands. Anna-Karin follows the movement and, next to her, Minoo, Ida and Linnéa do too.

The five judges enter. Two women and three men, all more or less ancient. One by one, they sit down at the judges' table.

'Please be seated,' the woman in the middle commands.

She is wearing a suit in a dark red color that makes Anna-Karin think of blood.

'Escort the defendant into the court,' the woman says.

Anna-Karin turns to look. Like everyone else.

Two guards enter from the library with Vanessa between them.

Anna-Karin has never seen herself like this. She wears Mom's funeral suit. Walks easily, with her head high. Her hair is pulled back in a bun at the base of her neck. She looks almost beautiful.

As she is led towards the judges' table, Vanessa's gaze stays steady. But Anna-Karin can see that she is nervous.

What have I done? Anna-Karin thinks. How could I land the others in this mess?

The guards leave Vanessa at Adriana's table. Alexander rises.

'Your Honors,' he says. 'You see before you the defendant, Anna-Karin Nieminen. She is accused of having violated the laws of the Council. I propose that she is heard first, may it please Your Honors.'

'As you wish, Prosecutor,' the woman in the blood-red suit says, then stands up with an ease that belies her advanced age. 'I hereby declare the trial of Anna-Karin Nieminen begun.'

CHAPTER 60

Vanessa sits down on the ice-cold, hard chair. The metal armrests have been worn shiny and she imagines the many hands gripping them, the bodies that must have been writhing in agony while occupying this seat. But she doesn't sense any magic.

Instead she feels all the eyes focused on her. She forces herself to meet them.

The judges. The people in the audience. Viktor, who watches her with absolute concentration. Alexander, who manages somehow to look cool and under control at the same time as being full of expectation. Adriana, who nods encouragingly.

Vanessa looks at Ida, Linnéa and Minoo, before letting her eyes rest on Anna-Karin.

I'll fix this, Vanessa tells herself.

She takes a deep breath and straightens up, as much as Anna-Karin's body will let her.

'Are you Anna-Karin Nieminen?'

Alexander is walking slowly towards her. He moves with self-assurance, as if his victory is already won and all that remains is a minor formality, soon to be dealt with. Vanessa presses her fingertips against the cold metal.

'Are you Anna-Karin Nieminen?' he says again.

Is 'yes' a lie? Vanessa doesn't know. Sure, Anna-Karin's

body is sitting on the chair. But does this make the whole into Anna-Karin?

'Yes,' she replies.

She waits. Her tense hands clutch the armrests. Nothing happens.

'Your defense counsel has informed you of the consequences of lying to the court. Are you prepared to swear that you will tell the truth throughout this trial?'

Now, it is definitely time for a lie. She steels herself against the pain. She can almost feel it already. She glances at Linnéa, trying to find strength in her.

'Yes.'

But still nothing happens. Her hands relax a little.

'You are charged with practicing magic without the permission of the Council,' Alexander continues. 'You are further charged with having employed your magic power with a degree of openness that put you at risk of being exposed to the non-magic community as a witch. In addition, we cannot exclude the possibility that you may have used magic to break non-magic laws. Do you understand the charges made against you?'

'I do,' Vanessa says.

'Last autumn, you grossly abused your powers,' Alexander states. 'You used your earth magic in order to influence the image many people had of you. Is that correct?'

'Yes.'

'Why?'

Vanessa can't help thinking about Anna-Karin at Jonte's party and how they had to stop her from practically raping Jari. And then she thinks about all the times they tried to stop her doing magic in school, tried to make her understand that she risked giving them all away to the demons. But Anna-Karin wouldn't even admit that she used her power.

Is it so impossible to imagine that I could become popular without it?

She had detested Anna-Karin for what she did then. But now it is up to Vanessa to understand her, so she can save her.

'I know I behaved egotistically,' Vanessa says. 'I was aware all along that it was wrong of me. But all I wanted was for people to like me.'

Someone in the courtroom tut-tuts.

'I've been bullied for as long as I can remember,' Vanessa says and steals a quick glance at Anna-Karin. 'Even in pre-school. And it carried on, right through school. That's how it goes in a town like Engelsfors. Once something like that has begun, you never get free of it. Every day was like hell for me, over and over again ...'

'So you were driven by a desire for revenge?' Alexander asks.

'Yes, but not that alone. I had been given an opportunity to make life seem a little fairer. I took the chance. And I believe you would have done the same in my shoes, all of you. At heart, you know you would have.'

Vanessa looks straight at the judges, but they appear to be utterly indifferent, almost bored. The Council despises weakness. Why be merciful to someone like Anna-Karin?

'Call it what you like,' Alexander says. 'The facts of the matter are that you used your powers for personal gain and, by doing so, you broke the law of the Council. The case against you is more damning since you are one of the mythical Chosen Ones. Your responsibility is therefore greater than that of others.'

Now that she knows he ranks the Chosen Ones somewhere on a level with Santa Claus, she easily picks up the contempt in his voice.

'Do you admit that you broke the law of the Council?' Alexander asks.

'When we spoke in Kärrgruvan, you said yourself that I could not be held responsible for what I did before I knew of the Council's law. I didn't know which law applied to us.'

He cannot hide a slight smile.

'True, you did not know. Not initially. But later, you were informed by Adriana Lopez, isn't that so?'

He so loves doing this, Vanessa thinks. He is utterly convinced that he has got Anna-Karin in the bag. Certain that we can't get out of this hole. He is ready to show the Santas who is in charge.

'Yes.'

'And why did you continue to use your powers afterwards?'

Time now to go for the big lie. The lie everything depends on. Vanessa hardens her mind and body once more, in readiness for her punishment, for a great, piercing wave of pain.

'I did not continue,' she says. 'As soon as I was told, I stopped.'

She feels nothing.

Well, something. A little tingle of triumphant delight.

Over at the prosecution's table, Viktor goes pale. The whispering in the audience dies down when an old man on the judges' table raises his hand to demand silence.

'I must ask you to try and think carefully,' Alexander says between his teeth. 'When did you stop using your magic powers inappropriately?'

'As soon as I was told that it was forbidden,' Vanessa says. 'When Adriana Lopez told us who she is. And who we are. And what the Council is. She told me right there and then that I must stop using magic.'

She pauses dramatically and looks at Alexander.

'So of course I did. Stop, that is.'

523

'She is lying,' Alexander says.

'How could I? You've worked quite hard to prevent it.'

'During the preparatory hearings, my assistant, Viktor Ehrenskiöld, definitely registered that you lied when you made this same statement.'

'I have no idea what I'm supposed to say about that,' Vanessa remarks calmly, while looking straight at Viktor. 'Maybe you had one of your off-days?'

Linnéa titters and Vanessa doesn't dare to look at her for fear she too might start laughing.

'Your family barn burned down,' Alexander goes on. 'And you're aware that the fire was magic, aren't you?'

'I am now, because you told me during the interrogation,' Vanessa points out. 'But when it happened I had no idea.'

Alexander's eyes narrow.

'Are you sure of this?'

'I don't know what you want me to say. But I won't lie. I know what the consequences are.'

Alexander comes closer. He is furious. About to explode.

Good, Vanessa thinks. You're showing yourself up more and more in front of everyone you want to impress.

'Have you ever experimented with magic without the supervision of the Council?'

'No.'

'She's lying!' Alexander exclaims and turns towards the judges again. 'I don't know how she's doing it, but she is!'

Adriana stands up and starts to speak.

'Your Honors, with all due respect, I did point out from the beginning that this trial is a waste of your precious time. As you can observe for yourselves, Anna-Karin is innocent of the charges made against her. I must add that, in my view, Prosecutor Ehrenskiöld is harassing the defendant to attempt to prove his baseless assumptions. I hereby request that this trial be declared invalid.'

The dinosaurs on the stage turn to each other and have a mumbling exchange. Then the woman in the red suit looks straight at Alexander.

'We concede that this is a most unexpected turn of events,' she says in her sharp voice. 'But this trial will continue. Does the defense have any questions for the defendant?'

'No, Your Honor,' Adriana says. 'I deem that to be unnecessary.'

'In that case, I now call Ida Holmström to the witness stand,' Alexander says. Then he adds, with a furious glance at Vanessa, 'You may stand down.'

Minoo looks at the closed shutters and wonders if it is dark outside yet. Inside the courtroom, time seems to have ceased to exist.

Linnéa is sitting on the witness chair now. She is the last of the Chosen Ones to be called for questioning. And she sails through it, just as the others have. Even Minoo.

As the day passes, the atmosphere in the courtroom has changed noticeably. The members of the Council are tired and fed up. The judges look increasingly impatient. That, in turn, makes Alexander more and more stressed. Makes him spit out his questions. Viktor is sitting silently at the prosecutor's table. He is staring blankly into the middle distance, as if he cannot, will not, believe what is happening.

Minoo has worked out how this has happened. It is thanks to that side effect of the body exchange, the short-circuiting of their magic, that lying is possible. When they swapped bodies, their powers were lost. They have no elements that can be turned against them.

'Thank you, Vanessa,' Alexander says finally. 'You may stand down.'

And wordlessly, Linnéa gets up and walks past him, so close that she almost touches him before going to sit down next to Minoo.

Alexander goes to speak quietly with Viktor for a while.

One of the old men at the judges' table coughs repeatedly, loud barking noises that echo in the otherwise silent room.

'Your Honors,' Alexander begins again. 'I would like to call one additional witness.'

Clearly irritated, the white-haired woman in the center of the row of judges looks at him.

'Do try to be quick,' she says and Alexander nods.

'I hereby call Adriana Lopez to the witness stand,' he says.

Minoo is suddenly wide awake. Adriana knows everything. And she cannot lie.

The chairs behind Minoo start to squeak and scrape as the Council members come back to life. Now they are stretching and whispering excitedly.

Minoo never even imagined that Anna-Karin's defense advocate would herself be heard. Terrified, she stares at Adriana.

But Adriana looks quite calm as she walks towards the witness chair and sits down. Then, just as calmly, she scans the audience. Waits.

'Can you confirm that you are Adriana Lopez, sent to Engelsfors on behalf of the Council in order to investigate the prophecy of the Chosen Ones?'

'Yes, I can,' she says and meets her brother's gaze.

'And that you will be speaking the truth during these proceedings?'

'Yes.'

Anna-Karin grabs hold of Minoo's arm and Minoo feels her nails through the sleeve of her sweater.

'Last autumn, you reported certain suspicions concerning Anna-Karin Nieminen. You believed that she misused her powers, even though you had informed her about the law of the Council?'

'Yes.'

'In other words, she has been lying to the court?'

'No,' Adriana replies.

Minoo realizes that she has been holding her breath ever since Adriana sat down, but she is almost too scared to let the air out again, in case she is heard to sigh with relief.

Alexander stands with his back to Minoo, but his body language is easy to read all the same. This was his last option. His last hope. And now it's gone.

But how is this possible? Minoo wonders. How can Adriana lie?

'I reported my suspicions,' Adriana continues. 'But I had no proof, at any time. And neither do you.'

Is there a hint of a smile tweaking one corner of her mouth?

'Adriana Lopez,' Alexander says. 'Are you loyal to the Council?'

'Yes, I am. Always.'

Alexander stands very still. The room is so silent the faint humming in the ventilation shaft is audible.

'Since your arrival in Engelsfors, have your reports to the Council always been honest?'

'I believe, Alexander, that my previous answer is sufficient. I am completely loyal to the Council.'

'That is all for today,' the leading judge pronounces. 'I have heard enough. We will deliberate and announce the verdict tomorrow.'

When they finally leave the manor house, the evening air almost gives Minoo an oxygen high. It also makes her even more aware how much she longs for a smoke. She finds the packet in Linnéa's bag and lights a cigarette.

'May I have one too, please?' Adriana asks. Amazed, Minoo looks at her.

'Of course,' she says and holds out the packet.

'I'm worn out,' Vanessa says.

'It's been such a long day,' Adriana says and puts her hand on Vanessa's arm. 'Especially for you, Anna-Karin.'

'Long, but a success from beginning to end,' Linnéa says.

'Yes, really,' Adriana says and lights up. 'And I don't want to know how it was done.'

She and Minoo drag on their cigarettes. Adriana must never know how they managed to get through the trial. She is already in possession of far too much information that could become dangerous for her.

'And we don't want you to tell us either,' Minoo says to Adriana.

It's not true. She would dearly like to know more.

'What happens tomorrow?' Vanessa asks.

'I doubt that Alexander will want to carry on with the prosecution,' Adriana says and looks fondly at her. 'He won't care to risk making even more of an ass of himself. The case will be closed. They have no proof.'

Viktor comes out and stands at the top of the steps. When he catches sight of them, his eyes darken to the deepest blue. As he walks towards them, Minoo feels triumph sparkle inside her.

'Well, congratulations,' he says and looks at Linnéa. 'You won. You humiliated us totally, just as you said you would. You didn't lie that time, anyway.'

Linnéa grins while she twists a strand of Vanessa's blonde hair.

'How did you do it?' Viktor asks.

'I've no idea what you're talking about,' Minoo tells him.

'Linnéa, listen,' he says plaintively and looks at her. 'I saved your life.'

'And for that, I'm very grateful to you,' Minoo replies.

'You presumably don't know either how they managed it?' Viktor says and turns to Adriana.

'No, Viktor. I truly don't know.'

He stares at Adriana, and Minoo realizes that he is reading her mind, trying to catch her out in a lie.

'And how did you do it?' he asks.

Not a muscle moves in Adriana's face.

Viktor sighs, turns away so abruptly that the gravel crunches under his heels and walks back into the house.

'Alexander must hate us by now,' Linnéa says with a little laugh.

'He certainly will,' Adriana replies gravely. 'You've humiliated him and Viktor in front of some of the most influential members of the Council. He will want to restore his reputation above all. I think it is over for now, though, and I feel hugely relieved and happy. But I know Alexander will be biding his time.'

'We won't ever be free of him, is that it?' Anna-Karin asks.

'For now, I'm sure we are free of him,' Adriana says and a cautious smile suddenly emerges. 'There's nothing left for him to do in Engelsfors.'

Minoo looks at the others, takes in their relief. She wishes she could feel the same. But she hasn't had any opportunity to tell them about her dream.

After the trial you must identify and then stop the Blessed One.

Time is running out.

CHAPTER 61

Minoo feels it is very peculiar to be in her own room together with all the other Chosen Ones. Most peculiar of all, to see herself sit on her bed. Actually, it's unpleasant to think that Ida has slept in that bed for the last two nights. Minoo hadn't even had time to hide her diary. She can only hope that Ida has had enough distractions recently to keep her from snooping.

Minoo has just told them about her dream and the task that Matilda gave them.

'Now, we at least have something to go by. We know that the person who controlled Diana is no ordinary witch, but someone blessed by the demons,' Vanessa says. 'We can't be sure, of course, but Positive Engelsfors seems like a good place to start looking.'

'Minoo! Any chance of giving me a hand?' Minoo's father calls from the kitchen.

Ida pulls her fingers through Minoo's hair so vigorously Minoo worries it might come off. Ida glances anxiously at her.

'I'll come along too,' Minoo says and they go downstairs together.

Dad is standing at the cooker, wiping his forehead on his shirtsleeve. Then he bends to sniff the steam rising from the saucepan.

Minoo has missed him. Not only these last two days while she lived Linnéa's life. Her sense of loss has been with her for longer than that. Ever since the time when everything was peaceful and normal at home. Before the fights. Before Mom moved away.

She wishes she could hug him this minute. Tell him how much she loves him. Obviously, it's out of the question. He would think Linnéa had gone out of her mind.

'Almost done now,' he says. 'Minoo, would you set the table?'

Minoo points discreetly at the cupboard where they keep the guest china. Ida opens it and takes out plates.

'Let me help,' Minoo says.

She picks six glasses from the right shelf.

'Good to have all these people eating with us,' Dad says and drains the potato pan. 'I've looked forward to this, you know. You can tell the rest of them to come down now.'

Ida calls up the stairs. Minoo distributes the cutlery while the others get seated. When Dad finally sits down, he has placed a still-steaming oven roast, potatoes, gravy, and a bowl of salad on the table. It looks so nice, Minoo can hardly keep her fingers off it, but Linnéa sends her a warning glance.

'I'm so sorry,' Minoo says. 'I forgot to mention that I don't eat meat.'

Dad stares at her, clearly stressed. Then he turns to Ida.

'Come on, Minoo, why didn't you say?'

'Sorry, I forgot.'

'It's not a problem,' Minoo says. 'I'll be happy with potatoes, gravy and salad.'

'Probably you can't have the gravy either,' Linnéa says quickly. 'Not if it's made with meat stock.'

'Oh no, that's true,' Minoo says and glances at Dad. 'But there's always bread and cheese.'

Fire

Dad clears his throat. Gestures at the food to show that everyone is to help herself. Anna-Karin dishes up a large portion for herself and Ida glances crossly at her.

'Well, now,' Dad says. 'How come you decided to go vegetarian?'

'Where would you like her to start?' Linnéa says. 'The evils of the meat production industry or the moral position in general?'

Involuntarily, Minoo makes a face. But Dad only smiles.

'That's straight talking,' he says. 'Good. It's important for you to form your own opinions and stand up for them.'

'Yes, indeed,' Ida says emphatically.

Dad looks quizzically at her. For quite a while, no one can think of anything to say. Linnéa shuffles a piece of meat around in the gravy and then tries to hide most of it behind some potatoes.

'This is really good,' Ida says.

Everyone agrees warmly.

'Thank you, that's nice. I enjoyed cooking something from scratch,' Dad says. 'It's been a while.'

'It's fantastic!' Ida says brightly. 'Have you all got what you want or can I fetch anything?'

Ida is far too ingratiating. Hopefully, Dad will just think that Minoo is nervous and that's why she acts like an over-anxious hostess.

'Anna-Karin, would you like some more water?' Ida asks.

Vanessa smiles stiffly and allows Ida to top up her glass.

'Has anything interesting happened at work today?' Ida asks and puts the jug down.

'Actually, I have a sad piece of news for you,' Dad says. 'Your old headmaster, Ingmar Svensson...Surely you all knew him?'

Minoo remembers a gray man who probably would have

preferred to be left alone with his office work than to have anything to do with people. Especially not fourteen- and fifteen-year-olds.

'He's died,' Dad says.

Vanessa spills water on her plate.

'Oh no, I'm sorry,' she says, trying to mop up with her napkin and getting gravy all over it. 'How did he die?'

'Some kind of electric shock,' Dad says. 'They don't know exactly how it happened, but think there was something wrong with the cables in his office. A most tragic business. It might be related to the constant problems with the town supply recently. The electricity company has started to investigate if the risk of accidents is greater than usual. After all, Svensson is not the first casualty.'

'What do you mean?' Minoo says.

'I'm thinking of Leila Barsotti. One of Minoo's former elementary school teachers.'

'Did she die from an electric shock too?' Minoo asks.

'Yes, she did, though the paper didn't report it.'

Vanessa turns to Ida.

'Minoo, later on, you really must show me that gadget … in your room,' she says.

Ida looks blankly at her.

'Of course,' Minoo says and meets Ida's gaze. 'We might go and check it out after the main course. Before dessert. Would that be all right … Erik?'

She almost said 'Dad' but stopped herself at the last moment.

He nods and has a second helping of the roast.

'Sure, go ahead,' he says. 'I won't try to interfere with your secret plans.'

The rest of the meal flows nicely and even grows fairly enjoyable, but Minoo can't wait for it to end.

Vanessa knows something and Minoo simply has to find out what it is.

Minoo's room is decorated in warmer colors than the rest of the house and Linnéa really likes it. She sits back on the soft bed, with Ida and Anna-Karin on either side. Vanessa stands by the desk, beautiful in the low lamplight. Linnéa felt so proud of her when she saw her speak from the witness chair today. She was so obviously *Vanessa* that Linnéa couldn't think how Alexander could possibly fail to see it.

'Listen to this, it's so awful,' Vanessa says. 'The other day, Mona told Svensson's future and she saw that he would die soon. And now, when Minoo's father started to speak about electric shocks, something else occurred to me. Last autumn, Nicke was going on about a psychologist who had died from an electric shock. And no one could work out how it had happened.'

Linnéa goes rigid. A psychologist. Who had died.

'Svensson, Minoo's old teacher and a psychologist,' Vanessa continues. 'Three people, all killed by mysterious electrical shocks. True, the town supply has been fucked up for ages but so what? This is Engelsfors. The deaths can't just be coincidences.'

Minoo nods eagerly.

'Remember, Matilda says that the demons' Blessed One had many more crimes on his or her conscience and that we would soon realize this. It must be the Blessed One who's behind the deaths. And if it's electricity that's killed them...'

She turns to Ida.

'Diana's amulet bore the sign of metal,' she continues. 'Electricity and metal magic belong together, right?'

'Thanks for the info,' Ida says sarcastically.

'So it seems reasonable to assume that the demons' Blessed

One is a metal witch who has been controlling Diana and has brought about the deaths of at least three people during the last year. Question – why those particular three?'

Linnéa finds it hard to take in what Minoo is saying.

A psychologist.

She thinks about Jakob and how depressed he has seemed all autumn. And recalls what went on in his mind the day she read it …

… she is dead…she truly is dead …

'You know CAMH? The Child and Adolescent Mental Health clinic?' she asks. 'My psychologist there was totally heartbroken last autumn. His coworker had died, you see…'

She suspects that she knows what the three dead people have in common. But doesn't want to say anything before she is certain.

'If it's her, the one Nicke was talking about, her name began with an R. Regina, I think.'

Minoo switches her computer on and opens up a website page.

'Look, you can search the classified obits here, all of which have been published in the papers anywhere in the country.'

'So that's the kind of thing you home in on when you're surfing?' Ida says.

'Regina is quite unusual,' Minoo says. 'Vanessa, can you remember roughly when Nicke mentioned that death?'

'We had dug up that grave the same evening.'

'August, then,' Minoo says. 'Here. I've found her. The date fits. And the ad was published in the *Engelsfors Herald*. She was only thirty years old. Could it be her?'

Linnéa swallows. It is so absolutely incredible. And yet so logical.

'It's her. And I know what links the three dead people,' she says. 'Elias.'

She looks at Ida.

'You started bullying him in elementary school,' Linnéa says.

Ida blinks. But she does not object.

'Helena and Krister clearly didn't want to admit that their son was hounded by their friends' children. But they couldn't get away from the fact that Elias had a hard time in school. Instead, they blamed the teacher. Leila. I know that they even tried to have her fired. Later on, his problems grew really bad. By then, there was no point in trying to have all the teachers fired, so they targeted Svensson instead. Elias told me about all this.'

'How does the psychologist fit in?' Vanessa asks.

'Elias used to see her. He liked her. She helped him…But Helena hated his going to see her. She hates all psychologists and thinks it's somehow damaging to "root around in all these negative things". Besides, I think she was afraid that Regina would turn Elias against her. Despite her being such a fantastic, perfect mom.'

Fury makes her eyes fill with burning tears and she falls silent. Another word and she will start crying. She doesn't want the others to see that.

'The demons' Blessed One must be Helena,' Ida says. 'All the pieces are slotting into place. We were right all along.'

'She wants to revenge herself on everyone who, in her mind, has hurt Elias,' Vanessa says to Linnéa. 'Do you think it was her plan for Erik and Robin to kill you as well? Did she control them the same way that she did with Diana?'

'Have you ever seen Erik wear a necklace?' Minoo asks Ida.

'No, I haven't. And he'd never accept one,' Ida says. 'He thinks jewelry on men is strictly for queers.'

Ida glances at Linnéa, who realizes that they are both thinking about the same events.

Like all the times when Erik shouted 'Fairy' at Elias. When he ripped off Elias's necklaces and bracelets. The time he tore off an earring.

And Ida would always be around somewhere, laughing or just letting it happen.

But Linnéa can't muster any hatred now. That time has passed, though she will never forget it.

'I don't believe that they were meant to kill me,' she says. 'They must have been sent out by Helena to make sure I was thrown out of the apartment. Erik and Robin went as far as they did on their own initiative. Though Helena clearly had no problems with lying and providing alibis for them when the police asked questions.'

'Perhaps she doesn't dare attack you directly,' Minoo suggests. 'If she's communicating with the demons they will surely have told her who we are. The same goes for Adriana. The demons must know that she's a witch too and they must also be aware that the Council exists. Perhaps they don't want Helena to attract attention from other witches.'

'Ruining our lives has to be satisfaction enough,' Linnéa says.

'But it doesn't have to be Helena, does it?' Anna-Karin points out. 'Couldn't it be Krister?'

'Regardless of which one of them it is, they work together in any case,' Linnéa says.

'But we've never noticed either of them using magic,' Anna-Karin says.

'That's not so strange, though. The demons are bound to have told them to be cautious,' Vanessa says. 'And remember, Ida sensed the magic in the center.'

Anna-Karin nods slowly.

Minoo's father calls to them to say that dessert is waiting.

'We'll be down soon!' Ida shouts back.

'We'll talk more about all these things after the trial,' Minoo says. 'We'd better stay well away from Helena and Krister now that we have no powers.'

They get up and everyone leaves the room. All except Vanessa who lingers. She has turned towards the window and seems to be staring out into the night.

'What's the matter?' Linnéa asks.

'I'm just thinking about Svensson. Mona said it was inevitable. But if only we had worked all this out a little earlier...'

'If Svensson hadn't died we wouldn't have figured it out at all,' Linnéa says and hears how cold she sounds. 'I didn't mean it like that.'

'I know,' Vanessa says.

She looks wonderingly at Linnéa.

'What's the matter?' Linnéa asks once more.

'It's so strange to see my own face like this.'

It's even stranger to see Anna-Karin's face and still be this much in love, Linnéa thinks.

'I want to know what it's like to touch me,' Vanessa says.

She holds out her hand. Linnéa shuts her eyes and feels Vanessa's hand gently stroke her cheek.

She doesn't dare to say anything.

When Vanessa's hand leaves her Linnéa reluctantly opens her eyes.

'Strange...' Vanessa says.

They look at each other.

So close together.

But Wille stands between them.

Can't stop remembering that kiss. I want more.

'We'd better join the others, I guess,' Linnéa says and walks away.

CHAPTER 62

It is a chilly, misty Sunday morning, but when Anna-Karin cycles through Engelsfors she senses something new in the air. A promise of spring.

She skids on the gravel, puts Ida's bicycle on its stand and hurries into the dully-lit manor house.

She pushes past all the people standing around in the lobby and enters the library. The other Chosen Ones are standing together by one of the windows. Adriana has joined them but otherwise they are alone in the room.

'Hello, Ida,' she says when she catches sight of Anna-Karin. 'The judges are deliberating. They'll call us in when they are ready.'

'How long will it take?'

'Impossible to say. Anything from a few minutes to several hours.'

Anna-Karin can't think how she can bear waiting. She looks at the armchairs, but doesn't feel like settling down in one of them. They remind her too strongly of the interrogation. Presumably, the others feel the same, since they are both unoccupied.

She has hardly slept a wink all night. She doesn't dare believe that they've got away with it. The verdict has not yet been announced. And then there is all this about Helena and Krister Malmgren, and the murders …

'What *are* they doing in there?' Ida says.

'You mustn't worry,' Adriana says gently. 'The proceedings are per usual.'

Ida sighs loudly. Anna-Karin watches her.

In the early hours of the morning, just when Anna-Karin had managed to fall asleep, Ida's phone had woken her. Julia was on the line. Drunk. Blurred speech. But sounding happy. Wanted Ida to guess who she had just been kissing. And then Julia handed the phone over to Erik.

'We wanted you to know that we're having a fucking great time without you. That's all,' he said. 'Like, *fucking* great.'

Julia was giggling in the background. Anna-Karin cut the call. Turned the phone off.

'They're probably just trying to wind us up,' Linnéa says and tips her head towards the closed door of the courtroom.

'In that case they're doing fine,' Ida says.

An hour passes. Then two. For Minoo, time is crawling.

Every minute ticking past is valuable time lost. They must stop Helena and Krister. Prevent them from killing anyone else. Prevent them from setting off the apocalypse.

But for as long as they are sitting around here, they can do nothing. Not even talk freely with each other.

And still not the slightest sign of life from the judges.

Minoo stops in front of the fireplace and drums with her fingertips on the mantelpiece.

She is thinking about the amulet that Diana had worn on the chain. Adriana also had an amulet. She had bought hers from Mona Moonbeam. Could Mona also have been the one who sold the metal sign amulet to Helena and Krister?

Minoo looks at Vanessa, who sits next to Linnéa on a windowsill. They must confront Mona, all of them together. Try to persuade her to tell them all she knows. According to

Vanessa, Mona always refuses to reveal anything about her customers. But maybe she hasn't realized that she has been trading with the demons' Blessed One?

If worst comes to worst, Anna-Karin must force her to tell, Minoo thinks.

She doesn't like the idea, but people's lives are at stake.

She needs a smoke.

'Is it all right if I go outside, just for a short while?' she asks Adriana. 'I really want…a little fresh air.'

Adriana looks troubled.

'The judges might rise any minute now.'

'I'll be quick,' Minoo says.

'I'll come with you,' Linnéa says and gets up at once.

As soon as they are in the driveway, Minoo pulls the packet of cigarettes from the top of Linnéa's boot and lights up.

'I've been thinking about something,' Linnéa says in a low voice. 'To do with what we were talking about yesterday.'

'Not here,' Minoo says and glances over her shoulder while she sucks on the cigarette.

She inhales the smoke so eagerly she feels nauseated.

'I know,' Linnéa says. 'But there's just one thing that's important. I've thought of two people we must warn.'

Minoo only has time to nod before the front door opens. When she turns to face it, Adriana stands in the doorway and waves impatiently at them to come back in.

'They're about to announce the verdict now,' she says.

Everyone stands when the five judges enter the courtroom and process to their seats. Today, the senior judge is wearing a black suit and a black blouse. This outfit makes Anna-Karin think of death.

'We have just had an appeal from the prosecution. They are asking to conduct one last witness hearing,' the judge says, having indicated that the audience may sit. 'And we have decided to allow it.'

Anna-Karin checks the prosecutor's table. Alexander is alone. Viktor is nowhere to be seen. Adriana stands.

'Your Honor,' she says. 'The defense has not been informed...'

But the old woman silences her with one glance.

'The case before us is of such a serious nature that we are unwilling to convict and sentence before every item of evidence has been thoroughly investigated,' she says and then addresses Alexander. 'Chief Prosecutor, you may begin.'

Alexander rises.

'Thank you, Your Honor,' he says. 'We call Adriana Lopez to the witness chair.'

The Chosen Ones exchange glances. But Adriana shows no sign of unease when she gets up and walks to the witness chair.

'Adriana Lopez,' Alexander says, but he isn't looking at her.

He turns towards the audience instead. And now Anna-Karin begins to feel fearful. Alexander's self-confidence has returned.

'You stated yesterday that you are loyal to the Council. Do you stand by that statement?'

'Of course I do,' Adriana says.

'You also swore that you would tell the truth. But did you keep to that commitment?'

'Yes.'

Alexander nods to the guards at the entrance. They open both doors.

Viktor enters the courtroom. He is carrying a birdcage. Black wings beat against the bars of the cage which is far too small and Anna-Karin feels every blow. She too wants to escape.

As if hypnotized, Adriana stares fixedly at Viktor and the bird.

'You have stored any compromising memories in your familiar,' Alexander says. 'This enabled you to lie to the court yesterday, is that not so?'

'I have no intention of replying to that question.'

'There is no need,' Alexander says.

He now nods to Viktor, who places the birdcage on the table and opens its door.

The raven crows furiously at Viktor, who fumbles inside the cage until he manages to grab hold of the bird's body. Using his other hand to hold its beak firmly closed, he hauls the bird out. He has to bend his neck to protect his face when the raven spreads its wings and flaps wildly in the air.

Alexander takes the raven from Viktor's hands and grips its head hard.

'Please, don't...' Adriana says in a strangled voice.

Anna-Karin looks down at the tabletop. She knows that Alexander will do it.

And then he does.

A hard, crunching sound. A moist thing ripping. For a short time afterwards, the wings keep beating. Then the room falls completely silent. Anna-Karin's gorge is rising; she holds it back, swallows several times.

She looks up again just in time to see Alexander hand the dead bird to Viktor. Stony-faced, he places the body in the birdcage.

'Let us begin again,' Alexander says. 'Adriana Lopez. Have you been loyal to the Council in everything you have done since you arrived in Engelsfors?'

Anna-Karin watches Adriana's face. Observes one eyelid trembling, almost unnoticeably.

'Yes,' she replies.

Her head is thrown back. A faint moan, starting far down in her throat, finally reaches her mouth. Her jaws clench. She begins to hyperventilate.

It is all unbearable and yet Anna-Karin cannot take her eyes off Adriana. It feels as if it is her duty to watch. It is Anna-Karin's fault that Adriana is being tortured.

'No!' Adriana finally screams. 'No!'

And her body sags in the chair.

'Can you clarify that answer?' Alexander asks.

Adriana looks at him. A drop of blood from one of her nostrils trickles slowly down to her upper lip.

'No, I have not been loyal to the Council.'

The judges sit up on their chairs.

'Have you permitted the Chosen Ones to practice magic on their own?' Alexander asks.

'No.'

Adriana's head is thrown backwards again. Her back twists spasmodically and the pain makes her scream loudly. Fire, her own element, is being used against her. It must feel like being set alight.

Anna-Karin cannot stand this any more. She must take responsibility. She must confess.

She tries to stand, but Linnéa immediately pulls her down.

'We need you,' Linnéa whispers. She seems to have understood exactly what Anna-Karin has in mind. 'The world needs you. Adriana knows it, too. Do you think she would have run this risk if she hadn't realized that?'

Anna-Karin starts to cry, then tries not to sob, afraid that she might irritate the judges and ruin things even more for Adriana.

Alexander gestures and Adriana's body relaxes.

'We can carry on like this for any length of time. Speak the truth now. For your own sake.'

He sounds almost saddened and this frightens Anna-Karin even more. How can he do this, if he has feelings at all?

'I will never say anything that might harm the girls,' Adriana says. Her breathing is heavy and labored. '*Never.*'

'In fact, you chose to take their side rather than the Council's?' Alexander says.

'I was not aware that I had to take one side or the other. I believed that the Council should support the Chosen Ones. Apparently, I was wrong.'

The courtroom fills with excited whispers.

'I will not answer any more questions,' Adriana says.

The old woman in the middle of the row of judges looks unmoved.

'No further questions are required. We are ready now to pass judgment on the defendant,' the judge says. 'Anna-Karin Nieminen. Please stand.'

Vanessa stands. Anna-Karin forces herself to look at her. Tears are running down her face, but she must be strong. Brave. Like Adriana.

The judge clasps her hands on the tabletop and leans forward.

'The world is facing a new magic epoch,' she says. 'But with magic comes power and power can always be misused. Therefore, the ideals of the Council are more important than ever. Control. Honesty. Humility. Selflessness. The defendant has proved herself lacking in all these virtues. Indeed, she has acted in opposition to them. She has spat at everything the Council holds in high regard or believes to be sacred.'

Now Anna-Karin realizes it is all over.

'Anna-Karin Nieminen,' the judge says. 'This court has decided to ignore all the accusations against you and to free you.'

Anna-Karin can hardly grasp what is being said. She has

to test the words repeatedly inside her head to make sure that they actually mean what they seem to.

'It is true that Anna-Karin Nieminen has shown poor judgment,' the judge continues. 'However, we do not hold her responsible for her rebelliousness and law-breaking activities, since she at no time received appropriate guidance. In this most distressing case, only one person is guilty. That person is Adriana Lopez.'

The judge points her bony finger at Adriana.

'Your treachery and acts of conspiracy have finally come to light. You have systematically falsified evidence in order to deceive your superiors. Your aim has been to induce them to believe in your ludicrous notions about exceptional, chosen witches, demons and apocalyptic events.'

If Anna-Karin had been empowered just then, if she had been able to use her power in this courtroom, she would have made them stop the entire trial and save Adriana. And to hell with the consequences. Now, all she can do is sit and watch. Helpless, worthless, passive while everything is collapsing around them.

'The proposition that there are "Chosen Ones" in Engelsfors is a deceit from beginning to end. What we are dealing with here is a group of powerful natural witches, who have been duped by a ruthless swindler. She has persuaded them that they are being hunted by an enemy who has been "blessed by the demons". Tragic cases of suicide have been presented as murders in attempts to corroborate her absurd tales. We even suspect that her fire magic is the cause of the blaze that burned down Anna-Karin Nieminen's family barn.'

Anna-Karin glances at the other Chosen Ones. Like her, they are all silent. Like her, they are powerless.

'Adriana Lopez showed her true self already as a young

woman, when she broke her oath of allegiance to the Council. She succeeded in manipulating her judges into showing mercy. Since then, she has coolly bided her time and planned her next act of sabotage.'

'This is untrue!' Linnéa says. She stands up. 'Adriana is right. We are the Chosen Ones. And, whatever you'd prefer to believe, the apocalypse will come.'

Looking terrified, Viktor stares at her. But the judge only smiles haughtily.

'This young lady, Vanessa Dahl, has just provided another proof of the corrupting effect that Adriana Lopez has exerted on young minds. Although we do not need any further evidence to reassure us that our decision is right.'

She fixes her gaze on Adriana and gestures for her to stand.

Adriana tries to get up, but staggers. Alexander goes to her and offers her his arm to lean on, but she waves it away. Leaning on the chair, she stands.

'Adriana Lopez,' the judge says. 'It is time for you to atone for your crime. You are sentenced to the most severe punishment laid down by the Council.'

Adriana's face is still. But Alexander's goes pale.

'The execution will take place one week from today.'

CHAPTER 63

A wind is blowing straight into Ida's face, roaring in her ears. She screws her eyes up even tighter. This, she supposes, is what it must be like to be thrown out of a plane 30,000 feet up in the air.

Suddenly, the wind dies down. The world seems unnaturally silent until someone clears her throat.

Ida cautiously opens her eyes. Now she is standing at the opposite position in the circle. She looks at Minoo. A moment ago, she was inside that body.

Ida lets go of the hand that holds hers. She looks down on her own body. Now that she has lived for three days inside someone else's body, she realizes how familiar her own is. It's so much ... *hers*. There is no good way of describing what she feels, but why should there be? It's only in her creepy life that it's needed.

'It worked,' Minoo says and sounds just as relieved as Ida feels. 'Is everybody herself again?'

The others nod. Ida watches them in the faint light of the torch they have placed on the stage. Linnéa pulls a packet of cigarettes from the top of her boot and lights up. Vanessa teases out her hair. Anna-Karin buttons her duffel coat over the black suit, presumably longing for her sweats.

No question about it, they are all back where they belong. *Can you hear me now? It's working again, right?*

Linnéa looks hopefully at them.

Vanessa responds by becoming invisible and then reappearing.

'Our powers are back, too,' she says. 'If anything, it feels easier to use them now.'

'We'll need them,' Minoo says. 'We've got to help Adriana.'

Ida remembers the scene when the guards led Adriana out of the courtroom, how she was shaking so hard she could hardly walk.

Before, Ida has far from *liked* the Council, but now she *hates* the whole crew. Repulsive Alexander, who sold his own sister out and killed that poor raven. Repulsive Viktor. Repulsive old hag of a judge.

No fucking way is it up to the Council to decide whether Ida is Chosen or not.

'But how?' she says. 'I can't work out anything we can do. Besides, they're likely to expect us to try something and be prepared.'

'That doesn't matter. We've just got to think of something,' Anna-Karin says. 'She's sacrificed herself for us.'

'I agree,' Linnéa says. 'We have to do something. But we have a week to work it out. There's something more urgent on just now. I think I know which two names are next in line on the Malmgren killing list.' She turns to Vanessa. 'Wille and Jonte.'

Vanessa looks as if someone has slapped her face.

'Why should they want them dead?' Anna-Karin asks.

Vanessa's voice sounds frail.

'They sold drugs to Elias.'

'Okay,' Minoo says. 'We must warn them. But first of all, let's go through everything that has happened these last few days. So that we can work out what to expect in our own lives.'

'My grandpa told me about this dream he had,' Anna-Karin says suddenly. 'In the dream, he met a girl who had lived hundreds of years ago. She had become stuck between worlds. You can guess who she is, can't you? She told him that it was important for us to trust each other. That we had to learn all about each other's secrets if we're to confront the demons' Blessed One.'

Anna-Karin is speaking so quietly that Ida has to lean forward to hear her at all.

'And maybe that was *another* reason for the body exchange,' she continues. 'That we should get to know each other even better than before. Remember, Matilda talked about this when we met her here in Kärrgruvan for the first time. You know, that it was important. So I think we've really got to tell each other about what happened. About everything.'

Ida remembers the evening hours with Gustaf in Minoo's house.

She doesn't want to share them with anyone.

Linnéa turns to Vanessa with her summary.

'And on Friday, Wille sent you a text,' she finally says. 'He wrote that he couldn't stop thinking about when you kissed.'

She sounds so bitter when she says this. Vanessa doesn't reply, just avoids looking at her. And Ida understands. Vanessa's old junkie boyfriend is Linnéa's ex as well. Linnéa must still be in love with him.

'We've been hanging out together around the clock, so you know practically everything,' Minoo says to Linnéa. 'But I guess your art teacher didn't make much of your drawings.'

'Speaking of school, I don't think your physics teacher will be especially impressed by your and Anna-Karin's results on the pretest,' Vanessa says.

Alarmed, Minoo stares at them.

'I didn't even understand the questions,' Ida says.

Part Three

It is Vanessa's turn to tell Anna-Karin about what has happened in her life. Ida feels depressed just listening to what Anna-Karin's mother is like. Maybe it's not so strange that Anna-Karin has become the person she is.

Anna-Karin looks nervously at her, knowing that she's got to be honest.

'Well, you know most of it,' she says. 'But I picked up a call from Julia last night...'

She seems embarrassed, looks away and doesn't say anything more.

'And, what?' Ida asks.

'She and Erik,' Anna-Karin says. 'They have sort of...like...I mean, I don't know how far they went but they've—'

'Good luck to them!' Ida interrupts.

'I'm sorry...'

'They so deserve each other. Do you think I care?'

Actually, she does. Not about Erik, but Julia...How could *Julia* do this to her?

Ida longs for Troja so much it might kill her.

'Now it's your turn, Ida,' Minoo says.

Reluctantly, Ida starts. She holds out as long as she can before mentioning the talk with Gustaf. But in the end, she has to say something.

'You and Gustaf are friends again, thanks to me,' she says. 'It would have helped if you'd let me know what you two had been arguing about.'

'I didn't think it was necessary,' Minoo says. 'We haven't talked for absolutely ages.'

'Now you have. He's grasped that PE is, like, evil. But he plans to hang on in there anyway and gather info to pass on to your father.'

'He mustn't!' Minoo exclaims. 'It's far too dangerous!'

She truly *is* in love with Gustaf. Ida doesn't doubt it any more.

'Don't you think I tried to convince him of that? But G is so stubborn,' she says. 'Afterwards, we talked about me for a bit,' she adds quickly. 'It wasn't my fault. I just felt I had to defend myself.'

'Against what?' Minoo says.

'He seemed to think that I was, you know, a bitch. And he seemed pretty sure that you thought so, too. I had to make him see I'm not quite as awful as everyone seems to think. And later on, I guess I got a bit emotional. Okay? Just don't be surprised if G assumes that you're pretty unbalanced right now.'

'What do you mean? What did you do?' Minoo asks, looking terrified.

'Oh my God, don't look like that. I just…cried a bit. And he kind of…comforted me. No big deal.'

An eerie silence falls over the dance pavilion.

'What?' Ida says. 'What's the matter now?'

'Ida, we know,' Linnéa says. 'We know why you talked to Gustaf about yourself.'

Ida fumbles for the silver heart, glad that it is there for her again.

'Since we're talking about secrets anyway…' Linnéa continues. 'Do you remember the time, way back, when you took the truth serum?'

'Of course I do,' Ida says and twists the silver chain so tightly around her index finger it hurts.

'But you can't remember what you said,' Anna-Karin says.

'No, I can't. And?'

'You said that you were in love with Gustaf,' Vanessa says. 'And that you'd loved him for a long time.'

It feels just the same as when Felicia blurted it out during the autumn party. The same feeling of being stripped in front of everyone. Except this time is worse. It is as if she has just realized that for a whole year she's been walking around naked.

'Why haven't you said anything?' Ida says. 'Have you been laughing at me behind my back ever since?'

'I'm sorry,' Minoo says. 'I truly mean that.'

The others mumble agreement.

'Yes, yes. Whatever,' Ida says.

She's still standing, unbelievable but true. Her secret is exposed and she can't do anything about it. They are free to think what they damn well please. She knows that she and Gustaf will be together in the end.

'Anyone else got anything to say?' Minoo asks.

Ida looks down at her boots. She does have one secret left. The book's promises to her. That she'll get rid of her power if she collaborates with the others until the apocalypse has been stopped. That if only she does her duty, she and Gustaf will become a couple.

But she has promised the book not to tell anyone. Surely that promise is worth more than some dream that Anna-Karin's grandpa had?

'We must leave now,' Vanessa says and speaks to Linnéa. 'I'll talk to Wille if you talk to Jonte.'

'What can we tell them?' Linnéa asks.

'We have to tell them that they're in danger.'

'You shouldn't go alone,' Minoo says.

'Maybe I can help?' Anna-Karin says.

Linnéa nods.

'Sure, if you like. It would be good if you could come with me. If only we can convince Jonte, we'll get Wille thrown in for free. He always does what Jonte says.'

Ida sighs under her breath. She could so easily opt out. This isn't her problem.

Fire

But that isn't strictly true. Even though Ida is Ida once more, she doesn't quite recognize herself. Something has changed in her. For the first time ever, she feels that she belongs with the Chosen Ones.

Not that she wants to or anything. But she has accepted her fate. From now on, this is her life. Or at least until they've saved the world.

'I can come with you,' she says to Vanessa. 'It seems I'm able to give people electric shocks now. And, besides, we could use my mom's car.'

Vanessa looks surprised.

'And I'll speak to Gustaf,' Minoo says. 'Check out anything he might have found out about PE during the weekend. I might show him the amulet and ask if he recognizes it. Though, above all, we should show it to Mona and get her to tell us if she sold it to Helena and Krister.'

'The Crystal Cave opens at noon tomorrow,' Vanessa says.

'Good,' Minoo says.

'How much will you tell Gustaf?' asks Anna-Karin.

'As little as possible. But I've got to persuade him to get out of PE.'

'I hope you'll do better than I did when I was you,' Ida says.

CHAPTER 64

They can make out Jonte's house behind the bare trees. There is a faint light showing in some of the windows on the ground floor. Linnéa tries to see if anyone is moving in there. She has called several times, but Jonte hasn't answered.

How many nights has she come here? And how many times has she left in the morning, hating herself? In this house, she has made some of the biggest mistakes in her life.

Linnéa stays in the shadows, close to the lawn. She listens hard, but the only sounds are Anna-Karin's footsteps coming closer.

Linnéa shuts her eyes, grateful that her magic is there for her again. And Vanessa was right. It *is* easier to use now. Easier to call up the power, easier to control it.

At first, she is only aware of Anna-Karin's thoughts. Her memories of seeing this house for the first time, how the garden was covered in snow, the moment Jari kissed her in front of everyone and then, later on, when Linnéa and Vanessa pushed her into a corner. Next, Anna-Karin's mind touches on the memory of herself in Jari's bed and the wave of shame is so overwhelming that Linnéa has to make a real effort to refocus. But she can do it. And almost picks something up from inside the house.

'Try not to think of anything,' she whispers to Anna-Karin,

who naturally starts thinking hard about how she mustn't think.

Linnéa concentrates. She blocks Anna-Karin and directs all her power towards the house. She manages to capture the thoughts. They are straying, incoherent, stumbling over each other, pervaded by terror.

... how can I what can I do how did it happen what if someone thinks it was me who should I who can I call I'll call granny I must get out of here should I leave what can I...

She can't sense who it is or if there are any others in the house.

'Someone's in there,' she whispers to Anna-Karin. 'And something has happened to that person. Are you ready to use your magic if it's needed?'

Anna-Karin nods.

Linnéa starts walking across the garden. The wet, muddy lawn is sloshy under her boots.

When they reach the small outside set of steps, Linnéa sees that the door is ajar. Her fingers grasp the chilly metal handle and she pulls the door wide open.

She steals quietly into the hall with Anna-Karin close behind. Now the thoughts come to her as a hysterical babble, a rushing stream of words.

...I promise to be better good I promise I'll never take hard stuff again never lie again never drink again if only it stops now I promise I promise I promise that if this only stops I will start over again from the beginning and then I will never do anything bad again I will do just everything you want dear God if only you do something so I get through this make it so it hasn't happened ...

It is impossible to work out where in the house the thoughts are coming from. Linnéa shuts her power down. The silence seems impenetrable.

They go into the kitchen. The counter is cluttered with dirty dishes. A plate with scraps of food on it is still on the pine table. The pitted tabletop is covered in burn marks and small dents.

Linnéa eyes the closed door to the cleaning cupboard, then the worn curtains that reach the floor. So many places where someone might hide and jump out from any second now.

They move silently towards the living room and Linnéa peeps through the open door.

The room looks almost exactly the same as always. Only the gigantic TV screen is new. When Linnéa sees the orange-brown fluffy rug, one of the evenings she spent here comes back to her. She and Elias had shared a bottle of stolen booze and that rug had felt like the world's softest carpet. They were rolling around on it, laughing like maniacs, trying to make out and instead laughing even harder. Olivia was sitting on the sofa, watching them while she smoked a cigarette right down to the filter. When she'd finished smoking, she'd turned to Lucky, who sat next to her, and groped him hard, as if it were some kind of competition she had to win. Elias and Linnéa laughed even more.

A thump from somewhere upstairs makes Linnéa and Anna-Karin stiffen.

Linnéa senses Anna-Karin's fear and it makes her more courageous, just because she has to be. She pulls Anna-Karin along to the bottom of the staircase and stands still for a moment, scanning the total blackness above the top tread, listening.

The thoughts are coming from up there. Someone is there in the dark.

Linnéa places one foot on the bottom step. It creaks under her weight.

... they have come back to get me they are back to get me I must hide must get away from here must hide ...

The fear inhabiting this mind washes through Linnéa and she feels suddenly certain that this person isn't dangerous. But she can't be as certain that nobody else is here. Someone who knows her powers and is able to set up a defense.

Linnéa glances quickly at Anna-Karin and starts walking upstairs.

The corridor is dark. Only a narrow strip of light seeps out from Jonte's room. Linnéa reaches it, pushes at the door with one hand, allows it to open slowly.

Remains of magic hover in the room. It is like a lingering smell in the air, like a still-echoing sound.

Jonte's bedside light is on. His phone lies on his bedside table, next to an open book. The bed is one big mess of pillows, twisted sheets and duvets. And, underneath, something else.

Linnéa approaches slowly. A bare arm shows among the sheets.

She tries to read more thoughts. Fragments of a dream. But he is not asleep. She knows that already. It is only a body that is lying there. Still, she must see this with her own eyes.

Linnéa cautiously pulls the duvet back, revealing Jonte's head and naked torso. His eyes are half open, as if he has just woken up. One hand is held in front of his chest, tightly clenched.

Linnéa's hand trembles as she reaches out and puts her fingers against the side of his neck. No pulse. But his skin is still warm. Gently she closes Jonte's eyelids. She has never before understood why this is done, but now she does.

She looks at him. It has been such a long time since she's seen him bareheaded. Since then, he has thinned on top. She used to say to him that if he felt so badly about going bald, he should simply shave it off. Surely better than walking around with a cap on day and night, year in, year out.

'Linnéa!' Anna-Karin whispers.

Part Three

Linnéa turns around. Anna-Karin is standing just inside the door. She looks very scared and is pointing towards the corridor.

Linnéa joins her, listening into the darkness until she hears it. A muffled sob, from the room opposite.

She walks across, opens the door. The room is pitch dark. She can almost hear someone holding his or her breath. Linnéa fumbles along the wall until she finds the switch.

Lucky is sitting on an old mattress, curled up as if trying to make himself as small as possible.

… don't kill me don't kill me don't kill me don't kill me…

Linnéa has to shut his thoughts out. Lucky is close to losing his mind and it feels as though he could drag her into his insane chaos.

'Lucky?' she says.

He doesn't respond.

'Lukas? It's Linnéa,' she says and gingerly moves closer to him.

He whimpers and lifts his arms to clasp his head, as if protecting himself against a blow.

'Relax, buddy,' she says. 'Don't be afraid, Lucky. No worries. It's only me.'

She reaches her hand out to touch him, but changes her mind. He is far too frightened. She has no idea how he might react.

Linnéa looks at Anna-Karin, who is standing nearby, her hands pressed against her mouth.

'Can you make him talk?'

Anna-Karin lowers her hands. Nods.

Anna-Karin crouches down in front of Lucky and tries to pull herself together. Jonte's dead body has upset her, but it is almost worse to see someone as shredded inside as Lucky.

He is so much more scared than I am, she tells herself.

'Lucky, it's me. Anna-Karin. Do you remember me?'

Lucky cowers even more.

Except for the training exercise with the other Chosen Ones, Anna-Karin hasn't used her magic for a long time and feels unsettled about letting her power free. It is so easy to abuse. And so far, it has never led to anything good.

But I'm not the same person any more, she thinks.

She takes a deep breath. Frees her magic, just a few drops that flow easily out into her body, permeate all of her.

'Lucky, look at me.'

She doesn't command. Only coaxes him, as gently as she can.

Slowly, Lucky lifts his head and meets her gaze.

'There's no one here who can hurt you, Lucky. You mustn't be frightened any more.'

He nods gratefully, straightens up a little. Now she can see the printed logo on his T-shirt. 'PRIDE OF ENGELSFORS'.

'Please, can you tell us what happened?'

Lucky opens his mouth, closes it, opens it again.

'I was. In…in the cellar,' he says. 'I was in the cellar. And I heard some people walking on the stairs.'

'Do you know who they were?'

'No. I went upstairs…I heard Jonte scream somewhere up there. His voice sounded angry at first. Like he was having a fight with someone. He isn't angry often, but when he loses it he gets so fucking furious…And then I heard other voices. I began to, like, worry it was the cops. But then he started to beg for forgiveness. Like, really *beg*. He kept saying forgive me, over and over again. And then I heard…'

Lucky stops. His consciousness is slipping out of Anna-Karin's grip, he wants to sink back into forgetfulness, hide in a place where he doesn't have to think about what has happened. Cautiously, she frees up a little more of her power.

'You're all right now,' she says. 'It's all over now. Tell me what you heard.'

'A kind of sizzling sound. Like when you put a piece of meat in a hot frying pan,' Lucky whispers. 'And the ceiling lights flashed. Jonte screamed again. But now he was screaming because he was in pain. He screamed louder and louder, stop-stop-stop...and I...first I ran to help him but then I didn't dare to. I...hid. Jonte died. And I didn't do a thing. Nothing.'

'There was nothing you could do,' Anna-Karin says and pats his shoulder. 'These voices, can you tell me anything more about them? How many people were speaking? Did you recognize any of them?'

'I don't know,' Lucky says. 'No.'

'Tell him to dial 911,' Linnéa says.

'No!' Lucky says.

'Do you have your phone with you?' Anna-Karin asks mildly and he nods. 'As soon as we're gone, you'll phone the police. Promise?'

'But the plants...Jonte would never...I mean, I can't call the pigs in...'

'You will phone the police.' Anna-Karin increases her power output a little more as she speaks. 'And another thing – you'll forget that we were ever here. Do you understand?'

'Sure. I will,' Lucky says and pulls his phone from his pocket.

'I can't stay here,' Linnéa says suddenly and runs out of the room.

Anna-Karin checks Lucky one last time to make sure he is holding his phone to his ear. Then she runs after Linnéa.

Outside, she finds Linnéa bending over in a shrubbery. She is vomiting.

Fire

'Are you going to be okay?' Anna-Karin asks.

Linnéa spits, straightens up. Wipes her mouth on her sleeve.

'We have to warn Vanessa,' she says.

Chapter 65

Jonte is dead. Jonte is dead. Jonte is dead.

Vanessa says these words over and over again inside her head but they still don't make any more sense. Her brain seems not to take the meaning in.

Maybe Helena and Krister are already on their way to Wille, right this moment – perhaps they've already arrived.

The road to Riddarhyttan is winding through the deep blackness of fir forest. The headlights illuminate the worn asphalt immediately ahead of the bonnet. The white road reflectors shine against the blackness.

Jonte is dead. Jonte is dead. Jonte is dead.

Vanessa turns to Ida, who drives straight-backed, her hands steady on the steering wheel. She looks like a model driving-school student.

'Can't you go a bit faster?' Vanessa says.

'No problem,' Ida says. 'And we'd be such a help to your ex if we killed ourselves on the road.'

Vanessa picks up her phone and tries to call Wille but, as before, just gets through to his voicemail.

'Why didn't we work this out before, like on Saturday night?' she says. 'We could have warned them straight away, before it was too late.'

'It won't be long now,' Ida says. 'See that?'

Vanessa checks where Ida is looking. A roadside sign emerges out of the darkness.

White letters stand out against a blue background:
'RIDDARHYTTAN'.

'Ida, please,' Vanessa says.

Ida doesn't say anything, but the car accelerates.

They find the turnoff to Elin's place and the car swings on to
a narrow gravel track. A low branch of a tree sweeps across
the windscreen. Something sharp grinds against the under-
carriage of the car.

'Jesus,' Ida hisses. 'Who the hell would want to live here!'

They drive on, and Vanessa tries to read the numbers on
the fronts of the houses. They are tucked away, half hidden
by trees. The forest seems about to swallow them all up.

Finally, on a white wall she sees the figures 1 and 6 reflect
the light.

'Stop here!' she shouts and Ida brakes so abruptly that
Vanessa is thrown forward.

'Fuck, you scared me!' Ida says.

Vanessa tugs the door open and runs along the flagged path
to the house. Next to the front door, an outside light is on. She
presses the doorbell hard. *Für Elise* is playing inside the house
at top volume. Vanessa keeps her thumb on the button.

Ida has come to stand behind her.

'How are you going to explain all this if his girlfriend
opens the door?'

Vanessa doesn't reply. She hasn't a clue how to explain to
anyone, even to Wille.

She and Linnéa agreed that she should try to avoid talking
about what has happened to Jonte. It is impossible to predict
how Wille might react. The important thing is to get him
away from here as soon as possible.

Steps are coming closer and she takes her finger off the
button. The last tinkling notes echo inside the house. The

locks clicks, the door handle is pushed down.

Let it be him, she thinks. Let it be him.

It is. Wille sees her and looks shocked.

'Nessa? What the fuck are you doing here?'

He stares at her, then at Ida.

'Wait here,' Vanessa says to Ida and pushes past Wille into the hall.

And she can't resist it. She throws herself at him. He puts his arms around her and holds her tight. His body is warm. Alive. She might have been too late. She might never have been close to him again. The thought terrifies her.

'Listen, you can't just turn up like this, out of the blue,' he whispers gently. 'Elin's with her mom but she might just as easily have been at home.'

Vanessa steps back, out of his arms.

'There's something I have to tell you,' she says. 'It will sound like I'm crazy. But you've got to believe me.'

He looks at her, worried now.

'What is it?'

'You've got to come with me now. I'll explain on the way.'

'Why? What is all this?'

'Please. Come with me now.'

'What are you talking about?'

'Some people who are out to get you. People who want to take revenge for Elias Malmgren's death. You've got to leave with us, now.'

'Come on. I had nothing to do with Elias dying,' Wille says, suddenly sounding defensive.

'You sold stuff to him!'

'Since when did you start caring about who I sold to?'

'This isn't about me,' she says, barely holding back from shaking him out of sheer frustration. 'The people who're after you think it's your fault Elias committed suicide.'

'Is this some kind of sick joke? What's the fucking idea?'

'Saving your life, you fucking idiot!' she screams. 'You've got to leave! Now! Go to your uncle in Stockholm, take that fucking trip to Thailand. Wherever, but go.'

'I see, that's the plan, is it? To make me leave Elin?'

He doesn't get it. She has to make him.

'Jonte is dead!'

Wille stares at her.

'Linnéa was just at his place. She went there to warn him. But it was too late.'

'You're going too far,' Wille says in a low voice.

'Call Lucky,' Vanessa says. 'So you don't believe me. But call Lucky.'

'Go away.'

She takes out her phone and dials Lucky. When it starts to ring, she hands the phone to Wille.

'I'm not going anywhere until you've talked to him.'

Reluctantly, Wille puts the phone to his ear.

Please answer, Vanessa thinks. Please, please …

Lucky does answer. Vanessa can hear his hysterical voice from where she's standing. And she sees how Wille's anger changes into fear.

Suddenly, Ida leaps into the hall. Wille lowers the phone.

'They're here,' Ida whispers at the same moment as all the lights flicker and go dark.

Then, clicking sounds as equipment switches off everywhere in the pitch dark house.

Vanessa senses the magic. The source is somewhere in the garden. But it is coming closer.

Actually, she's fed up with running. She would prefer to face Helena and Krister. But not with Wille there.

'Start the car,' Vanessa whispers and Ida slips out through the doorway.

Part Three

A scraping noise from inside the dark house. A slightly metallic, hissing sound, as if a door is being pushed open.

Vanessa grips Wille's hand. Before this, she has never managed to make anyone except herself invisible, but now her magic flows easily through them both. And both become invisible and inaudible. She hopes Wille won't notice.

'Come on,' she says, holding fiercely on to his hand as they wander uncertainly in the darkness.

She mustn't let go of his hand. Mustn't allow him to become visible.

Blindly, Vanessa and Wille run through the dark garden towards the car, almost stumbling over each other.

They throw themselves into the back seat and Vanessa releases their invisibility shield.

'Drive!' she shouts.

Ida starts the car and they race down the gravel track. Through the rear window, Vanessa has a last glimpse of the house.

The lights flash as the electricity comes back on. And, in the light of the outside lamp, she sees two figures standing on the lawn.

Helena and Krister.

The woodpeckers are back pecking at Minoo's brain as she walks down the road to Gustaf's house. A cold wind blows over the canal and the meadow, ruffling her hair.

She has just read Vanessa's text. Four dead now. It might have been five.

Could we have saved the other victims? Minoo wonders. Shouldn't we have realized earlier who the killers are?

And a week from now, Adriana will be executed. Yet another death they've got to prevent, but also another puzzle they haven't solved. Minoo had tried to contact the guardians again at the fairground, but it didn't work.

The world weighs on her. The sensation is so heavy she can hardly breathe.

She stops just outside Gustaf's house. She hasn't been here for a long time and she suddenly realizes how much she longs to be with him.

How she wishes that it really had been *her* he made peace with. Now, it feels as if she has missed an important episode of the TV series about her own life.

She rings the bell and Gustaf opens the door almost immediately.

'Hello, Minoo.'

'Hi.'

She steps inside, hangs up her jacket, takes her shoes off.

Gustaf hugs her and holds her for longer than he used to. Or does he?

'Is that Minoo?' Lage Åhlander calls from the living room.

'Please, go and say hello to my dad,' Gustaf mumbles. 'He was totally thrilled when he heard you were coming.'

Minoo smiles, goes to the living room and talks briefly with Lage before going upstairs to join Gustaf in his room.

'I'm glad you phoned,' he says and sits down on the bed. 'I've been worried.'

'Why?' she asks as she closes the door.

'At the PE Center, the talk is all about you and your friends. Most of it about Linnéa and Ida, of course. But you, too. Everyone hates your father because of the stuff he writes in the paper. That means that they hate you as well. And Vanessa and Anna-Karin, because they're hanging out with the rest of you.'

Minoo dumps her backpack on the floor by the bed and sits down next to Gustaf. The photograph of him and Rebecka is still up on the wall at the head of the bed. Rebecka, who tried to make the Chosen Ones understand that they must work together, get to know each other. Form a circle.

Rebecka would be proud of them now, she thinks.

'You should stay away from school tomorrow. I've got a strong feeling that Erik and Robin are planning something,' Gustaf says.

'We can't just hide at home. Besides, what can they do to us at school?'

'Do you think I'm exaggerating?'

'No, I don't,' she says. 'Honestly, I don't.'

'Promise you'll keep it in mind, then.'

Minoo nods.

'What did you want to talk to me about?' Gustaf asks.

She opens the outer pocket on her backpack and pulls out the necklace. She senses the remnants of the strong magic that has been channeled into the chain and pendant. Holding it, her fingers tingle slightly.

'Look at this. Have you seen anything like it before?' she asks.

Gustaf glances at the necklace, gets up and goes to his desk.

He turns back to Minoo holding a black box. He hands it to her.

'Open it,' he says.

She lifts the lid gingerly. There, on a bed of black mock velvet, lies a chain and pendant identical to Diana's.

'I was given it yesterday,' Gustaf says. 'After they had agreed to have me back as a member. Rickard thinks I might be allowed into the innermost circle.'

Minoo fingers the metal symbol. She cannot sense any magic radiating from it, but perhaps the amulet has to be activated first.

She shuts the box.

'It's meant to give admission to the spring party in the school tomorrow,' Gustaf says.

'Have all the members of PE been given these?'

'Only the high school students. And the teachers. PE reps handed out the chains last week. But Rickard has had one since last summer.'

Minoo stiffens.

'Rickard?'

'Yes, he has one. I've seen it every time we go for soccer practice.'

Rickard, who was the first at school to talk about PE. Rickard, who was never outstanding in any way, until this year when he suddenly emerged as a leader. He must be under their control, just like Diana.

'Is Rickard the only one who's had one of these necklaces for a while?' Minoo asks.

'I haven't seen anyone else.'

'But now they've been handed out to everyone? Everyone who's going to the spring party tomorrow?'

'That's right. Why are you so fascinated by the necklaces?'

If only she could tell him.

'What's so special about this party anyway?' she asks instead.

'It's just a party,' Gustaf says. 'Buffet foods, dancing. The usual, but with some extras. They're going to choose the Young PE Member of the Year. And celebrate the spring equinox. You know, like "we're moving into brighter days".'

It sounds utterly innocent and she can't tell him why it's so very dangerous. Actually, she doesn't quite know why anyway.

'Please don't go,' she says.

'Got to. If I don't, they'll never accept me into the inner circle. Where all the real inside info is.'

'They're more dangerous than you think...'

She falls silent. Why can't she say what it is most important for Gustaf to hear about?

'That's exactly why I can't stay on the sidelines. Like you said, you can't keep hiding.'

Minoo accepts that she'll never make him change his mind.

'I know this sounds crazy, but at least promise me that you won't wear the necklace,' she says.

He looks uncertainly at her.

'If it really matters so much to you...I promise.'

Neither of them speaks. It strikes Minoo that they're sitting very close together on the bed. She feels the warmth from his body. Their hands resting on the bedspread are so close they almost touch.

And suddenly, without warning, he takes her hand.

A familiar sensation is spreading inside her. Her wrists tingle and her arms go weak. Her cheeks are hot. She doesn't dare look at Gustaf. Her hand must feel all limp, like a sticky, dead jellyfish. But he still holds it for a long while. She wants this to end. She wants it never to end.

She pulls her hand back. Tries to work out what she is feeling. Words are far too risky. She doesn't even want to utter them in her mind.

'I've got to go home now,' she says and gets up.

'Sorry if I—' Gustaf begins.

'Oh, no,' she interrupts, with the blood hammering in her ears. 'I mean, it wasn't because of that...it's just that I...I have to go now.'

CHAPTER 66

Ida opens her eyes. A sense of dread wakes her instantly. She sits up in bed and checks the time. Just about half past five.

They took Wille to Västerås, just in time for him to catch the last train to Stockholm. Ida didn't get back home until the middle of the night. The house was dark and silent. No one was waiting up for her. No one had even bothered to send a text asking where she was.

She gets up and showers for a long time, in an attempt to wash away her anguish. And then she inspects her body, searching for signs of change, traces of Anna-Karin. She can't find any.

Back in her room she opens her wardrobe. And stands there, staring at the row of clothes.

All these everyday choices used to be a matter of course but now they don't seem at all straightforward. Presumably because *nothing* in her life is straightforward any more.

What to wear to school when you know everybody hates you? If she were Anna-Karin, she'd hide inside a shapeless sack, made herself unnoticeable. If she were Linnéa, she'd dress up in some insane outfit that would force everyone to look at her.

But as for *Ida,* what would she choose?

It is as if she's inside an alien body once more. As if she's not the real Ida, but still has to keep up the pretense. She slides her finger across the pile of neatly folded tops, across the dresses on their hangers. Her stock of 'Ida' disguises.

She tries on clothes for half an hour before making up her mind: a V-necked, pale blue sweater and jeans. She takes care with her make-up and scrutinizes her face in the mirror. The silver heart glints in the light from the ceiling lamp. Its surface is scratched and worn. Her mom gave it to her when she started elementary school, and since then she has worn it almost daily. It has grown into a part of her, so much so that she has hardly looked at it properly for years.

Ida touches the heart. She has to speak to Mom. Try to make her understand.

The whole family is seated at the breakfast table. It takes a moment before Ida spots what's wrong. Four people at the table, four occupied chairs. Ida's usual chair stands by a wall.

Dread is invading her again. She places the chair at the short end of the table. No one has laid a place for her. She gets herself a mug and a plate from the cupboard.

'Good morning,' she says.

No response. No one even looks at her. It is as if she's invisible. For one awful moment, Ida thinks that she has body-swapped with Vanessa.

But then she sees Rasmus sneak a glance at her and try to hide a grin, before he quickly turns away again.

'Aren't you looking forward to the Spring Revel at the center?' Dad says to Rasmus and Lotta.

They nod enthusiastically.

'I *love* the spring equinox,' Lotta says. 'Afterwards, the days are longer than the nights.'

'That's right,' Dad says and ruffles her hair. 'What better reason for celebrating, eh?'

Fire

'I'm sorry I came back so late last night,' Ida says. 'I simply had to—'

'I dropped in at the center yesterday and they've prepared everything so nicely for tonight,' Mom interrupts without looking at her.

'Can you hand me the butter?' Lotta says.

'*Please*, can you pass me the butter,' Mom corrects her before giving it to her.

'What's the idea?' Ida says. 'Why are you ignoring me?'

No one answers. Lotta smears lots of butter on her toast. And then wipes off what's left on the knife with her finger and pops it into her mouth.

'Christ, you're such a pig,' Ida says.

'You're not allowed to do that,' Mom says calmly and takes the knife away from Lotta.

Crunching noises from Dad's mouth as he chews his toast sandwich. No one speaks. But Rasmus looks fit to burst with laughter.

'Having fun, or what?' Ida says.

He stares at the tabletop and squashes a breadcrumb under his finger.

'By the way, I met Erik at the center,' Mom says, looking at Dad. 'He was looking forward to tonight, too. To the party at the school. Apparently they're going to choose the Young PE Member of the Year. I think he hopes that he'll be the one. Not that he said as much out loud, of course.'

She and Dad smile at each other, a complicit smile.

'Could anyone tell me what I've done? Or is that too much to ask?' Ida says.

She can't bear losing them as well. Without them, she has nobody standing by her, nobody at all.

No one answers her. Lotta sighs and chews slowly with her mouth partly open.

'Look, it's so obvious that you think I've done something wrong,' Ida continues and her voice cracks so that she has to swallow several times before she can carry on. 'It would only be fair if you at least told me what I'm being punished for.'

'You know that well enough, Ida.'

Mom doesn't look at her.

'No, I truly don't,' Ida says, barely managing to keep her voice steady.

'We have been informed that you have started to go about with criminals,' Mom says, coolly and factually. 'You refuse to talk to me or your father. Then you disappear for practically the entire weekend and take my car without asking permission. You come home in the middle of the night. Clearly, you can't be bothered with us. That's why we have decided not to bother with you.'

Ida feels torn apart inside. As if someone has stuck a knife into her and started to slit her open while still alive.

'What can I do?' she says, unable to hold back her tears. They drip on to her lap. 'Say I'm sorry? Please forgive me. I truly mean it. Forgive me. I...haven't been myself.'

'No, we noticed,' Dad says.

'But what do you want me to do? Start going out with Erik again, for your sake? That's so twisted!'

'You're taking part in a campaign of filthy gossip directed against the son of our best friends...' Mom begins.

'But what's being said is true!' Ida exclaims. 'All true! He did do it!'

She can't stop herself. Everyone is looking straight at her now. Mom, Dad, Rasmus, Lotta.

'You're deliberately closing your eyes to what Erik is like,' Ida continues. 'He's horrible! All his life, he's been bullying people. Do you know what he did to Elias Malmgren when we were all, like, twelve years old?'

'All boys fight now and then,' Mom says. 'It's human nature.'

'He ripped off Elias's earring so blood was spurting everywhere and then he shouted that people shouldn't touch or they might get AIDS from the queer—'

'That's enough,' Dad says coldly and nods in the direction of Lotta and Rasmus.

'—and I was with him!' Ida continues without a break. 'I laughed, too. And was just as repulsive as Erik. And so are you, sometimes. You insist that Erik's parents are your best friends, but you always say awful things about them behind their backs—'

'That's enough, Ida!' Mom shouts.

Ida, with tears running down her cheeks, meets Mom's eyes. Frightened, Rasmus and Lotta stare in turn at both of them.

'Listen, Ida,' Dad says. 'We're very worried about you. But you cannot be part of this family unless you pull yourself together. We require a *meaningful* apology. And, above all, a complete change in your behavior.'

Ida is crying so much she finds it hard to speak at all. She turns to Mom.

'Mom…please. Mommy…please…'

A hint of sadness in Mom's eyes. But she shakes her head.

Ida gets up from the table. Her whole body is trembling. She can barely control the shaking as she walks into the hall, puts her jacket on, picks up her schoolbag.

If only Mom would call her name. Ask her to come back. If only Dad would hurry after her to say that the punishment has gone too far.

Then, Ida would have been prepared to forget all this. It would be over and done with. Just an unpleasant memory that would never have to be mentioned again.

But no one comes. No one calls her name.

Ida stands with her hand on the door handle and waits for just a little longer.

The only sound is the clatter of plates as someone starts clearing the table.

She opens the door and steps outside.

Vanessa walks slowly across the schoolyard. Two neon-bright yellow posters have been stuck to the main entrance doors.

'PE!' one of them announces. 'SPRING PARTY!' shouts the other one.

She checks the screen on her phone. No reception all morning.

She wonders if Wille has tried to reach her.

He phoned Elin from the car while they drove to Västerås last night. He had told her that his uncle had fallen ill and that he was going to Stockholm to be with him, but didn't know for how long.

And Vanessa couldn't help noticing how plausible he sounded. How easily he told fibs. And how good he was at lying.

'Thank you,' he said later, while they were waiting on the platform. 'Not that I can get my head around what's happened. But I do believe you saved my life.'

He is safe now.

But Jonte is dead. Helena and Krister murdered him.

Vanessa walks up the steps and into the entrance lobby, which is decorated with yellow bunting and large paper suns.

A crowd has gathered in front of the bulletinboard. Vanessa hears a babble of voices. And, often, Linnéa's name. She goes closer.

The yellow party posters on the bulletinboard have been covered in graffiti. Someone has scribbled on one of them with a broad, black marker 'PE = MURDERERS'. Photos of Erik and Robin have been glued on the poster. Their eyes filled in with black and their smiling faces scored with something sharp.

'She's got to be a psychopath,' a voice says and Vanessa doesn't need to think for a second about who the 'she' is. The person who everyone believes has done all this.

'I've heard that they're going to have her locked up,' another voice says.

'About fucking time.'

Approving mumbles all around.

Disgusted, Vanessa turns away and catches sight of Michelle and Mehmet as they come in through the main entrance. While Michelle says something to Mehmet, she pulls down the zip of her jacket. And Vanessa spots something glittering at the neckline of Michelle's sweater.

A silver pendant, the metal symbol.

'Michelle!' she calls. The crowd in the lobby falls silent.

Michelle turns from Mehmet to look her way. That glance pierces Vanessa's heart like an ice pick.

Michelle whispers something to Mehmet and he shakes his head. Vanessa feels certain they are saying something about her.

Someone bumps into her, so hard she almost falls over.

'Can't you look where you're going?' she says as she turns to see who it is.

And meets Robin and Felicia's eyes. Behind them, the rest of the crowd stands in silence, staring at Vanessa.

She is used to being stared at. Lots of people don't like her and that's fine by her. She'd rather people reacted to her than failed to notice her.

But nobody has ever before faced her with such hatred. And there are so many of them. The whole cluster is like one single, many-headed creature.

She starts walking away and hears excitable whispers behind her back.

'She's such a slut,' a voice says.

'What do you think, how many abortions has she had in the last twenty-four hours?'

Felicia and some of the other girls start tittering. Vanessa doesn't want to hear another word. She gives them the finger over her shoulder and increases her pace.

Tommy Ekberg, arms crossed over his chest, is waiting for her by the lockers. His pea-green shirt is more unbuttoned than ever and the silver amulet is buried deep in his mat of curly hair. It's so thick, it looks as if his pubic hair covers him all the way to his collarbones.

'I want a word with you,' he says. 'In my office. Now.'

'Why?'

'Your friends are already there.'

'My friends?'

'You'll come with me now!' Tommy roars.

Vanessa is shocked. Tommy's shirts are normally the only noisy thing about him. She has never before even heard him raise his voice.

'Fine, I'm coming,' she says. 'But calm down.'

Linnéa jumps when the door is pulled open. Tommy Ekberg shoves Vanessa into the room, and then points wordlessly at a folding plastic chair that is waiting for her next to Linnéa. Minoo, Anna-Karin and Ida are crammed together on the sofa.

'When I heard about the rumors you have been spreading about two fellow students in the school, at first I didn't think it possible,' Tommy begins while Vanessa settles down. 'Such vicious gossip. Such blatant malice! And then I come in this morning and what do I see? That appalling poster. That was the final straw!'

Fire

Tommy stands, arms akimbo, eyes fixed on Linnéa. The contempt in his eyes, the hatred he clearly feels for her, almost frightens her.

Is it *his* hatred? she wonders, looking at the amulet. Or is it Helena's, or Krister's?

All Linnéa knows is that Tommy is convinced that she and the others are guilty. There is obviously not a trace of doubt in his mind.

'I want you to know that I take this close and very personally,' he says. 'Whatever you do to my students, my school, you also do to *me*.'

'But we haven't done anything,' Anna-Karin says.

'Lying will only make it worse for you. I know what you girls are up to. Do you think I haven't noticed how you try to sabotage the good atmosphere in this school?'

'They must have done the vandalizing of the poster themselves,' Minoo says.

'And why would PE members blacken the name of their own people?' Tommy asks sneeringly.

'In order to set us up just like this!'

'Do you think I'm completely stupid?' he shouts.

Minoo stares anxiously at him and Ida starts crying quietly.

'Do you really want us to reply to that question?' Vanessa says.

Tommy's rage has reached such a pitch he can't breathe normally.

'Look, the truth is that none of us has done any of this,' Linnéa says hurriedly. 'We are being harassed, for Christ's sake.'

Tommy marches up to her and puts his bright red face close to hers. His breath smells sweet like chocolate.

'You have to root out the weeds before they suck up all the goodness in the garden,' he says.

Part Three

They mustn't get away with this.

His thought echoes so loudly through Linnéa's head, it seems unbelievable that no one else hears it. Tommy straightens his back and storms out of the office.

'Don't even think about going anywhere,' he shouts before the door slams behind him.

'What's he going to do?' Minoo asks Linnéa.

'I don't know.'

She tries to up the range of her power, catch more of his thoughts.

Now she hears it again. The same thought as before. And yet, not the same.

They mustn't get away with this.

'Hang on, wait,' she says and gets up.

'Where are you off to?' Vanessa says, but Linnéa doesn't answer.

She opens the door and looks along the empty hallway. Stands still and listens. The only sounds are distant voices from the classrooms, steps of someone running in the stairwell.

She closes her eyes and releases more power than she has ever dared to do before, ever been able to do.

It is like sticking her head into a beehive. The sensation is as it felt in the beginning, before she knew anything about her power, when she still thought she was going mad, that all her years of anguish and chemicals had finally ruined her brain.

So many people, so many thoughts. But in the middle of the buzzing, the same thought recurs, over and over again.

They mustn't get away with this.

Above her, below her.

They mustn't get away with this.

It is a mantra repeated endlessly, from different directions, everywhere in the school.

Fire

They mustn't get away with this.
They mustn't get away with this.
They mustn't get away with this.

Hatred is such a temptation. How good it would feel to let go and enter into it, to be allowed to hate without limit, unthinkingly. Linnéa is almost pulled along and she shuts her power down. Opens her eyes. An eternity seems to pass before there is silence inside her head once more.

The soles of her shoes grind against the floor when she turns and looks back at the others.

'They're all thinking the same thing,' she says. 'We'd better beat it.'

She looks over her shoulder and sees Tommy and Backman at the far end of the corridor, approaching briskly.

'Come on!' Linnéa shouts and the others leap up from their seats, finally energized.

Like a herd of terrified animals, they rush out from the headmaster's office, down the spiral staircase and out into the ground-floor corridor.

They swing around a corner and there is Kevin, waiting for them.

They're here!

Instantly, the thought rattles onwards through the school, like a row of falling dominoes.

They're here! They're here! They're here! They're here!

Kevin grabs hold of Linnéa's jacket, but Vanessa gives him a push and Linnéa tears herself free.

They run into the lobby. Footsteps behind them in the hall. Footsteps coming down the main staircase.

They mustn't get away with this.

They push their way out through the main doors and keep running.

I deeply, truly detest this school, Linnéa thinks.

CHAPTER 67

When they get to the City Mall, Minoo has such a bad stitch it feels as though a red-hot iron stake has been plunged into her side. She can hardly breathe, except in little shallow gasps, and she stops, bending over with her hands on her knees.

'What are we supposed to do here?' Vanessa says 'The Crystal Cave doesn't open until twelve o'clock.'

'I thought we could hole up in there,' Linnéa says and points at Sture & Co.

Minoo turns and looks at the darkened pane in the glazed door. Remembers the talk about drug dealing and knife fights. The wasted figures who stumble into the street after an afternoon session, people who are banned from Götis but don't yet have to seek refuge in Storvall Park. She hopes Linnéa doesn't pick up what she's thinking.

'We could go to my place and wait,' Minoo suggests.

'No, too dangerous,' Linnéa says and shakes her head.

'What, do you think they'll come after us with pitchforks and burning torches?' Vanessa says.

'I wouldn't rule it out,' Linnéa says earnestly, before going along to knock on the door of Sture & Co.

A thin man, with a nose like a largish cauliflower streaked with red, comes to the door. He recognizes Linnéa and smiles.

'Hi. I know you haven't opened yet, but is it okay if we hang out here for a bit?' she asks.

'No problem,' he says and lets them in.

Once inside, Minoo looks around. The walls are covered in mirrors and flesh-colored woven wallpaper. When they walk on the wall-to-wall carpet it gives off the stink of cigarette smoke. Grubby curtains, originally in a yellow check, have been pulled across the windows and prevent any scrutiny from the outside.

Linnéa leads them right into the back of the space, where there are small cubicles with dark brown wooden tables, marked all over with scribbles and carvings.

Minoo sits down inside one of the cubicles. The vinyl upholstery creaks underneath her when she slides over to sit nearest the window.

'Has anyone got any money?' Linnéa asks. 'We'll have to buy something.'

They pool all their cash. Minoo pulls at one of the curtains and sneaks a look outside. The window faces into the Mall and from here they have a view of the Crystal Cave.

She lets the curtain drop back when Linnéa returns, carrying a tray with five cups of tea.

'Sture says we can stay here as long as we need to,' she says as she crams herself into the seat next to Ida.

They look at each other in silence. Minoo thinks about what's just happened and the full extent of it begins to sink in.

'What were they going to do to us?' she asks Linnéa. 'Did you sense anything?'

'I don't think they knew themselves. They hadn't had their orders yet.'

The hairs on the back of Minoo's neck are standing on end.

'It must be the necklaces,' Linnéa continues. 'It felt as if they were all connected to each other. If one of them spots us, all the rest of them will get to know at once.'

'How many do you think are going to the school party tonight?' Vanessa says.

'Must be more than a hundred,' Minoo suggests.

'I think it's more like two hundred,' Linnéa says.

'So if all of them are wearing the amulets, Helena and Krister have recruited two hundred pairs of eyes to keep a lookout for them,' Vanessa says.

'We aren't safe anywhere.' Ida's voice sounds dead, as if she has already given up hope.

Minoo thinks about Gustaf. He promised not to wear the necklace. But what if he gets it into his head that he should, after all, in order to blend in more easily?

'But remember the Council,' Vanessa says suddenly. 'We have to face two sets of enemies. Positive Engelsfors and the Council. What if we could turn them against each other? Helena and Krister have broken every magic law in the book. If we reported them – maybe, to Viktor – then the Council ought to try to stop them. Perhaps we could *use* the Council.'

'I think it's too big a risk so soon after the trial,' Linnéa says. 'Perhaps they won't just be happy with taking away our title of Chosen Ones. They might just be waiting to catch us out over something else. If we've learned anything about the Council it's that they use information whatever way suits them. We can only trust each other. Which is precisely what Matilda told us from the start.'

'I miss Nicolaus,' Anna-Karin says. 'I wish he were here.'

Minoo nods, then checks her cell. Still no signal.

'Do your phones work?' she asks.

The others shake their heads.

Minoo places the phone in front of her on the table. She would like to phone Dad and warn him, but she couldn't tell him what about. She would like to get ahold of Gustaf and stop him from going to the party. She would like to call Mom just to hear her voice.

Time moves endlessly slowly. Finally, it's twelve o'clock, but there is still no sign of Mona.

Stress makes Minoo's skin crawl. They have no time to lose. But they don't know what they can do. So by one o'clock, the Chosen Ones are sharing a big plate of fries that Sture has let them have on the house.

By half past three, Minoo is close to tears. She has turned all their problems over in so many ways she can't think at all any more. Anna-Karin keeps a silent watch over the Crystal Cave. Ida has fallen asleep at the table, her head resting on her arms.

Suddenly, she sits up. Looks around, dazed, then wipes a little saliva from the corner of her mouth.

'She's there now,' she says.

'Who?' Minoo says. 'Where?'

'Mona,' Ida says. 'It must be her.'

'But no one has gone into the shop,' Anna-Karin says.

'Maybe there's another way in,' Vanessa says. 'Actually, that would explain a great deal.'

Minoo peeps through the window and sees the lights go on in the Crystal Cave.

'There's somebody in there,' she says.

They all stand up simultaneously. They thank Sture as they hurry past and run towards the shop.

When Minoo enters, a nauseating smell hits her. The mixture of incense and cigarette smoke is so overwhelming it almost knocks out her other senses.

More than anything, the Crystal Cave resembles an overstocked gift shop. The shelving looks ready to collapse any time soon under the weight of china angels and pyramids.

Part Three

Behind the counter, a woman with big hair colored a yellowy blonde stands counting receipts. A cigarette is gripped between her glossy pink lips.

And Minoo understands why the Crystal Cave is the perfect cover for Mona's other activities. Nobody who sees her or her shop could believe that Mona is a *real* witch.

'Now what's up?' Mona asks, looking at them all.

Vanessa locks the door and flips the sign to '*CLOSED*'.

'What do you think you're doing?' Mona says.

'We need help,' Vanessa tells her.

Minoo opens up the backpack pocket again, extracts the necklace and holds it up.

'Do you know what this is?'

Mona grabs it irritably. Examines it.

'It's an amulet. Obvious to you too, I should've thought!'

She throws the amulet to Ida who catches it with one hand, looks at it for a moment and then pockets it.

'Do you sell these?' Vanessa asks.

'I've never seen it before.'

'She's lying,' Linnéa says. 'She has sold amulets to Helena and Krister.'

'You leave me alone!' Mona snarls, spitting her cigarette out. It lands on the counter and she picks it up again, dragging angrily at it.

'Get out of here,' she says. Then she turns to Vanessa. 'Mona would never narc on you. You know that.'

Minoo used to think that Vanessa's stories about Mona were mostly exaggeration. By now, she realizes there's no need for that.

'I'm beginning to think you have no idea what is going on in this town,' Minoo says, making an effort to sound sympathetic. 'Or what these amulets are being used for.'

'As long as my customers pay for their goods, it's none of my business what they get up to afterwards. I mean, you wouldn't go around hurling accusations at a car dealer because a fucking drunk driver runs somebody over.'

'We're not accusing you of anything,' Minoo says. 'But you should know that Helena and Krister use the amulets to exert control over people. They're controlling almost everyone at school.'

'And they've murdered four people already,' Vanessa says. 'For example, Svensson. Remember him? You saw in his future that he would die soon. You were right. He was one of their victims.'

Mona looks away. Minoo hears Linnéa's voice inside her head.

I can't read her mind any longer. She's blocking me. Shouldn't Anna-Karin get her to talk?

Minoo just shakes her head. Anna-Karin sends her a grateful glance.

'We're pretty sure that Helena and Krister get their power from the demons,' Minoo says. 'And we know that the demons are about hurrying up the apocalypse.'

'Surely you must've noticed that something's going on,' Vanessa says. 'And if the world goes under you won't have any customers at all.'

Mona glares at them, inhales so deeply that sparks fly from the glowing tip of her cigarette, and then blows out a cloud of smoke that makes Minoo's eyes sting.

How could I ever have liked smoking? she thinks.

'How did they die?' Mona asks. 'The four characters you're talking about?'

'The police are clinging to some crazy theory about "electrical accidents",' Minoo says. 'But we know that the deaths were magical killings.'

Mona sits down on the stool behind the counter.

'Okay. I'll make an exception, just for you,' she says with her eyes fixed on Minoo. 'But only because things are getting out of hand, not because you all are so fucking special, just because you're the Chosen Ones or whatever you're called these days.'

The combination of being clairvoyant and rude is amazingly unattractive, Minoo thinks.

'Actually, we don't give a shit *why* you do it,' Linnéa says.

'I won't hear another word from you,' Mona scowls. 'In the summer, Helena and Krister turned up and placed a large order for amulets. The spec was that they should be fit for control by a metal witch. It was short notice and I couldn't fill the whole order there and then. For a start, they bought what I had in stock.'

'How many?' Minoo asks.

'A dozen. Since then, I've been ordering new batches from China all autumn.'

'So you've no problem with selling any number of zombie-amulets to PE?' Vanessa says.

Mona snorts and lights a new cigarette on the stub of the old one.

'Come on. That type of amulet can be used for a lot of things. For instance, you can charge them with extra energy if you're planning to run a marathon.'

'And that's the kind of thing you really believed they were going to use them for?' Vanessa says.

'I believed nothing,' Mona snapped. 'Not my job, believing this or that. What was the thing about your school and the amulets?'

'They've doled out amulets to everyone who is going to the school party tonight,' Minoo says.

'What, do you mean the bash at the center?'

'No. They've arranged a separate party at the school.'

'At the school,' Mona repeats and stares thoughtfully at the pillar of smoke rising from her cigarette. 'Are you telling me that tonight, everyone there will be wearing amulets?'

'Yes,' Minoo says, trying not to sound impatient.

'Not so good. Fucking awful energies in that place. And today is the spring equinox.'

'So what?' Ida says hoarsely. 'Why is everyone going on and on about the damn equinox?'

'There's always been a lot of hocus-pocus talked about the spring equinox. Amateurs head out into the forests to find their inner child and howl at the moon. But people who know about true magic know that only one rite matters on this particular day.'

She falls silent, blows a large cloud of smoke through her nose.

'And that's human sacrifice,' she says.

Minoo feels an icy chill gripping her.

'What do you mean?' she asks.

'What do you think I mean? A sacrifice of a human being. Or, ideally, a lot of them.'

'But why?' Anna-Karin asks feebly.

'Magic potential is part of being human. It is part of our living energy. Kill one human being and the magic energy is set free. Kill many…it leads to a fucking huge freeing up, to put it simply. If you can make that energy your own, you can use it as you see fit. But only a powerful natural witch can carry this off.'

Minoo remembers what Nicolaus told them about the time when he murdered the members of the Council.

It was a wooden church and burned quickly down to the ground. I had drawn circles around it and for every life that was consumed in the flames, my own life was lengthened.

'Considering all the ecto I've sold to PE since last summer,

I reckon it's something along those lines that they have in mind,' Mona continues. 'They've connected all the people in your school into one big network. Next, all you need is to herd the victims into a room where the circles have already been drawn and leave it for the metal witch to chomp away at all the energy in the network.'

'But what would they want with so much energy?' Minoo asks tiredly.

'Haven't got a clue.'

'They won't get that far,' Vanessa says. 'How can we stop this?'

'Easy-peasy,' Mona chuckles. 'The ruling metal witch must also wear an amulet. Rip that off him or her and you short-circuit the network. All the amulets become worthless.'

'Who is it, Helena or Krister?' Minoo says.

Mona smiles, a strange smile. Minoo feels uneasy. It is as if she has missed something, and as if Mona thinks she's too stupid to get it.

'Neither she, nor Krister, is a witch. Not a natural witch, that's for sure.'

Minoo stares at Mona.

'It must be one or both of those two,' Vanessa says. 'I *know* it must. Ida and I *saw* them.'

'They definitely work with a witch,' Mona says. 'But uppity Mr. and Mrs. Malmgren are not practicing magic. Somebody else is.'

'Do you know who?' Minoo says.

'No,' Mona replies and suddenly looks serious. 'I regret to say.'

'It must be one of Helena's favorites,' Ida says. 'When I sensed the magic in the center, they were the only ones there. You know, Erik, Robin, Rickard, Julia, Felicia...Or maybe someone else was there. I can't be certain.'

Rickard, Minoo thinks. Perhaps he's not controlled. Perhaps he's the controller.

'Gustaf said that Rickard has had an amulet since last summer,' she says.

'But why should Rickard help Helena and Krister take revenge?' Anna-Karin says. 'Did he know Elias?'

'No, he didn't,' Linnéa says. 'But then, Helena might have brainwashed him in some non-magical way.'

Minoo glances at the dolphin clock on the wall.

'We've got to go,' she says. 'The party starts in a few hours. Is there anything else we need to know?'

Mona smiles her odd little smile again.

'*Need* and *want* are two quite different things,' she says.

She puffs on her cigarette, looking at Vanessa.

'It's time for you to wake up, sweetie.'

'What?' Vanessa says, but Mona ignores her and lets her gaze slide on to Linnéa.

'People do change sometimes.'

Minoo sees Linnéa's jaw muscles contracting. Mona shifts her gaze to Anna-Karin.

'Say goodbye when you can.'

'What do you mean?' Anna-Karin asks fearfully.

'There's still time. Use it well.'

She looks at Ida now.

'The year ahead will be dark and hard for you.'

'Are you telling me it's going to get *even worse*?' Ida says.

Mona shrugs.

'Still, you'll get what you were promised,' she adds. 'So plodding on is worth it.'

Then, finally, she turns to Minoo. Examines her.

'There's something wrong with you,' she says. 'But you know that already, don't you?'

Minoo's stomach churns.

'What do you mean, *wrong?*'

'Wrong. Unnatural. You positively stink of magic, but it's unlike any magic I've ever come across. Can't fucking identify it at all. And I don't like it.'

Sirens start howling somewhere outside the City Mall. The sound is growing in intensity.

'I think you should go to be with your dad now,' Mona says.

Minoo doesn't even stop to think. She throws herself against the door, unlocks it and runs from the Crystal Cave.

CHAPTER 68

Minoo rushes towards the exit of the City Mall.

She hears running footsteps behind her, hears Vanessa call out her name, but doesn't stop. At the automatic doors, she has to wait while they slowly slide open. Smoke seeps in, the sound of the sirens is stronger still and panic fills her whole body. She is just about to run outside when someone grabs hold of her jacket and pulls her back, making her slip on the shiny floor.

Vanessa hauls her into one of the darker corners of the Mall. Minoo's back hits a wall so hard she almost loses her breath.

'Let me go!' she says.

'What do you think you're doing?' Vanessa asks.

Minoo struggles to get away, but Vanessa, who is stronger, grips Minoo's upper arms firmly and presses her against the wall.

'Let me go!' Minoo says again. 'My dad...'

'Minoo, please. Think.'

Minoo blinks. Her common sense catches up with her. No one would benefit if she ran straight into the arms of a horde of PE members out on a witch-hunt.

'I've got to find out if my dad is all right,' Minoo says.

'The two of us will go together,' Vanessa says and lets go of her. 'I'm pretty sure I can make us both invisible. It worked fine with Wille.'

Vanessa holds out her hand and Minoo takes it. Vanessa shuts her eyes.

When they experimented with magic before, this never functioned and Minoo doesn't know what to expect. But she doesn't have to wait at all. A strange, wafting feeling goes through her body.

Vanessa opens her eyes. Then their eyes meet. They can see each other just as usual.

'How do we know if it's worked?' Minoo asks.

Vanessa nods towards the other side of the aisle. A large shop window reflects the empty space where they are both standing.

Hand in hand, they run outside. Minoo notices the smoke rising to the sky, where it seems to become part of the low rainclouds. The sirens are suddenly silent, but the smell of smoke grows stronger the closer they come to Storvall Square.

He'll be fine. Nothing has happened to him, Minoo tries to tell herself.

When they reach the middle of the square, she sees that the dark gray smoke is billowing from the windows of the *Engelsfors Herald*'s editorial office. Minoo holds Vanessa's hand even more tightly.

They slow down as they approach the crowd that has formed on the square. Minoo scans the fire engine, the slowly rotating blue lights, the firemen shouting instructions to each other. She observes the police and the ambulance. The ambulance. She takes it in and almost loses her grip on Vanessa's hand. But the paramedics are standing by an empty stretcher.

Is that a good sign or a bad one? Does it mean that no one has been injured or that they haven't managed to get anyone out ...?

Minoo cannot finish the thought.

A group of women wearing yellow PE jackets comes walking across the square. They stop to look curiously at the burning building.

'Of course, it would be wrong to think that they deserved anything like that,' one of them says, obviously meaning the exact opposite.

'Still, that's where negative thinking gets you,' another woman says and they all nod in agreement.

Minoo looks at them as they walk away. She had no idea it was possible to detest complete strangers so fiercely.

Minoo and Vanessa carry on walking across the square, zigzagging carefully between passers-by and local residents who have come outside to stare and exchange gossip. Even Leffe has left his kiosk and stands there sipping coffee from a paper mug. As if this is a thrilling show, a public performance.

They have almost reached the police tape when Minoo catches sight of two of the paper's reporters. Then Kim from reception. But she can't see her father anywhere.

The smoke prickles inside her nose and tears at her lungs. When a couple of firemen visited the school, they had said that it was the smoke especially that was a deadly hazard and killed most victims. Minoo thinks about all the electric stuff in the office, the plastic flooring that has been there since the seventies, all the toxic gases that will form...

'Look, there!' Vanessa says and points.

Minoo looks. The relief is so strong her legs almost fold underneath her.

Dad. In good shape. He has put on his worn winter jacket and is arguing loudly with Nicke. Minoo picks up some of his words.

'...a crime has clearly been committed...must investigate!'

Minoo pulls Vanessa with her to where her dad is.

'First and foremost, the fire must be put out,' Nicke says

in a didactic tone, as if Dad is seriously slow on the uptake or, alternatively, about two years old. 'Then we'll have a closer look for the likely cause.'

'The cause of this is celebrating just around the corner! Positive Engelsfors has instigated this! They have been threatening me constantly since the autumn and you haven't done a damn thing about it!'

'Now, I think we had better calm down, right?' Nicke says.

'Calm? Why should I be calm?' Dad shouts.

Minoo watches him anxiously. She doesn't doubt that PE is behind this. But when Dad loses his temper, he simply sounds paranoid.

'Afraid I've got a job to do,' Nicke says and walks off.

Dad stands there. Minoo can virtually see the anger drain away. All that's left is despair.

When he had finished journalism college, he immediately landed a post in Stockholm, at one of the national dailies. He made a good career for himself. But all the same, he chose to move back to his old home town as editor-in-chief for the local paper. Not because it was a prestigious job, but precisely because it was not. Because Engelsfors was a town in decline. A town without hope, where fear and bigotry thrived.

He has given his life to this town. And now, it has taken everything from him.

Minoo dearly wants to go to him. But she has spotted several yellow jackets in the crowd. Probably not amulet-wearers, but she can't be certain. And her father is safe, while hundreds might die tonight.

'Come on,' she says to Vanessa. 'We must go.'

'Nicke really is a fool,' Vanessa says when they start walking back to the City Mall. 'Inspector Clouseau has more fucking talent.'

'I can't get into my head that he's been your mom's boy-friend,' Minoo says. 'She seems like such a nice person.'

'I guess that's what attracts all the losers.'

The sensor at the automatic door doesn't respond to invisible people, so they have to pull them open and sneak inside.

The others are waiting for them outside the Crystal Cave. But they are not alone.

'Fuck,' Vanessa says and Minoo can't help agreeing.

Viktor is there. He keeps a lookout in Minoo and Vanessa's direction. And raises his hand hesitantly to greet them.

Vanessa lets go of Minoo's hand and the same wafting sensation as before runs through Minoo's body.

'Is your father all right?' Anna-Karin asks.

'Yes. But PE has burned down the office.'

She looks at Viktor. He looks as if he hasn't slept all night and the shirt under his unbuttoned coat is creased. Minoo is reasonably certain that he wore the same shirt yesterday.

'What are you doing here?' she asks.

'The Council has decided to deal with the whole Engelsfors incident immediately,' he says. 'They intend to execute Adriana this evening. I don't know the exact time.'

The pain in his eyes looks almost genuine, but Minoo can't bring herself to trust him. She is convinced that he never does or says anything without a hidden agenda. The creased shirt and the harrowed face could just as well be his costume and mask for a new role.

'So why tell us?' she asks. 'Is the idea that we should set out to rescue her and run straight into a trap? So that you and Alexander can arrest us and charge us with a new crime?'

'I understand why you would think that,' Viktor says wearily. 'But I am telling you the truth. And I do want you to rescue her.'

'Why should we buy that?' Vanessa said. 'Yesterday, you

were in there, helping to get her sentenced to death.'

Viktor looks away, as if he can't bear meeting her eyes.

'I know you think that Alexander is a monster. You are wrong. He doesn't want Adriana's death. She's his sister.'

'Sure, he obviously cares for her a lot,' Linnéa says. 'You must have noticed it from the way he tortured her.'

'He never thought her sentence would be that severe,' Viktor says.

Minoo recalls Alexander's face when the sentence was announced. He had looked truly shocked. But she has just as clear a memory of his detachment as he wrung the neck of Adriana's raven.

'I take it then that Alexander knows you're telling us?' Minoo says.

'No,' Viktor says.

In her head, Minoo suddenly hears Linnéa's voice.

The weird thing is, I think he's being truthful. About everything. He's allowing me to read his mind.

'They might act any moment now,' Viktor continues. 'Please. We must hurry.'

What he has told them is beginning to sink in. Adriana is going to be executed. Tonight. When Helena, Krister and Rickard have planned some kind of magic massacre in the school gym.

'She is being kept under house arrest,' Viktor continues. 'I can help you to get in. But then I can't do any more.'

'Are we meant to smuggle her out on our own?' Vanessa says. 'And where do we hide her from the Council? Any ideas?'

'Adriana can't escape,' Viktor says. 'They would find her in no time. Her bond to the Council is even harder to break than for ordinary members.'

'Can we break the bond?' Anna-Karin says.

Viktor shakes his head.

'There is only one way to save her. She must become innocent.'

'How do you mean?' Minoo asks.

'Adriana betrayed the Council when she was young. After that episode, her behavior stayed exemplary and she was regarded as fully rehabilitated. It was only after she arrived here that everything started to go downhill. If only it were possible to wind back time and make her once more into the person she was before coming to Engelsfors.'

'Oh, yes? What's the effing idea?' Ida sneers.

'We have been observing Max in the hospital, and studying him,' Viktor says.

He is now intensely focused on Minoo. And it dawns on her what he has in mind. She begins to see what he is after but doesn't want to know.

'We discovered that someone had been inside his consciousness,' Viktor continues. 'We couldn't identify the magic that had been used. Whoever exerts such power is able to do things we believed to be impossible.'

Minoo stays silent, only shakes her head.

'Are you telling us that if only someone magicked away Adriana's memories of everything that's happened since she came here, then the Council would forgive her? Like that?' Vanessa says and snaps her fingers.

'Yes, I'm almost certain of it,' Viktor says. 'It's true what I said about Alexander. He doesn't want her to die. If he were offered the chance to have her declared innocent, he'd jump at it. He is powerful enough to have her interrogated again and have the sentence revoked. It would suit the Council. A living, obedient member is preferable to a dead rebel, who might become a martyr.'

It sounds perfectly reasonable, Minoo thinks. Even though

the Council have managed to convict Adriana, she is proof that it's possible to trick them.

'Minoo,' Viktor continues. 'You did whatever it was to Max, isn't that right? And if you can do that, you are also the only one who can save Adriana.'

Minoo's eyes wander towards the facade of the Crystal Cave. The interior lights are off and all she can see is her own shadowy mirror image in the shop window.

There's something wrong with you. But you know that already, don't you?

'I understand that you'll want to talk this through together,' Victor says. 'I'm going outside the Mall to wait. But please hurry.'

He glances at Minoo one last time before walking away.

The Chosen Ones stand together without speaking until the doors have closed behind him.

'It could be a trap,' Vanessa says.

'I don't think It Is, somehow,' Linnéa says.

'Doesn't matter one way or the other,' Minoo says. 'I just can't do this. When I liberated Elias and Rebecka's souls, Max's memories just came along. It wasn't that I took them from him, I just saw them. I sensed that, if I'd kept it up, I could have pulled out all his memories, but then his soul would have followed, just like that. It's like I can only ... amputate. And what I'm asked to do now is brain surgery.'

'Since then, our powers have grown stronger,' Anna-Karin says to Minoo. 'And this is Adriana's only chance.'

'Okay, listen,' Ida says. 'I know you'll all think that I'm emotionally stunted, like you always do. But we already have plans for tonight. There will be a couple of hundred people in the school tonight. And Adriana is just one person.'

Anna-Karin's cheeks flush with anger.

'How can you?' she says. 'Adriana is our friend!'

Fire

'I know, I know!' Ida replies. 'I wish we could save her, too. Look, it isn't my fault that there's a clash with PE's spring sacrifice party! What if we need Minoo to stop them? Imagine, if she goes with Viktor and everyone in the school dies just because she isn't there with us? And it isn't even certain that she *can* save Adriana, she says so herself!'

It's like one of those conundrums they've discussed in philosophy. Is it right to harm one person in order to save hundreds? Is it right to save one person if it will mean the death of hundreds? Theoretical thought experiments that are intriguing to argue about in class. In fact, Minoo got top marks. But a different kind of dilemma to face in reality.

'That's true,' Linnéa says. 'We don't know how things will pan out tonight. We don't know exactly what PE's plans are. And we don't know if we'll need Minoo.' She looks at the others and continues. 'We can't decide on the best strategy. All we can decide is what is right and then try to do it. And it is not right to leave Adriana to die. We actually have a chance to save her and stop whatever PE is up to as well.'

'I don't trust Viktor,' Vanessa says.

'Nor do I,' Linnéa says and looks at Minoo. 'But we have no choice.'

And Minoo knows she is right.

She looks around at the others. The Chosen Ones. There is so much she would like to say to them. But a superstitious instinct refuses to let her. If she acts as if this is their last time together, then maybe she'll be able to make it happen.

I'm thinking like a PE enthusiast, she tells herself. My thoughts will not affect what will happen. Only my actions matter.

But still she cannot make herself speak to them. The words feel too grandiose.

'I'll come to the school as soon as I can,' she says. 'Please be careful.'

'You can do this,' Linnéa says and hugs her quickly.

Minoo's eyes fill with tears.

'You, too,' she whispers.

Then she hugs Vanessa and Anna-Karin, holds them for a little longer than usual. Finally she turns to Ida.

'I asked Gustaf not to put that necklace on,' she says. 'I hope he hasn't but if...'

Ida nods gravely. And in that moment, Minoo realizes that they understand each other perfectly.

When Minoo goes outside, Viktor is standing close to the door with his hands plunged in his coat pockets.

'I didn't think you'd come,' he says. 'Thank you.'

'It's not because of you,' Minoo replies. 'I came for Adriana's sake.'

CHAPTER 69

As they drive through Engelsfors, Minoo observes Viktor. His profile, his long, thick eyelashes, his nose that's in fact a little askew, the stubble that lies like a faint shadow across the sharp line of his jaw.

Viktor Ehrenskiöld.

Supercilious incomer. A twin soul when it comes to literature and hating sports. Also an enemy. Ingratiating spy. Sad orphan of society. Alexander's right hand. Linnéa's savior. Adriana's prosecutor. Traitor to the Council.

I have no idea who he really is, Minoo thinks.

'I still don't understand why you're doing this,' she says. 'I thought you were loyal to the Council.'

'I am loyal to Alexander,' Viktor replies.

'And that's not the same thing?'

He swings the car into a street in Lilla Lugnet. They are close now to the block where Adriana lives. A light rain begins to tap on the windscreen.

'When someone in the membership is eighteen, he or she can choose to stay in the Council or leave it,' Viktor replies. 'Those who choose to stay have to swear an oath of allegiance. That is, promise to follow orders, without thinking. I haven't taken that oath.'

Minoo keeps looking at him.

'Why haven't they thrown you out?'

'There aren't many natural witches around. I'm valuable to them,' Viktor says so naturally it doesn't sound boastful. 'They made an exception for me.'

They pass the fire-scarred ruins of a house and Minoo thinks about the night when the Chosen Ones were on their way to break into Adriana's home. Then, they believed her to be a deadly enemy. Now, Minoo is traveling the same road, ready to risk her life in order to save Adriana's.

'If your loyalty is to Alexander, why go behind his back now?' Minoo asks.

'I'm doing this for him. Because he wouldn't be able to live with himself if he were to be the one who caused Adriana's execution. I know that. He told me that he would always go with the decisions of the Council, but it was a lie.'

He glances at her.

'And I think you realize that I am certain of that.'

'Why didn't you tell him that you had worked out a solution?'

'Because the oath obliges him to obey the Council. He would be forced to choose between the Council and Adriana once more.'

The car turns into Adriana's street. He slows down and parks a block away from her house.

'What I'm doing now is not just for his sake,' Viktor says. 'I think Adriana's death would be an injustice.'

'I thought that the Council always made the right decisions,' Minoo says.

'No, that's not the case,' Viktor says, looking at her. 'I have never said this aloud, but – no, the Council is not always right. The fact is that they often make the wrong decisions and invest their energy in the wrong causes. But they are needed. Without them, the whole world would be chaotic. Those capable of managing magic powers would oppress those who can't. The Council does a lot of good as well, whatever you think.'

'Why not swear the oath of allegiance, then?'

'Because if I had, I would have become unable to change anything. I want to make the Council better. In order to do that, I must be inside the system but still free to act.'

It seems that there is yet another Viktor, someone Minoo has never taken into account. The idealist.

'Until now, I've been successful,' he continues. 'But I don't know what they will do to me after this. Maybe Alexander won't be able to protect me.'

Viktor the self-sacrificial goody-two-shoes? Viktor the hero?

Minoo is more confused than ever.

The rain is heavier now. Viktor takes an umbrella from the boot and holds it over them both. They walk close together, her shoulder pressed against his arm.

She suddenly thinks of Gustaf.

Gustaf, who is probably at the school party. He will either be alone among hundreds of zombies, or a zombie himself. Minoo can't work out which alternative seems the worst.

She remembers last night, when he took her hand and held it. She must not fall in love with him. He is Rebecka's boyfriend. He will always be Rebecka's boyfriend, even though she is dead.

The white house is standing out against the dark sky. With every step Minoo takes, her fear increases. They follow the white wooden fence to the gate.

'I don't know if I can go through with this,' she says to Viktor.

'Think positively,' he says.

'Great joke.'

He opens the gate and they follow the flagged path through

the garden, where a few snowdrops are popping their heads up in the borders. At the front door, Viktor pulls a bunch of keys from his pocket.

'Any guards?' Minoo asks quietly.

'No need,' he replies and puts one of the keys into the lock. Opens the door and gestures to her to step inside.

Minoo can almost hear Linnéa's voice.

Welcome to the House of Horrors.

'What's the matter?' Viktor asks.

'A moment of déjà vu, that's all.'

The light rain feels ice cold against Anna-Karin's face and she pulls up the hood of her duffel coat. She is with Ida, Vanessa and Linnéa, shivering in a clump of trees and watching the school, which is towering against the horizon.

'What are they doing?' Vanessa asks.

Anna-Karin closes her eyes and slips into the consciousness of the fox.

It is standing close to one of the windows of the gym.

The perspective from above is almost dizzying. Anna-Karin and the fox are watching the people milling around the hall below their level. The gray-green floor is full of dashes and lines. Different colors for different sports. Anna-Karin hates them all.

The fox's sensitive hearing picks up the voices of the guests, loud and jolly. Everyone seems to be saying the same thing. What *fun* it is to be there. How *terrific* the decoration is. And what a *fantastic* evening it's going to be. The only subject they can't agree on is who is going to be chosen as the Young PE Member of the Year. Most of them think it's going to be Erik, but Rickard is the runner-up. Some people have suggested Kevin. But all these guys are so *fantastic* it doesn't truly matter who is the number one choice. After all, being in PE means that any right-thinking person can be a winner.

Tommy Ekberg and Ove Post, the biology teacher, are standing by the entrance to the gym. They remind Anna-Karin of the guards at the trial. The same watchful expressions. Kevin fills a glass for each new arrival from the punchbowl. In front of the wall bars, a long line of tables has been set out with tons of buffet food and stacks of yellow paper napkins. Robin and Erik are together hauling a large amplifier up on to the stage that has been constructed under one of the basketball nets at the far end of the hall.

'They're still getting the place ready,' Anna-Karin reports and carries on looking for familiar faces in the crowd.

She catches sight of Gustaf. He's sitting in the stands, talking to Felicia.

'I've spotted Gustaf.'

'Is he wearing the amulet?' Ida asks.

Gustaf's yellow polo shirt is buttoned all the way up.

'I don't know,' Anna-Karin says.

She tries to read Gustaf's expression, but he looks as hysterically happy as everybody else. Is he just acting?

The very bright strip lights are level with the window. They make the fox's eyes feel uncomfortable. Now and then, an amulet catches the light as the guests mingle in the gym.

So many of them. And all the time, more and more arrive.

For as long as they're wearing the amulets, they are enemies. But enemies that the Chosen Ones are out to protect rather than to fight.

Anna-Karin opens her eyes and turns to the others.

'I think it's time to move,' she says.

'Right, let's go,' Linnéa says and picks up a large stone from the ground.

Chapter 70

In Adriana's house, everything is exactly the way Minoo remembers it. The smell that is unnaturally clean. The heavy antique furniture, in its proper place exactly to the millimeter. Minoo wonders if any of the people in the portraits are ancestral relatives of Adriana and Alexander. She follows Viktor through the dark rooms and up the creaking staircase.

What are the other Chosen Ones doing at this moment? Are they in danger?

Minoo and Viktor walk along the upstairs corridor and stop outside Adriana's bedroom. They stand looking at the closed door.

What happens if I can't do this? Minoo thinks. And if I succeed at all, what if I don't remove enough and leave remains of memories behind that prevent her from being declared innocent? Or what if I remove too much? Maybe she'll become somebody utterly different. Or a vegetable. Like Max.

What if I kill her?

'Stop worrying,' Viktor says.

Taken aback, she looks at him.

'No, I can't read your mind,' he says. 'But it shows in your face. You're getting worked up. I know you can carry this off.'

'You know nothing. Well, you know nothing about my powers anyway.'

'But I believe in you.'

Oh, goody, at least someone does, Minoo thinks.

'We've blocked the corridor with circles,' Viktor explains.

He stretches out his hand and feels his way cautiously in the air. An electrical hiss and lights flash at his fingertips.

'Ouch,' he says and shakes his hand.

From his pocket, he pulls out a small transparent spray bottle. It is filled with something that looks like ordinary water.

'But we must of course have access to provide her with food.'

He sprays into the air several times.

Where the fluid hits the power field, the air glitters. Viktor grabs Minoo's jacket and pulls her through the shimmering area. She glances over her shoulder. The shining particles are extinguishing behind them. The power field between them and the staircase is intact once more. She is locked in.

'We must hurry now,' Viktor says.

He walks to the bedroom door, finds the right key, twists it in the lock and opens up.

The only light in the room comes from a plain, stainless-steel standard lamp. Adriana lies on the bed, staring at the wall. Her clothes are the same as at the trial. Her eye make-up has smeared a little. Her tights have torn and a long ladder has streaked up one of her calves. Her high-heeled shoes are on the floor where she kicked them off.

'Has the time come already?' she says dully and turns around.

She goes rigid when she sees Minoo and Viktor.

'Minoo. What are you doing here? What are you doing here…with him?'

'I'll stand guard outside,' Viktor says, walks out and closes the door behind him.

Minoo sits down next to Adriana.

'They're coming for me any time now. You must leave at once,' Adriana says. 'Don't trust Viktor. He's tricked you into coming here. It's a trap.'

'I will not leave you here, simple as that.'

'Minoo,' Adriana says gravely. She sits up. 'Listen, I'm not afraid. I have made two choices in my life that I am proud of. The first was to leave the Council together with Simon. The second was to take your side and not the Council's. I have accepted my fate.'

'But we haven't. We have no intention of allowing them to murder you. We are going to rescue you.'

'I can't escape—'

'I know that,' Minoo interrupts. 'There is another solution.'

She describes the plan and Adriana listens with a troubled look on her face.

'Viktor thinks that if we succeed, the Council will revoke the sentence,' Minoo says. 'I must be honest now. I have no idea if I'm capable of doing this. But it's your only hope.'

Adriana shakes her head.

'No, I can't let you run such a risk. If something goes wrong, you'll have to live with it for the rest of your life. And even if you're successful, I'll become the person I was before. I'd rather die than live like that other self.'

'The woman you were then *became* the one you are now,' Minoo says. 'There's nothing to say that you won't change again. And we will do everything we can to think up a way for you to break your bond with the Council.'

'That's impossible.'

'Many things we thought impossible have actually happened.'

'I can't let you do this...'

'If I didn't try to help you, do you think I could live with *that* for the rest of my life?'

Adriana looks at her, in silence. Minoo listens to her breathing. Watches the pulse beating at the base of Adriana's throat. Her beating heart. Her heart that the Council wants to stop.

'I don't want to die,' Adriana finally admits. 'I do my best to act courageous, but I don't want to die.' She thinks briefly. 'Where will my memories go?'

'I don't know.'

Adriana nods.

'Doesn't matter,' she says. 'Go ahead. But, Minoo...don't remove him. Simon. Without him...'

Her voice breaks.

'I promise,' Minoo says.

Adriana nods again.

'I should have been able to predict the turn the trial would take,' she says. 'But I failed to realize how powerful the group of skeptics has grown.'

'How can they twist the evidence like that? Can't they get it into their heads that the world will soon go under? Don't they care?'

'They don't want to know. To admit it would also be to admit that there are powers stronger than themselves. Events that they cannot control.' She looks at Minoo. 'In a way, this could offer you new hope. Keep a low profile and maybe they'll leave you in peace. I truly hope that they will.'

She puts her arm around Minoo and holds her for a while. Traces of her perfume remain, a faint scent of roses.

'I won't remember this, will I?' Adriana says as she sits back.

Minoo shakes her head.

'I will miss you as you are now.'

'So will I,' Adriana says with a sad little smile.

She lies down on the bed and closes her eyes.

Minoo takes a deep breath and puts her hand on Adriana's forehead. Whatever happens, she hopes that Adriana won't be in pain.

She allows the black smoke to pour forth. It swirls around the bed, splits up and fuses again, forms convoluted patterns against the white walls of the room, enveloping them both in its ink-black whirlpool.

Minoo closes her eyes and allows herself to be swept along.

The rain has stopped. Ida leads the way as they sneak between the cars in the car park behind the school. She checks out the loading bay below the wide steel door that leads into the dining area. They accessed the school via that route just about a year ago. Entering the pitch black passage had felt like stepping straight into hell. At least the lights are on in the gym, she comforts herself. It doesn't help much. Last year, they only had to face one enemy, and this time there are a couple of hundred.

And Erik is one of them.

Ida had thought Minoo was an idiot not to have realized that Max was evil.

She has always refused to believe that karma exists but lately evidence to the contrary seems to be piling up.

They reach the brick wall and Ida presses herself against it. She studies the fire escape's spiral of black metal that twists up along the wall all the way to the top floor. It has a landing corresponding to each floor level.

'Nicolaus might have thought of leaving his keys to the school behind,' she mutters. 'He should have worked out that we would have to fight the demons here again sooner or later.'

'Better go for the door on the top floor,' Linnéa says. 'I don't think there's anyone around there.'

Fire

'Are they all thinking the same thing?' Anna-Karin asks.

'No,' Linnéa says. 'They're affected by something, but the effect is low-key right now.'

Ida has a look around. The shadows under the street lamps seem to be growing denser.

This is such a terrible idea, she thinks.

Cautiously, Vanessa starts climbing the spiral staircase. Linnéa goes after her. Ida pushes past Anna-Karin and puts her foot on the bottom rung. If somebody emerges out of the shadows and starts chasing them, she doesn't want to go last.

The slippery metal grids of the treads shiver under their feet. Ida passes the landing at the second floor and glances through the pane in the door.

Except for the spooky green light from an '*Emergency Exit*' sign, the empty hallway is very dark. She has a vivid image of how something will materialize as soon as she has turned her back. A decaying face, pressed against the pane, staring at her, grinning hungrily.

Hold it, Ida, she thinks. Isn't what you've got to do now more than enough? No need to invent more scary things, right?

She fixes her eyes on her feet and refuses to look up again until she has reached the fourth and final landing.

Linnéa is peering through the dirty windowpane.

'Fuck,' she says. 'It's alarmed. I didn't think the school could afford being wired up.'

They stand close together on the small landing. The wet, cold railing is hard against Ida's back. One look over her shoulder tells her just how far down the ground is. The entire staircase seems to vibrate under them, as if it could soon work lose from its attachments. She doesn't want to be here for a second more. She pushes her way to the door and looks in.

'What are you doing?' Linnéa says.

Ida immediately spots the little white plastic box on the wall just inside the door. A red light winks teasingly at her.

If everybody else's power has become stronger and easier to direct, so should hers. She takes her gloves off, puts her fingers on the glass and concentrates.

Her fingertips prickle. She has goose bumps all over.

'What shit are you up to?' Vanessa says.

Ida's fingers tingle so much now it almost hurts.

She notes the little flashes that spark on the other side of the glass, level with her fingertips. She focuses on the red, blinking light, imagines it to be a monster's eye that opens and shuts, opens and shuts. And the flashes are flying towards the white plastic box. The sizzling sound can be heard out on the landing. A slender coil of smoke rises from the scorched box.

The red light has stopped blinking.

Ida shakes her hands to stop the stinging sensation. The others look impressed.

'Since when have you been able to do stuff like that?' Anna-Karin says.

'Since right now,' Ida says

Linnéa pulls off her thin top, puts her jacket back on and uses the top to cover her right hand holding the heavy stone. It would have been helpful if Vanessa could have picked the lock, but it is too complicated for her hairpin technique.

'What are they doing in there?' she asks and Anna-Karin closes her eyes.

'Kerstin Stålnacke is there with the school choir. They're getting ready.'

'Perfect,' Linnéa says.

With the choir yelling their positive campaign songs, the risk that anyone will hear the sound of the pane breaking is next to nil. And she has scanned this place for unidentified thoughts, but picked up nothing unexpected. It's now or never.

'Move over,' she says and the others back down a few steps. 'Mind the splinters.'

Linnéa tenses her arm, shuts her eyes and turns her face away.

The glass cracks with a dull sound, muffled by the fabric. But a few shards fall to Linnéa's feet, clatter loudly against the metal grid and carry on down to the ground.

Linnéa raises her arm again. This time the inner pane breaks. Glass is falling on the floor inside the door. They all hold their breath.

Up here, only a very faint reverberation of the choir singing can be heard. Still, there is no mistaking the ecstasy in the voices.

Linnéa puts the stone down. She winds the top more tightly around her hand and arm before gingerly sticking her hand through the hole. Twisting the inside handle, she opens the door and steps into the corridor. Stands still and listens. Registers the swarm of thoughts buzzing far down inside the building.

She looks along the hallway that leads to the bathroom where Elias died. Where everything began.

Vanessa comes and stands close to her.

And suddenly Linnéa wonders if she dares. She would so very much like to kiss Vanessa the way loving couples kiss in films, just as stuff starts exploding and the action should be far too fast and panicky for tender feelings.

Usually, she despises these couples. But now she understands them. Because how is it possible to face danger without giving your beloved a kiss that might be the last? What could be more important?

Vanessa looks quizzically at her. Linnéa is suddenly aware that Anna-Karin and Ida are standing right behind them. The moment is lost.

'Ready?' Vanessa whispers.

Linnéa nods.

She might be too much of a coward to show her feelings for Vanessa.

But she is definitely ready to put a stop to Positive Engelsfors.

Vanessa wishes her power were enough to pull them all with her into invisibility.

Instead she walks ahead, checking that the coast is clear before the others follow her. If one of the amulet wearers spots them, all the others will know in an instant.

And if they're seen, it's all over.

The last notes of a song are ringing out, deep down in the innards of the school.

She hears Linnéa's voice in her head.

Anna-Karin says that Helena and Krister are stepping up on the stage now. They are not wearing any necklaces. At least not as far as the fox can see.

Just how absurd have our lives become when we think this is a normal piece of conversation? Vanessa thinks.

You mean, apart from the fact that the conversation is happening inside our heads? Linnéa replies.

Vanessa can't help smiling. She goes and leans over the railing to look down into the stairwell. No one in sight.

I'll go down to the second floor and look around, she thinks.

Fine, Linnéa responds. *Take care.*

Promise.

Vanessa starts walking downstairs. Over her shoulder, she sees Linnéa trying to place her feet as gently as possible.

Behind Linnéa, Ida's blonde hair glows in the faint light from the windows.

Vanessa could scream, tap-dance, do cartwheels, whatever came to mind. But the others are defenseless. And the slightest sound echoes against the dark stone of the stairs.

She reaches the third floor and scans the long hallways that disappear into the dark and seem to go on and on for an eternity. Still no one lurking. At least, no one she can detect. She is just about to carry on downstairs when Linnéa's thought stops her.

Wait!

Vanessa stops in mid-pace.

I hear them, Linnéa thinks. *Two of them. Maybe three. Directly below us. We'd better take the spiral stairs instead.*

I hear you, Vanessa thinks. *But wait a second.*

She walks into the hallways, moves in and out between the lockers with their Positive Engelsfors stickers. Bits of yellow paper bunting swish in the draft as she passes by.

She opens the door to the spiral staircase.

All clear? Linnéa asks.

Yes. I'll go down first, you follow.

She closes the door quietly and starts out downstairs.

The light from below is reflected on the walls but Vanessa casts no shadow.

Linnéa opens the door to the spiral staircase. Closes her eyes and sets out, with Ida and Anna-Karin close behind. To detect if anyone is nearby, she must try to orient herself in the humming haze of thoughts that fills the school.

Thank God for Alicja.

One thought that floats slightly above the rest.

After tonight, surely Helena and Krister will be pleased with me?

Linnéa instantly passes a thought on to Vanessa.

Someone is standing below.

I can see her, Vanessa answers quickly. *It's Kerstin Stålnacke. Come on down. She's standing in the main lobby and can't see you.*

Linnéa sends her message on to Anna-Karin and Ida and the three of them descend to the ground floor as silently as they can.

They go into the corridor leading into the main entrance lobby.

Is she alone? Linnéa thinks to Vanessa.

Yes, Vanessa thinks. *She seems to be standing guard. I saw her take over from our gym teacher, Lollo.*

A burst of applause from the gym. The echo finds its way through the corridor. Linnéa thinks she can distinguish Helena's laughter.

'They're about to choose the young PE member,' Anna-Karin whispers.

'Is Kerstin going to hang around all night?' Ida says quietly.

Linnéa looks towards the lobby. Somewhere in there, Kerstin Stålnacke stands alone. Before Linnéa shuts her eyes and dives into the cacophony of thoughts again, she tries to imagine the dance and music teacher. She gets a grip on Kerstin's thoughts almost at once. It feels a little like holding on to a loose thread in a piece of material and then starting to pull.

Perhaps I ought to have chosen the nice tune from that nice film about the nice choir from Norrland instead. I think Helena would have enjoyed that very much. But golly, how I ramble on! Now I must focus on what went really well. I am a good choirmaster. I am musical, ambitious and imaginative, but above all I am enthusiastic and can enthuse and if there's something these young people need it's—

Something breaks Kerstin's line of thought.

'Alicja!' she calls from somewhere far off. 'You have no idea how proud you've made me tonight!'

A frail small voice says something Linnéa can't make out.

'No, no, thank *you*,' Kerstin says. 'You were outstanding!'

Ida tugs at Linnéa's sleeve.

'Is she alone with Alicja?'

Linnéa nods.

'Great,' Ida says.

She slips away down the corridor and Linnéa stares after her, almost panicking.

Where are you going? she screams inside Ida's head, but Ida blocks her at once.

Ida presses herself flat against the wall while she moves sideways along the corridor. Now she can hear Kerstin clearly.

'You're a star!' she is saying, just as Ida with wildly hammering heart peeps around the corner to see into the lobby.

To mark the occasion, Kerstin is wearing a radiantly yellow poncho. Around her neck, with the chain entangled in a wooden African neckpiece, dangles the metal sign amulet. Alicja is chewing on a strand of her dark hair.

That baby has all the charisma of a wrung-out dishcloth, Ida thinks. And Kerstin is raving about *her* being a star?

Ida stays pressed against the wall. She is itching to make a move. Literally. Flashes spark along her hands.

'You sing with such *true feeling*,' Kerstin says.

Ida peeps out again. Stretches her hands out. Kerstin and Alicja have no time to react before Ida has thrown them right across the room. Both flop down on the floor in a faint.

Suddenly, Ida feels anxious.

Did she overdo it?

She takes one step into the lobby.

In passing, Vanessa's invisible shoulder gives her a push. On purpose, obviously. Ida watches as an invisible hand removes the chains from around Kerstin and Alicja's necks.

Anna-Karin and Linnéa join them now.

'I'd better get them both to want to go home at once,' Anna-Karin whispers and walks over to Kerstin and Alicja, who are twitching restlessly on the floor.

Linnéa looks at Ida.

You shouldn't have done that.

Ida shrugs.

So what? It solved a problem, didn't it? There's nobody to stand guard any more. Nothing to stop us from barging on straight ahead. Isn't that what you usually go for?

Linnéa snorts.

Ida turns and looks at Anna-Karin, who is talking quietly to Alicja and Kerstin. They get up on shaky legs and obediently hobble along towards the main doors. Ida wonders if their brains will be totally burned out, having been controlled by two witches in succession. And, in between, being zapped by a third witch.

She looks towards the door leading to the gym. New applause is thundering down there. Ida can feel it through the floor.

Anna-Karin, Linnéa and Vanessa come to stand beside her. Anna-Karin's eyes are shut.

'The three top nominees are asked to come up on stage now,' she whispers. 'Erik, Kevin and Rickard.'

'I hope Rickard doesn't win,' Vanessa murmurs. 'Then we'll never get at him.'

'He won't,' Ida whispers. 'Erik is Helena's favorite.'

More thunderous applause from below.

'We'll fix this,' Vanessa says.

'Yes,' Linnéa says. 'Come to think of it, this is just like any other day in Engelsfors high school. Only, people are a fraction more zombified than usual.'

CHAPTER 71

It feels like coming home.

A power much greater than anything Minoo has ever known is filling her and now she is no longer afraid. Her hand rests lightly on Adriana's forehead, where she senses the life force pulsating underneath the skull. Minoo could draw that force out of her, as she did to Max. But instead, she concentrates harder still and slides *inside*.

Adriana.

Minoo is with her, inside her, in her thoughts and emotions, everything that is Adriana's self. Then Minoo observes the latest memory. She sees her own face as Adriana saw it. She is aware of Adriana's fear, but also of her hope. She has come to believe that Minoo might save her.

Minoo lingers in that moment. She could have started to tug at that memory in order to pull out many remembered events, linked like pearls on a string. But she is suddenly aware that there are other ways.

She concentrates even harder. The first time she did this it felt like discovering a new sense. Now she realizes that she has several senses she can use.

It is as if blinkers are coming off, as if walls are tumbling down. Memories are not linked into an anchor chain, steadily leading downwards, steadily deeper, through ever murkier waters. Memories are like a woven cloth. Thousands – no, many hundreds of thousands – of threads pass in and out, running above and below each other, forming patterns, associating in every direction.

And they are not static, but changeable. Slowly slowly, the memories shift, join up, merge, subdivide, distort, alter. They grow, shrink, are moved out of the way and push themselves forward. Their dynamism is hypnotic to watch.

Out of this constant shape-changing, her task is to extract certain details, cut away years from Adriana's life.

It ought to throw her into a state of complete panic, but doesn't. If anything, she grows interested. It feels as if everything about Minoo that is anxious, small, weak, *human*, can no longer affect her. It is liberating not to be afraid any longer. She is in control.

Around her, memories are pulsating slowly. She chooses a strong one. Slides into it.

Burns.

The pain is so extreme that she thinks she will die. She *wishes* herself dead.

And it fades, no, it is just that it hasn't started yet, because now she has reached the moment before it will be done to her. Minoo sees Alexander's face through Adriana's eyes, sees him as Adriana does at the same time as she sees him as Minoo does. He is younger, but his face is recognizably as resolute, as stern. It doesn't give away any emotion as he raises the branding iron with the sign for the fire element. It starts to glow as he holds it and moves it closer to Adriana's bare skin.

Minoo lets go of that memory, disappears into the next one that insists on her concentrating.

A tall, imposing woman with an antique silver brooch on the lapel of her jacket. She looks like Adriana, and it is her mother. 'I so wish I could have done more. I did try my best,' she says sadly. Adriana doesn't believe her. She hates her mother. She hates them all.

Minoo sees a boy in his late teens, with black, crew-cut hair. He is seated on a chair just like the one in the courtroom. No, it is the very same chair, Minoo is sure of that. And she is also sure that the boy is Simon, because Adriana loves him. Her love for him fills all of her. It is a love that will sustain her entire life. She cannot live without him. She is vaguely aware of how others look at them, but everyone else is only a shadowy presence in her mind. Simon is all she sees. He is gasping for air. His element has been turned against him. He cannot breathe. When she sees him die, something inside her dies with him.

Minoo pulls away, moves on. Back in time.

Two circles with fire as their power sign. Drawn on the stone floor in a room without any furnishings. It is high-ceilinged and its narrow windows admit a bleak light. 'Try,' a boy's voice says just next to her. She turns and sees a young Alexander holding the *Book of Patterns*. 'I can't do it,' she replies. He slams the book shut and sighs. Looks at the circles. A blue flame flares up. He gazes at her. 'You're useless,' he says and leaves. She watches the blue fire. She will not give up. She is going to make them all proud of her.

Minoo follows the twisting memory threads forward in time.

A hospital bed, in a single room. Machines piping, pumping and hissing. Adriana approaches the bed and looks down at Max's immobile face. Now she knows who he is and she curses herself for not having seen the signs, despite working together with him for almost a year. She examines the respirator, contemplates pulling the plug out. But it would mean an end to his suffering. And that, he does not deserve.

Onwards.

Adriana enters the Crystal Cave. 'There, I knew you'd turn up sooner or later,' Mona says and sucks on her cigarette. Adriana detests asking Mona for help, but she must find some way of telling the girls what's what. She is prepared to pay any price.

Minoo changes direction and moves backwards.

Adriana is in her study in this house. She is turning over fragile, yellowing book pages, until she finds what she is looking for. An ancient, long-forgotten passage about how a witch can set about using her familiar to hide memories and at the same time be able to access them.

Backwards.

Nicolaus meets her walking along one of the corridors in the school. He glares disapprovingly at her and Adriana understands him. She likes him and wishes she were able to show it.

Minoo goes further back in time and comes across her own face again. She is in the passenger seat of Adriana's car. Adriana has opened her Thermos and is pouring tea into a mug. 'Drink some of this,' she says. 'Is it...magical?' Minoo asks. 'It's Earl Grey,' Adriana says. She is feeling guilty. Frustrated. She wishes it were possible for her to do more for the Chosen Ones. But the Council will not let her intervene. It orders her to wait.

Still further back.

Adriana sees the blood on the asphalt. Rebecka's body has just been removed. If only she had run after the girl.

Backwards.

Rebecka is in her office, sitting opposite her. Rebecka's eyes are tightly shut and Adriana tries to understand what is going on inside her head. 'We'd better start at the beginning,' she says. Rebecka opens her eyes. 'Rebecka, what did you think this meeting was about?' Adriana says. The girl gets up from the armchair. 'Excuse me, I have to go,' she says and runs away.

Backwards.

Strange memories. At night, a deep dark forest seen from above. It takes a moment or two before Minoo understands that this is something Adriana has seen through the eyes of her raven. It descends to fly at tree height, turning this way and that to avoid the treetops, zooms so fast that Minoo can't pick out any details. It suddenly lands in a pine. Hears a voice. Nicolaus is speaking. 'Welcome, O Chosen One, you who have come to this sacred place on the night of the blood-red moon. Behold! The prophecy has been fulfilled!' The raven flies closer and, once more, Minoo sees herself, looking so small in her pajamas and sounding so helpless when she says: 'Excuse me?'

Backwards.

Adriana is spreading out all the lists of tenth-grade students due to begin that autumn. Just on an impulse. She doesn't think this will work. But she lifts the pendulum and moves her hand over the pages, leafing through the sheets of paper. Suddenly, the pendulum starts swinging over one of the class lists. She stares at it. In the next moment, her hand is pulled down. The pendulum has come to rest on a name. Elias Malmgren.

Backwards.

Adriana places the lamp with the dragonfly shade on the desk in her school office, plugs it in. She is feeling curiously full of expectation. Until now, she has not dared to believe that she was right all along. But now it feels as though something is about to happen in the godforsaken dump. Something that will change her. Set her free.

Minoo retreats.

She knows that here is where she must begin.

Fire

She has them in front of her now.

Shimmering, glowing threads. She links them, welds them together. She cannot tear the memories out of Adriana without damaging her, but she can construct new routes, weave new lines of thought that pass by all that is forbidden.

The black smoke wells out and closes in around Minoo, who feels the magic of the guardians operating through her; together they are burying the dangerous memories deep in Adriana's subconscious, where neither she nor any of the interrogators can get at them.

And then, just as Minoo knows that her task is complete, she feels tiredness flowing into her.

She slips out of Adriana's mind.

She is not yet back in the physical world, only almost there. She is in between, as in the moment when she saw the blessing of the demons radiate around Max like a halo.

In front of her, Adriana lies stretched out on the bed.

Now do you understand?

Minoo looks up.

Matilda has materialized on the other side of the bed. Her face is shaded, but Minoo feels sure that the apparition is smiling.

Your powers can be used for good.

Matilda doesn't move, but Minoo senses something that sweeps through the air, feels like a caress against her cheek.

You must hurry away from here. The others need you.

'What is going to happen tonight?' Minoo asks. 'Have Helena and Krister planned to kill everyone?'

Yes. It is the last requirement.

'For what?'

Matilda is melting away into the shadows once more, but her voice lingers.

For the apocalypse to begin.

Vanessa cautiously opens the door leading from the girls'
changing room into the gym.

The stands are full of PE members and those without a
seat are crowded together around the walls. A short girl right
at the back is jumping up and down to catch a glimpse of
what is happening on the stage.

Entering is like stepping back into the summer heatwave.
Vanessa tries to breathe through her mouth to avoid inhal-
ing the smell of new sweat and of old, ingrained gym.

But, above all, the air is thick with magic.

Vanessa can't see any ectoplasm circles anywhere. But
that's not necessarily significant. She and Minoo saw no circles a year ago, when they broke into Adriana's study. Some
circles don't become visible until they are activated.

It feels as though the magic in the hall is set to standby.
Any time now, the witch in charge of the remote can press
ON.

Vanessa watches the stage. Rickard's eyes flicker anxiously as they scan the audience. The amulet hangs outside
his yellow T-shirt. Next to him, Erik and Kevin have their
eyes hopefully fixed on Helena, who stands behind the
microphone and is just slitting open an envelope.

'And the Young Positive Engelsfors Member of the Year
is...' Helena makes an artificial pause and throws a conspira-
torial glance at the audience. 'Imagine how wonderful it feels
to give you such a happy message, because – yes! Most of
you will have voted for him.'

Laughter fills the hall. Helena pulls a card from the envelope. Her smile broadens and she reads out the name in a
triumphant voice.

'Erik Forslund!'

A new burst of applause. Stamping feet make the stands

shake. Wolf whistling cuts through the air. Erik doesn't even try to act surprised. Calmly, he goes to hug Helena. Then he turns to Krister, who hands him a big bunch of daffodils and a framed certificate, then thumps him on the back so hard the amulet jumps on Erik's chest.

Vanessa observes Rickard. He is applauding like everyone else, but is obviously disappointed. Krister says something to him and Kevin, and they get off the stage together.

Rickard joins a group of guys who are nibbling directly from the buffet platters. He takes his glasses off and starts polishing them, tries to act as if he's not upset. Vanessa sets her sights on him, moving through the crowd very cautiously in order not to bump into anyone.

'This is really a surprise,' Erik is saying from the stage. 'A *positive* surprise, of course.'

The hall fills with laughter again. Many of the voices sound over the top, forced. There is hysteria in the air and it frightens Vanessa. As if the fun and games could in an instant topple over into either despair or rage.

'PE has not only changed Engelsfors,' Erik carries on. 'PE has changed our lives. My life.'

Vanessa catches sight of Gustaf. He is standing near the stage, smiling like everyone else. But he can't hide the anger in his eyes. She is pretty certain that he isn't wearing a necklace. She hopes nobody else has noticed.

'It isn't easy to change your life,' Erik says. 'When we develop as human beings, we can't count on everyone around us developing at the same pace. Often, they may resist change out of jealousy. Anger. Take my ex. I did try to make her understand, but she refused. She was simply not ready for change. A real energy-thief. And I realized in the end that I had to cut the bond between us. It was hard, but now I feel all the stronger for it. She held me back. She pulled me down.'

Vanessa thinks of Ida who is hiding in the girls' shower-room together with Linnéa and Anna-Karin. Hopefully, she can't hear all this.

'I think many of you know what I'm talking about,' Erik continues. 'I'm not the only one who has been betrayed by somebody I thought was close to me.'

A familiar sob from somewhere. A girl with dark hair stands with her back to Vanessa. The girl's boyfriend is stroking her bare shoulder to comfort her.

Michelle and Mehmet.

'Put these feelings aside,' Erik says. 'Concentrate on your own goals. Who knows, perhaps the day will come when the others understand what we are about and catch up with us. Until that day, we have each other. Everyone in this room is a friend of mine.'

Hundreds of heads nod in agreement and Michelle's is one of them.

Vanessa has to look away.

Rickard puts his glasses on again. Vanessa homes in on his amulet. If only she can get it off him, all this will be over and done with.

The dark shower-room smells damply of mold and old shampoo.

Linnéa can barely make out the shadowy shapes of the others. Ida, who is sitting curled up on the floor. Anna-Karin, who is standing next to Ida. Linnéa can't see her face, but knows that Anna-Karin's eyes are shut. She is with the fox.

Outside, in the gym, Erik carries on with the praise of Positive Engelsfors.

Linnéa so wishes that the sound of his voice wouldn't make her heart race. Wishes that he didn't have the power to make her afraid.

'I hate him,' Ida whispers.

'You're not the only one,' Linnéa says in a low voice and, then, to Anna-Karin: 'Has Vanessa done it yet?'

'No. With such a crowd it's hard for her to move about.'

Linnéa is glad that animals can see Vanessa when she's invisible to humans. But someone in the gym might be able to see her, too. The thought makes her utterly terrified.

She presses her hands against the tiled wall, drums against it with her fingertips.

Linnéa.

Linnéa turns to Ida and Anna-Karin. But she realizes that this is not either of their voices. A stranger's voice. Inside her head.

Say nothing to the others.

Linnéa opens her mouth, but the other person's thoughts are ahead of her.

Or else I'll kill Vanessa. I know she's in the hall. And I know where you are.

Linnéa shuts her mouth again. Switches off all emotions. She must keep a cold head. Not act on impulse.

Good.

Now she suddenly recognizes the voice. She hesitates. Can it really be her?

Michelle? she asks. *Is that you?*

A moment's silence.

Not any more.

A quite different voice. This time, Linnéa does not hesitate. She knows Backman's thoughts only too well.

I am everyone.

This new voice she only recognizes vaguely.

Rickard? Are you the one doing this?

Laughter.

And now Linnéa understands. He can leap between the

consciousnesses of others, steer their thoughts towards her.

I control everyone in here, Rickard's voice continues. *I can make them kill you.*

'Linnéa?' Anna-Karin whispers. 'Vanessa's just standing there. Can't you ask her if we can do anything?'

'Just wait a minute,' Linnéa says, just managing to keep her voice steady.

Tell me what you want me to do, she thinks.

Find an excuse for going away. See to it that the others don't follow you.

'Vanessa is calling me,' Linnéa says. 'Something I must do.'

'We'll come with you,' Anna-Karin whispers.

'No. She says that only I must come. You stay here.'

'Right,' Anna-Karin says hesitantly.

Good. Now come along.

Linnéa leaves the changing room. The harsh light makes the hooks along the wall shine.

She would like to send Vanessa a warning thought, but doesn't dare. It might expose Vanessa to even greater danger.

All she can do is hope and pray to all the gods she doesn't believe in that Vanessa will succeed against all the odds.

CHAPTER 72

Vanessa moves slowly towards Rickard. His entire attention is focused on the stage, where Erik is still holding forth. He seems able to trawl his bottomless store of PE clichés for hours to come.

'We are many. And we will grow bigger and bigger,' he is saying. 'Our journey has only just begun!'

Noisy applause bursts out again. Incredibly, Erik seems to be finished. He steps aside for Helena, who is also clapping. To prolong the moment, she steps forward to the edge of the stage and puts her hands together above her head.

Vanessa observes Rickard.

He looks so ordinary. So *normal*. But isn't that exactly what the serial killer's neighbors always say, once the psycho has been caught and the police have excavated fourteen carved-up bodies from his garden?

The guys near Rickard drift closer to the stage and suddenly he is on his own. She goes to him. Stops.

The amulet chain looks thick. She doesn't dare pull at it.

The clasp has slipped down on to his chest. Vanessa curses. It's going to be much trickier to undo it from that position. She has only one option. She takes another step, wipes her sweating hands on her jeans, raises them and moves them closer, ready to grasp the amulet. She is so close she can smell vinegary potato chips and disappointment on his breath. Her fingers almost touch the chain.

Rickard starts. And looks at her.

No, it's impossible, Vanessa thinks. I'm imagining things.

Before she can get her head around what is happening, Rickard has grabbed her wrists and is holding them in a vise-like grip.

Vanessa kicks him on the shin as hard as she can, but he doesn't even twitch. His knee hits her stomach like a sledgehammer.

Pain makes Vanessa black out. She can't breathe. When she flops to the floor, Rickard is still holding on to her wrists.

She feels herself becoming visible again and, in confirmation, hundreds of pairs of eyes turn to look at her.

The shock ejects Anna-Karin from the fox's consciousness.

'He's caught her!' she whispers and opens her eyes.

Next to her, she sees the shadow that is Ida stand up

'He's caught Vanessa,' Anna-Karin says. 'He...'

She falls silent.

Steps approaching from the gym. Ida has heard them, too. She is already on her way out of the shower-room.

'Wait!' Anna-Karin hisses and tries to catch up with her.

But Ida is so much faster than she is and disappears through the doors on the opposite side of the changing room, out into the dark corridor.

Anna-Karin realizes she oughtn't to be surprised, but is all the same. She had really believed that Ida had changed.

The door behind Anna-Karin is pulled open. The door to the gym.

She turns around.

Julia and Felicia step inside. After them many more PE members pour in, like a bulky yellow mass.

Anna-Karin backs away. The look in their eyes shows that each one of them shares in a single consciousness, has one uniform intent. To capture her.

She releases her power at full strength.

STOP.

Julia and Felicia carry on walking towards her and Anna-Karin backs into one of the low benches that line the room, then almost bumps the back of her head into a metal clothes hook.

STOP!

The mass flows on towards her.

STOP!

The problem isn't that there are too many of them. Anna-Karin has controlled bigger crowds than this. It is that they are interconnected. Her power is diluted inside the huge communal conscience. It's like filling a bathtub a teaspoonful at a time.

Julia and Felicia go to each side of her and take hold of her arms. Anna-Karin doesn't even try to struggle and allows herself to be led out and into the gym. If the other Chosen Ones have also been caught, maybe they'll have a chance if they act together.

CHAPTER 73

The beat of the pulse booms in Linnéa's ears, rising and falling.

It is like being in one of her recurring nightmares. She is walking along the dark corridor leading to the attic stairs. She knows that something terrible is about to happen, that she must not let it, but she doesn't know how and fears that it is already too late.

Linnéa stops outside the graffiti-covered bathroom door.

Go inside, the voice commands.

She pushes the handle down and opens the door.

The strip lighting is switched on and she has to blink before her eyes can tolerate the strong fluorescent light.

She can't quite take in the woman who is confronting her. Her face is one Linnéa knows well and yet it is not. It has aged so much. As if many years have passed since they last spoke, rather than just a few months.

But the expression in the dark-brown eyes is recognizable. And a few fading blue strands are still visible in her hair, which hangs limply around the emaciated face.

'Olivia,' Linnéa says.

Olivia laughs abruptly. There is a dark gap where one of her teeth should have been.

'Whatever, it's not Rickard Johnsson,' Olivia says. 'Honestly now, did you all really believe that?'

Under the white powder, her skin is gray. Linnéa looks at the amulet that gleams against Olivia's black camisole top.

'Don't even think about it,' Olivia says and pulls the zip of her hoodie up all the way to her throat. 'You surely realize what will happen to the others if you try anything on.'

'Do what you like with me but let the others go,' Linnéa says.

Olivia sighs.

'Oh my God, how paranoid you've gotten. I won't hurt you. I've brought you here to tell you about what's going to happen next.'

'Great, so I'm here now. Go ahead, tell me.'

'Elias is going to come back.'

Linnéa stares at her. Any other answer was imaginable. But not this.

'Impossible,' she says.

'No, it isn't,' Olivia says. 'He's coming back soon. Tonight.'

Linnéa glances at the bathroom stall where she found Elias's dead body. The blood. The shard of glass. His beautiful eyes that would never again see anything.

'It's impossible,' she says again.

'Not for me,' Olivia says, solemnly meeting Linnéa's eyes. 'I am the Chosen One.'

'Who are you?'

Minoo opens her eyes and sees Adriana looking at her. Without a trace of recognition. Minoo has succeeded in what she set out to do and it is an uncomfortable feeling.

'Do you really not recognize me?' Minoo asks.

Slowly, Adriana sits up in bed.

'I don't know...I'm not...No. I don't recognize you at all. I'm so sorry but...'

She looks both embarrassed and alarmed.

Part Three

Minoo gets up from the bed. Her mind spins when Adriana's memories come back to her. Simon. Max. Rebecka.

The sensation of being in control, being invulnerable, is definitely gone.

'I feel so strange...' Adriana says. 'Have I been asleep?'

She looks down at her clothes, pats with her hands to try and smooth her crinkly skirt.

Minoo looks anxiously at her. She has to hurry on to the school, but can she simply leave Adriana like this? Is there anything she can say to calm her down? Advise her that she has amnesia? Perhaps not such a reassuring thing to be told, but at least an explanation.

'Adriana...' she begins, but is interrupted when the door opens.

She turns around. Alexander stands in the doorway.

'I was instructed about this last summer,' Olivia says. 'I'm the only one who can stop the apocalypse.'

Linnéa feels she's watching herself in a funhouse distorting mirror. But it's not a funny sight.

'Who told you that?' she asks.

Olivia smiles even more broadly now and Linnéa notes two more missing teeth.

'Elias.'

Linnéa almost wants to believe her. But only for a moment. She understands of course who has been parading as Elias.

'He spoke to me in my dreams,' Olivia continues. 'At first, I didn't believe it was him. But then he told me things that only Elias could have known.'

Linnéa remembers when Max stood in front of her in the dining area, pretending to be Elias. He had known all about the boy he was impersonating. Details that no one else could have known.

'It wasn't Elias,' Linnéa says. 'It is the demons—'

'You don't get anything! We're supposed to *stop* the demons. Elias and I. And you, if you care to join us.'

'You don't understand—'

'You're the one who doesn't understand! When Elias told me that I was the Chosen One…it was as if I had known all along. I always felt I was different. As if I were stuck in the wrong life.'

'Everyone feels like that at times,' Linnéa says. 'That doesn't make it true.'

'What is it with you, can't you just trust me?' Olivia shrieks and her voice echoes in the tiled space. 'You've never trusted me! You've never taken me seriously!'

Linnéa can't argue. What Olivia says is true.

'I'm telling you, there were times when I almost envied you,' Olivia continues. 'Because of what happened to your mother and then what with your father…'

'Envied me?' Linnéa exclaims.

'Yes! You never had to prove anything. You never had to explain. But I could never get anyone to understand why I felt bad at times. I didn't even know myself. All I knew was that I always felt lonely, regardless of how many people there were around. But then I realized that I was the Chosen One. It made sense, the Chosen One is always alone. Like, your fate is incomprehensible to everyone else—'

'I am the Chosen One,' Linnéa interrupts. '*One* of them. We are a group.'

Olivia sighs impatiently.

'I know that you and your new friends are witches,' she says. 'But there's only *one* Chosen One. And that is me.'

This is the second time in two days someone has claimed that Linnéa is not a Chosen One. And for a moment, doubt flutters through her mind. But only for a moment.

'You're wrong,' Linnéa says. 'In the beginning, we were seven. Elias was one of us. That was before the demons killed him. The same demons who have been lying to you.'

'Lay off!' Olivia screams. 'Why can't you accept just for once that it's *me* who's special!'

'And how did you get your powers, Olivia? Did you allow the demons to bless you?'

'It was Elias who gave me my powers!'

'Did he tell you that you would have to kill?'

Olivia thumps her fist against one of the sinks.

'Yes, he did! He told me to take revenge for his death. Every time I kill someone who has hurt him, my powers grow stronger. Elias knows I love him and he loves me back. And you're just jealous!'

Linnéa stares at her. What is she to do? What can she say to reach her? Vanessa's life and the lives of the others are in Olivia's hands.

'It doesn't matter why you think you do it. It *cannot* be right,' she says slowly. 'You have killed innocent people.'

'They weren't innocent,' Olivia says. 'Besides, it wasn't just me. Helena and Krister have been in on it all the time. Elias started to talk to them a year ago. And then they got in touch with me. Elias told them that I was the Chosen One and that I could help them.'

'So, this is your joint plan?'

'To get Elias back, yes, that's right. Though I haven't told them about the apocalypse that Elias and I are going to stop together. He said not to tell because they wouldn't understand. He said you wouldn't understand either, but *I* trusted in you.'

She tries to touch Linnéa who backs away.

'Linnéa...' Olivia says. 'We've known each other for, like, ages and ages.'

'Just about as long as you've known Jonte,' Linnéa says. 'How did you feel about murdering him? What was it like to hear his screams?'

Olivia stiffens. Looks defensive.

'As a matter of fact, it wasn't me who picked the people we should take revenge for Elias on. It was Helena and Krister. They wanted me to kill you, too, but I said no.'

'Thanks,' Linnéa says ironically. 'I'm so grateful that you only had me almost kicked out of my apartment.'

'Look, I had to do *something* to satisfy them,' Olivia says. 'And it would've been so much better if you'd been locked up in some home by now. Then you wouldn't have had to get involved in what's going to happen here tonight. You would've been safe, and then Elias and I could have come to take you with us.'

'What about Canal Bridge? I didn't feel too fucking safe there.'

'That wasn't my fault! Erik and Robin just lost it that night. If I'd had it my way, I would've killed them already last autumn. But you know how things stand with Helena and Krister. They refuse to believe that Elias was bullied. And Elias said to me that it was preferable to use Erik and Robin. If they joined PE, lots more people would join, too. Besides, they will be punished. And so will Helena and Krister, only they don't know it yet.'

Somehow, she seems to be looking forward to all this.

'I see, you're going to kill them as well?'

'Everyone we've taken revenge on has been guilty, but Helena and Krister are guiltiest of all. They never understood Elias. Only you and I did. We were the only ones who cared for him.'

She smiles at Linnéa.

'It's really been so hard not to talk to you about everything.

I would so much like us to do this together.'

'What exactly are you planning to do?'

Olivia's smile widens again.

'Carry out perfect justice,' she says. 'You know yourself who is in Positive Engelsfors. Everyone who bullied Elias. And the rest of them are people who stood by and let it happen. They all deserve to die. And they will. Tonight. When they're all dead, Elias will come back.'

Linnéa shakes her head.

'Elias would never have taken part in all this. He would never have—'

'That's what you think,' Olivia snaps. 'Maybe you didn't ever know him as well as you thought. But of course you've always been like that about Elias. You always wanted to keep him to yourself.'

Linnéa looks at Olivia. Tries to work out what is happening with the Olivia she used to know. The old Olivia, who was forever looking for someone who would listen to her, take her seriously, love her. She was always trying too hard which made people feel uneasy. And she couldn't understand why.

She was a perfect prey for the demons and their lies.

But then, what would I have done? Linnéa thinks. If I hadn't known what I know, if I'd lost Elias and he had started to talk to me in my dreams, if he had asked me to take revenge for him and given me the powers to carry it out…would I have been able to resist the temptation?

'Olivia, you've got to believe what I say. You've been deceived. I don't know what will happen when you've killed everyone, but Elias will never be resurrected.'

Olivia shakes her head so that her lanky hair flaps around.

It must be the magic, Linnéa thinks. It's too strong for her. It's making her body decay. The way nuclear radiation does.

'Why can't you just understand?' Olivia says. 'Why can't you just look forward to being happy? Listen, soon we'll meet Elias!'

She is breathing heavily. Watching Linnéa.

'You've got to choose now,' she says. 'Yes or no. Are you with us or against us?'

Alexander goes and stands by the bed. He looks intently at his sister. He seems not to register that Minoo is there.

'Adriana?' he says.

She stares at him, looking confused. For one terrible moment, Minoo is afraid that she has removed too much.

'Alexander?' Adriana says. 'What are you doing here?'

Minoo relaxes.

'Do you know where you are?' he asks.

'Of course,' she says, sounding not the slightest bit sure of herself. 'I am in Engelsfors. In my bedroom in Engelsfors.'

'Do you know who she is?' Alexander says and points at Minoo.

Adriana looks quickly at Minoo again.

'No,' she says. 'I've never seen her before.'

'She isn't lying,' Viktor says. He has turned up in the doorway.

Alexander scrutinizes Minoo. As if he, too, is seeing her for the first time and needs to decide whether she is a friend or an enemy.

Then he turns back to his sister.

'You've been unwell,' he says.

'I feel as though I might have been,' Adriana says. 'I mean...I feel so very strange.'

'I understand. You have been in a bad state for a long time now,' Alexander says.

'Have I been neglecting my work? I came here to…Have you found the Chosen One?'

'All that is in the past,' he says. 'Just a big misunderstanding.'

She looks disappointed.

'I see…' she says. 'I was so certain that…'

Minoo remembers the last memory that Adriana is still aware of. How hopeful she had felt then, how she dared to finally believe that her investigations were going to lead to a major, meaningful finding. Now, at a stroke, Alexander has crushed her dreams.

But what Adriana had dared to believe still exists. Minoo hopes that she will find her own way again and that it will somehow lead back to the Chosen Ones.

'Try to sleep for a while and I'll be back to see you later,' Alexander says and looks at Minoo again. 'We'll talk for a longer time then.'

He steps outside into the corridor. Minoo glances at Adriana for one last time. She has settled back in the bed and is reaching for the switch on her bedside lamp.

'Sleep well,' Minoo says.

'Thank you,' Adriana says and turns the light off

'Linnéa. Please. Say yes.'

Olivia's large brown eyes are watching her.

And Linnéa feels grief welling up inside her. All this is so meaningless. So tragic. And altogether, so fucking wrong.

'Olivia, you've got to stop all this. You must have noticed what it's doing to your body? You must have realized that whatever's doing this to you can't be good!'

Olivia looks at Linnéa and seems to waver, before she makes up her mind. Her gaze hardens.

'I'll heal when all this is in the past.'

'You won't survive the act you intend to carry out.'

'Of course I will. I am the Chosen One.'

'You're wrong.'

'In which case, it's a risk I'm prepared to take for Elias's sake,' Olivia says. 'You may well say you love him, but what have you done for him? What do you think he would've said about you being so buddy-buddy with *Ida Holmström*?'

They look at each other in silence.

'Punish me,' Linnéa says. 'But let the others go.'

'No, I need them. Elias needs them.'

She looks at Linnéa and her expression is sad.

'He'll be so disappointed when he comes back and finds you gone,' she says.

Next, her thought fills Linnéa's head, a scream that cuts like a knife through the brain.

Get her.

It reverberates throughout the school, from mind to mind.

Linnéa hears their footsteps approaching. They must have been ready and waiting.

The door opens with a crash and before she has time to turn, strong hands grab her arms. Backman holds her firmly from behind and she tries to pull herself free, struggling and twisting in his grip.

'Let go of me,' she screams, while his hateful thoughts rush through her.

He enjoys feeling her body against his. His power over her gives him pleasure; he's got her now, that uppity chick whose way of looking at him in the classroom has made him feel so ill at ease, as if all the time she knew what he was thinking.

'Let go of me!' Linnéa screams again, but Tommy Ekberg goes for her legs; her feet leave the floor and she is lifted up in the air.

The entire hallway outside the bathroom is crammed full

of students, all wearing the same amulet around their necks. Excitedly, they watch Tommy and Backman carry her away.

Minoo walks out into the corridor and closes the door behind her. The power field is gone. Viktor stands with his head down, staring at the carpet. Alexander examines her with an inscrutable face.

'I've explained the situation to Alexander,' Viktor says without looking up. 'He is aware of what we've done.'

Minoo looks at Alexander. Has Viktor misjudged him? Will he turn them in?

'What is left of her memories?' Alexander asks.

'She is the same person she was just before we began tenth grade. I couldn't remove more than that, it would have left her too fragile,' Minoo says. 'But she is loyal to the Council once more. And innocent of the so-called crimes she's supposed to have committed here in Engelsfors.'

'That is an impossible form of magic,' Alexander says.

Minoo doesn't answer. She has no intention of discussing her powers with him.

'Will the Council revoke the sentence and free her?' she asks instead.

'There are no similar cases. But if what you say is true...' He falls silent, then nods. 'I can think of no reason why they shouldn't.'

'And what about Viktor? Are you going to charge him with having helped me?'

'It's ok, Minoo,' Viktor says.

'No, it isn't,' she says and looks hard at Alexander. 'There are no grounds for punishing Viktor. Isn't that right?'

Thoughtfully, Alexander meets her gaze.

'No,' he finally says. 'I believe the best thing for all of us is to move on from here.'

647

Fire

Minoo has time to notice the grateful glance Viktor sends her. Then she walks past them. Carries on downstairs, through the ground floor and out into the garden.

When she reaches the street, she starts running.

The others need you.

CHAPTER 74

Linnéa is downstairs in the gym. She has stopped trying to resist them. There are too many of them, their hands are too strong. And she must save her strength.

In her thoughts, she calls to Vanessa and the others. No one answers.

When she is brought into the gym, she understands why.

In here, the magic is so powerful that she has no hope of penetrating it on her own.

The crowd opens up and makes a gangway for the men who are carrying her. She looks into their faces.

Everyone looks individually different, but all their eyes have the same expression. Olivia's expression.

Gustaf is the only one there whose eyes are still his own. And he looks terrified. Linnéa looks away at once, afraid that she might give him away.

She catches sight of Anna-Karin, who stands surrounded, close to the stage. Linnéa is about to call to her when Backman and Tommy let go of her and she crashes to the floor.

'Linnéa!'

It's Vanessa's voice. And in the middle of all her terror Linnéa is filled with relief.

She tries to sit up but is shoved back down. Through the forest of legs, she glimpses Vanessa, held captive by Rickard and Mehmet.

Linnéa manages to tear herself free from the hands that pin her down, but instantly other hands are there to keep her in place.

'Let me through!'

It is Helena's voice.

Tommy steps aside and Linnéa sees that, behind him, a long hallway runs through the sea of people. Olivia, Helena and Krister stand at the far end.

Helena's eyes are shining with hatred as she and Krister start walking towards Linnéa.

'I must say, Linnéa, I'm very pleased to see you here,' she says. 'I am so glad that Olivia changed her mind.'

'If there is one individual who deserves what they're going to get, it's you,' Krister says.

Linnéa tries to sit up again and, this time, no one prevents her. Krister and Helena are towering over her now.

It would have been utterly devastating for Elias to see them like this. Despite everything, he loved them.

She must try to make them understand, she owes him that.

'Elias didn't take his own life,' she says. 'Demons murdered him. The same demons who are giving Olivia the power to do all that she is doing. The same demons who have made you believe that you have been talking to Elias. You have been misled by Elias's murderers.'

'You're lying,' Helena says and Krister nods in agreement.

'How can you believe that he is the one who drives all this?' Linnéa exclaims. 'Your son Elias? Elias, who took care never to hurt anyone? Who never even hit back? Do you really believe that he would want you to kill people for his sake?'

Helena and Krister just look at her. For one brief moment, Linnéa hopes that she might have got through to them.

Suddenly, the ceiling lights flicker.

Blue flashes spark around Olivia's hands. She is still standing at the other end of the hall. Krister and Helena turn towards her.

'Don't!' Linnéa screams but it is too late.

Olivia lifts her hands. The flashes of lightning swoop through the air and hit the chests of Krister and Helena. There is a sizzling sound. They scream in pain. Then, complete silence. Olivia lowers her hands. For a moment, Krister and Helena stay upright, but staggering. Leaning against each other, they collapse to the floor.

The crowd ripples as if agitated by a wind, but nobody does anything. They are completely under Olivia's rule.

'Oh God, how I've been looking forward to doing that,' Olivia says.

'Please, no more,' Linnéa says. 'I beg you, Olivia, stop it.'

Olivia smiles and Linnéa sees the ectoplasm circles gradually start to glow around her.

Ida has hidden under the stands and is peeping out, in an attempt to grasp what's going on.

So, it's that pushy chick, Olivia Henriksson, whom the demons have blessed.

Ida half thought she ought to break cover and go and zap Olivia into the nearest exercise frame. But then she saw what was done to Krister and Helena. Besides, Olivia can influence every single PE fanatic in the hall. Ida doesn't stand a chance.

Then again, it might be too late anyway.

Slowly, ectoplasm circles take shape on the wall behind her, on the floor around her. She senses the strong magic flowing from them. Mona Moonbeam's voice echoes in her head.

People who know about true magic know that only

one rite matters on this particular day. And that's human sacrifice.

Ida twirls her silver heart, twists the chain tightly around her finger. What else was it Mona had said?

They've connected all the people in your school into one big network.

Ida stares at the sign of metal in the ectoplasm circles.

The ruling metal witch must also wear an amulet.

The ruling metal witch.

Ida lets go of the silver heart. She plunges her hand into her jacket pocket, roots around for the amulet chain, finds it and holds the necklace up in front of her.

Any natural metal witch should be able to do this.

Of course, Ida isn't sure. But she is absolutely sure that if she doesn't act instantly, she will be a human sacrifice in minutes.

Ida moves her hands to the back of her neck. The amulet clinks when it strikes the silver heart. She snaps the clasp closed. Becomes part of the network.

And suddenly she can *feel* the entire hall. No need to see it in order to know that circles cover the whole floor and the lower half of the walls. They interact, reinforcing each other's power fields, and together turning the hall into a gigantic microwave oven.

All the PE members are there. Like popcorn ready to be popped. Their minds are like spots of light, portals open for her to dive into. She sees Olivia like a dark sun, glowing among the pale and distant stars. Olivia is the ruler of everything here. The circles. The PE membership. And her rule is mediated through the network of amulets.

First, I'll switch off the microwave oven, Ida thinks. Next, I'll switch off Olivia.

She focuses all her power on the circles, starting with the one drawn on the wall above the stage. She extinguishes it, slowly but surely. When it is done, she turns her attention to another circle. And another.

She knows that Olivia has registered her presence. She can feel it quite clearly; it is like a power surge running through the network. Olivia is trying to get a grip on everyone's consciousness but for now Ida is the stronger one. She controls the circles and that keeps the PE members in check.

'Stop it!' Olivia screams.

Ida opens her eyes.

The ectoplasm circles around her are all extinguished. In the ceiling, the strip lights flicker like strobes.

'Where are you?' Olivia shouts at the top of her voice.

Ida smiles. No need for her to hide any more.

Linnéa gets up from the floor. Backman, Tommy and all the rest of them are standing around, immobile and staring emptily ahead in the flashing light.

She sees someone step out from under the stands. Sees the amulet on a chain around her neck. Linnéa never imagined she would feel so happy about seeing Ida Holmström.

As Ida walks through the hall, people step out of her way.

'Stop it!' Olivia screams. 'You're ruining everything!'

'That's the general idea,' Ida says.

Moving like sleepwalkers, the PE members flock towards the walls. Ectoplasm circles still glow here and there on the floor.

'Can you get them to take their necklaces off?' Linnéa asks Ida.

'I've got another minor issue to deal with first,' she replies, a little breathlessly. 'And I'd like some help.'

Linnéa goes to Ida and takes her hand. Anna-Karin and Vanessa follow. Together, they form a chain and lend Ida all their powers.

'Don't!' Olivia wails. 'It's not fair!'

Then the ectoplasm circle nearest to them slowly fades out.

Endorphins are pouring into Ida's bloodstream.

She has fought her powers for so long, tried so hard to get rid of them. Now, for the first time, she feels that her powers are part of her. And that she loves exerting them. She even loves the other Chosen Ones. A bit anyway. She must be on a magic high.

Ida feels as powerful as a goddess as she extinguishes one ectoplasm circle after another, while all the time holding the PE members under her influence.

She looks at Erik. Robin. Felicia. Julia. Kevin. They are clustered along the wall, their dully staring faces bathed in the flickering overhead light. She could revenge herself on them all. Make them pay a high price for their betrayals. Set them against each other, make them tear each other limb from limb. The thought seems hugely seductive and she suddenly thinks that Anna-Karin is to be admired for not doing anything *worse* with her powers. Now she understands how strong the temptation must have been.

Gustaf.

When she sees him come walking towards her, Ida almost loses her grip on Linnéa's hand. He stares at her. Stops only a few yards away.

She notices how shocked he looks. How are they to explain all this to him?

'Ida, focus,' Linnéa says.

Ida sighs. But Linnéa is right. They have to complete this.

Olivia shrieks with frustration when the last ectoplasm circle goes out.

'Now, it's all over,' Linnéa shouts.

'You've ruined everything! Elias will never come back now! He'll never come back!'

Olivia's voice reverberates throughout the hall.

All the lights go off at the same time. Everything is in deep darkness.

Ida is gripped with dread. She listens tensely. The only sound is that of two hundred-odd people breathing in perfect time.

'Look,' Anna-Karin whispers.

A pale blue glow is spreading at the far end. It is emanating from Olivia. And it grows in strength until she is surrounded by a blue luminosity that sparkles and glitters around her as she slowly advances towards the Chosen Ones.

She raises her right hand. Blue flashes flare and coil around it, like a ball of writhing electrical snakes.

Ida looks anxiously at Gustaf, who stands as if turned to stone. She wants to shout at him to take cover.

'You're so good at spreading shit about others, Ida,' Olivia says. 'But there are rumors about you as well. Like, you're completely obsessed with Gustaf Åhlander.'

Ida doesn't dare answer her, doesn't dare look at Gustaf. She releases her own power. It feels unlike anything she has experienced before. The link to the other Chosen Ones makes her stronger. She raises her free hand. It too glows blue in the dark, more intensely than the light Olivia emits.

'You have taken the one I loved away from me,' Olivia says. 'I will never see him again now. I'll do the same to you.'

She aims at Gustaf with her hand.

Ida doesn't even think. She lets go of Linnéa's hand and jumps to get in front of Gustaf. A dazzling flash is thrown from Olivia's hand and flies towards Ida. Her own flash hits Olivia's in mid-air, they twist around each other and, for a second, form a sparkling ball until they split apart again.

Ida is struck in the chest and flung backwards. She falls heavily on the floor, goes breathless. A tingling feeling creeps through her body, through her limbs, all the way out into her fingertips.

A clatter from the lamps as the light comes on again.

Ida shivers and sits up slowly. Meets Gustaf's gaze. He is unhurt. Physically, at least.

Olivia lies immobile on the floor at the other end of the gym. Linnéa is already on her way to the body.

'Be careful!' Vanessa shouts.

Linnéa crouches to pull down the zip of Olivia's hoody. Then she undoes the clasp and holds up the amulet.

Ida takes off her own amulet. Disgusted, she throws it away at the stands.

The network is broken.

Minoo has come halfway across the schoolyard when the main entrance doors are suddenly opened and Kevin comes walking straight at her.

She stops, her pulse racing. More PE members are following him out. There is nowhere for her to hide.

But when they come closer she realizes that something is wrong.

Or, rather, something is right again.

These people aren't under remote control. They look uncertain. Afraid. They walk together in little groups, leaning on each other. Some of them are crying.

Minoo increases her speed, runs in the opposite direction from the crowds, and elbows her way past Hanna A who is pressing her phone against her ear.

'Mommy…' she sobs. 'You've got to come and pick me up…'

The lobby is full of people and more are pouring up from

the gym. Tommy Ekberg grabs hold of her arm when she tries to push past him.

'There's been an accident,' he says. 'Something to do with the electricity. Don't go down there, it might still be dangerous.'

She tears herself free and runs downstairs, pushes and squeezes past people until she reaches the doors to the gym.

The dead bodies that were Helena and Krister are the first sight that meets her. They are lying side by side. None of their acolytes so much as looks at them on their way out of the hall.

'Minoo!' Anna-Karin calls.

She catches sight of them over by the stage. Anna-Karin, Vanessa, Linnéa and Ida. Gustaf is with them.

Relief washes over Minoo. She rushes along to be with them, hugs one after the other.

'How did it go with Adriana?' Anna-Karin asks when Minoo has stopped hugging her.

'It worked,' Minoo replies.

They all look happy and relieved. All except Gustaf, whose face is a deathly white.

Minoo wonders what he has seen. She senses the remnants of strong magic in the air.

'How are you?' she asks.

'I don't know. I don't understand anything. It's all been like a very strange dream...'

She understands completely. Reality has just been turned upside down for him.

'I know. But it's all over now,' Ida says. She is standing close to him.

'Minoo, it wasn't Rickard,' Linnéa says and points.

When a cluster of seniors has drifted past, Minoo sees a body that has been placed on the floor in the recovery position. Minoo wouldn't have recognized her if it hadn't been for the blue strands in her hair.

She wonders how Linnéa feels. That girl was her friend.

'Is she alive?' Minoo asks.

Linnéa nods.

'Touch and go. The ambulance is on its way.'

'I came across Tommy Ekberg upstairs,' Minoo says. 'He was talking about some electrical accident.'

'That's what we told everyone,' Vanessa says. 'No one remembers a thing of what's happened … Just like it was with Diana.'

Vanessa catches sight of somebody.

'Oh, fuck,' she says. 'Goddamn fucking hell.'

Minoo looks up. Alexander is entering the hall. He has brought two of the courtroom security guards. The last bunch of PE members stands aside for this trio, which marches across the floor.

I should've guessed, Minoo thinks. He's changed his mind.

But Alexander doesn't even look at her.

He walks straight over to Olivia and kneels next to her. Minoo goes over to see. He is inspecting Olivia's head. A few drops of blood trickle from her closed eyes.

He gently takes Olivia's thin body in his arms and gets up.

'What are you doing?' Linnéa shouts.

'If we leave her here, she'll die,' Alexander says. 'We are the only ones who can give her the care she needs.'

'And then what? What will you do with her?' Minoo asks.

'Olivia Henriksson is no longer your problem,' Alexander says.

Minoo watches Olivia's booted feet dangle pathetically in the air as he carries her towards the exit doors.

Ida's body is racked with a feverish shiver. She feels so

exhausted it's hard to stay upright. The only reason why she's still standing is Gustaf, the fact that he is right next to her, very close.

'Who was that?' he asks, looking at the door through which Alexander has just disappeared.

'The police,' Ida says feebly, because nothing better comes to mind.

But Gustaf hardly seems to have heard her.

'I just don't get it...What happened? What did you do to her? Who are you, all of you, really?'

Ida opens her mouth to reply, but can't think where to begin. There is only one thing she wants to say to Gustaf. Only one thing she *can* say.

'I love you.'

He stares at her and she shivers again.

'You see, that psychotic creature was right about it, only that *one* thing,' she says. 'And I don't even know if you like me...but I...I'm really trying and I feel...'

Gustaf's face slips out of focus, then becomes clear again.

'Ida?' he says.

She shivers violently.

'Yes...'

Her knees are giving way under her and she falls. But she doesn't get hurt, because Gustaf is there to catch her. She lands in his arms, his strong arms, and he lowers her slowly to the floor.

'Ida!' Minoo cries out from somewhere far away.

They are all calling out her name, all the Chosen Ones.

Ida, Ida, Ida, Ida! they shout, as if she were deaf or something.

Ida! Ida, are you okay?

And she wants to answer them and say everything is fine with her, fantastic, really. Because Gustaf is looking at her, his hands are touching her, he's talking to her, saying her name over and over again. She can hear his voice quite clearly, but at a distance.

She's not breathing!

She is looking into his eyes now, his beautiful, wonderful eyes. At last, he is looking at her the way she has always longed for him to do.

She's not breathing!

Doesn't matter, she wants to say. Doesn't matter at all.

She is so close to him now. Very close to Gustaf's face. He places his lips on hers and they merge until she hardly knows where Gustaf's mouth begins and her own ends.

She wants him so much it hurts.

And she doesn't even notice when her heart stops beating.

Part 4

CHAPTER 75

The bus doors open and Anna-Karin climbs out. The sun has just risen and the chill of the night lingers. She puts on her woollen hat and gloves that Grandpa knitted for her many years ago.

She follows a sandy track, lined with tall, bare trees. The stables are at the end of the track.

Anna-Karin has only ever seen the buildings at a distance. When she was little, riding was a dream of hers, but the stables belonged to people like Ida, Julia and Felicia. And it was far too expensive, Mom said.

Anna-Karin opens the door and sneaks inside.

The air is so cold she can see her breath. Her eyes fill with tears when she takes in the smells of animals and straw, smells that remind her of their farm. She walks between the loose boxes, reading the names on the labels. And then she finds him. A gray horse with gentle eyes. Troja.

'Hi, Troja,' she whispers as she enters the loose box.

Troja snorts when she gently strokes his neck. She lets her hand wander up towards his ears and he closes his eyes.

'Yeah, you like that, don't you?' Anna-Karin says.

As always when she talks to animals, her voice sounds different. Almost as if she is singing the words.

'You're lovely, Troja. A fine horse, that's what you are. Ida loved you so very much.'

Troja doesn't react to Ida's name. Of course he doesn't. But does he wonder about where Ida's gone? Does he miss her?

'I made a promise once to Ida that I would keep an eye on you, make sure you were all right,' Anna-Karin says. 'If anything happened to her.'

Tears burn behind her eyes and she allows them to run down her cheeks.

Anna-Karin has no intention of turning Ida into some kind of saint just because she is dead. Not with all her many memories of Ida as her persecutor and tormentor. But by now, she has other kinds of memories as well and feels she understands Ida better. Besides, it is thanks to Ida that Anna-Karin is alive in the first place. And that the apocalypse has not begun.

The gate is suddenly pulled open and she turns around, almost expecting to see Ida standing there. But it is a short, dark-haired girl who looks about thirteen. She stares at Anna-Karin.

'Who are you?' she asks.

'A friend of Ida's,' Anna-Karin says. 'She used to be one of Troja's main riders.'

'I know who Ida was,' the kid says. 'But now I'm the one looking after Troja.'

'I just wanted to see how he was. He mattered so much to Ida.'

'No kidding. No one had a chance of getting near him.'

The girl steps into the loose box and strokes Troja's back tenderly. No one could mistake the love in her eyes.

He'll be fine with her, Anna-Karin thinks.

'I only knew her slightly,' the girl says. 'I didn't really, like, know her. Just met her here, and stuff.'

Anna-Karin nods.

'She was a total bitch,' the girl goes on before she realizes what she's saying. 'I mean, she was good with Troja...except, she groomed his tail with the curry comb. Do you realize how much it wears the tail out?'

She looks almost accusingly at Anna-Karin.

'Not really...'

'It does, you know. But otherwise she took such good care of him. Ida's dandy brushes were always the whitest.'

Anna-Karin hasn't got a clue what this means. The kid is leaning her cheek against Troja's muzzle.

'And Ida was amazing at riding,' she continues. 'She always had the best bridles and blankets and things. And her riding boots were made of real leather. I've got all her things now, her parents didn't want to keep it. Her boots are still too big for me. And it's like, kind of sick, wearing a dead person's boots, so I'm not sure what to do with them.'

Anna-Karin can't help smiling. This kid has got dark hair and brown eyes, but there is a lot about her that reminds her of Ida.

'I'd better go now,' Anna-Karin says. 'Take care.'

The girl doesn't say anything more until Anna-Karin has stepped out of the loose box.

'Are you going to the funeral today?'

'Yes, I am,' Anna-Karin says, scraping bits of straw from her shoes.

'Could you, I don't know, like, say hello from me? What I mean is, up there by the coffin. Or whatever. Just say that Lisa is looking after Troja and that he's fine.'

'I promise,' Anna-Karin says.

'Though I always use a water brush for the tail. It's *so* much better.'

It is early in the morning and the shadows of the trees are still long as they fall across the playground. But the sun is warm on Vanessa's face. Spring has come once more to Engelsfors.

She pushes Melvin's swing a little harder and he laughs so happily she has to smile.

'More!' he shouts. 'More!'

Easter vacation has started and Vanessa has taken Melvin off to play so that her mom can sleep in. But Vanessa's reasons for coming here aren't entirely noble.

Wille answered her text at once. He's on his way here from Riddarhyttan. And the fact that he's even awake at this time in the morning is a clear sign of change. Perhaps there is hope for the two of them.

He's going to break up with Elin. Soon. He would have preferred to do it right away when he came home from Stockholm, but Elin went so crazy about the way he'd just upped and left. His conscience was bothering him about that. Wanted to give her some space, just a couple of weeks before inflicting another shock.

A couple of weeks has passed by now.

'More, Nessa!' Melvin cries and she laughs.

'You can't go any higher,' she says. 'You might fly all the way to the moon!'

'I *want* to the moon,' Melvin says.

She loves him so much it hurts. Being with Melvin is like taking medicine. He is so full of life. Nowadays, she needs to be reminded that life really does goes on. That there are joys, that it is not forever dark and difficult.

'Did you see that Ida was going to die?' she asked Mona the day after the equinox. 'Did you lie to her, too?'

For once, Mona had no pat answer to trot out. She only shook her head, looking genuinely concerned.

'I said exactly what I saw,' she said. 'I can't explain it. Normally, I wouldn't miss this kind of thing.'

But apparently she had. In only a few hours, Vanessa will be attending Ida's funeral.

She still hasn't grasped that Ida really is dead. Even though she saw her die, that fact has not yet sunk in. During the last few weeks, when she has met up with the other Chosen Ones, she has now and then wondered when Ida would turn up. There are only four of them left now.

'I want down now,' Melvin announces, so she stops the swing and helps him wriggle out of it. He runs over to the sandpit and she goes along to see that there aren't any discarded syringes or other charming surprises buried in the sand. Melvin starts digging with his red spade.

Vanessa looks up when she hears a car drive across the gravel and pull up. Wille parks in exactly the place where she once saw Nicke with Paula. He climbs out and walks over to them.

'Hi there, kiddo,' he greets Melvin.

Melvin looks indifferently at him and goes back to playing with his plastic bucket and spade.

'Seems he doesn't remember me,' Wille says.

'Don't take it personally.'

Wille smiles. He is wearing a dark, woolly sweater and is so good-looking it takes her breath away. As always.

'Do I get a hug?' he says.

'Of course,' she says and wipes her sandy hands on her jeans.

She crawls into his arms.

Wille's smell is enriched with thousands of memories. She knows it so well.

Yet still, there's something that feels different.

'How are things with you?' he asks and kisses the top of her head before letting go of her.

'I'm fine,' she says. 'You?'

He shrugs.

'It's so damn difficult, dealing with Elin.'

'We're just going to walk over to the swings,' Vanessa tells Melvin.

He nods, not very interested, because he's engrossed in making sand cakes that he crushes to a mess afterwards. Vanessa and Wille start walking towards the swings, but she doesn't feel ready to start talking about Elin just yet.

'How's your mom?' she asks.

'She's off work completely. They're investigating whether she can be treated with surgery.'

'I hope so,' Vanessa says.

They pick one tire-swing each and sit down.

'I'm nervous about the funeral today,' she says. 'I've never been to one.'

'It'll be all right,' Wille says. 'I didn't know what to expect when I went to Jonte's. But…well, it works. You're forced to kind of stop and think about what's happened.'

Vanessa nods. She was probably being selfish, but she hadn't been able to face Jonte's funeral.

'Not that I understand a thing about what went on the night he died,' Wille says.

Vanessa looks away.

'I don't either,' she says.

'What are we going to do, Nessa?' he says gently.

She turns her face to the sun again. Shuts her eyes.

'What do you mean?' she asks, even though she knows.

'About you and me.'

She slides her fingers along the cold chains of the swing.

'When are you going to talk to Elin?'

Wille sighs heavily.

'I've got to wait for the right time,' he says. 'But what about you? Will you be there for me afterwards?'

Something stirs inside Vanessa now. An insight she would rather not have.

She wants to believe Wille. She wants to believe in *them*. She wants something good to hold on to now that this world's turning out so fucking awful.

But Linnéa's voice sounds inside her head, the memory forces itself on her.

You know very well that Wille can't stand being alone.

She looks at him.

He needs someone to look after him.

Suddenly she understands. Wille's smell isn't different. There is nothing about Wille that is different in the slightest.

'So you won't break up with her until you've got some kind of guarantee from me. That's right, isn't it?' she says.

Wille looks confused, as if he can't see the point of the question.

'You aren't prepared to risk being single. Rather than chance it, you'll stay with Elin. Even though you don't love her. At least, until you find someone else.'

'Where've you got all that from?'

'That's what you did to me, wasn't it? You confessed that you'd been unfaithful first, when you were sure that Elin would have you if I left you.'

'That's so fucking unfair,' he says.

'It's true, though.'

Wille sighs.

'I thought you loved me,' he says and looks away.

I thought so, too, Vanessa wants to say.

Instead she holds on, leaning back and looking up at the sky. Something she heard in a middle school lesson comes back to her. The earth, they were told, spins at more than 1,000 miles per hour. Vanessa almost had an attack of vertigo where she was sitting.

Everything can change suddenly, quickly. In a single instant, everything around you can be different. And maybe it's an effect of being in constant motion, even when you don't notice it.

'I don't get it,' Wille says. 'What are you trying to do, test me or something?'

'No, Wille. I don't need to.'

She looks at him again. Every detail of his face, his body, his mind is familiar to her. And yet, she feels that she is looking at him with new eyes.

Sure, they would be happy again together. At least, until he met someone new. This realization, the fact that she dares to realize this, changes everything.

She doesn't love him any more. She hasn't loved him for a long time.

'I'm so sorry,' she says. 'But it will never work out for the two of us.'

He gets up from the swing and looks angrily at her.

'So it's all over now? Finished, just like that?'

Vanessa could easily scream at him that it was all over when he started screwing Elin behind her back, but she doesn't have the energy. Already, it feels completely at an end. Totally fucking finished. Wille doesn't belong in her life now.

'Go home to Elin,' she says.

'You're such a bitch,' he says.

She looks at him as he gets into the car and drives off with the engine roaring. She probes deep inside herself, to see if she finds any upset, any regret or sadness.

All she finds is relief.

She watches Melvin who is absorbed by whatever his sandpit adventure is all about.

She thinks that she will never, ever again share her life with someone who she constantly hopes will change. Instead, she wants someone to respect, someone who can inspire her and who understands her without always going along with everything. A person who challenges her and makes her challenge herself. Someone to laugh and cry with, in whose company she wants to discover the world.

And, if that someone should also happen to look fantastic, that would of course be perfectly acceptable.

Time to go home. Time to get ready for the funeral.

Vanessa jumps off the swing. And stands still on the spot.

She already knows someone who fits exactly with her description of the person she wants.

Vanessa remembers her first visit to the Crystal Cave.

The love of your life isn't the one you think, but it's someone you've already met.

Fucking Mona. Always has to have all the answers.

Chapter 76

The yellow sign has already been taken down from the facade. Linnéa watches the empty windows and the dark rooms behind them.

The door has been left open. Now and then, people step outside to throw stuff, books and potted plants and bits of furniture, into a dumpster. Everything must go.

The center of Engelsfors has acquired yet another abandoned building, lonely and spooky. The movement it housed might never have existed now.

And that feels like a perfect metaphor for how the topic of PE is treated when people in Engelsfors talk to each other. Their chat has empty, ghostly gaps. They seem to share an intense wish to tidy up and remove all traces. After the 'electrical accident', the school was closed for a few days and, when it opened again, all the PE stickers had been scraped off the locker doors.

No one mentions the iron grip in which Helena and Krister held the town. You might well think that everyone has forgotten.

But Linnéa has been listening in, picking up thoughts now and then. Ashamed thoughts. Frightened thoughts.

Helena and Krister were buried yesterday. Apparently, a very small number of mourners turned up to honor them.

Nobody will ever find out the full truth about their crimes, theirs and Olivia's.

Olivia's parents have reported her as lost. Her photo is posted on the Internet. Linnéa, too, wonders where Olivia is. Has she been dispatched to some secret headquarters? Or is she being kept by Alexander and Viktor in the manor house? Is she still alive?

Linnéa has stopped blaming herself for not realizing that it actually was Olivia who the demons had blessed. But she can't stop wondering if she might have been able to help Olivia at a much earlier stage. If only she'd listened more to her, taken her more seriously, then perhaps all this might not have happened.

Björn Wallin comes outside. He is carrying a tall stack of plain wooden chairs.

'Hi,' Linnéa says.

He looks at her, surprised. Puts the chairs down next to the dumpster and straightens his back.

'Hi, Linnéa,' he says.

She glances at him, looking for signs that he has started drinking again. In the very beginning, there are tiny signs, unnoticeable to anyone who isn't Linnéa.

'I'm still staying sober,' he says.

She looks him in the eye, refusing to be embarrassed. She has every right to doubt him.

'That's good,' she says.

He nods. Then looks at her simple black dress under the spring jacket, her black, opaque tights.

'Are you going to that girl's funeral?' he asks.

'Yes, I am.'

'Were you close?'

'You could say that,' Linnéa says, thinks for a moment and then changes her mind. 'Actually, yes. We were close.'

'I'm so sorry. It was a terrible incident.'

Linnéa nods.

She wonders what her father makes of PE today. And if he ever heard the rumor that Linnéa had tried to blacken the names of Robin and Erik. And, if so, what he thought about it. Did he believe the rumor?

She observes him again. It would be so easy to read his mind. But, somehow, it goes against her instincts. Perhaps she doesn't want to know. Or else perhaps because, if they are ever going to have any kind of relationship, she mustn't take any short cuts.

'What are you going to do now?' she asks.

It is her way of asking if he is about to start drinking again, and she's sure that he knows that.

'I've got a job at the sawmill,' he says. 'A friend of mine in PE fixed me up. I start soon, just after Easter. After that, I don't know.'

He looks earnestly at her.

'I will not start drinking again. I realize now that the only way of convincing you is to carry on proving it, day after day, every day. When you feel ready, we'll talk about everything that has happened. You get in touch, whenever you feel like it. I want to be your father again, but I know I have no right to demand it.'

Too many emotions well up inside Linnéa for her to reply. He has said exactly what she once stopped hoping ever to hear him say. And she knows that hope is dangerous.

'We're going to take some of the furniture away in the van soon,' he says. 'Would you like a lift to the church?'

'No, but thanks,' she says, a little too quickly. 'I'd like the walk.'

'All right,' he says. 'Take care, Linnéa.'

Linnéa nods, tries to smile and hurries away. After one block, her tears start flowing.

*

Anna-Karin sits down on the chair next to Grandpa's bed, taking care not to crease her skirt. She has borrowed her mother's funeral suit and put up her hair in the same style as Vanessa did for the trial.

Grandpa lowers his crossword magazine and peers at her over his reading glasses.

'Has somebody died, sweetheart?' he asks anxiously.

'Yes, a friend of mine. Her funeral is today.'

She has already told him about Ida, but apparently he doesn't remember.

'How are you, Grandpa?'

He waves the question away with his thin hand and says something in Finnish.

'Nothing new to report from this place,' he continues. 'Tell me about you instead.'

Anna-Karin has begun to investigate the forest again. Something inside her is urging her to go there. She has been drifting around with the fox at her side, searching for something without knowing what it is.

But she doesn't tell Grandpa about that part. Instead, she talks about the signs of spring that she has noticed in the forest. And he smiles.

'And how is Mia doing?' he asks later on. 'It's been a long time since she came to see me last.'

Anna-Karin's chest is constricting hard. She would rather not talk about her mom.

'Everything's just as usual with her,' Anna-Karin says. 'Somehow she never changes.'

'Do you think she can?'

'I don't know. Maybe, sometimes. Most often when I'm not with her. If I'm walking in the forest, I tell myself that I ought to take her out for a walk to show her how lovely it is. But then I get back home and she's just sitting there. And I realize it's not even worth asking her,' Anna-Karin says. 'Do you think she can change?'

'I'm not sure,' Grandpa says. 'The thing is, she's got to want to, herself. And be brave enough to ask for help.'

Anna-Karin nods.

'And now I'm asking myself if you'd be brave enough to,' Grandpa says.

He takes his reading glasses off and looks intently at her.

'What do you mean?' Anna-Karin says.

'Be brave enough to ask for help.'

'I have you, Grandpa.'

'That you have. For as long as I last. But I believe you'll need more than that. Perhaps you can't help your mother, but you can still help yourself. You don't have to carry all these heavy burdens alone.'

'Are you saying that…I should kind of talk to someone?'

Grandpa nods.

'I love Mia. And I have often thought about what I might have done differently. How much I am to blame for who she is. But, Anna-Karin, you do not have to end up the same way. You are not the way she is. And you are not responsible for saving her.'

Suddenly, Anna-Karin sees that she has been thinking just like her mom. That this is simply who she *is*. That pain is something you have to drag along, always, something you can never get away from.

But perhaps that's not how it has to be.

She looks at her grandpa.

Say goodbye when you can, Mona had said. *There's still time. Use it well.*

'I love you, Grandpa,' she says.

'And I love you, my sweetheart.'

Anna-Karin gets up.

'I've got to go now. But I'll be back to see you tomorrow.'

'I hope your friend will be given a good funeral,' Grandpa says. 'I'll be thinking about you all.'

Minoo hasn't worn this black dress since Rebecka's funeral. She hopes that she will never, ever have to wear it again.

She zips it up at the back. Sits down on the bed and pulls out the drawer in her bedside table. Takes out the *Book of Patterns*. Her finger glides over the leather binding, across the circles embossed on the front cover.

The guardians have started to speak to her again through the book. Only to her, not to any of the other Chosen Ones.

They have told her that Olivia's magic murders made the apocalypse come closer than intended. Had she succeeded in sacrificing everyone in the gym, the end of the world would already have taken place.

Now, they have bought themselves some time. The question is, for how long?

And, of course, what have the demons got planned next?

Minoo opens the book and allows the black smoke to well out while she leafs through the pages.

She asks her question again. It will not leave her in peace; it keeps her awake at night.

If I had not gone to Adriana, could I have saved Ida?

The signs tremble on the pages, but the guardians stay silent.

Minoo closes the book.

Perhaps there is no answer.

Minoo walks downstairs to the kitchen. Mom and Dad look up when she comes in. They are sitting at the kitchen table, having coffee and reading a newspaper each. Everything is back to how it used to be. Except that Mom is returning to Stockholm in a few days' time.

Fire

Mom gets up and hugs Minoo.

'Are you sure you wouldn't like us to come along?' she asks.

Minoo nods. At least she won't be alone at this funeral. The other Chosen Ones will be there. And Gustaf is on his way here to pick her up.

'But I'm so glad that you'll be here when I come back,' Minoo says.

Mom strokes her hair.

She came as soon as she heard about the fire at the *Engelsfors Herald* office. Since then, she and Dad have been amazingly nice to each other. Sometimes they've even seemed in love, with the energy sparking between them that Gustaf had talked about last summer.

Of course, it's helpful that Dad is taking it easier these days. The *Herald* has borrowed a room at the editorial office of the *Fagersta Gazette* and Dad's articles about how PE took over the area have been given a lot of attention in the national press. Since then, the story has taken on a life of its own. The whole narrative about the rise and fall of Positive Engelsfors has everything one could ask of a juicy media story. Corruption, brainwashing, misguided teenagers, attacks against the local paper and, to cap it all, that strange accident that killed the leaders of the movement. Even last year's 'suicide pact' has been added to the mix. Was what happened in the gym a botched attempt at inducing a mass suicide? Or even a mass murder? Why does everyone who was there claim to remember nothing at all?

Dad moans about all the over-the-top speculation, but it is obvious that he is, above all, pleased to be believed at last.

Minoo hopes that it might also be Mom's presence that helps to calm him. Maybe they have both gained some insights since moving apart.

The doorbell sounds and Minoo goes to answer it.

Gustaf is taken aback when he sees the dress. He obviously recognizes it. And he is wearing the same suit as the day when Rebecka was buried.

'Are you ready?' he asks.

She nods, puts on her coat and picks up the bunch of roses from the hall table.

As she and Gustaf step out into the sunshine together, his hand happens to touch hers.

They both simultaneously move their hands away.

He is just a friend, she tells herself.

They walk along, silent at first. The birds are singing and she spots a blue tit flying past as she looks up at the sky.

'I went to see Rickard yesterday,' Gustaf says.

Rickard is the only one of the PE membership who has suffered any physical damage since the end of the movement. He was controlled by Olivia for so long, and so frequently, that his body, too, was beginning to break down. He has been hospitalized ever since. The doctors are baffled. They cannot diagnose what is wrong with him.

'How's he feeling?' Minoo asks.

'So-so,' Gustaf says. 'His body has begun to recover. But he's depressed.'

Minoo nods. She feels sorry for Rickard. She wonders why he was the only one to be selected as Olivia's tool.

They have reached the tree-lined avenue that leads to the church.

'I've thought about what you said about Ida that night when I came to see you,' Gustaf says. 'You said that she was trying to become a better human being. I think you were right.'

A searing feeling runs through Minoo when she thinks of how Ida died in Gustaf's arms while he was giving her mouth-to-mouth resuscitation. She will never forget that moment. But she has seen to it that Gustaf has.

'What are you thinking about?' Gustaf asks.

'Nothing special,' she says.

But she knows that she cannot carry on lying to Gustaf like this. It is unfair to him.

At some point, she has to tell him the truth. She can't think how, or when, but she must. He has every right to know what really happened when Rebecka died. He should be allowed to know that Ida is the hero of the story. He deserves to know how the world works and what is at stake.

Come to think of it, doesn't everyone deserve to know?

The Council insists that the world of magic must remain secret from the rest of mankind. But why restrict the truth to just a select few?

The gravel crunches under their feet as they walk along the path leading to the church doors.

Linnéa, Anna-Karin and Vanessa are waiting at the steps.

Minoo goes to them and they all hug each other. She hands out the roses. Six white ones. Four from the Chosen Ones and one from Gustaf. The sixth is from Nicolaus. Minoo knows he would have wanted that.

She looks up and sees Viktor come strolling along with his hands in his coat pockets. He tries to catch her eye. She avoids him and he enters the church without saying a word as he passes them.

He phoned Minoo a few days after Ida's death. He was parked outside their house and Minoo came out to sit in the car.

'Adriana has been cleared,' Viktor told her. 'It all went through faster than I'd dared to hope.'

'How is she?' Minoo said.

'Still confused. But our doctors have provided her with a

diagnosis that explains her loss of memory. So she has something to hang on to. She'll pull through.'

Hearing him say this was a slight relief. But at the same
time, Minoo wondered how much the Council's doctors could
actually know in this situation.

'Will she be staying here?'

'For the time being, yes,' Viktor said. 'And so will we.'

She turned to look at him. He was fiddling with the turn
signal switch. Avoiding meeting her eyes.

'Why?' she said. 'I thought you'd made up your minds
once and for all that everything you'd heard about Engelsfors
was a bluff.'

Viktor didn't reply.

'What do you make of it?' Minoo asked. 'Do you believe
that we are the Chosen Ones?'

'What I do think is that you are very special, Minoo,' he
said and smiled.

Suddenly, it was as if the old Viktor sat next to her. The
smart operator who tried to charm her.

'Stop that,' Minoo said.

His smile faded.

'What have you done with Olivia?' she said.

'It's a matter I cannot discuss with an outsider.'

'So, what about everything you said about the Council?'
she said.

'I stand by what I said. But if I am to change them, I have
to play by their rules as much as I can.'

'In other words, you're obeying their orders again?'

Viktor looks sadly at her.

'I don't understand how someone as intelligent as you can
be so naïve at the same time,' he said. 'To you, everything is
straightforward. Right or wrong, good or bad. But it is the
goal that matters, not the route you choose to get there.'

'Are you saying that the ends justify the means?' Minoo said.

'If that's how you prefer to put it. Yes, absolutely.'

'You're wrong.'

'Am I? Consider what you did to Adriana. Would you truly call that intervention *good*? Removing her memories, and turning her into someone she'd rather not be?'

'But I did it so that she would survive...'

'Exactly,' Viktor said.

Ever since, his words have pursued her. And if she is sure of one thing, ever, it is this: she will never trust Viktor Ehrenskiöld again.

'Minoo,' Linnéa says now and tugs at the sleeve of her coat.

Further down the path, Erik walks with his arm around Julia.

'How does he dare show his face here?' Vanessa mumbles. 'How come he's allowed to fucking exist?'

Because that's how it all works, Minoo thinks. There is no cosmic justice. No 'Let the punishment fit the crime'. People like Erik can and will forge on in life, regardless of what they've done. Maybe he sleeps badly at night. Or maybe he sleeps just fine.

The Chosen Ones watch him in silence. He notices, but refuses to look in their direction. Refuses, or does not dare to. The latter, Minoo hopes. And, although she knows this is not how the world is and although she knows that revenge solves nothing, she wants Erik to have to pay for what he has done.

Or, at least, not to be able to harm anybody again.

They wait until Erik and Julia have disappeared through the church doorway.

Then they look at each other.

Time to go inside.

Time to say goodbye.

CHAPTER 77

She looks upwards, at the ceiling of the church. It is arching so high above her head she becomes quite dizzy thinking about the people who once crept around up there and built it, hundreds of years ago.

Behind the altar, they have hung an enormous oil painting showing the crucified Christ. His sad eyes are looking up at a dramatic sky.

So many people in here. All dressed in black.

Linnéa and Vanessa come walking up the central aisle. They are carrying one white rose each. They meet nobody's eyes and slip into an empty pew in the middle of the church. Linnéa is just about unrecognizable. She looks almost normal. She is wearing a simple black dress and her face is free of make-up.

After them, Minoo and Anna-Karin, also carrying one rose each. Anna-Karin has put on the same suit she wore at the trial.

But then, at the trial, it was Vanessa who was Anna-Karin. Surely?

It is hard to gather your thoughts when you're dreaming. You simply can't trust anything. Sometimes, you remember things that haven't even happened, or are memories of a dream you have dreamed earlier.

And then, there is Gustaf.

She runs along to meet him, follows him down the aisle. 'Where did you go afterwards?' she says. 'You vanished. Or, was it me who vanished? I can't remember.'

But he doesn't seem to hear her. He sits down silently, next to Minoo and the others. It is almost as if he is one of the Chosen Ones.

Everything feels so strange.

Someone shuts the large church doors and the bells begin to toll above their heads. The whispering in the pews is dying away.

She turns and looks at the vicar. He is a young man and she doesn't recognize him.

He says that they have all gathered here to say goodbye to a beloved daughter, sister and friend. She scans the congregation and sees familiar faces everywhere.

Julia sits with her head bent low. Large tears are dropping into the open hymnbook in her lap. Erik sits next to her. One of his arms is wrapped around her. The expression on his face is strange. As if he, too, is dreaming.

Felicia and Robin sit hand in hand, next to Julia and Erik. Kevin is there as well, but he is sitting so far back from the rest of the gang that you might think he doesn't know them.

Sobs are echoing against the stone walls of the church. Erik's family and Robin's parents are also here. Åsa is discreetly patting some tears away with a tissue.

She walks towards the front of the church, seeing people she has known all her life. Her aunt, whom she hasn't seen for many years. And her little cousins. They aren't so little any more.

But there are also lots of people she doesn't know well at all, and some she has never seen before. They seem to weep just as much as everyone else.

Suddenly, she hears a voice she knows only too well.

When I am dead, my dearest, Sing no sad songs for me; Plant thou no roses at my head, Nor shady cypress tree.

Alicja. She is standing at the altar and singing.

Be the green grass above me, With showers and dewdrops wet; And if thou wilt, remember, And if thou wilt, forget.

Mom and Dad. They're in the front pew and she runs up to them.

'What's happening here?' she asks.

Mom is crying so much her whole body is shaking. Dad is staring straight ahead while the tears run down his cheeks. Rasmus and Lotta sit on either side of Dad, curled up close to his big body.

'Hello?' she says.

They are ignoring her. They still haven't forgiven her.

She turns towards the altar again.

The coffin. Its shiny, light wood. Its polished brass handles. The sea of flowers.

And there, the photograph of herself. It has been propped up on a large easel.

There have been times when Ida wondered who would come to her funeral, but she has never dreamed about it before. Now she wants to wake up.

'This is no dream.'

Ida turns around. Matilda is standing very close. It's so strange to see her like this. She looks so real, almost more so than the people in the church. She is wearing a long, white smock. Her face is serious.

'This is no dream,' Matilda repeats.

'Has to be,' Ida says. 'Or else I'd be dead.'

Matilda doesn't reply.

And Ida remembers.

The gym. Olivia. Gustaf. The kiss.

It wasn't a kiss.

She turns back.

'Mom!' she cries. 'Mommy!'

Mom is hiding her face in her hands and Dad has put his arm around her and Rasmus.

'Dad?'

'They can't hear you,' Matilda says.

Ida runs down the aisle. The Chosen Ones will hear her. She tries to give Minoo's shoulder a good shake but can't get a proper grip.

'Minoo,' she pleads. 'Minoo, I'm here! I'm here!'

Minoo doesn't answer her. She is sitting close to Gustaf. He doesn't notice her either.

Ida shuts her eyes tightly and concentrates as hard as she can.

Linnéa! Linnéa! I'm not dead! I'm here!

Linnéa doesn't react. Nor does Vanessa. Nor Anna-Karin.

She observes the faces of the Chosen Ones. None of them are weeping all that much, there are others in the church who cry more loudly. But no one can fail to see how genuine their grief is.

People are rising from the pews and starting to walk silently towards the altar to leave their flowers on the coffin and say their goodbyes. Among the Chosen Ones, Minoo is the first to get up.

Ida reaches her hand out towards Minoo, but she walks straight through it.

'Come now,' Matilda says.

'I want to stay!'

'You can't. We must hurry away.'

'What are you saying?' Ida says. 'Where are we going? Into the tunnel of light? Or what?'

'No,' Matilda says. 'That is not where we are going. But we must leave. Before they find us.'

'Who are they?'

'I will explain everything,' Matilda says. 'Now, take my hand.'

Ida looks at her coffin. Then at all the people who have played different roles in her life. Then at the Chosen Ones again.

They were the friends who knew her best.

'I don't want it all to be over,' Ida says.

'It isn't over,' Matilda says. 'Trust me.'

Ida takes the hand Matilda holds out to her and a dazzling light fills her.

EARTH

FIRE

AIR

WATER

METAL

WOOD

Acknowledgements

As we write this, we have just finished the last set of changes into the *Fire* manuscript. Almost a year has passed since we wrote the first chapter. And, what a year it has been! We have been in touch with so many fantastic people. If we were to mention all of them, the acknowledgements would be as big as the book itself. So, we must restrict ourselves.

First and foremost we want to thank the incomparable Marie Augustsson, our publisher, who has guided us through both the text and the amazing, but sometimes chaotic, adventure that began with *The Circle*. Thanks also to the incredible Olivia Demant, our editor, who weighed up every single comma on her golden scales. There are an awful lot of them in a book like this! Thanks to all the people at Rabén and Sjögren/Norstedts who have given so much of their time and commitment to Engelsfors.

Thanks to Grand Agency — Lena Stjernström, Lotta Jämtsved Millberg, Maria Enberg and Peter Stjernström — who have expanded the borders of Engelsfors far beyond Sweden and who always provide a safe haven on Tomtebogatan.

Thanks to our beta readers Måns Elenius, Gitte Ekdahl, Martin Hanberg, Siska Humlesjö, Linnéa Lindsköld, Karin Hesselmark, Anna Bonnier, Margareta Elfgren, Elisabeth Jensen Haverling and Anna Andersson. You have given us invaluable input from a wide range of perspectives.

Thanks also to Lisa Ekman, Björn Bergenholtz, Martin Melin, Erik Petersson and Emil Larsson, who shared their expertise with us.

And an especially big thanks to those who have kept us anchored in reality.

Mats' thanks go to Johan Ehn, who throughout the process has listened, supported and helped me to stay sane. Living in Engelsfors for a large part of my waking day often leaves me disoriented and feeling rather odd. Your patience is both unbelievable and incredible and I love you.

Sara's thanks go to Micke. Thank you for being our first beta reader and enduring the editing chaos and stress-induced panic. During this last year not a single day passed without me saying, "I don't know what I would do without you." And I really don't. I love you.

Thanks to our families and friends. You have always been our rocks. And we hope that we will have time to see more of you in the future.

Our last and perhaps our greatest thanks goes to all our readers who have let Engelsfors into their hearts. Your enthusiasm has meant everything to us during the writing of *Fire*.

Coming Soon
Book III in
The Engelsfors Trilogy

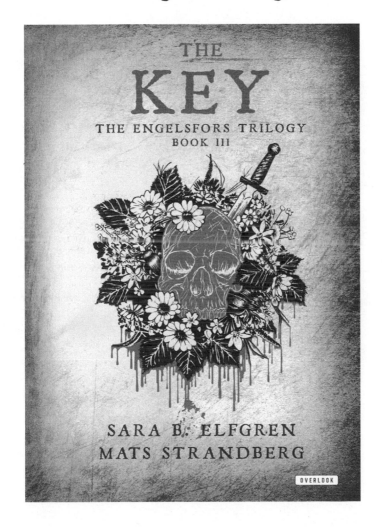

For news on
The Engelsfors Trilogy

go to

www.worldofengelsfors.com